OUR
GAL
CAL

OUR GAL CAL

BY

CHERYL JORDAN

A 4-NOVEL SERIES IN 1 VOLUME

BearManor Media

2011

Our Gal Cal
© 2011 Cheryl Jordan

This story is pure fiction. Any resemblance of the characters to real people, living or dead, is merely coincidental.

For information, address:

BearManor Media
P. O. Box 71426
Albany, GA 31708

bearmanormedia.com

Cover art by Blythe Russo

Typesetting and layout by John Teehan

Published in the USA by BearManor Media

ISBN—1-59393-371-1
978-1-59393-371-5

Dedication

Imagine, if you will, what the life of a Hollywood character actor would have been like in the mid-1960s. Even though this man didn't get top billing in the movie, he was oftentimes the one who was working steadily in Westerns and sit-coms while his superstar friends were idling at home, awaiting the perfect script.

In this story, Cal learns all about acting—and life—from Leonard Rhoads, a very busy character actor who is much wiser, more complex, and more dedicated to his craft than the average moviegoer might realize. Supporting actors like Leonard are the unsung heroes of stage, screen and television. These men and women are the sidekicks, the bosses, and the villains who give stories their flavor.

It is to these hard-working, under-applauded character actors that this novel is dedicated.

"This is a series of four novels featuring the same characters all in one volume. Because we get to know each character when they appear in the first section, they are generally not reintroduced or described again in later sections."

Table of Contents

PART I

A Whole New World

Chapter 1

APRIL, 1963

For once, Joe had abandoned his apron and was sitting at a table when he heard the familiar din outside. He looked at his watch to see if the clock on the wall was correct. Yep, it was only 2:48. *Cal must have messed with the school clocks again*, he thought as he finished his cup of coffee and offered another cupful to the attractively-suited woman across the table from him. She waved it away while expectantly watching the door for the approaching throng of high schoolers.

One after another, the kids made their noisy entrance into the diner that they had affectionately nicknamed "the Slop Shop." In the midst of the ruckus was its primary source—a diminutive, bright-eyed, fifteen-year-old girl with a mop of curly dark-brown hair and a seemingly endless supply of teacher jokes. She had been entertaining her cohorts with a spirited impression of their English Literature teacher when she noticed the stranger at the table with Joe. As her friends' guffaws died down and Cal took her usual place in the booth, she flashed a smile at the amused woman. *Hey!* Cal thought. *A grownup who laughs! That's a first. Joe's usually the only grownup around here and he's a grouch.* This time, though, Joe was actually smiling, too. *I wonder what he's up too?*

The woman looked at the proprietor as she discretely pointed to Cal. "Is that her?"

He nodded.

With a look of triumph, she motioned for the curious girl to join them at their table.

*   *   *

Thank goodness it was Wednesday! That was the only weekday that Cal's parents could both be counted on to be home at the same time. Time was a rare commodity for Dr. and Mrs. Thurman Ames. He was a pediatric surgeon with a thriving private practice and she was Director of Nurses at a major Dallas hospital, so this was the only day of the week in which they could have any semblance of a family life.

Generally, they depended on their housekeeper to take care of everyday matters involving their daughter, with strict orders never, ever to lay a hand on her. The Ameses had seen too many battered children come into the hospital and were determined that such a horrendous thing would never happen to any child of theirs. Even though working for this highly-respected couple was considered a prestigious thing, the Ameses seemed to have a more frequent turnover of housekeepers than would be expected.

On this particular Wednesday, Cal's parents were a bit disconcerted that she had brought a new friend home with her. Wednesday was their family day. What was this woman doing here?

Now, with all three Ameses assembled in the living room, Amanda Robinson showed them her Stagecraft Productions identification and told them about an upcoming motion picture and how it would affect them. It seems that high school drama teachers across the nation had been asked to submit the names and descriptions of their most talented students. From this list, eight lucky students were then chosen to fly to Hollywood for a screen test, for the purpose of appearing in a teen movie as a public-relations effort initiated by the Stagecraft studio, where it would be filmed.

"Nate Jenkins will be starring in it," Amanda said cheerfully to her young protégé. "Wouldn't you love to meet him in person?"

Cal asked eagerly, "How about Van Roman? Is he in it, too? Doris and Sue are nuts about Nate, but I want Van."

"No, Van's not in this one, but you can get Nate's autograph for your friends. I bet they'd love that. What do you think they'd say if they saw you on screen with him? Pretty neat, huh?"

"But she'sa just fifteen. That'sa so young," said Mrs. Ames, her accent clearly revealing her Italian origins.

"You were only *sixteen* when you came to America, Mom."

Amanda smiled. "All the kids will be about her age. She'll make new friends from all over the country on the set."

Impressing her pals and meeting famous people didn't appeal to Cal nearly as much as did being the first in her family to go on such an adventure. Her parents were always being recognized for meritorious things and being written up about in the newspapers, but now it was *Cal* who would spread her wings and soar. She would see things that her parents had never seen and do things that they had never done. She looked at her mother excitedly, "Please, Mom? I'll never ask for anything else as long as I live."

"I've heard that before," her father said, having remained silent until now.

"I really mean it this time, Daddy. You'll be proud of me. I'll do good. Please say yes. I want this more than I've ever wanted anything, and you're so good to me, Daddy. You always give me everything I want."

The couple looked at each other. Cal was right. They knew she would get her way. She always did.

"We'll take really good care of her," Amanda continued. "Stagecraft will pay all the expenses for Cal and her chaperone—meals, accommodations, and transportation. All she needs to do is pass the screen test to experience this adventure of a lifetime." Amanda opened her spacious purse and pulled out some official-looking documents. "Just sign on the lines that have a red X on them."

"What if she no pass-a the test? What then?" Mrs. Ames asked.

"We'd then pay your way back home but, believe me," Amanda nodded knowingly, "it was as if the kid was auditioning the minute she walked into the malt shop. She's a natural. She'll do great."

"I want to run these contracts by my lawyer first," Dr. Ames said with authority as he took the papers. "He handles all of our legal dealings."

Amanda nodded sympathetically, "Oh, I know how it is. I really do. These things are so complicated sometimes, but you know what? I've got an early flight back to L.A. in the morning, and my boss said I have to have the signed contracts in hand when I get there or I'll get fired." Then she explained that normally, this sort of thing is done far in advance. Production was set to begin very soon, and the cast and crew had been lined up and ready to go when one of the high-schoolers they had chosen broke her arm and couldn't do the film. Now they were scurrying around in search of a last-minute replacement from this part of the country. None of the others who had tested had been very impressive. Cal, however, should "knock their sox off," Amanda said with enthusiasm. She had seen the others and was confident that this girl had the charm, the sparkle that the director was seeking.

Dr. Ames had begun reading the contract carefully when his pager went off. "Excuse me, Miss Robinson," he said as he handed the contract to his wife and went into the next room to call the hospital.

Amanda then appealed to Mrs. Ames. "We're really in a time crunch here, I'm afraid. Cal needs to be at the Stagecraft studio Friday for her screen test. That's the last time they'll be doing them."

"Friday? *This* Friday? We cannot get away that soon. There'sa no way…"

"No problem," the woman said calmly. "She can stay with a family, and I know the perfect one for her. A wholesome family with kids and dogs and apple pie. How about that?"

"Dogs? Hot diggity! Mom, I've *got* to go now. I know we can't have pets 'cause of Daddy's allergies, but they've got *dogs*. Please, Mom. I want to throw a stick and they'll chase it."

Noticing the crucifix on the wall, Amanda added, "A nice, Catholic family. They'll treat her as their own."

Dr. Ames hurried through the living room to the front door. "I'll be back later, hon. The Madison baby's in trouble." He then left.

Amanda proceeded to give Mrs. Ames more details: Once Cal passed the screen test, she would then remain in California from three to four weeks for the filming of this incredible movie. "Believe me, we'll take really good care of her. I'll meet her at the airport myself and see that she gets the red-carpet treatment, just as any child of yours deserves. She'll have a great time."

Mrs. Ames took one more look at her daughter's ecstatic face, sighed, and took pen in hand.

*   *   *

"You did *what*?" asked an incredulous Dr. Ames after he returned from the hospital late that night.

"I signed-a the contract," responded his wife. "I'm a good judge of character, Thurman. Amanda is genuine."

"Maybe so, but tomorrow morning I'll have our lawyer contact that studio's lawyer. If there's really a movie being made there that involves amateurs, she can go. If not, then there's no way she's going to be on that plane Friday."

Chapter 2

CAL HAD NEVER FLOWN ALONE BEFORE. Today was truly a day of firsts for her. Not only was she flying alone for the first time in her life, but this was also the first time she had ever flown in the coach section. In times past, her parents had taken her with them to medical conventions all over the country, but they had always either flown first class or taken a chartered flight. *There sure are a lot of people in the coach section,* Cal noticed.

One of her parents would certainly have accompanied her had they been given more time in which to make plans. *Too bad I don't have more relatives,* Cal thought. Then she grinned as Antonio Pirelli, her mother's older brother and Cal's only other living relative, came to mind. Her mother called him Tony, but Cal got a kick out of calling him "Uncle Ant." *Poor ol' guy,* she thought. This perpetually-frustrated man had the sad misfortune of being the principal of the high school that Cal attended. Her eyes sparkled with delight as she thought about the pranks she and her friends had pulled on him. For some reason, it was always her friends who were given detention for those things and not the mischievous moppet herself. It was in the principal's office that Cal would be dealt with.

Through the closed door of his office, the school's administrative staff could hear his rantings. "Sono furioso con voi, voi mostro! Perché nascevate mai?" he would yell. Once Pirelli had regained control of himself and could speak with more civility, he would then switch back to English. "I find it really difficult to maintain discipline when you're always undermining my authority!"

"Yeah, yeah, yeah," she would sigh tiredly, after hearing that speech for the hundredth time. Grownups are such stiff-shirts. *Where's Uncle Ant's sense of humor, anyway?* So what if he had an urgent call to make to a misbehaving student's mother but couldn't because his phone had been unplugged? Or the timing system for the school bell had been advanced twenty minutes? Cal always saw that particular deed as a public service, but, for some reason, he didn't.

She wondered if it had indeed been Antonio who, as family legend had it, gave her the nickname "Calamity." Her real name was Stacy Maria Ames; but as long as she could remember, everyone had known her as simply "Cal." She had to admit, though, that Uncle Ant was probably the happiest of everyone when he had been told that Cal would be getting out of school a few weeks early this year to go to California.

To her friends, this fantastic adventure had seemed like a dream come true, a glamorous chance to become Dallas' own version of Annette Funicello. She would meet famous people and come back to Texas with many exciting stories to tell her friends. And, with her camera packed, she would have a photo album full of pictures of this very special summer to show them.

Cal's thoughts were interrupted when the plane touched down and was now taxiing in to the gate at Los Angeles International Airport. She was about to jump up so she could be the first one off, but the flight attendant announced the need for everyone to remain seat-belted until the plane had come to a full and complete stop and the captain had turned off the seatbelt sign. "Awwww," she groaned as she sat back down and buckled back up, wishing that she had sat in the front seat. Patience had never been Cal's strong point.

* * *

It seemed to take forever for the passengers in front of her to find and gather up all their carry-on items, then meander off the plane; but, eventually, she did find herself inside the airport and looked around for Amanda.

There she was. "Cal, hi!" Amanda waved. After a quick pat on the back, she led Cal to the baggage claim area, where they chatted until the luggage arrived. Once they were sure they had everything, Amanda then guided her into the VIP lounge, where a tall, brawny, sandy-haired man was standing with a cup of coffee. When Cal had caught the first glimpse of him as Amanda opened the door, she noticed that he seemed annoyed, like he wished he could have been anywhere but here. He then did a double-take as they walked in, and his expression softened. Cal wondered what that was all about. He looked so familiar to her. Where had she seen him before? He sure seemed to know her, too, judging from the way he was looking at her. *Maybe he's one of Mom or Dad's friends,* she thought.

Rising from her chair was a pretty lady with short, blonde hair and a gentle smile.

Amanda presented Cal to the couple. "Leonard and Jill Rhoads, this is Stacy Ames. Everyone back home calls her Cal."

Jill extended her hand, "It's so good to meet you, Cal. You're going to be staying with us for a few weeks while you're working on the picture. I hope you'll have a good time in California," she said warmly.

"Oh, I *know* I will. I promised my friends I'd take pictures of everything."

Leonard put his coffee cup down and took the luggage from both Cal and Amanda. "You look like somebody I used to know," he nodded to the child. "What's your mother's name?"

"Alicia Annabella Pirelli Ames. You probably know her or my dad. Mom came over from Napoli and she talk-a like an Italiano," Cal gestured grandly in the tradition of her mother.

He shook his head. Apparently, that name wasn't familiar to him.

"How about Dad? Dr. Thurman Ames, the pediatric surgeon? I just *know* I know you from somewhere."

Amanda turned to Cal with an amused smile. "Cal, where are we?"

"Los Angeles."

"Right. And what is Los Angeles known for?"

Cal thought, then guessed, "Movies?"

"Bingo! You've seen Leonard in movies and on television shows for years. He's usually the bad guy in Westerns."

"Ohhhhh, yeah," she nodded, and then looked up at Leonard. "You ride a horse like you've been doing it all your life."

"Only for a few years," Leonard answered as he led the way out of the terminal and to the car. He was carrying her four large pieces of luggage— one in each hand and one under each arm—as though they were empty. *He sure is strong*, she marveled.

"Do y'all keep your horses at your house?" Cal asked hopefully as she followed the adults out of the terminal. The prospect of having unlimited access to her favorite animal in the whole world filled her with excitement.

"No, dear," Jill smiled at her naiveté. "We don't own any horses. The ones you see him riding in those Westerns are loaned to the studios."

"Oh."

"Leonard's in the same picture that you are," Amanda told Cal. "I think you'll have a lot of fun. There will be several other kids your age in it, too. You'll probably make a lot of friends on the set."

Cal could hardly wait!

*　*　*

What a disappointment! She just couldn't believe it. At the airport, it wasn't all that apparent, probably because he hadn't said very much there. In the front seat of the car, though, Leonard and Amanda were discussing upcoming projects and the man was speaking with a distinctly *New York* accent! Surely, he was putting them on. On TV, his southwestern accent had been perfect. Until now, she would have bet money that he was a native Texan.

Cal leaned forward and tapped his shoulder. "Where are you from?" she asked.

"Long Island, originally." He pulled the car to a stop at the red light.

"Where's that?"

"New York."

Major disillusionment! Major! Maybe he's not the same guy she had seen on TV, after all. "Can you talk Texan?" she asked.

He turned around, draped his right elbow over the back of his seat, and, with a hint of a smile, drawled, "Well now, little lady, you ain't fixin' to bail outta this here car jes' 'cause I'm one of them damn Yankees, are ya?"

Yeah, he's the same guy, all right. "Wow!"

As he turned back around with a chuckle and the car proceeded through the now-green light, Amanda told Cal, "He can do a lot more accents than that. You'll learn a lot from Leonard."

Los Angeles sure is a big city, Cal noted, as they made their way along the various expressways through town. After about an hour on the road, they finally arrived at a group of buildings behind an open iron gate that proudly bore the Stagecraft Productions logo. Leonard waved at the security guard as they pulled into the studio parking lot, and then parked near one of the buildings.

"I'm sorry we have to jump right into it like this, Cal, without giving you time to freshen up," Amanda apologized, "but we need to do your screen test today."

Cal grinned, "And I didn't even study or anything."

Everyone emerged from the car, and then Cal was stopped by Amanda, who had withdrawn a small makeup kit from the vast expanse of her purse.

"Hold still a minute and close your eyes," she said as she quickly put some taupe eye shadow on the obliging girl's lids. Then she instructed, "Now look up at me," and applied some black mascara, then pink lipstick. Cal wondered what was next as Amanda again fished through her purse.

"Ya gonna pull a rabbit out of there?" Cal asked playfully.

Amanda then retrieved a soft, wide brush and a compact. As she brushed powder onto Cal's upturned nose and soft, smooth cheeks, she explained, "The lights would make you too shiny without this." Once she had added blush to her cheeks, Amanda stepped back and looked at her young friend with pride. The child's now-glamorous eyes glistened. "Yes, that'll do just fine." She patted Cal's loose curls into some semblance of order.

"What am I supposed to do in there?" Cal asked.

"Don't worry. Just be the same kid I saw at the malt shop, and you'll knock 'em dead."

The Rhoadses then followed the pair into the building.

*　*　*

After the screen test was completed, Cal was told to wait in the hallway. Amanda then went to her office in a nearby building while Jill and Leonard stayed with Cal and waited as development of the test film was hastily done. A while later, as three men passed them and went into the projection room, Leonard informed her that they were executives involved with the film. Cal wondered why such important-looking people would care about her screen test.

"Because there's a lot of money invested in this picture," answered Leonard, "and they want a good return."

All of this seemed so foreign to her. That making movies was actually a business seemed to take away from its magic.

*　*　*

Amanda's prediction was correct. Cal had done exceptionally well on the screen test and was told she had been awarded the part of Corky in the film. Amanda was notified and would ensure Cal membership in the screen actors' union by the time filming began. Next, they had to go to another building for her fittings. There, Jill went inside with her, and a woman measured everything of Cal's that could be measured, it seemed. Once that was done, they were then free to go.

*　*　*

The trio now pulled into the driveway of the Rhoads' home. Leonard gathered up Cal's luggage as Jill unlocked the front door and led her inside.

Cal let out a loud whistle and called, "Here, Poochie. Come on, boy!"

"What?" Jill asked.

"Your dogs. What're their names? I've always wanted a dog. Are they collies like Lassie?"

Jill said gently, "We don't have a dog."

"Yes, you do. Amanda said you do."

"No, sorry. Come with me and I'll show you around." She put her arm around Cal's shoulders and escorted her through the large, beautifully-arranged two-story Colonial-style house. It had one feature that Cal had never seen before, what Jill called a "media room." In this room were projection equipment and a big screen so that they could watch full-length movies from the comfort of an easy chair and sofa. They also had a television, stereo components, and recording equipment here. On shelves along the wall were dozens of cans containing 16mm and 32mm films of some of the movies and television shows in which Leonard had appeared, as well as others that he had found interesting.

"Wow! I *love* this room!" she exclaimed as Leonard set the luggage down in the hallway and joined them. Cal looked up at him gleefully. "We could really have a great party in here!"

"Every film has something in it that you could learn from," he said proudly. "You might find it helpful to study the different techniques that other actors use, then see how you could apply it to your work."

Work? It never occurred to Cal that being in a movie would be considered work. It sounded more like a social event to her, the way Amanda had been talking about other kids her age being there and everything. *Looks like ol' Len is just like a lot of the other grown-ups I know. They want to turn fun things into dull things,* she thought.

"You'll take the yellow guest room upstairs," Jill said as she then led Cal up the stairway to her new room. "I have it all ready for you."

Leonard followed with the luggage.

The room was beautiful! The pattern of the yellow floral bedspread was repeated in the priscilla curtains and the fluffy cushions of the French Provencal rocking chair. There was light-green wall-to-wall carpeting throughout. A matching white desk and chair were to one side, and a yellow lamp was atop the dresser on the other side. On the small bedside table was a yellow crocheted doily beneath an ornate white clock and a white telephone.

"Hot dog! My own phone!" Cal squealed. "Just like at home."

Jill pointed out the two keys on the dresser. "These are for you. One is to the front door and the other is to the back door, just in case you ever get back while I'm out." Then she nodded toward the hallway. "Our room is right across the hall from yours, in case you need us for anything. I hope you'll be comfortable here."

"All it needs is a record player; then I wouldn't have any reason to come out of my room."

"You can play records in the media room. Did you bring some with you?"

"No. Maybe your kids have some good ones. Where are they? I thought they'd be home from school by now."

"We have no children."

"No kids?" Cal was confused. "No kids, no dog. I bet that means there's no apple pie, either. But that's okay. I like brownies better."

Jill smiled uncertainly, not quite sure what Cal was talking about. "There *are* some young people in the neighborhood that you might want to get to know. Miles Mitchell and Nate Jenkins live nearby. They're both actors, too. You'll be working with Nate in this picture, but Miles usually works at another studio."

Leonard set the suitcases down and leaned against the doorway. "Nate's uncle is CEO of the production company you'll be working for. You'll want to be extra nice to him. It never hurts to understand the political structure of these things."

"My buddies back home made me promise to get his autograph for 'em. They think he's the grooviest. Not me, though. I'm a Van Roman fan myself. Does ol' Van live around here, too?" she asked hopefully.

"No, I'm afraid not," Jill said.

"Your housekeeper must be off today, huh?" Cal asked. "I haven't seen her anywhere. Ours is off Wednesdays and Sundays."

"We don't have one," Jill smiled. "Leonard's offered to get me a housekeeper a hundred times, but I always say no."

Leonard handed Cal a thick binder.

"What's this?" she asked.

"The *Campus Break* script. They said that your character in this picture is Corky Baxter, so you need to memorize all her lines as well as the lines of the people who give you your cues. Filming begins Monday."

"Golly, so soon?" she asked. "Guess I'll have to hurry up and make my rounds of the neighborhood over the weekend, then."

He shook his head. "I don't think so, Cal. You have quite a few lines to learn in a short amount of time. Once you've studied them, I'll cue you if you want."

Jill opened the closet. "You might want to hang up your dresses before they wrinkle. Let me know if you need anything pressed."

"I only have a couple dresses, but I have about twenty-five pairs of blue jeans. It took a lot of doing, but we finally got the administration to let us wear jeans to school." She looked up at Leonard. "Can I wear my jeans Monday?"

"Sure," Leonard said. "The wardrobe department will provide you with the appropriate clothes." He smiled at Jill, "Too bad this isn't a Western. She's already dressed for that."

True. Passengers and crew alike dressed up for air travel in the 1960s; but Cal had compromised, wearing a denim skirt and plaid shirt. That's about as dressed up as she cared to get.

"Yeah," Cal grinned. "All I'd need would be a sheriff's badge on my shirt and I'd be all set."

He patted her on the shoulder and drawled, "Ah, shucks, ma'am. They don't make li'l bitty kids like you sheriff, but I'll let ya be my deputy, if you're real good."

Yep, it looked like this was going to be a fun summer, even if they didn't have any dogs.

Chapter 3

"**See ya!**" Cal waved goodbye to her new friend and looked at the sky. It was starting to get dark. Maybe she'd better be getting back to the house. This had been her first full day here, a Saturday, and she had met quite a few of the neighbors. As she breezed into the front door of the Rhoads home, she found herself face to face with an irate Leonard.

"Where the hell have you been?" he asked.

"Just checking out the neighborhood. That Miles—golly! He's sure cute! And he's got a sister my age named Dottie, and their next-door neighbor Francis has a horse out in the country. We went over to look at him and he's gorgeous. All that's in one direction, too. I'd see who's living on the other side of your house, but just plumb ran out of sunshine and couldn't today. Maybe tomorrow." She looked up, noted his incredulous expression, and figured reassurances were in order. "I think I'm going to like it here." She started toward the kitchen. "What's for supper?"

He gripped her arm and jerked her back around.

"Hey, what're you doing?" she protested. "That's not allowed."

"Didn't I tell you that you had to learn your lines this weekend? Didn't you hear me say that? You've got to know your character when you walk on the set on Monday morning!"

"Cool it, man. I'll get it done."

"Have you even *looked* at the script yet?"

"A little. I like the orange cover."

"There will be no more socializing until you know those lines. For the whole day tomorrow, you'll stay in the house and study them so you'll be prepared Monday. Understand?"

She looked at him suspiciously. "Can I have my arm back? I'm hungry."

"All day tomorrow, you hear?"

"I can't. Miles and I have a date. I'll do it after we get back. How's that?"

He shook his head. "Not good enough."

"Okay. All night tonight, too."

"*All day* tomorrow. No date." He let go of her arm.

She looked at him with disgust. "I'm starved."

"Too bad. You missed dinner."

Cal went into the kitchen and got a banana off the table. "Got a Dr. Pepper?" she asked Jill, who had just finished loading the dishwasher.

"Dr. Pepper?"

"It's my favorite soft drink in the whole world. My parents buy it by the case."

"Well, we'll have to look into that. In the meantime, I kept your dinner warm for you." She picked up an insulated mitt and moved the plate from the oven to the quilted place mat on the table.

Cal put the banana down. "Oh, good! I *thought* I smelled fried chicken."

"Well, actually, it's baked. That's healthier." Jill filled the drinking glass with milk. "We're not accustomed to having a child around the house. This is the first time I've bought milk in a long time."

As Cal seated herself and picked up the chicken leg, she frowned, "You sure have a grouchy husband. Is he always like that?"

"No, not really. We were just worried about you."

"I mean here he is lecturing me about learning my lines and I haven't seen him doing his at all."

"Oh, he already knows his. He learned them before you got here. Then he'll review the lines for a particular scene the evening before they're to shoot that scene. Believe me, Cal, he does a lot of studying. He takes his work quite seriously."

"Yeah, I can tell."

"Don't let him bother you. Just learn your lines and he'll be fine."

* * *

Getting into bed that night, Jill was starting to feel like a referee. First it was Cal, now it was Leonard. "Now, dear," she said soothingly, "just give her a chance. All this is new to her. You need to set a shining example, and she'll follow your lead."

Normally, he would have been sound asleep by now, but he just couldn't relax. "Can't we give her back?" he asked.

"What do you mean?"

"I mean dump her on someone else. Why us?"

She thought she had explained it adequately before they went to the airport, but maybe her words didn't sink in. "She *needs* us, Leonard. With no chaperone, she has nowhere else to go. She can't stay in a hotel alone—she's only fifteen—and we have plenty of space here for her."

"Nobody in his right mind would mug her," he grumbled. "She'd frustrate him to death."

With a playful wink, Jill sat up and pulled her nightgown over her head, then draped it on the bedpost. Knowing exactly how to help her husband relax enough to sleep like a baby, she smiled slyly and turned off the light.

*   *   *

"Y'all don't go to Mass?" Cal asked, incredulously, the next morning. "I thought everybody did."

Jill shrugged, "No, we don't go to church. It would be distracting for them to have a recognizable actor in the congregation. If you want, you can watch some religious programs on TV."

"No, I guess I'll just go back to bed and sleep late. I've never done that on a Sunday before." *Life in California sure is different than Texas,* she thought as she turned around and went back into her room.

*   *   *

"Shhh," Cal said softly to Miles as he was walking her back to the house that night. "I'm going to go in the back way. Don't make any noise."

"I'm sorry I kept you out so late," he whispered.

"It's okay. I'll see you next time. 'Bye."

"Tomorrow night?"

Cal whispered, "Okay. 'Bye." She unlocked and slowly opened the back door, then inched her way in, closing the door softly behind her. She took off her shoes and tiptoed through the kitchen and down the hall to the stairway.

Leonard seemed to come out of nowhere, grabbed her by the shoulders and shook her. "Just *who* do you think you are," he roared, "that you can come here, do as you please, and ignore the rules?"

She had never in her life been treated this way by anybody, and was not about to let him get away with it. She gave his shin a hard kick, coming now to the painful realization that she should have kept her shoes on. "Who the heck do you think *you* are, bullying me around like that?"

"I'm the head of this house and the maker of the rules! And now you're forcing me to be the *enforcer* of the rules, too! You're grounded for the next week! Home and work, and that's all."

"Let go of me!" Leonard was still firmly holding her shoulders.

"Tell me what your first line is."

"No! Let go!"

"Your first line. What is it?"

She tried to punch him in the eye, but his arms were longer than hers and her fist missed its target. "Leave me alone!" she yelled.

"What's your first line?" he yelled louder.

"I don't know! I don't know! Now go 'way!"

"Just when did you plan to learn them?"

"I'll just read 'em off the cue cards. What's the big deal?"

"Cue cards? *What* cue cards?" he asked sarcastically.

"You know, the cue cards that they hold up."

"There *are* no cue cards," he said, releasing her shoulders. "I'm willing to bet yours will be the shortest film career in history. I wouldn't be surprised if they fire you on the spot."

"They can't do that," she cried. "I promised the people back home I'd be in this movie."

"So what're you going to do, then? You need to get enough sleep so you'll be alert tomorrow; and you also need to learn your lines. We have to leave for the studio in about seven hours. You've got a problem."

The seriousness of the situation finally hit her and she felt like a fool. "Help me?" she pleaded in a small voice.

"Then *neither* of us would get enough sleep."

Cal turned away from him and picked up the script from the living room table, where she had left it that morning. She had begun reading it then, but Corky didn't have any lines in the first few pages and that was why she had felt no sense of urgency. As she sat down in the overstuffed armchair to pick up where she left off, she heaved the most pathetic sigh she could manage. Leonard hesitated before going upstairs. His voice was more controlled now. "It's rare that they shoot the scenes in sequence because of logistics. Just study the third scene tonight, because that's the one you'll be doing tomorrow afternoon." Then Leonard sternly pointed his finger at her, "Every spare minute you have tomorrow, whenever you're not in the scene being shot, you better spend studying those lines. You hear?"

"Yeah." Deep, forlorn sigh. Cal, curled up in the chair, tucked her feet under her, turned to scene three, and sighed again.

Leonard had started up the stairs, then stopped and looked over at her. She really did look lost, contrite, almost pitiful. "Okay," he said softly, "just this one time, I'll help." He went back down the stairs and over to the sofa. "Come here. We'll do it together."

She joined him on the sofa, and he took the script. Turning to page forty-two, he pointed to a long dialog. "See this? This pretty much sums up your character. Read it carefully. It's really important to know your character inside and out before you set foot on the set. Build her from people you've known who are like her. It always helps to be able to visualize your character. The director will guide you a little further, but it's up to you to have the basic character down pat. In this film, you're Corky. Corky is a lot like you, Cal, so you shouldn't have much trouble there. She's full of energy and is very creative and sociable—but the problem is that she uses these otherwise admirable traits to get into trouble. Sound familiar?"

Cal shrugged innocently.

He continued, "Corky and her friend Mike are at loggerheads with Officer Stanton, my character. He's trying very hard to keep order, but the kids are trying very hard to keep things lively. I'm the frustrated character and you two are the ones causing all the commotion. It's the friction between our characters that provides the humor."

On into the night, they worked to build Cal's character and learn her lines in the third scene. By the time she went to bed, she was exhausted, but well prepared for the next day. Cal vowed to herself to never put off studying her script again.

Chapter 4

MORNING CAME MUCH TOO SOON. It seemed to Cal that she had been asleep only a few minutes when Leonard was shaking her awake. She looked at her clock. No, it had been several hours. He was already dressed and ready to go. "Hurry up. I let you sleep longer than I should have. We've got to leave in about twenty-five minutes. Don't worry about your hair or makeup. They'll do that there when the time comes."

As he went downstairs, Cal dragged herself out of bed, took a quick shower, and got dressed. Once in the kitchen, Leonard handed her a cup of black coffee, which she promptly downed. She grimaced at the taste. Sure, she needed caffeine to wake her up, but it would've been more pleasant coming from a Dr. Pepper. Cal grabbed a banana on her way out the door, and they were soon on the road. If it weren't for the excitement of actually seeing what it's like to make a movie, she probably would have fallen asleep in the car.

Cal expected to see a lot of famous movie stars that morning, but the only one she recognized, besides Leonard, was Nate Jenkins. There was no doubt when he arrived because the other girls' nervous giggles turned into excited whispers as he made his entrance. Cal couldn't figure out what they thought was so great about him. It wasn't like he was gorgeous or anything. Nice looking, maybe, but not drop-dead handsome—so the girls' reactions seemed way out of proportion to reality. Cal thought it odd, too, that instead of sitting with everyone else, Nate's chair was set back, away from the crowd, like he didn't want to have anything to do with the common folk. And he was always wearing those stupid sunglasses off-camera. *He must think he's a hot-shot or something,* she thought. *For Pete's sake, it's not like we won't recognize him with those things on.*

Leonard was teaching her the terminology. This large area within the garage-like building was called the sound stage, where three different sets had been constructed—a clubhouse, a bunkhouse, and a police station. It was sure a busy place! When the camera wasn't rolling, it was a noisy place, too! It was quite crowded with the big camera, sound equipment, lighting equipment, reflectors, chairs, and people. The floor was strewn with cables. She had been told that part of the filming would actually be done outside at a real beach, too, and was looking forward to that.

Even though Cal's first scene was scheduled for the afternoon, they had to be at the studio in the early morning not only because Leonard was in the first scene to be shot, but also because all of the teens had an early call that day. That was quite unusual, he told her.

It struck Cal funny to see Leonard come out of the dressing room area in a policeman's uniform. *Yeah*, she thought, *that's a* perfect *part for him—the bully policeman! That's sure what he's most like at home.*

And what seemed even funnier to her was watching him and the director interact. *How neat*, she thought, *that big, bad Leonard has to obey the director, who's only half his size!* How could anyone expect Cal to study her lines when there was such a fun show going on right in front of her? Seeing how much power the director wielded over Leonard made her determined to be one someday.

This wise director, Milan Royce, was shooting scene fifteen first for two reasons—it was short, and it would give the inexperienced young cast members the opportunity to observe professional actors at work before trying it themselves. Thus, the teens' early call. Leonard and Nate would set the precedent for proper behavior on the set.

It worked, too. Cal had to grudgingly admit, while watching the filming, that Leonard and Nate were real pros. On cue, as if by magic, they had transformed themselves into Officer Stanton and Mike; and they stayed in character, even while receiving instruction from the director. Leonard was no longer the obnoxious tyrant she knew. Instead, he was the rookie policeman, trying valiantly to maintain order in a hopeless situation—summer break for a couple of cabins full of rowdy high-schoolers. He even *looked* younger in this role! And Nate's character was fun-loving and lovable. What an acting job *that* was! The hours went by, but Leonard played his part with just as much energy at 12:30 as he had at 10:00. *For an old guy who hasn't had a lot of sleep*, Cal thought, *he's kind of amazing!*

"Cut and print," announced the director. "We'll work on scene three after lunch."

The assistant director continued, "Lunch break until 1:30. Jack, Pat, Cheryl, Judy, and Bob, you can go now, but we'll need you back here in the morning. Report to make-up at 7:00."

As the lights and camera were turned off and pulled back, Leonard came over to Cal. "We're both up next. You have an hour to review your part."

In the last few years, Cal had become adept at cramming for tests; and that's exactly what this felt like. About twenty minutes later, Leonard brought her a sandwich and Coke, then was about to leave when she grabbed hold of his arm. "You do yours and Nate's lines," she asked. "Let's see if I can remember mine."

He complied and was pleased that she needed no extra prompting. This was because of her excellent short-term memory, which had served her well throughout her academic career.

The scene they were to do next was to take place inside the police station. Officer Stanton was hauling Mike and Corky in for disturbing the peace at the beach. As his fellow officer was showing him how to fill out the paperwork, the kids slipped back out unnoticed, leading to the merry chase in the next scene.

After Cal ate her sandwich, Leonard then instructed her to change into the clothes the studio provided for the upcoming scene, and showed her where the dressing room was. Then he waited. And waited. He looked at his watch, then stood near the doorway and yelled, "What's the hold up in there, Cal? They're almost ready for you."

"I can't wear this," she complained from behind the door.

"Why not? Come on out and let me see."

She emerged, wrapped in a large towel from neck to knees. "It's a bikini, for Pete's sake! Mom would croak if she saw me in this thing."

"A real little one? I thought this was a family film."

"A family of letches, maybe." Cal went down the hall to the set, where director Royce stood talking to his assistant. She tapped the director's shoulder.

Leonard watched in confusion. He saw Royce put his hand on Cal's shoulder as he listened to her intently. Then, once the man gently took the towel off Cal, Leonard chuckled. That was no bikini; it was merely a two-piece swimsuit, quite modest by Hollywood standards. He then saw Royce smile and pat Cal on the back in a kind, paternal manner. Leonard couldn't hear the conversation, but the director was reassuring Cal that the other girls would be wearing similar suits for the beach scenes, and that his assistant would be glad to explain her wardrobe to her mother, if necessary. That seemed to satisfy her.

*   *   *

The rest of that day went smoothly, and they drove home with the feeling of a job well done.

"I was surprised to see you taking direction so well," Leonard commented. "Why can't you do that at home?"

"Well, I figured if *you've* got to do what the director says, I'd better, too."

"Good girl. I think you'll be okay after all." Leonard stopped the car at a red light and looked at the call sheet he had been given. "We're going to be doing scene seven in the morning, then scene four in the afternoon, and you're in both of them so you'll need to learn them; then get to bed at a decent hour this time. You have to report to make-up at 7:30." He set the sheet back down.

"I need to call Miles."

"Why?"

"He wanted to take me out tonight, but I just don't have time."

He nodded, then took out a cigarette and lit it, snapping the lighter shut and tucking it back into his pocket. "What did you say your mother's name was, again?"

"Alicia Pirelli Ames. Why?"

"Are you adopted?"

Cal looked at him in utter confusion. "Adopted? Me? No."

"Are you sure?"

"Positive. Why are you asking me this stuff?"

Leonard took a puff and slowly exhaled, then set the cigarette on the ashtray in the dashboard. "Just wondering."

"Why? What made you think I was adopted?"

He looked over at her and replied simply, "Because you look like Sheila Montgomery and you're bull-headed like me. I thought you might be my daughter." Noting her shocked expression, he added, "Don't tell Jill."

"Who's Sheila Montgomery?"

"A girl I went with in high school," he said. "Last I heard, she was still in New York. I haven't seen her in a long time."

"Since Jill?"

"Since long before Jill."

Cal breathed a sigh of relief. Having been raised in the Bible Belt, the idea of Leonard being unfaithful to his wife was unsettling to her. "How long have you guys been married?"

After doing a brief calculation in his head, he answered, "Almost six years."

"Gosh. That's not very long for old peop… . Uh, that's not very long."

He chuckled at her faux pas. When he was her age, he probably thought thirty-four was old, too.

*　*　*

She looked at the clock, then put her head under the pillow. "Just let me sleep a few more minutes, Len. It's so early."

"We *want* to get there early so we can see the dailies. You'll like that." He pulled the pillow off her head.

She rubbed her eyes. "What're dailies?"

"Sometimes they call them 'rushes'. It's the scenes we did yesterday. You'll want to see how you did."

"Oh, okay." She reluctantly left the comfort of her bed as he went downstairs.

*   *   *

"Ewww, I'm awful," she groaned after viewing herself in the previous day's scene.

"No, Cal," Leonard whispered. "For your first try, it's not that bad. It'll have enhancements added to it, music and everything, and the mic will be cropped out."

"But at least I don't look half bad in that bathing suit. I wonder if they'll let me keep it."

"Probably not."

"But they have three of 'em. That's how many are in the dressing room for me, and they all look alike."

"That's standard practice. They always have duplicate costumes, but they might want to use them again in some other film."

"I bet Dad'll buy it for me."

The other scene was now being shown and she enjoyed watching that. "You're pretty good in that, Len."

He shook his head. "Not good enough, though. I would've done better if I had had more sleep the night before."

Doesn't anybody like how they look in the dailies? she wondered.

*   *   *

"Oh, before I forget," Cal said to herself between scenes that afternoon. She got a sheet of paper and a pen from the script girl, and went over to where Nate was sitting. She pulled a chair over and sat beside him, tossing the paper and pen into his lap. "My friends want your autograph. There're eight of them, so you need to write eight different things."

He removed his sunglasses and asked, "I heard Leonard call you Cal. What's your last name?"

"It doesn't matter. None of those is for me. Do the first one for Doris. She's really got the hots for you. She said she wants you to write her name, then 'Thanks for an unforgettable night.'"

"But that would ruin my image," he protested.

"Too late. That's the image she already has of you."

Nate didn't quite know what to make of this newcomer. She certainly didn't act like the girls he had worked with in the past, nor did she blend in with the other first-timers. This spunky little pixie definitely stood out from the crowd. He put his sunglasses into his pocket and his script under the sheet, then scrawled out eight different messages, as Cal gave him the names of the recipients. Then he wrote a ninth one, addressed to Cal, inviting her to go with him to a charity banquet the following weekend. His press agent had him scheduled to give a large donation at this event, amidst much fanfare. *That's sure to impress Cal*, he thought. After all, his fame and wealth always *did* seem to have the effect of an aphrodisiac on girls; and, when they see him doing such a benevolent thing, they inevitably become putty in his hands. Being seen with him at such a highly-publicized event was bound to get her career off to a good start, too. She couldn't help but to be thrilled at a chance like that. *Yes*, he thought as he confidently handed the sheet back to her, *that's the least I could do for this PR project my uncle cooked up.*

"Thanks. See ya." She got up to leave.

"Wait a minute. Read the last one before you go. That one requires an answer."

Cal looked at the sheet and read the message. "Can't," she answered. "I've got to study my lines every night."

"It's on a Saturday evening."

"I don't go out with strangers. Why don't you take Doris?" Cal left him and went over to the far wall behind him, then proceeded to tack the sheet of autographs onto the bulletin board.

Nate jumped up from his seat and rushed over there. "What're you doing? Take that down!"

"Just showing everybody the right way to do autographs." She patted his cheek condescendingly. "There's a lot of new folks here who've never done one, you know."

He irately pulled the sheet off the bulletin board, as Cal grinned impishly and darted toward the other side of the room. He ran after her with the full intention of crushing that page of autographs into her smug little face. She ducked behind Leonard, however, and there she stayed. That necessitated an immediate change of plans as Nate came to an abrupt halt. He knew what everyone knew—that *no one* messes with Leonard Rhoads. He was big and he was strong. Everyone also knew that, off the set, he had quite a temper. Nate wadded up the paper and threw it to the floor in frustration, then went back to his chair.

Chapter 5

"SO WHAT'RE YOUR PLANS, CAL?" Leonard asked her at breakfast Saturday morning. This was the first time since last weekend that the three of them had had breakfast together, as Jill was usually still asleep when they left for the studio early in the mornings. "Would you like to do other pictures when this one's over?"

"I don't know," she said. "I hadn't really thought about it. I guess I thought this was just a one-time deal." Indeed, visions of returning home and showing her school buddies the snapshots she had taken in Hollywood was about as far ahead as her plans had gone.

"The producer said if this one's a success, they've got two sequels they could film. I'm sure that could involve some of the same actors, if they're available."

"I wish they'd get Annette to be in the next one. I bet she's a lot of fun to work with. And she's Italian, too, like me."

"So you'd like to continue in films?"

Cal shrugged, "I guess I could come back to do another one."

"You might get yourself an agent, then. Mine's Pete Harmon."

"What's an agent do?"

"He seeks out jobs for you and helps negotiate contracts."

"Should I call him?"

"Wait until Monday. He's not usually at the office on Saturdays."

"Okay." Cal refilled her glass with orange juice. "Bill Mayes is taking me out tonight."

"Who's he?" Leonard asked. "And where are you going?"

"The cute cameraman. We're going to a Hollywood party. I've always wondered what they're like."

Leonard and Jill exchanged looks, then he shook his head, "No, Cal. You're not ready for that. Does he know you're only fifteen?"

"I dunno," she shrugged. "If he had asked, I would've told him."

"And how old is he?" Jill asked. "A cameraman would be quite a bit older than you."

"I didn't ask him. Come on, guys. It's not like we're eloping or anything. I just want to see what those parties are like and he said he'd take me to one."

"No, Cal," Leonard repeated. "I'll call him and let him know you're too young for that."

"No! Don't do that. That's embarrassing, like I'm a little kid or something."

"Well, you are."

"I am not! I'm almost sixteen. How about letting him take me to a movie or something? Please don't call him," she pleaded.

Leonard looked to his wife for guidance.

"Maybe she's right, dear," Jill said softly. "That would be humiliating for her to be treated like a child. A movie would be all right, wouldn't it? It's just for one evening."

He looked from Jill to Cal, then back to Jill, and relented, "Okay, but I've got to see him before they leave."

Jill passed the platter of homemade cinnamon buns to their young charge. "Would you like to go shopping with me this morning, Cal? We can get you a pretty dress to wear on your date. I bet you'd look adorable in a dress with a matching ribbon in your hair. That can be our birthday present to you."

"But my birthday's not 'til September."

"I know. Your mother sent me a note, telling me about that. She said she's planning a 'sweet sixteen' party for you. Since we won't be there with you then, we can celebrate now."

* * *

Bedecked in her brand new green dress with matching bow that Jill had tied into her hair, Cal followed Bill to his car.

"You really look pretty tonight," he said as he held the passenger door open for her.

"I feel like a box of candy with this silly ribbon on my head."

"I think it's kind of cute."

"Where's the party? At a restaurant?"

He closed her door, went around and got into the driver's side. "It's at Paul Goldman's apartment. What film would you like to see?"

"I want to go to Paul's place."

"But Mr. Rhoads said I'm to take you to a movie tonight. He said you're too young for our parties."

"Heck, Bill, he'd keep me chained to the house until I'm forty if he could. I want to see what that party's like."

"Are you sure?"

"Yeah."

He turned the key in the ignition. "Okay, but don't tell Mr. Rhoads."

*   *   *

Later that night, Cal couldn't get back to the Rhoads house fast enough. After a hasty goodbye to Bill, she hurried into the house and headed toward the stairway.

"You're back early," Leonard said from the living room. "How'd it go?"

"Oh, okay I guess." She started climbing the stairs.

"Which picture did you see?"

She mumbled incoherently, and quickened her pace up the stairs.

"HOLD IT RIGHT THERE!" His booming voice seemed to shake the house.

She stopped and looked over the banister at him. He had lowered his newspaper and was glaring at her suspiciously.

"Where'd you go?" he asked. "And answer so I can understand you this time."

"Well, we could've seen *Tom Jones* or *Cleopatra*, but we knew you wouldn't want me seeing them, so we just went to a party instead." When she saw his expression change to one of anger, she broke into a run up the stairs and into her room, quickly slamming the door shut and locking it.

A moment later, there was a loud knock on her door. "Let me in, Cal!" Leonard said sternly. His tone of voice sounded to Cal like he was planning to break the door down if she didn't unlock it, so she sighed and opened the door.

He came in and swatted her hard on the rump. As she swung to hit him back, he caught her arm and roared, "I told you you couldn't go to that party!"

"It was the lesser of the two evils. You didn't want me seeing those dirty movies, did you?"

"There were other pictures you could've seen."

"Well, dadgum it, Len! I was curious, and now my questions are answered and I'm all done being curious, so everything's okay and I won't go to anymore parties."

He sat in the chair by the door. "What happened there?"

"At the party?"

"Of course at the party! Tell me everything. I want to know what happened."

"Haven't you ever been to a Hollywood party?" she asked incredulously.

"Pretend I haven't and describe it for me."

"Well….." Cal thought for a moment, then continued, "it smelled real bad in there because everybody seemed to be smoking. They wanted me to, too, but I don't smoke and never will. Dad says a lot of people die because they smoke. It makes their lungs real black and everything. The people at the party laughed at me when I told them that."

He nodded, "You did the right thing. Go on. What else?"

"How come you smoke?" she asked.

"Never mind that. Tell me the rest."

She sat on the bed, which was soft, so wouldn't further hurt her still-stinging derriere. "People were drinking a lot, too. One girl was reciting poems, and a guy went in another room with a couple girls. There were a lot of people just standing around and talking about stuff that didn't make any sense, and some of them started taking their clothes off, but it wasn't hot or anything, Len. One of the guys took the ribbon out of my hair, and that's when I wanted to leave. They were really weird. Bill brought me back here, and that was the end of that. I don't like Hollywood parties. Texas has better ones."

"I told you you shouldn't go there. Now will you listen to me?"

"Yeah, I guess so."

He stood back up. "You're grounded for a week."

"But you already hit me, and I said I'll listen to you and won't do it anymore," she said indignantly. "How come you're grounding me?"

"Because you disobeyed me. I'm glad you see the reasoning behind my rules, but I've still got to punish you for disobeying me."

"That's not fair!"

"I'm being more than fair. You'll understand someday."

Why do grownups always say that? Cal wondered. When they do something mean, they say "you'll understand someday." If she ever had kids, she was bound and determined she'd never say that to them.

*   *   *

Monday, Cal had conflicting feelings when she saw that the first thing Leonard did upon arrival at the studio was to approach Bill Mayes. Even though she didn't get close enough to hear what they were saying, she could tell that the younger man was being severely reprimanded for having taken her to that party. On the one hand, she felt quite embarrassed that Leonard would interfere with her dates like that; but, on the other hand, this made it easy for her to turn down any further dates with Bill. He lived in a world too different from hers and she didn't like it. She could just say that Leonard had forbidden her to see him again, which she was sure he would if she asked. Just to be on the safe side, though, she wouldn't ask.

That turned out to be a non-issue. Bill never asked her out again.

*   *   *

The next day, Cal came back from lunch and looked at Nate with a barely-concealed smirk. *Uh-oh*, he thought. *She must be up to something.*

The script had been changed again yesterday, and he glanced over it one more time before being called to the set. As the assistant director motioned them forward, Nate set the script on his chair and joined Cal on the sofa of the clubhouse set. The makeup artist put touchups on his face as the hair stylist went to work on Cal. Mrs. Schultz noticed that Leonard had gotten into the habit of mussing the child's hair when he was in a good mood, so she, again, had to tidy it back up. That done, Cal's makeup was refreshed a bit, then the extraneous crew cleared the area.

"Quiet on the set!" called the assistant director's voice. All noise ceased as Cal and Nate got into character, then a man held the clapboard before the camera. "Scene one hundred fourteen, take one." He snapped the arm down and returned to his position behind the director, who called out "Lights" and the area was softly illuminated, "Camera," and the camera set forth with a "Rolling" acknowledgment from Bill, and "Action!"

The summer was almost over. Mike and Corky had been "partners in crime" for almost two weeks, but this was the first time they had found themselves alone in a boy-girl situation, and it felt awkward. They looked to all the world like virginal adolescents on their first date.

He shifted position uncomfortably and cleared his throat, "Uh, Corky?"

"Yes?" she said softly as she studied her folded hands in her lap.

"Well," he fidgeted, "I've got to go back home tomorrow. We might never see each other again."

She looked away from him and sighed, "I'll miss you, Mike. Maybe we can write?"

"Really?" His face lit up. "You care about me? You'll write?"

"Um-hmm," she smiled at him coyly.

A self-confident air replaced his earlier discomfort. "Corky?" he asked as he gently turned her chin toward him and lightly kissed her lips.

"Oh, Mike! Don't go!" she pleaded with a melodramatic flair.

Now Nate knew what Cal was up to, and he abruptly stood up. "She's been eating garlic!" he said indignantly. "I can't work like this."

"Cut!" said Royce.

"You're absolutely right," Cal agreed with Nate. Looking over at the director, she added, "Let's get Miles Mitchell to fill in for him."

"Cal, behave!" Leonard said sternly from the far corner of the set.

Nate's indignation gave way to curiosity. "Where did you get garlic anyway? They don't serve that at the commissary."

With a grin and a mischievous gleam in her eye, she gestured dramatically, "Tony Roma's specialty, spicy-a sausage and linguini with just a little-a bit of oregano. She'sa justa down the street." Cal then added, "Tomorrow's special is ravioli, my favorite."

"Would you make her eat at the commissary like everybody else?" Nate pleaded with Royce.

The director motioned to one of the crew members, "Lisa, fix that, please. Nate, you can take a five-minute break."

As Nate returned to his canvas chair far behind the camera, Lisa scurried to the commissary for a couple items, then returned and picked up strong, minty throat spray from her supply cart. She handed Cal a large sprig of fresh parsley and a Styrofoam cup of milk.

"No, thanks. I already had lunch."

The assistant director started toward her, but Milan Royce intercepted and put his hand on Cal's shoulder. This time, he didn't look amused. "Eat the parsley and drink the milk," he said with authority. "They kill the bad breath. Then I don't want you to eat anything more with garlic or onions in it until the picture's completed. Understand?"

"Oh, geez," Cal sighed in defeat, then stuffed the parsley into her mouth as Lisa readied the throat spray.

Leonard had to duck out for a minute so they wouldn't see him laughing.

*   *   *

Cal was glad that she had a phone in her room and the Rhoadses allowed her unlimited use of it. In fact, Jill urged her to call her parents as often as she wished. That she did, usually catching them at home on a Wednesday night. She also called her best friend, Sue, at least once a week, and brought her up to date on her 'adventures in Hollywood.'

"Guess how many people are there when we're filming," Cal asked her buddy.

"Besides the movie stars, you mean?"

"Yeah."

"Oh, I don't know. Three or four?" Sue guessed.

"Heck, no!" Cal laughed. "Try fifty. Maybe even a hundred. There's people swarming around everywhere!"

"Are you kidding? How come that many?"

"Well, first off, there's the director and his assistant, and there's the makeup guy and script lady and cameraman. They use only one camera so we've got to do each scene two or three times so they can get it at different angles. There's people doing the lights and sound equipment, the costumers, the hair lady, prop people, the extras, actors who aren't in that scene but are just watching, family members and friends, set decorator, stunt men, stand-ins—Nate has a stand-in, but I don't."

"What's a stand-in?"

"They're people who just stand there, taking Nate's place on the set, while the technical guys move the camera and lights around. Those lights are hot, too. I wish I had a stand-in so I wouldn't have to do that. And there's a really great dog in a couple of the scenes and his trainer's there, and there's sometimes even a tour group and a carpenter or two. The guy that wrote the book was there for a little while, but he got mad and left. Len said writers do that a lot."

"Golly! How do they keep it quiet enough to get the movie made then?"

"They yell, 'Quiet on the set. Take one.' Well, actually, they sometimes say 'Take ten' because there's some kids who don't know their parts very well and we have to do the scene a lot of times until they get it right."

"Are you one of those kids?"

"No way! I study my lines every night. Len says I'm a natural, too. He says all I need is formal training, but I don't want to go to another school. Even one's too many. Anyway, when the guy says, 'Quiet on the set. Take ten', everything gets real still and quiet, like a library. And the director's a real little guy, but he's like Napoleon. Everybody does what he says, even Len."

"Well, sure they do. He's the boss, isn't he?"

"Yeah."

"Is he very mean?"

"No, not mean at all. He's kind of like your granddad. Len said that he's one of the most patient directors he's ever worked with and that's why they got him to do this film. There's about six of us kids in this picture, and none of us has ever done a movie before, so we're learning as we go. Len says that director must've been a nursery-school teacher before getting into show biz. And there's cables all over the floor. I've tripped over them a couple times and darn near broke my neck, but at least it wasn't on-camera."

"What's your part like?"

"I'm Corky and she's so funny. They've added some new stuff to my part, and now I get to handcuff ol' Len to his police car. We're going to do that scene tomorrow and I can hardly wait."

"That sounds fun."

"I wonder what would happen if the key I use to unlock the 'cuffs doesn't work. Hmmm, I think I'll take my house key and use that instead, to see what they'd do."

Each week, Sue got a better picture of what her buddy's new life was like; and each week, she missed her a little more.

Life in Dallas just wasn't the same without Cal.

Chapter 6

CAL HAD BEEN IN CALIFORNIA for three weeks, and she had grown really fond of Miles. They were back now from the concert, but were lingering on the porch for another goodnight kiss or two. Only three years older than Cal, he was the handsomest boy she had ever seen, and just as sweet as he was handsome. He didn't have a big ego like Nate or take her to weird parties like Bill. Gentle and caring, he was everything she loved in a boy. *"What a catch!"* she thought. She wished she could show him to Sue. *Why haven't we ever noticed him in movies before?* she wondered.

The front door opened and Leonard appeared. "It's past your curfew, kid. Get inside right now!"

"In a minute. Miles was going to ask me something."

Leonard took her by the arm and pulled her into the house. "Whatever the question is, the answer is 'No.' Goodbye." He then shut the door and bellowed, "I told you twelve o'clock! It's now quarter to one! Don't they teach kids how to tell time in Texas?"

Thoroughly frustrated, she kicked his shin as hard as she could. "Dadgum it, Len. He was fixing to ask me to go steady with him, I just know it, and you ruined everything!"

"I set the rules; you obey them."

"They're dumb rules!"

He gripped her by the shoulders and shook her hard. "If you can't be in by midnight, then you have no business going out at all! You're grounded again!"

She bit his arm. Full of fury, he smacked her across the face. She slapped him back and ran toward the kitchen. He ran after her, but she slung a kitchen chair into his path, causing him to stumble over it onto the floor. Cal then went back and triumphantly sat atop him, cheering, "Yay! Victory for the oppressed! I score two points for a take-down!"

"Think you're pretty smart, don't you?"

"Yep. Hooray for my side! The South shall rise again."

Leonard quickly bolted upright, causing Cal to topple over. Then he held her shoulders down to the floor. "But *I'm* the winner and still champion."

Being out of counter moves, she had to admit defeat. "Okay, okay. Let me up."

"Grounded for a week, you hear? If you try to sneak out, it'll be *two* weeks and we'll take your phone away."

"No! Not the phone!"

He nodded.

She sighed, "Okay. Let me up."

He stood and helped her up. "Curfew is midnight and not one minute later."

* * *

Jill arose the next morning and was making the bed when the telephone rang. She lifted the receiver to her ear. "Hello?"

"Is this-a Mrs. Rhoads?"

"Yes, it is."

"I'ma Mrs. Ames, Stacy's mother. How'sa my little girl doing?"

Jill broke out in a smile. "Oh, I'm so glad to be talking to you, Mrs. Ames. She's doing just fine. Leonard says she's becoming quite a good little actress, and she's certainly livened things up around here."

"Dr. Ames, he misses her so much and he say we shoulda fly there to surprise her. Would Wednesday be convenient?"

"That would be wonderful. I'm sure she'd be very happy to see you. Do you have your flight numbers yet? I can come to meet you at the airport."

"No, not-a yet. We make sure it's okay with you first. I'll do that-a right away. But be sure not to tell her we're coming. It'sa to be a surprise."

"All right. You'll need to get here in the morning. Sometimes they get home from the studio in early afternoon, and sometimes much later."

"Yes, I hang up and call-a the travel agent now. Thank you-a very much, Mrs. Rhoads."

"You're welcome. Let me know when and where, and I'll pick you up and bring you here. You can stay in our guest room."

"I call you back when I have-a the schedule. Good-bye."

"Bye, now." Jill returned the receiver to the cradle and smiled again. Now she understood where Cal had gotten her Italian looks.

* * *

Cal had finished in the makeup department and was about to enter the sound stage when she was joined by Amanda. That certainly brightened her day.

"Hi, Amanda! It's been so long since I've seen you. Did you come to watch me work?"

Without a word, the woman led her into a small room away from the others, closed the door, and seated her before taking a chair herself.

"What?" Cal asked. "What's going on? Are you okay?"

"I'm fine, and it looks like you're doing pretty well yourself, kid."

"It's a lot of fun. You were right about that. But did you know that Len doesn't have kids or a dog?"

Amanda leaned forward and put her hand on Cal's. "We're friends, aren't we?"

"Sure. Why?"

"I was sent to tell you something, and I'm also here to give you some good advice that I hope you'll heed."

Uh-oh, Cal thought.

*   *   *

She didn't really want to do this, but Amanda made her promise she'd let her parents know. She wanted to talk with Jill and Leonard about it first, though, since they understood Hollywood better than her parents did. This just didn't seem right to her.

It was dinnertime and they were all together, so she guessed now was as good a time as any.

"Len, is Leonard Rhoads your real name?"

"Yeah, why?"

"No one ever told you to change it to something else?"

"You mean in the business?" he asked, meaning, of course, the only business that existed for him—show business.

Cal nodded.

With an amused smile, he shook his head. "Now why would they want me to change a simple name like that?

"Well, mine's simple, too, but Amanda says the head honchos want to change it."

Jill was confused. "But why? Stacy Ames is a lovely name."

Leonard seemed unconcerned while putting gravy onto his mashed potatoes.

To Cal, though, this was serious. "Yeah, I like it, too, but they say it's not Italian. They say I look Italian so I've got to have an Italian name."

"And I bet they've already decided what that name will be," Leonard stated, matter of factly.

Cal nodded. "Anna Lucia."

He nodded while giving the name consideration. "That's kind of clever, rhyming with Santa Lucia."

"But it's not me."

"Yeah, that's true," Leonard said with a hint of a smile. "Italia Spitfire would be more appropriate."

"I don't want to change my name."

"It's just a stage name, Cal. You don't have to use it when you're not working."

"But I don't want to use it at all. Why do I have to?"

He shrugged, "You don't."

Cal's face lit up. "Really? Amanda made it sound like it was already a done deal. You mean I really don't?"

Leonard shook his head and reached for the plate of sliced roast beef. "Not if you don't want to. It's your decision."

"They won't fire me if I don't?"

He smirked as he looked over at Jill. "Firing Cal would not be a smart move on their part."

Cal couldn't believe her ears. Was Leonard actually giving her a compliment? Surely, he must not mean that the way it sounded. "You mean they'd be afraid I'd get mad and sue 'em?"

"No, because you're doing a pretty good job, Cal. I think this picture is going to be better than it otherwise would've been, because of you."

"Really?" It was so seldom that Leonard ever said anything good about her that she wanted to make it last a little longer. "What makes you think that?"

His demeanor changed back to one of disinterest as he took a bite of beef. "Just a hunch. Now eat your dinner."

*　*　*

When they're filming outdoor scenes, Cal found, there's sometimes a lot more waiting involved. Either the natural lighting has to be just right, or else they need to bring out the artificial lighting. Sometimes the light's just perfect, but they have to wait for an airplane overhead or a siren to pass. *But that's okay,* she thought. *It gives me time to tease Nate some more. It's been too long since I've done that and he's getting much too confident.* With an impish grin, she thought about how much fun he was to tease. His face would turn red and he would get so upset. Cal just knew, if there were nobody around, he'd really slug her good. But, as long as there were people about, she knew the most he would do was simply to chase her away. These Hollywood types sure are dramatic, she mused.

Cal strolled over to where Nate was taking a nap in a semi-reclining beach chair and assessed the situation. He was wearing a polo shirt, shorts, sox, and sneakers. *Hmmm,* she thought, *it's the oldest prank in the book and not at all original, but what the heck. It's just begging to happen.* She very slowly and carefully tied the laces of his two shoes together, then nudged him awake. "You're needed on the set, Nate. Up and at 'em!"

He jumped up and promptly fell face-down into the sand. "Cal, you idiot," he yelled angrily. While he untied his shoes, she casually sauntered back toward where the other people were. Instead of re-tying his shoes, though, he kicked them off, scooped up a handful of sand and ran after Cal. "We'll see how *you* like getting a mouthful of dirt," he threatened. She then broke into a run, laughing gleefully, and, again, found Leonard and retreated behind him, wrapping her arms tightly around his waist. Again Nate would have to get past Leonard to get to Cal.

Thoroughly disgusted, he returned to his chair and put his shoes back on, realizing now that naps on the set are out—at least, while Cal's around.

*   *   *

When Leonard and Cal got home from work that evening, Jill met them at the door. She was clearly distraught. She had Cal come into the living room and sit down before she told them what had happened.

"Your parents had planned to surprise you by being here when you got off work this evening," she started. "They boarded the plane early this morning and I went to the airport to meet them."

Cal's face lit up. "Hot diggity! Where are they?" She called out, "Mom? Dad?"

Tears made their way down Jill's cheeks as she gently told Cal that the plane never made it to Los Angeles. It went down in Arizona. All aboard were killed.

Cal was stunned. Her eyes grew moist.

Leonard put his hand on her shoulder as a gesture of support, while not knowing what to say.

Then Cal shook her head. "It's got to be a mistake. They're okay. Maybe other passengers had names like theirs. I bet they missed the plane. They're always late for stuff."

Jill said softly, "It was a chartered plane, and they were the only passengers."

Cal rose and started pacing. "I was going to call them tonight. They can't be gone. They just *can't* be!"

"I'm so sorry." Jill put her arm around Cal's shoulders.

Cal clung to her and sobbed, "Please make them look harder. They have the wrong people. Mom and Dad are somewhere else. They're okay. I know they are! Don't let them give up."

For once, there was a crisis in Cal's life that Jill and Leonard were powerless to fix.

* * *

At the studio, they rearranged the schedules to shoot the scenes in which Cal was not involved while she and Jill flew to Dallas. They were met at the airport by a morose Uncle Antonio and driven to the Ames house.

As they rounded the corner and her house came into view, Cal's heart leapt for joy. Her happiness turned to despair, however, when she unlocked the front door and came into the hallway. No one was there. She didn't know why she expected to see her parents in the living room. Maybe because that's where they were the last time she saw them together. The place was so different now. So quiet.

It seemed awfully strange for the place to be completely devoid of human life. Even Myra, their housekeeper, was gone. There were no smells of dinner coming from the kitchen. The chandelier that had always been such a majestic welcome in the front hall didn't seem so beautiful anymore. The rooms looked lifeless. Nothing was the same.

Lonely.

As Jill and Antonio settled into the Ameses' living room and began discussing funeral plans, Cal wandered from room to room. The kitchen looked darker than she remembered it. She fingered the heart-shaped magnet which held a photo of her as a Candy Striper to the refrigerator door. Her father had been so proud of her when he would chance upon her wearing that uniform and pushing a wheelchair-bound patient back to his room from the Physical Therapy Department. "That's my daughter," he would say to whomever was near. "That's my little girl."

"Heck, Daddy," Cal would say, "I'm not a little girl anymore. Hold out your arm and I'll show ya." She weakly smiled as she remembered the phony hypodermic syringe she kept in her pocket for just such occasions.

She drifted through the kitchen doorway into the dining room. The oval Chippendale table was covered by an ivory tablecloth woven in a Tibetan monastery. The table had four matching chairs with seat cushions skillfully worked in needlepoint by Cal's mother. Cal moved her hand slowly across the back of her mother's chair as she thought about all the Wednesday nights they had enjoyed dinner as a family. Dr. Ames insisted that neither his office, nor the hospital, disturb him on that day, except for dire emergencies. Other evenings of the week, Cal had dinner in the kitchen with the cook; but Wednesdays were different. The Ameses dined like royalty on that day, linen napkins and all, as Mrs. Ames presented her family with one of her homeland specialties. That was the only day in which she could indulge her love of Italian cooking from scratch. Her other day off, Sunday, was the Lord's day.

Cal sighed and ambled out of the dining room and back into the living room, bypassing the family room where she had spent many an evening watching Westerns on TV when she should have been doing her homework. On the antique table beside the sofa on which Jill was sitting was a small half-worked picture that Mrs. Ames had been cross-stitching. Cal had always teased her mother about working with needles all day at the hospital, then picking up an embroidery needle when she got home. That wasn't accurate, of course, since Director of Nurses was an administrative position. Mrs. Ames always seemed to be on the phone, embroidering as she talked to whichever of her friends or colleagues needed her advice that evening. Cal picked up the piece of cloth and looked at it as she sat heavily on the sofa beside Jill. Mrs. Ames had left the needle woven in and out of the cloth between rows so it wouldn't disrupt the weave of the material. *Now,* Cal thought, *this thing will never be finished. It'll stay half-done until the end of the world.*

Jill put her arm comfortingly around Cal's shoulders as she continued conversing with Antonio. Their voices sounded far away to Cal as she just sat, drained. With another sigh, she got back up. "I'm going to bed." Maybe the familiar comfort of her own bed would help the pain go away. She didn't have the energy for anything else.

"All right, dear," Jill said. "I know you're tired. I'll see you in the morning."

Cal disappeared up the stairs.

The adults resumed their discussion. Once they had made all the decisions they could at that time, the conversation turned to Cal. What was to become of her?

"Hell if I know," said Antonio with a shrug. "My sister told me she and Thurman willed everything to each other and, when last of them died, their house would be given to the hospital as a place for out-of-town families to stay while their children are receiving treatment there. The rest of their earthly possessions would go to Cal."

Jill asked, "What do their wills say about guardianship? Surely, they appointed someone."

He shook his head. "No one wanted her."

Jill found that exceedingly difficult to believe, but when she and Antonio met with the Ameses' attorney late that afternoon, he confirmed it. Because they had found no one willing to assume responsibility for Cal, that issue had not been addressed in her parents' wills. It had seemed logical to Jill that, after the filming was over, Antonio would allow Cal to move in with him. But he said no. He and Cal didn't see eye to eye on things. It just wouldn't be the environment either of them would need, he said. Jill tried to change his mind, but he wouldn't.

After Antonio returned Jill to the Ames house, she went into Dr. and Mrs. Ames' bedroom, closed the door, and spoke at length with Leonard on the phone. After much discussion, pro and con, the Rhoadses finally agreed that they should open their home to Cal on a more permanent basis. Jill was hoping that, sooner or later, their hospitality would make Antonio feel guilty enough to fulfill his duty to the child.

Jill and Antonio met with the Ameses' attorney again on Friday, and they arranged with the Court for the Rhoadses to assume temporary legal guardianship of Cal. Throughout the proceeding, Jill watched for any sign of second thoughts from Antonio. She saw none.

The funeral on Saturday was well attended by many of Dallas' most prominent citizens and the media. Cal couldn't care less about that. She asked that Jill and Myra sit with her and Uncle Antonio in the front pew. With Jill on one side and Myra on the other, Cal felt a little braver, more in control. She held their hands throughout the service. It was only when the alto soloist sang Mrs. Ames' favorite anthem, "Ave Maria," that Cal couldn't hold back the tears any longer. Saying goodbye, so unexpectedly soon, to the people who had given her life, love, and every creature comfort she could ever want, was the hardest thing Cal had ever had to do.

* * *

Jill thought it best not to tell Cal about her inheritance until the probation process had been completed. How much she would receive would not be known until all of her parents' outstanding bills, including funeral expenses, were paid and insurance policies were settled. As she and Cal flew back to California, Jill did let her know that she would be living with the Rhoadses indefinitely.

"Okay," Cal said grimly. What she was thinking, though, was *Oh, no. I have to live with that big ox 'til I'm eighteen?* But she thought that, unless she could earn enough money to live on her own, the only other alternative was an orphanage. As soon as they returned to L.A., she'd call Pete and tell him to line up as much work for her as possible. Then maybe she can afford her own place, and she and Miles would be able to stay out as late as they wanted.

* * *

Cal was eager to get back to work so she'd have something to occupy her mind. Back on the set, though, she noticed that everyone was treating her differently. There was no longer any lighthearted teasing or joking back and forth among the cast. Everyone was glum between scenes and they seemed to be uncomfortable in her presence. *That's no way to run a movie*, she thought. It then became Cal's mission to put an end to that stuffy atmosphere in the only way she knew—by becoming the resident clown. Her jovial antics immediately put everyone at ease and life at the studio was soon back to normal.

"I'm surprised she's not more affected by her parents' deaths," Cheryl confided to Judy on their way to the commissary.

Her companion shrugged, "Maybe she wasn't very close to them. She said once that they aren't home much."

It was only after work, when she was alone, that Cal had to deal with the reality of her situation. Jill noted that she spent an inordinate amount of time in her room, lying on the bed and listening to her radio. Her excursions around the neighborhood to see her friends seemed to be a thing of the past. Peeking in, Jill saw that there were numerous wadded-up tissues on the floor around Cal's trash can. *This isn't healthy*, she thought. *She's going to make herself sick if she keeps this up.* Now Jill had a mission, too—to help Cal through this difficult time by keeping her busy with chores and other diversions, and to keep things as upbeat as possible at home.

Chapter 7

"**Never look at the camera** unless you're addressing your audience directly," Leonard instructed. He and Cal were in the media room and he was showing her portions of films that would illustrate various points he wanted to make. "I've noticed you've done that a couple of times and the director didn't call you on it, but it's not at all professional.

"I've noticed something else, too," he added. "Since you got back from Texas, you're putting more emotion into your delivery. I like that. Don't ever lose it."

"Run that last part again," she said. "I can't believe such a little guy won that fight with you. How'd he do it?"

Leonard laughed. "Because that's how it was written in the script. Even *you* could beat me to a pulp with a feather duster if that's the way it's scripted."

Normally, it would have been like pulling teeth to get Cal to sit still for such sessions; but she was determined now to become so good at her craft that Pete would be able to find mountains of work for her. Leonard restarted the projector.

"Notice here the use of props," he continued. "Always be sure you hold the prop at such an angle that the camera can see it clearly. If it has a label on it, the audience must be able to read it. See how this actor handled the envelope—he picked it up, held it out so the camera could read the address on it, then tossed it back down."

"Yeah, I noticed Nate did that with the newspaper. At first, I didn't know why he held it up like that. Now I guess it's so the camera could see the headlines."

"Exactly." Leonard turned off the projector. "What *is* it with you and Nate, anyway? Why does he keep chasing you and why do you keep hiding behind me? Do you have something of his?"

"Naw, I just kind of tease him a little and he's trying to get me back. If he ever caught me, he probably wouldn't know what to do with me."

"Why do you do that?"

She shrugged. "He *reacts*. He's fun to tease."

"Well, don't do it anymore. Remember who he is."

"Are we done here?"

"For now."

"I've got to study my lines for tomorrow then."

"We have a scene together tomorrow. Would you like me to rehearse with you?"

"Okay."

"Like I said before, it's good to learn the lines immediately preceding your own so you'll pick up on your cues."

"I know, I know."

The dailies were getting less painful for Cal to watch now. She felt she was starting to get the hang of the job; and, she had to admit, Leonard's pointers were kind of helpful.

* * *

The next day, after getting her lunch at the commissary, Cal sat with Leonard and his friends, instead of her own.

"What's the occasion?" he asked as he shook some catsup onto his hamburger.

"I need to ask you about something, then I need to go to a bank."

She now had his undivided attention.

"How do I start a savings account?" she asked. "They make big money, don't they?"

"You mean interest?"

"Yeah, I guess so."

He nodded, "You get some interest on a savings account, but you get more on investments if you do it right. Why? What's this sudden interest in money?"

"I want to get an apartment and a car."

He mused, "You don't even drive yet, Cal. There's no sense in having a car. And without a car, it'd be foolish to have an apartment. You'd still be needing me to take you to the studio, anyway, so you might as well stay put."

"If I get investments, how fast would I have enough money for an apartment? Six months, maybe?"

"No, not six months."

Her eyes lit up. "Three months?"

"No, Cal. It'll be *years* before you have enough money to live alone. And, even if you *did* have enough money, it wouldn't be safe for you to live alone."

"Oh, Len, nothing bad happens to me. Crooks must know I hit back 'cause they've never bothered me. Will you take me to the bank after lunch so I can get some investments?"

"Don't need to. You already have an interest-bearing trust fund."

"I do? How come I didn't know about it?"

"Because you're not to touch it. Once I realized you were here for the long term, I opened an account for you and started putting your paychecks into it."

"You mean I earn more than the money you give me?"

"Of course you do, Cal. What I give you is just spending money. The rest of it goes into the bank. When you're twenty-one, then you can have it."

"But that's six whole years away, Len," she whined.

"That's right. Eat your lunch." He put the top bun back on his hamburger and took a bite.

Leonard thought the conversation was closed, but Cal didn't. "What bank's it in?"

"Doesn't matter. You can't take it out, anyway. Nothing can be taken out without my signature."

"Why? Why'd you do that, Len? Don't you trust me?"

He raised an eyebrow as he continued eating his hamburger and fries. His friends then drew him into their conversation, so Cal dejectedly picked up her tray and went to her own friends' table.

*   *   *

It had been two months now and filming was almost over. This would probably be Cal's last chance to pull a really good one on Nate.

She sought out the maintenance man and borrowed his screwdriver. While Nate was getting into costume, she loosened the screws in his favorite chair. Then she returned the screwdriver to its owner.

All morning, she waited for Nate to sit in his chair. But first he had a scene with Bob and Cheryl, then the three had a scene with Cal. It wasn't until they broke for lunch that he went anywhere near his chair. She would go get her lunch later. First, though, she wanted to stay here and watch the action. Dadgum it, he still didn't sit. He just put his script on the chair, then went to get some lunch. She sighed and followed. He went to the commissary, got a couple of sandwiches, then returned to the set to study the next scene. She followed at a discreet distance.

"Hey, Cal," Archie, another maintenance man, called as they re-entered the sound stage. "I found that screwdriver you were looking for." He held it up.

"No, that's okay. I don't need it anymore. Thanks anyway."

Would Nate suspect anything? He didn't seem to. He put his sunglasses into his shirt pocket, picked up the script, then sat in his chair. The chair immediately collapsed flat to the ground as Nate's lunch and script went flying.

Cal burst into gleeful laughter. "You look so funny, Nate! If you could run as fast as you fall, you might be able to catch me," she said as he got back to his feet. And off she went with Nate in hot pursuit—down the hall, out the door, across the patch of grass, and behind Leonard. Nate came screeching to a halt.

Leonard reached around and pulled her out by the arm. "No, Cal. I told you to stop that. You're not going to use me as a shield anymore."

She then darted the other way, running around a nearby building and looking for a door that she could enter, then lock behind her. It's the near misses—when he *almost* catches up to her, but not quite—that made this so fun. Spotting a lockable door, she sped toward it. With a burst of laughter, Cal grabbed the knob and pulled. Uh-oh, it's already locked! Her mirth came to an abrupt halt when Nate jumped her and they both tumbled to the ground. He then delivered a mighty blow to her back.

"Ow!" she yelled indignantly.

He then held her down with his knee on her back and pulled her head up by the hair. "I've had enough of you! Don't you *ever* pull those stupid stunts on me again or I'll sue you!"

"Okay, okay! I'll never bother you again as long as I live. I promise!"

"All right, then." He let go of her and stood up.

She got up, punched him squarely in the eye, then ran back around to the front of the building, joining the crew on their way back to the set.

As the afternoon wore on, Nate needed extra makeup to camouflage the progressive discoloration around his eye.

Cal had had to change to clean shorts and shirt, and stretched her back periodically. It sure did hurt, but it was still usable; so all was well.

* * *

This was Cal's last paycheck from the film that had just wrapped, so Leonard gave her a great deal more from it than he usually did, enough for the record player she'd been wanting. She and Jill then went to a department store and bought a stereo system for Cal's bedroom. Leonard noticed that now, with both the telephone and the record player to keep her busy, Cal was spending a lot of time in her room. More than once, he'd had to remind her to turn down the volume at night. Tonight was no exception.

"Okay, okay," she said, softening the noise level a bit. She had been sitting on the floor, reading.

Leonard came in and turned the knob to further lower the sound, then sat on her bed. "So what are your plans for the rest of the summer? Surely, you're not going to spend it loafing."

Cal held up the script that had been in her lap. "Look at this, will ya? It's a TV script Pete brought me and doggone if it isn't a little bitty thing."

He took it and smiled. "It's a half-hour show. Compared to a film, I guess it *would* seem pretty small." After looking through it and seeing that her parts had been highlighted by her agent, he gave it back to her. "It's a minor part, but will keep you out of trouble."

"I think I'm going to like this, too. Pete said it just takes six days to shoot."

"You can work that to your advantage sometimes. They let you get away with ad libs more on TV because they shoot on a tighter schedule than films do." His eyes sparkled with mischief as he recalled the ad libs he had sneaked in, in times past. "When does shooting begin?"

"Monday morning. Jill signed the contract, and Pete said they'll have a company car pick me up. I've got to tell Sue all about this. It sounds really neat."

Chapter 8

"Wʜᴀᴛ'ᴅ ʏᴏᴜ ᴡᴀɴᴛ ᴛᴏ sᴇᴇ ᴍᴇ ᴀʙᴏᴜᴛ, Bᴏʙ?" Leonard asked. This was the first time he had ever been called into the inner sanctum of Stagecraft's CEO. He took a seat in one of the plush chairs in front of the massive desk.

Very few people addressed Robert T. Stewart by his first name, and even fewer by its more informal diminutive, but he chose to overlook that detail for now. The rotund man flashed a smile that looked like that of a salesman. "Well, Leonard, I understand you and Jill have legal guardianship of Stacy now. Is that correct?"

He nodded, "That's right."

"Yes sir, I believe she's going to work out all right. She might benefit from some formal acting lessons, though, and maybe dance classes to help her develop a more graceful walk."

He nodded, "I thought she was damn good, considering it's her first picture. She's nowhere near professional yet, though. That will come after more time and experience."

"I think we can get her some lessons to help her improve those things and give her a better chance at success. And since we're going to be financing these lessons…"

"I'm teaching her myself. There's no need for the studio to do that. And Jill can teach her about walking."

"Now, Leonard, I know you're a busy man. Here at Stagecraft, we do things the old-fashioned way. Our contract stars don't need agents, managers, secretaries or anything. All they have to do is concentrate on acting. That's how it should be, and that's how we like to operate. Cal's a nobody now, but, with our guidance, she could have a pretty good career someday.

In return, all she needs to do is confine all her work to Stagecraft. We'll take good care of her."

Now Leonard understood what this was all about. "She's got an agent, and she's going to continue to have one. Not only that, but I act as her manager and advisor."

"Loyalty means a lot to us. We gave her her start, you know. If it weren't for us, she'd be just another obscure high school student."

"Don't worry, Bob. You'll reap a lot more of the benefits from *Campus Break* than she ever will. I noticed the contract her parents signed only got her a flat, minimum salary, with no percentage of the profits or any of the extras. That's a pathetic excuse for a contract."

"Because she's an unknown."

"Not for long." Leonard leaned forward. "You've apparently forgotten that I've been watching her, too, just as you have. I'm sure you saw the dailies, but I was on the set every day, all day long. I saw what a bang-up job she did, how well she took direction, and how much they expanded her role. Hell, by the time shooting was done, she had gotten almost as much screen time as Nate. I see her marketability as well as you do." Then he leaned back and smiled, "No sir, Cal's not going to be a pawn in any corporate games, and there's no way I'm going to let anyone overwork her or pump her full of drugs in order to increase their profits. She's an actress and she'll be a damn good one someday. She isn't owned by any studio. She'll work for whoever offers her the best role."

The executive leaned back in his well-padded chair and sized up the situation. Realizing now that he was dealing with a man who knew more than Bob thought he did about the business aspects of acting, he saw the need to use another tactic. "Well, you *could* do it that way. She could be independent talent with no steady salary and no guarantees. There's not much security in that. We need to think about her future. If she had a steady income now, that would enable her to go to college."

Leonard shook his head, "A steady income's not necessary. Money's not a problem for Cal. And besides, she's starting to do TV shows now and loving it. She might decide to confine all her future work to that."

Bob looked startled. "Television at another studio? No one told me she was doing that. We need her for some promotional work. That was in her contract."

"Her agent is Pete Harmon. You'll have to work it out with him." Leonard smiled in victory, rose from his chair, and left.

*   *   *

Cal could see that school here was going to be very different than it was back in Texas. Leonard and Jill had enrolled her in a private girl's school for the upcoming fall semester. She just couldn't imagine why anyone would want to go to a school that didn't have boys. When she protested, though, Leonard couldn't be dissuaded. "Once your film's released," he explained, "you won't be able to go to public school."

"Why?"

"Because Nate might be the one with box-office appeal that gets people to the theatre, but *you're* the one they're going to remember. You did a really good job as Corky, and I imagine you'll be easily recognized from the moment it's released. You'd be disruptive in a regular school."

She shrugged, "Shoot, I'm used to that. Uncle Ant was always saying I'm disruptive. That's no big deal."

"Trust me on this, Cal. It's the best thing for you."

Shooting on his last film had taken longer than expected and Leonard had only a few days before the next one was to begin, here in L.A. That was quite unusual, Jill had told her, to have two consecutive pictures filmed locally. Most of the time, they're made on location, sometimes in the United States, other times out of the country. While he'd been in the entertainment industry for over a decade, only now was Leonard really making a name for himself on screen. And already, he had gone on location in France, Aruba, Australia, India, England, Spain, and many cities throughout the United States. "It's an excellent opportunity for him to travel," Jill had said.

Agent Pete Harmon was working on Cal's behalf, too, and had lined up for her a few promotional appearances for *Campus Break* and two more television guest roles in the next two months. When she excitedly told Leonard that she was to appear on horseback in a Western, he took her to a dude ranch outside of town to practice riding. He was quite skillful at horseback riding himself, which had seemed odd to Cal, considering his origins. "They don't have horses in *New York*, do they?" she asked as they rode together on a Sunday afternoon.

He smiled at her notion of what New York was like. She apparently thought the whole state was just like Manhattan—tall buildings, big business, industry, overpopulation, hustle and bustle. "There are farms in upstate New York, just like in Texas. In some places, there's probably more cattle than people."

"Minus the oil wells, I bet."

He nodded. "Minus the oil wells."

"I'll race you to the top of the hill," she challenged him.

"You're on!" They took off in a cloud of dust. Cal was ahead at the beginning, but Leonard quickly overtook her and was waiting on top of the hill when she got there. "It's a good thing you're not in a race scene," he mused.

"I guess my horse doesn't like wind in his face," she said.

"Why didn't you tell me you already knew how to ride?"

"Because then you wouldn't have brought me here. I love horses. I'll get a faster one next time and then I'll show you some lightning speed. Speaking of which…"

He started his horse back down the hill and Cal followed.

"…I'm almost sixteen now. That means I can get a driver's license soon."

"You don't have a car, so why should you have a license?"

"I could always borrow your car or Jill's if you need an errand run or something. I bet Jill can teach me to drive. I've already got a copy of the driver's manual. Miles gave me his."

"In New York City, a person could go all his life without a car. They have every kind of public transportation you could ever need there."

"We're not in New York City, Len."

"True."

"So can I go for it? Jill said I had to have your okay."

He shrugged, "Go ahead. You might need it."

*   *   *

She wanted to get started right away, but the Stagecraft publicist had other ideas. *Now here we are in a totally weird situation,* Cal thought. A few days earlier, she and some of the kids were posing for a photographer as if they were doing scenes from the movie, but they were wearing different clothes than they had in the film; and now another photography session had been set up for just Nate and her on a couple of the studio's sets. One was arranged to look like a living room and the other like a lobby of some sort. The couple was instructed in one pose after another, with a change of clothing between the two sets; and the photographer was taking dozens of pictures. What that was all about escaped Cal, but it would've been more fun with Miles.

*   *   *

Jill took Cal to an empty parking lot. Now *this*, Cal could understand. She was finally going to learn to drive! Jill felt that the parking lot was a perfect place for her to learn the basics. Once Cal was proficient at that, she took her to a little-used country road to practice on-the-road driving. From there, she graduated to city driving.

"How'd you do today on the mean streets of L.A.?" Leonard asked from behind his newspaper that evening.

"Everything was great until I went the wrong way."

He lowered his paper. "Didn't you see the arrow that indicates a one-way street?"

"But it was a two-way street," Cal said.

He looked askance at her.

"I was coming out of an alley onto a street that only went left and right, and I didn't turn fast enough," she explained. "We blocked traffic for a little while, until I got the car to go in the right direction."

Leonard resumed scanning the newspaper. "Sounds like you'll fit right in."

* * *

They had done it again. When Cal and Miles were together, the evening seemed to fly. It was usually past her curfew before they realized it, and tonight was no exception. Miles had been away working on location for two weeks, so they felt the need to make up for lost time. Starting the evening early, she had dinner with his family. Afterward, the couple had gone to a movie, then to the ice-cream parlor, where they lingered over banana splits. Cal was delighted when some fans recognized him and asked for his autograph. It had been quite a full evening.

Now, it was long past midnight, and Cal knew what was awaiting her when she got home. She knew it wouldn't do any good to sneak in the back way; the man was born with radar. There was no way to get past him, unless…

Cal came to a halt on the sidewalk and looked up at the second-floor window of her bedroom.

"What?" Miles asked.

"Do you think I could climb up there?"

"I don't see how." Indeed, there were no trellises or pillars for her to climb. No trees were close enough to the window to be of any use. "You'd need a ladder."

She shrugged, "Yeah, I guess you're right." She kissed Miles goodnight, then came into the house through the front door.

"Well, it's about time!" roared Leonard.

"Time just got away from us."

"It always does."

"But it's Friday night. I don't have anywhere to go tomorrow and can sleep late. It's dumb to have such an early curfew on a Friday!"

"Rules mean nothing to you, do they?"

"This one, especially."

He took her by the shoulders and looked her in the eye. "Cal, this is going to be your last warning. The next time you stay out past midnight—the *very* next time—we're taking your telephone out!"

"But I *need* my phone."

"Then you'll have plenty of incentive to get home on time."

"But I don't have a watch. How can I know what time it is?"

"I'll buy you a watch."

"What if I forget to wear it?"

"Tough! Now get to bed." He locked the front door and turned off the lights.

She went upstairs and into her room. Something was missing. She shut the door and changed into her pajamas. Oh, yes! The shoving and hitting—*that's* what was missing. Coming in late just didn't seem the same without some knock-down, drag-out activity afterward. What had come over him? He'd been the epitome of self-restraint lately. Was he drunk or something? She didn't smell alcohol on his breath, so that couldn't be it. Ever since she and Jill had come back from her parents' funeral, these sessions had been much less dramatic.

She went to bed confused. "I'll never understand guys."

Chapter 9

TELEVISION WORK WAS REALLY FUN. Cal had enjoyed doing the Western. On horseback and in a ranch setting, she was right in her element. True, in her hometown of Dallas, she hadn't lived on a ranch; but her Uncle Antonio did, and her mother had taken her there often to visit. Not that Cal particularly wanted to see *him*, but she loved his horse, Winifred. It was there that she had learned to ride and care for horses. While her mother was having a nice visit with her brother, Cal could always be found either in the stable or riding Winifred in the field. Antonio found that he could get along quite well with Cal during these visits; she would always behave when her mother was around.

Now that this TV show and the *Campus Break* promo spots were finished, she sure hoped other opportunities to go riding with Leonard would pop up. That seemed to be where they were most compatible. He wasn't a hothead on horseback like he was in the living room after midnight on a weekend. In fact, he actually smiled when they were riding!

One thing Cal really enjoyed about this past week, aside from working with horses, was that it wasn't dragged out nearly as long as filming a movie would have been. You do it, and within a few days it's finished. A few weeks or months later, you'll see yourself on TV. Neat-o!

Her other television appearance would be filmed in a couple of weeks. She was to play a high-schooler again. Cal yearned to play something more sophisticated, but Pete impressed upon her that the image to be promoted for her was that of the little sprite next door. That, he said, is what would work best for her because of her short stature and winning smile. A heavier role just wouldn't work for her, he said. Well, okay. Maybe for a while but, sooner or later, she's bound to start looking older and can have some really serious roles, like the kind Leonard does.

Yeah, she thought, *exactly like his!* The roles in which she had noticed him the most before coming out here were those of the "bad guy." They were a lot more colorful than the hero and looked like a lot of fun to play. And they get to ride horses fast as they make their hasty getaways! Yep, she definitely wanted to be a television "bad guy."

Maybe taking some vitamins would make her grow taller.

* * *

"For me?" she asked as the postman handed her a package.

He looked at the label, again. "For Stacy Ames. This is the right address, isn't it?"

"Yeah. That's me. Thanks." She took it inside and opened it. It was a box of chocolates. "Hot digs!" A tiny card was inside. It read 'To the sweetest girl around, from a fan,' followed by an unfamiliar name. She grinned and went to find Leonard or Jill. He was in the study. "Hey, looky here. I've got myself a fan." She handed him the card and took a piece of the candy out of the box.

"DON'T EAT THAT!" he said so emphatically that it startled her.

"Why? You want one?" She held the box out to him.

"No! Give that to me." Leonard took the piece of candy from her, as well as the box. He then threw them into the trashcan.

"Hey! Don't do that." She went after them.

He pulled the trashcan out of her reach. "Don't you *ever* eat anything given to you by a fan. You don't know what's in it."

"But Len," she whined, "it's *chocolate*."

"I don't care if it's filet mignon."

Why did she come in here? Why didn't she just enjoy her candy in solitude? This guy was bound and determined to ruin every good thing about being a movie star.

Seeing that Cal obviously didn't understand the situation, he put his hands on her shoulders and looked her in the eye. "I'm not trying to be mean, Cal. This fan might have all the best intentions in the world and they might be perfectly good chocolates. But, then again, they might be laced with arsenic. There's no way for you to know the difference by looking at them, so it's best to throw them away."

"What's arsenic?"

"Poison."

She shook her head in frustration. "Fans don't put poison in candy. They *like* us, Len."

"You'd be surprised what fans will do. They've been known to kill. It's happened before, and it'll happen again."

Doggone it, Cal thought as she turned and left the room. *Why does he have to always be so dadgum dramatic?*

Leonard uncharacteristically emptied the trash himself, taking the contents of that trashcan to the large bin outside. He then got the garbage container from the kitchen and took that outside, too, dumping its contents atop the candy. That would guarantee that, should Cal find the chocolate, she wouldn't retrieve and eat it.

*   *   *

"Golly," Sue said over the phone, "it looks like you've had some terrific dates with Nate. Why didn't you tell me?"

"What're you talking about?" Cal wondered.

"*Screen Today*, of course."

"What?" She still didn't understand.

"You know. The magazine, *Screen Today*. There's an article with lots of pictures of you and Nate in it, and it shows y'all playing records and dancing in your living room and going to a movie and everything. Gosh, he's so cute! This'll drive Doris nuts!"

"I've never been on any dates with Nate."

Why is she playing dumb? Sue wondered. "Aw, come on, Cal. The pictures are right here—you and Nate dancing and having Cokes and going to the movies and everything. It says y'all met on the set of *Campus Break* and have been a hot item ever since. There's one goof, though. It says here that you were born in Italy."

Cal shook her head, "The whole thing's got to be a mistake, or...hey, wait a minute. Was I wearing a green shirt in that living room scene?"

"I can't tell. They're black-and-white pictures."

"Oh. How about in the lobby, then. Was I wearing a plaid dress?"

"Hmm. Yeah, you are. I guess California's changed you a lot. You never wore dresses to movies when you lived here."

Now Cal understood what had happened. "I still don't. We weren't really on dates. It's just publicity. All those pictures were taken on the same day at Stagecraft on a couple of their sets. The guy with the camera told us how to pose. We were supposed to look like we were having a good time, but all I was really thinking about was wondering how many photo sessions it would take to earn enough money to get an apartment."

"They paid you for that?"

"I think so. Len gets my paychecks and puts them in an account for me. As soon as I get enough, I'm going to get my own place."

"Neat-o!" Sue squealed. "You get to have a good time with Nate, and get paid for it, too. I want your job."

* * *

The next day, Leonard glanced over at the pictorial spread she was holding in front of him and shrugged, "Yeah, good publicity. So what?"

"It's a big lie, that's what." Cal said angrily as she closed the copy of *Screen Today* that she had gotten at the drugstore.

"Welcome to Hollywood, kid."

"Can't we sue them for malpractice or perjury or something?"

He tried to hide his amusement. That she was a doctor's daughter, and a very naive one at that, was obvious. "Stagecraft's publicist gave that story to the magazine. It wouldn't be smart to sue Stagecraft. Just look at it this way, Cal—it's great publicity, not only for the film, but for you, too."

"But it isn't true. None of it is, except the part about us meeting when we did *Campus Break*. And I was born in Dallas, not Italy. They've even got *that* wrong."

Leonard put his hand on her shoulder. "Cal, you've got to understand that, in Hollywood, celebrity is only ten percent substance. The rest is hype. The only time it does damage is when you start believing it yourself." He shrugged, "Hell, the studio is going to build up this story as much as they can because it brings more people to the theater to see the film. They did the same when Jill and I assumed guardianship of you. This picture is getting lots of publicity—some planned, some not. I'd be surprised if it *doesn't* score big at the box office."

She mumbled. "But it's just lies. That's all it is."

"If you want truth, go to Broadway. The stage is acting at its purest and most honest."

Oh geez, here we go again. Every time he gets on the subject of the Broadway stage, it turns into an impassioned speech, Cal thought. *Well, at least guest appearances on TV shows don't have as* much *hype.* She sure wished her parents were around to see her in that television Western. They would've loved it. The horse that the studio provided for her was a gentle filly named Alexandria the Great. Someday, she'd sure love to have a horse of her own—one just like that one.

She sighed as she went upstairs and into her room. *I'd better mail that page of Nate's autographs to Sue,* she thought. It didn't look like she would be getting back to Dallas anytime soon, and she was too distraught to remember it last time. Cal had really hoped to deliver them to her friends in person and tell them all about her Hollywood experiences. She had envisioned going to see the movie with her buddies and them all cheering and clapping when

Corky made her entrance in scene three, but it now looked like this lovely scenario would never happen.

As she dug around in the drawer of her desk, she sighed again. She sure missed being able to call her parents. They were excited for her when she used to give them a week-by-week report of her experiences here. Her mother, especially, was very pleased that Leonard had introduced Cal to Vincent Price. Cal didn't even know he was anyone famous until Jill told her. Until then, Cal thought he was just a nice man who knew a lot about art.

Ah, here it is. After Nate had thrown the crumpled-up sheet of autographs to the floor and left, Cal waited until she was sure he wasn't looking, then had retrieved it. She then had brought it home and stuffed it into her drawer. Now, she smoothed it out on her desktop. It's not in the best shape in the world, but Doris will think it's worth a million dollars, regardless. Cal tore the last note off and threw it away. Then she picked up a pair of scissors and cut the sheet so that each note was separate. After tearing a page from a notebook, she jotted a brief note to Sue, then put them all into an envelope and sealed it shut. Cal had Sue's address memorized. She had spent many a night at her house, staying up most of the night comparing notes about teachers and boys, and plotting new ways to annoy Uncle Ant. Cal addressed the envelope, then took it downstairs to Jill.

"Where can I get a stamp?" she asked.

"Oh, I'll mail that for you. Are you keeping in touch with your friends?"

"Yeah. They probably didn't have this address, so I wanted Sue to have it."

"That's good. Why don't you go see your new friends in the neighborhood? Since school's out, they would probably be home all day now, too. You really need to start getting out more, the way you used to. You must get bored when you're not working, don't you?"

"Yeah, kind of." She got a banana off the table, then went outside.

Cal began eating the banana as she strolled down the sidewalk to see which of her peers was outside today. It was a beautiful day in southern California. There wasn't any smog today, and she hadn't seen a dust storm or heard of any tornados happening around here the way they did in Texas. There sure were advantages to living in California. The earthquakes she had seen here so far were much preferable to tornadoes.

About two blocks down the lane, Cal encountered someone who appeared to be about her age, sitting on the large porch of a beautiful house, reading a book. When the girl looked up from her book, Cal yelled, "Hey, there!" and waved. The girl tentatively waved back.

Cal went over to greet her, stuffing the banana peel into her pocket. "Hi! I'm Cal Ames. You're probably the only kid around here I haven't met yet."

"Nice to meet you. I'm Becky Stewart, but I'm not really a kid."

"You don't look old."

"Well, I'm twenty, but pretty much on my own these days."

"You mean you own this house all by yourself?"

"Yeah."

"Wow! You must make big bucks! What do you do? Whatever it is, I want to do it, too. I'd love to have my own place."

"I do volunteer work part-time in a museum, but my dad's the one who bought me the house."

"Oh. How about letting him know I'm up for adoption?" Cal smiled innocently.

Becky dusted off the chair beside her. "Sit down. Would you like some iced tea?"

"No, thanks. What're you reading?" Cal asked as she sat in the chair beside Becky.

"*Joy in the Morning,* by Betty Smith, the same author who wrote *A Tree Grows in Brooklyn.* It's pretty good."

Neither book rang a bell with Cal.

Becky set the book down and looked her companion over. "Did you just move here? You don't sound like a Californian."

"I'm from Dallas and am here doing some TV and film work. I live a couple blocks away."

"So you've met all the kids in the neighborhood? There are a bunch of them."

"I've met Dottie, Miles, and Francis. Are there more?"

"Oh, yes! There's Maxie and Jennifer. And I'll have to introduce you to Nate Jenkins. Everybody loves him. He just lives a block away from here."

Hot diggity dog! Cal thought. *It won't be a boring summer, after all! I can torment poor ol' Nate for the rest of my life now—or at least until I get rich and move away.* "Yes, I'd like to meet him," she said as casually as she could.

"You know who he is, don't you? He's in films, too."

"The name's familiar."

Becky got up. "Well, come on. He just finished work on a picture a few weeks ago and doesn't have another one anytime soon, so we can probably catch him at home. He never travels if he can help it." She led Cal down the sidewalk in the direction of the Rhoads' house.

"Oh, so he lives between your house and mine," Cal noted. "I must've gone right past it a minute ago."

They went down the sidewalk a block and stopped at a wrought-iron fence, which was largely obliterated by hedges. From the street, all one could see of the property were the tall bushes.

"There's a house here? It looked like woods to me," Cal said.

"Uh-huh. There's a trick to this." Becky reached around to the other side of the gate. "You turn the knob clockwise on the inside, then push the button in the middle, and voila!" The gate opened. The girls went through, then Becky closed and relocked it.

Once they were a few steps beyond the gate, the greenery parted and the house came into view. It was a two-story house with a cobblestone walkway leading to the front porch. It had a well-manicured lawn and perfectly-symmetrical landscaping. Tall hedges surrounded the property on all four sides and now all she could see over the greenery were the tops of his next-door neighbors' houses.

"It sure is a big house," Cal said. "Must be a lot of Jenkinses living here."

Becky rang the doorbell. "No. Just Nate."

When a middle-aged woman opened the door, Cal's new friend went inside, saying, "Hi, Mrs. North. I don't have my key with me. Nate's here, isn't he?"

"Yes, ma'am," Mrs. North said. "He's in the den."

Becky yelled, "Nate! Come here a minute." Then she turned to talk to Cal and realized she was still out on the porch. "Come on in, Cal," she beckoned.

"Uh-uh. I don't go in strangers' houses." Cal then heard Nate's voice inside say "Hi, Becky." With a mischievous grin, she pulled the banana peel out of her pocket and dropped it right in front of the door.

Becky took Nate's hand. "We've got a new neighbor that you need to meet. Cal, come on in. He's not a stranger."

"Yes, he is. He'll have to come out here."

"Did you say 'Cal'?" Nate asked, as he stepped out onto his porch, followed by Becky. His foot slipped out from under him and he landed with a thud, accompanied by Cal's laughter. "One of these days, Cal, I'm going to *kill* you!" he warned bitterly as he got back on his feet.

"That'll never happen. You'd have to catch me first," she chided as she stepped behind Becky.

"I did once. I could do it again."

"That's only because the door was locked. You were just lucky that time."

"Okay, so you two *have* met," Becky said as she dusted off the back of Nate's pants, then she looked around at Cal. "I thought you said you haven't."

She grinned. "I didn't say that. I just said his name sounds familiar. It still does."

"Just my luck that *you*'d live around here," Nate said dryly.

"At Len's house." Cal's eyes twinkled.

Things were now coming clear to Becky. "You're not the 'Stacy Ames' they've been reporting about in the newspaper, are you?"

"In the newspaper? I thought it was in *Screen Today*."

Nate answered for Becky. "In the entertainment section of the newspaper and even in the gossip columns, they've been going on and on about how wonderful Leonard is to take you in when you were orphaned. They've really been playing it up big. You would think he's the most benevolent soul in the world, the way they talk. It's going to ruin his image."

"But it was Jill's idea, not his. Len probably wishes I'd run away or something."

"Well, he's the one getting the credit for it."

"Figures. I guess he'll have to play sheriffs now instead of bad guys."

"So you really *were* orphaned," Becky concluded as she digested the meaning of all this. "You weren't kidding when you said you're up for adoption. That's awful!"

"You bet it is! What makes it worse, I have only one living relative left in the whole wide world, my Uncle Antonio, and he doesn't want to have anything to do with me."

"Gee, I wonder why," Nate said sarcastically.

Cal grinned wickedly. "Yeah, he's a lot like you, Nate, only he yells in a different language."

He looked over at Becky, "Keep Cal away from me. I always seem to end up on the ground when she's anywhere near."

"Oh, Nate, that banana peel must have just fallen out of her pocket," Becky said soothingly. "I'm sure it wasn't intentional."

"Yeah it was," Cal piped up. "I figured he should get to know the floor of his porch as well as he knows the ground at the studio and on the beach."

"Well, anyway, I'm going back home. Just thought you'd want to meet the new neighbor. Sorry. Come on, Cal." She started back down the sidewalk.

As Cal turned to leave, Nate silently grabbed her by the back of the collar, punched her hard on the arm, then let go and went back into his house.

Cal was not about to let him have the last "word," but he had already gone inside and closed the door. She looked back around and saw that Becky was approaching the gate, completely oblivious to what had just occurred behind her. Cal yelled, "I've gotta' go home. I'll see you later, Becky."

Becky looked back and waved. "Okay. I'll leave the gate open for you. Be sure to latch it back. See ya." She then proceeded homeward and was soon beyond the hedges and out of sight.

Cal then went back to Nate's front door and rang the bell.

He opened the door and asked irritably, "What do you want now?"

"Just this." She punched him sharply in the eye, then turned and haughtily walked away. When Cal heard Nate's door slam and his quick footsteps behind her, though, she broke into a run. She knew that, once beyond the gate, there would be people around. Before she could get that far, however, Nate caught her by the arm and the back of her shirt, and threw her to the ground. He then fell atop her and tugged hard at her jeans.

"I'm going to kill you, Cal! I swear I am!" he yelled. The manic, out-of-control rage in his eyes and the determined set of his jaw startled her. It then became obvious that his intent was not only rape, but a brutal one. Terrified, she pushed against his chest with all her might. That didn't deter him, so she kicked her knee into his groin as hard as she could. Nate doubled over onto his side in agony.

Shaking uncontrollably, Cal scrambled to her feet, zipped her jeans back up, and ran all the way home. Once inside the house, she raced up the stairs to her room, locked her door, and fell onto the bed, sobbing into the pillow. What had started out as just good fun had turned into a nightmare!

A few moments later, her phone rang. Thinking it might be Sue, she dried her cheeks on the bedspread and forced herself to calm down, then answered it. It was Nate and he was livid. "If you try anymore of your stupid stunts," he warned, "I *swear* I'll make you sorry you ever knew me!"

"How'd you get our number? It's unlisted."

"I've got my ways," he said. "You'd better not breathe a word about this to anybody—and I mean *anybody*—or you'll *really* get it next time. You hear?"

Cal didn't know what to say. She had never let anyone intimidate her before, but was too frightened to defy him.

"Answer me!" he yelled hysterically.

That scared her even more. "Okay, okay!"

"If you dare say anything to hurt my image, Cal…"

"I won't," she said. Then she hung the phone up and buried her head under her pillow. More than anything in the world, she wished that she could go home to her parents now.

*   *   *

Leonard was surprised to see their gardener still there when he got home from the studio that evening. "Working kind of late tonight, Jack?"

"Yes sir, Mr. Rhoads. I wanted to get the bushes trimmed before the storm comes tomorrow. Can't work in weather like that."

"Well, that makes sense."

"Speaking of storms, looks like Cal's got one brewing, the way she went tearing into the house a while ago. She didn't even stop to say hello. Looked like she was crying. You might want to check on her."

Leonard shook his head, "At that age, Jack, everything's a crisis."

"That's true. Once people get my age, though, they realize very few things are worth getting that upset about."

"You're a man of wisdom, sir," Leonard smiled. He went into the house and looked through the mail on the table. Nothing urgent. He set it down, then went upstairs. Cal's door was shut. He knocked on it. "Cal, you in there?"

"Yeah." Her voice sounded different, kind of faint and dull.

"Are you decent?"

"Yeah."

He tried to turn the knob, but it was locked. "Let me in."

A moment later, Cal opened the door.

He came into the room and looked around. Her eyes were red-rimmed and her bedspread askew. "What's this I hear about you coming home crying? What happened?"

"Who told you that?"

"Jack."

"Oh." She sat on the bed, seemingly devoid of all energy.

He waited, but she didn't offer any explanation. "Well?"

Cal just shrugged. "It's nothing."

"You don't come running home crying over nothing, Cal. That'd be completely out of character."

"Maybe I was practicing for a part. Sometimes my characters might do stuff like that."

He folded his arms across his chest. "You don't want to tell me what it was all about?"

She shook her head.

"Why?"

"I just don't. That's all."

"Are you okay now?"

"Yeah."

"Whatever the problem was is solved now?"

"I guess."

"Okay." He mussed her hair and left.

*　*　*

The storm Saturday was enough to keep everyone indoors. Cal didn't want to go anywhere anyway. Except for an occasional clap of thunder, it was a quiet day. Leonard was up in the study, memorizing another script.

Jill looked into the media room. Cal had been there all morning, watching one film after another. "You really shouldn't have this equipment on during a storm."

"But I need it."

"Need it? Why?"

Cal shrugged, "I don't know. I just do."

Jill noticed that it was one of Leonard's films she was watching, one in which he played the sheriff who kept everything under control in his Western town. "Turn off the projector and come with me, Cal. I want to show you something."

"What?" She turned the projector off.

"It's time you learn to apply your own makeup. I'll show you how."

Chapter 10

THE FOLLOWING MONDAY, the studio car picked Cal up and took her to Stagecraft's Studio D for the taping of her next television guest appearance.

Having watched this situation comedy at home in Dallas many times, she recognized a lot of the people with whom she would be working. What seemed kind of strange, though, was that they just looked like regular, everyday people as they entered the studio that morning without makeup on. Cal made a mental note to buy an autograph book and bring it with her the next day. Her friends back home would be thrilled to receive it in the mail, every page filled with signatures of people they've seen on screen for so long.

As the week progressed, Cal realized that the director wanted her to play her character in this show exactly like her "Corky" character. That sure made it easy!

*   *   *

Before long, Leonard's film had wrapped and he was home all day again, preparing for his temporary move to Florida. While filming the series, he would be there all week, then fly home for the weekends.

As Leonard and Jill were getting ready for bed, he asked, "Why don't you and Cal come with me? Then I won't need to commute."

"Then *Cal* would be the one commuting. All her work is here in L.A. They're really keeping her busy, and giving her a lot of publicity, too, I've noticed."

He nodded, "She shouldn't be travelling alone at her age."

"Now, if you could get her some work on your series… ."

"Since I'm not the star, I'd better wait until my character is well established before making requests like that. I guess I'll just do the traveling until something comes up for her."

"I wonder why she wouldn't go to the party Stagecraft held for those kids. It was done to introduce them to the press and publicize the picture, I'm sure, but Cal absolutely refused to go. I assured her that Nate would be there, too, but she wouldn't change her mind."

Leonard chuckled. "Remember the party she wanted to go to with that cameraman a while back?"

"Yes."

"They ended up going there instead of to a film and turns out it was a pot party in some punk's apartment. Cal decided then and there that she doesn't want to go to anymore 'Hollywood parties.' She thinks they're all like that."

"Aren't some parties required, though?"

"Politically speaking, I guess they are. But she doesn't have to play by Hollywood rules. I don't. Staying away from parties might help to keep her out of trouble."

Jill smiled in agreement. "I guess we should just count our blessings."

"I'll go along with that."

*   *   *

Miles stroked Cal's cheek. "I'm going to miss you." At the end of their evening together, they were spending a few quiet moments parked in front of the Rhoads house.

"Yeah, I bet."

"Well, things like this happen. She wants an exclusive relationship. Don't be mad."

"Don't give it another thought. I'll be fine." Imagining Miles with Sherry was more than she could take. She was everything Cal wasn't—tall and beautiful, with the long, silky, blond hair that was so much the rage those days. She had a sweetness about her that reminded Cal of Jill. Sherry was the kind of girl any boy would want. "See ya." She opened the car door and got out. Miles got out of the car, too, but Cal motioned for him to get back in. "There's no need for you to see me to the door. I think I can manage to get that far by myself. Bye, Miles. Have a good life." She tried to hold back the tears until she got inside the house. Once inside, she closed the door, set her purse on the table, looked up, and gasped!

Leonard was standing there with her phone in his hands. The cord had been cut and was wrapped around the phone.

"You *didn't*!" she cried.

"Oh, I did."

She grabbed her purse off the table and threw it at him. "How *could* you? I need that phone!"

"You did it to yourself, Cal. You know the rules. You have a watch. It's past midnight. You chose to break the rules, so out the phone goes. You can't say I didn't warn you."

She ran to him and beat him on the chest with both fists. "I *hate* you! I *hate* you!"

He put the phone down and took hold of her arms. "If you want to get phone privileges again, you'll have to earn it. You'll have to come home before midnight four times in a row. Then, and only then, will you get your phone back!"

"Don't you ever get tired of being the cop?"

"Don't *you* ever get tired of being the delinquent?"

She pulled at her arms and he let go of them. Cal then left the living room in a huff, and went into the kitchen. She was badly in need of something chocolate. As she got a brownie and poured a glass of milk, Leonard came in. He got a can of beer from the refrigerator, then sat across from her at the table.

She took a bite of the brownie. "What're you staring at me for?"

"I was just going to ask you the same thing."

"I just can't believe you'd be so heartless."

"It's the people who let you have your own way for fifteen years who were heartless."

She slammed her hand on the table. "They are not! Don't talk that way about my parents!" She couldn't hold back the tears any longer.

"Well, they apparently didn't realize they were doing more harm than good. You never learned to respect authority. That's an extremely useful thing to know if you plan to go anywhere in life. The prisons are full of people who don't respect authority."

"My parents are good people!"

"I'm sure they *were*. But, to a certain extent, it takes a selfish person to raise a good kid."

"How would you know? You've never raised one."

"I am now. You have no concept of the enormous responsibility that's been put on us."

"If you don't want me, either, I'll just go away. I'll go sleep on a cot in an orphanage, or in a park somewhere." Her eyes were blurry with tears. "That's where unwanted people go."

"You're not unwanted, Cal," he said tiredly. "Save the melodrama for the studio."

"Well, what the heck do you want from me?"

"Obedience, that's what! A little respect would be nice, too. You'll find that you'll get what you give. If you give respect, you'll get respect."

"If I obey you, will you obey me?"

"Don't be a smart mouth." He set his beer down. "Once I start work on this series, I'll be home only one or two nights a week. I don't want to spend that time arguing with you. Do you think you can behave like a reasonable person and get home before midnight?"

She took another bite of the brownie, pondered the question for a moment, then sighed. "I'll do better than that. I won't go out at all." Then the floodgates opened and tears started streaming down her cheeks. "Miles is going steady with Sherry now." She put her head down on the table and sobbed.

This turn of events took Leonard aback. Why did this have to happen on the night he took her phone away? To give it back now would weaken his authority. He reached over and patted her head. "It's okay, Cal. You'll be all right."

"But I wanted him to be *mine*."

"I know. You'll survive." He took a handkerchief out of his pocket and handed it to her. "How about we get in another afternoon of horseback riding before I leave?"

Her sobs quieted down. She looked up and wiped her tears away. "Really?"

"I think we can work it in."

She sadly finished the brownie and picked up another one. Chocolate always made her feel better.

*   *   *

Campus Break was at last being released; and Leonard, Jill and Cal went together to its premiere. It was fascinating to Cal to see how all those scenes that had been filmed in such a disjointed way were put together to tell the story. And Leonard had been right—the music and other enhancements made a huge difference. It was a lot better than the dailies. Cal couldn't hold back her excitement as she saw herself and Leonard making their entrances. It was just incredible! It was amazing! It was also over too quickly.

"Wait a minute. Where's the rest of it?" she asked as the house lights came back on.

Leonard looked at her in confusion. "What d'ya mean 'Where's the rest of it'?"

"You know. The beach scene where the girls and I buried Nate in the sand. And the part of the dance scene when Jack and I were doing the Watusi. I wanted my friends to see that."

"On the cutting room floor, Cal. They don't use everything they film."

"But they left out the best part!"

"That's the way it goes, kid."

"And they filmed the water fight and used it for the intro. I didn't know they were going to do that. That's kind of neat," she grinned as she looked over at Jill. "That wasn't in the script."

"I know. Leonard told me about that."

Hmm, Cal thought, *it looks like the person who works in the cutting room decides what's in a movie. Maybe that's what I oughta' be someday. Then I could be sure it's done right.*

* * *

Cal's autograph book was starting to look quite impressive. The first page was Leonard's and the second had been Miles'. She had gotten all of the regular characters from that TV show to sign pages, then she had even gotten Becky to have Nate sign one. She made Becky promise not to divulge who the owner of the book was, but Cal knew that her friends wouldn't consider it complete without his autograph. She hoped she would have the book with her next time they bumped into Vincent Price.

And who knows what Pete would line up for her next? Leonard almost always seemed to have really famous co-stars, so maybe she will, too. She'd asked Leonard if he would take her book with him and have the other actors in his series sign it, but he refused. Yeah, she couldn't envision him asking people for autographs. He left without her autograph book.

A few weeks later, she got the long-awaited call from Pete. He had another film for her—an Italian character, a poor-little-rich-girl sort, the best friend of the lead character. Cal could hardly wait to do this one. It was quite natural for her to mimic her mother's accent—she did it quite often for fun—and now she'd even get paid for it! This film was to be shot in New York. Jill agreed to go with her since Leonard was tied up with the series. So the autograph book was packed and, ten days hence, to Manhattan they went.

They stayed in a hotel and a car picked Cal up each morning. In the evenings, Jill would help her practice her lines for the next day. On the weekends, Leonard would visit them there; and the three would go to a Broadway show. It was then that Cal fell in love with live plays. She had been in two in school, but they weren't nearly as resplendent as those on Broadway. She was simply dazzled!

"You think watching one is so great, you ought to try being *in* one," Leonard said, his eyes aglow. "The acoustics, the symphonic-like orchestra backing, the professional choreography, the best directors and playwrights on earth, the massive choices of lighting. It's out of this world!"

"No way! I'll be the audience. *You* be the Broadway star, if you want."

"Why not? You've been in plays before. What's different about this?"

"What's different between a school play and a Broadway one? The size of the audience, for one thing."

"The audience is so large because these actors are professionals. You'll be that way someday, I guarantee it."

"Not on Broadway, I won't. There's no way you're going to get me on any of *those* stages."

An extra bonus from these weekends in Manhattan was that Cal's autograph book was being filled up much more rapidly now, thanks to Leonard's willingness to take her backstage to meet some of the cast members after each show. Some of their names were quite familiar to her, from having seen them on *The Ed Sullivan Show*, on game shows, and in movies—so she was sure her friends would recognize them, too.

The actors who played her parents and friends in the film on which she was now working also signed her book. Cal could hardly wait to finish it and mail it to Sue. There was only one page left.

"I know the perfect person for that page," Jill told her. "She has fans all over the country and everybody loves her. I'm sure she'll be happy to sign it."

"And she's here in town? Who?"

"The star of the silver screen, television, and, someday—according to Leonard—stage, Stacy Ames!"

"Oh, yeah!" Cal had forgotten that she was now qualified to sign the book, too. So she made an elaborate autograph on that last page, then packaged up the book and mailed it to Sue.

*　*　*

While they were still in New York, Jill got a call from Pete. Cal's "Corky" character was needed again. The first film she did was grossing enough in ticket sales to warrant investing in filming the sequels, and the producers asked that Cal come back to reprise her original role. They wanted to film these two back-to-back, before she outgrew her character. A contract, committing Cal to work exclusively for Stagecraft Productions appearing in up to three pictures a year for the next seven years was sent post haste to the hotel in mid-week and Jill signed it as her guardian. As she put the signed documents in the hotel's mail chute, Jill smiled. Cal will certainly be excited when she learns how much Stagecraft Productions values her as an actress. So young and so new to the business, and yet she's already got a seven-year contract and a very good salary, with extra benefits, to boot!

Chapter 11

IT WAS GOOD TO BE BACK HOME AGAIN. Sleeping late was a luxury that Cal relished between projects. Having a sit-down breakfast every morning with Jill was nice, too.

The script arrived for the first sequel, which was tentatively entitled *Spring Fling*. It was vacation time again for Corky and the gang. As Cal read over the script, though, she inwardly groaned. Nate's character was in it, as well; although there was always a possibility that someone else would play it if he were tied up. None of the other characters were repeated from last time, so Cal wasn't sure who else would be in it. She *had* been told that Milan Royce would return as director, though, which suited her just fine. She liked him a lot.

The big worry in Cal's life right now, though, didn't involve her work. It seemed that Jill had been pale and fatigued a lot lately. At her age, that wasn't a good sign at all and was quite unlike her. In times past, it seemed to Cal that Jill had always had plenty of energy. Such a change in her health troubled Cal profoundly and she couldn't help but to fear the worst. Her parents had been suddenly taken from her, and now she was scared half out of her mind that it would happen again—this time to the beautiful woman who had become her surrogate mother. In her prayers every night, Cal promised God that she'd be good if He would only make Jill healthy again.

The day of Jill's appointment with the doctor arrived. She wouldn't let Cal go with her and, afterward, she returned home looking worried. Cal wanted so badly to know what the doctor had said, but Jill wouldn't tell her until she had spoken with Leonard. *Oh no!* Cal thought. *It must be really, really awful!*

"If you're real sick and need someone to take care of you, I'll take time off from work to do that," she offered. "Do you need an operation or something? Come on, just give me a hint."

"Later."

"Does it get worse or better?"

"I'll tell you later."

"It's not leukemia, is it? I had an aunt with leukemia once."

"No, not leukemia."

"Good. She died."

Cal's fears were driving her crazy, so Jill called Leonard early that evening instead of waiting for him to call her. She used the phone in their bedroom and had closed the door so their conversation would be private.

They must have had that room reinforced or something, Cal thought. *When the door's closed, I can't hear a single word from in there, even when I put my ear against it.*

The conversation with Leonard lasted a lot longer than past ones had. *What are they doing,* Cal wondered, *making out their wills?* Finally, Jill opened her door again to find Cal pacing the hallway.

"Okay. *Now* tell me," Cal pleaded. "Is it diabetes?" Jill put her hand on her young charge's shoulder, reassuringly. "We're going to have a baby."

Cal felt immense relief. It was as if the sun had started shining brightly again after a week of thunderstorms. Then excitement welled up within her. "Hot diggity! A little bitty person running around here. I can hardly wait!"

Cal had no idea what it was like to be pregnant. Being an only child, she had never seen her mother pregnant and none of her friends had been. Was it painful, she asked Jill. No, she just felt nauseated sometimes, but the doctor said that probably won't last very much longer. Jill assured Cal that she would keep her advised of any developments. If anything hurt, she'd be sure to let her know.

"If it's a boy, will you name him Len, too?"

"Len? I don't think so."

"Leonard, I mean?"

"Maybe."

"Leonard, Jr. Boy, ol' Len would love that! I'll teach Junior to ride a horse."

"What if it's a girl?"

"I'll teach her, too. She'd need a seatbelt. When you're on a horse, you do a lot of bouncing. She might bounce right off without a seatbelt."

The thought made Jill smile. She could see that the next six months would be long ones for Cal as she tried to take care of Jill without really knowing how. Thank goodness for *Spring Fling* coming up! That will give Jill some peace and quiet during the day.

*   *   *

"Keep it down in there. We're going to bed," Leonard said as he passed Cal's room on the way to his own that Saturday night.

She obligingly lowered the volume of her stereo.

"Maybe we should've put that thing downstairs," he said as he joined Jill in their bedroom and closed the door. Leonard took the bank book out of his pocket and tossed it on the bed. "Here. You'd better take care of that while I'm away." He then took his shirt off.

"What is it?" She picked it up. "Oh, Cal's savings account."

"It's a trust fund. I've been giving her twenty dollars a week spending money and putting the rest into this account. With the money she's earning now, residuals she'll get in the future and inheritance from her parents, she should have a pretty nice little nest egg when she's twenty-one. If you need money to buy her anything, just take it out of our own account. Hers requires my signature."

"I'm sure she'll be mature enough to handle it herself once she's eighteen. She wants to get her own apartment then."

He shook his head. "I don't think so. The money I give her now is gone in a matter of hours, usually at the record store. She's awfully impulsive. We'll just have to wait and see if that improves."

As Jill settled into bed, she looked anxiously at Leonard. "I'm a little worried about something."

"What's that?" he asked, as he sat on the bed and untied his shoes.

"To be perfectly honest, I'm worried that you might take out your frustrations on our baby, the way you do Cal. You know how concerned I've been about your rough treatment of her."

"I don't take out frustrations on anyone, especially babies. Why on earth would you ever think I'd abuse a baby?"

"From the very beginning, you told me you didn't want any children, and now I think I know why. Seeing how you treat Cal, I think you probably don't trust yourself to be gentle enough with them."

He turned around to face her. "You've met my brother. *He's* why I don't want kids. Autism is thought to be an inherited condition. I wouldn't wish that on anyone."

She looked at him sadly. "Just promise me you'll never harm the baby."

"You've got my solemn word on that. If it makes you feel any better, I won't even touch the baby."

"Make me another promise?"

"What?"

"That you'll never harm Cal, either."

"I don't harm her. Jill, you've got to understand that that kid went fifteen years without an ounce of discipline. It wasn't until she got here that she was ever given any rules."

"But I've heard you two banging around downstairs. Discipline doesn't have to be so physical, Leonard. I'm afraid you're really going to hurt her one of these days."

He shook his head. "Cal's tough. Don't worry about her. You want to know the truth? All I've ever given her is bruises. She's given me scars—real scars, Jill, on my shins. She reacts to discipline the way a two-year-old would, by kicking me in the shins. She's a physical person who's finally met her match. Being physical is the only way to make any impression on her."

"Well, I don't know..."

"I do. Trust me on this."

"But it's like you're trying to break her spirit. Please don't do that. She's got a beautiful spirit."

"No, I'm not. It's that spunky spirit that will get her places in her career. What I'm doing is bringing her under control."

"Control! That's it! It's like you're wanting her to be completely under your control. But she's not a possession, Leonard. She's a person in her own right."

He shook his head. "You just don't understand. I know what I'm doing. I know from firsthand experience how to handle an undisciplined child, because I *was* one, once."

She found that difficult to believe.

"Of course, that was long before you knew me; but it's true. I used to be very much like that. It takes firmness, consistency, and, yes, sometimes force to straighten a person like that out. In my case, it took a few police officers, one of which very wisely took me to see what prison was like. Believe me, Cal will thank me someday."

* * *

Now that autumn was well underway, a tutor had been assigned to Cal during the filming of these two pictures. Last spring, it had been so close to the end of the school year they didn't concern themselves with school or tutors for the kids. This year, however, they realized Cal's work for the studio would be ongoing and the law required her to continue her education. Between films, she would be going to a private girls' school; but while she was working, Mrs. Weinstein held class at the studio every weekday. They would go into the studio classroom, and Cal and two others would get private instruction. Usually such classes would contain more students, but Stagecraft had only three people under the age of eighteen actively working at the moment. This time, the actors who played her buddies were beyond high-school age in reality, but, like Nate, looked much younger.

And, yes, she found that she was, indeed, working with Nate again. Her pranks had ceased, however. She no longer had any desire to upset him, especially since Leonard wasn't around to protect her.

After the initial read-through on the first day, the actors involved in scene two were asked to stay; the rest were given their call sheets for the next day and dismissed. While the technicians were getting all the equipment arranged in accordance with Mr. Royce's instructions, Cal sat on the sidelines and looked over her script. *Yeah,* she thought as she scanned scene two. *I have that whole scene pretty much memorized already.* She put the script down and looked back up at the activity around the set. They were still positioning the lights and setting out all the props. Then she looked around and noticed that Nate was in his chair about twenty feet away from hers and was keeping a close eye on her. *Looks like he doesn't trust me,* she thought. *Well, I've got news for him. I don't trust him, either.* Throughout the filming of this picture, she would make sure that she was always near other people when Nate was around. Now that she had been made aware of how dangerous his anger could be, she had no intention of ever being alone with him again.

Everything was now ready and the director's assistant was calling the actors to the set. As she took her place, Cal was thinking that now would be a good time to have one of those out-of-body experiences she'd been hearing about. Whenever the script called for her to make any physical contact with Nate, she could simply depart from her body and be somewhere else. Why do people only seem to have those things they don't want to? Being anywhere near Nate now made her nervous. And the worst part of it was that he *knew* he now had the upper hand.

For the first time, Cal was sure wishing Leonard were here. When he's around, it seems almost nothing's so bad it couldn't be fixed. Just his very presence seemed to keep things under control. No one else around here had that ability—not even director Royce.

* * *

"Hey, kid," Leonard said Sunday morning as he passed Cal in the hall and mussed her hair. "How's the film going?"

"Okay, I guess."

"You guess? Don't you know?"

She shrugged.

"Haven't you been watching the dailies?" he asked.

"No."

He put his arm around her shoulders. "That's okay. Sequels usually aren't as good as the original."

"It's not that. It's just not the same without all those other kids we had the first time. They have older people playing high-schoolers now. It's just not very realistic. I mean who would believe Nate's seventeen? He's twenty-three, for Pete's sake! I think they ought to give his part to someone younger."

"Yeah, Cal, *you* be the one to tell his uncle that," he laughed. "Seriously, though, they don't have to worry about Child Labor Laws when they use adult actors. I'm sure they saw how expensive it was the first time to pay for airfare, meals, transportation, and accommodations for all those kids and their chaperons—and they only got one star out of the whole deal after going to all that expense. They probably thought they'd be credited for discovering more. And this time, they have the added expense and inconvenience of schooling. You *do* have a tutor at the studio, don't you? You don't want to get behind academically."

"Yeah. It's a lonely class. And it's only for twenty minutes at a time, then I'm needed on the set again. I miss being in a real school with a lot of real kids. When will filming be over on your series?"

"Okay, I can see something's really bothering you. Come on, we'll talk about it over breakfast."

They went downstairs and joined Jill in the kitchen. She was making waffles and sausage this morning, one of Cal's favorite breakfasts. As they sat around the table, Leonard helped himself to the sausages, then gave the platter to Cal. "Okay, what's the problem?"

She set the platter down. "Do I have to finish this film? Can I get out of it? I don't want to do the other sequel, either."

"Why?"

"I want to do more TV shows. And I want to do them somewhere else, away from this studio."

"I'm afraid that's out of the question now that Jill signed that contract."

"Well, will you be finished filming your series before they start the next Corky film? They really need you in it."

"You're hemming and hawing around, Cal. Tell me what the problem is."

"I can't."

"Why not?"

"I just can't."

"Then what can we do about it?"

"Finish your series and be in the set when I'm working."

"The only way I can do that is if they do your film while we're on hiatus. You've done a picture without me before and it seemed to go okay. What's different about this one?"

"I can't tell you."

Jill handed Leonard the platter of waffles and he took four, then passed it to Cal, who set the platter down without putting anything on her plate. She emitted a deep sigh.

"Aren't you hungry, Cal?" Jill asked. "You're not sick, are you?" She put her hand on Cal's forehead.

"No."

"But it's your favorite breakfast. Just have a little, okay?" she coaxed.

"Okay." Cal reached over and took a sausage. "I think I need to go back to Texas. I don't belong here."

Both Jill and Leonard looked at her with concern.

"Of course you belong here," Jill reassured her. "I need you to look after me. Don't you want to be here when the baby comes?"

"Yeah, but I think I'm in the wrong job. Maybe I ought to be a librarian or something." She took a bite of sausage.

Leonard was growing impatient. "Stop this right now, Cal, and get to the point! Did Royce criticize your work or what?"

"No, he's fine. I'm full." She got up. "I'm going back to bed. It's too early to be up." She scooted her chair away from the table and went back upstairs.

Leonard looked over at Jill. "What's that all about?"

Jill shrugged, "I don't know. She seems awfully discouraged, but I don't know why."

Having an actor's innate ability to interpret body language told him it was much more than that. "Something on the set is scaring her," he said. "She's trying to avoid something, but we can't do anything about it if she won't level with us."

"I can't imagine what would scare her."

"If the director was anyone but Milan Royce, I'd suspect he was being too hard on her. Has she said something to you about anyone at the studio? Is a technician coming onto her or something?" As Jill shook her head, he thought of other possibilities, "Another young actress who's jealous of her might be sabotaging her, or maybe she's in a scene she thinks is dangerous."

"There are a few beach scenes in it. Is she afraid of the water?"

He rejected that idea, "Can't be that. She's a good swimmer. We had a hard time keeping her *out* of the water in *Campus Break*. In fact, she's the one who instigated the unscripted water fight that was being shown behind the opening credits."

Jill nodded, "No, dear, I don't think Cal's afraid of anything. She probably just had a hard day yesterday. Monday will be better, I'm sure."

* * *

Oh, it was so great to be on horseback again! Cal and Leonard had been trotting single-file along the country road. Now that the road had straightened out and they could see any cars that might be coming, Leonard slowed his horse until Cal's was alongside. "Feeling better, now?"

"Yeah, lots. I wish I could live on a horse farm in Wyoming."

"You don't like my house?"

"Well, yeah, I do. Maybe I could become a horse trainer or a jockey or something."

"Let's race." He turned his horse off the road and into the field, as Cal's followed. "To the fence over there."

She positioned her horse, "You're on!"

"Ready, set, GO!"

They took off and were neck-and-neck for a little while, then Cal's horse had a burst of speed and got to the fence first. "I did it! I beat!" she said excitedly.

"Guess it's your lucky day. Dismount."

"I beat! I be--What?"

"Get off your horse. We've got to talk."

They both dismounted, and Leonard led Cal to a grassy mound, where they both sat.

"That's the first time I've ever beaten you," she grinned. "See? I'd be a good jockey."

"What's all this nonsense about leaving the business? I want to know what's *really* bothering you. No one else is around, so you can tell me."

A shadow of gloom came over her, banishing her high spirits. "No, I can't."

"Why not?"

She looked down and shrugged, "I just can't."

"Okay, if you won't tell me the problem, tell me the solution."

"Do you have to stay in that series the whole time? What if it lasts as long as *Gunsmoke*? Can't you leave it before it ends?"

"Give me a good reason why I should. It's starting to get good ratings."

"Because I need you here."

"Why?"

"I can't tell you."

He was quite exasperated. "Cal, if you ever want to know what drives a man crazy, just listen to yourself for a minute, will you?"

"I need more of those sessions in the media room. I need to know better ways to act. I'm not doing it right anymore."

"Why aren't you?"

"I've forgotten what you told me."

"That's a lot of bull and you know it."

She got back up. "Let's race some more."

"No, Cal." He took hold of her arm. "Sit down."

She sighed and sat down again.

"I don't want to leave the series," Leonard said. "It's a good series, I'm getting good exposure and making good money. But I *will* leave it if you can give me a compelling reason."

"Really? You'd do that for me?"

"If you have a *really* good reason."

She fidgeted.

"Out with it!" he said impatiently.

"Len," she looked at him pleadingly, "Nate's gotten weird and I need you around to keep everything under control."

"I thought *you* were the one making *his* life miserable."

"Well, that was back in the good old days. Everything's different now, and I don't like it."

"Sounds like he turned the tables and taught you a lesson, huh? Good for him! I didn't know he had it in him."

"You don't understand."

"Well, you know you had that coming. What'd he do? Tie *your* shoes together, for a change?"

"Len, he scares me. Every time the script has me getting close to him, I start shaking. Can't you be on the set when it's filming? I could do my job better if you were right there, so I'd know nothing bad would happen."

"I'll think about it." He stood up and went back to his horse. Cal did the same. They mounted and rode back to the road. "You really feel safer with me around?" he asked her.

"Of course, I do. Anyone would. Unless you're mad at *them*, that is. You could kill someone with your bare hands if you wanted."

"I've been mad at *you* before, and that didn't seem to bother you one whit."

"Aw heck, Len. I knew you wouldn't kill me."

"How could you be so sure? There have been times I've been awfully tempted."

She looked at him. "Well, I mean I know I can trust you. You're not a bad person."

"Shhh!" he said teasingly, in an effort to distract her from her fear. "Don't spread *that* nasty rumor around. It's my bad-guy image that paid for that house you're living in."

Chapter 12

"**Put your hand right here,**" Jill said as she guided Cal's hand to her mid-abdomen. "Do you feel it?"

"A little bit. Junior's moving around in there, huh?"

"A lot." In her sixth month of pregnancy, Jill was now in maternity clothes and Cal thought she had never looked more beautiful. She was so glad to have the opportunity to see the miracle of developing life, right here in the same house.

Just recently, Cal had gotten an advance on her allowance to buy a Christmas present for the baby. Of course, that meant she wouldn't get any more money for a few weeks, but it was worth it. Getting that advance from Leonard was no easy task, either. Cal had seen that super-deluxe rocking horse in the store, and it was on sale for only two more days. After that, the price would go back up. Once he understood the situation, he gave her the advance, along with a lecture about the advisability of saving up for something you want.

"Only a few more months," she said to Jill. "I wish we could make time hurry up. I can hardly wait to hold him."

"Or her," Jill reminded Cal.

"Yeah. You're still not hurting anywhere, are you?"

"Just a little backache now and then. The nausea is gone."

"Want a backrub? I'm good at that. Mom taught me how to do it."

"Okay. That would be really nice." She turned around and Cal started massaging her shoulders. "Right around the waist is where I need it." Cal obliged. "Oh, yes!" Jill purred. "That's wonderful."

"Can we put the crib in my room?" Cal asked. "When I'm not working, I can take care of the baby during the night. That way you can get a full night's sleep. Becky told me that babies want to be fed every few hours. This way, you can sleep at night and I'll sleep in the day."

"That does sound like a good arrangement, but Leonard wants to hire a nanny and maybe a part-time housekeeper to help out during the first year."

"You don't need a nanny when I'm here."

"Well, we'll think about it."

"I'm starting to think that's what you and Len say when you mean 'no.' He says that to me a lot, and he still hasn't quit his series."

"It doesn't mean 'no.' It means we're undecided at the moment. Is everything going okay on the set? This picture should be finishing up soon, shouldn't it?"

"Yeah. We have just a few more scenes to do. Today we had to do yesterday's scene over again. Mr. Royce didn't like the dailies of that one this morning. I sure wish Len was here. I'm supposed to do 'suspicion' tomorrow, and I'm not real sure how's the best way to do that. If Len were here, he'd find just the right film that would have that very thing on it and he'd tell me how it was done. And when we don't have a good example of it on a film, he just does it for me himself. When he's gone, I feel like I'm groping around in the dark about these things."

"Maybe the director can help you."

"Yeah, maybe. This TV-series business is for the birds. I don't like him being gone all the time, do you?"

"No, I don't either. But at least the house has been a lot quieter."

"What do you mean? He doesn't make a lot of racket."

"No, not by himself. But you and Leonard tend to have a lot of arguments when he's home every day."

"That's only because he won't see things my way."

"And you won't see them *his* way, either."

"But that's because I'm right."

"Cal, sometimes you need to compromise. There are some things he'll never change his mind about."

"He should, though."

"Maybe so, but he won't. You just have to come up with a compromise that will suit you both."

"Well," Cal smiled, "I'll think about it."

* * *

It had been a nice Christmas day. Everyone was home and spent the day together. At dinner that evening, Leonard had an announcement that served as the best Christmas present Cal had ever received. "I'm quitting the series at the end of the season."

Cal whooped with joy.

Jill was shocked. "Why, dear? I thought it was doing so well."

"I'm getting bored with it."

Cal was looking forward to life getting back to normal. Now, when she didn't know how to play a part, help would be available much sooner. Best of all, though, she would feel safe and secure again.

Off screen, she had kept her distance from Nate throughout the filming of *Spring Fling* and everything had worked out all right. She was hoping working in the second sequel would be similar to this one. It better be—it was due to begin in the second week of January, while Leonard would still be away.

Chapter 13

IT WAS DIFFICULT FOR HER, but Cal had to go to work on that Monday morning. Jill had given birth to an adorable baby girl the previous Thursday and Leonard was to bring them home today. Cal wanted so badly to be there when they got home and to hold that little baby in her own arms but, while Leonard's studio would allow him time off to be with his family, hers wouldn't.

The day went slowly for her, as was becoming painfully evident to the people around her. The normally-patient director finally threw his hands up in exasperation. "Cal, for the love of Pete, it's only ten minutes later now than it was the *last* time you asked what time it was! As soon as we finish with this scene, you can go home. But if you don't concentrate on your lines, you'll be here until midnight working on it."

That was all the incentive Cal needed to do her very best job ever. She psyched herself up to be completely focused on the scene at hand, and the next take was done to the satisfaction of all. Mission accomplished. She was now on her way home.

*　*　*

The moment Cal had long been awaiting was here at last. After she was comfortably seated, tiny Stacy Michelle Rhoads was placed into her eager arms. She had felt so honored when Jill had named this child after her, and now she was being allowed to feed her. After gently stroking her fuzzy hair and soft cheek, Cal took the warmed bottle and offered it to her little bundle.

"Hey! She sure knows what to do with this!" Cal said gleefully, as Stacy immediately got down to business. What a profound feeling of contentment it was to feed a baby whose tiny hand was wrapped around her pinky and whose trusting blue eyes gazed into Cal's. It was at that moment that she decided that someday she'd like to have a whole houseful of kids of her own.

* * *

Cal just couldn't seem to get enough of Stacy. All her life, she had wished she had a sibling. Now, it felt as if she finally did. Each day, she would hurry home to play with Little Stacy.

"The kid can't even get in a decent cry," said Leonard. "All she has to do is whimper a little, and you're right there to give her whatever it is she wants. She might never learn to talk, at this rate."

Nevertheless, Cal continued to enjoy the baby. It was a delight every time Stacy learned something new—rolling over, sitting up, picking something up with her tiny fingers. Once she had become adept at crawling, Leonard discovered Cal on her hands and knees, too, as the girls were exploring the various nooks and crannies of the house together.

"Taught you to crawl, did she?" he teased Cal. "Good girl. You'll be walking before we know it."

"Hey, Len, the world looks a lot different from down here. You ought to try it sometime." Then she added, as she looked way up at him, "You sure look like a skyscraper!"

He chuckled to himself as he proceeded to the easy chair to read his newspaper.

* * *

Cal was so glad that she was not working this week.

"Where's a doggie?" she asked the tot in her lap.

Stacy pointed to the picture of the dog in the book.

"Good girl! How about the horsie? You see a horsie there anywhere?"

The child looked the animals over and finally pointed to the horse.

"Yeah! And someday we'll ride a horsie, you and me. You want to ride one like Daddy does?"

Stacy looked at Cal and smiled. Then she refocused on the book.

Cal continued, "Okay, I see a cow there. Where's the cow?"

The little tyke turned around and pointed to Cal.

Taken aback, it was a moment before Cal realized that her nickname was pronounced like the animal. She laughed, "I mean the moo-cow." Cal pointed to the animal in the book. "See? The difference is this cow goes 'mooooo' and I go 'booga-booga-booga,'" she said as she tickled giggling Stacy's tummy.

She then set Stacy gently on the floor and put the book back in the bookcase. Cal then stood, looking out of the living room window. "I wish it was sunshining today so we could go outside," she sighed. Then she watched Stacy pull herself up into a standing position at the coffee table. That gave Cal an idea and she sat on the floor.

"Come on, Stace, come to Cal. You can do it," she coaxed, reaching out to the toddler a few feet away. When Stacy made her way along the length of the table while holding onto it, Cal shook her head, "Hey, that's cheating." She then scooted back away from the table so Stacy would have to walk on her own to get to her. Stacy flashed a sweet smile at Cal, and Cal grinned back, holding her arms out. "Come on. Come to Cal."

The child excitedly stiffened, then fell backward onto her derriere.

"Oops. Wrong way," Cal said as she lifted her back onto her feet. Once Stacy was steady again, Cal again scooted back a couple of feet and reached out. "Come on. I can catch you if you come over here."

Stacy held one arm out to her as she held on to the table with the other.

"Uh-uh. This time, *you* come to *me*. I know you can."

After a moment's hesitation, Stacy took a tentative step toward Cal.

"Yeah! Yeah! That's right. Come to Cal. I've got you."

Stacy took another step forward, then started wobbling. Cal steadied her, and sat back. Stacy then took one more step into Cal's waiting arms.

"You did it! You did it!" She gave the child a big, happy hug. "Jill! Come see what Stacy can do!"

A moment later, Jill came into the room. "What'd you do, sweetie?"

Cal then turned Stacy around to face her mother, and let go. Stacy then sank to her knees and happily crawled over to Jill.

"Hey, hey, hey," Cal said as she retrieved her and stood her upright again. "She can walk, Jill. She took three steps all by herself a minute ago. Go on, Stacy. Walk to Mommy." As Jill knelt down and held her arms out toward her daughter, Cal held onto Stacy's hands for her first step forward, then let go for the next one. Stacy had made that second step before she realized that Cal wasn't holding onto her.

Jill smiled broadly and scooped her child into her arms. "Good girl! You're getting to be a big girl, yes you are."

Cal felt a sense of achievement. Pretty soon, they would be walking to the park together. She could hardly wait.

Chapter 14

It was bedtime, but three-year-old Stacy was watching at the window, waiting for Cal to come home. Cal had been on location in Flagstaff, Arizona, for over six weeks and the film was finally finished.

"Come on, sweetie. You need to get your bath," coaxed Jill.

"Where's Cal?"

"Oh, I'm sure she's on her way. You'll see her before you go to bed, I promise you."

"Is she in the airplane?"

Jill looked at her watch. "No, baby. Her plane must have been late, but I'm sure she's in her car on her way home right now. By the time she gets here, you'll be squeaky clean and ready for bed." She picked up her little girl and took her to the bathtub.

* * *

When Cal opened the front door, Leonard looked up from the newspaper. "It's about time. You're late."

"Yeah," she said as she set her luggage down and closed the door. "The plane circled around for twenty minutes before finally landing. I thought I'd be spending the rest of my life in the air. Is Stacy still awake?"

"Yeah, upstairs."

Cal ran up the stairway. "Where's that little Stacykins?" she called.

She heard a squeal of delight and water sloshing; then the naked, sudsy child came running down the hall and bounded into Cal's outstretched arms.

"Oooh, Stacy, you're all wet!"

"What'd you bring me?" Stacy asked.

Cal held her with one arm and reached the other hand into her pocket. "A little bar of soap that has your initial on it! See the S? S stands for Stacy. Isn't it cute?" She handed her the souvenir from the Sheraton Hotel.

"Yeah!"

"It's just your size." She kissed her soft little cheek. "I think we'd better get you back in that bathtub now." She carried her to the bathroom. "Hi, Jill. Sorry about that."

"Look, Mommy. My own soap," Stacy showed Jill excitedly. "It has my name on it."

"That's very nice, sweetie."

Cal put her back into the tub, took a towel from the rack, then dried her arms and the front of her clothes as she went downstairs to the living room. Leonard set his newspaper down. "This isn't a very good time of year to be in Arizona, is it?"

"No. It's awfully hot, and we had a lot of outdoor scenes. I wonder if our skin was a different shade by the time we were done. We probably won't match from one scene to the next. If I were the director, I would've shot our scenes in sequence for that reason."

"I'm sure the Makeup Department took care of that."

She sat on the sofa and propped her feet up on the coffee table. "I was working with one of your old friends, Alex Stevens. He said to tell you 'hi.'"

"I haven't seen him in—I bet it's been fifteen years. We did a play together back when we were both new in the business."

"He was playing my love interest in this picture. Can you believe that? He's your age!"

"It's not all *that* unbelievable, Cal."

"I guess guys don't age the way gals do on screen, huh?"

"I don't know why it is. A love scene between an older man and younger woman works well, but the public doesn't seem to accept an older woman with a younger man, as a general rule."

"Well, at least I was a college girl this time; just a freshman, though. But for a while, I was afraid they'd have me playing kids forever. I'm glad to be home. I don't like working on location for such a long time."

"But you see? You were afraid to make this trip all by yourself, but you did it and everything turned out just fine, didn't it?"

"Yeah. I'm glad you told me step-by-step what I had to do, though. I wouldn't have known who to call for transportation or anything once I got there."

"It's a piece of cake, Cal. Don't ever be afraid to try new things."

"Well, I'm doing something new in the show we start working on next week. I play a kid on crutches who's a whiz at the piano."

"Have you ever used crutches before?"

"Nope. That's why I said it's new."

"We'll have to rent you some, then, so you can get used to them. We'll do that first thing in the morning."

"Okedoke. And I guess I'd better learn how to play the piano, too."

"Did they say you had to?"

"Well, no. I just assumed… "

"Don't worry about it, then. It'll be dubbed." He started lifting his newspaper back up, then stopped. "Oh, you *did* miss something while you were gone. My dad and brother came to visit. This is the first time they've ever been here."

"From New York?"

He nodded. "They consider that a long trip. That's why they don't come out here more often."

"How old is your brother? Does he look like you?"

"He's six years younger than me, and I don't think we look at all alike. People say that Dad and I look alike, though. Darrell looks more like our mother."

"I'd like to meet him. Is he single?"

Leonard smirked, "Yeah, he's single all right. I don't think he's your type, though."

"Oh, I don't know about that. He might be."

Leonard became more serious. "Cal, he's autistic."

"What's that mean?"

"It's a developmental disability. He's physically healthy, but he doesn't perceive things the way we do. I don't know if his behavior is because of his perception or not, but he doesn't behave like we do, either."

"Oh," Cal said with a mischievous glint, "you mean he's nicer than you?"

He gave her a lighthearted scowl.

"Oh, and guess what," she said. "Alex and I went horseback riding while we were there in Arizona. He said it'd be a shame to be in ranch country with a Texan and not go riding. So we did."

Leonard's smile faded. "What else did you and Alex do?"

"What do you mean?"

"Go out to dinner? Go to a show?"

"No, nothing good like that. We had trailers during the outdoor shots because they were shooting so far out in the boonies, and he entertained a bunch of us in his trailer. He plays guitar really well."

"That's good."

"And he came to my trailer a couple times."

"What for?"

"He said I needed help with my part, so we went over it. I guess since you weren't there to coach me, I'm glad he was."

Leonard eyed her with concern. "What kind of help did he think you needed?"

"He said I wasn't being emotional enough."

"Just what emotion did he want you to demonstrate? Was he alone with you in your trailer?"

"Good grief. You sound like Perry Mason. I feel like I'm on the witness stand."

"Answer my questions."

"Well, yeah, he came when I was alone."

"And?"

"Nothing, Len. Like I said, we went over my part. What's the big deal?"

"What kind of part was it? What kind of scene?"

"I don't remember." She got back up. "I'm going to bed. It's been a long day."

"A love scene?"

She didn't answer, because she knew exactly what he would say if he knew the truth—that it had, indeed, been a love scene and Alex had tried to take it further than the script did. Cal was sorry she had mentioned him now.

Leonard got up, too, and grasped her by the shoulders. "Be careful, Cal. Guys like him have been known to take advantage of girls like you."

"I can take care of myself, Len. I'm eighteen now, not a kid anymore."

Jill came down the stairs. "Stacy is temporarily in bed. Next time, will one of you put her back in?" she asked. "I want to polish my nails tonight. Cal, did you have a good flight?"

"It was a little bumpy, but they served a good dinner. We had lasagna and chocolate cake. No movies, though. I'll see y'all in the morning. G'night." Now would have been a good time to go to her room, but she couldn't move. Leonard was still holding her firmly by the shoulders and looking her in the eye, as though the interruption had not taken place. Cal returned his stare.

"Just remember what I said," Leonard continued. "Be careful around him. If he ever does anything inappropriate, let me know and I'll take care of it." He released his grip on her shoulders.

"He won't." Cal picked up her luggage and went upstairs, as she was thinking, "Inappropriate by whose standards? Yours or mine?"

* * *

Becky and Cal had been swimming in Becky's pool the next morning, and were now lounging in the reclining chairs nearby.

"I met the cutest guy at Dad's lawyer's office while you were gone," she excitedly told Cal. "His name's Johnny."

"Did he ask you out?"

"A couple times. He's a really nice guy. I've got to show him to you one of these days."

"Sounds serious."

"Well, not this soon. But it does show a lot of promise," she grinned. "Now you need a boyfriend, too."

"I've given up on guys. I'm through with them."

"Oh, you can't mean that. One of these days, someone will come along who will make you forget all about your vow of celibacy."

"Forget my what?"

"I was hoping it'd be Nate."

"No way! Whatever that means, it won't be Nate."

"What? You don't want him to be celibate, either?"

"Heck, no!"

Becky smiled at the joke, knowing that Cal had no idea what the word meant. "What a shame. I was hoping we could have a double wedding."

"I'm going to stay single forever," Cal said emphatically.

"If Miles were a little older, *I* could really go for him."

"Go ahead and go for him, anyway. Age is just a number. It shouldn't keep you from going out with him. He's one of the nicest guys I've ever known, and really cute, too. And he sure can kiss! I really miss that."

"So you're going to be Miss Prude now? No more boys and no more kisses because you want to be single forever?"

"Well, I *did* kind of have a good time with a guy in Arizona. He even likes to ride horses."

"That sounds like the way I envision Arizona natives."

"Oh, he's not from there. We were just making the picture together there."

"Oh, another actor. It must've gotten hot and heavy then, huh?"

"Just a little. The only trouble is Alex is almost forty. I don't know why I was attracted to him."

"Well, like you say, age is only a number."

"Yeah, I guess so. Then I made the mistake of mentioning him to Len, and he started lecturing me again. He thinks I'm still a dumb kid."

"Got to cut the cord sooner or later."

"Yeah. Now if we can only convince *Len* of that."

*   *   *

Cal returned home at the same time that Leonard did. After retrieving a set of crutches from his car, he walked with her into the house. "I want you to use these for the rest of the weekend so by the time you walk onto the set Monday morning you'll have a good feel for them," Leonard said.

Once inside, she took the crutches, put them under her arms and started walking with them.

"No, not like that. People don't move crutches the way they move their legs. You're supposed to move them together." He took them away from her. "To the media room."

Cal followed him into the familiar room and settled on the sofa. Leonard chose three film cans from the shelf and sat beside her. As he loaded the projector, he instructed, "Watch this closely for crutch technique."

* * *

As Jill was frosting a cake for that night's dinner, she heard what sounded like glass breaking in the living room. "Is everything all right in there?" she asked.

"I'm sorry, Jill," Cal answered, "I didn't mean to break your lamp."

Leonard gave Cal further instruction, "Don't use the crutches to point with and our furniture will last longer. Use them just for ambulation, that's all. Try it again."

"It's not as easy as it looks."

"When you're doing it, Cal, it *doesn't* look easy. Try it again."

She hobbled the length of the living room, turned around, then returned to her starting point.

"You're starting to get it. Do it again."

"My arms are getting tired."

"That's okay. Your character's arms will be tired, too, so you'll understand how it feels. Do it again."

Again, she made her way to the other end of the room and back. "We need to get you a set, too" she said, "so we can have a race."

"Come on," he said heading toward the door. "We'll try it outside, on an uneven surface."

She carried the crutches and followed him.

"No!" He stopped her. "Come out here on crutches. I told you I want you to use them *continually* all weekend. I don't want to see you walking at all until Monday morning. Even if you sleepwalk, I want you to do it on crutches."

She sighed, tucked the crutches under her arms, and hobbled out onto the porch. When she got to the four steps, though, she abruptly stopped.

"Go on. You can do it," he urged.

"Heck no! I'd fall on my face."

Leonard went down the stairs. "Take it one step at a time. I won't let you fall." He stood on the bottom, with his arms outstretched, in case she needed to be caught.

Cal gingerly placed the crutches on the first step, then carefully swung her feet down.

"That's right. Keep coming." He took a step backward, to give her more room.

She came down the next step, and the next, until she reached the bottom, then proceeded along the sidewalk.

Leonard backed out onto the grass. "Now come out here. Let's see how you do on this terrain."

"Isn't it lunchtime yet?" she asked, plaintively.

"Not yet. Come on."

She came out onto the grass, but the tips of the crutches sank into the soft ground.

"No, that's not going to work." He went back onto the sidewalk. "Just practice going up and down the walkway, then. The cobblestones will be uneven enough."

Leonard had wanted Cal to know not only the physical feeling of being crutch-dependent, but the emotional feeling, as well. To demonstrate that, they went into town. Once there, they posed as shoppers, going from store to store. This jaunt was interrupted by fans here and there who recognized them and asked for autographs. Cal had fun with the people who expressed concern for her condition, asking how she had injured her leg. Her lighthearted explanations ranged from having had a skiing accident to a sky-diving scene going bad. Many people just stared at them, but it was the people who had not recognized Cal and Leonard that were the ones from whom she learned much. She found that they either had pity in their eyes, or they avoided looking at her at all. If they spoke, it was usually to Leonard, not her. Being ignored in such an obvious way annoyed Cal. Once, she had gotten the saleslady's attention by tapping her derriere with her crutch, but had been reprimanded by Leonard for that. She wondered how people who were permanently on crutches dealt with such treatment.

By the time Monday morning came, Cal's underarms were quite sore but her crutch-walking technique was very good. She had learned to convincingly ambulate forward and backward, up and down stairs, on carpet, tile, and cobblestone surfaces.

* * *

Thanks to Leonard, the ensuing week went very well. The show's director complimented Cal on the realistic portrayal of her character. She was believable, he said, but not overly sentimental, which was exactly what he wanted.

Her lack of skill at the piano was no problem. When she sat down at the instrument between scenes and mimicked a concert pianist, absolutely no sound was produced. Cal then lifted the top and discovered it was hollow inside, with nary a string or hammer to be found. Leonard had been right, again. The beautiful music was, indeed, to be dubbed in by a professional.

She returned home that Friday evening convinced that she had done a fine job.

Chapter 15

CAL RIPPED THE ENVELOPE OPEN and read its contents eagerly. It was Sue's graduation announcement with a letter enclosed. As a graduation present, Sue's parents were treating her to a trip anywhere in the country she wanted to go; and she chose California. Would it be all right, she asked, if she and her parents visited for a few days?

Cal waited until everyone was together for dinner, then excitedly asked Jill and Leonard if they could let Sue's family stay there at the Rhoads house. "We have a couple of guest bedrooms and there's only three of them, Sue and her parents. Please?"

But those bedrooms were for *their* guests, people they knew personally, Leonard explained. They couldn't open their home to strangers. But they would be happy to make reservations for them at a nearby hotel.

"But *I* was a stranger," she countered.

"That was a completely different situation," he answered.

"How about if I let them stay in my room and I sleep in the guest room?"

"No, Cal."

"Boy, you can sure tell y'all aren't Texans," she complained. "We'd *never* make a friend stay in a hotel."

Leonard had his business manager, George, make hotel reservations for Sue's family; and Cal met them at the airport. When Sue appeared at the gate, the girls ran together in a big bear hug. They chatted and laughed all the way from the airport to the hotel, a twenty-five minute drive.

During their three-day visit, Cal drove them to the sites that they had wanted to see—Grauman's Chinese Theatre, the corner of Hollywood and Vine, and Warner Bros. Studios.

"This is really neat that you have your own car now," Sue said the next day when they were alone. "It's pretty, and so big. Mine's a little sports car."

"Yeah, yellow reminds me of sunshine and daffodils. I wanted one of those cute little Mustangs, but Len said the only way he'd co-sign for my car is if I got a full-sized one. He says they're safer. And I'm paying for it myself. I handle my checking account and he takes care of my savings."

"Can you please, *please* introduce me to that dreamboat Nate Jenkins?" Sue gushed. "Doris will just die if she finds out I met him in person. She's got pictures of him all over her bedroom wall."

"But he's better looking on the screen than in person. You don't want to be disappointed, do you?"

"There's no way he could disappoint me. Please?"

"He's only three feet tall, you know. He has to do his scenes standing on a box."

"Oh, he does not," Sue good-naturedly scolded. "*Movie Fan* magazine said he's five foot ten, has dark-brown hair and beautiful brown eyes. Doris calls them 'bedroom eyes.' And he's got broad shoulders and a cute butt, too. I wish I could give it a little pat," she grinned.

"*Movie Fan* magazine said *that*?"

"Well, I added the part about the shoulders and butt myself."

"He's really got all those things? I never noticed."

"All that and more. And charities love him. He's always donating big wads of money to them, so he must be a really nice guy."

"I don't even know if he's in town this week. Actors do a lot of work on location, all over the world, you know. Len's made movies overseas sometimes. Hey!" she remembered. "Len's a better actor than Nate. You want to meet him?"

"Yeah, maybe him, too. But especially Nate. What was it like to kiss him? Was it heavenly?"

"Oh," Cal shrugged, "he's the same as any other guy."

"If it had been me, I would've kept messing up my lines so we'd have to do that scene a hundred times in order to get it right," Sue grinned. "You're so doggone lucky."

"I can't remember how many takes it took. Probably just one or two for each camera angle, I guess, since the other kids weren't in that scene."

"I brought my camera so I could get some pictures. Would you take a picture of Nate and me together?"

"Oh, okay." It looked like Cal wasn't going to be able to get out of this one, unless he was out of town. She could hope, anyway.

* * *

With Sue along, surely he'll act like a movie star and not like his real self, Cal thought as the two girls went through the wrought-iron gate and up the sidewalk to his house. It seemed funny to her that Sue was so excited at the prospect of meeting Nate. Leonard would've been much more impressive.

Cal rang the doorbell and looked over at Sue, who had her hand over her heart and was looking skyward. "Pledging allegiance to the flag?" Cal asked.

"No, just wishing my heart wasn't beating so hard. Oh, gosh, I hope I don't faint. That would be so embarrassing."

"Want to call the whole thing off then?"

"No!"

Nate's housekeeper answered the door. "Yes?" she asked. "Can I help you?"

"Nate's not in town today, is he?" Cal asked, hopefully.

"Who may I tell him is calling?"

Darn! "Tell him that Cal Ames has brought a fan to meet him."

"Oh, Cal," she smiled. "Good to meet you. Please come into the sitting room and wait there. I'll tell him you're here."

Cal had the uneasy feeling of being lured into a trap.

Mrs. North led them to the appropriate room, then left through the tall double doors, closing them behind her.

"I've seen doors like that on *The Loretta Young Show*," Sue said.

Cal looked around and saw some elaborately-framed photos on the wall by the fireplace. She went over to take a closer look, then came back. "They're just pictures of him with famous people."

"What famous people?" Sue asked as she went over to see. "Ooh, Elizabeth Taylor and Richard Burton in this one! And Dyan Cannon here. How neat!"

The double doors opened and Nate came in. "Oh, I thought it was another of your tricks," he said to Cal.

"Nope. This is Sue. She's from Dallas and wanted to meet you. Sue, here he is," Cal grinned to her buddy. It was fun to see Sue's dream come true, misguided though it may be.

Nate reached out and shook Sue's hand with a pleasant "How do you do?"

After a moment, Sue found her voice. "I've seen all your movies and you're great in them! Really great!"

"I appreciate that. It's fans like you who make everything worthwhile. Which film was your favorite?"

"The first one you did with Cal, *Campus Break*. You looked *terrific* in that swimsuit."

"You think so?"

"Oh, boy, do I ever!"

"How about you, Cal?" he asked wryly. "Do you think I looked terrific in that swimsuit?"

Cal smiled pleasantly, but didn't comment. She wanted to make this a happy experience for Sue, so she was determined to be civil to Nate.

He turned back to Sue. "Cal's always telling me I ought to be showing more skin in these flicks. She has a hard time keeping her hands off me."

"I do not!" Cal objected. She could go along with this movie-star charade only to a point.

"Did you see me my latest release, *The Midnight Caller*?" he continued to Sue. "That's the picture I'm proudest of."

"Yeah," Sue said eagerly, "it's a mystery and you turned out to be innocent. Everyone thought you were the guilty one!"

"That happens so much in life, doesn't it? Things aren't always as they seem."

"I'll say!" Cal said pointedly.

Sue agreed, "I guess so. Cal and Doris and I used to see your movies together back in the ninth grade. Cal might have been drooling over Van Roman, but Doris and I definitely had our eyes on you, and so did half the other girls in school. Cal's always had weird taste."

"Hey, Sue, didn't you want to give him a pat?" she grinned mischievously at her friend. "Now's your chance."

"Oh—no, no, that's okay," Sue said uncomfortably.

"You sure? What was it, again? His cute what?"

"Cal!" she yelled. "Stop it!" Sue wouldn't *dare* faint now. She had to stay conscious to keep Cal's mouth shut.

"So you're from Dallas?" Nate asked. "What brings you to sunny California?"

"This trip is her graduation present," Cal answered. "She makes straight A's, so I used to sit beside her on test days."

"Is that why?" Sue asked. "I thought you sat beside me because I was your best friend."

"Yeah, that too. Didn't you want me to take a picture of you two with your camera?" Cal asked.

"Oh, yeah!" Sue agreed. "But first let me take one of you and Nate together, then you take one of him and me."

"You don't want me in your pictures," Cal said. "Give me that camera."

"Yes, I do. You get over here for a minute. I want a Corky-and-Mike picture," Sue said as she stepped back a few feet and looked through the viewfinder at Nate.

Cal took a step toward Nate, then looked at the camera and smiled.

"Oh, come on, Cal. Get closer than that. It looks like y'all are strangers or something," she admonished her friend. "You can't fool the kids back home. They know y'all are buddies and make movies together all the time."

"Yes, come on, Cal," Nate joined in. "Get nice and close. Don't be shy." He took her arm and pulled her in front of him so they were both facing the camera, then he wrapped his arms around her waist so tightly her ribs hurt.

Cal whispered to him, "Ow! Stop it." When he didn't, she covered his arms with her own and discreetly dug her fingernails into his flesh.

"Smile for the camera," he said, without changing his hold on her. "How's this, Sue?"

Sue smiled. "That's more like it. Smile, Cal."

Cal knew that if she didn't force a smile, she'd have to stand here and be squeezed to death all day, so she smiled gaily for Sue, who snapped the shutter, advanced the film, then handed the camera to Cal and announced, "My turn."

Nate released his grip on Cal, and she was finally able to take a deep breath again. She looked the camera over as she switched places with Sue. "It's just like mine. Okay, you ready?"

Nate put his arm around Sue's shoulders and smiled obligingly at the camera. Sue had an ear-to-ear grin. "This'll really make Doris green with envy!" she giggled. "She said she wishes she could be Cal's stand-in when y'all do a love scene together."

Cal snapped two pictures, then lowered the camera. "Okay. All done. Can we go now?"

Sue turned around and shook Nate's hand again. "I'm so glad to have met you. I'll see you at the movies."

"Good meeting you, too. Tell Doris hello for me," he said as Cal gave the camera back to Sue and headed toward the door.

Sue reluctantly followed. As they went out the door, back down his sidewalk and toward the gate, Sue looked back and waved once more as Nate acknowledged her wave, then closed the door. "What did he mean when he said he thought it was another of your tricks?" Sue asked. "Cal, *please* tell me you don't pull any of your shenanigans on *him*."

"I don't anymore," she replied. "Now you want to meet a *real* actor?"

"I just did."

"I bet Len's home. I want you to meet him."

"Tell me again who he is. In the movies, I mean. I know you live in his house and everything, but what movies has he been in?"

"That's the problem with being a character actor. People recognize you when they see you, but they don't know your name. Len was the policeman in *Campus Break*, and he's been in lots of Western movies and a guest star on just about every Western TV show there is, and he was a regular on *Chisholm Trail* for a year. He played Duke. You'll know him as soon as you see him. He taught me everything I know about acting."

"You were acting all the time at school, whether you were supposed to or not."

"Well, I mean the professional kind. That's a whole different ballgame." She led Sue down the street and cut through the front yard to the Rhoads house.

"Golly, everybody around here has such big houses," Sue noted.

"And the funny thing is it seems the biggest houses only have one or two people living in them. Nate lives alone."

"Golly, really?"

"Yeah. Len tells me that people usually make enough money to buy a house after they've been acting for about ten years or so. That's what I'm saving for. He told me a house is a lot safer than an apartment for a single girl. He said apartments get broken into a lot."

"I bet Nate hasn't been acting for ten years," she said as they got to the front door of the Rhoads house.

"Well, he probably earns a lot more than most people because his uncle's such a hot shot."

"So is he."

They went through the door, into the living room, then to the kitchen. "I really didn't think Len was in *here*, but I'm hungry." Cal took a banana off the kitchen table and offered it to Sue.

"No, thanks."

She then peeled it and took a bite as they continued looking through the house. "Oh, I want to show you something first. Come here," Cal said as she led Sue into the media room. "Isn't this the most perfect room you ever saw? All this neat stuff in here, but they won't let me have a party. What a waste!"

"What *is* all this stuff, anyway?"

"Projection equipment mainly, so we can watch movies right here. See all those metal containers on the shelves? They're his films, and mine, too. And he has all his TV shows on film. And, of course, the usual TV set and stereo and all that stuff. He has video and audio recording machines, too. Maybe we can watch a movie tomorrow if your parents don't need you for anything."

"Mom planned a couple of those guided tours tomorrow and they want me to go along."

"Aw, shoot." They continued their journey through the house. Cal started going up the stairs.

Her friend hesitated. "Shouldn't I stay down here?" Sue asked. "It's bedrooms up there, isn't it?"

"Yeah, but his study's there, too. He spends a lot of time in his study. That's where he goes to learn and practice his lines. He's doing a TV show next week, so he'll probably be in there. Come on." They proceeded up the stairs.

Leonard was at his desk and looked up from his script when he heard them enter.

"Len, this is Sue." Then she looked at her friend, "Recognize him now?"

"Oh, yeah! I've seen you a hundred times in movies and on TV."

He stood up and shook Sue's hand. "Good to see you."

"Say it, will you," Sue asked him eagerly, "what you said to Corky when she handcuffed you to your police car?"

Leonard set his script down and instantly became an irate Officer Stanton…

> *… grabbing Corky by the collar with his free hand. "You little hoodlum! Get out of here, right this minute! Get out of town. Hell, I'd blast you to the moon if I could!" Then he let go of her collar and became calmer. "But first," he cleared his throat, "uh, where's the key to the cuffs?"*
>
> *Corky shrugged and held her hands out innocently, "Why, I don't know. Don't you have it?"*
>
> *"You know you lifted it from my pocket!" he roared. "If you don't get these cuffs off me right this minute, you'll be spending your next semester in reform school!"*
>
> *"Oh, okay." Corky took the key out of her pocket and released her nemesis from the car.*

Sue laughed gleefully. "He sounds just like your uncle, doesn't he?" she asked Cal.

"It just isn't the same, though," Cal grinned. "He doesn't turn purple and yell in Italian."

"Yeah." Sue laughed.

"I can't imagine why they wanted me to play Corky, can you?" Cal asked, with a smirk.

"Only because you're exactly like her, that's all," Sue nodded.

"Len used to be in plays, too. We both got our start the same way, except his was on Broadway and mine was at school.

Leonard nodded at Sue, who was now looking at him through the viewfinder of her camera. "I've heard about the trouble you used to get into at school because of this kid here," he said, mussing Cal's hair. "I understand that you were no stranger to the detention hall."

Sue snapped a picture of the pair.

"And this is why my hair always looks like I stuck my finger in a light socket," Cal complained good-naturedly. "He keeps doing that. In that first Corky movie, he'd sometimes mess up my hair between takes, so the hair lady would have to come and make it look good all over again. I bet she didn't like you very much, Len."

"So goes life," he replied.

Cal took the camera from Sue, "Go stand by Len so you can prove to the kids back home that you were here and met the greatest actor of all time. Smile." She snapped the photo, then gave the camera back. "Okay, Sue. Now you've seen what a real, live movie star looks like—almost like a real person, huh?"

"*Two* movie stars—Mr. Rhoads and Nate," Sue corrected.

"Three!" Leonard countered.

Both girls looked up at him.

"Don't forget *Cal*," he added.

Cal grinned.

"Well, you *did* sign the autograph book," Sue told Cal.

"Jill told me to do that. Come on. Len's got to study. I want to show you my room." Cal led Sue down the hall and into her bedroom. "Isn't it gorgeous? I don't know how Jill knew that yellow's my favorite color, but she has everything matching yellow in here."

"Wow, it sure is! It looks like a professional interior decorator did it."

"Jill did it all herself. She's so smart about these things. She even made the curtains herself. She sews a lot."

"He sure is big," she whispered, while tipping her head toward the study. "Len?"

"Yeah! We look like a couple of shrimps beside him."

"Yeah, I know. If he ever wants to get out of show-biz, he can be a bodyguard or a bouncer or something."

"And what a hunk! I wouldn't mind living with him. He's hunkier in person than he is on TV."

"You should see him in swimming trunks. For a guy his age, he still looks really good—and he doesn't have to work out to stay that way like Dad did. With Len, it's just natural, I guess."

"Oh, man," Sue said dreamily.

Cal shrugged. "But he's married and Jill's gorgeous. Sorry, kid. Now, *Miles* is the hunkiest guy I've seen in these parts."

"Can I meet him?"

"We aren't going together anymore."

"I know, but he's so cute."

"Yeah, I know. I wish you could stay longer so I could let you see a show being taped."

"That's one of the things we'll see on that guided tour tomorrow."

"Cool!"

*　*　*

Sue and her parents spent all of the next day on their tours. The following morning, Cal drove them to the airport and hugged them all goodbye before they boarded the plane for home. It had been so good to see her friends again after all these years! Maybe next time, they could stay longer. And, maybe by then, she would have her own house and they could stay with her!

Chapter 16

AS CAL CAME INTO THE STUDY, Leonard was ending what appeared to be a disturbing phone conversation. "Just don't call her anymore, you hear?… You know damn well why.… That's my worry, not yours.… Bye, Stevens." He slammed the phone down.

That last word got her immediate attention. "*Alex* Stevens? Why'd you *do* that?" Cal punched his shoulder.

Until now, he hadn't realized she was standing there. "Because he has no right to come on to you like that, that's why!"

"Why not? He's not married."

"He's trying to take advantage of you, Cal. He knows how naive you are."

"He is not, and I'm not naive! I've got to call him back!" She reached for the phone.

He clamped his hand over hers, "No, you don't!"

"I'm not a little kid anymore, Len! I can take care of myself!"

"You don't know what you're getting into. He's trouble."

"No, he isn't. Let go of my hand!"

"Come here, Cal. I'm going to give you a history lesson." He led her to the sofa. "Alex makes a fine friend for me, but not for you."

"You're wrong!"

"Listen to me. It was about five years ago, maybe more, that Alex was arrested for molesting a minor. He must have political connections because it was swept under the rug, but that doesn't change what happened. And I'll be damned if I'm going to let him get his hands on you!"

"Maybe he was framed."

"Don't make excuses for him. He's a sick man.

Tears welled up in her eyes. "So anyone who comes on to me is a sick man? Anyone who likes Cal Ames has got to be crazy, huh?"

"No, no. That's not what I'm saying."

She clung to him and sobbed.

"It's okay, Cal. You'll be all right," he said, patting her on the back.

Jill brought Leonard the mail and stopped short when she saw Cal in his arms. "What happened?" she asked.

Leonard nodded to her, "It's a long story. I'll tell you later." Then he looked back down at Cal. "Are you okay now?"

"I'm going to my room."

"Don't make any calls," he said sternly.

She got up and went to her room.

Leonard followed, unplugged her phone, and took it out of her room, closing her door behind him on his way back to the study. From past experience, he had learned that if Cal didn't actually *say* she'd comply with his order, she didn't intend to; and he had better take extra precautions to be sure it was carried out.

* * *

It was quite early on a Tuesday morning. Leonard had just finished his breakfast and would be going to the studio in a few minutes.

"Daddy?" Stacy asked, as she climbed onto his lap, "I wanna be a cowboy."

"A cowboy? Why?"

"So I can ride horses and shoot guns like you."

"When have you ever seen me shoot a gun?"

"On TV last night."

He had been in the study for most of the evening, oblivious to Stacy's activities. "What show did you see?"

"I dunno."

"What did I do in it?"

"You shot at lots of people and wore a black hat."

"Stacy, you know I don't really shoot people. It's just pretend."

"But they fell down."

"They were pretending, too."

"And you rode the horse good."

"That part was real."

"Can I have a horse, Daddy?"

"You're too young to have your own horse. But maybe next time Cal and I go riding, we'll take you with us. How's that?"

"Okay. Let's go today."

"I've got to go to work today. Maybe Saturday."

She put her little hands on his cheeks and giggled. "You're fuzzy!"

He smiled. "That's because I'm pretending to be a mountain man this week. Guys like that sometimes don't shave." He set her on the floor and finished his coffee.

Cal came into the kitchen and got a box of cereal out of the cabinet.

"Hurry up," Leonard told her. "We've got to leave in a minute."

This week, they both were working on television shows in the same studio complex, but different areas; so they would be riding together.

"Daddy's gonna' be a mountain goat," Stacy told Cal.

"A mountain man!" he corrected.

"Oh, and I'm gonna be a cowboy," Stacy informed her.

"Well, then, you'll need a cowboy hat, won't you?" she said, then hurriedly ate her cereal. Leonard handed her a cup of coffee, which she polished off quickly. "Okay, let's go." As they headed out the door, Cal looked back and saw tiny Stacy standing alone in the kitchen. "Wait a minute, Len." She went back and picked the child up. "Let's go keep Mommy company, okay?" She carried the child upstairs and laid her beside Jill in the bed. "We'll see you tonight, Stacykins. Bye, Jill." She kissed Stacy goodbye, then went back downstairs and out the door, joining Leonard in the car.

*   *   *

"What's so great about nineteen?" Cal asked as her birthday cake was brought out at dinner that night. "Eighteen's the biggie. After that, nothing until twenty-one."

"Well, it means you're a year closer to twenty-one," Jill offered. "I don't know if that's good or bad."

Leonard added, "At twenty-one, you can do just about anything, Cal. Two more years, then you'll be a full adult. Something to look forward to."

"What were you doing at nineteen, Jill?" Cal asked.

"I was in college."

"Really? I didn't know that. What did you major in, Home Ec.?"

"No, actually I was an Elementary Education major, with a minor in English. I was a teacher, until this thespian swept me off my feet and changed all my plans. I met Leonard when I took my third-grade class to the theatre to see a scene of a play that was being reenacted for them."

"Oh, how romantic!" Cal grinned.

"He insisted that no wife of his was going to work. So, consequently, I wash, iron, dust, vacuum, cook, and do various other forms of recreation instead," she said.

Leonard and Cal looked at each other. Was Jill complaining or joking? Sometimes it was hard to tell.

"I've told you, Jill" Leonard said, "we can get a housekeeper if you want."

"No, I'd rather do it myself. I like it done a certain way, and have found it quite satisfying to keep our home running smoothly."

Cal asked, "What were *you* doing when you were nineteen, Len?"

"I was in the military, defending our country from every calamity except you," he said facetiously. "You were born that year, I believe."

Stacy couldn't stand it anymore. "Blow out the candles, Cal! I want some cake."

"Yes, ma'am." She obediently extinguished the candles, then cut pieces of the cake for everyone.

* * *

Once all were finished with their dinners, Leonard scooted his chair back. "Okay, Cal. Into the media room." He got up and headed in that direction.

"Good dinner, Jill, as always." Cal said before following Leonard.

They seated themselves on the sofa directly in front of the big screen. He, as usual, was in control of the equipment.

"Now," he began, "you say you're having a problem with timing."

"No. What it is, is that my character is startled, and the director says I'm waiting for it."

"That's a timing problem. He means that your body language is alerting the audience that something's about to happen. You don't want to do that. You want them to be just as startled as your character is. I've got several films here that show you the right way to express surprise, and notice the timing." He started a film and advanced it to the proper spot. "Now watch this one." They observed as his character was watching people transact some business when a gunshot rang out. "Did you see? I was totally absorbed in the dialogue, as though I had no idea anything else was going to take place. I willed myself to concentrate on what was happening right before the gunshot."

"Yeah, but how do you get yourself to jump right then without doing it too soon or too late?"

"Tell yourself that, if that second thing happens, it would be *catastrophic*. While you're concentrating on the first thing, you keep your ears open for the second, then react naturally. You'll actually feel your heart skip a beat if you're doing it right." He took that film off and replaced it with another. "Here's a different scene in a different picture, but with a similar situation. Notice how I'm focusing in on what happens immediately before." He advanced the film to the right place, then ran the scene twice for her. "You see?"

"Yeah. I think so."

"Here's something else, too. I've noticed you don't seem to have an understanding of the physical nature of 'action and reaction.' For every action, there is an equal and opposite reaction. Look here in this one." Again he changed films and advanced it. The actress was standing when an earthquake suddenly occurred. "Notice she steps back, then forward, as though she had to do that to keep her balance. In reality, of course, the floor was stationary, but she had to give the illusion of movement." He ran the scene again. "See?"

"Yeah."

"The same is true in other forms, too. Because my character is so often the bad guy, scripts have me grabbing people a lot. When they break loose…"

"*That's* a laugh!"

"What is?"

"In real life, if you didn't want someone to break loose, they couldn't. And if you *did* want them to, you wouldn't be grabbing them in the first place."

"This scene is an altered reality, where a suspension of disbelief is necessary. Look at the example of 'action and reaction' here." He prepared the film and started running a portion of it. "Notice I don't just open my hand and let go." He stopped the film. "Better yet, let me demonstrate. Here, grab my arm tightly and no matter what, don't let go."

She complied.

"Now watch your hand." He pulled his arm free of hers. She watched as her hand jerked backward. "See, up until that point, you were pulling against my arm to keep it from getting away. When it finally did, the pulling motion you were originally making caused your hand go backward when my arm was no longer there to pull against."

"Oh, yeah."

"So next time, remember that. Action and reaction."

"Pete sent over a movie script for me. It'll be filmed next year overseas."

"Have you read it over?"

"Some of it."

"How's it look?"

"I like the story."

"Let me see it before you get back to him about it."

"The only trouble is *where* it's being filmed—in Spain."

"What's the problem?"

"It's overseas!"

"A lot of films are made overseas."

"I've never been there before. I've never been outside of the U.S. before and I don't know Spanish."

"It'll be next year. You have time to learn."

He didn't seem to be getting the message. "I'd be on the other side of the world for a couple months, Len! It's a place that has different customs and everything. I'd be so far away for so long."

"If you don't want to do it, tell him no," he shrugged.

"Just like that?"

"Sure. I've turned down lots of work, but that's mainly because I already had other projects scheduled for the same time."

"So if I turn this one down, Pete won't stop giving me scripts?"

"No. The decision is always yours, not his. And he's obligated to make you aware of every bona-fide job offer you're given."

"Cool!"

*　*　*

"Let's go, Daddy! Get up."

What time was it? Leonard looked at the bedside clock. 5:52 a.m. "Go where?"

"To ride horses and be a cowboy! It's Saturday!"

He groaned and closed his eyes.

Jill said gently, "Baby, the horses are still asleep. Go back to bed."

"Aww," Stacy whined as she shuffled back to her room.

A few minutes later, she went into Cal's room and climbed into bed with her. She reached over and opened Cal's eye.

"Don't do that," Cal said as she turned to her other side.

"But it's Saturday."

"I know. That's the day we sleep late."

"I wanna ride horses."

Cal turned back to face Stacy. "Let's play train. You lie down and turn over. You'll be the engine and I'll be the caboose."

Stacy complied and Cal put her arm around her. "Now our little train will go to Dreamland. Nighty-night."

Grown-ups sure sleep a lot, Stacy thought as she tried to go back to sleep, too.

*　*　*

"We're a Stacy sandwich!" Cal said as she rode one horse with Stacy sitting in front of her and Leonard rode the other in front of them. The sun was high overhead and it was getting quite warm for the beginning of autumn.

"I need a gun, Daddy!" Stacy said.

"No, you don't," he replied.

"I'll get you a cowboy hat next time I'm in Texas," Cal promised. "That's better than a gun. Daddy always wears a cowboy hat when he's riding horses on TV."

"I want a black one like Daddy's."

"I had a red one when I was little," Cal said.

They rode slower than usual because of their passenger. But such a tame ride was anything but pleasurable to Cal and Leonard; so after about ten minutes of that, Cal took her horse over to the fence, where she dismounted and lowered Stacy to the ground.

"Now you stand right here by the fence and be the judge. Daddy and I are going to race, and you tell us who the winner is."

"Okay."

Leonard backed his horse up even with Cal's as she got back in the saddle. "Around the lake and back," he said, with a twinkle in his eyes.

"Stacy, you say 'ready, set, go.'"

With all the Rhoads authority she could muster, Stacy shouted, "Ready. Set. *Go!*"

And they were off! The sound of the horse hooves was loud to Stacy at first, then grew faint as they neared the lake. They were neck and neck as they circled the water, with Leonard on the outside. Then as they came down the home stretch, Leonard came out ahead and won by a nose.

"Daddy beat!" Stacy clapped.

"Ah, it's good to hear applause again," Leonard said to Stacy. "Cal, you're getting good at this."

"If I were a horse, it sure seems I'd run faster with a light person on my back than a heavy one." She leaned over, "Come on, Stacy. Hold onto my hand and I'll pull you back up here."

"No, Cal," Leonard said. "That's not a good idea."

"Sure it is. I've seen people do this before." She took hold of Stacy's hands and pulled. Instead of Stacy coming up, though, Cal lost her balance and went down, landing on her shoulder.

"Ow!" she yelled. "Ow, ow, ow!"

"You should've listened to me," Leonard admonished her. "Are you okay?"

"It hurts."

"Where?" He dismounted and went over to her.

"Right here," she said, indicating her left shoulder.

"You'll probably just be bruised for a while," he said. He reached out to help her up. "Come on."

As she extended her arms to take his hands, she yelled and put her hand back on her shoulder. "It hurts! There's a bump there."

"Uh-oh. Let me see." He knelt down in front of her. "Move your collar over so I can take a look at your shoulder."

She unbuttoned just enough of her shirt to uncovered her shoulder. He felt along her collarbone, which caused her to flinch. "It hurts like the dickens, Len! Don't touch it."

"This bump wasn't there before?" he asked.

She shook her head.

"It looks like the collarbone has a dislocated break. Let's go get it taken care of. Come on." He stood and helped Cal onto the back of his horse, behind the saddle. He next lifted Stacy up onto the horse, in front of his saddle. Then he got into the saddle while holding onto the reins of Cal's horse. "Hold on to me with your good arm," he told Cal, as they started back toward the farm with Cal's horse walking alongside.

"Now we're a 'Daddy sandwich'!" Stacy noted enthusiastically.

* * *

"Oh, my goodness! What happened?" Jill asked as the trio returned home late that afternoon. Cal's clothes were dusty, and her left arm was in a sling.

"It's the story of her life," Leonard said as he closed the front door. "She didn't listen to me and suffered the consequences."

Jill looked at him crossly. "What did you do to her?"

"Nothing! I didn't do it!" he said. "She fell off the horse and broke her collarbone. I told her not to pull Stacy up like that, but she wouldn't listen."

"Daddy took her shirt off, too," Stacy added.

"No, I didn't!" he quickly corrected her. "All I did was…"

Cal reassured Jill, "He had to see my shoulder in order to know it was hurt enough to go to the hospital about, so I just opened the top part of my shirt so he could do that. He didn't do anything wrong. It's the nurse at the hospital who took the whole thing off. You should see the sling *under* my shirt. It feels like a girdle or something."

"That's probably going to keep you from working for a month or two, Cal," Leonard said, "unless you can get the part of a klutz. It's just a good thing you weren't in the middle of making a film."

"What would've happened if I *had* been?"

"If they could, maybe they would've written it into the story. If they couldn't, and it was near the beginning of filming, they would've replaced you. If neither of those was possible, then they would've loaded you up with drugs, taken the outer sling away, and told you to do your job."

"What kind of an inhumane business *is* this, anyway?"

"One where the bottom line rules, in most cases."

The business aspect of filmmaking was getting more distasteful to Cal all the time.

*   *   *

Cal and Becky were sitting by her pool. Since she couldn't work, Cal found she had a lot more time for her friends now, and she could sleep late every morning. She was happy for that. She was unhappy, though, at the fact that she couldn't go swimming because of her broken collarbone. Instead, the two girls had taken their shoes off and were sitting on the side of the pool with their feet in the water.

"Dad's making some big plans," Becky said. "I think he should've been a marketing man because he's always coming up with new promotional ideas."

"It's not too late. He can always change jobs."

"Well, he probably likes it better the way it is. He comes up with the ideas, then has his staff carry them out. Maybe that's not such a bad job for him, after all. I don't think he'd have the fortitude to do the scut work himself."

"I wonder if I'll ever work again," Cal thought out loud.

"Why do you say that?"

"Because I have car payments to make."

"I mean why do you have any doubts that you'll be working again?"

"Well, Pete says if I'm out of the public eye for any length of time, everybody'll forget who I am and I'll stop getting work."

"Oh, don't worry about that. It'll only be a couple months."

"Len said something to be funny, but maybe it's a possibility. He said I could play the part of a klutz now, with my sling and everything. Or soap operas deal with the down side of life a lot. Maybe Pete can get me on one of them."

"For goodness sake, just enjoy your time off. That'll give us time to do some shopping."

Cal grinned. "I bet you want to get something romantic for Johnny for Christmas, huh?"

"Sure do, and I have a couple months to find just the right present for him. I really think he's 'the one,' Cal. I'm not interested in dating anyone else now that he's in my life."

"That *does* sound serious. Can he support you in the manner to which you're accustomed?" Cal winked.

"Gad, Cal. Nobody except Dad can do that. Dad's the one who got me used to all this high living in the first place."

"You own the house, though, don't you?"

"Yeah."

"So Johnny can move in with you instead of the other way around—when you get married, of course."

"Oh, Cal. No one waits that long anymore."

"I do."

"Believe me, kiddo, you're in the minority. You'll probably be the last virgin bride in America."

"I'm not going to get married."

"Oh, yeah. I forgot. But one of these days, someone's going to come along and change your mind. Mark my words."

"All the good ones are off limits to me."

"Are you talking about Alex?"

"He's one of them. Why didn't you tell me about him?"

"I didn't know about it."

They sat silently for a while, then Becky pulled her feet out of the water and stood up. "It's probably better that you're not able to go swimming today. It's pretty cool and probably will stay that way until spring. I've got to have this thing drained before long."

"What time's it getting to be?" Cal asked.

Becky looked at her watch. Almost six-thirty."

"I better go." Cal said as Becky helped her up. "I'm late for dinner."

"Let's spend tomorrow shopping, okay? Be sure to wear sunglasses or something so we can shop in peace."

Cal picked up her shoes. "Okay. See ya." She headed home.

*   *   *

Several days later, Cal had been singing along with her stereo at top volume when Jill came to the door.

"You have a phone call."

The vocals continued, oblivious to her presence.

Jill came into the room and lowered the volume on the stereo. "You have a phone call."

"Oh! Hi, Jill." Cal turned the music off and picked up her phone. It was Pete, and he sounded excited—so excited, in fact, that it was hard for Cal to get a word in edgewise. Stagecraft Productions wanted her to go on a tour with a few of its other stars, he told her, and the pay would be quite good. The purpose was to promote the films that they would be releasing in the next six months. There would be two troupes of stars making tours, each taking half of the states in the continental U.S. They would make an appearance in the capitol city of each of those states, so it would be a twenty-four day tour. He understood that Cal was out of commission for a while due to her injury, but this wouldn't begin until March fifth.

Hmmm, she was thinking. *Both the slings will be off by then, so I'll at least look* normal. Cal told him she would discuss this with the Rhoadses and let him know.

* * *

"Don't you love me anymore?" Stacy asked Cal, with a pout.

"Of course I do, but I just can't pick you up right now. It makes my shoulder hurt."

"It's my fault that you got hurt."

"No, Stacykins, it's *my* fault. Daddy was right. I shouldn't've tried to pull you up."

"Can I sit on your lap?"

"Yeah, as long as you don't lean against my shoulder."

"Will you read me a story?"

"Sure. I've got enough time now to read *War and Peace*."

"Okay. Come on." Stacy took Cal's right hand and led her to her bedroom and the rocking chair that had been a part of her room since she was a baby. "Sit here."

Cal sat.

Stacy went to her bookshelf, picked up *The Little Red Hen*, and brought it to Cal. She then climbed into Cal's lap.

"Careful," Cal said as Stacy got situated.

"Can I kiss it and make it well now?"

She smiled. "Well, it's all covered up. Maybe you can blow it a kiss. Would that work?"

"I don't know."

"We can give it a try."

Stacy put her hand up to her mouth, kissed it, and blew the kiss to Cal's shoulder.

"Ah! I felt that! It feels better already," Cal said.

Stacy grinned. "I did good."

"Yes, you did." Cal hugged Stacy with her right arm and kissed the top of her head. "You know, I've never in my life had a sister and I always wanted one. Would you be my honorary sister?"

"We can be sisters?" she asked excitedly.

"*Honorary* sisters. That's even better than regular ones."

"Okay!"

Cal then proceeded to read Stacy's favorite story, and then another one. Before Stacy could get a third one out, dinner was ready.

*   *   *

"So what do you think of it, Len?" she asked that night at dinner, after relating to him what Pete had told her. Stacy had already finished her dinner and gone into the media room to watch TV.

"Sounds like it'll be a lot of hard work, but it'd be good exposure for you. They'll probably work up an act for you to do. It sure doesn't hurt to learn another form of entertainment. The more versatile you are, the better."

"What kind of act? Like a skit or something?"

"A monolog, or a musical number, or something."

"I used to be in the church choir back home. Maybe all of us together can be a choir and maybe do gospel songs or something. That'd be neat!"

"I'd be willing to bet they'll want you to do individual acts, rather than a collective one."

"Why don't you get out of whatever's on your schedule and come along?"

He shook his head. "I'll be in Illinois, working on a film that I've been looking forward to for a long time. I don't want to get out of it."

"Phooey! So you think this tour would be a good career move for me?"

"Definitely."

"Okay. I'll do it, then."

"Good."

"That will affect life at home quite a bit," Jill commented. "With both of you out of town at the same time, Stacy and I will be alone. That's the first time that's ever happened."

"You'll have time to kick off your shoes and relax," Cal said. "You won't have to do our laundry or anything, so you can go to Burger Bar every night if you want to."

Leonard laughed. "That's something I just can't envision her doing."

"Stacy, yes. Jill, no," Cal agreed.

Chapter 17

WITH THE TRAVEL ARRANGEMENTS MADE, Cal was starting to get excited about the upcoming tour. While Leonard was unable to make the trip with her, two of her castmates from films-past would be. She found that musicians would also be travelling with them, which made her suspect she may be called upon to do a musical number, just as Leonard had guessed.

About a month before their scheduled departure, the plans were firmed up and she was given an itinerary, as well as the music and script for the acts they had written for her and—*Oh, good grief,* Cal thought. *I'm paired up with Nate again.* They'd be doing the acts as Corky and Mike. *Don't people ever get tired of that?* she wondered.

She looked over the itinerary. Once they're flown to their first stop, buses would then be used to get the actors and musicians to their destinations until it was time to fly back to California. The technical staff and director-manager would have a separate vehicle. Her group would be taking the eastern half of the country. Hot diggity! Even though she was disappointed that a stop in Dallas wasn't on the list, at least she *would* be doing a show in Illinois, where Leonard would be doing his location work. Wouldn't that be great if he could see the show? He had never seen her sing and dance. She knew she could do it, too, because she did in her high school play. And it looked like her shoulder would be in fine shape by then.

There would be a show in a different state every night, beginning in Florida. The coolest month would be spent mostly in the south. She was hoping their stop in Illinois would be on Leonard's birthday. That would've been so great. But, alas, the Illinois show would be on March 18th. Too soon. *Guess that* was *a bit much to ask,* she thought.

Rehearsals were to begin at the studio next week for all the acts. It would be like an *Ed Sullivan Show* on wheels, they said. Some stars would be doing a magic act; some would be doing a dramatic reading; others would be doing comedy, singing and dancing. "*What?*" she wondered with a giggle, "*No plates balancing on top of poles?*"

"It looks like it's going to be a lot of fun," she told Leonard as she showed him the plans. "You'll have to come to Springfield on the 18th to see us."

He looked over the itinerary and the instructions. Then he read her script and looked at the music. After studying them for a number of minutes, he set them down on his desk, leaned back in his chair, and looked at Cal.

"Well?" she asked.

"You're going to be exhausted when you get back home."

"Hey, I'm young and have lots of energy. It'll be a piece of cake," she shrugged. "At least I'm working again and travelling, too. I love being paid to travel."

"And travel you will!" he said emphatically. "Just be sure to leave time between the tour and your next project to rest up." He looked again at the itinerary. "I'll try to make it to Springfield on the 18th."

"Doesn't it look like it's going to be a great show?" Cal asked enthusiastically.

"Yes, I think so."

"If you had been able to come, too, I wonder what kind of acts they would've put you in."

With just a trace of a smile, he answered, "Well, when you first came to live with us, I felt like a lion tamer."

"Hey, that's right. Ed Sullivan sometimes has animal acts. But it doesn't look like we will. How about if I do a lion-taming act, only with kittens? Wouldn't that be neat? Instead of loud roars, the audience would hear little meows."

"I think that's already been done."

"Yeah, I think I saw that on the *Sullivan* show once, too. Well, I think I know why we're going on buses instead of by plane."

"Because it's cheaper."

"No, Becky told me Nate's afraid to fly. Isn't that a scream?"

"A lot of people are."

"I wonder if Cleveland Amory knows about that. He could fill up his whole column with a gem like that."

He looked at her sternly. "Keep mum about it, Cal!"

"Aw, shucks. Why?"

"It's just good business to have nothing but good things to say about your co-stars. Nate might be a world-class jerk, but whenever anyone's around who will be quoting you, for Pete's sake, act like he's your best friend."

"Why can't we be honest?"

"Nate's the type who can be either your best friend or your worst enemy. There doesn't seem to be any middle ground with him. He's got powerful connections. Believe me, you want to be his friend."

*   *   *

After the first rehearsal, Cal was a bit less enthusiastic about their act. That song and dance number wasn't as easy as it had seemed! It *was* a good act, though, as was the comedy act. That one reminded her a lot of the George Burns-Gracie Allen routines she had seen on TV.

The troupe was working with a choreographer and piano accompanist for now. During the actual shows, though, they would have a band behind them. The song assigned to Cal and Nate was a romantic number, a variation of "Spanish Eyes" known as "Moon Over Naples," with lyrics written especially for them to play up both their fictional image as young lovers and her Italian background.

It tickled her to see Nate singing and dancing. She didn't know he could do that, but she had to admit he had a nice tenor voice. In fact, he seemed to be catching on to the choreography more quickly than she was. That just didn't seem right to her. *After all*, she thought, *my brain cells are seven years younger than his.*

As they were headed back to their cars, Nate asked, "Do you want to get in some extra rehearsal time? There's a room in my house that would be perfect for practice."

"Yeah, but let's do it in my house. The study would work pretty well for that. There's a lot of room to move around in there." No way was she going to be alone with him in his house.

"Okay. I'll ask Dana to make a recording of his accompaniment for us to use."

During the next two weeks, they practiced in the study four times. Each time, Cal asked Jill to watch and give them her opinion. Jill seemed to enjoy the acts. Seeing them together, she told them, she could now understand why the producers insisted on putting them together for public appearances. They made a cute couple, in both the musical number and the comedy routine.

After Nate had left, Jill asked, "I've been wondering for quite a while why you and Nate don't go out together sometime."

She shrugged, "We're just not each other's type, I guess."

"That's hard to believe. There definitely seems to be chemistry between you two when you're performing."

"That's just an act, Jill. We're actors, remember?"

"Well, what type is he looking for?"

"Probably someone who spends the whole time telling him he's wonderful. When Sue was doing that, he was just eating it up."

"And what type are *you* looking for, Cal?"

"Oh, I don't know. I guess I'm not looking for anybody."

"Don't you want to get married and have a family someday?"

"Uh-uh. I don't give guys much thought, anymore."

"I hope, when Leonard gave you a hard time about you and Miles coming home late, that didn't make you afraid to start dating again."

"Heck, no! I'm not scared of Len."

"That's good, because I can tell that Nate really cares for you."

"No, he doesn't. And I don't care for him, either."

"Sure you do, Cal. He's a nice boy."

"I bet if Sue were going to stay longer, he would've taken *her* out. He's definitely *her* type."

Jill put her hand on Cal's shoulder and asked earnestly, "Could it be that you've already found the one you want, and that's why you're not looking? Someone who's unavailable, maybe?"

"No, I don't think so. Why?"

"Just wondering." Jill sighed and went back to the laundry room to finish her ironing.

Who's she talking about? Cal wondered. Miles, maybe? He's unavailable. Sherry's wearing an engagement ring these days. It couldn't be Alex. He *is* available, but Cal didn't think Jill knew about him.

*   *   *

March fifth was here at last. Their acts were polished and ready. They had had a dress rehearsal at the studio, with the band and the technicians present. The modified lyrics and lighting for "Moon Over Naples" were very romantic. The stage would go dark, then a large moon would glow in what appeared to be the starlit sky behind them as the pink spotlight showed Cal and Nate strolling slowly onto the stage, arm in arm. They'd stop and gaze at the moon, then, overcome with love, Nate would start his serenade, to be joined a few bars later by Cal's alto harmony. They would slowly dance around the stage during the instrumental interlude, then sing the final verse facing each other, holding both hands, until the last note, when they'd melt into a tender embrace, silhouetted against the moon. Curtain down. *Corny,* Cal thought, *but the lights make all the difference in the world. The audience might not even notice that we hate each other.* In fact, she would never admit it to herself or anyone else, but his beautiful tenor voice and graceful dancing style made her understand now why so many girls would swoon over Nate.

Why's he working as an actor when his talent's clearly in the musical realm? she wondered.

The costumes were a real treat, too. For the musical number, Nate would be wearing a white tuxedo and Cal a flowing, pink chiffon gown. In the comedy routine, they wore matching red satin suits.

Janice Jergens and Sean Millerton were the other stars who were performing on this tour. Cal and Nate's, Janice's, and Sean's acts would be performed between previews of the various Stagecraft films that would be at the neighborhood theaters that summer and fall, making it a very full and entertaining evening for their audience.

Everything was ready. Their adventure would soon begin.

Cal gave Jill and Stacy a big goodbye hug. Leonard had already left for Illinois a few days earlier. She then loaded up her car and left for the airport.

The Stagecraft instruction sheet directed her to go to the VIP lounge to await her flight. There, she joined the other stars who were making this journey with her. The musicians, she was told, had already left on an earlier flight.

"What're *you* doing here?" she asked Nate. "I thought you were afrai..."

He quickly put his hand over her mouth and led her away from the others. "Don't you dare!" he whispered vehemently. When Nate realized how confused she was, he calmed down and whispered, "I was going to take the train, but they've gone on strike, so I had no choice but to fly." He lowered his hand. "I need your help, Cal. If you'd keep me distracted during the flight, I'd appreciate it."

*   *   *

Their flight to Florida was one of the more unusual ones she had ever taken. When the other passengers realized that they had not *one* movie star in their midst, but *four* of them, Cal suggested they try out their routines on this captive and quite-interested audience. Nate quickly agreed and organized the others. Since the musicians weren't on this flight, they sang *a capella*. None of their fellow passengers would soon forget the superb entertainment that was theirs that day. Enjoying it most were the entertainers themselves. Once they got started, they didn't want to stop. It was just the distraction that Nate needed. No one but he and Cal were aware of his fear of flying. The movie that the flight attendants had planned to show was put away for later.

Arriving at their destination seemed almost an anticlimax. They were met at the airport by a limousine and transported to their hotel. Cal and Janice shared a room, as did Nate and Sean, next door. This would be their only "day off," they were told. Publicity will have already been done prior to their arrival at each stop. The first show was scheduled for the following evening at eight o'clock. They were to have a brief run-through on that stage in the early afternoon, then give their performance that evening. After the show, they would sign autographs and perhaps do a brief interview, then head back to the bus, where they would be driven to the next state. This would be their routine for twenty-four days. Cal figured they'd probably be doing all of their sleeping on the bus.

It was early evening now and they had had room service bring their dinners to the room. The two couples had dinner together, then played cards for a couple of hours. Cal had never played bridge before, but caught on to the rules fairly quickly. Her strategy wasn't all that clever, though, and she became the least-desired partner. "At least I'm good at being the dummy," she admitted.

"We *could* play poker," Sean suggested.

"How do you play that?" Cal asked.

"In that case, let's make it strip poker!" he said with a grin. Nate seconded that motion.

Janice vetoed that idea with, "Does everyone know how to play Hearts?"

Music started coming from the room down the hall. *It must be the men from our group,* they thought, as they got up and followed the sound. Sure enough, their musicians were there and had decided to have a jam session. They set a time limit: "until either nine o'clock or the hotel management complains, whichever happens last," they said.

Yes sir, Cal decided, *this is really going to be a fun tour!*

* * *

The jam session had started out good enough, Cal thought, *but now it's starting to get downright strange.* Max, the trombonist, was serving as bartender and the drinks were flowing freely. One by one, the other crew members had joined them until almost everyone on the tour was crammed into this room. Cal had sung and danced with the rest of them at first, teaching them a hardy rendition of "Angelina, the Waitress at the Pizzeria." It seemed, though, that the more people drank, the more inclined they were to shed their clothes and the rowdier they got. Cal was glad that Max had plenty of Dr. Pepper on hand, and she discovered that Florida soft drinks tasted better than California or Texas ones did. She was on her third glassful when she noticed that the clarinet player was stroking her derriere.

"Just trying to figure out what kind of underwear you've got on," he explained. "None, right?"

"Uh, I forget," she replied, pulling the waistband of her slacks out to see what was beneath. Then, she triumphantly announced, "Yeah, they're there, all right."

She then spotted the trumpeter going toward Janice with a pair of handcuffs in his hand and a mischievous gleam in his eye. Cal left the clarinetist to check that out. "Why're you arresting her, ossifer?"

"Oh, it's okay, Cal. He's just teasing," Janice assured her.

All of a sudden, the lights seemed to dim and Cal's head started buzzing. She blanched, then handed Janice the glass of Dr. Pepper and made her way through the crowd to the door.

From across the room, Nate noticed and set his drink down.

Cal held onto the wall for support as she went down the hallway to her own room. It was more difficult than usual to unlock her door, but she finally got it opened. Once inside, she dropped onto the bed. *If the floor would just hold still,* she thought, *I'll be all right.*

Nate had been following from a discreet distance, and now came into her room. "What's the matter? Feeling a little dizzy?"

"The room's moving," she complained. "We're having an earthquake."

He was reaching to close the door when Janice appeared in the hallway and joined them in the room. "You must've had too much to drink, Cal. I guess you're not accustomed to alcohol."

"All I had was Dr. Pepper."

Nate shook his head, "Max was putting rum into your drinks. I saw it."

Cal groaned.

"I thought you knew."

She slowly shook her head, "Crazy Hollywood parties."

Janice got a blanket from the bureau drawer and covered Cal with it. "Why don't you just take a nap? That might help. You want to be in good shape for the show tomorrow night."

"Okay." Sleep was exactly what Cal wanted most right now. She closed her eyes.

"Goodnight. Sweet dreams." She patted Cal's back, then took Nate's arm and led him back to the party.

Chapter 18

The show was getting better and better. Each night, it was just a bit more polished than it had been the night before. Cal and Nate's musical number seemed to put the audience in a hypnotic trance. Almost without fail, the ending of the song would be followed by a few seconds of silence, then thunderous applause. Their comedy act was a big hit, too. It was so fun to make the audience laugh that Cal had a difficult time keeping herself from joining in with them.

They had now gone almost two weeks without a day off. The tour was halfway finished, but that didn't give much comfort to the tired troupe. Except Cal. This was the day she had been anticipating. Leonard would be there for the show tonight. It'll be terrific to see "family" again! *Wouldn't it be great,* Cal thought, *if Jill and Stacy would fly out here to surprise me, too? Then we could all be together.* But a feeling of dread hit the pit of her stomach. No, on second thought, she didn't want them to come. The last time her family had flown somewhere to surprise Cal, they had been killed in a plane crash. In just an instant, she had gone from pampered daughter to orphan. She'd rather Jill and Stacy be safe at home than to risk that. She'd already lost her family once; she didn't want it to ever happen again.

They arrived in Springfield before ten a.m. Cal watched and waited for Leonard. *Surely, he won't forget,* she thought. The buses were parked right beside the auditorium, so he couldn't miss them. *Maybe he had to work today and will break away just in time to see the show,* she thought. *Yes, that's probably what happened.* The troupe went into the auditorium to go through the routines so they could see what modifications had to be made for that particular stage. Cal, Janice, Sean and Nate weren't bothered at all with the idea of modifying their acts. If it can be done in the narrow confines of an airplane, they reasoned, it can be done anywhere. As rehearsal of Cal and Nate's comedy act came to its end, they heard applause from the back of the auditorium, followed by a very familiar, robust, "Bravo! Encore! Encore!" Cal grinned. The figure standing in the back was shaded, but she knew instantly who it was. She jumped off the stage and ran toward the back of the auditorium, arms outstretched, crashing into Leonard in a big bear hug. His embrace lifted her off the ground, then returned her to earth.

"Oh, wow! It's so good to see you again, Len!"

"Same here, kid! You haven't dropped from fatigue yet, I see."

"Nope! I'll make it the whole twenty-four days, just like I said."

"And how would you like to have a little vacation after the tour? We could take a cross-country drive."

"Noooooo! I don't think so."

He laughed. "I didn't think you would."

She yelled toward the front of the auditorium, "Mr. Dean, are y'all through with me now?"

"You're done until tonight. Be in the green room at six-thirty, and don't be late!"

"Okay." She turned toward Leonard, "Let's go somewhere."

"Where?"

"Anywhere that's not a bus, a hamburger place, or an auditorium. That's all I've seen for thirteen days. You should see the people in the hamburger places when we all go in. You'd think they were being invaded by ghosts the way they stare. They just stop eating and stare."

He put his arm around her shoulders as they left the building. "How many more days on the tour?"

"Eleven days and twelve hours."

"It *does* get old after a while, doesn't it?"

"Kind of, but it's fun, too. The guys have taught me to play poker and Janice taught us bridge. And we get serenaded by the band. They've written a few new songs, too, one with Janice's and my names in it. Going to Dad's medical conventions would've been more fun when I was a kid if we'd taken our own band with us."

"Did you see the Everglades and Stone Mountain?"

"Well, actually, it was nighttime when we went by those places, so we didn't see them. Mainly, the bus is for sleeping and playing cards and strumming the guitar. Larry's teaching me to play the guitar. How's your picture going?"

"Fairly well. The weather's cooperating, so everything's on schedule."

"Are you the bad guy again?"

"No, Cal. You'll get a kick out of this one. It's a comedy, and I'm a spy who just can't seem to get it right. I blow my cover on the first day, and lose my briefcase of weapons and maps, picking up a briefcase of Avon samples instead!"

Cal laughed with delight. "How do you play it?"

"Gently. He's a likable character who wants to do a good job but doesn't quite know how."

"Boy, that's sure a switch! I've got to see that."

"It'll probably be at your neighborhood theatre in about eight months."

"And in the media room soon after that. Will we get to go to its premiere?"

"Most likely."

They got into his rented car and proceeded around town to do some sightseeing, then to an Italian restaurant for the best meal she'd had since her hotel stay in Florida, which seemed so long ago.

"Psst, Mom! It's Corky and Officer Stanton!" said a teen at a nearby table.

The duo attracted quite a bit of attention in the restaurant, but they didn't care.

*　*　*

This had been one of the best shows they had ever given. Cal gave it her all, and the rest of the troupe followed suit. They were all playing to Leonard, who was sitting incognito in the back of the auditorium. Afterward, he waited backstage as they signed autographs and visited with the fans, and the stage hands and musicians loaded their gear onto the bus. He then spent some time on the bus with the troupe until it was time to pull out and head to the next state. Cal and Leonard gave each other a long, sad goodbye hug, then he exited the bus. He then leaned on his car and waved as the bus started its trek down the highway toward Des Moines, Iowa.

Once Leonard was out of sight, Cal got a blanket off the overhead rack and covered herself as she pushed her seat into a semi-reclining position. That was as far back as the seats on this bus would go. It sure would feel good to get back in her own bed again. Then she lay there in her bus seat, waiting for sleep to come.

Janice looked over at her and saw tears trickle down her cheeks. "What's the matter, Cal?"

"I guess I'm just a little homesick, that's all."

"I think we all are. Eleven days and three hours to go."

*　*　*

Day sixteen: Tomorrow would be Leonard's birthday, Cal remembered. He had given her an address and phone number where he could be reached in case of emergency, so she asked the bus driver to take them by a Western

Union office when they got to the next town. Once there, she went in and ordered a telegram to be delivered to Leonard the following day. It was to say, "Happy birthday, Len! The last one home is a rotten egg!" Worded that way, she knew there would be no need to sign her name.

* * *

On day eighteen, they had passed through a town that was in the midst of a riot. Fortunately, that was happening in the downtown area, rather than ten miles farther away where their show would be held. It was sad that there was so much discord in this country, the girls commented. The Vietnam War was at the root of all the tension, according to the guys. Would it ever end, they all wondered. It seemed that at any time the youngest of these men could be drafted into the military and sent into that hell.

With this war and their President's assassination a few years earlier, it was certainly a bleak part of American history.

* * *

Day twenty: Only four more days to go! They were coming down the home stretch. Their last stops were in the New England states, and they found that area quite attractive. In body, the troupe was getting weary; but in spirit, they were starting to revive. The end was in sight.

The last few nights, Cal couldn't believe how relaxed she had felt with Nate actually in the seat right beside hers. But all four of them had been so close and congenial on this tour that the fear Cal had felt toward Nate just a few years earlier was all but forgotten now. Sure, in close quarters and with such continuous proximity to each other, each of the four had had their spells of irritability; but there had been no major disagreements or unpleasantness. Humor had always saved the day, and members of the band could be counted on to come through with plenty of that, even though Cal didn't always understand their lingo.

This quiet night had brought them almost six hours of blessed sleep. Through the bus window, there was a trace of sun coming up over the horizon. Cal was still half asleep when she thought she felt a soft kiss on her lips. "Miles," she whispered. She put her arm lazily around his neck.

"No," he whispered back. "Guess again."

She opened her eyes. It was Nate, in the seat beside hers. "Oh, I'm sorry," she said as she withdrew her arm. "I guess I was dreaming."

"No, you weren't dreaming, Cal." He leaned over and tenderly kissed her again.

If anyone ever had any romantic feelings for Cal, early morning was the best time to express them. That's when her guard was down and she was feeling the most relaxed. She leaned toward Nate and rested her head on his shoulder, as she closed her eyes and went back to sleep.

* * *

Janice arose from the seat two rows in front of theirs and made her way toward the lavatory in the back of the bus. As she passed by their row, she caught a glimpse of Cal, asleep in Nate's arms. "Aha! Just as I thought," she whispered triumphantly.

Nate had been dozing, too, until then. He put his finger up to his lips, "Shhh."

Janice patted him on the shoulder and proceeded to the restroom.

* * *

Rehearsals on the Concord stage were winding down. They now had some time to kill before they needed to put on their makeup and costumes for tonight's show.

Cal was checking out the green room backstage. Nate followed. "Let's take a walk," he suggested.

"Yeah, as far away from that bus as we can get," she agreed.

The pair put on their jackets and exited the building. Nate donned his sunglasses and gave her a pair, which she then put on. Even though it was almost April, it was still quite cool in New England. *L.A. is nice and warm by now,* Cal thought. Before going any farther, though, she ducked back into the bus to retrieve her camera. The original idea of bringing her camera along was for the purpose of getting great shots of the different landmarks through-out the eastern half of the country. So far, though, she had seen very few of them. Maybe she'll have better luck today. *Isn't this where the Liberty Bell or something is?* she wondered. They ambled down one street and up another in search of something interesting to pass the time. Ah! A movie theatre!

"Let's go in here, Nate. *The Graduate* is playing, and I've never seen it."

"We don't have enough time to see the whole thing, but at least we can catch part of it," he agreed.

Nate got their tickets and they went in. Cal took a side trip to the con-cession counter and got a big bag of popcorn, while he bought two Cokes. Nate then beckoned for her to follow him upstairs to the balcony. Cal always preferred sitting right up front, but felt obligated to sit with Nate this time since he had paid for her ticket and was carrying her Coke. As they reached the balcony, they found that the theater was already darkened and the movie had begun. Skillfully holding both Cokes in one hand, Nate removed his sunglasses and put them in the pocket of his shirt. Cal did likewise, putting hers in his pocket, too. He then led her to two seats in the back row. "Good grief," she mumbled. "We couldn't get farther away from the screen if we tried." After setting the Cokes on the floor, he shed his jacket and helped her with hers, then put them in the seat on the other side of his. As they settled in, he handed her her Coke, then put his arm around her shoulders.

"Want some popcorn?" she whispered, holding the bag out to him.

He whispered back, "No."

Cal then focused on the leading man, Dustin Hoffman. Leonard had told her that he predicted great success for this young actor, whom Cal had never heard of until this film came out. When Leonard referred to someone as an 'actor,' rather than a 'star,' he was giving that person a very high compliment.

Just as if Cal were in the media room with Leonard, she noticed some of the signs of good acting that he had told her to watch for and to emulate in her own work. In fact, she was so engrossed in the details that she had very little idea of what the actual story line was. Anne Bancroft was also very good, Cal noted. Very believable, worldly. Action and reaction—for every action there is an equal and opposite reaction. *Their timing is just perfect. Why can't my timing be like that?* she wondered.

So absorbed in these details was Cal that she had not noticed that Nate's hand had climbed from her upper arm, to her shoulder, then to her neck. When it burrowed under the collar of her shirt and caressed her bare shoulder, though, she snapped back to reality. "What're you doing, Nate? Stop it!" she whispered. She would have pulled his hand away but her hands were holding the popcorn and Coke.

He then leaned over and kissed her fervently. When she then turned her head away from him, he put his Coke on the floor, then grasped her chin, pulling it back toward him as he kissed her long and hard. Cal tried to pull free of him, but his lips were insistent as he pulled her close to him. If he would just let go for a minute, she could put her Coke and popcorn down, too; then she could fight him off—but he wouldn't stop. He was becoming more and more passionate as the moments passed. She dropped her popcorn and tried to push him away, but he wouldn't be discouraged. Her drink spilled, so she let that drop to the floor, too. With both arms now, she pushed with all her might and freed herself of his grasp.

"Leave me alone," she whispered emphatically. "We're in public, for Pete's sake!"

He was still breathing heavily. "I saw a hotel about a block away." He looked at her pleadingly.

"No!" Cal stood up and went downstairs to a seat near the front of the theater, where she would be able to see the rest of the movie in peace. She was very glad Nate hadn't followed her to the front. It would have been downright embarrassing if he had acted like that in front of people. And now on the screen was a striptease dancer. He certainly didn't need anyone putting more lusty ideas in his head! Cal couldn't take her eyes off the screen, though. How did that dancer *do* that with the tassels? Wow! They were going in opposite directions at the same time. That was amazing. Cal sure wished she had her popcorn and Coke now. She and Leonard always had popcorn on hand when they were viewing films, so it just didn't seem right to be here without it. Once the mesmerizing dance was over, she went back to the lobby for another box of popcorn and more Coke.

"Hey, it's Corky!" remarked a lanky boy who had just come in.

The girl beside him looked up and said excitedly, "Hey, yeah! Can I have your autograph? Right here, on my ticket stub?"

Well, Cal thought, *it's nice to be appreciated.* She chatted with these two enthusiastic fans for a while until they were joined by a few more eager kids. When she saw she was attracting a crowd, she bought the popcorn and Coke and returned to her seat in the front, followed by her little impromptu fan club, who then sat in the row behind her.

"She has an entourage now," Nate noted from above. "That's fast."

Cal ignored the nervous whispering behind her and refocused on the film. She saw that Dustin's girlfriend was getting married to someone else. How'd that happen? A lot must have transpired while she was in the lobby! As the scene progressed, it became quite apparent that Leonard was right. In this most poignant and dramatic scene, Dustin's character was expressing heartbreak and rage. He was so very convincing! The emotions seemed to come from the very depths of his soul. What an actor! She had heard that he was a method actor. *How on earth did he psych himself up for this scene?* she wondered.

When the film was over and the house lights came back on, Cal went back to the balcony for her jacket and camera. They were still where she had left them, but Nate was nowhere to be found. Oh, no! How would she ever be able to find her way back to the auditorium? She had absolutely no sense of direction and would most likely get lost. Nevertheless, she tried to retrace her steps. She left the theatre and went down this street and that, looking for something familiar. It was getting dark now, and their show was bound to be beginning soon. Everything looked different now. Where was she? Where was the auditorium? Where were the police and fans when she needed them?

"You're lost," came a voice from behind her.

She turned around, hoping it was a police officer. It was a seedy-looking stranger, who reeked of alcohol.

She mumbled, "Oh, I'm okay. I don't need any help."

He took hold of her arm. He might have been trying to be helpful, but she didn't want to take any chances. The night was scary enough already. She slung her camera around and hit him in the head with it. When he let loose of her arm, she ran down the street to put as much distance between them as possible.

When she turned the corner, Cal did, finally, see a familiar sight—the movie theatre! Heart pounding, she went back in and asked to see the manager. He was summoned and was soon by her side. A look of recognition crossed his face and he pointed at her, "You're Stacy Ames, aren't you? I heard you and Nate Jenkins would be in town."

"Yeah, and, boy, do I ever need help!"

"Let's go into my office before the next crowd gets here." He ushered her down the hall and to a chair in his small office.

She poured out her story to him and asked if someone could drive her to the auditorium for the show tonight. He looked at his watch and noted that it was already eight thirty-six. Because of the time crunch, he drove her there himself, just in time for Cal and Nate to do their comedy act before the show was over.

The stars dutifully signed autographs, then got back onto the bus. For the first time, Mr. Dean got on their bus, too, and proceeded to loudly reprimand Cal. "Your comedy routine was not meant to be the closing act! You had no right to force us to make it one. You were over two hours late! Nate had to do the 'Moon Over Naples' number alone. Thank God he was enough of a professional to know to do the original version, rather than the modified one, since *you* were nowhere to be found! And how *dare* you come onstage looking like that! You and Nate are supposed to project a wholesome image. Nate fulfilled his image, but you looked like an alley cat! If we weren't so close to the end of this tour, I'd send you home tonight!"

Normally, she would never argue with a director, but Cal was at the end of her rope. "Nate's the reason all this happened! He abandoned me there at the movie theater and I got lost trying to get back."

All eyes turned to Nate, who coughed, then shrugged, "I think she's been working too hard. The poor kid's having delusions."

Cal stared at him in disbelief.

"Don't you remember, Cal?" Nate asked patiently. "*You're* the one who left *me*."

"Whatever your game is," Mr. Dean said, pointing to Cal, "don't you *ever* do that again!" Then he got off the bus.

Nate left his seat and came up front to sit beside Cal. He put his arm around her shoulders as though to comfort her and whispered in her ear,

"All you had to do was join me in that hotel and you would've gotten lost in ecstasy."

She pushed him away, "Get out of my life!" Tears of frustration were streaming down her cheeks.

He got back up, patted her condescendingly on the head, and went back toward his seat.

She took off her shoe and threw it at him, hitting him on his back.

"Don't be so mean to him, Cal," said Janice. "He's just trying to give you moral support."

"Yeah," echoed the others on the bus.

The trumpeter a few rows back pulled out his instrument and played a tender rendition of "Wonderland By Night" as the bus lumbered down the highway toward Montpelier.

Cal threw her other shoe at the trumpeter.

Chapter 19

CAL HAD GOTTEN IN AT 7 A.M. and had never been so glad to see her own bed in her life. As soon as she got all her luggage up to her room, said hello to Jill, and gave Stacy the tiny bottle of shampoo that had been in her hotel room that first day, she went right to bed. When she finally woke up, it was already evening. Then Cal showered, dressed, and came down the stairs chanting, "There's no place like home. There's no place like home."

Leonard was carrying his suitcases in the front door. "Appreciating home now, are we?" he asked with a knowing smile.

"I'll say! I'm never going to go on a tour again. If I ever forget that, chain me to the house, will you?"

"How long did you sleep? I can tell you've had some now." He set his luggage down and picked up the mail that had accumulated while he was gone.

"What time is it?"

He looked at his watch. "Almost 7:40."

"About twelve hours, I guess."

"Remember what I told you before you left?"

"I know, I know."

"Say after me, 'You were right, as usual, Leonard.'"

She brightened, "But at least I'm not a rotten egg."

He mussed her hair. "Thanks for the telegram, kid. You brightened my day."

"Hey, how'd you know it was from me?"

"Just a hunch."

"Well, I don't know about you, but I'm starved," Cal said as she headed for the kitchen. She picked up a banana off the table and peeled it.

Leonard came in, poured himself a cup of coffee, and sat at the table as he opened the mail.

Jill closed the oven door and kissed Leonard. "Welcome home, dear." The wonderful aroma of roast beef filled the room.

"It's good to be back," he acknowledged.

"I never want to work on another project with Nate ever again," Cal said. "Can we move to another neighborhood?"

"No. Why?" he asked.

"Because he's obnoxious, that's why."

"Let Pete know, then," Leonard instructed as he opened and examined each piece of mail. "He can make sure you don't get in anymore pictures with Nate if it's that important to you."

Cal finished her banana and put the peel in the trashcan. "Len, one of the fans at the end of the show said she already had my autograph. She said I already sent her an autographed picture. I sure don't remember doing that."

"A secretary handles all that. She has an office near the studio and responds to all your fan mail."

"I have a secretary? Since when?"

"Almost from the moment your first film came out."

"How come? It's my mail. I want to read it myself. I didn't even know I was getting any fan mail."

He nodded as he looked closely at the fine print of a document that had come in the mail. "Yes, Cal. Of course you do."

"Why don't I ever see it?"

He put the document down and looked at her. "Do you *want* to see it?"

"Yeah! If it's addressed to me, I need to read it and answer it myself."

The thought made him smile. "Okay. I'll take you there tomorrow."

Cal got a Dr. Pepper out of the refrigerator and sat at the table with Leonard. "Can you fix my camera? The film won't advance anymore."

"I'll take a look at it, but I'm no handyman. Did you drop it in water or something?"

"No, I hit somebody with it."

He took the document in hand again. "Nate?"

"A stranger. It was nighttime and I was walking around in Concord and a guy grabbed hold of me. There was nobody around to help me, so I just belted him with the camera."

Leonard dropped the document. "What were you doing walking around in Concord alone at night?"

"It's a long story."

"A lot worse than that could've happened to you, Cal."

"I know. I'm glad I had my trusty camera along."

"Don't *ever* go out alone at night anymore, you hear?" he said sternly.

"Okay, okay. That looks like a legal thing you're looking at."

"It's a contract. I'm changing agents."

"Why?"

"I'm not satisfied with the kind of work Pete's been getting for me."

"But you said you'd been looking forward to that comedy you just finished."

"I arranged that myself. I've been doing a lot of the work myself, and that's not my job. So I'm getting a new agent."

"Pete's been doing a good job for me."

"You think so? I don't."

"Why?"

"You have too much time between projects and your roles are all very similar to each other. I'll see how Michael works out. He comes highly recommended. If he's good, you might want to switch, too."

*   *   *

The next morning, Leonard drove Cal over to the office of the Correspondence Secretary, a branch of Stagecraft. She was a pleasant middle-aged woman who had four assistants to help her handle not only Cal's fan mail, but that of other clients, as well. Some stars chose to use the service, and some chose not to. Fan mail had been one indication to the agent of which stars and combinations of stars appeal to the fans and which ones don't—and why. As for Cal's fans, Mrs. Ralston said, the majority of writers appear to be under the age of twenty, and they have the most favorable comments to make about the films in which she appeared with Nate Jenkins.

Cal asked to see the fan mail that had come in for her. Mrs. Ralston led them to a room in the back of the building, where the letters were filed after a response had been made. They were first sorted by star, then by the nature of the correspondence and date. Cal didn't realize there was more than one type of fan letter, but she was assured there were many. Usually, fans just asked for an autographed picture, which Mrs. Ralston and her assistants were happy to send. Some, however, asked for other things, such as loans or a lock of her hair.

"Darn," Cal laughed, "I was hoping they could give *me* a loan. Don't any of them send money?"

"Play a poor college student one of these days, Cal, and they might," said Leonard.

"They sometimes ask for dates, too," continued Mrs. Ralston.

"Fans have been asking me for a date?" Cal asked incredulously.

"Oh, yes indeed! That's not unusual. Some go so far as to propose marriage."

"Has any of those been from a guy named Miles, by any chance?"

"Cal," Leonard said, "just give up on that, will you?"

"Well, what do you tell them? Am I engaged yet?" Cal asked Mrs. Ralston, ignoring Leonard.

"We respond with thanks for his kindness, but tell him that your heavy schedule prevents you from following through with his request. On the other hand, many of the girls ask when you and Nate will be getting married."

Cal grimaced. "The answer to that one is when hell freezes over."

"We say that no marriage plans have been made. Then there's still another type of letter we get periodically, and the police are notified of them."

Leonard held his hand up. "That's okay. She doesn't have to know all that."

"Yes, I do. What is it that you tell the police about?"

Mrs. Ralston looked up at Leonard, who looked over at Cal. "I know you, Cal," he said. "It's going to upset you."

"Tell me."

The woman sighed, then continued, "Threats of one kind or another."

"Like what?"

"Kidnapping threats, death threats, things like that."

"Why would a fan send a letter like that?" she asked the woman, who didn't respond. Cal then looked to Leonard for an answer. "Why?"

"I guess there's as many reasons as there are people," Leonard replied. "They're mentally unstable, though. They're people you don't want to deal with."

Mrs. Ralston added, "When a fan sees you on his television set in his own house, it's as though you're visiting him. He feels a personal connection with you. That's why they feel they know you well enough to ask you on a date, or things like that."

"But I mean why would they want to kidnap me or kill me when I've never done anything to them?"

She shrugged, "Jealousy, I guess. Maybe they think by harming a famous person, they could become famous, too."

"If they only knew what a headache fame is, they'd change their minds pretty fast. Having to disguise yourself just to go to the corner store, for Pete's sake! And not being able to have an uninterrupted meal in a restaurant. And it's such a weird feeling being stared at all the time."

"I know," Mrs. Ralston agreed. "I hear that all the time."

Cal was afraid of what the answer would be, but had to know, anyway. "Has anyone made any threats to me?"

She nodded. "But we always alert the police, and Mr. Rhoads is told about it, too, just in case extra precautions are necessary."

The amazed girl turned accusingly to Leonard. "You've known about this, Len, and you didn't tell me?"

He looked skyward. "I *knew* it would upset you. Would you just forget it, Cal?"

"How can I? Someone's going to do something bad to me."

"No, they're not. Most people never follow through with their threats."

"But how about the one who does? It just takes one, you know."

"Then we deal with it when it happens. It's not worth losing sleep over because it'll probably never happen." Then he turned back to Mrs. Ralston. "Tell her how much *positive* fan mail she gets in a week."

She looked in her data files. "Of course, it varies from week to week. During the first three months after one of your pictures is released, the amount of mail goes up sharply. Generally, you get anywhere from fifty to two hundred fifty in a week. When you're in a picture with Nate Jenkins, that will push it up to over a thousand."

"Wow!"

"So, how about it, Cal?" Leonard asked. "You want to answer all those letters yourself? Should we have them sent to the house?"

"No, I guess not."

He started toward the front of the building. "And those figures are why Stagecraft keeps pairing you up with Nate in your films and public appearances. Come on. Let's go."

"Bye, Mrs. Ralston," Cal waved. "Keep up the good work."

*   *   *

"I don't want to be dead," Cal said on the way back home.

"You're not going to be dead, Cal."

"I don't want to be kidnapped, either, unless it's by a really cute guy."

His first instinct was to impress upon her the seriousness of a kidnapping—that it's not a joking matter. Leonard knew that as her fame grew, the danger increased. But making her aware of this, he knew, would just serve to make her even more apprehensive than she already was about it. Cal wasn't aware of it, but he had hired undercover protection for her several times in the past. That stranger she hit with her camera could very well have been one of them, except for the fact that none were on duty while she was on tour. It just didn't occur to Leonard that she would wander away from the rest of the troupe. If he had known, he would have hired someone to watch over her. So, in response to her comment, he just said what he thought would ease her mind. "Sorry kid, you're not very likely to get kidnapped, either."

She asked, "I wonder if your fans ask you for dates, too."

"Probably."

"I guess they don't know you're married. You ought to tell them. Does your secretary tell them about that when she writes back to them?"

He shook his head, "I can't believe how naive you are."

"I am *not* stupid!"

"I didn't say you were."

"Yes, you did."

"No, I didn't. I said you're naïve."

"What's the difference?"

"Naive means that you don't see things as they actually are. Your thinking that women care if an actor's married when they want to get close to him is naive, not stupid."

Cal looked at him with a question in her eyes.

He felt her eyes on him and looked over at her. "Well, you're right, Cal. They should. But they don't—not in today's world."

"That's scary," she said, more to herself than to him. "Len, you've never cheated on Jill, have you? Please say no."

"No, Cal, I never have."

"Really?"

"Really."

"And there's lots of guys like you, aren't there?"

"That don't cheat?"

"Yeah."

"More in Small Town, USA, than in Tinseltown, I'm afraid."

"How come you're different?"

"Because I come from strong stock with high standards. It's my heritage, contrary to my screen persona."

"I don't want to ever get married."

"Why?"

"Well, how could I be sure I'd get a guy like that? How can a girl know ahead of time?"

He took a cigarette out of his pocket and lit it. "Cal, believe it or not, I don't have the answers to all of life's mysteries. That's one of the tough ones."

"I think I'll just stay single."

"Okay with me. In fact, you can stay with us indefinitely, if you want. There's no need for you to ever feel you need to get married."

"No, I need to get my own place as soon as I have enough money. How much money do I have, anyway?"

"Not enough."

"How much longer?"

"Oh, I'd guess five or six more years."

"That long? How come?"

"It costs a lot to own a house. Not only do you have to consider the initial cost of the house, but there's also furniture, utilities, maintenance, insurance, and taxes. And I know *you*'ll need a housekeeper and cook."

"I heard you say once that your business manager makes investments for you and they're bringing in as much money as your films are. Why don't we ask him to invest mine, too?"

"Why are you so anxious to get out of my house?"

"Because Jill said people are supposed to be on their own when they're nineteen. Y'all were. I feel like I'm dragging my feet and not doing what I should be doing."

"She was in college and I was in the military at that age. We were both being governed by outside forces. I wouldn't call that being on our own. There's no rush, Cal. You're much safer here with us than you would be living alone. I'll keep the big, bad murderers away."

"That's true," she grinned. "If anyone tried to break in here, you'd pick 'em up and throw across the state line, wouldn't you?"

"More or less," he smiled.

* * *

He answered on the second ring.

"Pete, it's Cal. What's this newspaper article about? It's on the AP wire and the whole world will read it."

He smiled, leaning back in his chair. "Pretty good, isn't it? Your publicist released that."

"My what? And why? I wasn't born in Italy, I was never in my life an A student, and I'm not kin to royalty."

"It's promoting your image. That'll help your career."

"But Pete," Cal said, with exasperation, "how am I going to live up to that? I don't know the first thing about royalty."

"Don't worry about that. You just concentrate on acting."

She sighed in resignation, then asked hopefully, "Got anymore work lined up for me this month?"

"No, I thought you said you wanted time off after the tour."

"Yeah, but it'd be nice to know there's something coming up that'll help me make those car payments."

"You mean all that money from the tour is gone already?"

"No, it's in my trust fund and I can't touch it."

"Oh. Well, as a matter of fact, there *is* something being discussed by some of the bigwigs at the studio; but I wasn't going to tell you about it yet. The only reason I know is because they checked with me on your availability."

"What? Another film?"

"A television series."

Her eyes grew huge. "A series? I'd be working every week? That's great!"

"You and Nate were such a hit on the tour, they're tossing around ideas for a TV show that you two can star in, based on the comedy sketch you did." He was getting excited now, "They're looking at different formats, but it'd likely be a sit-com."

Cal's face fell. "No, not with Nate. I don't want to work with him anymore."

There was a long silence.

"Pete? Are you there?" she asked.

"I'm here and wondering who would want you without Nate."

"Oh, come on. I've worked without him before and it turned out good."

"But he's the best thing that's ever happened to your career. When the public thinks of you, they automatically think of him. You're a set in their minds, like Sonny and Cher."

"Let's change their minds."

"Why?"

"Because I don't want to be in anything with him anymore."

"Why?"

"I just don't, that's all."

"I've heard that you were awfully rude to him. I'm surprised *Nate* isn't the one making this request."

"Why does he always come off looking like the good guy and I'm the bad guy? Nobody believes me when I tell the truth."

"Because he's a gentleman to his co-workers and fans. My sources tell me that he tries to be nice to you and you respond with rudeness. You need to change your ways, Cal. People don't get very far in this business behaving that way. And Harold Dean tells me that you were quite irresponsible on the tour. I can't believe you almost missed the whole show."

"Just that one time, and it wasn't my fault. I got lost and it took forever to get back to the auditorium."

"What were you doing away from the troupe, anyway? Everyone else was there on time."

"For Pete's sake, Pete. I'm not on the witness stand and you wouldn't believe me if I told you, anyway. No one does."

"Try me."

"Okay. Nate and I went to a movie to pass the time. He wanted to make out, right there in the theater, and I didn't, and he was really getting carried away and wouldn't leave me alone, so I changed seats and, when I got back to where he was after the movie, he was gone and I had to find my way back alone and it was dark and I got lost."

"I don't believe that for a minute, and I'll tell you why," he said irritably. "Number one, Nate's quite aware of his public image and has worked hard to build it up. He's worked for and earned the respect of his fans, so I know for a fact he would *never* do something like that anywhere, much less in a public place. Number two, he could have any woman he wanted. He'd have no reason to resort to such adolescent behavior. Number three, he's too honorable a person to just leave you there to find your way back alone, especially in the dark. He cares about people, Cal, and would *never* do that. If you go around spreading rumors like that, you're setting yourself up for a lawsuit. You'd better change your story, and fast!"

"Are you *his* agent, too, Pete?"

"You bet I am."

"I thought so. Just get me work without him."

"You're passing up a golden opportunity. A TV series would be excellent exposure for you, and you'd earn a lot of money."

"It's not worth it."

"You're crazy, Cal."

"Just get me something else. I don't care what, just something a hundred miles away from Nate."

He sighed. "I'll do what I can."

∗　∗　∗

It'd be good to see her buddy, again. Cal took the long way over to Becky's, going a couple of blocks out of her way to avoid walking by Nate's house. She rang her doorbell, but there was no answer. She looked in the driveway; Becky's car was gone. That was odd. This wasn't one of her work days. Maybe she had gone over to Nate's. She *is* his friend, too, after all. But he lived only a block away. Why would she drive?

Cal turned around and went back home. She'll try again later.

∗　∗　∗

Leonard hung up the phone and went upstairs to Cal's room. She was sitting on the floor, listening to records on her stereo while reading a script, and didn't hear him come in. He turned the stereo off.

"Hey!" she objected, "Why'd you do that? It wasn't *that* loud." She reached out to turn it back on.

He pushed her hand away from the machine. "Put your shoes on. We're going to the hospital."

Her eyes grew huge. "What's the matter? Did Jill or Stacy get hurt?"

"No." He handed her a sandal and looked around for the other one.

She put it on. "Are you having a heart attack or something?"

He looked under her bed, pulled the other sandal out, and handed it to her. "Now do I *look* like I'm having a heart attack?"

"I don't know. What's a heart attack look like?"

"Not like this. Come on." He went back downstairs and out the door.

Cal put her other sandal on, then followed him downstairs. She looked in the living room, then the kitchen. There they were—Jill was ironing and Stacy was watching TV in the media room. Thus assured that they were all right, Cal went to the car.

As she got in and closed the car door, she asked, "So what's going on?"

"Nate's in the hospital with pneumonia and they aren't sure he's going to make it. He asked for you," he said as he started backing the car out of the driveway.

Cal opened the car door back up and started getting out.

Leonard grabbed her arm and pulled her back inside. "Close that door, *right now!*"

"Dadgum it!" She closed the door and rode in silence for a while. Then she wondered aloud, "How'd he get pneumonia, anyway? Syphilis would be more believable."

He looked askance at her. "How do you know about syphilis?"

She shrugged, "My dad was a doctor and my mom was a nurse. They talked about medical stuff sometimes."

Leonard changed lanes. "I don't know how he got it. Maybe a result of the tour or something."

"And why on earth would he ask for me?"

"Your guess is as good as mine."

"Maybe he thinks it's contagious and he wants to give it to me."

Leonard was clearly upset. "Cal, I don't care what your relationship has been with him in the past, but you've got to be a friend to him today."

"I'm not *that* terrific an actress, Len."

"If it's as serious as they say, his uncle is likely to be there; and he's a powerful man. He could make or break your career."

"Not to mention yours."

"No, not so much mine. I've got more than one iron in the fire. That studio is just a small part of my livelihood. But most of your work—in fact, *all* of your film work—has been produced by that company. If you alienate Bob, you'll never work for them again. And that would make it difficult for you to get work anywhere."

She was resigned to the inevitable. "Okay. Set the scene. You're the director."

At a stop sign now, Leonard pulled out a cigarette and lit it. He took a long puff as he pondered the situation. "You're a concerned friend. What you want most in the world is for Nate to get well. Nothing else matters to you as much as that does. You'll take him a gift of some sort, which we'll get at the shop in the lobby. You're distraught that he's feeling bad and you'll be worried that he might get worse. You'll hold his hand…"

"Len, not that," she whined.

He looked at her sternly, "… and you'll *keep* holding his hand all night, if need be!"

"Are you sure he's really sick? He's probably just faking it."

"I don't think Becky would have called if it weren't important."

"Oh, Becky told you about this?"

He nodded. "She called from the hospital."

Cal stopped and thought for a moment, then asked softly, "Is he going to die?"

"It would surprise me if someone that young died of pneumonia, unless there were complications that we don't know about."

They pulled into the hospital's parking lot.

*   *   *

She pointed to the sign on the door and looked at Leonard. "It says 'No visitors.'"

"That doesn't apply to us." Leonard pushed the door open for Cal.

With a potted plant in hand and Leonard behind her, she tentatively took a step inside. Sitting in a chair beside the bed was Becky and in the chair at the foot of the bed was a portly man who appeared badly in need of a cigar. They both looked worried.

Becky looked up. "Cal! I'm so glad you came. Come on in and sit here." She rose from her chair. As Cal went to stand beside Becky, she set the plant down on the bedside table. "Go on, Cal. Sit down." Cal sat. Then Becky beckoned to Leonard and the other gentleman as she started walking toward the door. They followed.

"Hey, wait a minute! Where're y'all going?" Cal asked.

Becky turned back around. "We'll be outside in the hall for a minute. We want to talk to Leonard about something."

"Leave the door open!"

"Okay." They exited the room and stood in the hallway.

Cal turned her attention to Nate. He looked awful—so pale and tired! His eyes had a dullness to them. His hair was damp. There was an oxygen tent over him from the waist up, and he had an intravenous tube taped to his arm. He looked so harmless! "If you were always like this, Nate, we could get along just fine."

He didn't answer, but looked over at her.

She glanced toward the doorway and saw Leonard right outside. He motioned to her, pointing to his hand. Picking up on the cue, Cal took Nate's hand in hers. It was very warm. "I brought you a plant."

Nate didn't look in the direction of the plant, but uttered a brief, "Thanks." Breathing seemed to be difficult for him. His chest was going up and down in an exaggerated manner. With each breath, she heard a rattly sound. *Could that be the 'death rattle' I heard Mom and Dad talking about once?* she wondered. Maybe he really *was* dying! But how could that be? He had scads of energy in the balcony of that theatre, and was in fine shape just a week ago when they had gotten back from the tour.

"What's pneumonia feel like?" she asked.

He took a couple shallow breaths, then said hoarsely, "Like hell."

"Your hand feels hot. You must have a fever."

He nodded.

She didn't know what else to say. Thinking back on the directions that Leonard had given her, she put her other hand on top of Nate's and stroked his hand. "I hope you get better real soon. This is no place for you—there's no cameras here."

He smiled weakly and closed his eyes.

"You want to go to sleep? I'll leave you alone if you do."

"Don't go," he said softly, still holding onto her hand. His eyes remained closed.

The other three came back in the room, and Leonard stood behind Cal with his hands on her shoulders. "It looks like all this company is wearing him out. Do you need to be alone, Nate?" Leonard asked.

"I offered to leave, but he wanted me to stay," Cal told him.

"You want me to come back later to pick you up, then?"

"Okay."

He reached down and took hold of Nate's arm. "Hang in there, buddy. You'll be better in no time." Then he patted Cal's shoulder, "I'll be back in a half hour."

"Okay."

Then he left.

How could Nate have gotten so sick so fast? she wondered. She looked over at Becky. "When did all this happen? He was fine on the tour."

"He had a cough when he got back, and it got progressively worse. I think it's all the coughing he's been doing that has him so worn out, not the company."

"When did he come here?"

"This is his third day."

"Have you been with him the whole time?"

"Yes."

"If y'all want to go have some supper, I'll stay with him," Cal suggested.

Becky looked over at the man. "You want to eat something, Dad?"

Oh, Cal thought, *that's her dad.* She had thought he was Nate's uncle. "Yeah, Mr. Stewart," she said, "you look like you need a break. I'll take care of things while y'all go get a bite."

He stood back up. "I do have some business to attend to. Let's have dinner, Becky, then I'll go to the office for a while, then relieve you about nine o'clock."

"That sounds good," Becky said as they headed toward the door. "I'll be back in a little while, Cal. Is there anything we can get for you at the cafeteria?"

"No, I'm fine."

They left.

Cal would have gone over to look out the window to see what kind of view he had, but Nate was still holding on to her hand. He seemed to be asleep, though. He was so manageable when he was this sick. *What a shame he can't be this calm when he's healthy*, she thought. Cal scooted the chair a little farther back, then leaned back in it and propped her feet on the edge of his bed. She reached for the remote control with her other hand and turned on the television, keeping the volume low so it wouldn't wake him.

* * *

"I've never seen anybody get so sick so fast," she told Leonard that night on the way home.

"Becky told me he had rheumatic fever as a child. That weakened his heart, which, I guess, makes things like this more devastating."

"Really? I didn't know anything was wrong with his heart. In fact, I didn't even know he had one."

"Stop it, Cal! She said that he hasn't shown any improvement since being admitted to the hospital. His fever hasn't gone down at all. He just seems to be getting worse, and doesn't even show any will to live. That's why they called us."

"I wonder what she figured *we* could do about it."

He shrugged, "Beats me. But if he was asking for you, I guess it makes him feel better for you to be there."

"He slept most of the time I was there, though. I don't think I did much good."

* * *

The next morning, Becky called and asked Cal to come back to the hospital.

As Cal drove herself there, she worried that perhaps he might have taken a turn for the worse—if, indeed, that was possible. Otherwise, why would Becky have made that request? It was hard to believe, but Cal was actually hoping Nate would get better. First, she wanted him to recover completely, *then* stay out of her life forever. But the first order of business was to get him well. If he died, she'd be feeling guilty for the rest of her life.She walked into Nate's room not knowing what to expect. The first thing she noticed was that *Becky* was looking better. She didn't look as drawn as she had the day before. She smiled and took Cal's hand. "His temperature's starting to go down—*finally!* And he got a good night's sleep last night, for the first time in a week."

Cal looked over at Nate. He didn't look quite so pale, but everything else was still the same. The IV and oxygen tent were still there. He was still rattling.

"Hi, Nate. You feeling better today?" she asked as she went over to his side.

He reached his hand out and she took it. "Better," he said.

Cal returned to the chair and propped her feet back up on his bed. "Want to watch TV? Maybe they'll run an old Corky movie or something." She picked up the remote control.

"Mike movie," he said with a weak smile. Then he started coughing.

Catching his joke, Cal smiled as she turned on the television. "No movies on yet this early. Feel like tuning in to a soap opera and seeing who's married to who this week?" She looked over at him to get his verdict. He shook his head. She flipped to another channel. "Okay, how about a game show?" He focused on the television. She looked up at the screen. *The Match Game* was on. *Maybe he knows some of the celebrities,* she thought. She set the remote control down and watched the show with him.

Hand-in-hand they remained through the next few hours, until Cal went downstairs to get something to eat. At the cafeteria, she bought a sandwich and Coke, then found an empty table. She had only gotten started on her sandwich when a woman with a tape recorder took the seat across the table from her.

"You're Stacy Ames, aren't you?" she asked.

"Yes, ma'am."

The woman extended her hand in greeting. "My name is Erin Day, and I understand that Nate Jenkins is a patient upstairs. Is that correct?"

"Are you a reporter?"

"Yes, I am," she said.

Cal tried to remember whether anyone had told her to keep Nate's confinement a secret. She didn't recall that ever coming up. "He's got pneumonia. But it looks like he's starting to rally now."

"And you rushed to be by his side, I see."

Cal shrugged, not having a good answer for that.

"Did he have a brush with death?"

"I don't know. He was looking pretty awful at first, but now he's watching TV. He's acting more human today. He matched a couple of the stars on *The Match Game*, but he's still not ready to run in the Olympics or anything."

"Tell me," she leaned closer, "is there any truth to the story that you two secretly got married while on tour last month?"

Cal did a double-take. "Where'd *that* story come from?"

"There were reports that you and Nate snuck out one afternoon while you were in Concord, New Hampshire. When questioned about it soon after you left, no one knew where you two had gone."

"We went to see *The Graduate*. Have you seen it? It's pretty good. Dustin Hoffman and Anne Bancroft have terrific timing and everything."

Erin gave her a sidelong glance. "Are you sure that's where you went?"

"Hey, Len and I disappeared for a couple hours, too, in Springfield, but no one makes a big deal out of that."

"Is he one of the musicians?"

"Leonard Rhoads. I live at his house here in L.A. We went sightseeing in Illinois."

"Leonard Rhoads, the actor?"

"Of course!"

She looked confused, "So you're living with one man and married to another?"

"No! No! Len and I aren't 'living together' like *that*. He's married, for Pete's sake! And I'm *not* married to anybody and never will be." This was getting uncomfortable! "You're not reporting for a tabloid, are you?"

"No. The daily newspaper."

"Whew! I could just see the scandalous headlines from being misquoted about that! I better keep my mouth shut."

"The angle I'd like this story to take is your coming to his side in Nate's hour of need."

"Well, actually, I'm not that saintly and he's not that needy. Why don't you just report that he has pneumonia and is doing better?"

"We'll see."

* * *

Uh-oh, she thought on her way back up to Nate's room, *what've I done now? If that reporter makes it look like I'm going around trying to make myself look like a do-gooder, that could hurt my career worse than not going to see Nate at all.*

At Nate's door was a nurse and a man with a notebook. The nurse was explaining that the patient inside was very ill and was allowed no visitors. *Another reporter?* Cal wondered. While she waited for them to settle their dispute, Cal noticed for the first time that Nate's name wasn't on the door. When they had first come up here, Leonard knew Nate's room number; so she hadn't noticed the lack of a name on the door then. *Double uh-oh,* she thought. *If that nurse isn't mentioning the patient's name and they don't have his name on the door, does that mean Nate didn't want the media to know he's here? If so, I blew it.*

* * *

After another several hours of hand-holding and television-watching, Cal got up to stretch.

Nate's grip tightened. "Don't go."

"Hey, you're getting your strength back, Nate. You weren't holding my hand that tight yesterday. But I've got to go. I've got to study my script tonight and go to work in the morning."

He let go of her hand. "Come back after work?"

"Okay." She went over to Becky. "It'll probably be kind of late when I get in—maybe about eight-thirty. I'll grab a bite to eat, then come here."

"See you tomorrow," she said. "Thanks for coming, Cal."

"It's nothing. I'm sure he would've done the same for me." With that, she left. On her way back to the car, Cal thought, *Yeah, he'd do the same for me, all right. The only difference would be that, instead of sitting there holding my hand, he'd probably end up in the bed with me. I'd have to put that oxygen tent around my whole self to keep his hands off me.*

* * *

As Cal was getting a hasty breakfast, Leonard was seated at the table, reading the morning newspaper. "What's this?" he asked. "Stacy Ames and Leonard Rhoads living together?" He looked over at Cal, then back at the article.

She went over to him and read over his shoulder. On top was a file photo of Nate. Under Erin Day's byline, the article at first told of Nate's illness, then went on to describe the complicated love affair he was having with Stacy Ames, who was living with Leonard Rhoads, a married man. "Oh my gosh! How could she get it so wrong?"

"How did she get it at all?" he asked.

Feigning ignorance wouldn't work, Cal knew, because Ms. Day had written that she had talked to her. "She wrote this like it was a tabloid, Len! She misquoted me."

"Why did you talk to her?"

"Because I don't snub people. She came up to me in the hospital cafeteria and asked me some questions. I thought the worst that could happen would be that she'd make it look like I was trying to make myself look good for coming to see Nate."

"Now it looks bad for both of us! For me, it's no big deal; but it could ruin your squeaky-clean image, which, on second thought, might not be a bad thing."

"At first, she seemed to think it was the 'living together' kind of thing, but I explained to her that it wasn't like that at all because you're married. I thought she understood."

He shook his head, "Apparently not."

"But surely everyone will remember the publicity that came out when my folks died and y'all took me in. They'll know that's what this is all about."

"People have a poor memory for honorable things. The scandalous things, they remember for decades." He put the newspaper down. "And what's this about a love affair with Nate? Is that what you told her? A week ago, you never wanted to see him again. Have you gone to the other extreme now?"

"No. Once he's well, I *still* won't want to see him anymore."

"But right now, what?"

"Good grief, Len! *You're* the one who made me go see him! You're the one who told me to hold his hand! I'm just doing what you told me to! Now I'm getting in trouble for it?"

"You don't have to go overboard, Cal! You don't have to *live* at that hospital! You were there most of the day yesterday!"

"Because he wanted me to stay!"

"That's what the word 'no' was invented for! You have no trouble using it when you're talking to me. Try using it on *him*, for a change."

"Since this is a regular newspaper and not a tabloid, maybe they'll print a retraction or something."

"It wouldn't hurt if you'd write a letter to the editor, straightening everything out. Let me read it before you send it."

"Okay. And Len? She *did* spell our names right. She didn't put an extra 'e' in yours. You always said that's the important thing."

* * *

"Hey, where's your tent?" Cal asked. "Now you can't go camping."

Nate was looking *much* better this evening. The oxygen tent was gone and he was starting to get the sparkle back in his eyes. So was Becky. After she had settled into her usual routine, Cal found that Nate wasn't rattling anymore and was more conversational. All that was left of the bad stuff was the IV. So why did he insist on holding her hand again tonight, she wondered. He was out of the woods now, wasn't he?

The doctor came in, looking at the chart. "Well, Mr. Jenkins, I see that your temperature is almost down to normal now. Let's see how your lungs sound."

Cal and Becky took this opportunity to take a walk down the hallway.

"It's a shame he isn't married," Becky said. "He has nobody to look after him once he gets home."

"That's what Becky-buddies are for," Cal grinned. "I bet he'll be going home pretty soon, too. He's doing a *lot* better now, isn't he?"

"I'll say! Do you know what he told me when he was real feverish?"

"What?"

"He said you're the only girl he'd ever loved and he wanted to see you once more before he died. That's when I called Leonard. At that point, I didn't even know if Nate would make it another day."

"Yeah, I can see why if he said that. He was *really* out of it, wasn't he?"

"No, he was never delusional or anything. I'm sure he meant what he said."

Cal shook her head. "Love is probably the *last* thing he feels for me when he's healthy. Lust, maybe, but not love."

"Well, Cal, I think his male pride gets in the way. If it weren't for that, he'd be a lot easier for you to get along with. If something makes him feel ridiculed or hurts his pride, he'll lash out. He's been that way all his life."

"Does he get pneumonia a lot? Len told me about the rheumatic fever."

"Oh, every few years, but this time was by far the worst. Probably, the tour tired him out and lowered his resistance."

"Yeah," Cal nodded. "He put a whole lot of energy into his performance." While she maintained an innocent expression, Cal inwardly laughed at her inside joke. *...at the movie theatre's balcony in Concord*, she was thinking.

Becky saw Nate's doctor leaving his room and caught up with him. "Do you think he'll be ready to go home soon?" she asked him.

"Let's give him a couple more days to rest up. I understand there's no one at home to take care of him."

"He has a housekeeper and cook, and I could drop in on him every day."

"He needs complete rest. If he keeps improving like he is now, I'll probably be discharging him day after tomorrow." With that, he left them and went to his next patient's room.

The girls went back into Nate's room. Cal picked up her script from the window sill, turned to the page at which they would be starting in the morning and folded the pages back. She felt a nudge and looked over in that direction. Nate was reaching out for her hand again. "Okay." She took his hand and sat in her chair, reading over the first few lines.

"What's the script for?" Nate asked.

"I'm doing a TV show this week. Guess what part I play."

"A nuclear physicist?" he answered.

"A schoolmate of the daughter. It's a sit-com. The big problem for them to solve this week is the crush the daughter has on her substitute teacher, who is a really gorgeous hunk of man, played by Kevin Norris. The parents will have the problem solved in exactly twenty-six minutes, not counting commercials."

"Oh, a half-hour show."

"Yeah. How come substitute teachers don't really look like that? I would've paid more attention in class if there was something worth paying attention to."

"Becky showed me the newspaper. Did you know we're having a love affair?"

Cal leaned toward him. "Nate, guess what that reporter thought at first. Remember when we went to the movies in Concord? All she knew was that we disappeared for a while and no one knew where we went. So where's the most logical place we could've gone? They figured, where else? The Justice of the Peace!" She burst out laughing. "Can you believe that? Isn't that where *everybody* goes when they have a couple hours to kill?"

He smiled.

"But I think I spilled the beans without meaning to—about you being here, I mean. I had to plow my way through some reporters in the lobby tonight." She picked up the remote control and turned the television on. "Let's see what movies are playing."

*   *   *

It was almost midnight when Cal walked back into the house that night, but Leonard hadn't gone to bed yet. He lowered the newspaper and looked at his watch. He then gave her a disapproving glare.

"He's getting a lot better now," Cal said, ignoring the time issue. "The doc says he'll let him go home in a couple days."

"When were visiting hours over?"

"I don't know. They said we don't have to pay attention to that. His uncle must carry a lot of weight, even at the hospital."

"Remember I told you not to go out alone at night? Do you remember that? Why did you?"

Cal shrugged, "He needed me."

"Not *that* much, he doesn't! Not enough to risk your life!"

"Oh, Len, I just can't keep myself away. I mean, he's so helpless and harmless. It's like *I'm* in the power seat now. I'm enjoying this. Although this hand-holding business is getting doggone inconvenient. I have to do everything one-handed."

"Nevertheless, if you're going to be out alone at night, I have to know about it ahead of time."

"Why? You can't worry about me unless it's officially on your calendar or something?"

"Don't be a smart-mouth."

"Then how about if you go with me tomorrow night?"

"I just might do that. Did you study your lines?"

"A little. He wanted to talk a lot, though."

"Did you write that letter to the editor?"

"No."

"Do it now."

"But it's so late, Len, and I have to go to work in the morning."

"You should've thought of that before you decided to stay out so long." He put his newspaper aside, got up and pushed her by the shoulders upstairs into the study. He pulled the desk chair out and retrieved a clean sheet of paper from a drawer. "Sit!"

She sat.

He handed her a pen, then stood back with his arms folded.

"What should I write?" she asked.

"The truth. That there's no love affair going on between you and Nate and never will be. And that you're living as a guest in our house and nothing more."

"But Pete tells me that the public thinks there *is* something going on between Nate and me, and he says that's good. He says that's the image Stagecraft wants us to project—like a wholesome kind of love affair."

"But there's no truth to that, is there?"

"No, there's nothing wholesome at all about it."

"What?" he looked startled.

She grinned, "Just kidding."

"Okay. There's no harm in letting them think that, but we *do* need to straighten out this 'living together' business for the sake of your image. It has Jill pretty upset, too."

"Yeah, okay. I'll say that y'all saved me from the evil clutches of the orphanage. If I make it real dramatic, maybe the public will remember it for longer than ten minutes."

*   *   *

Leonard did, indeed, go with Cal to visit Nate the next evening. He was amazed at the younger man's physical improvement in just a few short days. And Cal was glad that, for the first time, Nate didn't take her hand. It was good to have full use of it for the entire evening. The pair stayed about twenty minutes, then took their leave.

On the drive home, Leonard said, "Now *that's* the way to make a hospital visit. Short and to the point."

"He'll be going home tomorrow, so now things can get back to normal around here, again."

*   *   *

The doctor had imposed a two-week confinement at home for Nate to ensure his complete recovery. During this time, a nurse had been hired part-time, and Becky came by morning and afternoon to oversee his care. She got reports from the housekeeper and cook, took his temperature, fluffed his pillow, and did anything else she could think of to make his recovery time more pleasant.

"Why won't Cal come see me anymore?" he asked her.

"I don't know. She said something about being alone in your house, but I'm not sure what she was talking about. I assured her you *were* alone and would like some company."

"But I'm *not* alone! Tell her about the housekeeper, cook, and nurse. I don't think she's concerned that *I'm* alone, but that *she* would be alone with me. I think that idea makes her nervous."

"Oh, yeah. Our little nun and her virtuous lifestyle. I forgot about that." So later that night, Becky telephoned Cal and asked, "Can't you just drop by to see Nate? He's been asking for you."

"No way!"

"Why?"

"He's too well. If he's well enough to be home, he doesn't need me."

"He says he does."

"What he needs, every girl has. He'll have to get it somewhere else."

"He's not *that* well, Cal. The doctor says he needs two more weeks of rest."

"So I'm doing him a favor by staying away."

"He wants you to know there are plenty of people around. He's got a nurse taking care of him, and the housekeeper and cook are still there."

"So he's got enough company. He doesn't need me."

Becky realized there was no use arguing with Cal. Her mind was made up.

*　*　*

"It's for you," Jill said as she handed the phone over to Leonard.

"What time is it?" he mumbled, still half asleep.

She looked at the bedside clock. "6:30. It's Antonio Pirelli, Cal's uncle."

He sat up and took the phone. "What can I do for you, Pirelli? Don't you realize we're two hours behind you here?"

Jill got out of bed and went into the adjoining dressing area, where she washed her face and started getting dressed.

"You know we've got legal guardianship of her," she heard Leonard say. "You gave up all rights to her."

Apparently, her uncle is finally coming to his senses and agreeing to take responsibility for Cal, Jill thought. *And it's about time, too.* Then, she heard Leonard say, "Well, that's just too bad. You blew it, pal."

She looked around the corner at him. Surely, he can't be trying to discourage Antonio from re-establishing a relationship with his niece!

"There's no way you're going to get her."

"Leonard," she whispered, "no!"

"Look, Pirelli, you're not fooling me for one minute. I know what you're really after. Sure, you want her now, now that she's worth big bucks. Where were you when she needed you, huh?"

Jill sat on the bed beside Leonard, wishing she could hear the other end of the conversation.

"She's mine now, not yours. She's going to stay here; and if you contact her in any way, I'll have the law on your tail so fast, you'll rue the day you tangled with me." He slammed the phone down. "The nerve of that guy! When she was orphaned and in need of a home, he was invisible. But now that she's an heiress who's pulling in five figures for her films, he's suddenly decided to be an uncle again. The jerk!"

"But, Leonard, he *is* the only blood relative she has. You can't deny him contact with her."

"When he gave up rights to her, that should've been the end of it for him. She's mine now, and neither he nor anyone else is going to take her away from me!"

"From *us*, Leonard. We're *both* her guardians," she said softly.

"Whatever," he mumbled, as he got out of bed and started getting dressed.

"And it's all academic, anyway," Jill added. "After all, she's over eighteen."

"The guardianship's in effect until she's twenty-one."

"Really?"

He nodded. "I had them put that clause in there. Because of her special circumstances, she needed a guardian longer than most kids would've."

"And when she's twenty-one, then what?"

"I'll deal with that when the time comes."

Something about the way he said that made Jill feel very uneasy.

*   *   *

Okay, Cal figured, maybe the phone isn't the best way to impress upon Pete the importance of getting her more work. She drove to his office. It's the first time she had ever been there, and she was disappointed at its lack of elegance. It was a small office suite, with two rooms. One in back for him and another, smaller one, in the front for his secretary. On the wall of the secretary's office were framed portraits of Pete's clients. She noticed that he didn't have one of her alone but, rather, it was a portrait of both Cal and Nate, as Corky and Mike, taken from her first film. *Apparently, that's the only way he can visualize me,* she thought.

Now she was sitting in the red vinyl chair in front of his desk. "Got some shows lined up for me yet, Pete?" she asked, hopefully.

"I'm still working on it. *Let's Party* would've been interested if Nate could've been on with you. So would *Teen Time.*"

"Why can't I go on them alone?"

"And do what? You're not a soloist, Cal."

She thought for a moment, then her eyes lit up. "Hey, you can team me up with Van Roman!"

"He's under contract with another studio."

"Can't they loan him out?"

Pete shook his head, "Not likely."

"What about Frankie Avalon? He does movies with Annette. Maybe he'll do it with me, too."

Pete shook his head. "The public wants to see him with her, not with you."

She figured as much. "How about if Len and I work together?"

"Do you think you can talk him into working one of these teeny-bopper shows?"

She shrugged and sighed. "Probably not. He likes adult stuff."

"Face it, Cal. With Nate, you're hot property. Without him, you're hard to place."

"But it shouldn't be that way. Len's taught me to be a really good actress. Why can't casting directors see that?"

"Because there's hundreds of good actresses in town, and most of them are willing to *motivate* the producers to hire them, if you catch my drift."

"What do you mean?"

How Pete wished he could educate Cal in the ways of Hollywood—after all, it would greatly increase his own commission if she would follow the unwritten rules of the profession—but he knew word would get back to Leonard if he did. He certainly didn't want to risk Leonard's wrath. "Never mind. I'll see what I can do for you, Cal. Just be patient."

"Look out the window, Pete."

"What?"

"Look at that yellow car parked in front of your building."

He looked down at the sedan two flights below. "Yeah? So?"

"I've got payments to make on that car. If I don't make them, they'll repossess it, then I won't be able to get to *any* of my jobs."

"With the money you've made on your past jobs, you should've had that car paid off by now."

"Well, I don't. I need work, Pete. Please? How about if I motivate *you*?"

He looked at her skeptically. "In what way?"

"By giving you fifteen percent instead of ten?"

"I'll see what I can do, Cal. That's all I can promise."

She sighed.

*　*　*

That evening, Cal got an excited call from Becky. Nate had been nominated for an Omnus Award, and the presentations would be the following month. It would look so good, she said, for Cal to be at the table with them that night. Would she, please? As a favor to her best friend?

"Oh, okay, I guess," she replied. She had never been to Omnus presentations before and knew there would be many, many superstars there. Maybe she'd even get to see Van Roman.

*　*　*

"What'd you want to talk about?" Leonard asked Jill as she closed the bedroom door.

She sat on the bed and beckoned for him to sit beside her. He did. "I think we ought to legally adopt Cal," she said.

"But that doesn't make sense, as old as she is."

Jill shook her head slowly, "The poor child doesn't really feel like a part of any family, Leonard. This would show her that she's one of us, that she's wanted. She said that she's always wished she had a sister. This way, she'd have one."

"She's already like a sister to Stacy. We don't need a piece of paper to tell us that." Leonard stood back up, took a pack of cigarettes out of his pocket, and shook one out. "No, I'm not going to adopt her. That's out of the question." He lit the cigarette.

"Don't you care about her, Leonard?"

"Sure I do."

"But she *needs* a father."

"It's not going to be me."

The softness had left Jill's voice. "So exactly *what* are you to her?"

"Not her dad, that's for sure."

"That's how she thinks of you, you know. You're nothing more to her than a father figure."

"I'm her mentor. She looks to me for guidance."

"Like a father."

"I don't want to talk about it anymore. No adoption, and that's that." He left.

Chapter 20

IT WAS NEARLY IMPOSSIBLE FOR CAL to keep herself from staring. All around her were absolutely beautiful people, world-famous people, people she never dreamed she'd ever see in the flesh. Because the Omnus Award Presentations was one of the most-watched broadcasts of the year, the participants were all here in their finest, exquisitely coifed and glittery with jewels, to see and be seen.

A few of the people at their table were familiar to Cal from previous films. Among them were Becky's dad and also director Theo Malone, who won an award himself the previous year.

They, of course, saved the lead actors' awards for last. Nate's nomination was for his starring role in *Green Grass of Home*. Everyone at the table held hands as Bette Longworth opened the envelope and paused, dramatically, before reading the winner's name.

"And the winner is… Nate Jenkins, *Green Grass of Home*."

Becky screamed and gave him an excited hug as the crowd around them roared their approval. Nate was beaming as he rose from his chair and noted Cal's thumbs-up signal. He leaned down and gave her a joyous hug, too, then advanced to the stage to receive his award.

*　*　*

Instead of going right home after the ceremony, Nate and all his guests went to The Diplomat, the ritziest restaurant Cal had ever seen, where they dined and danced the night away. Many of the people she had seen at the award presentations were there, too. Early in the evening, Nate had led her to the floor for a soulful waltz. Quite a few flashbulbs went off during that dance, she noticed. Cal knew she shouldn't have been surprised at how well he danced, but she was anyway. Later in the evening, while she was at the buffet, she glanced up and saw Nate leaving the room with a beautiful young woman. They were gone for about thirty minutes. *So what?* Cal thought. *I don't care what he does.* If Cal wanted to dance and no one had asked her, she went to whoever appealed to her and asked him. She hardly sat down at all that night.

In the back seat of the limousine on their way home, Becky asked Cal, "Why were you dancing with so many old men?"

"I wasn't."

"Well, you know—guys in their thirties and forties. There were plenty of guys our age there. Why didn't you ask *them* to dance?"

Cal shrugged, "I don't know."

"And how about you, Nate?" Becky turned to him. "Where did you and Mimi go? I saw you two sneaking out. Does The Diplomat have bedrooms upstairs or something?"

"What *are* you, a one-woman vice squad?" he asked, good-naturedly.

"Just looking for some explanations, that's all. It was your party and you disappeared. I thought there must be a good reason for it."

"Well," he shrugged, while smiling to himself, "I thought it was a good reason. She just wanted to congratulate me—in her own sweet way." Then he leaned across Becky to look at Cal, "Did you miss me?"

"I didn't even notice you were gone."

"Yeah," Becky agreed, "she was too busy dancing with every old guy she could find."

"They weren't old!" Cal corrected her.

"You did *too* know I was gone," he told Cal. "I saw you watching us leave."

Caught in a lie, she simply shrugged and mumbled, "Who cares?" For having had such a good time, Cal sure was feeling grouchy now—and she didn't know why. *Probably the late hour,* she thought.

Chapter 21

"Knock, knock," Stacy said with a giggle.

Cal had been sitting on her bedroom floor, listening to records, when this Honorary Little Sister of hers came running in and draped herself over Cal's shoulder with her latest "knock-knock" joke.

"Who's there?"

"It's me!"

Cal pulled her over her shoulder and into her arms, where she held her and nuzzled her face into Stacy's tummy, causing a new cascade of giggles. "You silly kid! Guess what, Stacykins!"

"What?"

"Your mommy signed you up for kindergarten today. You're going to be a real schoolgirl in September!"

"Will I get to ride a bus like the big kids do?"

"Well, not to kindergarten. But when you start first grade, I bet you will."

"Will I be in first grade next year?"

"Your birthday's in June, so you'll be the right age two Septembers from now."

"Mommy used to be a teacher."

"That's right. And did you know she used to be your age? She was a little bitty girl once just like you, and I bet you look a lot like she did."

"And Daddy, too?"

"Well, I don't know. I think Daddy was born forty."

Stacy's trusting eyes grew large. "Really?"

Cal laughed, "No. I'm kidding. But I can't imagine Daddy being little, can you? He's so *big*!"

"Yeah! Shirley said he's the tallest man in the whole world."

"Okay, I'll buy that."

"Girls, dinner!" called Jill from the foot of the stairs.

They looked at each other and grinned. "Let's go," Cal said.

* * *

"*Of course* you need to move around during the dialog," Leonard said during dinner. "You've been doing it for over five years now."

"Yeah, I know, but *why?*" Cal asked. "People don't do that in real life. We're supposed to be realistic, aren't we?"

"Only to a certain extent. Movement adds to the interest. Look at everyone here at the table now. We've all stayed in the same spot throughout dinner. The only thing that's changed is the dialog. Imagine you're an audience watching this. Would it sustain your interest?"

"I guess as long as we pass the platter to them, too, they'd stay awake."

"Come with me." Leonard got up from the table and went into the media room.

Not as much as a nod of appreciation to the cook. Cal never could understand that.

"Good dinner, Jill. I'm stuffed," Cal said as she got up and followed Leonard. She sat in her usual place, beside him on the sofa in front of the big screen.

He picked up a film and put it on the projector. Advancing it to the proper position, he continued, "This demonstrates what I'm talking about." The fictional family was at a table. After making a comment, one member moved from one seat farther from the main character to the spot right beside him on the pretense of showing him something more closely. Then the mother got up and poured coffee into the father's cup while contributing to the conversation. "And when there's a lack of movement in the scene for one reason or another, that's when they sometimes resort to close-ups or other movement from the camera." He stopped the projector, then changed films. "This one's even better. You'll see how cleverly movement can be incorporated into the scene." This was a scene with several characters standing and conversing. Cal noticed there was almost constant movement in this one. As each character spoke a line, he moved to another place, relative to what he was saying. After a few minutes, everyone was in a different position; but the movement was quite relevant to the dialog. "If the viewer is not particularly observant, he might not notice exactly what's happening. All he knows is that it holds his interest."

"Okay. You made your point. Real life is dull."

"Sometimes."

"Tomorrow, my character will be hearing things that only she can hear. How would *you* do that?"

"First, the movement of the eyes will hint that you hear something. Then you'll turn your head toward the sound." He got another film out and put that on the machine. After setting it to the proper place, the scene showed just that. "See how he did that?"

"Show it again. It went past me too quick."

He rewound it and started it again, this time in slow motion. "The eyes first. See? Blinked and to the right. Now the head, toward the sound."

"Okay. I think I've got it now."

"Do you know all your lines for tomorrow?"

"About half of them."

"You better get busy then. I've got stuff to do, too. Michael's lined up some really good roles for me in the next eighteen months."

"Wow! That far ahead?"

"That's the best way to do it. Planning goes more smoothly. Ideally, I know at least several months in advance what I'll be doing so I can prepare for it. Michael's really good. You ought to think about changing agents, too."

"But I don't need to."

"Pete leaves big gaps and doesn't like to take chances. You have potential that's barely been tapped yet, Cal. You need an agent who will dare to reach for the stars—metaphorically speaking, of course."

"I better go study those lines." She got up and left.

*   *   *

After sleeping late on a Saturday morning, Cal had a leisurely breakfast while Jill held a partially-assembled dress up to Stacy in the next room.

Stacy had been in casual clothes most of her life and had very few nice dresses to wear to kindergarten. Jill knew it would be quicker and simpler to just buy her a new wardrobe, but she so enjoyed sewing that she was determined to make five new dresses for her before September. Such creativity always gave Jill a feeling of achievement.

"It's a pretty day outside, Jill," Cal said. "Why don't we have a picnic in the park?"

"That's a lovely idea, but I'd like to finish this dress today. When I'm so close to being finished, I really don't want to stop."

"Yeah, I know the feeling."

"In a minute, I'll be finished with Stacy, so you two can go to the park, if you wish."

"Can Becky come, too?" Stacy asked.

"That's a good idea," Cal agreed. "Let's go ask her. We'll be going right by her house on the way."

Cal put her shoes on while Stacy finished up in the sewing room. Then they left for Becky's house. Becky was home and invited the girls in. They followed her to the utility room, where she loaded the clothes washer and pressed the "start" button.

"How come you do your own laundry?" Cal asked. "You have a house-keeper that comes every day."

"She keeps the house clean, but I prefer to do my own laundry because I've seen how household help will sometimes find out intimate details about the people they work for, then blab them to a tabloid for big money. Laundry for one person's not that hard to do, anyway."

"Why would a tabloid want to know about *your* laundry?" Cal asked. "Because you're Nate's friend, you mean?"

Becky nodded, "Partly. We're close."

"Yeah, but ... *laundry*?"

Her friend smiled at Cal's naïveté. "Sometime when we're alone, I just might tell you about that and why I never have live-in help." She winked at Cal while tilting her head toward Stacy.

"Oh. Well, anyway, you got time to go with us to the park? It'll be a while before that load's done."

"Yeah," Stacy tugged at Becky's sleeve. "Come with us."

"Okay, sure. Let's go to the park." She picked up her portable radio and house key, then the three girls went out the front door, bumping into Nate, who was coming to see Becky. She invited him to join them, which he did. Becky locked her front door, then the foursome walked the two blocks to the park, amidst the stares of many passersby. Being constantly watched, once outside the home, had become a very predictable part of Cal's life ever since the first installment of the trilogy was released. She had just learned to accept it and go about her business.

"This is just like *The Wizard of Oz*!" Stacy said gleefully.

"How's that?" Cal responded.

"I'm Dorothy, and y'all are the scarecrow and the cowardly lion and the tin man."

Cal began, "Weeeeeee're off to see the wizard..." and the rest of the group joined her in unison. By the time they reached the park, they looked like a chorus line, arms around each other's shoulders and singing to the top of their lungs. The two stars may have been the famous ones, but Cal felt it was the tiny chorus girl in the middle who stole the show with her "Lions and tigers and bears, oh my!"

Then Stacy broke away and ran toward the sliding board, while her elders seated themselves on the park bench. Becky turned on her radio and set it on the sidewalk beside her feet. The strains of "Leaving On a Jet Plane" were coming from the small, blue box.

"I've sure been doing enough of *that* lately," Cal noted. A few weeks earlier, she had returned from filming in Nevada. Being homesick and knowing no one in that location, she flew home almost every weekend.

"That's why I prefer making films at the studio," Nate said. "It seems to be the ones with the Western or exotic themes that rely most on locations with terrains you don't find around here."

"But they have Western towns on the studio back lots, too."

A man who had been walking by did a double-take when he saw Cal and Nate in conversation on the bench. He then went up to them with a request.

*   *   *

"Y'all should've seen it," Cal told the family that evening at dinner. "The guy didn't have any paper, but he insisted on getting our autographs. We didn't have any paper and no one else around there did, either. So he turns his back to us and wants us to write on his *shirt*. Why on earth would he want to ruin a perfectly good shirt? Anyway, I refused to do it and he started yelling at me, saying I was a big phony and everything else he could think of. Then, out of *nowhere*, this big guy comes up and takes him out of the park, just like that. He wasn't in uniform or anything—just a good Samaritan, I guess."

Jill looked over at Leonard, who smiled and took a second helping of veal.

Cal continued, "He looked a little familiar—that big guy, I mean. I've seen him before, but I can't remember where."

"Doesn't matter," Leonard said. "All's well that ends well."

"Boy, I'll say! But how come fans are so unreasonable sometimes?"

"I guess they get so excited that they aren't thinking straight," Jill replied. "They don't understand that people who make movies are just like anyone else."

"Nate said that sometimes they'll throw hotel keys at him. Why would they do that?"

Jill tried to suppress a smile as she looked down at her plate. "Care to take that one, dear?"

"Not with Stacy sitting here, I don't," Leonard replied.

Stacy piped up, "I know why! It's in case he gets locked out of his house, so he won't get cold at night."

"Yeah," Leonard said, "you're partly right. He wouldn't get cold."

Cal mused, "Throwing a little thing like a key would hardly faze him. They ought to throw something bigger, like a piano, then he'd get off the stage."

*   *   *

Later that evening, Cal came downstairs for a Dr. Pepper, then noticed a light on in the media room. *That's odd,* she thought. She went to turn it off and saw that Leonard was sitting there, watching a film made several years earlier.

She joined him on the sofa. "I haven't seen this one in a while."

"Have you ever noticed how the choice of music influences the way the audience reacts to a scene?"

"Yeah. Sometimes the music they pick gives it a completely different mood than what I would've chosen."

They watched in silence for a moment.

"Is Stacy in bed?" he asked.

"Yeah."

"I can answer your question now—the one you asked at dinner." He lowered the volume on the movie, then set the remote control down. "Those girls are throwing Nate a key to their hotel room, hoping he'll pay them a visit."

"Why do they think he'd go visit a stranger? And why would they want him to, anyway?"

He looked at her in disbelief, then shook his head. "You're amazing."

"What do you mean?"

"You *really* don't know why they want him to?"

"No."

"They want to go to bed with him, Cal."

She looked at him as though he had turned into an alien. "With *Nate*?"

He nodded.

"But it's *Nate* we're talking about, not Miles."

"I know. He's quite popular among moviegoers, Cal. A lot of girls find him appealing."

"I thought Doris and Sue were his only fans."

"Not by a long shot. Why do you think he's got a fence and tall hedges around his house and someone to answer the door for him?"

She shrugged. "I dunno. And I don't even think *Doris* would be *that* forward—to throw him a key." She stopped and thought for a moment, then, "And those fans expect him to do that with a perfect stranger?"

"So it appears."

Her eyes glazed over as she became deep in thought.

"Sorry to disillusion you, kid, but you have to grow up sometime." He turned the volume back up and focused his attention back to the screen.

She scratched her head. "I wonder if he does."

"Goes to the hotel rooms?"

"Yeah."

"Why don't you ask him?"

"Because I don't want him to think I care, because I don't." She looked over at Leonard. "Do ladies throw you keys?"

He reached around to the table behind the sofa and retrieved the bowl of popcorn. "Want some?"

"No. Well, maybe." She took a handful.

He took some, too, then returned the bowl to the table.

"Do they?" she asked again.

"If they do, I don't notice."

Content with that answer, Cal smiled and enjoyed her popcorn as Leonard's bad-guy character instigated yet another barroom brawl on screen.

*   *   *

After the movie was over, Cal went to her room and telephoned Becky.

"I can't believe girls would do that with their hotel keys! Does Nate take them up on it?"

Becky laughed. "I didn't know you knew about those kind of things."

"Of course, I do! I'm not stupid, you know."

"I know."

"Well, does he?"

"How should I know? I don't follow him around."

"Well, I thought he told you everything."

"If he does, he's living a pretty dull life. And I don't think he is."

"Oh."

"He *has* told me that he keeps asking you out and you've turned him down every time. Even right after he recovered enough from pneumonia to go out again, you refused to go with him. Boy, that really confused him!"

"That's because he was back to normal by then."

"But when you came to see him in the hospital every single day and spent so much time with him, he thought that meant you really cared about him. He was floating on air. Then he gets well enough to rejoin the land of the living, and you won't go out with him. I think that's rotten. He'd really be good to you, Cal, if you'd only give him a chance."

"So, Becky, how are you and Johnny getting along? Hasn't he popped the question yet?"

"Not yet. No one can accuse him of jumping into things too soon."

"Why don't you ask him, then?"

"I don't know. Guess I'm not as hip as I want to think I am."

"I'll ask him for you."

"No, I can wait. Sometimes, we just have to let nature take its course."

Chapter 22

"**You're not my only client, Cal.** I'm doing the best I can."

"Well, how about a sci-fi, then?" she asked Pete over the telephone. "Or *Laugh-In*? Yeah! I could do *Laugh-In*. I'm not too young for that. Get me on that one. Come on, Pete. My calendar's empty again!"

"*Laugh-In* is really popular. Everyone wants to be on that show. They're booked up for a long time, but they might could squeeze you in if you and Nate do it together."

"Then get me an adult role on something. I'm almost twenty-one, Pete. I'm old enough."

"Your image isn't. You've still got five good years left in you as a teenager. After that, I don't know."

"How about films? Any films need someone like me?"

Leonard came into the study. Finding Cal at his desk, he took his script from the desk and went to the sofa and sat down.

"None at the moment," Pete answered. "I'll call you when something comes up, Cal."

"Don't forget my car's not paid off yet. I need work."

"I'll see what I can do."

"Bye."

"Goodbye."

She hung up and looked over at Leonard. "Why's he dragging his feet? I'm getting better, and he's finding less and less work for me."

He set the script down. "Probably because you're looking less like a kid and more like a woman now. He thinks you're only capable of playing a kid and he knows you're becoming less believable as one."

"Don't they write screenplays about twenty-one-year-olds?"

"Sure they do. Would you like *me* to get you more film work?"

"Yeah!"

"If I do, though, it won't be as a teenager."

"Good."

"Michael's negotiating on one for me that will begin shooting in a few months. This one's a very special opportunity I didn't want to miss. Not all the roles have been filled yet, but I warn you—by your standards, it's a *very* adult film."

"I can do it."

"Nothing at all like what you're accustomed to."

"Okay by me. I've got to have work, Len, or else they'll repossess my car."

"Okay, kid. I'll see if we can work in some negotiations for you, too. We'll have to get Stagecraft to agree to loan you out, though. This isn't one of their productions."

"Whose is it?"

"Triple Star's."

"Can they pay me ahead of time?"

"You don't have to ask them to do that."

"But I don't want *you* to make any of my car payments. It's mine."

"Okay, I'll loan it to you. You can pay me back when you get paid."

"Okay. What's the film called?"

"*Henson of Manhattan*. It's quite sophisticated, with some nudity in it. That's just in one scene, though."

"That's okay. I can handle it."

"*I* know you can, but I'm surprised to hear *you* say that. Usually you resist trying anything new."

"I've *got* to do it. If I don't, I won't have a car."

"Okay. I'll get you in that film, Cal, one way or another."

"Thanks, Len."

"A film like that could change the course of your life. If you do it really well, you'll gain respect as an adult actress. They'll forget all about your Corky image." He smiled and nodded, "That's exactly what your career needs right now."

*　*　*

Cal couldn't believe her ears. "*You*'ve got a horse? Since when?"

"I bought him last month and he was delivered this morning," Nate informed her over the phone. "Want to come see him?"

"You better take good care of him!"

"If you knew what I paid for him, you'd have no doubt that he'll get good care."

"Do you have a saddle and everything?"

"Sure do. Come on over and take him for a ride."

"But you don't have a pasture on your property."

"No, but there's plenty of room for him here. My back yard goes on forever."

"I'll call you right back."

Cal hung up and dialed Becky's number:

"Does Nate *really* have a horse?" she asked.

"He does, and it's beautiful. You're going to love it. He's been studying up on raising horses and feels they're a good investment. You'll have to teach him how to ride, though. He got all the accessories and everything, but has never ridden one."

"I need to call him back, then. What's his number?"

Becky gave it to her.

"Okay. I'll talk to you later."

She hung up again, then dialed Nate's number:

"Okay," she said. "I'll be right over."

*   *   *

He was, indeed, beautiful! He was solid black and strong and seemed to be quite sweet-natured. She stroked his silky mane. "What's his name?"

"His former owner called him Zeus."

"Zeus! Is that your name, sweetheart?" she asked the animal, as she lay her head affectionately on his neck. "He needs to keep that name. It'll confuse him to be called something else." She checked to be sure the saddle was on securely, then climbed up onto it. Cal rode him toward the back of Nate's property, then around its perimeter. "He rides like a dream. You can tell he's used to being ridden," she reported to Nate, who was watching from a distance. She then urged Zeus into a faster pace, then a gallop for a couple laps around Nate's back yard. After returning to a trot, she asked, "Can I ride him over to my house sometime? I want to show him to Len."

"You can right now, if you want."

"He's not home now, but he will be in about an hour." Cal and Zeus returned to Nate's side, and she dismounted. She returned the reins to him.

He led Zeus back into the stable that had recently been built on his property, and Cal followed. "I'll make you a deal," he said.

"What's that?"

"I'll hire you to take care of Zeus. You can groom him, feed him, exercise him, and everything else that's necessary to keep him in good condition."

"But sometimes I'm off doing location work out of town."

"We can work it out so we're not both out of town at the same time. That way, one of us will always be around to take care of him. You'll need to show me how, though."

"Okay. And I'd get to ride him every day I'm in town, wouldn't I?"

"That's right."

"You got yourself a deal! Where do you keep all his stuff?"

"Back here." Nate led Cal to the back room, where Zeus' supplies were kept. He seemed to have everything.

She took the brush and started grooming the beautiful horse. "Golly, I wish I had one like him. Or, heck, I'm not *that* picky. I just wish I had a horse, period. How'd you get past the city ordinances, anyway?"

"When you know the right person to approach and give him proper incentive, anything can be accomplished." Nate watched carefully to see how Cal cared for Zeus. Even though he had done quite a bit of research before purchasing him, he still lacked experience in handling such an animal. For the next hour, Cal demonstrated her method of grooming, feeding and exercising Zeus, and encouraged him to take a ride himself. He declined, but promised he would sometime in the next week.

"Can I ride him over to show Len?" she asked. "He's bound to be home by now."

"Sure. Let me know when you bring him back."

She planted a grateful kiss on Nate's cheek and got back up on Zeus.

*　*　*

Just for the heck of it, Cal tried the front steps. He did it! Zeus could even climb stairs! What a fantastic animal! She rode up to the front door and rang the bell with her foot. It sure felt strange for the bell to be so low! Come to think of it, Cal remembered, she had never rung that bell before.

When Jill opened the door, she was quite startled to find herself face to face with a horse.

"I'm up here, Jill. This is Nate's new horse and he hired me to take care of him. Isn't he gorgeous?"

"He certainly is. So you'll be going over to Nate's every day, then, won't you?"

"Yeah, unless I'm out of town, of course. Then he'll take care of Zeus by himself."

Leonard heard the conversation from the living room and came to the door. One look at Zeus and he was by his side, taking stock of the animal. "Where's he going to keep him?"

"He's got a stable behind his house. I've got *two* jobs now, Len. I'm in charge of taking care of Zeus. He's going to pay me to do that, so I can afford my own place faster. Isn't that great? You want to take Zeus for a spin, too?"

"Just for a minute. Let's take him around back first."

She rode Zeus to the back of the house, then dismounted. Leonard got into the saddle and smoothly led him around the back yard, first slowly, then at a faster clip. Then they came back to Cal and he dismounted. "He's a good horse. Do you know how to take care of him?"

"I watched Uncle Antonio with his, and I helped him out. So I know *his* way of doing it."

"And his animals were kept healthy and content?"

"Yep."

"Okay. I guess you know what you're doing then."

"I've got to take him back to Nate's now. Just wanted you to see him." She got back up in the saddle, and rode him around to the front of the house, then one block down the street to Nate's house. Seeing the gate of the iron fence closed, Cal was awfully tempted to try to take Zeus overtop it in a smooth jump, but decided against it. There wasn't enough level ground in front of it to reach the proper speed, and she didn't know if he'd been taught to jump yet. She got off, opened the gate, led Zeus to the other side, then latched the gate and walked the horse to the back yard. She put Zeus back into the stable, took the saddle off of him, and brushed him down again. She made sure he was fed and watered. Then she went to Nate's back door and rang the bell. His housekeeper answered the door. "Would you tell Nate that I brought his horse back? I'll see y'all tomorrow," she said as she gaily headed home.

Chapter 23

"It looks like Cal and Nate are developing a good relationship now," Jill said cheerfully, "and it's about time!"

"She never could resist a horse. I wonder if he's figured out that it's Zeus she's crazy about, and not him," Leonard mused.

"Well, you never know. This may lead to something bigger."

"Don't worry about playing matchmaker, Jill. It'll never happen in this case."

"But she spent so much time with him in the hospital. Maybe she doesn't realize it, but she really does like him. When I watched them rehearse for that tour, I could tell they had special feelings for each other. And what a good match that would be! He's got status, money, and connections. He could give her a good life. If you really care about Cal, you'd encourage her to take Nate seriously. He has a lot to offer."

"She doesn't care about all that. He's not her type."

"You might be right. She might consider him too old for her," Jill reflected. "She said he's seven years older. She's still carrying a torch for Miles, you know. He's closer to her own age." She studied his face to see if he had caught the deeper meaning of what she just said. It was hard to tell. If only he weren't such a good actor, it might be easier to know what he was thinking.

* * *

"Do I look like a school girl?" Stacy asked her father that morning. She and Jill had gotten up an hour earlier than usual in preparation for her first day of kindergarten. All dressed and ready for breakfast, the little girl looked adorable in her red plaid jumper and white ruffled blouse.

Leonard was doing a television show this week and was almost ready to leave for the studio. He stopped and smiled at his daughter. "You're the prettiest school girl I've ever seen!"

"Will I get a desk of my own in school?"

"You will in first grade. I don't know if they use desks in kindergarten, though."

"Can I put it in my bedroom?"

Jill interceded, "You'll use the desk while you're in that classroom, but it belongs to the school."

"Do you *need* a desk in your room?" Leonard asked Stacy.

"No, she doesn't," Jill said.

"It'd be neat to have a desk like Cal's," Stacy corrected. "I want a white one, like hers."

"I'll tell you what, young lady," Jill pointed to her. "When you start having homework, we'll get you a desk."

"Okay. Will I have homework today?"

Her mother smiled. "Not this soon. Come on, sweetie. Have some breakfast."

Leonard lifted Stacy and put her in the chair beside his, then left for the studio.

*   *   *

The sun was starting to go down before Cal was finished exercising Zeus that evening. That would be beneficial, though, as the air was cooling off a bit now. *Wouldn't it be neat,* she thought, *if I could teach him to jump the fence!* She could just hear Leonard's voice echoing in her ears, "No, Cal. That's not a good idea." *For a guy who's willing to tackle anything—absolutely any kind of role in creation—he sure is sometimes hesitant to let* me *do stuff,* she thought. Or, at least, stuff she *wanted* to do, like jumping fences. It's funny—when it came to film or TV work, she could do anything and he'd be fine with it. But in her personal life, it seemed he wanted her motto to be "caution above all else." That just reinforced her belief that the male mind was not meant to be understood by females.

After a few more laps around Nate's property, Cal rode Zeus back to the stable. Nate was unloading a new shipment of supplies in the back room. "What do you think of me teaching Zeus to jump?" she asked as she removed the saddle from the handsome stallion.

"Don't do that," he replied. "I don't want to risk his breaking a leg. He's too valuable."

"You don't break a leg when *you* jump." Cal took the brush and started grooming Zeus.

"Don't, anyway. My groundskeeper is already having fits about the craters you're leaving in the yard when you run Zeus." He leaned against the doorframe and admired his horse. "You've been doing a good job with him, Cal. He's healthy and strong. And I appreciate your teaching me how to take care of him."

"It's easy. Just takes some time, that's all."

Nate took another brush and worked on Zeus' other side. "And many hands make light work, huh?"

"Yeah. This must feel so good to him, kind of like when we get haircuts. My mom used to love it when I'd brush her hair. She used to ask me to do it sometimes when she was bone tired from working at the hospital. She said she didn't care how her hair ended up looking; she just liked the way brushing felt."

"You really miss your parents, don't you?"

"A lot. At least now I can talk about them without getting all teary-eyed. For a while, I couldn't."

"My dad died, too."

"I didn't know that. Was he in a plane crash?"

"No, he had a heart attack. My mom's an alcoholic who has no room in her life for anything but booze. We never got along, so I left home."

"Wow, that's awful. How long ago?"

"About eighteen years, when I was ten. Uncle Bob and Aunt Marian raised me as their own after that."

"So your dad never got to see your first picture. Mine didn't see mine, either."

"No. My film career started later."

They had finished with the brushes and put them back on the shelf. "Well, I guess I'm done for another day," she said.

"Come over here. Let's talk a little." Nate went to where the bales of hay were kept and sat on one.

Cal took the clipboard off the wall and sat beside him, checking off the items on the list. "See? This shows everything we need to do for Zeus every day. I keep a list to be sure I don't forget anything."

"That's a good system. I think I picked a good caretaker for my little pride and joy."

She set the clipboard down. "Well, yeah, I think so."

"Thank you, Cal." He kissed her tenderly, then whispered, "I really appreciate it."

She whispered back, "You're welcome."

Nate took her in his arms and kissed her again.

Oh, what the heck. Why not? Cal thought, as she put her arms around him, too. *I wanna see what those girls in the hotels saw in him. I'll show him what a Texas kiss is like... Uh-oh!* Already, he was back in the emotional state he had reached at the movie theatre in Concord. She tried to push away from him, "No, Nate. Don't get carried away, again. Let's just keep it light, okay."

"Oh no," he said, breathing heavily. "You're going to finish what you started." He held her tightly and kissed her with tremendous passion, while easing her down backward onto the hay.

She pushed against him. "Quit it!"

"Don't be afraid. I'll be gentle."

"I've got to go. Let me go!"

"You'll enjoy it. Just relax." He reached down and unbuttoned her top button. "I'm going to show you what life is all about."

"Stop it!" She pushed his hand away.

"What are you so scared of? Everybody does it."

"Not me!"

"You will now. There's no turning back now, babe." His lips hungrily sought hers.

Cal struggled to get out of his clutches, but he definitely had the strength advantage. Finally, though, as he was going for the second button of her shirt, she was able to catch him off balance and pushed him onto the floor. She got up and started to run out, but he grabbed hold of her ankle as she sped past, causing her to trip and fall.

"By God, I'm going to have you if it's the last thing I do!" He pulled her back over and ripped her shirt, his hand disappearing under it as he kissed her hard.

When she was at last able to come up for air, Cal protested, "No, you're not!" She saw no other way out of this situation than to kick her knee into his groin again, as she had done so long ago. That immediately cooled his ardor and gave her time to get away.

She ran all the way home. Once inside, she slammed and locked the front door.

Leonard, in the living room chair, looked up from his newspaper. "What's *that* all about?"

Cal rested her forehead against the door as she took a moment to catch her breath. Then, "I never want to see Nate again as long as I live."

"I've heard that before."

"This time I really, really mean it." She went over and collapsed onto the sofa. "Never again!"

He was startled at what he saw. "Cal! What happened to your shirt?"

She looked down. Three buttons had come off and her shirt was open halfway down to her waist. Cal pulled it closed. "That guy just can't seem to stay vertical!"

He threw the newspaper down. "What, exactly, did he do?"

"He wouldn't let me go. He was all over me, Len. He gets turned on faster than any guy I've ever known! And it wasn't my fault, either! I didn't do anything wrong. I mean, just one Texas kiss is all it took."

"*You* kissed *Nate*?" He couldn't believe what he was hearing.

"Just once."

"Why?"

"Well, I don't know. I guess I miss being kissed. I mean, it's been so long since Miles."

"Cal, you don't understand the first thing about men. If you kiss a man, especially a young man like Nate, you're leading him on and giving him all sorts of ideas. Now go change your shirt."

Cal arose and headed toward the stairs.

"Uh," Leonard said as he retrieved his newspaper, "did you say a 'Texas kiss'? What *is* that, exactly?"

"Well, it's like Texas—bigger and better."

"Then, *of course* it got him excited, Cal. What'd you expect?"

"Len, does 'having me' mean what I think it does?"

"Having you?"

"He said he's going to have me if it's the last thing he does."

That did it. "Don't go anywhere *near* Nate's house anymore, *ever*!"

"I guess that answers that question."

"'Having you' means going all the way."

She nodded, "That's what I thought."

"How far did he get?"

"From my head to my waist. He would've gone farther than that if I hadn't kicked him. Before I came out to California, Myra, our housekeeper, told me to kick a guy there if things ever get out of control, but she said don't make a habit of it. She said it really, really hurts. It looks like she's right."

"Stay away from Nate, you hear?"

"Why did God make guys stronger than girls? It's just not fair. And if all those girls throw their keys at him, why's he picking on me?"

"Maybe he likes a challenge. But, for whatever reason, you just stay away from him until he develops some interests elsewhere. Someone else will have to attend to his horse."

"No, Len." Her tears started flowing. "Not *Zeus*."

Leonard came over to her and put his arm around her shoulders. "Everything will be okay, Cal. You call Pete and tell him to be sure you're never signed onto any project with Nate again. And I'll tell Nate you won't be able to take care of Zeus anymore."

"But Len..."

"We'll have to get you some work at another studio."

Jill came into the room. "What's all the commotion?"

"Your theory about Nate and Cal has been shot to hell," Leonard said. "Look what he did to her." He stepped back so she could get a good look at Cal, but Cal didn't want Jill to see and turned away. "Go ahead. Let her see." He turned her back around to face Jill, as Cal clutched her shirt and wiped away a stray tear. "He tore her shirt!"

It was so humiliating to Cal for Jill to see her like this. Beautiful Jill—who led such a flawless life, always under control, every golden hair in place—would never understand the lack of control in Cal's life. The two were such opposites in so many ways, and it made Cal feel woefully inadequate. Everyone treated Jill like a lady. Why didn't they treat Cal that way?

Jill came over and took Cal into her arms. "You poor dear. I'm so sorry this happened to you. Whatever could have possessed him?"

"A Texas kiss, that's what," Leonard replied with disgust.

"But Miles never reacted that way," Cal said.

"What? You did that to Miles, too?" he asked, shocked. "And *he* dumped *you*?"

She nodded.

"Guess you overloaded the poor guy's circuits, kid."

Jill picked the hay out of Cal's hair. "You can go back to your newspaper, Leonard. I'll take care of this." She said to Cal, "Let's go into the kitchen. I just took a batch of brownies out of the oven."

They went into the kitchen.

Leonard was quite confused. What did brownies have to do with this, and why did that make Cal's tears stop?

*   *   *

The next day, it was driving Cal crazy to know it was time to exercise Zeus and she wouldn't be the one to do it. All day long, she had visions of him getting fat and lazy because no one would run him, or maybe getting so skinny his ribs would show because no one was feeding him. He'd look sloppy because no one would brush him and love him. She tried to busy herself with other things, but her thoughts kept coming back to Zeus. He needed her and she needed him.

She didn't care what Leonard said. She was going to go see Zeus!

Cal waited until Leonard had gone into his study, then she ran down the block, through the gate, and into the stable. She didn't care if she saw Nate or not. She did make a mental note to never again let him kiss her, though. That's when he would start getting revved up, so all she had to do was avoid any kisses and everything would be fine. Leonard was just overreacting to the whole situation. Come to think of it, overreaction must be a male trait, she figured. Leonard and Nate sure had that in common. In fact, even Jill told her that there was nothing unusual in the way Nate was behaving. She said that's the way California boys are. She said it just meant that Nate found Cal very attractive. It was to be considered a compliment.

"There you are, baby," she cooed to Zeus. "Did you miss me?" She hugged his neck.

"You better believe it!" came a voice from the back room. "But my aim will be better next time."

"I wasn't talking to you."

Nate came to the doorway and leaned against it with his arms folded across his chest. He looked angry. "If you try that stunt with your knee one more time, I'm going to kill you, Cal! I swear I will!"

She got the brush off of the shelf and started grooming Zeus.

Nate was confused. "Leonard called and said you weren't going to do this anymore."

"He was wrong."

"Kind of possessive, isn't he?"

"That's not what I would call it."

"Have you ever felt like running away from there?"

She shrugged.

"That was pretty nervy of him to tell me off like that. He knows I could have him banned from the studio."

"He works at all the studios. He doesn't need yours."

"But you do. Maybe you ought to get away from him before he ruins your career."

"I can't. I don't have enough money to buy a house yet."

"You could stay at mine."

"I'm not *that* stupid."

He took the clipboard off the wall and checked off two items. "You're still going to come here every day to take care of Zeus, then?"

"Depends."

"On what?"

"On whether you leave me alone or not."

He put the clipboard back on the wall. "You know you're hooked, Cal. Zeus and I are a winning combination; you can't stay away from either of us."

She walked around and started working on the horse's other side. "Oh, I could stay away from you easy. It's Zeus I'm hooked on."

"I don't believe that." He followed her and took the brush out of her hand. "I get propositioned by girls every day."

"Propositioned? What's that?"

"They're perfectly willing to do what you're too scared to."

"Am not. I'm not scared of anything."

"Oh no? Prove it."

She got the saddle and put it onto Zeus, fastening the straps securely. "No."

"Told you."

"So let *them* have you. I'll take Zeus." She started getting into the saddle, but Nate pulled her off.

"You can't ride him anymore."

She pushed him away and lifted her foot to the stirrup again. He pulled her away more forcefully this time, and she fell to the floor. "It's a package deal, Cal. Zeus and I come together."

She got back to her feet and punched him in the arm. "That's not fair!"

"Too bad. He'll miss you. I think maybe I'll sell him to a dog food company."

"You can't do that!" Tears came to her eyes, and she put her arms protectively around the animal's neck.

"So what are you going to do about it?"

She buried her face in Zeus' neck for a moment. Then she looked over at Nate. "What would it take?"

He leaned against the wall, crossed his arms, and said with a sly smile, "Every day, after you take care of him, you come into my house and take care of me."

"No way!"

"I'll let you have weekends off."

"No!"

"Well, if you insist, you can work weekends, too."

"No!"

"Too bad. He's gotten really attached to you." Nate strolled toward the door. "He'll miss you."

"Hey, wait a minute," Cal called after him. "How about if I buy him from you?"

"You have a spare two hundred grand lying around somewhere?"

"My gosh! Is *that* what he costs?"

"I won't take any less for him." He left.

Cal looked back at Zeus. *Dog food companies pay that much for a horse?* she wondered.

* * *

"What *is* he?" Leonard asked in amazement. "A Triple Crown winner or something?"

"He's the most beautiful horse I've ever seen in my life and the sweetest, and I want him so bad, Len. I've got to have him! I've wanted a horse since I was a kid. If I put all my savings and earnings and everything together, would I have two hundred grand? And, what I don't have, can you loan me?"

"Maybe."

"What's a grand, anyway?"

"A thousand dollars."

Cal gasped.

Leonard advised, "This wouldn't be a good place for him. We don't have any pastureland for him."

"Maybe he could stay on that farm where we go riding."

"That's a possibility. The initial cost of a horse is only *part* of the expense, though."

"I know. Can we get him? Please, Len? I'll never ask for another thing as long as I live."

He mulled it over for a moment, then asked, "Is he really worth all that money to you?"

"Yeah!"

"You know you won't be able to sell him for anywhere near that amount."

"Oh, I'd *never* sell him. He'll be mine forever."

"Okay. I'll call Nate and tell him it's a deal. He'll have to keep him at his place until we make arrangements." Then he added emphatically, "And you stay away from there until those arrangements have been made and we go to pick Zeus up."

Her face glowed with happiness. "Hey, maybe I can ride Zeus to work."

Imagining Cal riding Zeus along the Santa Monica Freeway made Leonard laugh.

*   *   *

"Saturday night? No, I'm not busy, but I don't want to date you," Cal said into the phone.

"It's not a date," Nate insisted. "Becky can go, too, if you want. I just want to show you something."

"Show me what?"

"A club meeting. I want you to see it. We only have to stay maybe a half hour," Nate said.

"What kind of club?"

"You'll find out when we get there."

Cal didn't know what to think. What kind of club could it possibly be? Nate didn't seem like the club type. "It's not the Ku Klux Klan or anything like that, is it?"

"No, nothing bad. I'll pick you and Becky up at 8:00." He hung up.

*　*　*

Jill closed their bedroom door to ensure privacy, then turned to Leonard. "Why on earth did you agree to such a thing?"

"It's her money, and that's how she chose to spend it. She's an adult now and can make those choices."

"Not yet. She hasn't had her twenty-first birthday yet. And you *know* that means she won't have enough money left to move into her own house. She'll have to stay here until she gets married."

"Is that such a bad thing? We're the only family she has, Jill. If she lived in her own place, she'd be completely alone. Can you imagine being completely alone at her age? Would you want our Stacy to ever be in that situation?"

"Well, no."

"And Cal has more reason to need people around than Stacy would. Now and then, when a fan gets a crazy idea, she needs protection. Not only that, but she needs to be protected from her own naïveté, too."

"Why don't we encourage her to keep her horse at Nate's then? As long as he's there, she'll keep coming in contact with Nate."

"That's *exactly* the thing we want to avoid! Don't you remember what he did to her?"

"Oh, Leonard, boys *do* that kind of thing. I dealt with that all the time when I was her age. She wasn't crying about that. She's able to handle Nate just fine. It's the thought of not seeing that *horse* again that got her upset."

"Guys did that *to you*? I just can't picture that."

She nodded. "I chose you because you had more class. You were more mature than most of the others."

"It must be rough being a pretty girl."

"Sometimes it is, but I still think Cal needs a home of her own."

"She'll have enough money to get the horse and still be saving for her own place."

"Sounds like you'll be loaning her the whole two hundred thousand dollars."

"No, actually she has a lot more than that in her trust fund now. I've mainly been putting money in; very little has been taken out. For the last two years, I've been paying all her expenses myself, except for the car."

Jill looked at him in disbelief. "But why?"

"I wanted to be sure she'd never have to marry in order to have financial security. She'll have plenty of her own money."

"If she has that much money, she should've had her own house long ago! She could have paid cash for it!"

"You know as well as I do that she's not ready for that."

"Oh yes, she is," Jill said with eyes flashing angrily. "I think *you're* the one who isn't ready for her to move out."

"I don't know what you're talking about."

"Like heck you don't," Jill said, leaving the room and thereby ending the conversation.

*   *   *

It was almost 9:00 on Saturday night, and Nate was driving Cal and Becky back to their homes.

"So what do you think?" he asked.

Cal was in the passenger seat, while Becky rode in the back. "I think they're crazy," Cal said.

"Crazy about me. That's what a fan club's all about."

"You put on your humble-movie-star act, and those stupid girls believed every word you said. Boy, are they ever dumb! And the way they act so silly whenever you do the least little thing, it's sickening."

He smirked, "Yeah. All I have to do is look at any one of them, and she's ready to hop into the sack with me. Not only that, but she'd consider it an honor." Then he leaned over to Cal and whispered so Becky wouldn't hear, "*They're* not scared."

"Of what?"

"You *know* what."

"Where do they get all those people? It was like a whole roomful of Dorises!"

"That's not all of them, either. There's fan clubs for me in twelve states."

"They're nuts."

"A few of them tonight seemed to be a little put out that I brought you girls. I guess they wanted me all to themselves."

Cal wasn't impressed. "I think I'm going to puke."

"I think you're jealous."

"Jealous? Me? Of what?"

"Because they got so much of my attention while we were there. Did you see how they fell all over themselves to get me a chair, and stammered when they tried to talk?"

"Why don't you just drop Becky and me off, and then you can go have a good old time with those weirdos."

"What do you suppose they see in me? What makes them fall in love with me so easily?"

"'Cause they don't know you, that's why."

"Hmm," he mused. "I think I'll follow your advice."

"What's that?"

"After I let you and Becky off, I'm going back, and I'm going to spend the night with one of those girls."

Cal just stared out the window.

"Maybe with two of them," he corrected himself. "Now, *that* would be interesting."

"You can spend the night with *all* of them, for all I care. You just passed my house. Stop the car."

"Don't you want to see Zeus?"

"Len told me not to go to your house anymore."

"Since when do you do what he says?"

"He'll kill me if he finds out I'm at your house."

He looked at her with disbelief. "Let me get this straight. You can't come to my house, but it's okay for me to take you places? I could've taken you to a hotel, for all he knew."

"He doesn't know I'm with you. He was in the study when you picked me up."

He smiled.

"Stop the car. I'm getting out." She opened the door of the moving car.

He slammed on the brakes. "What'd you do that for?"

Once the car was stopped, she slid out. "Because I've got to go home. Give all your girlfriends a big, sloppy kiss for me. Bye, Becky." She slammed the door shut and ran home.

Chapter 24

CAL COULDN'T BELIEVE HER GOOD FORTUNE! She was now the proud owner of the most beautiful stallion in the world! The animal trainer they knew from the studio, Mr. Knapp, agreed to let Zeus stay on his farm with the other horses and, for a fee, he would take care of him. He would get all the supplies necessary, too, and would bill Cal once a month.

What a great deal, she thought. All they have to do is pay his bill, then just go and enjoy Zeus whenever they want. When he was in town, she and Leonard were going over there to ride about twice a week now; and she felt she had saved that gentle soul from the dog-food factory.

Cal was trying to talk Leonard into buying a horse of his own, too, instead of always using one of Mr. Knapp's; but he seemed perfectly content with things just the way they were.

Now she was especially glad that Leonard had gotten her a role in *Henson of Manhattan* because it paid well. Of course, the kind of acting involved wasn't what she was accustomed to—it had much more emotion in it, but, now that she had a car *and* horse to maintain, she was quite grateful for the promise of a larger paycheck in the not-too-distant future. The timing of this new film couldn't have been better, too—an adult picture to begin filming soon after her twenty-first birthday. And Pete had come up with television shows for her to do in the meantime.

"Here's our scripts," Leonard announced as he opened the large packet that had been delivered while he was at work. He handed Cal one. "Read it over carefully and let me know where you're going to need extra help."

She flipped through it. "It's sure a thick one!"

"I'm sure some of the scenes will have to be cut; otherwise, it'd be about three hours long."

"Who do I play?"

"Veronica Myers to my Howard Henson."

"Hey! We've got the *leads*? They're not supporting roles?"

He beamed, "That's right, and I get to use my natural accent. But they'll have to change your name to Daisy Mae if you can't lose your Texas drawl by then."

"I'll just talk like you."

"The vowel sounds are different."

"And New Yorkahs talk fastah."

Over the years, Leonard had noticed that Cal had a special talent for mimicking others' speech patterns. He smiled as he mussed her hair. "I'm glad you agreed to do this picture, Cal."

*　　*　　*

"Another new outfit?" Cal asked as she joined the others in the kitchen. Jill had just finished brushing Stacy's blonde tresses in preparation for another day of kindergarten. "You're the best-dressed little lady in L.A. this year."

As Stacy seated herself, Jill put bacon and scrambled eggs onto her plate.

"Do you have a desk in school?" Cal asked.

"We have a big table, just like our kitchen. No, it's bigger than this. It's like the one in the dining room, only not tall."

"What did y'all do yesterday?"

"We marched to music. I got to lead the parade!"

Leonard smiled with pride. "Jill, did you hear that? She's a leader, just like her old man."

"And, Daddy, Miss Gardner said that we'll have a Christmas program and our families will come watch. I asked her if my honorary sister can come, too, and she said okay."

He nodded approvingly. "Maybe you'll get the lead."

"Hey, Jill," Cal said, "I just *know* they're going to need you on the Costume Committee. I can be the ticket taker, and Len will throw out all the hecklers."

Thus, with such family support, Stacy's academic career was off to an illustrious start.

Chapter 25

SEPTEMBER 20, 1969

The much-awaited twenty-first birthday had finally arrived!

As Jill was slicing the cake that evening, Leonard said, "After we get done here, you'll have to get dressed up nice and pretty, Cal. We have a surprise for you."

"What?" she asked, looking first at him, then at Jill.

Jill looked over at Leonard, who beamed, "We're taking you to a nightclub to celebrate your coming of age."

"You're officially adult now, Cal. Leonard thought a nightclub would be symbolic of your new status."

"Hog diggity! Can Becky come, too? She's over twenty-one."

"No. Just the three of us," she said. "Becky's going to babysit Stacy."

"What do people wear to nightclubs, Jill?" Cal wondered.

"How about that nice lavender dress we got you for Nate's award ceremony?"

"Oh, real fancy, huh?"

"This'll be a night to remember, kid," Leonard said.

"Becky knew about this and didn't tell me? That little sneak!" Cal said with a grin.

*　*　*

This was exciting! The trio seemed to have the best seats in the house. Leonard and Jill looked so sophisticated in their nightclub finest. They had given her a locket with a diamond in the center, and she wore it with pride.

A stand-up comic was the opening act, and Cal thought he was fantastic. Then the headliner, a singer whom she had admired for several years now, took over. All three at Cal's table enjoyed his show immensely. It was a special treat when he pointed out to the audience that Leonard Rhoads, his lovely wife Jill, and Stacy Ames were present to celebrate Stacy's twenty-first birthday.

"How'd he know that?" Cal asked Jill.

"You need to stand and acknowledge their applause," instructed Jill. Leonard and Cal then stood; he nodded and she waved to the smiling audience.

Once they were seated, again, Cal restated her question, "Jill, how did he know?"

"Leonard told them when he made the reservations. That's how we got such a good table."

"Oh." Until then, Cal thought the choice table was because he was Leonard Rhoads, a man whose very presence commands respect.

Once the entertainment was over, Leonard ordered a chilled bottle of champagne for the occasion, poured some into a glass and handed it to Cal. "Your first legal drink." As she began to take a taste of it, he took hold of her hand and lowered her drink. "Wait! We haven't made the toast yet." He poured some into two more glasses, then he and Jill held theirs up and Cal did the same. "To the screen industry's brightest and most promising new *adult* star!" he said proudly.

"That's me, all right!" Cal grinned, as they sipped their champagne.

"It's been a long, tough road, kid, but we made it."

"I'm sorry I used to be such a pain, guys."

"Oh, you weren't that bad," Jill said consolingly.

"From now on, you'll be working as an adult," added Leonard. "There will be no more of those kiddie shows for you. You will be a highly-respected and desired adult actress in your own right."

"Sounds like you have big plans for me."

"That's right. Your life will be changing now—professionally and personally."

Cal lifted her glass to her lips.

"Take it slowly, dear," Jill advised. "Champagne's to be sipped."

Cal looked over at her. Her happy smile faded as she noticed how sad their lady looked. "You're not getting sentimental on me, are you, Jill?" she asked, taking a sip of the champagne.

"No, not really."

"What were you doing when *you* were twenty-one?" Cal asked her.

"I was in my final year of college and doing some student teaching. That's when I knew I had chosen the right profession. I really enjoyed that year."

"Len, you need to let her go back to teaching. She loves it, don't you, Jill?"

"She doesn't have to work for a living. I make plenty for both of us."

"But she *wants* to, don't you, Jill?"

Leonard shook his head. "No, she's got plenty to keep her busy."

"But… "

"It's okay, Cal," Jill said softly. "Don't worry about me." Then she smiled, "It's your birthday. We're here to celebrate *your* being twenty-one."

"Okedoke." Cal took another sip of champagne, then set it back down the way Jill had been doing. "Doggone, this stuff's good. How about you, Len? What were you doing when you were my age? Were you making big bucks yet?"

"That's when I was learning my craft. I hadn't done any film work yet at that age, and it took a few years more before the accolades started coming. It takes time and hard work, but it's worth it."

The orchestra started playing a tender ballad. Leonard set his champagne down, stood up, and held his hand out to Cal. She grinned, put her hand in his, and rose to her feet. He escorted her to the dance floor, and they came together for a beautiful waltz—the first one of her adult life.

* * *

Cal had never seen Leonard dance, or be this gallant, before. Everything tonight had been perfect—absolutely perfect! When they got home, she excitedly told Becky all about her evening. "The show was terrific!" she said. "Len and Jill looked so gorgeous all dressed up; and with high heels on, I could see over his shoulder!" For the first time in her life, Cal had been treated like a lady; and it felt wonderful. "Look at the beautiful locket they gave me. That's a real diamond. And we had champagne and hor d'oeuvres and everything."

After sharing Cal's excitement with her and giving her a congratulatory hug, Becky gathered her book and purse and went to her car.

From the porch, Cal watched her go, then looked up to the infinity of the star-filled sky and sighed contentedly. "Mom and Dad, I'm all grown up now. And Uncle Ant was wrong—I didn't end up in jail."

What could easily have been a *multiple* tragedy, leaving her in an orphanage, a ward of the state, was the very thing that made it possible for her to become a part of this very special family. So many coincidences had worked together to make this highly unlikely scenario a reality. Who would have guessed that Thurman and Alicia Ames's little girl would grow up to be seen in movies and on television, to live in a beautiful home in Los Angeles, and to hobnob with people known throughout the world? Was all this simply coincidence, or was there a master plan? And was that master plan not finished yet, but rather, still in the process of being fulfilled?

What did life have in store for the adult Cal Ames? No matter what the future held, she knew that, with the love and support of this family, life would be good!

PART II

Jill

Chapter 1

It was almost 4:00 P.M. and Cal was getting home from the studio earlier than usual. Savoring the freedom to use the extra time any way she wished, she could hardly wait to actually have dinner with the whole family for a change and maybe ride Zeus for a while, then read Stacy a bedtime story. As she approached the house, though, she noticed only Leonard's car in the driveway. She hoped she hadn't missed a family outing.

Cal had been working on a television show this week, one which again played up her Italian heritage, this time by making her the leading star's cousin from the Old Country, seeing America for the first time. She was enjoying his role.

She entered the house and hung up her jacket. "Hey, y'all, I'm home early today!" she called out as she looked around. "Where's that little Stacykins?"

Silence.

Cal went into the living room, and the kitchen. No one was there. She looked in the media room, then went back into the hallway to the stairs leading to the second floor. "Anybody home?" she yelled.

"In here." It was Leonard's voice, from the study upstairs. But he sounded different; there was a weariness in his voice.

Cal bounded up the stairs and entered the study. One glance was all she needed. Something was very wrong. Leonard was seated at his desk, which was uncharacteristically littered by papers in what appeared to be a random hodgepodge. On top was a legal document of some sort. To one side was a bottle of Jack Daniels, and in Leonard's hand was an almost-empty glass.

"What's going on?" she asked. "Where is everybody?"

He finished the contents of his glass, then leaned back and looked at her in disgust. "Gone."

"Gone where? And how come you're drinking that stuff? I thought you liked beer."

"Not strong enough." He said, turning his attention back to the document. "Take a look at this." He handed it to her.

She took it. "What is it? Looks like legal stuff."

"A petition for divorce. Jill's gone and she took Stacy with her."

Cal had to sit down quickly before her knees gave way. *No!* she thought. *That can't be right. Divorce? That doesn't make any sense at all.* She looked at the document. The wording of the petition didn't answer any of her questions. She turned page after page, but it seemed as though written in a different language. "What do they mean, 'irreconcilable differences'? I've never in my life heard y'all arguing about anything. It's you and me who do all the fighting."

"She doesn't believe in having arguments in front of kids."

"But what on earth? I can't believe this, Len. I can't." A tear made its way down her cheek.

"Divorce is almost as common as marriage in this town," he said flatly.

"What're we going to do now?" She got up and started pacing. "We *need* Jill and Stacy. We're not a family without them."

"I know, I know."

She came to a halt and studied his face intently. She had never seen him look so depressed before. It seemed to Cal that the light had left Leonard's life, so he *had* to be feeling awfully rejected. It might not have been his fault, though.

"Len, have I been such a pain that she couldn't take it anymore? Is it my fault?" The possibility that Cal herself might have done this to him grieved her. "That's why my parents' housekeepers left."

"That would be an oversimplification."

"My birthday. Was that it? She seemed kind of upset at the nightclub. Did I do something there that made her go?"

"Stop blaming yourself, Cal. It's more *my* fault than anyone else's. She's been unhappy for several years." He stood up and went over to the window.

She followed. "But how could that be? You always treated her like a queen, and I thought she adored you. She was always taking your side on things."

"Only when other people were around."

This just wasn't making any sense. "Oh, Len," she cried, "let's go find them and make them come back. Tell her you're sorry and won't ever do whatever you did again." Tears came freely now for them both as they held onto each other tightly. Jill and Stacy had been the mainstay in their lives, and they were feeling utterly abandoned. For as long as Cal had known them, Jill had always been there for them—someone to talk to, someone who would understand, someone to smooth away life's rough spots. How could she do this to them, just out of the blue, to leave like that? And to take Stacy away from them—that energetic, golden-haired, bright-eyed little bundle of silliness who liked to wait up for Cal when she was working. No more bedtime stories, or piggyback rides, or knock-knock jokes. "Where'd she go, Len? She can't keep Stacy away from her daddy, can she?"

"I don't know where they went. I'll have to have my lawyer work something out about Stacy."

*   *   *

The house was awfully quiet without that precious child around, and the void was painful to Cal. When the laundry remained untouched, the litter on the floor only grew greater, and they were reduced to order-in meals every evening, Cal and Leonard started realizing how hard Jill had worked every day to provide a comfortable and attractive home for them.

Looking with uneasiness at all the clutter around them, she concluded, "We need a wife, Len."

"Well, the first order of business is for you to learn how to do the laundry," he decided. "The dry cleaner can't do everything."

Cal realized he was right. "Becky can teach me that. She does her laundry every Saturday."

So Cal made a point of visiting Becky that Saturday morning to learn the basics. "There's nothing to it," she reported to Leonard later that day. "Sort the colors from whites and delicates, put the washer on the right setting, then put the loads in with however much detergent the box says, and you're all set."

From then on, Cal adopted the same schedule as Becky—Saturday was laundry day. And she learned that if she hung the clothes up the moment they were finished drying, she didn't have to iron nearly as much. Ironing was one chore she loathed and would do anything to avoid.

Leonard's contribution to the running of the home was to pick up after himself. As Cal gleefully watched him retrieving and throwing away all of the back issues of the newspaper, she couldn't help but to imagine how elated Jill would be to witness this. "When she comes back and sees what we're doing, she'll never leave us again. I might even keep doing laundry, so she won't have to work so hard." Cal then joined Leonard in tidying up the room. From now on, she decided, she would sleep on top of the sheets and spread so the bed wouldn't have to be made up all over again every day.

*   *   *

Cal was so glad that she had acting work this week. Having anywhere to go would help keep her mind off the crisis at home, but the work of an actor has a special blessing. At the studio, whenever the cameras were rolling, she wasn't Cal Ames anymore. Instead, she was able to concentrate fully on portraying a completely different person. This week, she was Paulina, a schoolmate of *The Davis Clan* daughter.

It was after she got home and things were quiet again that the loneliness gnawed at her. She kept listening for signs of Jill and Stacy in the driveway. On the way to and from the studio, her heart leapt if she saw a car that looked like Jill's—then sank when she realized it belonged to someone else. Many a time, Leonard found Cal in the media room late in the evening, watching home movies of the two people who had been such an important part of her life. *Surely they'll come back*, she thought. *Why are they staying away so long? Don't they miss us?*

Leonard knew better than to harbor such hopes. When she moved out, Jill had taken with her all the clothing and personal items that belonged to her and Stacy. It was obvious to him that she had no intention of ever returning. While he was trying to keep everything going as though nothing untoward had occurred, every now and then Cal would notice a lonely, faraway look in his eyes that hadn't been there before. She wondered what thoughts were going through his head, but knew not to ask. He would probably deny any of the remorseful or sentimental feelings that he was bound to be having.

*   *   *

Cal's guest appearance on *The Davis Clan* was over now and she was left with only one more job on her calendar, the movie entitled *Henson of Manhattan*, which was scheduled to begin shooting the following month. "I like TV shows," she told Pete. "They only take a week to do. How about lining up a few more for me after *Henson* is finished?"

"There just aren't that many Italian teenager roles on TV these days."

"I'm twenty-one, Pete. It's okay for my characters to grow up now. I can do grown-up things."

"But your public knows you as a teenager. That's your image, and that's the only way they'll accept you."

"And it's my mom who's Italian, not me."

"To the public, you're Italian."

"Does that mean no more work?"

"That means your choices are limited. But I'll see if I can get you in another film that's coming up in a few months. It would be perfect for you."

"Okay, but I've got car payments to make, Pete. I need those paychecks. It's not fair for Len to have to pay for it."

"I'll see what I can arrange. I just hope your *Henson* role doesn't ruin everything. I wish you had talked to me about it before accepting that part."

That was a depressing thought. She, like Pete, was hoping that such a drastic change in her image would not bring her career to a screeching halt.

Chapter 2

LEONARD WAS ON HIS WAY to the study to work on his lines for the upcoming film. As he passed Cal's room, he noticed she was lying on her stomach on the floor, reading a magazine while listening to a record on her stereo. "Do you know your lines in *Henson* yet?" he asked her. "We'll be starting that soon, you know."

"I've got my first two scenes memorized."

"Have you scanned the rest of it? I know you'll need help with some portions because they're a lot different from what you're accustomed to."

She sat up. "Like what?"

"You have some emotional scenes, Cal. They deal with some feelings you've never done on-screen before. Read through the whole thing to get a good idea what's needed, then I'll help wherever I can."

"What kind of emotions?"

"Jealousy, for one. Fear is another. I doubt you've ever felt jealous in your life. Do you know how to do that?"

"Yes, I have. I'll just think about Sherry."

"Who's that?"

"The gorgeous model who got Miles. I thought they would've broken up by now—after all, this *is* Hollywood—but they're still married."

"Okay. How about fear?"

She looked off to the side, then slowly nodded. "Yeah, I know what that feels like. I can do fear."

"I guess you're set for your first few scenes, then. Do what I say, though. Read the whole thing over so you'll be well prepared." He took the script off her bedside table and tossed it on the floor beside her.

* * *

The first few weeks filming *Henson of Manhattan* went fairly well. The director was not particularly obliging, but Leonard was a tremendous help to her when she encountered a glitch in her role because she wasn't sure how to play nervousness. She knew how nervousness felt, but she wasn't sure how to show it so the audience would recognize it as such. That was an emotion that she had only seen Don Knotts do, and his comic style would not be appropriate for this very serious drama. After a session in the media room in which Leonard showed her films with several examples of the emotion, she was able to proceed with confidence. Cal was very glad that she was working with Leonard again—until the middle of the fourth week:

It had been a long, frustrating day at the studio, and they were now driving home. Tension still lingered in the air. Cal was sitting as close to the passenger door as she could and staring out the side window, as Leonard's eyes never left the road ahead. Until now, they had been riding in silence.

"Just answer me one thing," Leonard finally said, while trying to control his temper. "Am I all that repulsive?"

"It has nothing to do with that. When I read the script and saw that *I* was the one who was supposed to do that scene, I told them to get a stunt double and I'd do the voice-overs. I just can't do it myself."

"It's not a dangerous stunt. It's just a love scene, for Pete's sake, and it's on a closed set."

"But it's you and me, and that's weird. I want a double."

"That'd be impossible. To shoot it from a distance would detract from the mood. It wouldn't work with a double. What's the big deal about a double anyway?"

"It's like doing it with your own parent. Would you make out with your mom? Tell me that."

"'Making out' is what hormonal kids do. In this scene, our characters are making love. There's a world of difference."

"Whatever," she mumbled.

"We're actors, Cal! It's not real! The actors don't *really* go all the way in these things. You know that."

"We might be playing parts, but you're still you and I'm still me."

"No!" he adamantly corrected her. "You're wrong! When the cameras are rolling, I'm Howard Henson."

"Well, you might be able to fool yourself, but I just can't do that, Len."

"How can it be like doing it with your own parent, anyway? I'm *not* your dad! We never adopted you, so we're not even *remotely* related!"

"But you've been *like* a dad to me. For years you have been, and that's how I think of you. I got you a shirt on Father's Day and everything."

"I warned you about that scene before you accepted the role, and you had no problem with it then."

"That's because I thought someone else was going to be doing it. I thought you were telling me about that scene so I'd know how adult the film was. It didn't occur to me that *I'd* be expected to do it."

He shook his head in frustration. "Cal, this is the first romantic lead I've ever had in film. I've wanted a part like this for years and I'm not about to let you blow it."

"I don't want to blow it. There's got to be another way."

"You don't have to be experiencing a feeling in real life in order to play it, you know. Just remember back to a time when you did feel it."

She shrugged.

They rode on in silence. Then, it suddenly occurred to him. *Of course!* he thought. It all was starting to make sense to him now. "You've never done it before, have you? You've never made love."

"No," she said quietly.

"Both Alan and Jeb told me if you're not ready to do that scene by tomorrow afternoon, you're out. And what they say goes," he added. "They're starting to think you're too juvenile for this role, but I know you can do it."

"Please don't let them fire me, Len," she said earnestly. "I've got car payments to make. I need the money."

He thought for a moment, then took out a cigarette. "Okay, I'll take care of it."

"What're you going to do? Sue them for breach of contract?"

"There was no clause in the contract about any double. You'd be the one breaching the contract." He lit the cigarette and took a long puff, then let it out slowly. "No, Cal. Tonight you're going to experience it 'for real' so you can play it."

"*What?!*"

"You don't know *how* to make love. That's what the *real* problem is. You want method? You'll get method." Equally important, he knew, was to get rid of that paternal image she had of him. This would surely do that.

"No, Len!"

"There's no need to feel threatened. This is rehearsal. We're protecting your job."

They were in the driveway now. The car hadn't quite stopped yet when Cal scrambled out of it. At first, she headed toward the house, but when Leonard followed, she turned and held her shaking hand out. "Stay away from me."

"Am I touching you? Am I anywhere *near* you? I'm going into my house, Cal. My <u>own</u> house. Is that permissible?"

She sighed. Once inside, she asked, "Can't they change the script? Just that one part?"

"If it weren't so important to the story line, they probably could. But it's an integral part of the story. It's at that moment that Henson realizes he loves Veronica, and that influences the rest of the story."

"Can't she do something else lovable instead, like give him a backrub or something? I can do that."

He laughed at the absurdity of that, as he leafed through the mail.

Cal gave up and went into the kitchen. "We need a wife around here!" she yelled to Leonard. "Someone to have dinner waiting for us when we get home." Dirty dishes filled the sink and counter. She opened the refrigerator, perused its meager contents, then closed it again and mumbled, "Someone to do the grocery shopping, too."

"Looks like we'll have to order in, again," Leonard said as he came in and checked the refrigerator, too. "How about a couple hoagies?"

Good, she thought. *A distraction.* "Yeah, hoagies are good. I wonder what's on TV tonight."

*   *   *

Now that the hoagies were finished and the mail read, Leonard stood up, turned off the television, and rested his hand on Cal's shoulder. "Come on."

"Len…"

"For an actress, you've been far too sheltered; and I admit I was probably just as much at fault as Jill was. Here you are twenty-one years old and still ignorant about many important life experiences. I'm going to teach you how to make love like an adult, so you can play it for the camera. I'll take it as slow as I can; but remember, we only have until tomorrow to get you over this."

"Don't we have some films I could study or something?"

"That wouldn't get you over your hang-up about me."

She remained seated, but was clearly in a quandary.

"Okay, Cal. We won't go all the way, just as far as we would on the set tomorrow. No further, I promise."

There seemed to be no choice if she wanted to keep her job. She sighed and stood up, filled with dread. He took hold of her hand and led her upstairs. *This is going to be really, really weird,* she thought.

*   *   *

Much later that evening, Cal just couldn't believe it. *I didn't know he could be this tender and gentle,* she marveled to herself. Indeed, this was a side of Leonard she had never known before. If he weren't already married, she might have even have found herself falling in love with the man.

Because of her trepidation and inexperience, they had first gone through the scene fully clothed. Once Cal was comfortable with that, he then gradually set the scene more like it would be on the set the next day. As the hours passed, he taught her all she needed to know to play the scene convincingly.

Leonard had saved Cal's job again. And this time, once she accepted the basic premise, she found this homework to be kind of fun! It left her with a hundred unanswered questions, though. Leonard was right—making love as an adult *was* a whole lot different than the way she and Miles had shown affection. If "everyone did it," as her friends kept telling her, why didn't Miles? And, my gosh, Leonard could be so doggone loving! Why on earth would Jill have ever left a guy like that? But the question that Cal tried not to dwell on too much was "What's the rest of it like?"

Chapter 3

CAMERAMEN LOU AND RAYMOND were packing up their gear the next evening. It had been mostly an ordinary day, considering the intensity of the afternoon's shooting, with one exception:

"Did you see it coming?" Lou grinned.

"Uh-uh."

"I did. I was watching them and she was trying hard not to."

"She must've been out partying last night or something. All Alan had to do was stop shooting long enough to adjust the lighting. Next thing you know, ol' Cal's sound asleep."

"Well, at least she was in the right place if she wanted to take a nap," he chuckled.

"Who was giving a party last night? I don't remember hearing about any."

Lou shrugged. "Beats me."

*   *   *

"I did it! I did it!" Cal was jubilant as they made their way home earlier than usual. "And they liked it, too. Did you hear the applause from the crew when Alan said 'Cut and print'?"

Leonard was more pensive. "Yeah."

"I won't be afraid of scenes like that anymore. It's easy!"

Silence.

She looked over at him and playfully punched his shoulder. "Thanks, Len."

"Okay."

She expected him to be tired after having had so little sleep the night before, but something else seemed to be bothering him. "What's the matter?" she asked.

"I'll tell you later."

"Why not now?"

"Because it's dangerous for you to jump out of the car while it's speeding down the freeway."

"Yeah, right. Don't fall asleep at the wheel."

"Not a chance."

Being clueless as to what he was talking about, Cal just leaned back and savored having had such a victorious day on the set.

* * *

Once they were inside the house, Leonard closed the front door, then dropped the mail onto the hallway table without looking at it. "Whose coaching is responsible for today going so well?" he asked Cal.

"Yours, of course."

"And what would've happened if you had gone to work this morning the way you left it last night?"

She shook her head, "Well, I guess Jeb would've fired me, and they'd have to reshoot my scenes with someone else, and my car would be repossessed."

"Don't you feel you owe me something for saving your job?"

She felt a bit confused. "Like what? You make a lot more than I do."

"Cal," he said as he took her by the shoulders and looked her in the eye, "doing that scene over and over last night, then again with even more intensity this afternoon, does something to a man. It's like hours and hours of foreplay without ever getting to the main event. You know what I mean?"

Uh-oh. "But, Len, it's not real. We were just playing parts. You were Howard and I was Veronica."

He looked at her impatiently. "Let's go upstairs and finish what we started."

"The kitchen's where *I* want to go." Cal tried to pull herself away from his vise-like grip, but couldn't.

"You said yourself that the scene was fun," he reminded her, "and I could tell last night that you were ready to go the full distance. I didn't take it that far, though, because I promised I wouldn't. I'm not bound by any such promises now."

Cal felt embarrassed that he could read her mind so accurately. Last night had, indeed, left her longing to experience lovemaking in its entirety, and Leonard would be the only man she trusted enough to lead her through it; but she had quickly banished those thoughts from her mind, knowing that to follow through on them would be to betray Jill. She just couldn't bring herself to do that to the woman who had been her advocate for so many years.

"You owe me big, kid, and I'm calling in that debt right now." He gathered her up into his arms and carried her to the stairway.

"Fiddle-dee-dee, Rhett," she said in her southernmost manner, as they ascended the staircase. "Let's think about this tomorrow. After all, tomorrow *is* another day."

Once they were inside his bedroom, he kicked the door shut and set her down. Leonard stationed himself between Cal and the door, then began shedding his shirt and jeans. Momentarily distracted, Cal watched with interest. She couldn't help admiring what she saw. He was a very strong, solidly built man, but without the grossly bulging muscles of a body builder. At age forty, he was still looking good.

But when he then came toward Cal, she snapped back to reality. She took a step backward, holding her hand out to stop him. "Len, I can't," she pleaded.

"Sure you can. You were made for this." He unbuttoned her shirt, pulled it off and tossed it aside.

She backed away from him. "No, I mean *we* can't. You're still married."

"Face it, Cal. She's never coming back. You've lived here all these years because of my generosity. I've been supporting you all this time, even though I didn't have to. That's something else you owe me for. Get *back* here." He took her arm and pulled her back toward him, then unzipped her jeans, pushing them over her hips. The jeans then dropped to the floor. Leonard lifted her back up, carried her over to his bed, and set her onto it. He then lay beside her.

She put her hand on his chest. "Len, we can't do this. It's wrong, you *know* it is."

"Don't worry about that, Cal. You won't go to hell. For the first time in your life, you're the innocent one." He kissed her fervently on the neck.

Her heart was pounding so hard she could hear it. "But I don't want *you* to go to hell, either."

"I'll be in *heaven* in a few minutes, and so will you if you'd just calm down."

"Len, I'm scared."

"You'll be fine. Trust me." He kissed her passionately on the lips, melting away any further protest.

*　*　*

The atmosphere had been fraught with electricity, but the room was now restored to its original calmness.

"Feel better now?" she asked.

"*Much* better!" He reached for a cigarette. Cal started to get up, but he took hold of her arm. "Stay here."

She lay back down. "Dadgum it, Len. Last night you were Joe Cartwright, but tonight you're Yosemite Sam! Bring Joe back. I miss him."

"No, Cal. Last night I was Howard Henson because that's the character you'd be relating to on the set. What you have tonight is Leonard Rhoads. You deserve honesty from me when it's real."

"Forget honesty! I want Howard Henson."

He lit the cigarette and took a long puff. "The difference between an actor and a movie star is that an actor can take on whatever persona is necessary to get the job done. That's what last night was all about. Remember that. You'll be a real actress someday."

"Now you're insulting me? I'm just a job, and I'm not a real actress?"

"No insult's intended. I'm just giving you an acting lesson so you'll someday graduate from movie star to actress. You have tremendous potential, but haven't developed it. The talent is there—I see it every day. You feel things more keenly than most people, just as all great artists do, but until now…"

"Great artists?" she asked. Was she hearing right? Had he actually given her a compliment?

"Yes, Cal, you're an artist of sorts. Until now, the films you've done have been about characters very much like yourself but without any true emotional depth, so they haven't called for any real acting. That's why you're having more trouble with this one."

"How about the scenes I've done with Nate? That was real acting. I can't stand that guy, but you couldn't tell it on the screen."

"Yes, you could. If you're as observant of human nature and knowledgeable about body language as an accomplished actor is, you can tell."

"How?"

"After work tomorrow, we'll study film clips and I'll show you what I mean. But not now. I'm worn out." He snuffed the cigarette out in the ashtray. Then he held Cal close, gently kissed her forehead, and closed his eyes.

Within a few minutes, they were both sound asleep.

Chapter 4

Leonard loved this business. Where else would you legally be able to impersonate someone else and get paid big bucks for it? He had been perfecting his style for twenty years.

It was now the next evening, and he and Cal sat in the media room, viewing excerpts from various films and TV shows, as he gave her wise instruction:

"You need to get *completely* wrapped up in your character. Study her and become her. Create a history for her. Think like she would. For the time, you *are* your character, and your real self doesn't exist.

"When you're to deliver a line in a drinking scene, say it first, then lift the glass and take a drink, so your words won't echo in the glass.

"Look at this scene. You'll notice that, even though the camera is focused elsewhere, the actors in the background are very much involved in the action. They are reacting to what's going on just as much as the actors in the foreground are. And reacting at the *right time*—never anticipating it.

"In this film, the actor plays identical twins whose lives went in opposite directions—one completely sadistic, the other a man of the cloth. Notice the difference in the portrayals. Look at the body language, the walk, the talk, the way they stand and move, their grooming, voice, facial expressions. Everything's different.

"Okay. Here's one of the later films you did with Nate. See the way you took a half-step backward when he came near? You weren't supposed to do that. Your character wouldn't have done that. But, in one way or another, you did it throughout the whole film—sometimes subtly, other times it was more obvious. I'm surprised your director didn't catch it when he was viewing the dailies. Now compare that with the scenes of your first picture." He switched films. "Your relationship with Nate, the person, was better then and you leaned *toward* him as you were talking to him. That was good, because your character would have done that." He turned to Cal. "You should *never* let your own personal feelings show on-camera, unless they match that of your character. If you do, you're not acting. Remember that, on-camera, you are your character, not Cal."

"I see what you mean," said Cal. "So you can tell what I was really thinking."

"That's right. You give off signals, body language. They tell an observant person a lot more than words do. When the words conflict with the body language, it's usually the words that are false."

"Okay. I'll tell my body to shut up."

"Oh, here's something. Look at this scene. She appears to be looking at herself in the mirror, doesn't she? She's not. At that angle, she can't see herself at all. In reality, the camera sees her reflection in the mirror and she sees the camera's. You have to be aware of the audience at all times, and be sure that they see what you want them to see. Gestures are vitally important, but they're meaningless if the audience doesn't see them."

It wasn't until the last couple of years that Cal started appreciating the extent of Leonard's devotion to his craft. She had been living under the same roof with this man for six years, and this was the second film in which she had appeared with him; but it was only gradually that she had learned the subtleties involved in his work, that good acting is not only an art, but a science too. She *had* noticed that his whole demeanor seemed to change as he was getting into character, but only now did she realize how and why. And from the very beginning, it had been apparent to her what a master of dialect he was. There was nary a trace of his own Long Island accent when he was doing a Western.

"Here, I want you to watch this all the way through." He prepared the next film for viewing and it began. "This is what TV acting was like in the good old days. This was a play done *live* on TV in the '50s. It was a lot like the stage, except instead of an audience there were cameras."

As the first scene began, she was incredulous. "My gosh, is that *you*? You're so young!" This was a revelation to Cal. "Were you really as innocent as you looked?"

"My character was."

"That's not what I'm asking."

"Well, that's the only answer you're going to get. Remember what I've been telling you about body language as you watch this and you'll learn a lot." He got up and stretched. "I've got an early call in the morning, so I'm turning in. You've got the day off. Enjoy." With that, he mussed her hair, then left.

Cal sank down comfortably into the plush sofa. "Wow!" she said to herself, "He was sure cute back then." Looking around, she found the popcorn and put the bowl in her lap.

As the play unfolded, Cal was caught up in both the story line and the superb acting. It was a tremendously poignant portrayal, and Leonard was simply amazing in it. He never seemed to miss a line and he was right on cue, every single time. His concentration was total. Never before had she seen work of this caliber by anyone in a live production. This character was completely different from any other she had ever seen him do—with an irresistible innocence and vulnerability—and she was simply mesmerized. It was all in the body language and the mindset, just as Leonard said. The story came to its sad conclusion too soon, and left her sobbing. It took a few minutes for her to get herself back together, drying her wet cheeks with the hem of her shirt. She rewound the film, then turned off the projector and took the empty popcorn bowl back to the kitchen. How did he *do* that, she wondered. How could he be so convincing as a character so different from himself? And on *live TV*, too!

Cal turned off the downstairs lights and climbed the stairs. Leonard's bedroom was directly across from hers. She peeked in. He was asleep. She sure wished he were awake. She had so much to talk to him about, so many things she wanted to ask him about that show. But he had an early call tomorrow and needed his sleep. Cal gazed at him. "All that talent in one person," she whispered to herself. And the irony of it was that the general public was completely unaware of it. He made it look so easy, they assumed it was.

Cal went into her room and changed into her pajamas. She started toward her bed, then stopped and looked back toward the door. After pondering the situation for a moment, she turned off her light and tiptoed into Leonard's room. Cal slowly lifted the sheet a bit and slipped into bed alongside him. She gazed at him for a long moment, then whispered, "You're awesome."

His eyes opened drowsily. He noted her look of admiration and smiled slightly. "Got to you, did it?" He once again held her close, and they fell asleep in each other's arms.

*   *   *

"Me? Why me?" she asked the next morning.

"Because you're here and you have the day off."

"Well, how's it work?"

"Beats me. That's for you to figure out." He mussed her hair and left for work.

They were alone now—Cal and the dishwasher. She and Leonard had reluctantly resorted to washing the dishes by hand once about a month ago and it needed to be done again; but the dishwasher was there to be used, he said, so from now on it would be. She opened it and peered inside. There were already a few plates there, having been left by Jill almost two months ago. Taking her cue from the way they were arranged, she put the rest of the plates in. The remainder was a mystery, however, so she put everything in the best way she could. It took some creative maneuvering, but finally she got every last item in and closed the door.

"Now what?" she wondered. She moved this knob, then that, until she heard water running. "Hey, that wasn't so hard."

Next, she attacked the second chore of the day—getting groceries. Leonard had given her enough money for a year's worth, it seemed. Now was the best time to be in public, Cal knew, because most of her fans were in school in the mornings. Their parents probably wouldn't know her from Adam. So she hopped into her car and looked for a supermarket. Ah, a Safeway. Going into the store brought back some happy childhood memories of times her mother's housekeeper had taken her along as she did the shopping. At the produce department, she knew that Myra would squeeze some fruits, but not others. "How do you know which are which?" she asked herself. Squeezing a tomato, the juice squirted her in the face. "Oh. That's how." Later, pushing her cart down the aisle of detergents, she noticed some made specifically for dishwashers and stopped in her tracks. "Uh-oh! I bet I was supposed to put detergent in that dishwasher!"

*　*　*

"Come look at the kitchen," she urged Leonard that evening.

He went to inspect her work. The counter was clear and clean for the first time in weeks. He looked in the cabinets. "Where are the dishes?"

"Well, they're in the dishwasher. I had to do them twice because I forgot to use detergent the first time. But look in the 'fridge. There's lots of goodies there now."

Sure enough, he found three cartons of Dr. Pepper, one six-pack of his favorite beer, several tomatoes (one of which had a hole in it), a can of marinated artichoke hearts, a chocolate meringue pie, and chocolate milk.

"*Marinated artichoke hearts?*" he asked.

"Well," she shrugged, "it looks good. We're supposed to have lots of veggies every day. That's what my health teacher said."

Opening the freezer, he then discovered cartons of chocolate and chocolate-marble ice cream, a Sara Lee chocolate cake, and several pizzas.

"Are you sure you got enough chocolate?" he teased.

"They didn't have any chocolate doughnuts."

He found several large bags of chips in the bread box and two bunches of bananas on the table. In the pantry were four large boxes of cereal and some Pop Tarts. "You plan to put chocolate milk on your cereal?"

"Oh," Cal thought aloud, "I forgot about that. We'll need to go back and get some of the regular kind."

"What's for dinner?" he asked.

"You like-a the pizza? We have-a the cheese, we have-a the sausage, and we have-a the combination," Cal grinned.

"I don't like pizza."

He had to be kidding. "Aw, come on. Everybody loves pizza."

"Not me."

Looking around her, she realized that there wasn't much else here that would make a real dinner. "Frito pie? We've got Frito chips. I think that's what it's made of."

"Okay. Make it."

"I don't know how."

He walked out of the kitchen, shaking his head. "I think we've got a problem, Cal."

She followed him. "We can have hoagies delivered."

"Where's my change?"

She went back into the kitchen, then returned to him and put three one-dollar bills and several coins into his outstretched hand. "The price of groceries has gone way up," she said

His shock was quickly replaced with resignation.

"But look at it this way, Len. We won't be running out of football-game goodies for a long time. We're all ready for a Super Bowl party."

"I'll tell George to hire us a housekeeper and cook."

"Okedoke," she grinned. Another victory.

Chapter 5

Up until now, it had been a peaceful, quiet Sunday afternoon.

"Dadgum it, Len!" Cal burst into the study, where Leonard had been memorizing his next day's revised script. "Why do you have to keep dying?"

"What on earth are you talking about?"

She wiped a tear away. "In almost every film you made, you end up dying, almost *every single time*. Why?" She dropped heavily onto the sofa beside him.

"I've gotten pretty good at it, haven't I?" he smiled. "And I don't have to stick around until the filming's over. I make a dramatic exit from one picture, then start on another one."

"But why? Why?" she asked impatiently. "It hurts to see you die."

"Because, Cal, I play the bad guy."

"Why's the bad guy got to die all the time? It's stupid."

"For Pete's sake, what do you expect? You want the bad guy to live happily ever after?"

"Yes!" she sobbed as a fresh supply of tears made their way down her cheeks.

He pulled a handkerchief from his pocket and gave it to her. "The bad guy always gets his comeuppance. The good guy saves the day. It's the bad guy's job to make the good guy look virtuous."

"Why do they keep making you the bad guy? You're not really that way—not usually."

"Just look at me, Cal. I'm big and can make myself look like a desperate criminal when I want to. I have no problem getting into that mindset."

She shook her head.

"It doesn't matter that I'm not really that way. That's what acting's all about. It's convincing people that you're someone else."

She dried her cheeks again.

"Which film were you just watching?" he asked.

"The one where you got shot."

"Which one? I've gotten shot dozens of times."

"Why do they have you using guns all the time? What is it with guns?"

"They're *Westerns*, for Pete's sake! Everyone has guns in those shows. What else is a bad guy to do his dastardly deeds with? A slingshot?"

"But I'm from cowboy country, and not everyone has guns in Dallas."

"Westerns are stories of the *old west*, Cal. Guns were necessary for survival back then."

She gripped his arm earnestly. "Don't leave me. Promise you won't die before me."

"How can I promise that? I'm a lot older than you."

"I don't care how. Just do it. You can do anything."

"You know what that means then, don't you?"

"What?"

He tapped her nose. "That you'll have to die young."

"Okay."

Puzzled, he studied her pleading, tearful eyes intently. Then it hit him. *Oh, of course!* he thought. All he had to do was put the facts together—her parents had died suddenly, her only other relative had turned her away, and now Jill and Stacy were gone, too. It's the classic fear of abandonment. He saw now that she was afraid he would disappear like everyone else had, leaving her all alone. Leonard set his script down and held her tenderly in his arms. "I'll never leave you, Cal," he murmured softly.

"Get rid of your guns?"

"No."

"Why?"

"I need them so I can keep in practice. I've got to look like I know what I'm doing when I threaten a good guy with a gun. My aim needs to look accurate. Who would be afraid of a bad guy who isn't at one with his gun?"

"I'm afraid they'll give you bad ideas. I'm afraid you'll get so used to people you've shot getting back up after the scene's over that you'll forget that it doesn't really work that way and you'll shoot somebody and they'll shoot you back."

He had to laugh in spite of himself. "Don't you have any more faith in my aim than that? Hey, if I shoot somebody, they're not going to be in any condition to shoot back."

"But then you'll go to jail."

This was getting rather silly, he thought. "Sorry, Cal. They're tools of my trade."

Chapter 6

THE DRIVE HOME FROM WORK each day was a good time to unwind and talk shop. Today, Leonard had some pleasant news for her: "When we get home, there should be a new person there. George got us a housekeeper, a Mrs. Morris, I think."

"Hot dog! Another female in the house. Now I won't be outnumbered anymore."

He looked askance at her. "How do you get 'outnumbered' when you're one and I'm one?"

"You own the house, and you're twice my size. Your vote counts more than mine."

He smiled to himself. "Good point. You're still outnumbered."

They rode in silence for a while, then Leonard cleared his throat. "Cal, we may have to do a little acting at home, too, when she's there."

"What do you mean?"

"George told me quite a bit about her, and she sounds like a terrific housekeeper and cook. The only drawback is that she's a devout Southern Baptist."

"She won't preach at everybody, will she?"

"No, I don't think so. But she may have problems with the fact that we're living together, unsupervised, and not married."

"What's bad about that? Dads and daughters live together."

He looked at her and raised an eyebrow.

"Oh, yeah. I forgot," she said. "But how would she know about that, anyway?"

"If you come over into my bed, unmake yours first and mess it up a little, then maybe she *won't* know."

"Okay."

"Actually, I'm surprised that the tabloids haven't caught on yet. Once Jill and Stacy moved out, that left us wide open to scandal. Just watch what you say and do around her, okay?"

"Okay."

Silence enveloped them, each thinking their own thoughts. Then Cal started fidgeting.

"Len?"

"What?"

"Do you think I ought to get my own place? I can afford a little one, can't I?"

"Not yet. Stay at my house as long as you want."

"It *is* an awfully big house—too big for one person."

"That it is."

They pulled into the driveway and saw that George's car was already there. Once inside, Cal looked from room to room, while Leonard sorted through the mail.

"We're in the kitchen," called George. "I was giving her a tour of the house."

Cal, then Leonard, joined them in the kitchen and were pleasantly surprised to find that Mrs. Morris was a very charming lady. In her fifties, she had graying hair, lively eyes and a warm smile. She reminded Cal very much of her own mother. After introductions were made and pleasantries exchanged, Leonard departed for the study to work on his lines for the next day, while Cal followed George and Mrs. Morris through the house. The new housekeeper-cook's work schedule would be weekdays, from 11:30 to 7:30 p.m., George told her. This would enable her to have the house cleaned and dinner waiting for them when Cal and Leonard got home about 6:30. She would begin the next day.

Cal waved goodbye to them as they left, wishing Mrs. Morris could start work right now because she was hungry. She closed the door and bounded up the stairs to the study. Leonard had been leaning against his desk, reading his part aloud. When Cal arrived, he stopped and lowered the script.

"This is going to be great, Len. Dinner will be waiting for us every night! A real dinner, just like in the good old days."

"Can she make Frito pie?" he asked with a trace of a smile.

"Gee, I don't know. I forgot to ask."

He handed her his script. "We've got this scene together tomorrow. Let's go over it."

She scanned it. It was a very dramatic scene that would require a lot of concentration and the attention to technical details that Leonard had taught her about.

He went to the other side of the room. "The scene hasn't been blocked out yet, but let's assume I'll be downstage right and you'll be center stage when it begins."

"Gee, Len. You make it sound like Broadway. Next, you'll be telling me it's curtain time."

"Sometimes, I miss stage work. There's nothing to match it—having to get it right the first time, a live audience…" His eyes were aglow with pleasure. "Their reactions and the curtain calls are manna for the soul." Leonard grew silent for a moment, savoring fond memories of his early career on the New York stage. Then he added, "That's *real* acting, at its purest and best. That's where we both belong."

"Oh, no. Not me. I like knowing I can do a retake if I mess up."

"Well, anyway, let's go over this scene. You've never done one like this before, so we need to get some of the basic points down before we get to the studio tomorrow." He returned to the desk and got her copy of the script, then took it back with him to the other side of the room. Flipping over to the correct page, he instructed, "The mystery is building. You're getting more worried by the minute. It seems to you that all the evidence of guilt points to me, but you're trying hard to deny it. But, at the same time, you're afraid it's true. You don't know whether you can trust me or not."

"Well, then, I'd say this calls for some chocolate. I wonder if Mrs. Morris can make brownies like Jill."

He grew impatient. "Come on, Cal! Get your mind off food!"

"Hard to do. We're going to have real dinners again."

"Forget about that. We've got work to do! Let's pick this up from the top of page 115."

"Steaks. Spare ribs. Fried chicken…."

Leonard threw the script to the floor. He stormed over to her, gripped her shoulders and shook her hard, with fury in his eyes. "If you don't stop that and concentrate on this scene right now, I'll fire Mrs. Morris before she even starts!"

She shrank back from his hold. "Okay, okay, Len. Let go."

He released her, and returned to his place across the room while keeping his eyes on Cal. He picked up the script.

"Where do I start?" she asked in a small voice.

"Top of page 115."

After that, Cal did the scene with such emotion that even Leonard was impressed. Her voice trembled as she took on her character's personality. The complexity of her character's feelings was evident, and Cal handled it well…

…just as Leonard had planned. *All it takes is a little inspiration*, he inwardly congratulated himself, while maintaining a stern exterior. The next day, on the set, he would have to remind her of his threat right before they did that scene for the camera—repeating a variation of his performance, in order to provoke hers.

Chapter 7

THE DISHWASHER WAS AGAIN being used every day, but not for everything. Tonight, Mrs. Morris was hand-washing the Teflon cookware and Cal was happily drying. Leonard was leaning against the kitchen doorway. Normally, he would have been elsewhere, but this time felt he should stick around—mainly to be sure that Cal maintained the discretion he had warned her about. Sure enough, it didn't take long for sensitive issues to surface.

"How did you come to live in this lovely home?" Mrs. Morris asked Cal. "I understand you're not related."

Leonard said, only half jokingly, "She was an orphan, left on my doorstep. What else was I to do?"

"You are such a kind man," she smiled, then turned to Cal. "George told me that your parents passed away in a plane crash. I'm so sorry."

"The worst part about it is that I never had a chance to say 'goodbye.' And they never got to see my first picture. They would've loved it."

"Well," Mrs. Morris winked. "You'll all be together again someday. I have no doubt about that."

"My only relative is my Uncle Antonio, but he didn't want me. He's a high school principal. He said working with kids was one thing, but living with one was another. I was already here with Len's family while we were working on my first film, so Len just let me stay here forever and pretty much kept supporting me since I'm not employed as steadily as he is. I've just been lucky to be able to make my car payments and maintain my horse on what I earn."

"Oh, you have a horse?"

"Yeah," Cal's eyes lit up. "His name's Zeus and he's so gorgeous. We keep him at a farm, right outside of town."

"I keep telling you, Cal, you need a better agent so you'll have more work," Leonard advised. "Pete didn't do a thing to get you this part in *Henson*. I had to do it myself. He's utterly useless to you now."

"We used to have the same agent," Cal told her new friend, "but Len switched to a different one a few years ago."

He added, "It made a big difference, too. But how do you get kids to listen to their elders, Mrs. Morris?"

She chuckled. "I've found that our children realize how right we were once they have children of their own. That's when a parent—or, in your case, a guardian—begins to get the respect that's due." Dishes finished, she put the dish rack and drain-board away and tidied up the sink. "'Cal.' What an unusual name for a female. Where did that come from?"

"Well, actually my real name's Stacy Ames and that's how they list me in film and TV credits. But nobody calls me that, unless they don't know me very well."

Leonard explained further, "You see, when Cal first came here, she was an adolescent who had had very little discipline in her life. She was headstrong and prone to be rather mouthy, what Jill called 'incident-prone.' 'Cal' was a shortened version of the word 'Calamity.' We tried hard to reprogram her, and succeeded somewhat."

"But the way you went about it, Len," Cal objected. "Like a bulldozer!"

"Well, that's what it took. Nothing short of that would've fazed you. You were a tough customer back then, Cal. You have no idea."

"But you know what, Mrs. Morris? We might've broken some furniture with our roughhousing, but at least it showed me that somebody cared about me."

Mrs. Morris smiled warmly. "And now you've blossomed into a delightful young lady."

"Really?" Cal stood a little straighter and grinned. "You really think so?"

"Certainly. Well, I think my work is done for the day," Mrs. Morris said. "It's been lovely chatting with you two. Have a good evening and I'll see you tomorrow."

They walked with her to the door, and Cal waved goodbye as their new housekeeper backed her car out of the driveway. After she was gone, Cal turned to Leonard. "Did you hear that? I'm a 'delightful young lady.'"

"You'll be high on that for a few days." He shut the front door and headed toward the media room.

Cal followed. "Aren't you going to go study your lines?"

"I'm not in any of the scenes tomorrow. That'll give me some time to talk to my lawyer about Stacy." He sat on the sofa, picked up the remote control, and turned on the television. "You know, it's ironic that Jill named Stacy after you. She sure did like you those first couple of years."

"What do you mean 'first couple of years'?"

"Well, I thought it was silly myself, but a few years ago she started thinking that there was something going on between you and me."

Cal asked incredulously, "What made her think that?"

He shrugged. "She said that, almost from the beginning, I couldn't keep my hands off of you."

"You mean when you kept hitting me? Every time Miles and I came home late, you'd whack me. You mean she was jealous of *that*?"

"Your guess is as good as mine. Any man who claims to understand women is only fooling himself."

"How come you were so rough with me, but not with anyone else?"

"Hey, I wasn't the only one. You packed a pretty good wallop yourself and left scars on my shins.

"Well, why not? You hit me; I was obligated to get you back. Serves you right."

He flipped the channels.

"What scenes are scheduled tomorrow?" she asked.

Leonard pulled the call sheet from his pocket, unfolded it, then found the answer. "The cellar and bridge scenes."

"I'm in the bridge one. Morning or afternoon?"

"Afternoon."

"I'll work on the lines later then. Anything special I need to know to do it?"

"No. Your character's pretty sedate in that scene."

"Good." A movie was starting on TV. Once the title and credits confirmed that neither Cal nor Leonard was in it, she said, "I'm going over to Becky's," and left.

*   *   *

Cal and Becky were sitting on the patio, sipping Cokes and enjoying the balmy evening. Cal had described in detail the wonderful dinner Mrs. Morris had made, and now Becky had some news of her own.

"Johnny's cousin is coming to visit, so maybe we can all go out together this weekend, the four of us."

"Oh, I don't know," Cal said.

"Oh, come on, Cal. You haven't had a date in ages."

"What's his name and what's he like?"

"I think Johnny said his name is Jeff. I don't know much more about him. But you know if he's Johnny's cousin, he's got to be dreamy."

Cal laughed. "Not that you're prejudiced or anything."

"Right." She set her drink down. "Cal, how come you haven't dated much since you and Miles broke up? That was so long ago."

"Oh, I don't know. Haven't felt much need to, I guess."

"Well, I consider it my job to find you a new boyfriend. That'll be my mission in life. I won't rest until you're madly in love, just like I am."

"After Jill left Len, I'm wondering if it's worth it. You think people are in love, they commit their lives to each other, get married and have a baby together. Everything seems to be terrific, then you come home and they've filed for divorce." She sighed. "What's the use?"

"It doesn't always end up like that."

"I mean you live with these people, you see them every day, and they seem so right for each other. How could that happen? And why isn't Len fighting it? Why isn't he trying to get her back? I don't get it."

"Well…"

"It's not like him to just accept an injustice. When something's wrong, he's always the one to fix it."

"There must be more to it, something that you don't know about."

"Like what?"

"I don't know."

"I hate to see him hurt, and he was real hurt the day he got the first notice about the divorce. I've never seen him like that, before or since. It like to killed me. I hope he never has to go through heartache like that again."

Becky turned her chair to face Cal's, bringing the girls eye to eye. "Tell me something. And I want to know the truth. What's going on between you and Leonard?"

Cal squirmed, uncomfortably. "What do you mean?" she asked, hoping to goodness that Becky couldn't read her as easily as Leonard could.

"Well, when you used to talk about him, it was like a kid complaining about her dad. But it's not like that anymore."

Cal shrugged. "When's Jeff coming? Friday?"

"Cal," Becky pointed her finger at her, "don't change the subject."

"I don't want to talk about it, Becky."

"Why not?"

"If I knew the answer, maybe I'd tell you; but the truth is, I just don't know."

"How can you not know?"

"I'm just confused about some things, that's all. Nobody knows everything." Cal got up and handed her glass to Becky. "I have to go study my lines. I have the bridge scene to do tomorrow. See ya."

"Okay, sit back down. We won't talk about it anymore." Becky returned her chair to its original position.

Cal settled back into her chair. "Have you seen Dustin Hoffman's new picture? Len swears he's going to be one of the greatest actors of our day."

"I never heard of him before *The Graduate*, and now everybody's talking about him. He's pretty good."

They sat in silence. There was the sound of crickets in the air, and the sweet smell of honeysuckle. Cal leaned back and closed her eyes. "I love this time of year. And this time of day. It's so peaceful."

"Yeah," Becky sighed. "After a hard day at work, it would feel good."

They let the serenity of the evening wash over them for a few moments.

"Well, is it Friday?" Cal asked.

"Is what Friday?"

"When Jeff is coming."

"I think so."

"Let's go see that new Dustin Hoffman movie."

"Sounds good to me."

Chapter 8

"**Where are you going?**" Leonard asked. Friday evenings were usually spent unwinding in front of the TV with a bowl of popcorn, but Cal had just come into the media room wearing a dress.

"Got a date."

"With who?"

"Becky and I are going to the movies with Johnny and his cousin."

He picked up the remote control and flipped channels, coming to a stop at the nightly news. "Don't leave until I meet him."

"Oh, Len. I'm not a kid anymore."

"You heard me." He flipped to another network.

Cal was about to protest when the doorbell rang. She hurried to the door and opened it wide. It was them. "We can't go yet," she told them. "Y'all need to come on in first."

Becky pushed Jeff toward the front. "This is Jeff, Cal. He's visiting from Canada for a week and wanted to meet a real movie star. So here you are, Jeff. Cal's been in several movies and TV shows under the name Stacy Ames."

He had a shy smile and soulful, brown eyes. "Glad to meet you." He held out his hand. Cal took hold of it and led him to the media room.

"You've got to meet Len. He's been not only in a zillion movies, but on stage and TV, too. He's the *real* star of the family."

Becky and John followed close behind, as they all entered the room in which Leonard had been watching television.

"Here he is, Len. This is Jeff somebody." She looked at Jeff. "What's your last name?"

"Fullerton."

"And you probably recognize this guy—Leonard Rhoads. He's in a lot of Westerns and, depending on which character he's playing, would either shoot you or arrest you."

Leonard stood up and shook hands with the young man and nodded to his companions. Cal couldn't help but notice how Leonard's presence seemed to overpower everyone else's. He was not only more physically imposing, but also exuded an air of confidence and control that the others didn't have. There was no doubt that he was king of his domain. "Get her back here before midnight," he instructed.

"But it's Friday, Len," Cal whined, "and I'm *twenty-one*, for Pete's sake."

"Okay, one o'clock. But no later."

"Yes sir," Jeff said.

Cal then herded everyone back out into the hall. "Where's the orgy? We better go there first, since I have to be back so early."

"What!?" came Leonard's booming voice from the media room.

"Just kidding. Bye," answered Cal with a grin and a mischievous sparkle in her eye, as she closed the front door behind her.

*   *   *

It was one o'clock on the dot when they returned. After Cal bid the trio goodbye, she shut the door and started toward the stairs.

"See? It's not so hard to get in on time," said Leonard from the living room. "How'd it go?"

She turned to join him. "Oh, pretty good. You're right. Dustin Hoffman is one terrific actor. This movie was even better than the last one."

"Sounds like you had a good time. Were Becky and John with you the whole time?"

"Of course."

"That's good." He put the newspaper down and went over to lock the front door.

"Jeff and I are going out to dinner tomorrow night, just the two of us. And the timing is good since Mrs. Morris won't be here to cook, so I won't miss anything good."

"When are you going to work on your lines? You can't go out every night when you're working."

"I'll have time for that Sunday." She headed toward the stairway.

"How long will he be in town?"

"Just a week."

"Okay. Just be sure to keep Sunday open. You'll be in big trouble if you show up on the set unprepared Monday."

"I know."

Leonard turned off the downstairs lights as Cal ascended the stairs, went into her room, and closed the door. After she had changed into her pajamas, her phone rang. It was Becky.

"So what do you think of him?" she asked Cal breathlessly. "Isn't he cute?"

"Yeah, he's real cute. I can't get over those beautiful brown eyes of his. He's so shy, though."

"Johnny tells me that it was uncharacteristically bold of Jeff to ask you out on a single date tomorrow night. He said he doesn't usually move that fast."

"Well, he only has a week. I guess that makes a difference, huh?"

"Guess so. And I think your 'movie star' status impressed him, too."

"Has he seen any of my films? I couldn't quite get that out of him."

"I don't know. Maybe it's just the principle of the thing."

Cal laughed. "The less people know about this business, the more impressed they are."

"Guess what." Becky sounded excited.

"What?"

"Johnny said while you and Jeff are out tomorrow night, he and I should go look at engagement rings."

Cal squealed, "Really? Oh, boy! It's about time!"

"I've got to go now, but I had to tell you the news. I can hardly wait to have it on my finger and show it to you."

"It won't be long now. I'll talk to you tomorrow. 'Bye, Becky."

They hung up, and Cal turned off the light and went to bed.

* * *

Cal was so glad that Mrs. Morris was here these days so she didn't have to spend Saturdays doing laundry anymore. Becky did, though; so Cal hopped into her car and went to see her beloved Zeus.

"There you are, baby," she greeted him with a hug. "Did you miss me?"

He nuzzled against her, then pushed his nose against her right hip.

Cal laughed. "You know what I have in there, don't you?" She put her hand in her pocket and pulled a sugar cube out. She held it out to him on her flattened hand, and he ate it. "You think *that's* good? Too bad you can't have one of Jill's brownies. They're even better."

She took the saddle and reins off the post and put them onto Zeus, strapping them on securely. Cal then put her foot into the stirrup, climbed on, and they were off.

It was really tempting for her to try to take Zeus over the low hedges, to see if he could jump them; but she knew better than to take a risk like that when she was working on a film. If he were to suddenly stop, rather than to jump the hedge, Cal might fall off and, perhaps, break a bone. So any risks, she figured, had better be taken when she's between jobs. But at least Zeus never shied away from a fast gallop, and he was a good racer when Leonard was with them on another horse. "The Long Island cowboy," she laughed to herself as thoughts of Leonard on horseback accompanied Zeus' trot down the country road. Considering how different their worlds had been, it was amazing how much she and Leonard had in common.

This is one of those times Cal missed Stacy the most. Stacy loved to go with her when she went to see Zeus. "I sure hope we get visiting rights," Cal sighed. "I sure miss that little rug-rat."

Chapter 9

"YOU DON'T HAVE TO WAIT UP for me every time, Len," Cal said when she returned from her date that night. "I can remember to turn off the lights and lock the door."

"It sure took you two a long time to have dinner."

"Well, we went other places, too."

"Where?"

"We went walking in the park. It was a nice evening for it. I had my sunglasses on most of the time so no one recognized me or anything."

"The park? You could've gotten mugged! That little squirt couldn't protect you from a Chihuahua."

"Oh, Len, you sound like a dad."

"I *am* a dad."

"Yeah, but not mine! I'm a grown-up woman now and can take care of myself. You don't have to treat me like I'm ten."

He put out his cigarette. "Tomorrow, we work on our lines."

Cal hesitated. "Uh, Len?"

He didn't like the sound of that. "What!" he said, rather than asked, more testily than he intended.

"Jeff's taking me bowling tomorrow."

"No!"

"What do you mean 'no'? I already told him yes. I haven't been bowling in years."

"Too bad. Tomorrow is going to be spent working on our parts."

"I can't go back on my word!"

"You already did! You told me just last night that you would devote Sunday to learning your lines!"

They were both yelling now. "He's only going to be here a few more days, Len!"

"Tough!"

She glared at him.

He glared back. "You're not too old to be grounded, you know."

Her frustration was overwhelming. She threw her purse at him, wishing it were much larger and heavier. "I hate you!"

"Don't forget to turn off the lights when you're through down here." He locked the door and went upstairs.

Fuming, Cal flipped off the living room lamp, ran up the stairs, slammed her bedroom door shut, and changed into her pajamas, while muttering, "I'll show him. I'll sell Zeus and get a place of my own. I don't care if it's dinky and little and dangerous. I've just *got* to get out of here!" She paced the floor, getting angrier by the moment. "I'll move far away from here so I won't ever have to see him again! I'll go back to Texas, that's what I'll do!" She got into bed. "And I won't tell him where I'm going. And I'll change my name so, even if he searched from now until doomsday, he still won't be able to find me." She tossed and turned. "And I'll never watch another film with him in it! Never! I never want to see his face again!" There's no way she could go to sleep in this frame of mind. She got back up, grabbed the pillow off her bed and stormed into Leonard's room. He had just settled into bed when Cal rammed the pillow against his face. She straddled his stomach and put all her weight onto the pillow. "I'll smother you, that's what I'll do! I won't ever take this off you until you're dead. Then you'll be out of my life forever!"

Quick as lightening, he pushed the pillow aside and flipped Cal over, then pinned her down by the arms. Now it was *he* who was looking down at *her*. "You're going to do *what* to me?" he laughed. "I'm oh-so-scared."

Utterly humiliated, she kicked his shin, hurting her own bare foot a lot more than him. "I hate you!"

They looked at each other intensely for a minute, neither quite sure where to go from there. Then Leonard leaned down and kissed her lightly and tenderly. When he looked at her again, the fury had disappeared from her eyes and her fists were no longer clinched. He murmured softly, "There's a fine line between love and hate, baby. A very fine line." He then kissed her again, this time passionately. He released her arms and she wrapped them around him, returning his ardor.

Tonight would mark the first time that they truly made love.

*　*　*

When Cal awoke the next morning, she looked over at Leonard. He was on his back, sleeping peacefully beside her. She snuggled up to him and sighed. Could she have really been the source of Jill's unhappiness? And is she the reason Leonard had not contested the divorce? If so, why didn't Jill tell her? And could she continue her relationship with him with a clear conscience?

"Doggone conscience, anyway," she mumbled.

"What?" Leonard asked as his eyes opened and he turned toward her.

"Oh, I was just thinking out loud," she said, stroking his hair. "Were you being Len last night, or was Howard Henson back for a visit?"

He smiled and kissed her nose. "That was me. Henson taught me a few things."

"What would I do without you, Len? I'm sorry I tried to kill you."

He laughed. "If that was a serious attempt, it was pathetic. Next time you want to suffocate me, I'd advise you to tie up my hands first. Take it from an experienced bad guy, you'll get much better results that way."

"Well, I was plenty mad at the time, but I guess you were right. I did promise to work on my part today."

"So you'll tell that guy to get lost?"

"I'll tell him I can't see him today because I've got to study my lines. He'll understand."

Leonard got up on an elbow and looked at her. "Tell him you can't see him anymore."

"Never again? Why?"

He looked at her as though the answer were obvious. "Because you're *mine*, Cal."

"What?" she asked incredulously.

"I've taken care of you for six years. I gave you a home, supported you, and assured you a career. You're mine."

"I belong to *me*, Len. You can't buy or sell me."

"You know that's not what I meant." He drew her close and kissed her on the neck.

"Again? You're kidding," she asked.

"Hey, I'm an animal."

"Are all guys that insatiable?"

"Dunno. Why don't you take a poll and find out?"

"Golly, for an old codger you sure have a lot of energy!"

Chapter 10

Mrs. Morris had become more than just a housekeeper and cook to Cal. She seemed to be the most stable part of her life. Regardless of the circumstances, Cal always found Mrs. Morris to be calm, wise and optimistic. Until this woman had come into her life, Cal had had no one in California with whom she could discuss religion. It just didn't seem to be a big part of anyone's life out here, as it had been in Texas.

"Oh, no!" Cal said, wide-eyed. "Are you serious?"

"That's my understanding," said Mrs. Morris.

"We're no longer male and female in Heaven? That's awful!"

"Why do you say that, dear?"

"Because Len is so *good* at being a guy!"

Mrs. Morris laughed out loud. There was something so engaging about Cal, and she had developed an affection for her. She finished ironing a shirt and hung it up. "He told me that his next picture will be filmed on location in England."

"Yeah. That's one place I'd sure love to see someday," Cal sighed.

"Oh, I would, too. But we can find enough to keep us busy here."

"I bet he's going to get an award for *Henson of Manhattan*, the film we're doing now. He's got the lead and is *so* good in it. I can't stop being amazed by that guy. He can do absolutely anything! Have you seen his work?"

"I've seen some of his guest appearances on TV shows. But I don't get out to the movies very often."

"You're lucky. He keeps getting killed in the movies. That irritates the daylights out of me."

The woman chuckled as she put another shirt on the ironing board.

"But he doesn't in this one. We'll have to take you with us to the premiere. I'm not so great in it, though. Len's trying to help me because it's so different from any of the other pictures I've ever done. He's really taught me a lot, but he still outshines me by a mile when it comes to acting."

"I'm glad you hold him in such high esteem. So many young people don't learn to do that until they're much older. That's a credit to your maturity, young lady." Mrs. Morris beamed. "And I imagine when you have as many years of experience as he does, you'll be just as good at your work as he is."

"He really throws his whole self into a role. I have a hard time doing that. He keeps telling me I've got to actually *become* the person I'm playing and to think like she does. Wouldn't it be funny if I played a really horrible character and couldn't let go of the role, even after I came home? He'd have a hard time living with me then, huh?" she laughed.

"I've seen that happen to some actors."

The phone rang. "I'll get it," Cal said as she went to the next room. After a few minutes, she returned.

"Good news and bad news. That was my agent. He's got me lined up to do another picture right after this one, but it's a lot like the ones I usually do. It won't be real challenging, but at least I'll have no trouble knowing how to do it, and it'll help me with my car payments. But Len will probably be pretty disgusted by it because he likes me to try new things. He'll probably tell me again to change agents."

"Why don't you?"

"Well, Len thinks it's because I don't like change but, really, I'm being loyal to the people who gave me my start."

"Could he be right, do you think?"

"No, I'm just being loy… Oh, I guess maybe. Change *is* kind of scary."

"A lot of people feel that way. But quite often change can improve the quality of your life. If I were you, I'd trust Leonard. He's been where you are now, and he can help you avoid making some mistakes that he might have made."

"You know, I would swear you're a mother."

She smiled. "As a matter of fact, I am. I have two grown children."

"Yep, I thought so."

"When Leonard told me about his going on location next month, he asked a very special favor."

That sounded intriguing. "Are you going to airmail him some of your dinners?" she asked.

"No. It's quite a different kind of thing. He told me that he was concerned that you'll get lonely while he's gone and he asked that I find a pet for you to keep you company in the evenings."

Cal's face lit up. "In addition to Zeus? Hot diggity! Maybe now I can finally get a dog."

"He didn't specify what kind of pet, but a cat would probably be easier to keep indoors than a dog. Would you like to go with me to make the selection?"

"I sure would! When can we go?"

"Today would be good."

*   *   *

Leonard was in the study when they returned. Cal carried in a little white kitten and Mrs. Morris brought in the accessories for it.

"Isn't he the most precious thing, Len? I think I'll call him Luigi." She sat on the sofa and set the kitten on her lap. "He doesn't know how to say 'meow' yet—it's more like a little squeak. I think he needs speech therapy."

Leonard came over to where she was sitting and gently stroked the little animal. "Well, Cal, I guessed wrong. I was sure you'd come home with a dog."

"Well, I figured if we're both away at the same time, a cat could take being alone better than a dog could. Uncle Ant has both cats and dogs, and the cats are more independent. They're self-cleaning, too."

"Good point."

She took his hand and looked up at him. "Thanks, Len, for letting me have him."

"I didn't want you to get lonely while I'm away next month."

She let his hand go and stroked the kitten. "Did I tell you that Pete got me another picture? I'll be starting it about the time you start yours."

"He did? What kind?"

Cal looked at Mrs. Morris, then back at Leonard. "Well, it uses skills I already have, so I can handle it myself while you're away. See Len," she looked at him intently, "I really need your help when I'm tackling something new."

"Okay. But why don't you ask him to get you something that's completely different next time—maybe science fiction, or pure comedy? I'll help you with it. The more versatile you are, the more work you'll get."

"Too bad *The Twilight Zone* went off the air. Something like that would be fun."

"Exactly! TV exposure on a show as popular as that would be perfect. *The Twilight Zone* had a huge audience."

"Okay. I'll ask him to do that."

"Where's your picture being shot?"

"I haven't seen the script yet, but, from what he said, it sounds like the whole thing can be done at the studio and on the back lot."

He looked at her in disbelief. "You accepted a part without seeing the script?"

"Why bother? They keep revising it anyway."

"Who else will be in it?"

"He didn't say."

"Who's directing?"

She shrugged.

"You're taking a big chance, Cal. It might turn out all right. It might not."

"Well, I know the title of it. It's called *Campus Dreams*. Guess I'm in school, again."

He turned to Mrs. Morris. "What I'd *really* like to see her do is a play. Now *that's* a challenge; and, whether she realizes it or not, she can do it."

"Oh, I know she could," Mrs. Morris agreed. "With her youth and vitality, Cal can do anything."

"Oh, Len," Cal said, "don't get started on that again. Professional stage work scares the daylights out of me."

"Remember the tour? Performing live on stage in a variety-show setting didn't bother you."

"Well, gee, that's kind of different. That was fun. I love to be in musical shows with a band behind me and everything."

"Not much different at all, Cal. How about if we do a play together? Would you consider it then?" he asked.

"I don't know."

"Well," he returned to his desk. "That would have to be pretty far into the future. I already have commitments for the next eighteen months or so."

She heaved a sigh of relief.

Chapter 11

Cal and Becky were strolling along the quiet street between their houses.

"Isn't it beautiful, Cal?" Becky flashed her sparkling new engagement ring to her friend. Then she polished it on her shirt, and looked at it from different angles. It glistened in the sunshine.

"It sure is. Did y'all set a date yet?"

"Not yet, but I want you to be my maid of honor."

"Sure!"

"Hello, girls," came a familiar voice from behind them.

Cal whizzed around. It was Nate. She hadn't seen him for quite a while. She was hoping that he'd fallen off the face of the earth. No such luck.

"Hi, Nate," said Becky gleefully. "I was just showing Cal my engagement ring. Johnny finally came through. See? Isn't it gorgeous?"

"Congratulations," he said. Nate then smirked at Cal, who ignored him and kept walking. "I think I know something you don't," he told her.

"So what?" Cal replied.

"Don't you want to know what it is?"

"No."

"Well, then, you'll really get a big surprise the first day you step onto the *Campus Dreams* set."

Uh-oh. How'd he know she was doing that film? "Why?"

"Because," he pinched her cheek condescendingly, "we're co-starring in it, you sweet thing! It uses the same main characters as the last two installments of the trilogy."

Cal's heart sank as she pushed Nate's hand away from her face. She had hoped they'd never have to make a joint appearance again. Now she wished she had listened to Leonard and found out more about the picture before agreeing to it.

He couldn't resist taunting her further. "I was surprised to see that we'd be working together again. You must've pulled some strings to make it happen."

"I did not! Pete didn't tell me who was in it."

He whispered in her ear, "And we have a *really* hot scene in it. I bet you helped them write it, too."

"Get lost!" Cal shoved him away, and ran for home. It seemed to take forever before she reached the front door. She ran through it, up the stairs and into her room, dropping onto her bed and covering her head with a pillow. "No, no, no. I can't believe it's happening again," she moaned. Then, she pulled the phone over onto the bed and called her agent. "Pete? It's Cal. I told you I don't want to ever work with Nate again. Why'd you do this to me?"

"For the good of your career, that's why. You've been nagging me to get you work. Well, I got you work. The only way you're going to be able to have as many jobs as you want is by working with Nate. That's all there is to it. Believe me, you'll thank me someday." Then, he added, "And this time, be *nice* to him, you hear?"

"You've got to get me out of it. I can't do this film."

"It's too late. Everything's firmed up. They start shooting in a week."

"Well, can I have a different part, then? Let someone else be Corky and I'll take a smaller role."

"You *are* Corky, Cal. No one else can play that part."

"Ask them right now. Or maybe Corky can have a smaller part so another character can do whatever Corky was going to do."

"Don't get your heart set on it. I'll try but I don't think it can be done at this late date."

After a few more pleas and non-committal responses, they hung up.

Cal searched around her room for the script, which had been delivered last week. Finding it, she thumbed through it, looking for that "hot scene" Nate was talking about and hoping that he was lying. As she progressed through the script, she felt a little better. So far, so good. It was all pretty tame stuff. She got engrossed in the story line and laughed at her character's antics, until - "Oh, no. No!" There it was on page ninety-four. She read it carefully, and a profound feeling of dread overwhelmed her. "I can't do that with him. Len, yes. Nate, never! Not in a million years!"

It was a passionate bedroom scene. The trilogy had been family fare. Why was this one so different, she wondered? Their characters were in college now, rather than high school, but still…. . Don't they have chaperones in college?

Cal took the script and searched through the house for Leonard. He'd fix it. She found him in the study, at his desk, getting his personal business wrapped up prior to leaving for England. She opened the script to the offensive page and dropped it in front of him. "This scene is *not* important to the story line. It only sensationalizes it. Can you make them take it out, or use other characters to do it?"

He read it over, then shook his head. "You can do this, Cal. Remember how well you did it just a few months ago?"

"But, Len, it's with Nate!"

"*Nate*? How'd he get in it? I thought you told Pete to make sure you two are never in the same picture again."

"I did. He says he did it for the good of my career. He said I'll thank him someday, the jerk!"

Leonard looked at her with disgust and shook his head again.

"I know, I know," she said. "I need to change agents."

"That's right. Don't you wish you had listened to me now? When are you going to realize that the advice I'm giving you is for your own good?"

"I know," she agreed. "But can't you fix it? This scene doesn't have to be done by the main characters. One of the others could do it."

"Who's directing?"

"Sidney Erickson."

"I'll give him a call tonight. Maybe something can be arranged."

She gave him a hug. "Thanks, Len." Maybe it would be manageable, after all. Cal went back downstairs as Leonard got his address book out.

* * *

As he hung the phone back up, he shook his head. During the course of his career, Leonard had taken many chances. Some had paid off, some hadn't. He had gambled with Cal's career only a few times, though. This time, he had taken what he knew of the studio at which she worked and used it to her advantage. He knew that no film they had ever produced with either Cal or Nate separately had been nearly as profitable as the ones they did together. He knew that the studio would do just about anything to keep them both in this picture, so he threatened them with a walk out. He told Sidney Erickson emphatically and without any doubt in his tone that Cal would certainly walk out if the love scene were not given to the minor character in this film. Sue her for breach of contract, if you want, but that's the way it has to be. So, rather than risk Cal's walking out and ruining their opportunity to have a hit film, Erickson agreed to do what was necessary to keep Cal involved with this project and happy. He would get with the chiefs and work something out.

Chapter 12

"**Good night, Mrs. Morris.** I'll see you tomorrow," Cal waved as her friend pulled out of the driveway. She then went into the living room and looked around, pondering what to do now.

This was the first night she had ever spent alone in this house. Leonard had left that morning for England. All the times he had had out-of-town work in the past, Jill and Stacy were here to keep her company. Now she was alone.

Or so she thought.

Luigi appeared at her feet, and squeaked a cheery "good evening." Cal smiled and gathered her furry pet into her arms. "Now I see why Len got you for me. You're good company." She carried him into the media room. Cal turned the TV on and sat in the recliner, placing Luigi on her lap. The late news was coming on. She stroked the kitten as they watched the news of the day. A few minutes was all she could take of that. "Too much violence," she sighed, as she turned it off and put on one of Leonard's films instead. As it progressed, she mused over the irony of the situation—as the 'bad guy' in the film, Leonard had provided plenty of violence, which didn't bother her at all. But there *was* a huge difference. If Cal had analyzed it, she would have known that the violence on the nightly news was so bothersome because it was entirely real and happening to innocent people. Not so with the film version.

She watched the movie as Luigi was taking a nap on her lap. This was one of Leonard's better Westerns, and also in it were two of his character-actor buddies. *It must have been like a reunion when they filmed this one*, Cal thought. She watched it almost to the end, but stopped and rewound the film right before the part where Leonard's character was killed. She still couldn't bear to witness that, real or not.

Maybe it'd be wise to work some more on her *Campus Dreams* lines. A rewrite had been delivered, and she discovered that Leonard's efforts had paid off. They did, indeed, switch the offensive scene to a minor character. So

Cal's character would now remain at arm's length from Nate's. *That won't be so bad*, she thought. She set Luigi on the sofa beside her and took the script upstairs to her room, then lay across her bed as she turned to her first scene.

She tried to concentrate on the script, but her eyes were getting heavy. She looked at the clock. Normally, 8:35 wouldn't seem so late to her, but she had gotten up very early that morning to see Leonard off. She put the script down and decided to go to bed.

Cal went downstairs and checked all the outside doors to make sure they were locked, just as Leonard normally would do. Then she turned off the downstairs lights and went upstairs. Luigi followed her. He might be small, but he was quite athletic and climbed the carpeted stairs like a pro. Cal put on her pajamas, then settled into bed. There was no need to set her alarm tonight, since they told her she's not due on the set for another two days.

The house seemed so quiet, so empty. Even with Luigi curled up at her feet, the loneliness was pervasive. Cal shut her eyes and tried to sleep, but sleep wouldn't come.

The jangling of the phone on the nightstand startled her. *It better not be Nate,* she whispered to Luigi as she gingerly lifted the receiver. "Hello?" she asked cautiously.

"Good morning, Cal. The sun's just now coming up over here!"

Her face lit up. "Hi, Len! It's nighttime here. How was the flight?"

"Pretty good, but awfully long. Guess what movie they had on board?"

"What?"

"Remember when you played Letitia, that little Italiano?"

"I had no trouble coming up with *that* accent. I just became my mom."

"And with all those grand gestures, you were quite convincing. Could your mom talk without using her hands?"

"I don't know. I never saw her try."

"So how's everything at home? Is your kitten keeping you in line?"

"It sure is quiet around here without you. I'm awfully glad Luigi's here."

"See? I take care of you, even when I'm on the other side of the world."

She smiled. "Yeah, you sure do. And tomorrow, I'll have all day to ride Zeus. It's just not the same, though, horseback riding without you."

"I'll be there in spirit; and I'll beat you to the finish line again, this time by proxy."

"No, you won't. I'll throw a proxy banana peel in your path," she grinned.

"What did Mrs. Morris fix you for dinner tonight?" he asked.

"Fried chicken and mashed potatoes with brown gravy on top. I hadn't had that in a long time. And chocolate cake for dessert. But it seems silly to make a whole meal just for me, so I made her eat dinner with me."

"Good for you! Well, I've got to catch a few winks before meeting with some people later today. Just wanted to make sure all is well there."

"It is."

"Goodnight, Cal."

"'Night, Len."

She hung up, and sighed. Now she knew what she'd have to do in order to get to sleep. She got out of her bed, picked up Luigi, and went into Leonard's room. She got into his bed, on the side where he usually slept. She set Luigi beside her, turned off the light, and went right to sleep.

Chapter 13

It was Cal's first day on the set of *Campus Dreams,* and she felt quite smug. *Once I see Nate,* she thought, *I'll tell him all about the switch in scenes that Len arranged. Then I'll have the last laugh while Nate'll fume. I can hardly wait.*

He arrived at the studio a few minutes later and came directly to her. "You just couldn't stand for someone else to have that scene with me, could you?" he asked with a sneer.

Hey, wait a minute, she thought. That wasn't right. "What're you talking about?"

"Well, first they change that hot scene so I'm doing it with another character, and now I find out that *Corky* is now that other character."

"*What?*"

"Corky and Patty have switched lines. Patty is now my accomplice and Corky is the minor character. But never fear, Cal. It's still Corky who gets to do the love scene with me. Pete told me you asked him to make Corky the minor character. He sure earned his ten percent this time, didn't he?"

"Oh, no! He told me he didn't think they could do that." She sank down into the nearest chair and felt sick to her stomach.

He put his arm around her shoulders. "Don't you worry. I'll save all my goodies for you."

She pushed his arm off. "Go away!"

Nate leaned over and whispered, "Just you wait 'til I get you under those sheets. I get hot just thinking about it."

Cal couldn't take anymore and punched him in the eye. With any luck, it would produce a shiner that couldn't be covered with makeup. Then they'd have to postpone his first scene that day, and that would set the whole schedule back.

He left her alone the rest of the day.

She was fined for disruptive behavior.

* * *

It had been a long day on the set, and all Cal wanted to do was have dinner and relax. Luckily, her new part didn't have as many lines to learn each day, so she would have more time for other things. She was quite troubled by the turn of events, though, never really thinking that Pete could actually get her part changed. And now Leonard was away and couldn't get them to give that scene back to the major character. *But* Cal had a plan. If she played her cards right, the problem would solve itself. This was a different director than had done the trilogy. Judging from the low tolerance he had for her behavior this morning, it should be pretty easy to just slug Nate a few more times and get fired from the picture. Maybe that would even get in the gossip columns and the public would finally realize they're not a lovey-dovey couple after all and would stop insisting on seeing them together.

She and Mrs. Morris enjoyed a leisurely pot-roast dinner this evening, and Cal helped her clean up afterwards. After the woman finished her work and left, Cal settled into the media room with Luigi and turned on the television to a situation comedy. *It's so good to just sit back and let someone else do the entertaining for a while,* she thought.

The doorbell rang. She continued watching the program. When the bell rang a second time, Cal then remembered that Mrs. Morris had already left; so she went to answer it herself. Too late did she realize that it was Nate. She tried to slam the door closed, but he was already halfway into the house and pushed it back open.

"Hello, Cal," he said as he came the rest of the way inside. It gave her a degree of satisfaction to note the bruise around his left eye.

"What're you doing here? You'd better get back home and study your lines. You have a bunch of them for tomorrow."

"Oh, I already know the whole thing—my own part and everyone else's, too. My favorite is when Corky says, 'Mikey, now that we're finally alone, I've got a surprise for you.' Then you'll coax me over to the bed and I'll get to sample my favorite Italian dish, with the blessing of Stagecraft Productions."

"I think I'm going to puke."

"They're really going to be amazed at how realistic our love scene will look under those sheets. Can you guess *why* it's going to look so realistic?"

"I've got stuff to do," she said crossly. "What'd you come here for and when are you going to leave?"

"I just thought I'd drop by and torment you a bit. Our much-anticipated scene will be shot in a couple of days. I bet you can hardly wait. You're probably having all kinds of fantasies about it."

"Would you just go away, for Pete's sake?"

"I really don't have to. I happen to know that Leonard's gone for two whole months, and you're all alone."

"Who told you that?"

"Becky."

"That stinker!" she cried. "She knows better than that."

"No, she doesn't." He came close. "Becky likes me. She knows what a nice guy I am. She was glad when I volunteered to check in on you now and then to be sure you're all right. She just can't imagine me ever doing anything bad to a buddy of hers. In fact, she apologized for your rudeness the other day."

Cal backed away. "Maybe I ought to set her straight."

"You do that. She'll just think you're jealous. She'll think you don't want her to be around me anymore so you can have me all to yourself." He stepped closer to her and fingered one of her curls. "I think we need to get in some extra rehearsal time, so we'll know our scene really well. Don't you?"

"I'm not going to touch you until I have to, now go away!" She wished with all her being that Leonard was here. He could get rid of Nate in two seconds.

"So which shall it be, your bed or mine? You'll like mine. There's a lot of room to play on it."

"If you won't leave, I will." She started toward the door, but he pulled her back by the arm and shut the door.

His smirk faded, and he became serious. "It would be to your advantage, Cal, to cooperate with me on the set."

"What are you talking about now?"

He pointed to his darkened eye. "My uncle could ban you from Stagecraft for doing this."

"I wish he would. Then I wouldn't have to be in this stupid picture!"

"And I happen to know plenty about you and Leonard that could ruin both of your careers."

"You do not!" *Surely he's bluffing,* Cal thought. *I didn't tell Becky our naughty secret, so how on earth could Nate know?*

He looked smug. "You'd be surprised."

She shook her arm free from his grip and reopened the door. "Len always says, 'Just be sure reporters spell my last name without the e.' Threats don't bother him."

"Don't you think a criminal case against him would bother him?" He shut the door again.

She stopped short. "It's not criminal, is it? I mean… what're you talking about?" She *was* twenty-one, after all.

"Child abuse is definitely criminal. I saw the bruises he put on you when you were a teen."

Oh, that. She breathed a sigh of relief. "You have no proof. They're all gone now."

"The make-up artists could testify. They had to hide those bruises when they were preparing you for close-ups. Do you know what the penalty is for child abuse?"

"Get out of here!"

"Okay, but I expect *full* cooperation on the set from now on. You know what'll happen if you don't. Leonard will go to jail." He left.

Cal slammed the door, locked it, and ran upstairs. She went into the study and dropped onto the sofa. What was she going to do now? Why do these things keep happening to her? She wanted so badly to call Leonard so he would tell her what to do. She got up, went over to his desk, and picked up the phone. He had left his contact phone number there, and she started dialing it. Then she abruptly stopped and hung up the phone. This would really upset him a lot. It not only would jeopardize his career, but could also sabotage the custody hearings for Stacy. Having this weighing on his mind would keep him from being able to fully concentrate on his work. She'd be doing him no favors to unload her problems on him now.

Cal sat back on the sofa, curling up into a ball. She had never felt so alone in all her life as she did now.

*   *   *

One advantage of having a smaller role was that she had the next two days off. While Mrs. Morris was cleaning the upstairs, Cal sat in the media room, viewing one of Leonard's old movies. She told herself that she needed to study his acting methods more closely. But what she really wanted was to see Leonard again, to feel a connection with him. When he was around, she felt protected; and she desperately needed to feel his protection right now. The first film she chose was one in which he played the authority figure, the sheriff. "At least he doesn't die in this one," she sighed. Hour after hour was spent watching Leonard's films.

Mrs. Morris was concerned. Having finished the upstairs (and having noticed that Leonard's bed had been slept in and Cal's hadn't), she peeked into the media room. "Are you all right? You seem to be awfully quiet today."

"Oh, I'm okay. I'm just kind of missing Len."

"He'll be back before you know it. Would you like to go with me to do the grocery shopping?"

"No, thanks. I'll just stay here." *Nate's at the studio,* Cal reasoned. *There's no chance he'd show up here during the day.* "I just wish you worked here during the evenings when Len's away. That's when this house gets spooky."

"Well, I could work later hours, if you wish. Would you like me to come in at 2:00 and stay until 10:00?"

Her face lit up. "Would you? That'd be great!"

"I'll be happy to, dear. Leonard said we might want to adjust my hours while he's away. Turns out he's right about this, too, isn't he?"

Cal smiled and nodded. *Score another point for good ol' Len,* she thought.

Chapter 14

THE DAY SHE DREADED WAS HERE. This was the day that that scene was scheduled to be shot. She had tried to think of a way out of it, *any* way out of it, but had come up with nothing. Nate's dire threat, and the phrase "full cooperation on the set" kept haunting her. She was physically sick from worry and dread. Then she brightened, "That's it! I'm sick! I can't go in when I'm sick." She went to the phone and called the studio office. When the receptionist answered, Cal explained that she wouldn't be in today because she was ill. The receptionist took the message. Cal hung up, grinning. "That was easy."

She felt much better now, and finished her breakfast and fed Luigi. She stacked her dirty dishes on the sink counter for Mrs. Morris and hummed as she put the cereal away. Then she plopped down onto the sofa in the media room, propped her feet up, turned on the television with the remote control and watched one of her favorite game shows. Cal played right along with the contestants and figured she would have won about $500 by the time she heard the doorbell ring.

She opened the door a bit and peeked around it. It was Nate! Her heart sank. He pushed the door open and confronted her. "Calling in sick will only delay the inevitable. Come on. You're going with me to the studio."

"I can't. I'm really sick. My stomach hurts. You don't want to catch the bug from me, do you?"

"I'm not buying it, Cal. Come on."

"No! On the set, I'll cooperate. But I'm not on the set now. I'm staying home."

"If you don't come to the studio right now, I'll go to the DA's office and report Leonard."

"You said 'cooperate on the set!' You said nothing about cooperating here!"

"So I lied. See you in court."

She longed so much to smash his face. "Okay, okay. I'm coming, you jerk."

He got into his car while she grabbed the keys and locked the house door. He leaned over and opened the passenger door of his car, but she went the other way—toward her own car. She got in, started the engine, and drove past him to the studio.

* * *

Once in the building, she went right to the director, who was surprised to see her. After a moment of intense conversation, he and Cal went into an adjacent room and shut the door. Everyone on the set was curious, and discussed among themselves what might be going on behind that closed door. The producer was summoned to join the two in the little room. About fifteen minutes later, the three emerged, and Cal looked much happier. She then joined her coworkers before heading toward the makeup room.

"What was that all about?" asked Georgene.

"A victory for decency. I convinced the guys that this should be a family film, just like the original trilogy because it'll have the same audience and that I should keep all my clothes on in the scene we're doing today. And it won't be under the sheets, either."

Georgene was amazed. "How on earth did you do that? I thought skin increased the box-office draw."

"Well he said we'll try it my way and see how it looks. I promised him I'd make it really good. Ol' Nate won't know what hit him."

"Why don't they let me do it? I can do it the way they want."

"Well, I mentioned that. He said since they had already switched stuff around, they didn't want to do it again."

Georgene shook her head. "It would've been okay by me. I still don't know how you did it. You must have connections or something." What she was thinking, though, was "What an oddball she is! I didn't know Cal was such a prude."

* * *

Except for the creepy feeling of having Nate's hands all over her and having to give what she felt was a performance deserving of an Oscar, everything went fine. She would be eager to view a copy of this film with Leonard and show him what a great acting job she did. Cal was sure she hadn't betrayed her real feelings on camera at all this time. She simply internalized what Leonard had taught her—to completely disassociate her own self from the character. For that moment, she was Corky—and Cal didn't exist at all. She wanted to get this scene over with in one take, so she gave it her all, acting as she would have if it had been Miles doing that scene with her.

As she walked to her car that evening, she thought, *If Cal had existed and realized who she was doing that scene with, she* really *would've gotten sick.*

And, sure enough, ol' Nate didn't know what had hit him.

*   *   *

She was hoping that Leonard would call that night and, by golly, he did.

"Hey, Cal. How's it going?"

"You wouldn't believe what happened at work today. It's kind of complicated, so I'll wait until you're here, then tell you the whole story. But what it amounts to is fighting City Hall and winning. I can't believe it worked!"

"That sure whets my curiosity."

"And wait'll you see the super-duper acting job I did today. You'd be proud of me. So, how's it going there?"

"It's been raining a lot, but England's a very nice place. Filming is a little behind schedule because of the weather."

"Oh, no. How much?"

"Hard to tell. Might take just a few more days than planned. That'll make it go over budget, and the big guys never like that."

"When do you think you'll be back?"

He paused. "Why? Are you missing me?"

"Well," she admitted, "kind of."

"Just a little?"

She hated to admit how much, but she hated lying to him even more. "Okay, okay. I'm missing you a lot."

"How much?"

"Don't do this to me, Len. You know it kills me to grovel."

He laughed. "What's your work schedule look like in the next week?"

"I have one day of filming on Thursday, and then that should be it for me."

"Are you kidding? They must've given you a *bit* part."

"It's okay. I don't mind."

"How about flying out to join me once you're finished there?"

Her face lit up. "You really mean it, Len? I'd be coming to England?"

"That's right."

"How come?"

He hesitated. "Don't do this to me, Cal. You know I don't like to grovel."

It took a moment for the significance of this statement to sink in. Then she smiled, "Are you saying you're missing me a lot, too?"

"Bingo."

She grinned. "It's nice to know the feeling's mutual, Len."

"Believe me, baby, it is."

"This'll be terrific! I've never been outside the U.S. before."

"Call George tonight. His phone number's on my desk. He'll make the arrangements and get your passport and everything lined up."

"And Mrs. Morris can take care of Luigi for me."

"I'll call again tomorrow to get your flight schedule. Plan to stay a few weeks."

"Hot dog!" Cal could hardly contain her excitement.

"Well, I've got to leave in a minute for work. I'll talk to you soon, okay?"

"Okay. 'Bye, Len."

"Goodnight, Cal. Sweet dreams."

She hung up the phone, then leapt for joy. This is the first true vacation she will have had in years. And it afforded the double opportunity not only to be with Leonard again, but also to be many thousands of miles away from Nate.

Chapter 15

THIS IS THE LAST TIME I'LL SEE THIS SET, Cal thought as she entered the studio Thursday morning. Tomorrow, she would get up bright and early to catch the plane. There was a bounce in her step this morning. All seemed right with the world.

There are many advantages to playing a minor part, she found. While she would be finishing up today, the major characters still had at least two more weeks to go. While they were toiling over their lines, the lighting, the blocking, and all those details, Cal would be with Leonard in jolly old England. The idea of going to any foreign country was intriguing to her, and England held a particular charm. The Beatles were very popular at this time, and they had increased Americans' interest in the United Kingdom. Many things that were related to England—their fashions, customs, phrases—were showing up on more and more television shows these days. This was Cal's chance to see it in person. She could hardly wait for tomorrow morning to come.

"So you're back for more," Nate chided. "Couldn't stay away, hmm?"

"After today I will." Not even Nate could spoil her mood. She headed toward the makeup department. He followed.

"We really ought to redo that last scene we did—only this time, the way it was written originally."

Just one more day, Cal thought to herself. "Guess the head honchos wanted to go for quality, rather than cheap thrills."

"It was better before they changed it."

"That's the way it goes."

He stopped and took her arm. "I think they might have to retake that scene. I think Uncle Bob will insist on it."

"Too bad. I'm leaving town tomorrow, and nothing in the world's going to change those plans."

"You can't do that! The picture's not finished yet."

"It is for me. And not a moment too soon, either."

"Where are you going and when will you be back?"

"That's none of your business."

He looked at her hard. "Remember 'complete cooperation'?"

"Only when I'm in town." She shook loose from his grip and continued to the makeup department, leaving him behind.

* * *

"Why didn't you tell me you were going away?" Becky asked that evening on the phone.

"Because it seems like everything I tell you goes straight to Nate these days, and the other way around, too, apparently."

"He's not that bad, Cal. I don't know why you don't like him. I've never seen you treat anyone the way you treat him."

Cal was in a quandary. If she told Becky about the blackmail Nate was using against her, then she would have to admit that some wrongdoing had occurred between her and Leonard. But she couldn't bring herself to agree with Becky about him, either. She remained silent.

"Well, where are you going and when will you be back? I won't tell."

"I'll call you when I get back. Then you'll know."

"Why are you keeping it a secret? I thought we were buddies."

"We are," Cal said, "but I've got to go, Becky. I have a lot of packing to do."

"Okay. Send me a postcard."

"Will do!" She'll be sure it arrives at Becky's about the time Cal gets back home.

* * *

She was too excited to sleep that night. Several times, Cal had gotten back up when she thought of one more thing she wanted to pack. Mrs. Morris had taken Luigi home with her last evening and would take care of him until Cal got back. It felt strange now not to have him curled up at her feet.

Morning finally came. She wolfed down a bowl of cereal, then packed the car. The mail that had accumulated for Leonard was on the table in the front hallway, so she gathered it up and put it in her carry-on bag. She stopped, looked around her to see if anything more needed to be done, then, assured that all was well, locked the door behind her, started her car and headed to the airport.

This is one of those times that Cal, with sunglasses and floppy hat on and makeup off, was very happy to blend in so well with the rest of the human race.

Once at the airport, she checked all but her carry-on bag, then sat in the waiting area at the appropriate gate. George had gone with her Wednesday morning to get her passport. She didn't know how he did it, but all went very smoothly and quickly. Then yesterday evening, he had given her her tickets and boarding passes, arranged in proper order. George sure knew how to get things done! Leonard was smart to have him as his business manager.

Boarding for her flight was finally called, the passengers found their seats, and the flight attendants made sure all the overhead bins were closed securely. As the plane started taxiing to take off, the attendants began their safety monologue. "Yeah, yeah, let's get on with it," Cal kept thinking. They were taking the polar route and, try as she might, she couldn't get the plane to get to England any faster. But eventually, many, many hours later, they made their descent into London. It was nearing midnight California time, but, in London, it was morning, although an overcast one. *Well, just this once*, she thought as she put on a little lipstick and eye shadow, then temporarily covered back up with sunglasses and hat. They now were on the ground and taxiing in to their gate. The plane slowed, then stopped. Cal tried to be patient as the passengers ahead were getting their luggage out of the overhead racks and gathering their coats. She got off the plane and followed the crowd through customs, then continued on into the main portion of the airport. She took off her sunglasses and looked around. The area in front of her then cleared.

There he was! Leonard had a broad smile as he stood there with outstretched arms. In his hand was a single yellow rose.

"The yellow rose of Texas," Cal grinned as she broke into a run and soon felt those strong arms holding her tightly. How she had missed him!

They were receiving confused stares by some of the American passengers who had also deplaned, but Cal was completely unaware of it.

"That sure looked like Stacy Ames," said a sixteen-year-old passenger excitedly.

"Just because we live in L.A. now," her mother sighed, "you're always imagining people you see being movie stars."

"But that was Leonard Rhoads she was hugging, I think. That's weird. Nate Jenkins is her boyfriend, not him."

"So what're ya' gonna' do? Report it to Earl Wilson? Come on," she said tiredly, leading her to the baggage claim area.

*   *   *

It was quite a distance from the airport to the hotel. Leonard carried her luggage up to room 314, and Cal followed. Once they were inside the room and the door was shut, Leonard then dropped her luggage and took Cal into his arms, kissing her tenderly. "It's been a long two weeks, hasn't it, Cal?"

"I'll say. Don't go on location anymore, okay?"

"Can't promise that. Maybe you can come with me next time."

"Yeah," she readily agreed. She gave him a bear hug, with her head resting on his chest. It was good to hear his familiar heartbeat again. Then she noticed that his luggage was there, too. "Are we staying in the same room?"

"I don't see why not."

"But we have to be careful of what people see.

"It's okay. We're not subject to bad press, since we're not as well known here as we are at home. For all the Brits know, we're married."

"Don't people wear wedding bands in England?"

"Well, yes, I suppose they do."

"I better get one, then." She flashed a wicked smile at him, then started unpacking.

"I've got the day off," he said, "so we can gad about today and do whatever we want. Where would you like to go?"

"I want to see Big Ben and Buckingham Palace and Westminster Abbey and the Victoria and Albert Museum. And I want to see cricket and rugby matches, and see what a pub is like."

"Hey, one thing at a time! Let's just walk around and see what's here first. We have three weeks to do all those things."

They strolled, hand in hand, down some of the streets. It seemed so odd to Cal to be able to walk freely through public places together without being stopped by autograph seekers.

They browsed through some stores, and Cal got a postcard for Becky. She'd be sure to mail it a day or two before she returned home. Then they took a ride on one of the houseboats through the canals. "I thought only Venice had canals," she marveled. The villages were so picturesque that Cal yearned to do a painting of one. They ended the day with a stop at the jeweler to buy Cal a wedding band.

They then returned to their hotel room and had dinner there. It had been a wonderful day for Cal.

After the dishes had been taken away and they were once again alone, Leonard turned down the sheets of the bed. "You've still been taking your pill every day, haven't you?"

"Yeah, but don't tell the Pope."

"Then, for reality's sake, we really ought to consummate this marriage, my dear," he said in a very convincing British accent.

She brightened, "I love method acting!"

* * *

Leonard had to go to work early the next morning, so Cal used the time to get caught up on her sleep. She finally arose, ready to start the day, around noon local time. Then, with English currency that Leonard had given her, she went to the art-supply store a few blocks away and bought everything she needed to do a painting of that small English village they had seen yesterday. Once back at the room, she set everything up and began painting. This would be her routine most days that Leonard was working. Being able to see new sights and paint scenes she had seen was quite fulfilling to her.

Leonard returned around 7:30 that evening, and they went to a restaurant together for a late dinner. True to their nature, he ordered a dish unique to England, while she stuck with American fare.

Back at the hotel, Cal remembered the mail she had brought and gave it to Leonard. He looked through the envelopes, took one out and put the rest on the table. It was from his attorney. He opened it, read it and the attached documents carefully, and smiled. "This is the final divorce decree, Cal; and we get Stacy on alternate weekends and two weeks in the summer. We won! That little girl will remain a part of our lives for years to come!"

"Yippeeeeee!" she cried.

They hugged each other in victory, and ordered a bottle of champagne from room service to celebrate.

*   *   *

This had been Cal's dream vacation. The three weeks sped by as they spent off-time sightseeing, shopping, taking long walks, and simply enjoying being together. Too soon, though, it was time for her to board the plane for the trip home. Leonard still had a few days of shooting left, then would follow.

*   *   *

"So you went to England?" Becky asked. "I never got that postcard."

"You will. I mailed it before I left."

"What's this?" she pointed to Cal's finger.

"Oh!" Call took the wedding ring off. "Nothing."

"Who'd you marry?"

"Nobody. It's just a ring, that's all. Lots of people in England wear them."

"Well, tell me what it's like. I've never been there."

Cal eagerly began telling Becky all about her adventure. "I found out that Strawberry Fields is an orphanage right next door to where John Lennon grew up. Did you know that?"

"No."

"And the pubs there are a lot different from bars here. 'Pub' is short for public meeting house, and it's a real social place. And Len even got me to be an extra in his picture. If you watch it without ever blinking, you might see me in a couple crowd scenes if I don't end up on the cutting-room floor. I got to get all dressed up in 17th century clothes and everything. It was really neat! But they couldn't pay me for it because I didn't have a work visa. I just did it for fun. Don't tell the actors union, though. They don't allow us to work for free."

"Sounds like you had a great time, while Nate was looking all over the place for you."

"Why?"

"Something about a scene needing to be reshot."

"Oh, no. When they couldn't find me, did they just go ahead and do it without me? That scene could be done with any of the characters. It didn't have to be mine."

"That's not what Nate said."

"Don't tell him I'm back, okay? Maybe he'll give up."

"Too late. As soon as you called, I let him know because I knew he was looking for you."

"Doggone it!" she said irritably. "Would you stop squealing everything to Nate? That's why I didn't tell you where I was vacationing." Cal went to the back door and motioned for Becky to follow her. "Let's get out of here. If he knows I'm back, he's bound to be here soon. And I don't want to see him until Len gets back."

The girls returned to Becky's house by the back way. They spent the rest of the day together, then Cal returned home as the sun was setting. She had unlocked the door and was opening it when she felt a shove from behind that propelled her into the house. The door then closed behind her. She turned around to find Nate between her and the door.

"Get out of here! I didn't let you in."

"They're going to reshoot that scene, Cal, and you're going to do it right this time."

"Not in a million years!"

"Your contract said your commitment to the film is up when shooting is complete. It's not complete yet."

"Both the producer and director agreed to the way we shot that scene. They're the ones who decide, not you."

"Well, it seems they've changed their minds."

What to do now? Why did she ever get mixed up in this crazy business anyway, she wondered. Then Cal got an idea. "How about we take care of this in a week? My schedule is free next week."

Nate stepped back and looked at her suspiciously.

Cal just smiled serenely.

"What do you know that I don't about next week?" he asked.

"Oh, gee Nate. Probably nothing. You seem to know a lot more about most everything than I do."

"You're not going out of town again, are you?"

"Not that I know of."

He reached over and opened the door. "Okay. Next week." Then he looked at her hard and pointed a stern finger at her. "And you know what will happen if you don't cooperate, and I mean completely!"

"Right. 'Bye now," she waved pleasantly.

He looked at her another minute, then left. Cal shut the door behind him and grinned. "Len'll be here in a couple days, and he'll take care of this. *Gotcha', Nate!*"

*   *   *

"No, not another delay! Len, you've *got* to get home quick!" she practically yelled into the phone that night.

"Sorry, Cal. It'll just be about ten days longer. You can live that long without me, can't you?" There was a benevolent tone in his voice.

"You just don't understand. You don't understand," she sobbed. "You don't."

"What is it? What's the matter?"

"Oh, Len. That last picture got real complicated. They switched that awful scene to a minor character all right, just like you told them to. But then they switched *Corky* to that character, too. So I had to do it anyway. I refused to take any clothes off for it, and they agreed to that. But now they're saying we've got to do a retake of it the way it was originally written. Len, you've *got* to come home and fix this! It's a mess!"

"Aw, baby, they're wanting to change the rating of the picture to an "R" so it'll sell more tickets. Just do it and get it over with. You know you can do a bedroom scene with shorts on—what's under the covers doesn't show."

"But, Len, it's with *Nate!*"

He thought a moment. "Well, just refuse to do it then. What can they do, fire you? The film's about ready to wrap anyway."

"Well, this is where it gets a little more complicated. It seems Nate remembers pretty vividly how things were several years ago, when you were putting some bruises on me, and he said if I don't do this scene with him the way he wants it, he'll report you to the D.A. for child abuse."

"He's just a lot of hot air. How could he prove it, anyway? That was a long time ago."

"He said makeup artists would testify. He said it's a criminal offense."

"No they won't, Cal. Don't worry about it. Just do whatever you want about this scene. Don't worry about me."

"Really?" she brightened. "You really don't think he would do it?"

"No. He's a lot of talk, that's all. If it weren't for that hotshot uncle of his, he would probably just be pushing a broom for a living."

She gave a sigh of relief. "Okay, Len."

"You're all right now?"

"Yeah."

"Did you have a good time in England?"

"Oh, yeah. It was a trip of a lifetime. Brought home some pretty good paintings, too. I've got to get some frames for them."

"Hey, most people take snapshots. But not you."

"I don't have a camera, anymore. My old one broke."

"Well, we'll have to do something about that. Do you miss me?"

"A lot. Do you?"

"A lot." Noticing the time, he said, "Well, Cal, I've got to go now. I'll be talking to you in a couple of days."

"Okay. 'Bye Len."

"Goodnight, Cal."

*   *   *

"I just won't do it. That's all there is to it."

The producer's assistant had brought Cal the revised script for the remaining scene of *Campus Dreams*, only to be completely rebuffed. "I'm confused, Cal. Nate said you'd be ready to do it Monday."

"No, I told him I'll take care of it next week. I didn't say I'd participate in a reshoot. Why don't you get Georgene to do it?"

"He insists on it being you. And, after viewing the way you two did the scene last month and showing it to the execs, they've decided to go back to the way it was written originally with Corky and Mike. They've added a couple more things to it, too."

"Well, I guess you'll just have to change their minds because you're sure not going to change mine."

He took the script back. "Okay, Cal. I'll tell them what you said, but they're not going to be very happy."

Chapter 16

THE FOLLOWING WEEK, Mrs. Morris appeared concerned as Cal and Leonard were having their dinner. "We had a visit from the District Attorney while you were gone this afternoon. Here's the card he left."

Leonard looked at it, then asked, "What'd he say?"

"He wanted to talk to you and Cal. He said you need to give him a call."

Leonard and Cal looked at each other in disbelief. *Nate wasn't bluffing, after all!* they both were thinking.

*   *   *

The call was not made. Instead, Leonard consulted with his attorney.

After a while, he was back to his usual routines. "What will be, will be," he told Cal.

She still worried, though. "What am I going to do, Len? If I refuse to testify, they could put me in jail. If I do testify—and I'd *have* to tell the truth—they'll put *you* in jail. I don't want to testify at all, but you say if they subpoena me, I've *got* to. What'll I do?"

"Well, let's see," he said. "You don't have to be the one to press charges in a criminal case. The state does that. But you *would* be their key witness. And if they subpoena you, you're required to testify and tell the truth, unless..." He pointed a finger at her.

"What?"

"A woman's not required to testify against her husband."

"We could get those rings back out. Would that work?"

"Only if we're *really* married. They would find out if we weren't."

She sat on the sofa and mulled the idea over. That would be another of her dreams shattered. If she was to ever marry at all, she wanted it to be to someone who loved her more than life itself; but Leonard had never, even once, said he loved her. In fact, she knew she'd been a downright pain-in-the-neck to him sometimes. "I don't know. What do you think, Len?"

He thought for a moment, then nodded. "It would work."

"Would you want it to be a short thing? I mean like just stay married until the trial's over?"

"Oh, I don't know, Cal." He left the desk and sat beside her on the sofa. "I don't like divorce. No matter how amicable it is, divorce is still an ugly thing."

"Yeah, it's against my religion, too." She put her hand on his shoulder. "But, Len, you don't love me, and that's what marriage is all about."

"How can you say that? Why else would I have taken care of you all these years? Why else would I miss you so much after only *two weeks* that I would fly you to England? Do you know how much it costs to make spur-of-the-moment transcontinental flight plans like that?"

"No, Len, this is important. You're the best actor I've ever known, but I've seen you use that to get things done in your personal life. In looking back, I can see that you've acted like you were this way or that in order to get me to do something. Please don't act like you love me if you don't really mean it."

"Look back again and take note of *when* I did those things. Wasn't it always for your own good? In order to get you to give a good performance and further your career?"

She stopped and re-thought those things. He was right. She couldn't think of a single time that he had done that for selfish reasons, except maybe one. "How about when you didn't want me to blow your opportunity in a romantic lead?"

"Okay, but think for a minute, Cal. Who made sure that you were my love interest in that picture? It was me. Pete had absolutely nothing to do with that. In fact, he didn't think you could do it, but I knew you could. You wanted an adult role and I got it for you. As much as I wanted the lead, I accepted it only with the provision that you would be my co-star. They had to either hire you or lose me. It was a huge gamble, but it paid off. That picture is going to do more for your career than all those teeny-bopper films you've done in the past put together." Then he gently stroked her cheek and said softly, "And, Cal, that's why I never adopted you. Jill wanted to, but I said no. I wasn't sure why at the time, but I am now. I don't want to be your father; I want to be your husband."

She became silent, and her eyes grew moist. "And all this time I thought… . Do you *really* love me, Len?" She looked earnestly into his eyes.

"Of course I do." He held her close. "I thought it was obvious."

She put her arms around him, too. "Okay, let's do it. Let's tie the knot real tight."

He smiled. "We'll go get the marriage license, then. Where are those rings?"

"Let's have Becky be our witness. She'll tell Nate and that'll just *kill* him," she grinned.

Chapter 17

IT WAS BRIGHT AND EARLY on a Saturday morning, and Becky was taking advantage of her day off from the art museum to sleep late. The ringing of the phone startled her awake.

"Hello?" she said groggily.

"Hi, Becky. It's me. You don't have anything planned for today do you?"

"Just laundry, Cal. But let me sleep a few more minutes. It's Saturday. What time is it, anyway?"

"It's 9:30 already. You've got to get up now. We're taking you someplace in twenty minutes."

"Where?" she yawned.

"Can't tell you, yet. But you'll find out pretty quick. Just be ready in twenty minutes."

"Come on. Give me a hint."

"Okay. You'll be really, *really* surprised."

She waited. Then scratched her head. "Is that the hint?"

"Yep. Twenty minutes, Becky. Be ready." Cal hung up.

Becky reluctantly left the warm comfort of her bed, washed her face, combed her hair, and got dressed.

"Okay, where are we going?" is how she greeted Cal when she arrived.

"I'll tell you when we're in the car and it's too late for you to squeal to anybody who might try to stop us."

Leonard was in the car waiting for the girls. Becky's curiosity was growing by the minute. "What're you going to do? Kidnap me? I wonder how much ransom Johnny would put up for me?"

"Oh, it's better than that. Hop in," said Cal as she opened the back door for her. Once Becky was settled in the car, she closed the door and joined Leonard in the front seat. They then headed west. "Well, Becky, it wasn't planned this way, but it looks like I'm going to beat you to the altar."

Becky's eyes got huge. "Today?"

"Yep."

"At least I'm glad you're not keeping it secret from Leonard. Who are you marrying?"

Leonard chuckled. Cal leaned over and kissed his cheek, then looked back at Becky with a sparkle in her eye.

Becky looked confused. "What are you telling me?"

"That I'm marrying the man who took me in when no one else would, and who is the best doggone drama coach in the world, and who has moved mountains for me."

"You're marrying *Leonard*?" Becky asked in a whisper.

Cal grinned. "Yep."

Becky stared for a minute, then looked out the window. "I can't believe it. This is really bizarre."

"Why?"

"Well, I don't know. I guess I just didn't know you had that kind of a relationship."

"Yes, you did, Becky. Remember when you asked me what was going on between us? Shoot, you knew it before I did."

"Well, maybe so," she remembered. "But I thought it was just my imagination."

"You're going to be our witness."

What Becky said was, "Sure." What she was thinking, though, was *But, Cal, why? Sure he's a hunk, but he's so old!*

"In this case, being a witness is just as good as being a maid of honor."

"What I want to know, though, is why is it so sudden? Why don't you have a regular wedding like I am?" Becky said. "If you were anyone in the world but Cal Ames, I'd suspect you were pregnant or something." Becky mused silently that Leonard would be lucky to get to first base with Cal, even on their wedding night. *But maybe, at his age, it doesn't matter*, she thought.

* * *

As it turned out, Becky enjoyed the day almost as much as Cal and Leonard did. After the minister performed the ceremony, Leonard treated the girls to a celebratory seafood and champagne dinner at the marina. This was one of the few exceptions Leonard made to his practice of avoiding public American restaurants. A reporter for a local news program was at a nearby table and noticed the attention that the couple had attracted. He sensed a story and interviewed them on the spot. Sure enough, it was an excellent story; and he left the restaurant with a notebook full of details before his dessert had been served.

"What do you want to bet it'll be on the news tonight?" Cal asked as he exited the building.

"Probably will," Leonard agreed. "The local news, anyway."

"I wish I could see Nate's face when he finds out," she continued. "Becky, take a camera with you when you tell him, okay?"

"Oooh, you're a wicked one, Cal," she scolded. "It'll break his heart."

"Yeah, and not for the reason you think, either," Cal added.

After dinner, they took Becky back home. She got out of the car, looked back at them and smiled. "See you later. Thanks for letting me be a part of your big day." Any skepticism with which she had started that day was gone now. Until today, she had never seen Cal and Leonard together for more than a few minutes at a time. Now, after spending a few hours with them, she had a clearer picture of their relationship. There was a strong bond between them that she had never seen before. While they sometimes joked about their age difference, it didn't really seem to be a barrier. He was only forty, after all, and it was now evident that there was nothing 'old' about him. And, most importantly, it had become obvious that they were soul mates. Becky rested assured that her close friend was in loving hands.

*   *   *

"Well, Mrs. Rhoads," Leonard said, as they walked toward their house. "We've already had our honeymoon, haven't we?"

She grinned. "And *what* a honeymoon, too! In England!"

After opening the front door, he scooped her up and carried her over the threshold. Cal felt an unexpected and overwhelming rush of love as they gazed into each other's eyes. Maybe her dreams had not been destroyed, after all. He gave her a tender kiss, then, once inside, set her down.

She looked around and wondered silently, *Now what?* Back to the scripts, she guessed. As she ambled into the living room, she heard a voice behind her say, "I'm going to catch you." She looked back and saw a playful glint in Leonard's eye.

Cal grinned. "Uh-oh, I'm in trouble now," she responded, taking off toward the kitchen with the lightning speed of a track runner.

He sped after her as she ran past the living room, through the kitchen, down the hallway, into the media room, around the sofa, out of the media room, farther down the hallway, around the corner and up the stairs, gleefully laughing the whole way. "And *when* I catch you..." he continued, as he took the stairs two at a time, chased her into the bedroom, and grabbed her as they both fell onto the bed, "I'm going to hold you and never let you go!" They held each other tightly, taking a moment to catch their breaths. "My lord, you're fast!" he said between breaths.

"Gave you a run for your money, didn't I?" she asked with a big, pleased smile.

"That you did," he agreed. He gave her a kiss, then said happily, "Now you're mine—*all* mine—and woe to any man who ever tries to take you away."

"You're mine, too, and no lady better try to get her hands on you," added Cal, as she gave him another hug.

"Whatever happened to 'I belong to me'?" he teased.

"Oh, hush. Tell me my new name again."

"Mrs. Leonard Rhoads."

"Cal Rhoads. Sounds like a street sign."

"It means you're going in the right direction."

"Touché."

*   *   *

The very next weekend was their first visitation from Stacy. It was so wonderful to see that little girl again! After clearing up the confusion of Cal now being Daddy's wife, they realized she was much more interested in the new kitten in the family.

It was hard to believe, but Stacy's fifth birthday was approaching. That would be during one of their visitation weekends with the child, so Becky and Cal got busy planning a gala birthday party for her.

Chapter 18

JILL WAS SITTING AT HER FRIEND'S kitchen table, sharing coffee with her now that the children had been put onto the school bus and the two women were alone. She folded the newspaper and set it aside. "Stacy was right. It's in the news."

"You still love him, don't you?" Alice asked sympathetically.

"Yes, I really do. But once Cal turned twenty-one, I knew I had lost him."

"What do you mean?"

A tear made its way down her cheek. "It didn't start out that way. Practically from day one, he was really rough with her. I couldn't figure out why until Leonard mentioned once how much she looked like a girl who jilted him in high school. Maybe it was a subconscious thing. He was taking out on Cal his frustration and hurt from that long-ago experience. I heard them downstairs when she and Miles got in late from a date, and I heard Leonard smacking her. It was odd, but I could have sworn I heard her hitting him back." She stopped and thought for a minute. "In fact, I *know* she did. They both always had a couple bruises on them, almost all the time. Leonard's were usually on his shins. Alice, children never hit adults when I was growing up."

"We wouldn't dream of it."

"But they would really be going at it for a while, yelling and banging around, then they'd calm down. At first, I felt so sorry for Cal and wondered how I could have married such a brute. So during one of their louder fights, I couldn't stand it anymore and went downstairs to stop it. I was taught that the man is the head of the household and the wife shouldn't interfere with the way he chose to do that, but I just *had* to this time; and, Alice, you'll never believe what I saw!"

"Uh-oh. What?"

She leaned forward and intimated, "The kitchen chair was knocked over, Leonard was sprawled out on the *floor*, and Cal came over and *sat* on him, cheering "Victory for the oppressed!" She was quite pleased with herself. I couldn't believe it! It was then that I realized that little girl could handle Leonard quite nicely without any help from me. She had clearly won that battle. I don't know *how* she did it, though."

"How could such a little person get the best of Leonard?"

"I haven't the faintest idea! They're both such emotional and volatile people, though. I begged and begged him to get counseling to help him control his temper, but he refused. Please understand, though, he never laid an angry hand on our daughter or me. Never. Just Cal. Then, when Cal's parents died in the plane crash, the violence suddenly stopped. I never again heard any fighting, physically, between them. They argued a lot, but that's all it was. Then I noticed that there was still a lot of physical interaction going on, but it was of a different nature now. He couldn't pass her in the hall without mussing her hair or giving her arm a playful punch. If he was talking to her, he'd have his hands on her shoulders or he would take hold of her arm. He seemed to feel that she was his own personal property. He controlled her money, her career, everything. When he found out that I had signed that contract that gave Stagecraft exclusive rights to her, he blew up. It was only then that I learned that he wanted her to work on an independent basis so she could accept the best roles, wherever they may be. We hadn't discussed it before then, so I didn't know." Jill finished her coffee. Then she continued, "Leonard really knows what he's doing. He knows the business inside and out. Cal sees that. She's always looked up to him…"

"Literally!" Alice smiled. "The man's a giant. What is he? Six foot five?"

"No, just six-three. But she has a great respect for his work. Of course, she's much more into the performing arts than I am, and they spend a lot of time bouncing ideas off each other and talking shop, discussing career moves and directors. He's been a good mentor to her. He's spent a lot more time with her doing that than he ever spent with Stacy or me."

"Aren't most guys like that, though? If they have somebody to talk shop with, it'll be hours before they come up for air."

"Yes, but with Cal it was different. As she grew up, he became more and more focused on her. It makes me ashamed to think what I was trying to do. I tried to redirect Cal's attention from Leonard to Nate, even though they've never gotten along."

"Cal and Nate not get along?" Alice laughed. "You've got to be kidding. Everyone knows they were sweethearts."

Jill shook her head and said, "She doesn't like him at all. Nate's been trying to get her in bed for ages and, probably out of frustration, was becoming overtly aggressive and ugly to her. I still encouraged her to continue seeing him, though. I thought that if he somehow succeeded and they eventually *had* to get married, that would save *my* marriage." Jill acknowledged Alice's look of astonishment, "I know, I know. Cal trusted me and I betrayed that trust. It was selfish of me."

"That doesn't sound like you at all."

"I know, but that just shows how desperate I was feeling. I'm not at all proud of it." Jill looked down for a moment, then shook her head. "I know now that it was a mistake, but I gave Leonard an ultimatum—either Cal moves out or I do."

"Oh, no. What did he say to that?"

"He said she was going to stay right there, and that was that. He insisted on celebrating her twenty-first birthday at a private nightclub; and while I sat there alone, watching them dancing together, I was thinking about how very much alike they are. They're both strong-willed and determined individuals, thoroughly entrenched in the show-business world that I'll never understand. As they were dancing, they appeared to be perfectly in sync with each other—not only physically, but emotionally, too. They looked so happy. I felt like an outsider. It hurt too much to watch, because it was obvious then that he was in love with her. So the next morning I just moved out and filed for divorce. I thought by forcing his hand like that, he'd come to his senses." She shook her head sadly, "I was hoping he'd come look for me and try to change my mind, but he never did."

"Did you tell him where you went?"

"No, but the first place most people would look for a missing wife is at her parents' house. That's where Stacy and I were for a few weeks, but he never called or came by. That pretty much told me that my suspicions were right. And, now, this newspaper confirms it."

"What's it say?"

"Leonard and Cal got married Saturday. The minute he was free to marry her, he did. He probably planned it that way all along, but I wonder how he talked her into it. She said she didn't want to ever get married." Jill lifted the cup, then realized it was empty and set it down again. "I bet I was barely out the door before he decided it was time to teach her that bedrooms are for more than just sleeping." Her eyes flashed angrily. "He's taught her everything else, so I'm sure he was quite happy to teach her that, too."

"Oh, Jill. She probably already knew all about that."

Jill shook her head. "No, I don't think so."

"She was twenty-one and still a virgin? In Hollywood? That's unheard of."

"I'm almost positive she was."

"How'd she get so far in the business, then?"

Jill shrugged, "The public loved to see Cal and Nate together and clamored for more. That's why they made that first movie into a series of films. I understand there's still talk about doing a TV show, based on that. It seems there's a lot of chemistry between those two on screen."

Alice refilled Jill's cup. "What an ungrateful child! After all, it was *your* idea to have Cal stay at your house in the first place. And now, she shows her thanks by stealing your husband."

"No, it's not like that at all. Cal doesn't have a malicious bone in her body. The whole thing was controlled entirely by Leonard, and he knew better. She went wherever he led her. Once she wakes up and realizes he's keeping her from a normal life with a boy her own age, she'll probably leave him. If Miles came back into her life tomorrow and wanted her back, I bet she'd leave Leonard in a second. I don't think she ever got over Miles."

"Jill," Alice asked, fingering the rim of her cup. "Are you okay financially? Do you need any help?"

"Oh, no, everything's fine, thanks. I don't really need to do this, but I'm going to get recertified so I can go back into teaching. I've been wishing I could do that anyway. Since I inherited so much of my grandparents' estate, I didn't even need to ask Leonard for alimony or child support, but he's been sending me checks through my lawyer anyway. I've got plenty to live on."

"You're a classy lady, Jill. Most women would go for the jugular."

"I think he's doing that to keep me from getting the courts involved in our finances; but I figure if I can play along and keep communication open and friendly, he might come back to me someday. There's a very real possibility that, sooner or later, he'll be divorced again."

*   *   *

"Come on, Pete. Just a couple TV shows. How hard could that be?" Cal asked impatiently over the phone.

"I told you before, the squeaky-clean sit-coms are reluctant to have you because your image has changed. They know you were in *Henson of Manhattan*. We've got to undo the damage that film's going to do."

"Forget my image and use your imagination, man! It doesn't have to be a sit-com. How about a soap opera or *Medical Center*? I can do those."

"They're out of your league, Cal."

"They are not." She hesitated for a moment, then mumbled, "I think I need a new agent."

"Okay with me. Child stars are awfully hard to accommodate, once they age."

"I was never a child star, Pete. I was fifteen when I made my first picture. That's not a child."

"You weren't an adult either."

"That's the way it'll be, then. Pete, you did terrific things for me in the past, but as an adult, Len says I need an agent with a bold streak. You'll see. I'll be just as successful in adult roles as I was in the young ones."

*   *   *

Later that evening, when Cal told Leonard of her conversation with Pete, he was overjoyed. Finally, she would let his own agent, Michael, represent her, too. Michael had been very good for Leonard's career, having arranged a wide variety of roles for him. This kept him from being typecast, which would have limited his options. Since Leonard had appeared so often in Westerns before hiring Michael, becoming typecast had been a very real danger for him. Now, thanks to roles in the comedies, science fictions, murder mysteries, and dramas Michael had set up, there was no such barrier to Leonard's future employment. And now Cal would have Michael working in her behalf as well.

Chapter 19

The couple was in the media room, again studying films.

"Now, Cal, look at this and tell me what the adult character's thinking after he's been told the truth." Leonard started the film. This character was an authority in a boy's home, and one of the boys had finally confessed to a misdeed. Very slowly, the man began to smile as he looked at the young man approvingly. Leonard stopped the film. "Okay. What did you see?"

"At first, I think he was real surprised that the guy finally 'fessed up. Then he was glad. Then he kind of looked like he admired the boy." Cal looked up at him. "Am I right?"

"Exactly! That's what I mean when I say you can communicate just as much by silence, using body language, as you can with words. *Never* be afraid of silence. It can be a powerful tool."

Then he looked at the label of the next film. There was a gleam in his eye as he continued, "Okay. Here's another bit of nonverbal communication. Tell me what my character's thinking here." After changing the films and advancing it to the intended scene, he slowed it to normal speed.

As the scene unfolded, Cal grinned. When he stopped the film, she said, "Hey, I've seen *that* look on you before. He's horny as anything!"

He roared with laughter. "Cal! I've never heard you use language like that before. Where'd you hear that?"

"It's one of the things Nate would say when he was whispering in my ear on the set and everybody else thought he was being so gallant. But Len," she intimated, "the first time I saw that look on *you*, it like to scared me to death."

"I'm glad you got over that."

"Oh yeah, did I ever!" she grinned. The sparkle in her eyes matched Leonard's.

He smiled as he put another film on and took it to the scene he wanted. "Here's a very impressive example of an actress transforming herself from one character into another. This is about a woman with a multiple personality. Part of the time, she is very introverted. Other times, she's a party-girl. Opposite personalities. In this scene, she's switching from one to the other. Watch how she does it."

As the scene progressed, Cal was spellbound. The woman seemed to grow a couple of inches taller as she became the party girl. Her very plain face became radiant and beautiful. "Wow! How'd she do that? Was that camera tricks?"

"No tricks. It was her posture, facial expression, the focus of her eyes. She pulled her hair forward, rather than tucking it behind her ears. She smiled, which really lights up a person's face. But most of all, changes like that have to come from within. She threw out the timid mindset and replaced it with the adventurous one."

"Golly, she's good!"

"She is. Here's one that's very different." He switched films again, then started. "I'm not very happy with the way this character is portrayed."

"Is it one of mine?"

"No, it's mine. See? Here I play a person with manic-depression, but I wasn't given enough time to do much research on it." They watched it carefully. Then he pointed out, "Even the dialogue isn't quite right. Parts of it contradict other parts. I should have either insisted that both the screenwriter and I be given more time to prepare, or else turned down the part."

"How would you've researched it?"

"By watching two or three people who have that ailment and seeing how they deal with it, what effect medication has on it, and how it affects their relationships with others." He stopped the film. "Of course, all people with any given disability don't behave and think the same, but you can get a general idea of what's realistic and what's not." While rewinding the film, he continued, "You know, I wish the disability this character had was autism. My brother Darrell is high-functioning autistic, and I could play that like a pro since I observed him for ten years. You really get to know a lot about a particular person by spending time with him and shadowing him. Remember that when you're given a role that's not familiar. And I hope that will happen more and more now that we're showing the casting people that you're capable of playing a wider range of characters." He switched films and restarted the viewer. "Here's another pointer for you. Look at this one. In this film, a lot of the camera angles were such that I had to use my non-dominant hand as though it were dominant. It's really a good idea to learn to use both hands well so that the audience can see what you're doing. Sometimes using your dominant hand would hide some of the action."

As the film progressed, he noted, "Your roles generally aren't as physical as mine, but this might be good for you to know, too. Most of this scene was done by stuntmen. Watch the way this character falls." He started the film. It depicted the beginning of a fight. "Look at that. He didn't just hit the ground, but, rather, landed on his shoulder and rolled."

"Ouch! And he just got hit in the face. That's got to hurt!"

"Fight scenes are meticulously choreographed. It looks like he hit the guy in the face but, in reality, his fist was about a half-inch away. Frank jerked his head back to further confirm the illusion."

"Oh, that's Frank? I didn't recognize him."

"That's because he's made up to look like the bad guy, and that's Bruce McDonald doing the star's fighting. You've got to be really sharp to do a fight scene realistically, and sometimes injuries do happen. That's why some actors insist they use stuntmen in those scenes, and the studio goes along with it. They don't have as much of a financial investment in the stuntmen as they do in the superstars."

"Then why don't you use stuntmen for your fights?"

"I do, sometimes. If it's something I can handle myself, though, I like to do my own." He looked over at Cal. "And, besides, I'm not a superstar and never will be."

As the screen fight progressed, she had another question. "They're right there on the cliff. How come Frank doesn't just push Bruce over the edge? That would've been easier than all that scuffling."

He smiled. "Because that would've made the fight end too quickly. And besides, Bruce is supposed to be the good guy. Rule #1 is you can't kill the good guy. Keep watching, though. In a minute you'll see Frank go over the edge. But that's okay. He's the bad guy."

"No, I don't want to see that. Stop the film. I like Frank."

He complied. "It's okay, Cal. He had a soft landing on a few mattresses." As he started rewinding the film, Leonard said, "That's a good series to work on. I've guested on it several times."

"You must work cheap," she teased.

"Not at all. I'm a professional. A true professional will give them their money's worth every time. They like that."

"Okay, Len, now let's look at *Campus Dreams*. I want to show you what I did." She reached across him and got that film. As soon as the previous film finished rewinding, Leonard replaced it with this one. "Go about forty-five minutes into it," she instructed. He zip-advanced it until she told him to stop. Then Cal pointed to the screen. "Okay. Look. There I was hopping into bed with that jerk, and this time you really *cannot* tell that he repulses me, can you?"

"Fully clothed, I see," he mused. "You don't see many love scenes like that anymore."

"Yeah. Remember I mentioned fighting City Hall and winning? That was about this scene," she grinned. "That's why it was done on top of a made-up bed. They originally wrote it to be under the sheets. My way is a less-drastic change from the original trilogy. They later changed their minds, but I wouldn't do it again and Nate wouldn't do it with anyone else, so they had no choice but to leave it the way it was."

He watched the scene carefully, and his amusement faded. At scene end, he put it on pause and turned to her. "What on earth were you envisioning when you did that?" His tone of voice had an edge to it.

Cal grinned. "Why? Can't you tell we hate each other? I thought an observant actor could always tell."

He shook his head, incredulously. "It looks like you were having one hell of a lot of fun."

"Believe me, I wasn't; but I wanted to get it done in one take, so I gave it everything I had. What do you think? Did I do good?"

He rewound it and watched it again. He then turned it off and switched back into the teacher mode. "You did much better in this one than in the last one you did with Nate. What were you doing mentally?"

"Just what you told me to. I completely disassociated my real self from the role. I psyched myself up to think I was really Corky and he was Mike. Corky was crazy in love with Mike."

Leonard nodded. "It looked like he never stopped thinking he was Nate."

"But I was so psyched up, I was able to ignore that." She then put her hand on Leonard's knee. "Have you heard anything more about the investigation? When are they going to set a court date?"

He rewound the film and turned the lamp back on. "Nothing yet. But the two best witnesses—you and me—are of no use to the prosecution now. We'll have to see who else they find to testify."

Chapter 20

THE BIRTHDAY PARTY WAS A HIT. Becky and Cal hosted six pre-schoolers, who seemed to have unlimited energy and enthusiasm. They loved Herman the Clown, as he made balloon animals for each child and told a few age-appropriate jokes to a delighted audience. Leonard was content to observe for a few minutes from a distance; a room full of excited young children was not his favorite place to be. After the pizza, cake, eight flavors of ice cream cones, and a variety of soft drinks were polished off, the parents came to pick up their children. As Cal and Becky gathered up the remaining debris, Stacy followed them around the room, happily chattering away. She had obviously had a very good time, and didn't want the day to end.

"How old are you now?" Cal asked.

"Five! That's almost grown up, isn't it?"

"Well, I always thought grown up was eight."

"Oh." She thought for a moment, then, "Well, five's almost eight."

After disposing with the last of the trash, Becky collapsed into a chair. Cal and Stacy sat on the floor and began playing with Stacy's new toys.

"We've set a date," Becky said.

Cal perked up. "Oh, good. When?"

"What's that mean?" asked Stacy.

"Becky and Johnny are going to get married, and they've decided on their wedding date," answered Cal, as she looked back up at Becky, "and it's about time, too. Y'all have been going together for a zillion years."

"It's going to be on Saturday, November 15th. You won't be out of town doing location work then or anything, will you?"

"Not that I know of. I only have a few TV shows lined up between now and then, but nothing that will take me out of town in November."

"Good. That takes care of that. It'll be at the church near my house. A wedding in a church always seems a little more real, and I know this is a marriage for life. I want to start going there on Sundays, so they won't think I'm just using them. How about going with me tomorrow, Cal? I want to show you the place. It's really big and beautiful. I can just envision myself walking down that aisle."

"I wanna' go, too," said Stacy.

"Okay with me. Okay with you, Cal?"

"Sure!" The opportunity to bring church into Stacy's life was like a present for Cal.

*   *   *

Leonard had been reading the Sunday newspaper when Cal and Stacy returned. "How'd it go?" he asked.

"Really great, Len. I like the minister a lot, and the music's out of this world!" Her eyes glowed with excitement. "They had an adult choir and children's choir singing a duet, from opposite sides of the sanctuary. It was wonderful! I'd love to sing in a church choir again, like I used to back home."

Stacy joined in Cal's praise of their outing. "And they had Children's Church, too, Daddy!"

"What's that?" he asked Cal as he set the paper down.

Cal explained, "Right after the children's sermon, they led the kids out of the sanctuary to go to another place in the church where they can have a little service on their own level."

"That's a good idea."

"Why don't you come with us next week, Len? I bet you'd like it."

He lifted the newspaper and opened it back up. "Oh, maybe sometime."

Cal knew a hopeless case when she saw it. "Come on, Stace. Let's get out of these icky ol' dresses and put on some *real* clothes. Last one upstair's a rotten egg." The child ran as fast as she could up the stairs while Cal ran in slow motion so Stacy would win the race.

*   *   *

They were each in their rooms, changing into jeans now. Cal couldn't stop thinking about the service. It had been too long since she had been to church, and it felt so very good to go today. She had been raised Catholic, but the Protestant church she had attended today suited her very well, too. At least, she felt, if Leonard wouldn't go with her, Becky would. Cal wanted to be a regular churchgoer again. That, she felt, was the most important thing that's been missing in her life since she left Dallas.

Chapter 21

LEONARD HUNG UP THE PHONE. This was good news. He didn't really think there had been anything to worry about, and now that was confirmed. The relief he was feeling came as a surprise to him. "Cal! Come here!"

She followed his voice into the study. "What?"

"It's not going to trial, after all! Insufficient evidence! It's *over*!"

It seemed too good to be true. "They dropped the charges?"

"No one could testify against me. The makeup artists couldn't remember anything, and Jill told them she never saw anything abusive happen. All they had from Nate was conjecture—he never saw me do anything. So that kills Nate's hope for a criminal case, plus the lack of damages and time that has elapsed make it a moot point as far as a civil case would go. All charges are dropped."

She whooped for joy as he picked her up and swung around with her. Tears of relief flooded Cal's eyes as she planted a big kiss on his cheek and hugged him tight.

Stacy walked in, cradling Luigi in her arms. "What's going on?"

"Let's celebrate!" Cal cheered. "Where's that champagne?"

The trio drank toasts to freedom, the American justice system, and poor memories—the adults with champagne and Stacy with soda pop in a champagne glass. Life, once again, was good.

* * *

"But why? The one I have is just fine, Len."

"You deserve better. I want to get you a *real* wedding ring, one with diamonds in it."

"But I love this one. It reminds me of our vacation in England."

"Okay then, how about this—I'll get you a ring that matches that band, one with a huge rock in it. Let's go."

"Right now?"

"Right now. I've got to work tomorrow."

They got into his car and he drove her to one of the finest jewelers in Los Angeles. After inspecting their whole line of diamond rings, Cal and Leonard finally agreed on one with a rectangular center diamond and a baguette on each side. The base was of the same two-tone gold that her original band was, resulting in a perfect match.

As they headed home, Cal kept looking back down at her left hand and moving it back and forth in the sunlight coming through the passenger window. How it sparkled! It looked like something her mother would have worn. Never did she ever expect to see such an exquisite piece of jewelry on her own finger.

Chapter 22

Preparations for Becky's wedding were well underway. The church and minister were reserved for the big day, and invitations were chosen and ordered. Today, Cal and Becky had gone to Mon Cherie Bridal Shoppe on ritzy Rodeo Drive to choose the bridal gown and the attendants' dresses. After a delightful afternoon of shopping, they returned to Becky's house for a quick, refreshing swim. Becky was now walking Cal back home.

"I like your choice of colors, Becky. My gown being green with pink trim, and the bridesmaids wearing pink with green trim is beautiful!"

"I thought so, too, and green looks so good on you."

"And your gown is fabulous! I can hardly wait for Johnny to see you in it. He'll fall in love with you all over again."

Hearing footsteps some distance behind them, Cal felt a strange uneasiness. She looked over her shoulder. It was Nate. He looked different though. Gone was his taunting smugness. His pace quickened, and he now seemed to be consumed by rage, on the verge of being out of control. She had seen that look on him only once before, years earlier in a situation that had given her weeks of nightmares. Something deep in the pit of her stomach told her that she had better get away from him *now*. "Becky, I'll see you later. Bye." Then she bolted for her house, which was only a block away.

"Oh, no you don't!" Nate yelled as he sped after her.

Becky followed, wondering what was happening.

Cal was almost home and was cutting through the yard to get to the front door when Nate lunged at her. They both tumbled to the ground and rolled. As she tried to get up, his arm went around the front of her neck and yanked hard, bringing her back to the ground.

"You're not going to get away this time," he said menacingly into her ear as his arm tightened around her neck. He was cutting off her air; she couldn't breathe. Cal tried desperately to pull Nate's arm away, but it wouldn't budge. Tighter and tighter it got as her fingernails dug into his flesh.

When Becky caught up to them and saw what was happening, she screamed, "Nate, stop it!" She tried to separate the two, but couldn't. He was more determined than she had ever seen him before. Then she got behind Nate and pulled on his shirt. That just served to rip the material.

Cal was rapidly losing consciousness.

"Help! Somebody, help!" Becky cried out as loudly as she could. "Make him stop!!"

Leonard heard the screams and looked out the front door. When he saw Cal and Nate, he shot out of the house. He grabbed Nate by the collar and forced his arm away from Cal. Once she was free, Leonard cast a fierce blow to Nate's jaw, then one more to the head, knocking him unconscious. "Go in my house and call the police," he told Becky. "This bastard deserves to be hung!"

"We need an ambulance," she said, as she rushed into the house.

"And the police!"

He knelt down and looked at Cal. She didn't look good. She was breathing again, but appeared to be in a daze. "Are you all right, Cal?" he asked. "Say something."

She appeared to be trying to talk, but her voice wouldn't come. She still seemed disoriented.

In a few moments, Becky returned. Her cheeks were wet and her hands were shaking. "Is she okay?"

"I don't know," he said, brushing the hair out of Cal's face. "She can't seem to talk."

"She needs to go to the hospital. I called the ambulance."

"No, I'll take her." He lifted Cal and carried her to his car. Becky followed and opened the car door, then he lowered Cal into the front seat. Leonard went around to the driver's side as Becky secured her friend's seatbelt and closed the door.

"You stay here and tell the police what happened. Tell them if they want to talk to us, we'll be at St. Mary's Hospital."

"Okay."

He backed the car out of the driveway and sped to the hospital. Becky went to check on Nate, as he started coming to. She knew Nate had broken the law, and violently, too, but she just couldn't bring herself to report the incident to the police. That didn't matter, however. The hospital would.

* * *

"Will she be okay, doc?" Leonard asked.

"It's hard to say yet. We'll run a couple of tests to see if there's been any damage to her brain or neck. Then we'll have a better idea of what we're dealing with."

"Her brain? From lack of oxygen?"

"Yes. How long was she without air?"

"I don't know. I wasn't there the whole time."

"We'll let you know what we find out," the doctor said as he left the room.

Leonard went over to Cal. She seemed to be sleeping. He put his cheek close to her nose to be sure she was still breathing. She was. He softly kissed her forehead and stroked her hair. "You'll be okay, baby. Len's here." Cal opened her eyes and reached for his hand. He grasped it.

A nurse came in with a wheelchair. "Can we sit up?"

They helped Cal to a sitting position and transferred her to the wheelchair.

"Why don't you wait in the lobby and we'll let you know when we're finished running the tests," the nurse said as she wheeled Cal out the door.

Leonard watched them as they went down the hall and turned the corner, then he wandered into the lobby as the ambulance attendants brought Nate in.

*   *   *

Leonard had been waiting for about ninety minutes, with no word yet from the hospital staff. Time seemed to drag on and on. He kept looking at his watch, then halfheartedly checking to see what was on the television in front of them. He stood up and stretched. "I'll be back," he said to Becky as he went down the hall and into a room on the left.

Becky continued to wait. Every time a nurse came through, she looked expectantly at her, hoping she was bearing some news. But none had been. Finally, the doctor returned.

"Where's Mr. Rhoads?" he asked.

"I'll get him." Becky ran down the hall and saw that Leonard was sitting silently on a pew in the hospital's small chapel. She tapped him on the shoulder. "The doctor wants to talk to you."

He quickly got up and joined the doctor in the lobby, followed by Becky. "How is she? Will she be okay?"

"There appears to be no permanent physical damage to either the neck or the brain, so I think she'll be all right. But she's been quite traumatized, and I would suggest we admit her for observation for a few days. We can have a psychiatrist check her over tomorrow."

Leonard and Becky were enormously relieved. "Can she talk yet?" Becky asked.

"She's not making a whole lot of sense, but she can talk."

"Where is she?" Leonard asked the doctor, who then ushered them back into the emergency room. Cal was in a wheelchair near the nurses' station. Leonard and Becky followed the doctor to the desk, where he told the head nurse to go ahead and admit Mrs. Rhoads, gave her instructions, then left to see the next patient.

"We reported the incident to the police, so you should be getting a visit from them soon," the nurse informed them. "They'll want to know all the details."

Cal was admitted to a private room on the third floor. Once she was comfortably situated, hospital personnel left. Leonard remained with Cal throughout the evening, during which time they were visited by a police investigator, who jotted down notes in a small notebook. Leonard told him all the details he knew about the incident while Cal listened.

"It was at least assault, possibly attempted murder, then," the investigator said. "Ma'am, did you feel that your life was in true danger?"

"Almost home. Just a few more steps," she said hoarsely.

Leonard answered for her, "She's still dazed, but I can tell you she was actually turning blue by the time I got him away from her. There's no doubt in my mind that murder was his intent."

"Will you sign an affidavit, testifying as to what happened?"

Cal looked over at Leonard as he nodded, "Absolutely!"

"Okay," she said.

"When you're able to tell me what happened, ma'am, I'll get your statement, too."

The officer gathered up his supplies and left. Leonard then sat on Cal's bed. "Will you be okay without me? I'll be back in the morning and I'll bring you a decent nightgown."

"Gotta get away from Nate!" she said, eyes wide with fear.

Until now, he had not even thought about what might have become of Nate. There was a strong possibility that he had been admitted as an inpatient here, too. If he was, that could be a big problem. "I'll find out where he is."

He went to the nurses' station and talked to the nurse. She telephoned the admissions office, then the emergency room. After hanging up, she reported, "He was treated and released."

After explaining the situation to her, he got the nurse's assurance that they would guard Cal's room zealously to keep not only Nate, but also any reporters, out. Then he returned to Cal's room and took her hand as he reassured her, "Nate's not a patient here, so you're safe. I know I broke his jaw," he smiled at Cal. "He won't be able to eat anything solid for quite a while."

"Okay," she said.

"So you'll be okay if I leave? If you need anything, just press that button for the nurse."

"Okay."

"I'll be back bright and early in the morning." He started to leave, but the look on her face gave him second thoughts. "Cal, what day is this?"

"Are we late for Becky's wedding? I'm wearing green."

Leonard came back into the room and sat down. "Never mind what I said, Cal. I'm not going anywhere."

It's a good thing the hospital personnel had already been told to make an exception to their visitation rules for Leonard. He had no intention of leaving Cal all alone in this condition, simply because some executive committee somewhere had decided that visiting hours should end at 8 p.m.

* * *

On the afternoon of the second day, Cal was much more lucid when the investigator had returned with the affidavit for Leonard's signature. After Leonard signed it and the officer also signed as witness, they listened as Cal told them her version. He came back the next morning and she signed her affidavit. Cal was released on the third day, in good condition. There were bruises on her neck, but she was otherwise in good physical health. Her voice and memory were almost back to normal.

The officer had assured her that she was safe. After receiving treatment for a fractured jaw and concussion, Nate had been charged with attempted murder and placed in the county jail.

This bizarre incident, because it involved three celebrities, made its way into most of the major U.S. newspapers. The facts had been distorted, however; and it wasn't made clear exactly how Nate had harmed Cal or whether it was intentional. The notices were mum about his whereabouts. This led Leonard to suspect that Nate's uncle had had some influence on the media, again, as he had when some of his studio's other valuable stars had gotten into trouble.

When Cal read one of the accounts, she confided to Leonard. "What's really scary," she said, "is that while you were in England, Nate came over when I was alone in the house. He could've killed me then and no one would've been around to stop him. I didn't know he would go that far."

"Me, neither. He must have just snapped."

"I smelled alcohol on his breath. He'd been drinking, but that didn't seem to slow him down any. I hope they locked him up good so he can't get out. Because, golly, if he does…"

"Believe me, Cal, you're safe. The law and I will see to that."

* * *

Leonard and Cal were lingering at the dinner table that evening, while Mrs. Morris was in the adjoining kitchen cleaning up after the meal. "You know, Len," Cal said, "just a couple months ago Nate was trying to ruin our careers. Now it looks like he's the one who might never work again."

He nodded. "Maybe there *is* justice in the world. His big-shot uncle might be able to sway the media, but not a jury. Nothing's going to get Nate out of this one. He'll be in prison for a long time."

Mrs. Morris hung up her apron and joined the couple in the dining room. "I think, Cal, that maybe you're still aptly named. You still seem to be 'incident prone,' don't you?"

"Yeah, and why is that?" she asked. "Why do weird things keep happening to me? Becky's life is so peaceful, compared to mine. Why?"

"You don't really believe these things happen randomly, do you?" Leonard questioned.

Cal looked at him. "What do you mean?"

"Well, I'm not saying you're one hundred percent to blame, but it's evident that you might have contributed quite a bit to it. For instance, most actresses would have gone ahead and done the scene the way it was written, regardless of how they felt about their co-star. And I've heard reports that you were downright hostile toward him on the set. He over-reacted, yes; but you've got to admit what he did was a reaction to what you did."

"I can't believe that you're defending him!" She got up and started pacing. "He tried to kill me and you're taking his side!"

"No, I'm not! What he did was inexcusable, and now he's getting just what he deserves. But don't you see what led up to it?"

"But I couldn't just sit still and take it! He was doing everything he could to make me mad on the set—he was always whispering crude things in my ear, so only I could hear them. Everybody else thought he was being such a gentleman because they couldn't hear what he was saying to me. And he dragged me to the studio when I was sick, and he kept threatening me. Everything I did and said to him, he deserved. Everything!" She held onto Leonard tightly and began to sob.

He held her securely. "It's okay, Cal. Don't get all worked up over it. It's over, and he's locked up." Then he admitted, "I feel partly to blame, too. Our getting married was probably the final straw, ruining all his plans." He kissed her forehead. "I guess it'll take a long time for you to get over this, won't it?" Wanting to comfort her, he stroked her hair. "You'll be okay, baby. I won't let anyone hurt you ever again."

Mrs. Morris motioned to Leonard that she was leaving. As she exited the front door, she was dismayed to see a reporter coming up the walkway. "Oh, please don't bother them now," she pleaded. "Another time would be much better. Please."

After he tried, unsuccessfully, to get some information from her, he left.

* * *

The two studios involved took advantage of the free publicity involving their stars and released *Campus Dreams* and *Henson of Manhattan* earlier than they had originally intended. Even though Cal had a minor role in *Campus Dreams*, she was given prominent billing. Ticket sales of *Campus Dreams* were almost triple and *Henson of Manhattan* were double, what had originally been expected. Practically overnight, the public's appetite for more and more news involving the three began to make life difficult for Cal and Leonard. No longer was she able to browse through a store with Becky or take Stacy to the park relatively unnoticed. A floppy hat and sunglasses weren't enough anymore. George had to hire staff to guard the premises and to escort Cal when she ventured outside without Leonard.

"Maybe we ought to move to England or somewhere," Cal suggested.

"You've got to stop running away from problems, Cal," Leonard replied. "I imagine this would follow us wherever we went, but it's not forever. Fame, especially this kind, is fleeting. Just as soon as some other celebrity causes a stir of some sort, they'll forget all about us and start hounding him."

"Well, can we take a vacation then? I want to get away from here."

"No. We both have guest appearances to make on TV shows in the next few weeks, and you wouldn't want to miss Becky's wedding, would you?"

"No."

"She's counting on you."

"I'll be there for her. Oh, Len," she said. "I'm sure glad we didn't have a big wedding like hers. Too many details, too many things to remember and do. Flowers, gown fitting, photography session, invitations, planning the reception, renting the church. Whew! Too much for me."

He smiled. "There *was* a certain novelty to ours, wasn't there, kidnapping our witness and all?"

"Yeah," she smiled at the amusing memory. "And she thought you were just being our chauffeur for the day. The look on her face when she realized you were the groom was priceless. Golly, these girls with their puny, half-baked boyfriends don't know what they're missing."

* * *

Because Leonard and Cal were to be at Becky and Johnny's wedding, security personnel were stationed around the church. Only those bearing invitations were allowed to enter, so the ceremony and the celebration afterward would be private. No one would be asked any questions by reporters as long as they remained inside the church. Entering and exiting, though, was another story.

"I'm so sorry, Becky. I hope your guests don't mind," Cal apologized.

"Hey, no problem, girl. Our wedding will be reported about in more newspapers this way. Let's you, Leonard, Johnny and I pose for a picture outside and maybe our friends and relatives far away will see it in their own newspapers."

One thing Cal loved about Becky was her optimism.

All went well at this much-anticipated event. It was a wedding that would be remembered for many years. And, sure enough, the foursome posed for photos outside for the loved ones who were unable to attend; and it, indeed, had the desired affect.

Maybe Becky ought to be my agent, Cal thought. *She sure recognizes opportunities when they happen!*

* * *

She couldn't find them anywhere. They had simply disappeared. "We've been robbed!" Cal lamented as she went into the living room where Mrs. Morris was dusting.

"How could that be?" asked a now-perplexed Mrs. Morris. "No one can get in here unnoticed anymore."

"I don't know, but I can't find my England paintings anywhere. I'm sure I left them in my old room, but they're not there. Did you maybe move them when you were cleaning?"

"Yes, I probably did. I'll look for them in the morning."

The phone rang. Cal took it in the den. She was gone about ten minutes, then rejoined Mrs. Morris.

"That was my new agent. He's not having a hard time finding work for me the way Pete did. It seems I now have a choice of several pictures to do. Isn't that great?"

"It certainly is. Leonard will be pleased."

"And this time I got smart. I told him I want to see every script first and know who's already lined up to be in each picture. Of course," she shrugged, "that part doesn't really matter anymore since Nate's out of commission. He's the only one I never want to work with again."

"Just reading through all those scripts ought to keep you busy for a while."

"He said that it'd really be a winning picture if Len could be in one of them with me. But he's already got him booked up for the next two years. I want to do something really good completely on my own, anyway. I was hoping *Campus Dreams* would be that, but it turned out to be a real bummer. Maybe one of these new ones will be just right. One's a murder-mystery. That might be fun."

"That would be something new for you, wouldn't it?"

"Yeah. Len keeps telling me to branch out. He's done just about everything there is. He even did a horror film once. That's something I'd never have guessed in a million years that he would do."

"He certainly is versatile."

"He says that's the advantage in being a character actor, rather than always the leading man who gets the girl. I guess I see it differently than everyone else, though. I keep thinking he ought to get the girl, too."

"You sound like a woman in love."

"Well, I guess I am, but he's such a cute bad guy."

* * *

Michael brought three scripts by the house that evening. One was the murder-mystery, one a comedy, and the other a drama. Cal and Leonard were both pleased that all three were more adult fare than most of her past films. Michael informed them, however, that none of them would be filmed in town. Two would be on location in various parts of the U.S., and most of the other one would be filmed in Spain.

"So that means that, unless you're on location with me, I've got to pick one that doesn't have anything new in it," Cal said.

"Not necessarily. It depends on the director. There are some who are very helpful to an actor if he's having trouble with his part." He held up the comedy. "The director of this one would be good in that regard," he said. "My next picture begins in January and will be filmed in Lexington and Ft. Worth, so I probably won't be with you while you're working."

She got excited. "Texas! Oh Len, take me with you. I haven't been home in years. I want to see my old friends again, and the old neighborhood. I wonder what Uncle Ant's doing these days. Please let me go with you."

"It's okay with me. You just have to pick the film that doesn't conflict with it." He held up one of the scripts. "Did Michael say when these are going to start?"

"No. But he says the sooner I can get started on one, the better. He's afraid the public will forget about me if I'm not constantly in front of them."

"Timing is really important. In six weeks we start shooting in Kentucky, then a few weeks later in Texas. See what he can arrange."

* * *

Work began almost immediately on *Lee's Follies*, a Civil War comedy being filmed mainly in Virginia, near Richmond and, later, in Manassas. This was a good experience for Cal in many ways. It was only the second time she had done a picture completely away from her home studio, and she was very glad her old friend Adrienne Starkey was in the cast, too. Adrienne and Cal shared a hotel room for the duration, which suited them just fine. She helped Cal develop better methods of disguise, so on their off days they were able to go sight-seeing together, unencumbered. At Adrienne's urging, Cal bought a wig, which changed her appearance drastically. And she made a point of not wearing any makeup on their jaunts. With the wig, she was able to avoid those sunglasses altogether.

Since Cal and Adrienne were in many scenes together, they usually had the same days off. Their off days were most plentiful at the beginning of filming, so they took advantage of them. They rented a car and visited area museums and Civil War memorials. Richmond's Monument Avenue, especially, intrigued Cal. They later decided to check out other cities nearby that would be of historical significance. They spent a day in Charlottesville, taking a tour of Monticello; and later enjoyed Colonial Williamsburg. History was coming alive for them during these visits.

Cal befriended a local film processor in town and spent many hours with him and his assistant in their back room. When her coworkers asked about that, all she told them was that the trio was working on a special project. The secretiveness generated some gossip, but Cal didn't care. She knew that if she confided in them, word would get out. It would then appear in print, and Leonard would find out. That was to be avoided at all costs.

At the end of their second week, the girls had a three-day weekend so they drove to Roanoke. Adrienne had heard people calling it the "Star City of the South" and wanted to see what that was all about. It turned out to be a beautiful valley. High atop Mill Mountain was a huge neon star that could be seen all over the city. Most evenings, the star would glow white. Saturday night, though, it was red. They asked the hotel clerk about that. It shines red, he said, when there is a traffic fatality in town.

"What a great idea!" Adrienne said. "That memorializes the person who was killed, and reminds the local people to drive carefully."

There was an eatery there that tickled Cal's fancy. With a name like Texas Tavern, how could it not? A little bitty white building, it served "a thousand people, ten at a time," and had chili to rival any she could find in her native Dallas.

Cal fell in love with Roanoke. It was a medium-sized city, but had a small-town feel. The people were very friendly, but in a reserved way, not at all the way Texans were instant buddies with everyone they encountered.

When she called Leonard that evening, Cal gushed the praises of Roanoke to him, lobbying for that to be the city in which they would someday live, maybe in their retirement years.

"We'll see when the time comes," he said. "By the way, your paychecks are starting to come in, so I've been depositing them in your checking account for you."

"I like having more work and lots of money coming in, Len. We went shopping and I bought a wig last week. How would you like me with long, straight, blond hair, like Sherry?"

"Who's Sherry?"

"Miles' wife."

"Not too good. It'd just make you look like every other starlet in town."

"Well, at least when I wear it with no makeup, people don't seem to recognize me. Adrienne wears a short auburn wig and sunglasses. No one has any idea who we are. It's like the old days."

"How do you like doing comedy, again?"

"Well, Len, it's more fun to watch a comedy than it is to film one. The gags and stuff get awfully old by the time they wrap the scene, and no one's around to laugh at the funny lines, so we forget they're funny."

"*Aha!*"

"What?"

"That's precisely why I love doing stage work, Cal. The audience. Their reactions. It's a great feeling, I'm telling you. You've got to try it."

She was silent for a moment.

"Are you still there?" he asked.

"Yeah. I was just thinking. If you want to line up a play, I'll do it—but only if you're in it with me. At least then we won't be on opposite ends of the continent anymore."

That's exactly what he was hoping she'd say. "As a matter of fact, I know of a magnificent play coming up. I'll check into it."

"How's Luigi?"

"He's been sleeping at my feet. Two males in one bed seems awfully strange to me."

Cal laughed. "He'll keep your feet warm on cold nights, anyway."

"Do they have any idea yet when your picture will be finished?"

"Well, it's staying pretty much on schedule, so I guess it won't be more than a few more weeks. We ought to be done by Christmas. Why don't you fly out here and I can show you Roanoke?"

"I could come, but it wouldn't be to see Roanoke."

She couldn't help but to smile. "You miss me?"

"It just isn't the same with Luigi sleeping with me."

"If it weren't for Adrienne, I think I would've gone crazy missing you, Len. But she's kept me so busy on our off-days that I don't have time to mope around."

"Good. Tell her to find something else to do next weekend because you'll be busy."

"Doing what?"

She heard some paper rustling at his end. "My plane lands at 4:43 p.m. Friday. I'll get a car and meet you at the hotel when you get off work that evening. We'll be in room 612 for the weekend, then I'll have to come back here Monday to do some research for another film."

"You already had it all planned, then."

"Sure did."

They both smiled with satisfaction.

*   *   *

All week, Cal was looking forward to Friday evening. In preparation for his arrival, she and Adrienne went shopping for a glamorous peignoir. "Wear this little number," Adrienne said, waving the bag in the air, "and he'll forget to go home on Monday."

"Hey, that'd be neat," Cal added. "Golly, I miss him."

"Okay, Cal, tell me something. I've never worked with Leonard. Which most closely matches his personality—gentle as a lamb or rough and tough?"

"Well," she thought out loud, "there's a little of both in him. He's a really complex person and it depends on his mood. But I'll tell you what. I'm glad Westerns are going out of style, because they always seem to cast him as the bad guy in Westerns, and he's not at all like that. He's more like the sheriff than the bad guy."

"I wonder if he'll use his lasso to round you up into that big bed."

"Oh, Adrienne. That's corny. He's not really like that."

*   *   *

"Well, little lady," Leonard said in his best southwestern drawl, with a playful glint in his eye, "I think I'm gonna have to arrest you and handcuff you to this here bed so you don't escape."

Cal had just emerged from the bathroom in her new peignoir, and it seemed to be having the effect that Adrienne had predicted.

"Oh, don't you worry none, Sheriff. I'm not fixin' to go nowhere," she said with a grin.

"Not even if I do unspeakable things to you, like this?" He swept her up into his arms and kissed her neck passionately.

"Oooh, especially if you do things like that."

Life was so good.

*   *   *

Leonard and Cal spent most of the first day in their hotel room, having room service bring their meals up. The next day, it started snowing. This was something that Cal hadn't seen in years. They took a walk in the snow, and did some window shopping. When they spotted sweatshirts bearing one of the state's slogans, "Virginia is for lovers," they bought Cal one; and she wore it for the rest of the day. Leonard, ever the pragmatist, declined when she offered to buy him one. "I won't have any need for a shirt that warm at home. And when I'm doing location work, it wouldn't be good PR to wear a shirt advertising another state."

The guy's too doggone logical, she thought, as she scooped up some snow and patted it into a ball.

"What're you planning to do with that, Cal?"

"I've give you two guesses," she said, with a twinkle in her eyes.

"If you throw that at me, you'll be sorry."

Almost before he got those words out, the snowball hit him in the chest.

Growling, Leonard playfully picked her up and draped her over his shoulder. "I'll dump you into the next trash bin I find." He carried her back to the hotel and through the lobby in this manner, to the amused delight of the onlookers, many of whom had recognized the couple.

"Hey, look at that. Officer Stanton finally got Corky!" one of the spectators quipped. "Are ya takin' her to jail?"

"Len, this is embarrassing. Let me down."

"Can't yet. There's no trash bin around here."

"Come on. Please?"

He acquiesced, setting her down right as the elevator door opened.

*   *   *

The weekend was over much too soon. Cal always thought tearful goodbyes were pure drivel; she had no patience with people who were such slaves to their emotions. Until today. She tried hard to prevent the onslaught of tears, but finally succumbed to it. She put her arms around him in a bear hug and buried her face in Leonard's chest so he wouldn't see her cry. He lifted her chin to give her a goodbye kiss, and noticed her wet cheeks.

"You're not getting all mushy on me, are you?"

"No."

"It's only for a couple more weeks."

"I know."

"Kind of makes you look forward to doing a play together, doesn't it? Then we'll be working together every day. You'll probably be sick and tired of me, then."

"Maybe doing a play wouldn't be so bad, after all. I don't like long-distance relationships."

"That would be the ticket, then, ma'am," he replied, giving her a grand and passionate goodbye kiss.

*　*　*

Cal was ready to get back to work Tuesday morning. Work, she found, kept her mind occupied so she wouldn't get so homesick. Sometimes, though, there was a lot of waiting involved, while the cameras and lights got situated and re-situated, or sometimes waiting for a cloud or a jet to pass during an outdoor scene. Those not involved in the adjustments found creative ways to stave off boredom. There was always something going on. Gregory, one of her co-stars, used the time to show his friends card tricks. Cal loved to watch such things and tried to get him to tell her his secrets, but he refused.

Lee's Follies finally wrapped on December 22nd, just in time for the cast and crew to get home for Christmas.

It was good to be home again. Cal was amazed at how much Luigi had grown. He was looking like a cat now, even though she still thought of him as a ball-of-fluff kitten.

On Christmas Eve, Cal and Leonard went to the midnight service with Becky and Johnny, sitting in the back in order to be as unobtrusive as possible. All went well, and they found the service quite inspiring. Cal loved belting out Christmas carols in a large church, and it felt wonderful to have Leonard sitting beside her there. There was a bounce in their step as they left. Afterward, the four went to the Rhoadses' house for coffee and a slice of Mrs. Morris' delicious homemade chocolate-chip cake with mocha frosting atop. They had a fine time.

After Becky and Johnny left, Leonard told Cal to go ahead upstairs because he had something to take care of. Yes, he would put the dirty dishes in the kitchen, he assured her, if she would just go. She reluctantly went. Once upstairs, she washed her face and changed into her nightgown. Then there came a sound of hammering downstairs.

"What's going on?" she called from the top of the stairs.

"I'm building you an ark. Go to bed," he answered.

She went back to their room. "It's a good thing I wasn't alone in the house during the last couple weeks. There wouldn't be any surprises in the morning if I had been," she said to herself, knowing her curiosity all too well.

* * *

The "mystery of the missing paintings" was solved on Christmas morning. Leonard had had all four of them professionally framed for Cal, and they were now hanging on the living room wall.

"Wow! Those frames make them look *beautiful*, Len! People might think I actually have artistic talent now!" she said excitedly, as they stood hand-in-hand, admiring them.

"You do. You mean no one's ever told you that before?"

"Not really. Now look what I made for you in Virginia." She handed him a gaily-wrapped box.

Upon opening it, he found a reel-to-reel movie, entitled *The First Half of Leonard Rhoads' Illustrious Career*. They went into the media room and he put it on the projector. It was a medley of excerpts from the films he had made and Cal's loving narration of his twenty years of achievement since starting in this business. The scenes that had been so impressive to Cal were all included, as well as the ones in which Leonard took pride. The clips began with that first TV drama he had done live in the 1950s, and ended with their big love scene in *Henson of Manhattan*. When it was over, he turned off the machine. "How'd you do this? And when did you have the time?"

She grinned. "Did you notice that your films were gone while I was away?"

"No. I had no reason to look at them then."

"Good. I found a film processor named Mr. Redmond in Richmond, and he showed me how to put this together. His assistant helped me write the narration and do the voice overs. The tough part was the plays you did at the very beginning of your career, since there's no stills or clips from them. Mr. Redmond had the playbills, though, because he's always been a Broadway buff, so we used them." She turned the light back on. "So what do you think? Do you like it?"

"I sure do." He hugged her close and kissed her forehead.

Cal said, "I wonder if we could get one of the networks to show it."

"Well, that would probably be expecting too much. Maybe after we die, they might find it valuable; but not yet. Then *they* can be the ones to deal with the copyright infringement." He rewound the film and re-boxed it. "We ought to make one of these showing all the different ways I've been killed off over the years. We could call it *Adios Amigo*."

"I don't want to think about that."

"Let's see. I've been shot, stabbed, hung, dragged to death, thrown out a window, exploded in a car… what else?"

"That's enough."

"But most of the time, the writers aren't very creative and just have me shot."

"Stop it, Len."

"Whenever it gets you down, Cal, just imagine the director saying 'Cut!' and me coming back to life again. You know that's the way it always happens."

"I had a really strange dream about dying last night, Len. Instead of being a nightmare, though, it almost seemed like a beautiful love story."

"What happened?"

"I dreamed first you kissed me, then you shot me."

"Must've been the result of a demented playwright."

"Well, in my dream, a doctor had just said I had six months to live and I was telling you I didn't want to live that long because it hurt so bad. So you gave me a big, long kiss, then you shot me." She sighed and looked up at him. "It was sad, but beautiful."

"That's the kind of role I'd like to play on screen someday. A story like that requires real acting."

"You don't think you'd really do that to make my pain go away?"

He thought for a moment. "It's hard to say. I guess if I had to watch you in agony, day after day, I might be very tempted to fix it for you. When my mother was dying of cancer, she asked my dad to help her die sooner, but he just couldn't bring himself to do it. She suffered for two more months before dying. It was miserable for us all to watch that."

"I can imagine. I guess my parents were lucky to have gone so fast."

"Mom's biggest worry wasn't about herself, but about Darrell. She was afraid he wouldn't get the care he needed if she wasn't around." Leonard became more pensive. "We ought to go see Dad and Darrell sometime."

"Oh, let's do. We've got a while yet before we're due in Ft. Worth, and I've never been to Long Island before."

Chapter 23

THE PLANE HAD JUST LEVELED out after takeoff and the "no smoking" sign was turned off. Leonard got a cigarette out.

"What's Darrell like?" Cal asked.

"Well, he's different. But not as different as a lot of people think. He tends to obsess about things sometimes, though."

"Like what?"

He lit the cigarette and took a puff. "He collects menus from restaurants. He has hundreds of them, and memorizes them all. Years later, he'll still remember all those details and gets upset if he goes to that restaurant and something on its menu has changed. If we had a memory like his, we'd have to read through our lines only once."

"He has *hundreds* of menus? How'd he get so many?"

"I've sent them to him when I'm traveling. Family and friends do the same thing."

"Is there anything I should or shouldn't say to him? You said once that he has tantrums. I don't want to cause one of those."

"It really sets him off when someone teases or makes fun of him. He definitely doesn't like that. But that's not something you'd do to a guy like him, anyway. I would suggest that you take it slow when you're first getting to know him, though. He feels threatened when someone comes on too strong at first or tries too hard to get him to interact. When you're introduced, just say 'hello' to him, then let him make the moves after that."

"Okay. I should've brought him a Mama Rosa's menu."

"He already has one."

* * *

Mr. Rhoads held the door open wide for them as they entered his Cape-Cod style home. He looked very much like an older version of Leonard. Cal liked him instantly. "This must be the new missus," he said, holding out his hand in greeting. She responded with a warm handshake and a smile.

"Yes, Dad, this is Cal. I think you've heard quite a bit about her, haven't you?"

"Over the last five years, quite a bit," he agreed. "You're not going to be like those movie stars that have a different wife every few years, are you?"

"Not a chance. This one's a keeper."

"Glad to finally meet you, Cal. And how are you doing, Lennie?" The men shook hands.

Leonard tried to ignore the smirk on Cal's face. He knew she was inwardly laughing at such a juvenile nickname.

"Okay, Dad. It's not easy to maintain a macho image when people are still calling me Lennie in front of Cal," he kidded.

"Oh, don't pay attention to that, Cal. Around here, he's been Lennie since he was a toddler, and he'll still be Lennie when he's got a long, gray beard."

"And there's my baby brother," Leonard said. "Hi, Darrell. This is Cal. Remember I told you about her?"

Darrell had been standing in the doorway to the living room. His eyes downcast, he nodded and waved.

Cal turned and waved back. "Oh, hi Darrell." Then, remembering Leonard's advice on the plane, she turned back to Mr. Rhoads. "I hear you're an expert woodworker."

"Well, that's my favorite hobby. I've been making cut-outs this week for the residents of the old-folks home to paint. They have a craft show every spring and sell the things. Come on in and take your coats off." He led them into the living room.

"Len had to buy me this coat when I was getting ready to go on location in Virginia in the winter. He warned me that it would be awfully cold in New York this time of year, too. He sure was right."

Mr. Rhoads took their coats and handed them to Darrell, who took meticulous care to hang them up just right in the closet. That done, he came into the living room and sat beside his father on the sofa.

Cal and Leonard sat across from them, and she tried hard not to stare at Darrell. He was quite a handsome man. From what Leonard had told her, she figured he was about thirty-two. He never quite looked anyone in the eye but, rather, seemed to be looking around or through them. He was very well dressed. *He doesn't look very disabled to me,* she thought. *Just maybe a little shy.*

"Darrell," Leonard said, "let's show Cal your menu collection. She doesn't believe you have so many of them."

"Okay," Darrell said. He arose, took Cal by the wrist, and led her into his bedroom. She was amazed. Two of his walls were completely lined with shelves containing hundreds of menus of all sizes.

"Wow! How many do you have?"

"Three hundred and fourteen."

"Do you have any from Florida?"

"Yeah." He reached high above them and retrieved a Lobster House menu. She didn't know how he found it so quickly. They weren't arranged in any particular order that she could ascertain, and yet he knew exactly where that one was.

Leonard joined them. "Watch this, Cal." He gently took the menu from Darrell and opened it so that he and Cal could see what was inside, but Darrell couldn't. "What's the third item down on page two?"

"Cod fillet platter. $7.99."

Leonard looked proudly at Cal. "See? The guy's amazing."

"Golly, you're right," agreed Cal.

"We like to play this game, don't we, Darrell?" Leonard asked.

"Yeah."

Leonard gave the Lobster House menu back and picked up another one. "This one is from Billy Bob's Diner in Lake Charles, Louisiana. What was their special that day? "

"Pot roast and vegetable soup combo. $12.50."

Cal was in awe. "Unbelievable!" she said.

Darrell took the menu from Leonard and put it back on the shelf, exactly as it had been before.

"What kind of work do you do, Darrell?" Cal asked.

He didn't answer.

Mr. Rhoads was in the doorway. "He goes to the workshop every weekday. They were putting plastic utensils and napkins into bags for a fast-food place today."

"But, with a memory like that, he could do a lot more," Leonard said. "The workshop's holding him back."

"Now son, we've been over and over that. There's no other choice for him at the moment."

Cal piped up, "I bet he could deliver newspapers and remember which houses on each block have subscriptions!"

Leonard nodded. "Yeah, things like that, Dad. He can do that on his bike. Don't they have people at the workshop who can teach him to do a real job?"

"Theoretically, they do. But they said there's a waiting list of their clients who are ready for competitive employment. He just has to wait his turn."

Leonard shook his head. "He needs to live in a place with more opportunities."

"Yeah," Cal agreed.

* * *

"This was my room when I was a kid," Leonard told her as they prepared for bed that night. "I'm glad Dad took my old single bed out and replaced it with a double. It would've been awfully crowded for the two of us in that little bed."

She couldn't help but to smile. "I can't imagine you as a kid. In my mind, you sprang to life as a gorgeous hunk of man. And I can't imagine you fitting into a single bed, either. You almost take up the whole double bed now and ours is bigger than most."

"What do you think of my family?"

"They're pretty swell guys." She sat on the bed. "And you're right—Darrell needs to live in a city like L.A."

"I've tried to talk Dad into moving out there, but he refuses. He's lived all his life here and plans to stay forever."

"Maybe Darrell can live with us."

"No, Cal."

"Why not? It's a big house."

"Not big enough." She didn't understand. "Cal, you don't know what you're asking. It's harder than you think to live with Darrell."

"I don't know why. It's not like he needs a wheelchair or someone has to feed him or anything."

"Just take my word for it."

She changed into her nightgown. "And he's neat as a pin. He keeps his room real tidy."

"No, Cal! Forget it!"

"But why? He's…"

The steely look in his eyes made her realize this conversation shouldn't go any further while they were guests. At home, they could discuss things as long and loudly as they wished, but not here.

*　*　*

"Good morning, Cliff. I just had to meet Lennie's new wife," gushed Aunt Mildred, as she came into the kitchen and joined them at the breakfast table. She smiled at Cal and poured a cup of coffee for herself. "We just live across the street and I saw you arrive last night. I thought I'd better wait until you got settled before coming over to say hello. You're a precious little thing! She looks *exactly* like Sheila, doesn't she, Lennie?"

Cal's ears perked up.

"Maybe a little," Leonard said as he buttered his toast.

"Yeah, I saw that right away, too," Mr. Rhoads interjected. "She looks just like a young Sheila."

"Tell me about Sheila," Cal asked.

"She's the one that got away," Mr. Rhoads said.

Aunt Mildred added, "She was Lennie's girlfriend throughout high school. Everyone thought they would get married when they graduated, but she up and married someone else. Broke poor Lennie's heart. She treated him pretty badly, though, so I'm glad it turned out the way it did. It wouldn't have been a happy marriage."

Maybe bringing Cal here wasn't such a great idea, Leonard was thinking.

Aunt Mildred put cream and sugar in her coffee. "I don't know if you were such big news all over the country or just here because this is Lennie's hometown, but they had articles about you two almost every day for a while in our paper. Our boy is certainly a hero, isn't he?"

Cal nodded. "He saved my life."

"The news out of California was kind of fuzzy," Cliff said. "I called the local paper and told them what really happened."

Leonard broke in, "That's all over and done with now. How's Uncle Bob?"

"Oh, he's as stubborn as ever," Aunt Mildred said. "I keep telling him he should retire, but does he listen? No. He'll keep working until he drops dead of a heart attack, mark my words."

"Is stubbornness a Rhoads trait, Aunt Mildred?" Cal asked, with a side glance at Leonard, who returned her glance.

"Oh, my, yes! I believe Cliff invented it, then he passed it on to his brother."

"*Me?*" Mr. Rhoads asked indignantly. "Why do you say that?"

"As many times as Lennie's tried to get you to come to California, you steadfastly refuse. You *know* that would be a good move. Not that I'd be happy to see you leave New York. I wouldn't. But you'd be close to your son and granddaughter. I'd jump at a chance like that if I were you."

"Yeah, Dad," Leonard added.

"Better yet, son, why don't you move here? You could work on Broadway again. You always loved that kind of thing. Doesn't it pay as much as those hotshot movies do?"

"Well, as a matter of fact, it doesn't, but Cal and I have decided to give the New York stage another fling. I have to honor my previous commitments first, though."

Mr. Rhoads' face lit up. "You're going to move back east? When?"

"We don't know. We have a lot of months of film and TV work lined up. My agent's negotiating an agreement for us to appear in a play around here in about a year, but that's not firm yet."

"If you get it, will you move here permanently?" Aunt Mildred asked.

"Probably not. Sometimes plays don't last very long. We'll just have to see how it goes."

"Well, that certainly gives us something to look forward to, doesn't it, Cliff?" she smiled.

"Indeed it does."

Darrell came quietly into the kitchen and got a plate out of the cabinet and set it on the counter. Very methodically, he retrieved the bread from the table and took two slices out. He put them into the toaster, then got two hard-boiled eggs out of the refrigerator. He peeled the eggs and cut them in precise quarters. He set a spoon and knife at right angles to the table's edge, filled a glass with orange juice and set that on the table as well. Right then, the toast popped up. He put them just so on his plate, then put the plate on the table and sat down. He concentrated on buttering his toast and seemed completely oblivious to the other people at the table.

"I wish I were that well organized," Cal said to no one in particular.

* * *

"Can I go with you, Lennie?" Darrell asked that afternoon, as Leonard was putting their luggage into the rented car for their return to the airport.

"Not this time, Darrell."

"When can I see your house again?"

"Keep asking Dad to bring you to California. Then you can see my house."

"Cal smiles like an angel."

"She likes you, too."

"Can she come live with us?"

"No, Darrell. She lives with me."

"Where's Jill?"

"She moved away. I don't see her much anymore."

"Did she get another big house?"

"A medium-sized house. She says she doesn't need a big one."

"Where's Stacy?"

Leonard looked at Darrell in confusion. "Have you ever seen Stacy?"

"On July 10th, 1967. It was a Monday. Dad and I came to your big house."

He nodded, "Oh, that's right. Stacy's living with Jill. She visits me sometimes, though."

"I want to come with you today and see your house and see Stacy."

"No, Darrell. Not today."

Darrell's face clouded over and his voice took on a darker tone. "I want to be in crime. I want to be a street gang."

"No, you don't."

Cal reached out to Darrell. "Is it okay if I give you a goodbye hug?"

"Okay." He stood still as she hugged him.

"I'll see you again sometime. Take care," Cal said.

As she then got into the car, Leonard shook Darrell's hand. "Take care of Dad for me."

"Okay."

Leonard then joined Cal in the car, waved to his father in the doorway of the house, and started the car on its trek to the airport. Once they had turned onto the highway, Cal asked, "What was that about? The crime and street-gang thing?"

"Oh, whenever he can't have what he wants, he says that." Leonard couldn't help but to smile. "A one-man street gang, that'd really be a sight to see! I wonder how he would surround his victim?"

Just the opening Cal needed. In this car, without any family around, they could argue as loudly as they wished. "Why are you being so hard-hearted about having Darrell stay with us? In L.A. there's bound to be a lot of opportunities for him. He can hold a real job there."

"It's not hard-heartedness, Cal. I'm just being realistic."

"'Just being realistic' is what cynics say."

"Cal, I lived with him for twelve years. You didn't. Trust me on this."

"But that was a long time ago. It's got to have been at least twenty years. You seem to have forgotten any of the good things about it. I mean, just look at this morning—he didn't need anyone's help getting his breakfast."

"That's a good example, Cal. He has had that exact same breakfast every single morning for years, at the same time of day, on the same plate. If Dad runs out of hard-boiled eggs, he has a tantrum and it takes hours for him to calm down."

"So we can keep a good supply of hard-boiled eggs on hand. What's the big deal?"

"It's not just that. He's a stickler for routines, hundreds of them. When we take him to get a haircut, we must take the same route every time to the same barber. If there's construction going on and we have to make a detour, he goes into orbit again. If one of his favorite TV shows is pre-empted, or if the bus is late to pick him up, it's tantrum time. Cal, it's a very difficult thing to live with a person like Darrell. I don't know how Dad does it."

"How about if we hire someone to help him through those things—like a job coach, only for day-to-day living stuff?"

He pointed his finger at her sternly. "I'm only going to say this one more time. He is *not* going to live in the same house with us! Get it completely out of your head right now!"

"Then what kind of future does he have? There's nothing for him where he is."

"Cal, *no!*"

They rode in silence for a while. Then Cal brightened, "They're not too far from Manhattan. There's *got* to be lots of options for him there."

"There are. They have a myriad of group homes and supported-employment agencies in the New York City area. I've already checked that out."

"So why isn't he there?"

"Because Dad doesn't want to let him go. He sees putting him into a home as 'giving up on him.' He thinks he can give Darrell everything he needs at his own house."

"What does he suppose is going to happen to Darrell when he gets too old to take care of him?"

"Amazing as it is, that doesn't seem to bother him. I think he's too close to the situation to see it realistically. Another problem is that I don't think Darrell would do well in a group home. You noticed that he talks to himself a lot?"

"Yeah. He says the same phrase over and over."

"That's called perseveration, and it's a common characteristic of autism. If the other people in the group home are trying to sleep or watch TV, his perseverating would cause a lot of problems. And he follows his routines rigidly. That would probably interfere with the activities at the group home, too. So I can't see how that would work for him."

"So now we're back to square one."

"I think he'd do all right in his own apartment."

"Really? Is he *that* independent?"

"Of course, he'd need someone to check in on him every few days to be sure he's okay. But, yes, I think he could handle it. Dad's taught him to cook, and he's done his own laundry for a few years now. He has his own checking account, but someone else would have to reconcile it with the bank statement."

"Wow! It sounds like *he* could take care of *us*! I don't cook." She glanced at him. He flashed her a severe look that made her slink down in her seat. "That was just a joke, Len. I wasn't saying he needs to live with us."

They rode on in silence.

*   *   *

When they arrived home, one of the messages on the answering machine was from Michael. It sounded urgent, so Leonard called him back immediately, while Cal took their suitcase upstairs. Normally, she would have put the clean clothes away and put the dirty ones in the laundry basket. This time, though, everything that was clean stayed in the suitcase since they would be leaving in a couple days for Dallas. She gathered all the dirty clothes together and took them downstairs to the laundry room. While she was putting them in the washer, she heard Leonard excitedly calling her, "Cal! Cal! Where are you?"

"In the laundry room."

When he came into the room, she saw he was beaming. "Michael says I've been offered a lead in the play called *Legends* on Broadway! There's still a couple parts unfilled, so you need to audition for it."

"You're back on Broadway?"

"That's right." He could hardly contain his joy. "And I'll teach you what you need to know to wow them at your audition."

"When does it start?"

"Rehearsals begin in April."

"*This year*? But, Len, you're already committed for this year."

He shook his head. "Look, this is an opportunity of a lifetime. It's a lead in a great play. If we can't do this one, we'd probably have to settle for an off-Broadway production next year. Michael's going to rearrange as many of my obligations as possible so I can do this. Appearances on TV shows can be done at other times, and they can find other actors for the films."

"Oh, okay." She continued to load the washer.

"Cal," he turned her around to face him, "didn't you hear what I said? You'll get a part in it, too. I'm sure of it."

"Yeah, I heard."

"Why aren't you happy about this? It's a golden opportunity for us both. We'll be able to work together again. We won't have to be working in different parts of the country. Isn't that what you wanted?"

"Well, yeah."

"But?"

Not wanting to spoil his exuberant mood, she was reluctant to say it; but she just couldn't lie to him. "Broadway scares me. The audiences there are so big and unforgiving. They expect perfection. Can't we do summer stock, instead?"

His hands on her shoulders suddenly felt like vises. "Don't you *dare* back out of this, Cal! Michael and I worked hard to set it up for you."

"I won't."

"You'd *better* not!" If the past six years had taught him anything, it was that the basic laws of human nature don't apply to Cal. Leonard knew that most people are somewhat reluctant to try something new; but with Cal, she has to be dragged, kicking and screaming. Once she gets used to the new way of doing things, she often will grow to embrace it; but it's getting her to that point of acceptance that had always been so nerve-wracking to him. For a long time, he couldn't understand what was behind her attitude. After all, she had been the epitome of boldness when she first came into their lives. Then he realized that the changes had begun when her parents died so suddenly and unexpectedly. This probably did more than anything to undermine her sense of security. And perhaps he was unaware of her feeling of vulnerability—for years, she had known that if the Rhoadses turned her away as her uncle had done, she had nowhere to go.

"I don't want to see the audience," Cal said earnestly. "I want to just look at you and pretend they don't exist. Then maybe I won't be so scared. That's what Cher used to do. She didn't look at the audience; she just looked at Sonny."

"In this play, only the narrator would be looking directly at the audience. I guarantee you won't be the narrator."

"Well, maybe it'll be okay then."

"You bet it will! You can do whatever you set your mind to."

Chapter 24

LEONARD AND CAL ARRIVED IN DALLAS the evening before location shooting was scheduled to begin on his next picture. The furor surrounding the Nate-Cal-Leonard incident was now dying down, so they were able to have dinner in peace at Reunion Tower, a revolving restaurant high above the city. During the course of the evening, it had revolved several times, giving them a complete and awesome view of the greater Dallas area at night. Cal spent a lot of that time pointing out to Leonard the places that had special significance to her, places like the hospital in which her parents had worked and the church the family had attended.

She had been back to Dallas only once—for the funeral of her parents. Now that the sting of her loss had been lessened by the passing of years, Cal was eager to see her old friends again.

The next morning, after Leonard left for work, she telephoned Sue, who was now married and had a baby boy. Sue whooped with delight when she realized who was calling and that Cal was in town. Cal excitedly told her about the latest developments in her life, and questioned her about hers. By mid-day, the two friends and baby were sharing a group hug in the lobby of the hotel. They spent the afternoon together, getting caught up on each other's lives and strolling around the area. Before they parted, Sue promised to get a babysitter the next afternoon and drive Cal around to their old haunts. Cal was bubbling over with happiness that evening when Leonard arrived back at their room. She told him all about her day, and said that she and Sue would be together the next day until late, so Leonard should go ahead and have dinner without her.

Tuesday was a big day for her. She and Sue stopped first at the Slop Shop, and Cal was glad to see that it hadn't changed much. Joe had aged, but, then again, so had Cal and Sue. The duo shared a banana split, just like in the good old days. They almost expected to see all their pals come through the door, arms loaded down with textbooks, after another day of school. Instead, it was eerily quiet.

Next, they visited their old high school; and Cal's Uncle Antonio had escorted them to the teacher's lounge, where they were reunited with many of their former teachers. "Being here feels really weird," Sue said. "Last time I was at school, we weren't allowed in this room." Cal was so glad to see Mrs. Hanfield again! Of all her teachers, Mrs. Hanfield had been the most patient and understanding. *A lot like Mrs. Morris*, Cal thought. "Thanks for insisting we use proper grammar, Mrs. Hanfield," she said, "instead of always using Texas jargon. If I were in Westerns a lot like Len is, it wouldn't matter. But I'm not, so it's a good thing that doing it right doesn't seem wrong to me. It makes it easier to learn my lines when they make sense."

"The only colloquialism you wouldn't give up was the contraction 'y'all,'" the woman acknowledged with a knowing smile.

Cal grinned, "Hey, I've taught that word to Len's little girl. People think she's a southern girl, now."

Ninety minutes later, the girls were back in Sue's car and heading toward her parents' house. "I'm so glad we went to the school today," Cal beamed. "I had such a good time."

"Yeah, me too. Did you see old Mrs. Gummel? She's still her same cranky self. Wouldn't even crack a smile. I thought she would've retired by now."

Cal giggled. "You remember the time in ninth grade when she left the room and we turned her clock ahead fifteen minutes? We got out of class early that day. I bet all the rest of her classes that day did, too."

"I wish you'd come when we have our ten-year class reunion. It'd be really neat to be together to see all our old friends again. A lot of them have moved away."

"That'd be fun. We'll have to see what my work schedule is like then. Len and I are hoping to be doing a play together soon. He says sometimes those things last one performance, sometimes years."

"Tell me, Cal, what's he like? When you introduced me to him in California, I wasn't around long enough to get a good idea of what he's like. He's such a manly hunk! I can't believe you landed him."

"Oh, Sue. He's not at all like his characters, but he is definitely 'manly.' You've got that part right."

"Alice is a psychology major at SMU now and she was telling me that you married Leonard because you needed a father figure in your life after your dad died."

Cal shrugged off the idea. "That's ridiculous. I married him because I love him."

"A couple of our friends were so sure you'd end up marrying Nate since y'all've been in so many movies together, but I told them what you told me— that it's only a working relationship between you and him."

"And not even that anymore."

"Yeah, that was in our newspaper, too, but it didn't give very clear details. You couldn't tell who did what to whom."

"Well, like I told you on the phone, Nate got it in his head that he wanted to kill me for some reason. And he would've, too, if Len hadn't been nearby."

"I know, and that didn't surprise me. I know a couple other people who wanted to kill you, too. Remember Tommy? You used to tease the daylights out of him. I kept telling him that, if he'd just ignore your jabs, you'd stop, but he wouldn't do it."

Cal grinned mischievously. "Yeah, that was fun. Whatever became of ol' Tommy, anyway?"

"He's studying for the priesthood."

"Oh, man! I'm in trouble at headquarters now," Cal said, pointing to the heavens.

They pulled into the driveway of Sue's parents' house. Seeing them again was a joy. They had been very kind to Cal during the many evenings she had spent with Sue at their house, years before, as the girls did their homework together and plotted their various antics. Tonight, the four had a delicious meatloaf and mash-potato dinner, then played Canasta afterward. At 8:30, Cal thanked them for their hospitality, bid them goodbye, and pushed Sue out the door.

They then drove back to the hotel. When they got up to the room, Leonard was there, reading the newspaper. Cal re-introduced Sue to him, and told him all about their day. The two girls took turns excitedly telling him the details of their visit to their old school, and he obligingly listened. After they had run out of news, he sat back down with his newspaper and Cal walked with Sue back down to the lobby.

"Golly, Cal. He doesn't act like a famous star. He's more like a regular person."

"Yeah, he combs his hair and shaves in real life, unlike all those bad guys. Did you see *Henson of Manhattan*? He's not made up like a bad guy in that one. He looks more like himself. I just love his character in that."

"Oh, Cal, I *did* see it, and I couldn't believe you were really in a movie like that."

"Why not?"

"Well, it was so, uh, grown up. You were naked for Pete's sake!"

"No, I wasn't. In that love scene, I still had shorts and sox on under the sheets, and so did Len."

"Well, you couldn't tell it."

"Of course not, dummy! You're not *supposed* to tell it. And Len made sure the audience didn't see *too* much of me. Did you notice he was between the camera and me when it was a front shot?"

"No, but I don't want to watch it again to find out."

Cal laughed. "I'm outgrowing my teen image, Sue, and if I didn't do something about it quick, I was going to be out of work. Len got me the role in *Henson* so I can show moviegoers that I'm an adult now and can handle adult roles."

"Yep, you looked adult all right."

"It's like Patty Duke doing *Valley of the Dolls*. I'll probably be doing more pictures like *Henson* from now on. It took some doing to get Stagecraft to agree to loan me out for it, but now I think they're glad they did. It made me more valuable to them. They even wanted me to be naked as a jaybird in a *Campus Dreams* scene, but I wouldn't do it that way." She grinned at Sue. "I don't think *they* see me as a kid anymore."

"I kind of hate to see your old image go, though. It was so wholesome." Sue paused, then brightened. "So, Cal," she asked, "when are y'all going to start a family?"

"Gee, I don't know. I haven't thought about it. He's already got an adorable little girl, and it's almost like she's mine. I've been around her all her life."

"But nothing is as wonderful as having your very own baby. I never knew such a strong bond existed until my Brandon was born."

"Don't pressure me, Sue. I'm not ready for that, yet."

"Well, just think about it, okay?"

"I figure we have the best of both worlds right now. We get Stacy every other…"

"Stacy?"

"Len's little girl."

Sue's eyes grew huge. "You mean his first wife named her daughter after his second wife?"

"Well, Sue, none of us had any idea I'd be his second wife way back then. That was five years ago. Things were a lot different then."

She laughed. "So now both the females in his life, though totally unrelated, have the same name. That's funny. Only in Hollywood could something like that happen, huh?"

"Anyway, we get her every other weekend and on holidays, plus a few weeks in the summer, except when Len's working out of town. So it's like we get to be with her for special, happy times; then Len and I get to be alone the rest of the time."

"I guess that *is* a pretty good arrangement. You can have a child around, and Wife #1 gets the stretch marks and takes care of the pediatrician appointments. Kind of like being a grandmother."

"Exactly! The best of both worlds."

At the hotel's front door, the girls hugged goodbye and promised to get together once more before Cal left. Sue then departed. Cal returned upstairs.

"Well, Len, she was duly impressed. She gave you a high compliment—said you were like a real person."

"Yeah, I play that part pretty well, don't I?" He arose and took off his shirt. "I need you to do something for me. My back is sore from the work we did on the rodeo scene today. It's been a long time since I've done that kind of thing." He lay prone on the bed, and Cal knelt beside him and massaged his shoulders. "Ahhh, that's good. Perfect."

"Do you think the filming of this picture will be done by April?" she asked.

"Oh, sure. No problem there. Did you get Stacy a cowboy hat today? She asked us to get her one while we're here."

"I forgot. I'll do it tomorrow. Maybe I can find her a little Indian dress, too, and a turquoise necklace so she can pretend she's a beautiful Indian princess."

"She'd like that."

"One of my friends in school was Indian—Cherokee, I think. She had the most beautiful black hair I've ever seen. It looked so silky."

"I'm getting Friday off next week so we can fly to New York for your audition."

She startled. "So soon?"

"Yes."

"Why can't they come here?"

"Cal, you don't ask the producers of a Broadway play to come to Dallas to audition someone who's never done professional stage work before. It's just not done that way."

"Oh." She moved down to his mid back. "Sue thinks we need a baby."

"Why? Does she want to give hers away?" he teased.

"No. She's just so in love with motherhood, she thinks I ought to give it a try."

"I don't think so."

"How come?"

"Autism might be genetic."

"But even if we did have a baby with autism, it wouldn't be the end of the world."

"There's a wide range of functioning for people with autism. Darrell is one of the lucky ones. At the other end of the spectrum are those people who are totally nonverbal and profoundly handicapped. They require around-the-clock care for their whole lives. If you want to know the truth, Stacy was an accident. Jill and I weren't going to have any kids for that very reason."

"Ohhh," she grinned. "I bet I know what happened."

"Tell me."

"You must have been filming a steamy love scene that day and came home all hot, and it turned out to be the wrong time of month to prevent a baby."

He turned toward her with an incredulous expression.

"You mean I'm *right*?" she asked.

They both burst out laughing.

"Very close," he said. "I wonder how many show-biz babies were conceived under those circumstances," he said.

*   *   *

It seemed they were getting on and off planes a lot these days. The New York airport was beginning to feel like home to her now, as she and Leonard again walked through LaGuardia to the car-rental area. Cal was quite nervous, never having auditioned for a play on a professional level before; but Leonard had coached her intensively. He felt confident that she would do well. Cal wished she could be that sure.

They met later that day with the producers and director of *Legends*. In order to reduce Cal's jitters, Leonard asked that he be allowed to read with her the scene that would be used in the audition. They agreed, and all went smoothly. Ever since *Henson of Manhattan*, Cal had found it easy to relax when Leonard was in the scene with her. His convincing portrayal encouraged hers. The decision makers were apparently quite impressed, because later that evening the phone call for which Leonard had been waiting came to their hotel room, offering Cal one of the major roles in the play.

It was with a tremendous feeling of a job well done that Leonard boarded the return flight to Dallas the next day. As for Cal, she was cheered that she had merited a good part in the play; however, the little insecure part of her was hoping that perhaps the world would come to an end prior to opening night.

Chapter 25

Throughout the filming in Texas, Cal busied herself with various projects while Leonard was working. She rented a car and visited her old neighborhood twice. It was a wonderful feeling for her to see the neighbors from years ago and to learn how their lives had being going. The filming was also being done in Amarillo and then in Kentucky. She was glad to see what those places were like. Recreational travel had not been a priority with the Ameses as she was growing up. The travelling they had done was mainly centered around medical conventions. Cal felt as though she was making up for lost time now.

Filming finally wrapped in early March.

When they returned home, their *Legends* scripts were waiting for them. Leonard handed one to Cal.

"I've been thinking, Len. Are we going to rent a house in New York?"

"Maybe. Why?" He glanced through the pages of his script.

"Can we find one with an attached apartment?"

He looked at her, confused. "Why? You want a place to go when we have an argument?"

"Well, you said Darrell could handle having his own apartment. Maybe your dad would let him try that if we were nearby and would check in on him every day. In New York City, he wouldn't be too far away from your dad, so they could visit each other whenever they want. "

"Cal…" he said.

She held her hand up. "Don't yell at me again. I'm just trying to help."

"I wasn't going to. I was going to say that's a brilliant idea."

"*Really?* You're not mad?"

"Yes, really. No, I'm not mad."

Feeling bolder now, she continued, "And maybe we could find a job for him in the play. Maybe he could help with sound effects or be in the crowd scenes. A real job, Len. One that he can do with regular, everyday people and take pride in."

Leonard put the script down and thought for a moment, then slowly nodded. "He would need a job coach for something like that. Someone who would show him how it's done and explain things to him in a way he would understand."

"They're bound to have hundreds of them in New York City. Maybe thousands."

"It would need to be a job that's predictable and the same every time. He could pass out the playbills, or be a prop man," Leonard added.

"Or how about a ticket taker at the door? Or an usher?"

"If we were doing a film, he could be a stand-in while the technical crew prepares for a scene. The possibilities are numerous." He went over to her and put his arms around her. "Why do you care so much about Darrell?"

"Because he's a sweet guy. And he's your brother and *you* care about him."

He nodded his head and hugged her close. "I love you, Cal."

It felt like her heart was leaping clear out of her chest. This was the first time Leonard had ever said those words to her. Feeling now that she could let down her guard, she put her arms around him. "I love you, too, Len."

"So many people are afraid of Darrell, just because he's different. Even Jill was wary of him, but you're not."

"We should've looked for a house with an apartment while we were there."

"No. If people know it's us who are house hunting, the prices will go sky high. George will do it. All we have to do is tell him what we want it to have. He'll find it and get a good deal for us. Believe me, a good business manager is an excellent employee to have, Cal. He earns his salary many times over."

* * *

There were no indications that the world would come to an end before April; so, bracing for the inevitable, Cal started looking over her lines. "There's so much dialog in this play! You ought to tell these folks about the value of nonverbal communication, Len."

"That works better on the screen than on stage. On stage, the audience can't see the subtle things. Or they may be looking at another character at the time. The stage doesn't offer the advantage of close-ups."

She looked through the script. It seemed she had lines on almost every page. "Why did they give me such a big part? I'm new to this business. They should've started me off with something small."

"Oh, stop your griping. Do you want me to read with you? I could do Claudius to your Antonia."

She continued her perusal through the entire script. "You've got even more lines than me. It'll take forever to learn all these."

"Not only our own lines, but everyone else's as well. We have to know the whole thing, Cal, so we can cover, if and when someone forgets a line."

She looked quite unhappy as she put the script down.

"Don't be discouraged," he said consolingly. "That's why they brought us the scripts so far ahead. We have plenty of time to learn it. And we're not expected to be off book during the first few rehearsals."

"But they start in only one month."

"I, for one, can hardly wait for opening night. I want you to know what it feels like." His eyes were aglow with dreamlike pleasure. Like in the *Green Acres* sit-com when Oliver Douglas began talking about the virtues of the American farmer, Cal halfway expected to hear a fife playing "Yankee Doodle" as accompaniment to Leonard's seeming soliloquy. "The reactions of the audience. Knowing you're keeping them spellbound in their seats. There's nothing like it in the whole world!" He patted her on the back. "You'll see. Once you've done it for a few weeks, you'll be hooked. Film work will seem too tame after that."

"I can't believe this is how you got your start. How come you started with the hard stuff, then went over to movies and TV?"

"That's the best way to learn. If you can "wow" them on Broadway, you can do any form of entertainment under any circumstances."

She picked the script back up.

"You're going to like this format, Cal. It's five plays in one—each spotlighting a different person in history who made an impact, good or bad. So we each get to play five different characters. It'll be a good way to show the world how versatile you are."

"But I'm *not* versatile," she lamented.

"You *will be* by opening night. Let's go over the first scene you're in. You read all the female parts and I'll do all the men. As time goes on, it'll get easier. I promise."

And so the hard work that preceded the April rehearsals began. This, she was to learn, was the least enjoyable part of doing a play, but the most important. Without such a solid foundation, it wouldn't work.

In early April, Leonard and Cal moved to the house on Long Island that George had found for them. It was perfect for their needs. They brought Luigi with them, and Mrs. Morris agreed to relocate to New York so she could continue as their housekeeper. Once rehearsals began, Cal's circle of friends expanded to include four other actors—Carole Sherman, David Duke, Renee Gladstone, and Mel Davis. This core of six would each take on the personalities of five very different people in order to tell their stories. She had never met any of these other actors until the first day of rehearsals. It's then that Cal realized that many very excellent actors were limiting their work to the New York stage with something akin to a religious fervor. Actors who work primarily on the New York stage are well known there, but are oftentimes relatively unknown to the rest of the country. Working together with Carole, David, Renee, and Mel, day after day, created a family atmosphere; and they grew very close. In the process of bringing this script to life, Cal felt a special kinship with Mel, who was young and relatively new to the stage, too. A member of an elite actors' group in town, he had been in only two Broadway plays previously, playing small parts. This was his chance to shine. There were also other actors playing minor roles, a couple of whom also served as understudies.

After a couple weeks of intensive rehearsal, they were all completely off book, much to Cal's amazement. Run-throughs had become much easier now. For the dual purpose of providing more challenge and being prepared for any unforeseen event, they swapped roles for one run-through. The results were quite comical, especially when an actor had the part of another gender. It was interesting to Cal to see how the others reacted when a prop wasn't where it should be. *You can tell these guys are pros,* she thought. *The audience'll probably never know anything's wrong.* From them, she learned how to cover for such occurrences. And she learned to not be afraid of them, but to use creativity in working around them.

Technical and dress rehearsals began one week prior to opening. The play had been written in such a way that the actors in the final part of one mini-play would not be in the first part of the next one. This allowed enough time for costume changes. Make-up, Cal found, was different in plays. The colors were brighter. This, she was told, is because the lighting on stage would make a subtly made-up face appear washed out to the audience. If a character were elderly, the actor actually had lines drawn on his face. This would appear to the audience to be wrinkles. Until she got accustomed to this, Cal felt ridiculous to be so garishly made up. As soon as dress rehearsals were over, she and her cast mates would scrub the make-up off before going outside. "So we won't be mistaken for hookers," Renee said.

Soon, the day Leonard had been eagerly anticipating had arrived. It was opening night! For the first time, Cal understood the adrenaline rush that he had been telling her about. They were all made up and costumed for the first scene. They had had the traditional 'break-a-leg' sendoff and were all in their places. Waiting in the wing for their cues, Leonard reached over and pinched Cal. When she looked up at him, he winked at her and whispered, "It's curtain time." As the curtain slowly started rising, they got into character and the play began. Once the now-very-familiar dialog had begun, Cal's opening-night jitters were quickly replaced by conditioned response.

* * *

Cal and Leonard were on their way from the theatre to the cast party that evening. She could hardly contain herself. "Four curtain calls, Len! Can you believe it? And the audience—they were great! They laughed at all the right places, and I heard them gasp at the execution."

"What?" he feigned surprise. "Are you telling me that stage acting is actually *fun*?"

"Okay, okay. You were right about that. And I missed a line, but I bet no one in the audience knew it. Carole covered for it and it went smooth as silk. And the flowers that came! I'm glad I didn't have to look at the audience until the curtain calls. There were so many people there! When are your dad, Darrell, Uncle Bob and Aunt Mildred coming? Didn't he say they would? Or were they here tonight?"

"Dad always stays away from opening night on purpose. Says it's a rat race. He has tickets for later in the week."

"When will we know if it'll run long enough to move Darrell here and get him a job?"

"The reviews will be one indication. Ticket sales will be another. I think it's best to wait a few weeks, at least. We sure don't want to uproot Darrell, then a week later have to take him back home because the show closed. Any changes in his life need to be long-term."

"I have his apartment all ready for him."

"I know you do, but don't be disappointed if he redecorates it complete-ly. You noticed all the magazine clippings on the walls in his room at home? I would bet he'll want to replace the paintings you hung in the apartment with his clippings. He has his own unique style."

"What about Stacy? We haven't been able to see her since we came out here."

"You know she's too young to fly alone."

"Yeah, but I miss her, and she must miss us, too."

"We'll figure out something, Cal. Don't worry."

They arrived at the restaurant where the cast party was being held. Once inside, a festive atmosphere prevailed and they were immediately given glass-es of wine. Stage actors often wait until after the show to eat their large meal of the day, and they were now famished. Consequently, the bulk of the crowd was hovering near the buffet tables.

Renee spotted the couple and rushed over. She took Leonard's arm. "I want you to meet Gregory Moore over here. He's a drama critic and was re-ally impressed with your performance tonight." She led him across the room to a portly, tuxedoed gentleman.

Cal took a sip of her wine and looked around for some other familiar faces. Everyone seemed to be in groups except Mel, who was sitting alone and gazing out the window. She went over and sat at his table.

"So how do you think it went tonight, Mel?"

He brightened. "Fairly well, I guess. I can't believe this is your first stage experience. You're really good. Where'd you get your training?"

"Oh," she smiled proudly, "I learned at the knee of the master. Len taught me everything I know."

"Really?"

"Yeah. He got formal training, years ago. So I guess he just passed everything that he's learned on to me."

While still in conversation with Mr. Moore, Leonard discreetly glanced around to see where Cal was. He spotted her at a secluded table with Mel. His smile faded.

Cal set her wine down. She had rarely been able to empty a glass of anything with alcohol in it. "How come you're over here by yourself? And don't you want to load up a plate over there at the buffet? You must be really hungry, like I am. We don't eat much before the show."

"I guess I'm just a little down. My family could have come tonight, but they didn't. I sent them tickets. But they've never come to any of my plays."

What jerks they are! she thought. *Poor Mel!* Cal patted his hand. "Oh, I bet they're just waiting until the hubbub of opening night is over. They'll probably come later in the week, I bet. And when they do, they'll see what a great job you're doing. I like your Crown Prince the best."

Leonard excused himself from Mr. Moore and went over to Mel's table. "Mind if I join you?"

"Not at all," Mel motioned to an empty seat.

"Looks kind of cozy over here. Is my wife making passes at you, Mel?"

The young man replied, "Oh, no sir."

"I'm going to get something to eat," Cal said as she arose and made her way to the buffet, where she was joined by Carole. As they took plates and started going through the buffet, Carole invited Cal to a party at her boyfriend's apartment later that evening. "He doesn't have a fancy buffet like this, but he does have something that'll make you higher than this wine will."

"Oh, no thanks, Carole. Len and I don't go in for that kind of thing."

"I wasn't inviting Leonard. Just you and Mel. We like to party with people our own age. The older folks kind of put a damper on things, if you know what I mean."

Cal put her hand on Carole's shoulder. "I can't this time. But maybe Mel would like to. Why don't you go ask him?" She looked over at the table. The men seemed to having an intense discussion. "I think he'd probably like to be rescued about now."

Carole looked over at Mel and Leonard. "Rescued?"

Cal instantly regretted having said that. "Oh, I was just kidding. Sorry." As she finished filling her plate, she was asking herself, *Why did I say that?* She then returned to Mel's table and the men's discussion came to an abrupt halt. "Don't you guys want anything? They have shrimp."

Mel got up. "That sounds good. I like seafood." He left them and went over to the buffet.

Leonard suddenly became serious. "I saw you holding his hand, Cal. Don't think you're getting away with anything."

"Holding his hand? When?"

"Right before I came over here."

"I don't remember doing that."

He looked at her reproachfully.

"It was probably just a subconscious thing, Len. I don't remember holding his hand."

He took her glass of wine and finished it, his eyes remaining steadily on her.

She ate the best part, shrimp, first, having a feeling they would be leaving early. "And what the heck difference does it make, anyway?" she added. "We're in show biz, for Pete's sake. I should've been hugging and kissing him. That's what show people do." She looked around at the crowd and noticed that Mel was taking his filled plate to Carole's table.

"That's not what *we* do, Cal. I expect you to behave like my wife, not like you're on the prowl."

She couldn't believe this. "Since when did it bother you that I talk to another guy? You were even gung-ho about me doing a love scene with Nate, and that's a lot worse."

"The scene with Nate was acting. A rendezvous at a party is not."

She stood up and gathered her things. "I'm going home. You can stay out all night if you want. I don't care if you never come home." She popped the last shrimp into her mouth.

"You shouldn't be driving in this traffic."

"I'll take a cab."

"I wouldn't advise it." He arose, too. With a steel grip on her arm, he led her out the door and to the car.

They drove back to their rented house in stony silence.

*   *   *

Once inside the house, she punched him in the arm. "Why were you being such a jerk tonight? You ruined my evening!"

He gripped her shoulders so tightly it hurt. "Because you were out there in public coming on to that young punk! That's why!"

"I was not! I was just sympathizing because no one in his family has ever bothered to come to his plays. He needed someone to talk to."

"How did he know they weren't there? There were a thousand people there. If he was looking that much at the audience, he wasn't doing his job."

"You know what this reminds me of, Len? Do you? This is just like when I was fifteen and came in late at night. You acted crazy then, too."

"*You*'re the one who makes me crazy! How do you suppose that looked to everyone there tonight?"

"I did nothing wrong, darn it! You're always blaming everything on me." She threw her purse onto the hallway table and started toward the adjoining living room.

Leonard grabbed her by the arm. "Get back here! Don't walk away from me."

"Let go!" She gave him a swift kick to the shin.

"Don't ever wander off like that again, do you understand? When we're at a party, you stay with me."

"No! I'm not your puppet!" Cal tried to pull her arm free.

"That's right. You're not. You're my wife, or did you forget that?"

She stopped struggling and became suddenly calm. "Wait a minute. You said I was coming on to that 'young punk.' I remember, you specifically said 'young.' Would it have bothered you if I had been at the table with David? Does Mel's age have something to do with this?"

Leonard let go of her arm and went into the living room, reaching into his pocket for a cigarette. "That's a distinct possibility."

She followed him. "Why?"

Leonard sat in the easy chair and lit the cigarette. He took a long puff, and slowly exhaled it. Then he said softly, "Because it seems to me that you would be more attracted to someone Mel's age than mine, that's why."

"Oh, Len," she said as sat on the arm of his chair. "You're ten times more attractive to me than anyone my own age. I want a man, not a boy. And no one's more of a man than you, Len. I love you."

He snuffed out his cigarette and pulled her onto his lap. "Show me."

"With pleasure," she said as she smoothed his hair back and gave him the most passionate kiss he had ever had, on- or off-stage.

Coming up for air, he took a deep breath and mused, "Are you sure you're only twenty-three?"

"That, my dear, is a genu-wine Texas kiss. You might always be the bad guy in movies, but, by golly, you got the girl in real life."

* * *

Most of their cast mates had stayed at the restaurant until the morning newspaper, with its play reviews, arrived. The reviews were mostly good and the ticket sales remained high. Three weeks into the *Legends* run, Leonard was confident enough of its future to propose their idea for Darrell to his father. For that reason, they had brought Mr. Rhoads, Darrell, Aunt Mildred and Uncle Bob back to their rented house after they had attended the play during the first week of its run. Cal and Leonard had deliberately shown them the attached apartment without telling them their purpose for it. Now, with Cal beside him, he was disclosing that purpose to his father on the phone.

"What do you think of our idea, Dad?"

"Well, I don't know."

"Cal and I would check in on him every day to be sure he's doing okay. You've already taught him a lot of the things he needs to know to live independently. This would be a good, safe way to see what more he needs to be taught."

"But he's got the workshop here. He'd have to start all over on the bottom of some waiting list if he moved."

"We've already taken care of that. They've agreed to let him help the prop men at the theatre, and an organization here has promised a job coach for him."

"Well, son, what can I say? It's a nice apartment. I'll ask him what he thinks and let you know."

"How about letting me talk to him now?"

"Um, okay. Just a minute." He called Darrell to the phone.

After a moment, Darrell answered, "Hello?"

"Hi, Darrell. This is Lennie. Would you like to come live next door to us here in Long Island?"

"In your house?"

"You remember that apartment we showed you and Dad? The one with the blue couch and little TV?"

"Yeah."

"That's where you would live. It's right beside our house."

"Okay."

"And would you like to help us do the play? That would be like a job for you. You'd get a paycheck and everything."

"Do I have to talk loud like you do?"

"No, you don't have to talk at all. When the curtain comes down, you would then put the table on the stage and the telephone on the table. Things like that."

"Okay."

"Good. Let me talk to Dad again."

When his father got back on the phone, Leonard said, "It's fine with him, Dad. When can we arrange the move?"

Cal was cheering silently.

* * *

Jill was overjoyed when Leonard told her that his relocation to New York would be long term, and possibly permanent. This, she felt, gave her the freedom she needed to move back to Connecticut, where her extended family lived. Her parents did the same. Now Stacy could visit her father on the east coast without difficulty.

* * *

Within a week, Leonard and Cal were helping Darrell settle into his new apartment. At first, he seemed a bit apprehensive. After a few weeks, however, he had gotten accustomed to his new surroundings and felt comfortable there. Little by little, they noticed the place was being personalized in his own inimitable style with magazine clippings and posters on his walls. From the beginning, they made sure his menu collection was a part of his décor.

Once his living situation was established satisfactorily, they engaged the job coach and Darrell's first true vocational training began. Because of the sameness of the routine each night, Darrell caught on to his duties quickly. Mr. Rhoads found himself attending the play several times a month now, in order to watch both of his sons and his daughter-in-law at work. He frequently brought friends or relatives with him.

After one of these performances, Mr. Rhoads had taken Darrell back to his apartment while Cal and Leonard changed out of their costumes and makeup. They later rejoined the men at the apartment.

"This place looks just like home, Darrell," Mr. Rhoads had commented.

"Yeah," he agreed.

"Hey, Dad, didn't Darrell do a great job with the props?" Cal interjected. "Everything was exactly where they should have been. He's the best prop man I've ever worked with."

"That's good. There are a couple times when the curtain is up during the scene changes, and we can see him on stage. Even though it's dark, I can tell it's him by the way he walks."

Leonard added, "They have the prop men wear black so they aren't as easily seen. But, if your eyes are accustomed to the darkness, you can still see them."

"And Len told me that in one play there had to be scene changes while the lights are still on and curtain up, so then they had the prop men wear costumes, like the cast. I thought that was kind of neat. Wish I could've seen it."

"Why don't you stay overnight with us, Dad?" Leonard asked. "Stacy will be coming over tomorrow, and I know she'd love to see her grandpa."

"Oh, boy! Stacy!" said Darrell as his eyes lit up.

*   *   *

"Uncle Darrell!" Stacy squealed when he opened the door to his apartment. She had been on her grandpa's shoulders, but Mr. Rhoads lifted her over his head and set her down in front of him.

"Stacy! My Stacy!" Darrell gave her a bear hug, lifting her a couple of feet off the floor.

Cal looked over at Leonard, who told her, "Darrell loves kids. And they seem to love him, too. Their parents—well, that's sometimes another story."

Darrell put Stacy down and retrieved an item from his bedroom. "I have your puzzle for you." He brought it into the living room and put it on the floor. Uncle and niece sat on the floor and spread the pieces out, then began putting them back in, one by one.

"Is it okay if we have some coffee, Darrell?" Leonard asked.

"Yeah."

Leonard motioned for Mr. Rhoads and Cal to follow him into the kitchen, where he got three cups out and poured the coffee. "He always keeps a pot of coffee on, just like you do at home, Dad."

Cal got the cream out of the refrigerator, then the trio sat around the table.

"Well, Dad. What do you think of Darrell's new life?" Cal asked.

"I couldn't be happier. I'm learning to 'never say never' these days. If, a year ago, someone had told me that he would be in his own apartment and working in a regular work setting without any other disabled people around, I would've thought they were crazy. I thought he'd spend the rest of his life in that workshop."

"I *knew* he could do better, Dad," Leonard smiled, feeling quite victorious. "This job is perfect for him, especially if *Legends* runs for a couple of years. After that, he'll have a good work record and can be prop man for another play."

Mr. Rhoads poured cream into his coffee and stirred. "You know, when your mother was expecting Darrell, all we wanted was a normal, healthy child. We got an autistic child. I figured I could either let it drive me crazy, or I could modify my expectations. Once I decided on the latter, everything got easier. I came to appreciate the quite extraordinary people both my sons have become. And now, Lennie and Cal, I'm pleased as punch that you are all working together and he's getting such good care while being so independent." He looked at Leonard. "Your mother would be proud."

"She would," Leonard agreed. "I know she'd have her whole bridge club in the front row, cheering the prop man on every time there was a scene change."

The men shared a chuckle.

"So, she was a bridge player, huh? My mom was, too," Cal said. "Tell me more about her."

"She would've loved you, Cal," Mr. Rhoads smiled. "Lennie told me that the apartment was your idea. That sounds like something she would have thought of. You're a lot more like her than Jill was."

"I sometimes wish I could be as ladylike as Jill. She always looks so gorgeous, and I've never seen her lose her temper."

"Oh, ho! My Kato had a temper. I think that's where Lennie got his. Isn't that right, son?"

"If I have one at all," Leonard teased, "it had to have come from the Rhoads side."

Stacy and Darrell came into the kitchen. Stacy climbed onto her grandpa's lap as Darrell got a cup of coffee. Then, he approached Cal. "I sit there."

"Oops, sorry." She moved over.

"That's his routine," Leonard smiled at her.

It was quite a revelation to Cal to discover that she had so much in common with Leonard's mother. How she would love to have gotten to know such a woman!

*　*　*

Doing the play every day put new demands on Leonard and Cal, not the least of which was now an altered lifestyle. It had been many years since he had been in the habit of sleeping until almost noon, but having the bulk of their work schedule now occurring in the evenings made later sleeping and waking times necessary. This was no problem for Cal, however. She had never been a "morning person" and did her best work at night. When they got back from the theatre, she was still in the "go" mode, with energy to spare. This was due, in part, to the creative and emotional fulfillment she was experiencing in stage work. The part that meant the most to Leonard, audience feedback, was an important aspect of this. Another factor was the continuity she found in the very nature of the stage—they were telling a story from beginning to end, without interruption except for brief scene changes and the intermission. This is quite different from making a television show, which was spread out over a week, or a movie, which was often filmed a little at a time, usually out of sequence.

Leonard and Cal found this to be a way of life that suited them both.

Chapter 26

1980

"Please say yes, Daddy. Cal thinks it's a good idea," said a very excited Stacy, as she showed Leonard the letter from her high school.

"What is it?" he asked, taking the letter.

"A chance to be an exchange student for a semester in France. My grades have been good and French is my favorite subject. Please say yes."

Cal tried to swing his verdict in Stacy's favor. "Doesn't it sound great, Len? What an experience that would be!"

"But she's so young."

"Remember how old I was when I came to California for the first time? And I was traveling alone."

He turned to Stacy. "What's your mother say about this?"

"I don't know. I haven't asked her yet. They just gave this to me in French class today, then Cal picked me up at school for the weekend."

"Well, let her know as soon as you get back home. I'll call her later next week, and we'll discuss it." He gave the letter back to Stacy and went upstairs, motioning for Cal to follow.

"Go get a snack if you want, Stacy," Cal said, "but not too much. Mrs. Morris is going to make lasagna for dinner tonight." Then she went up the stairs and into the study. "What?" she asked.

"You don't think she's too young?"

"Uh-uh."

"But, Cal. This is about *France,* and Stacy. I don't know."

"I guess you'll just have to wait and see what Jill thinks. Maybe she'll go with them. She likes to travel, doesn't she?"

"I don't know. We never did much traveling together."

"It'd probably make you feel better about it if she went, too. Maybe we could pay her way or something." Cal started for the door, then turned. "By the way, Michael called this morning. He wants you to call him back about a film that'll start in April. As for me, he has another play lined up."

"Another play?" he asked wearily.

"Yeah."

"Here in New York?"

"Yeah. Off-Broadway. It's called *Once in a Lifetime*."

"But you know a play could tie you up for a long time. Remember *Legends*? That went on forever, it seems."

"Yeah, but I like plays, and this one's a musical. That's what I've been wanting to do."

"When does it start?"

"Rehearsal begins in March."

"Good. That gives you time to do a few TV shows. Be sure he arranges a good variety of them for you."

"No Westerns, though," she teased.

"May they rest in peace."

"And that's a shame, too. Right when I was starting to get guest shots on the good ones, they died. And don't tell me that's *why* they died."

Leonard chuckled, then went over to his desk and picked up the phone.

Cal went back downstairs. She joined Stacy and Mrs. Morris in the kitchen. Mrs. Morris was snapping fresh green beans for that night's dinner.

Stacy smiled triumphantly at Cal. "Mrs. Morris thinks it's a good idea, too. That's three against one."

"But Dad's vote counts as four," Cal warned. "After all, it's going to be coming out of his pocket."

"You really think he'll let me go?"

"Well, I'll tell you what. He'd probably agree in a second if it were England. He's spent a lot of time working over there and likes it a lot. But France might be a bit harder to sell him on. You know the reputation of those lecherous Frenchmen. And you'll always be a little girl to Daddy, no matter how old you get."

"Yeah," Stacy sighed. "I know."

Mrs. Morris agreed. "I don't think any father thinks his only daughter is ever old enough to go to France."

"Ask your mom if she'll go with you, Stacy. Don't they need chaperones for these things?"

"I don't know, but I'll find out. That would be neat if she and I could go together. She sure needs to get away. She's been kind of depressed lately."

"How come?" Cal asked.

"I don't know. I mentioned something about your tenth anniversary, and she got kind of grouchy. But I don't know if it has anything to do with that or not. It might be totally unrelated."

"Maybe a trip to France is just what she needs to help her feel better again, then. She's so pretty and kind that I'm surprised she hasn't remarried."

"Oh, she's had offers, but turned them all down. Guess she'd rather be single."

* * *

Late that evening, Cal was in the media room when Stacy returned from a date.

"How'd it go?" she asked, putting her film on pause.

"Oh, pretty good. We went to see *Superman II*, but I liked the first one better."

"Yeah, that one's going to be hard to beat. Chris Reeve is sure a hunk, isn't he?"

"A what?"

"Oh," Cal stopped herself. "Girls probably call them something different nowadays, but a hunk used to be a good-looking guy."

"Oh that. Yeah, he sure is." She sat beside Cal on the sofa. "What're you watching?"

"You'll never believe who this is." She released the pause button, and watched Stacy for a glimmer of recognition.

"Which one?"

"The guy with blond hair."

Stacy scratched her head. "He looks familiar, a little bit like Uncle Darrell. Who is he?"

Cal gave a hardy laugh.

"Who is he? Tell me."

"That, my dear, is your father, when he was twenty-three years old."

Stacy's face broke into a grin. "That's *Daddy*?"

"Sure is. Wasn't he adorable? Who would've guessed back then that he'd turn into a bad guy? He must've fallen in with the wrong crowd somewhere."

"Where is he? I've got to show this to him."

"Hey, *he's* the one who showed it to *me*. At the time, I was so impressed that this was a recording of a live TV broadcast." Cal said. "In fact, I'm still impressed at how well he did his part. But I'm not all that surprised anymore that he actually enjoyed getting in front of a zillion people and performing live. He's gotten me hooked on doing that now."

"Golly. He's been acting a long time, then. What's he now, sixty?"

"Fifty-one. He's been in the business about thirty years. And I'm still totally blown away by this production. What gets me is that that's not after thirty years of experience, but it's in the *first few years*. I watch this every year or so to see if I come close yet to measuring up to his standards. I still have a long way to go."

"Would you back it up? I want to see the whole thing."

"Okay." Cal rewound it, then started it again. The two sat silently together, eyes glued to the screen for the entire show.

*   *   *

Cal cuddled up to Leonard, who had already gone to bed by the time the girls had finished watching the film. She put her arms around him and whispered in his ear, "You're *still* awesome."

He opened his eyes. "You've been watching it again, haven't you?"

"Yeah, and the less-experienced you can still act rings around the more-experienced me. I've reached the conclusion that a person either has it or he doesn't. I think you have the natural talent and training. I just have… I don't know what I've got."

"You're too critical of yourself. I've heard some pretty good comments about your work from some of your directors."

"Really?" She brightened.

"Sure, and don't forget that Emmy nomination you got a few years ago."

"But I didn't win."

"That means nothing. The nomination is the important thing."

"I love you."

He smiled and kissed her forehead.

"What did Michael want?" Cal asked.

"He's got three films lined up for me so far this year. And the year is young yet. Looks like it's going to be a busy one."

"You're still hot, Len. Four films and all the TV guest shots you can shake a stick at."

"I also let him know you're available to do guest appearances before play rehearsal begins.

"Okay."

Leonard put his arms tightly around her and his leg across hers. *This is weird*, Cal thought. She could barely move. "What's this all about? Are we into bondage now or what?" she asked.

"I'm bracing you for news I got today."

"Uh-oh. What?"

"Michael's wasn't the only call I got from California today. There was another one, telling me that Nate's being released from prison next week."

"What!!?" She would have bolted upright, but Leonard's stronghold prevented that. "But it's only been ten years! He was sentenced to thirty."

"He was. There are some inadequacies in our judicial system, and early parole is one of them. Be careful, Cal. You're going to hyperventilate."

She strained against his arms. "But that was a violent crime! Early parole should be for the non-violent ones."

"It should be, but it isn't."

"Let go of me!"

"Not until you calm down."

She summoned every ounce of her acting skill, and forced herself to breathe normally again. After a moment, she was able to say, "Okay. I'm calm."

"No, you're not."

"What makes you think that? And *don't* give me another acting lesson, for Pete's sake!"

He kept a firm hold on her. "I can feel your heart beating hard and fast."

"Do you have any idea how frustrating this is, Len, to not be able to move when I want to tear the room apart?"

"I think we're going to have to spend the whole night like this."

"I can't sleep. I need to take a walk or something. Let me go take a walk."

"Not yet. You're liable to break something—like your hand when you ram it through the door."

She gave up the fight. "Len, how can they do this?"

He shook his head. "I know it doesn't make sense, but it's done all the time. I knew Nate would take advantage of that, sooner or later."

"But…"

"Shhh. It's okay, Cal. He's clear across the country from us. He'd have no reason to follow you here. I imagine he'll be plenty busy just trying to rebuild his life."

She looked unconvinced.

"Ex-cons frequently return to crime because no one will give them a job. Nate's got a benevolent uncle, though, who will make sure he starts getting roles in pictures, again." Then Leonard smiled, "And don't forget—Nate's afraid of flying. He won't come here."

"Well, you better believe from here on out I'm going to know who else is in the picture before I agree to do one. And I won't work at that studio again."

"Good girl." He looked at her closely. "Are you ready to be let loose?"

"Yeah."

"You're really and truly calm?"

She nodded.

He slowly released her. She lay still for a moment, then she grabbed her pillow and hurled it across the room. "I can't believe this is happening!"

"Remember, Cal, Stacy's down the hall. However you choose to vent, do it in a way that won't upset her."

"I'm going downstairs."

"Don't break anything."

"I won't." She put on her robe and went back to the media room. Unwelcome memories came flooding back, bringing tears to her eyes. Ever since their move to New York, the pain of these memories had been dulled by sheer distance and a busy schedule. *Becky!* she thought. *If he wants to find me, Becky's the person he'd ask.* She reached for the phone and dialed Becky's number. While it was ringing, she tried to remember how many hours behind them California was. It was only 10:00 there. Good.

"Hello?"

"Becky, hi! It's Cal."

"Well, hi Cal. I haven't talked to you in a few months. How are you?"

"I was great until Len told me Nate's being paroled. Is he out yet?"

"No. Monday's his big day."

"Please, Becky, whatever you do, don't tell him where I am. Please?"

"Okay."

Whew! Cal thought.

"But that probably won't make much difference, though. The trade papers mention you and Leonard now and then. He'll probably find out one way or another."

"Thanks, Becky. You really brightened my day," she said sarcastically.

"Well, I'm sorry. That's just the way it is. But I'll tell you what. I'll feel him out and see if he even *cares* where you are. There's a very good possibility that he would have other things on his mind these days, like surviving."

"I sure hope so."

"I mean, it's been a very long time, Cal." Becky then asked about Stacy. They talked for a few more minutes about other things, then Becky promised to call again in a week, after she'd found out what's happening with Nate.

Cal put the phone back down and went into the kitchen. She lifted the lid of the cookie jar. It was full of homemade chocolate-chip cookies. "Thank you, Mrs. Morris," she whispered, as she took several out. Then back she went to the media room, where she watched television for the next two hours. She had no idea what she was watching; her mind was elsewhere. Slowly, as time went on, she became calm and her eyes began getting heavy.

Leonard then came down the stairs and into the room. He put his hand on her shoulder. "Come to bed now, Cal."

For the time being, she felt she had come to terms with the Nate situation. So she turned the television off and walked over to Leonard, putting her arms around him and resting her head on his chest. Being so close to him almost always made her feel safe and secure. He returned her embrace. Then she silently thanked God for him as they ascended the stairs together.

*   *   *

The following Monday afternoon, Cal was reading over her script when she felt a tug at her foot. She looked down. One of her shoelaces had become untied and Luigi was pulling at it, so she took her shoe off and waved it over him. He took a few swipes at the dangling shoelace, then seemed to remember that he's too old for such antics and started grooming himself instead.

The phone rang. Mrs. Morris answered it, then handed it over to Cal. "It's Becky."

"What'd you find out?" Cal asked.

"Oh, I'm fine, thank you, Cal. And how are you?"

"Okay, okay. Hi, Becky. How are you?" she complied.

"That's better. Well, Cal, I think you can rest easy. He didn't bring your name up and neither did I. We talked about lots of things, too. He's happy as a lark to be out of the slammer, though."

"Yeah, I bet."

"He's back at his house in our neighborhood, so I'll be seeing him now and then. I'll let you know if anything develops. I'm assuming he'll go back to doing films, but I'm not sure. He'll probably just spend a while enjoying his freedom before going back to work."

"So you really feel everything's okay? He didn't seem mad or anything?"

"Not that I could tell. He just seemed glad to be out. He said that place was hell."

"Still, though, don't tell him where I am. Don't say anything to him about me, okay?"

"It's *okay*, Cal. Stop worrying, will you?"

Easy to say. Hard to do.

*   *   *

Cal returned to the house after checking in on Darrell. They would soon be working together again, once rehearsals began on *Once in a Lifetime*. His good work reputation made it quite easy for Cal to talk the producers of her plays into hiring him as one of their prop men. Darrell was always on time, paid strict attention to his work, never haggled over money, and was well-liked by his coworkers. His job coach had taught him to hold his perseverating until he got back home. Once inside his apartment, he would talk to himself constantly, as though making up for lost time. "Apparently," Cal had told Leonard once, "he must have a quota or something. It's like there's a certain amount of talking that he simply *must* do each day before he can relax enough to go to sleep."

Leonard wasn't home yet this evening. They had just finished a joint sitcom appearance, and she had enjoyed every minute of it. He was now doing a guest spot on another show, while she had the week off. This past week was the first time they had both guested on the same television episode. It was such a pleasant experience that she was wondering if it would be feasible for the couple to have their own television show so they could work together all the time. Cal soon dismissed the idea, however. Working together on *Legends* every day for a little over two years was good in some ways, but not in others. She found there was such a thing as *too much* togetherness. Maybe it's better for them to go their separate ways during the day, then come together in the evenings. At least for the time being.

Another idea she had been considering, but one she felt would definitely *not* be pleasing to Leonard, was the possibility of her changing careers altogether. Watching Darrell's job coach at work, Cal felt that she could easily do that. *Being able to help other people like Darrell to achieve success in the real working world would be so fulfilling,* she thought. *But then,* she realized, *Len and I would have less in common—less to talk about at the end of the day.* Being in the same business as he had given her a definite advantage over Jill in years past. Cal had seen subtle hints in the messages brought to them by Stacy that Jill was still very interested in Leonard. In the past few years, she noticed Jill making herself more and more accessible to him; and she was calling more often now, asking him for advice.

No! Cal thought. *No matter how rewarding another career would be, I'm going to stay in show biz.* After living with Leonard this long, living permanently apart from him was unthinkable. "Jill *chose* to leave him," she said to herself. "She had her chance and she blew it. She has no business changing her mind now."

* * *

What was I thinking? Cal wondered. *Jill can have him. He's driving me crazy!* "But I *like* plays," she said. "You got me hooked on them, and now you're telling me to stop. Make up your mind, will you?"

"I wanted you to *try* them, not devote your whole life to them! Why do you have to be so obsessive?"

"Why don't *you* get on *my* schedule? Why do I have to be the one to change?"

"I want to keep loving stage work, and the way to do that is to perform in a variety of venues, so burn-out doesn't happen. Now go ahead. The phone's right behind you. Call Michael and tell him you want film and TV work from here on in."

"No!"

"If you don't, I will."

"Don't!"

"Call him!"

"No!"

He walked around the sofa to the phone and lifted the receiver.

"Stop it!" Cal yelled as she climbed over the sofa and leaped onto his back.

He started dialing. "Get off."

"No." She clung to his back like a leech.

After replacing the receiver, he reached over his shoulders to grasp hers and pulled her over his head, back onto the sofa. He then walked away from her and took the phone with him, dialing as he went. She jumped up and followed.

"Michael, it's Leonard Rhoads."

"Ignore him, Michael!" Cal yelled.

He quickly set the base of the phone on a nearby table and put his hand over Cal's mouth, wedging her head firmly against his chest. "As soon as *Once in a Lifetime* is over, Cal's to get back into film and TV work. No more plays."

Cal reached for the receiver, but he propped it between his head and shoulder, and, with his newly-freed hand, grabbed her arm and held it out of the way.

"Yes, that's right. This is her last play for a while. It's back to the screen, just as soon as this is over."

She struggled to free herself, but in vain.

"She likes TV work best, so focus on that."

Cal struggled with all her might.

"Okay, Michael, see what you can do. Thanks, pal. Talk to you later." He let go of her arm and hung up the phone. Keeping his hand over Cal's mouth and putting his other arm across her to hold her still, he looked back down at her. "Now this is more like it. A quiet female. This is the way it *should* be."

Her angry response was muffled.

"Remember, you promised to 'love, honor, and obey.' *Obey*, Cal! You seem to have a lot of trouble with that one."

She tried to pull his hand away from her mouth, but couldn't.

"Ask that preacher of yours," Leonard continued. "He'll tell you the wife is subservient to the husband. What's that word they use? 'Submit,' that's it! Wives are to submit themselves to their husbands." He released his hold on her. "Remember that."

"Paul wrote that. He was a bachelor, and that's probably why." She grabbed the phone.

"Oh, no you don't." He took the phone away from her and held onto her arms. Each stared stubbornly at the other, neither wanting to yield. It was then that Leonard realized the need for another approach. His expression softened. He kissed her lightly on the forehead. "Cal, just think about it. Give it a day or two of thought. You'll understand then that I'm right. It's not good for a marriage when the husband's on one schedule and the wife's on another, like ships that pass in the night. Look around us. How many couples in this business stay together? Not very many, and it's because of that very thing. I don't want that to happen to us, Cal."

"But I like plays."

"I do, too, but not constantly. Maybe it would be okay every few years to do one for a few months. But not *all the time*."

She sighed and looked at the floor. He was starting to make sense again. "But filmmaking is so boring."

"Then concentrate on TV work. There's plenty there to keep you busy. And many of those are with a live studio audience these days."

"Not on the east coast."

"Good point." He took a cigarette out and lit it. "We might want to look into moving back to California. That's where most of my work is, anyway."

"But what about Darrell?"

"We can keep renting the apartment for him, and his job coach will keep him employed. Dad can check in on him since they live in the same city, so Darrell will be fine."

"And, Len—Nate. He's back in the old neighborhood again."

"We could move into another neighborhood, clear across town. L.A.'s a big place, Cal. If it makes you feel better, we can live up in Santa Barbara." Seeing that she had no argument with that, he added, "You can't let fear run your life. That's no way to live."

"Then if you have to go on location, can I go with you? I don't want to be home alone. If he'd strangled me when I was alone, I'd be dead now."

"Sure. I like it when you're with me on location."

Maybe it wouldn't be so bad then, she thought.

Chapter 27

THE PLANE RIDE WAS SMOOTH SO FAR. Jill looked over at Stacy, who was devouring the teen magazine her sponsoring family had sent her. It was entirely in French, so Stacy had been translating some of the parts she thought her mother would be interested in.

Funny, Jill thought, *that Leonard offered to pay my way to France, as well as Stacy's.* The program had no need for volunteer chaperones, but Jill decided to take Leonard up on it and go anyway. In trying to figure out *why* he had extended such a generous offer, she came up with two possibilities: 1) he felt uneasy about his little girl going so far away, or 2) Cal had put him up to it to get Jill out of the way. The second possibility made her somewhat uncomfortable, that perhaps her strategy to get Leonard back may not have been as subtle as she thought it was. It certainly seemed to her that he would welcome the kind of companionship she could offer—loving, calm, and stable. Stacy was aware of the arguments that were once again going on between Cal and Leonard, even though they had done their best to shield her from them. While they rarely displayed their fiery tempers in front of her, she had heard their neighbors talking about it a lot and had told her mother what they had said. *Things haven't changed much in seventeen years*, Jill thought. She was hoping that Leonard might have grown weary of the conflict by now—that this thing with Cal had been nothing more than a midlife-crisis situation—and he would, once again, be ready for the mature stability that Jill could offer. If so, Cal, being an adult now, undoubtedly with money of her own, would not be living in the same house with them anymore and they could have some semblance of normality again.

* * *

Once In a Lifetime was a moderate success, but Cal stayed with it for only three months. Acknowledging that Leonard was right about the theatre's becoming a wedge between them, she chose to leave the play of her own volition. After her final performance, the troupe gave Cal and Leonard a goodbye party before their move back to California. Also invited to the party was Leonard's family, who had been given special front-row seats that evening for the show. It's a sad reality, Cal realized, that a move means leaving some good friends behind. But, then again, she would probably be seeing some of her old coworkers again in California. In her years in the business, she had made many friends and was always happy when their paths crossed again. She knew that, when Leonard had been doing primarily Westerns, many of the same character actors showed up in the same films over and over, and strong friendships developed as a result. He found himself working time and time again with Ray Cooper and Doug Medford, perhaps because these three were considered among the best character actors in the business. Such repetition wasn't as evident in other types of pictures, however. So when Cal learned she was in a picture with someone she had worked with in the past, it was quite a treat.

Saying goodbye to her stage career was very difficult for her. Leonard's suggestion, though, that she go back to it for a short time now and then helped her in the transition. At least it was not a final and complete farewell.

Once again, Mrs. Morris agreed to move with them. "Whither thou goest, I will go," is how she phrased it. A more loyal employee was not to be found anywhere.

As Leonard, Cal, and Mrs. Morris boarded the plane to take them to their new homes, which had been secured by George, Cal was thinking with a tear in her eye how appropriate the lyrics were to "Give My Regards to Broadway."

* * *

"I'm so glad you're back for good!" Becky said excitedly when Cal greeted her at the door.

"Wow, Becky, you're looking great! How're the kids?"

"Oh, doing good. Let me see your new place. I'm sure you have a media room somewhere, and a study for Leonard."

Cal laughed. "Yeah, I guess all our houses have to have those things. The kitchen is the next-most-important feature." She gave her a guided tour of the two-story white brick house. "Did you notice the blue shutters? I've always wanted a blue and white house, and now I finally have one. Len said he'll even have the door painted blue, too."

"And, Cal," Becky said, with eyes wide, "when I talk to Nate, it seems he couldn't care less where you are."

"You didn't tell him we moved back, did you?"

"No, but I'm sure you'll see him around. He's back in the industry. He had a small part in a film last month. But I really and truly don't think you have a thing to worry about. There seems to be no malice in him at all anymore. He seems almost serene, if you can imagine that."

"I've never seen him like that."

"Me, neither, until now. I wish you didn't live so far away from me. We can't walk to each other's houses anymore. You want me to let you know next time your old house is for sale?"

"No, that's okay. I like this one. Blue trim, you know."

"Tell me about Stacy. I can't believe she's so grown up now."

"Yeah, she's an exchange student in France for a semester. Wasn't it only a year or two ago that she was a little bitty thing? I remember when she was learning to walk."

"Yeah. You remember her first word?"

"Damn," they said in unison. They both laughed, then Cal winked. "That's when Len figured he'd better stop using language like that at home. Thank you, Stacy!"

*   *   *

"Eeeewwww, Len. How could you play such a detestable character?" Cal asked that evening after he had related to her the story line of his new picture, to begin production soon.

"Why, Cal Rhoads, whatever could you mean?" he asked with mock innocence. "I'm the mayor, a public servant. How could I be detestable?"

"A crooked one! You fix the elections, you ruin people's businesses, and you take bribes. That's got to be the worst character you've ever played. They packed everything bad into one person."

"The writers really outdid themselves this time, didn't they? I wonder why they wanted *me* to play it," he smiled good naturedly.

"Okay, okay," she acknowledged his mirth. "You're going to enjoy this, aren't you?"

"Well, like you say, film work can be boring. At least, when I'm the bad guy, I can liven things up a bit."

"I've noticed that. If the script isn't colorful enough, you improvise and make your character even meaner, don't you?"

"Sometimes. Once you get to know your director, you can tell whether or not you can get away with things like that. In fact, some of them even welcome it."

"I'm probably the only one who watches your pictures and roots for the bad guy." She thought a minute, then, "Hey, Len?"

"What?"

"You think I could play a bad guy?"

"You couldn't be convincing as *any* kind of a guy." He looked at her from different angles and frowned. "Nope, not even from the back."

"You know what I mean. An accomplice, maybe. Or even the main bad person, the one who thinks up the bank robbery and carries it out."

He then realized she was serious. "I don't know. Can you dredge up some venom? Can you completely—and I mean utterly, fully, totally, *completely*—forget who you really are and become a person like that?"

"I think so."

"While you're a much better actress now than you were ten years ago, I think you still keep a tentative grasp on reality when you're working. You never seem to quite lose sight of who you really are."

"Wish I could get over that."

"If you want to play parts that are contrary to who you are, that would be advisable. On the other hand, look at Pat Boone. He holds fast to a certain ideal and has had a successful career. His options are limited, though. You've accepted more diversity than he would already."

"I think I could play an accomplice, though. Maybe not the thoroughly evil person, but I could play the person who goes along for the ride."

"And you could easily play the person who is doing something bad for an honorable reason. Something like that would fit in with the image most people seem to have of you."

"Like stealing food in order to feed my family?"

"Exactly. In fact, doing something like that would be a good career move for you. It combines what the audience already thinks they know about you with a new side, a darker side. You see, Cal, the public has finally accepted you as an adult, but they still see you as a good person. You need to take them with you on your journey from respectable woman to desperate criminal. They will accept it if they understand it."

"I wish I were a screenwriter. Then I could make my part to order."

"Tell Michael what you have in mind. Maybe he knows of something coming up with a role like that."

"You remember that clip we watched the other day of the guy on a horse getting hung? What would happen if the horse, in reality, would bolt? What keeps the actor from really getting hung? Surely, they have safeguards, but what are they?"

"Three things. First of all, the rope around his neck probably wasn't fastened to anything so if he fell, it would go down with him. Second, his hands probably weren't really tied behind him. If they showed the tied hands at all, you'd notice they're not tightly bound. Also, most of the scenes were close-ups, so you couldn't see when there was a trainer down there controlling the horse. No, Cal, a good production company wouldn't risk a valuable actor's life by neglecting those safeguards."

"Whew!" she sighed with relief, as she thought of the tightrope scene she was to do in the next picture Michael had arranged for her.

*   *   *

Mrs. Morris answered the phone. "Yes, she's right here. Just a moment." She held the phone out to Cal. "It's Becky."

"Hi, Becky. How's it going?"

"Pretty good. Is Leonard there, too?"

"Yeah. He's upstairs."

"Good. Nate wants to come see you both."

Cal almost dropped the phone. "Why? And how's he know we're here?"

"Everyone knows you're here, Cal. I didn't tell him, but he found out. He says he wants to talk to you both and he asked me to set it up."

Silence.

"Are you there?" Becky asked.

"Yeah."

"I can come with him, if that would make you feel better."

"I don't want him to know where we live."

"Okay. You come to my house, then."

"I'll have to ask Len."

"Ask him now while I'm on the line. I'll hold."

"Becky? Are you *sure* he's not mad, anymore? Is he really serene?"

"Yes, Cal. He is. Really!"

Still unconvinced, Cal mumbled, "I don't know. I just don't know."

"You're going to encounter him sooner or later anyway. You might as well do it in a controlled environment."

She sighed. "I'll go ask Len." She put the phone down and went upstairs.

*   *   *

"I'm glad you came," said Nate as he shook Leonard's hand and ushered them to Becky's living room. Cal took her husband's hand as they moved toward the sofa. Once Leonard had seated himself, she sat very close to him, holding onto his knee; and he put his arm around her shoulders protectively.

"Drinks, anyone?" Becky asked.

"No, thanks," Leonard said. "What's on your mind, Nate?"

"I wanted to apologize to you both. I am so sorry I caused you such grief and pain. And I want to thank you, Leonard, for intervening when you did. You prevented a disaster."

349

Leonard and Cal looked at each other. She didn't know what to say. Becky was right—Nate's demeanor now was utterly peaceful. The resentment and animosity was gone from his eyes, replaced now with good will.

Nate continued, "I've had ten years to think about what I did, and I regret it more than you'll ever know. Every day of my life, I thank God that you were there, Leonard."

"Me, too," Cal said.

"If I could rewrite history, I would. Please accept my apologies. Please forgive me."

"See, Cal?" Becky asked. "I told you."

Nate added, "I left prison smarter. I don't plan to ever go there again." He looked back at Cal and Leonard. "I see I'm going to have to earn your trust. It was kind of naïve of me to assume you'd be this quick to forgive." He got back to his feet. "I'll work hard to earn it, Cal. In time, you'll realize I really mean what I'm saying. So long." He left, closing the front door behind him.

Cal glanced out the window and watched as Nate walked down the sidewalk and out of sight.

Becky asked, "Well? What do you think?"

"He's like a completely different person," Cal replied.

"Yes! He seems sincere to me."

Leonard lit a cigarette. "Must be. He's not that good of an actor."

Chapter 28

CAL COULD HARDLY WAIT for Leonard to come home. As soon as he stepped in the doorway, Mrs. Morris starting putting dinner on the table and Cal ran to meet him. "Guess what? Michael found me a bad-guy role."

"A film or guest spot?"

"On a TV detective show. Doing a crime for a good reason, just like you said."

"Great!" He thumbed through the mail, then set it back down. "When?"

"Next month. My part's about finished on the picture, so now I can get back to the TV stuff I like."

They strolled together into the dining room and sat down for dinner.

"This might be the start of a whole new image, Cal. One that you can really have fun with."

"And he's got me another guest spot as a teacher on a sit-com next week. I guess, now that I'm in my thirties, I can't pass as a student anymore."

"He's a good agent, Cal. I'm really glad we moved back out here because he's getting us so much work. Otherwise, I'd be gone a lot."

"Yeah. It's a good move. I liked New York a lot, but California seems more like home to me."

As Mrs. Morris finished bringing the meal to the table, Leonard rubbed his right ear. "There's still a ringing in there."

"A ringing in your ear? Why?" Cal asked.

"It's a scene we did today. Doggone if that woman didn't spend the whole time screaming in my ear. A shrill, high-pitched scream. I got that scene over with as soon as I could. If my character hadn't killed her, I would've."

* * *

Cal found her way into the studio where the television sit-com was to be made. It wasn't very far away from the studio where she had made many of her first films. The script was interesting. She had never played a school teacher before and tried to remember all she could about the ones she encountered during her student days. She decided, if the director was agreeable, to pattern her character after Mrs. Hanfield.

Cal looked around to see if there were any familiar faces among the cast and crew. Jonathan was the first to catch her eye. He was the same cameraman with whom she had worked on a *Prairie Days* episode so many years ago. Then, there was Maxine, who refreshed their makeup between takes. Someone was standing in the back behind the lights and raised his hand in greeting. Who was it? She took a few steps to get a better view, then gasped. It was Nate!

"Its okay," she said to herself. "Calm down, Cal." It didn't do any good. Her heart was beating too hard.

He saw her discomfort and rushed to reassure her. "I didn't mean to upset you, Cal. I just wanted to watch you at work. Becky told me you've gotten really good and I wanted to see. If it bothers you for me to be here, I'll leave."

"It might be kind of hard to concentrate on my work with you around."

"All right. I understand." He patted her on the back, then went behind the lights, gathered up his things, and left.

She watched him go and wondered—He *seemed* trustworthy. Was he really? She wasn't sure.

"Hey, Cal!" came a voice from behind her. It was Shirley, one of the regulars on the show. She had worked with her once in a short-lived play several years earlier.

"Hi, Shirley. It looks like you've landed a better role this time, huh?"

"Oh, yeah. This is our third season. How come you're shaking? There's nothing to be nervous about here. Not like standing in front of eight hundred people and doing a play, that's for sure."

"We have a couple scenes together, don't we?"

"Yeah, and you stinker! You're going to give me detention," she joked.

Cal grinned. "Well, then, don't pass notes to your boyfriend and I won't."

"You just can't reason with substitute teachers," Shirley good-naturedly mumbled as she headed toward the conference room. "Come on. This is where we go on Mondays."

Cal followed.

* * *

The rest of the week went smoothly. Unfortunately, the director didn't want her to play the part like Mrs. Hanfield but, rather, more like Mrs. Gummel. This might have been a blessing in disguise, though, Cal reasoned. Being less than likable in this show might help the audience accept her next character, who would end up committing a crime. She enjoyed working with Shirley, Jonathan and Maxine again; and Nate did not return after that first day.

*   *   *

"Hey, Michael, can you line up lots of TV shows for me like you do for Len? They're a lot of fun, and I'd love to have steady work like that."

"Would you be agreeable to some less-savory parts than what you're accustomed to?"

"Sure. The way I'm feeling these days, I think I can handle any kind of role."

"Okay. There's one open for an abusive young mother. How about that?"

She hesitated. "Anything else available? I'd rather not do that one."

"Let's see. Oh, here's one for an operatic prima donna. You'd need padding for that one."

"Would I have to do my own singing? I can do choir singing, but not solos."

"That could be dubbed."

"I think I could do it, then."

"She's an obnoxious character, Cal. Are you sure?"

"Yeah, as long as it doesn't conflict with the detective show I'm doing next month. Len can teach me how to be obnoxious."

"Okay, I'll see if I can set it up."

"And other ones, too, Michael. I want to work every week if I can."

"I'll do my best."

*   *   *

"An operatic prima donna? How would *I* know how to play that?" Leonard asked.

"Because he said she's an obnoxious character. You specialize in obnoxious."

"But I know nothing about opera. You need to do some research."

"Where? How?"

"At the opera house. Go to opera rehearsals, get to know the performers, observe the most temperamental ones and listen to what their coworkers say about them."

"But I've only got two weeks."

"Good luck," he shrugged.

Cal asked George to help her find such information, but came up short. There were no operas scheduled in that part of the state in the next two weeks. They went to the public library and found much information about operas in general, but nothing specifically about the temperament of prima donnas. Retired opera stars were reticent about such things.

"What should I do, Len? There's nothing. Do you think I'd be able to bluff my way through it?"

"Let me see the script," he said. She handed it to him and he leafed through it. After a few moments, he shook his head and gave it back to her. "It leaves a lot of the details up to individual interpretation. If you knew a lot about the subject, you could interpret it just fine. But you don't. I'd advise you not to attempt it."

"But I'm trying to branch out."

"That's fine, but don't hang yourself. Do only those roles you're prepared for. Remember the disaster I showed you when I tried to play a manic-depressive without being well prepared?"

"Yeah."

"Don't make that mistake."

"I hate to admit to them that I can't do it."

"That's better than *showing* them that you can't do it. At least this way, they still have time to find an actress who knows the subject."

She sighed. "Okay."

Leonard handed her the phone and dialed Michael's number. "Next time, don't get yourself into a situation like this."

*　*　*

Cal confessed to Michael that she was unable to do that role, so he worked to get other ones for her. As usual, he did a fine job. She now had a half dozen appearances lined up, sometimes on consecutive weeks; and most of these shows needed no extra preparation. The one she was looking forward to the most, though, was the detective show. The billing was great and the script was excellent. She would be the special guest star, playing a nurse in a terminal-care unit who, in order to shorten her patients' time of suffering, would overdose them on drugs. Cal felt she could play that part well because it dealt with an issue about which she felt keenly. Her character would end up going to jail because of her compassion.

*　*　*

The time for work on the detective show had come. Leonard's film was over and his next one was to begin the following month, so he went with Cal each day and watched the show's filming. They were now on their way home after the final scene had wrapped.

"I think this show will start people thinking," Leonard said. "It dealt with the issue fairly, stating both sides."

"Yeah. The opponents say mercy killing is a crime because people might do it when the patient is not all that terminal. So why don't they write some guidelines? Make it mandatory for two or three doctors to agree that it's a hopeless case? Then that person can be put out of his misery."

"They would probably argue that by saying nothing is truly hopeless. Miracles happen every day."

"Well, yeah, but it seems that if God wants to miraculously heal that person, He could do it no matter what we do. I mean, He's mightier than people are."

"Another argument is that mercy killing is 'playing God.'"

"So is abortion, but they seem to have no problem with that. And that's another thing—Why is it perfectly okay in the eyes of society for people to kill an innocent unborn baby who has no way to defend itself, but it's a crime to go next door and shoot your neighbor, who *can* defend himself?"

He said, "The reasoning on the other side is that a woman should be able to do whatever she wants with her own body."

"So why can't she go next door and squeeze her trigger finger? That's doing whatever she wants with her own body, too."

Leonard reached over and patted her on the knee. "You better keep your opinions about such a hotly-debated issue to yourself if you don't want to lose half of your fan base."

"But this is America. We have the freedom of speech."

He shook his head. "No, it's Hollywood."

Sometimes she missed being just plain ol' Cal, one of many Dallas residents who could enjoy America's hard-won freedoms.

Chapter 29

LEONARD LEARNED THAT HIS NEXT FILM was first being shot in France, then later in Belgium. They were relieved that the ringing was gone from his ears now, and he made a mental note to avoid scenes like that in the future. He was now packing for his early-morning flight, while Cal was sitting on the bed, watching.

"You'll be gone a long time," she noted.

"It sure looks that way. How's your schedule? Can you make a visit or two while I'm gone? I know you've got a lot of TV work lined up."

"Golly, I really want to, because I've never been to either of those countries before. But I don't think I'll have enough time to do it. Michael has me doing a different show every week for the next few weeks. Maybe, by the time you're in Belgium, I'll have more than two days off at a time."

He nodded. "Sure. We don't know the exact date we'll be going there yet. Depends on how quickly we can get the parts done in France. I'll let you know when I know."

"Maybe you'll see Stacy while you're in France."

"I plan to give her a call and maybe meet her for dinner somewhere. I'd like to meet the family she's staying with, too."

Cal nodded, "That's a good idea." She watched in silence as he put a dozen pairs of sox in the suitcase. Then she asked casually, "Is Jill still over there?"

"I think so. Why?"

"Just wondering."

He looked around. "Where's my script?"

"On the dresser." She watched him pack the script and his electric shaver. "What if she calls and wants to get together with you. Would you do it?"

"Who?"

"Jill."

"Oh. I guess I would. Why?"

She sighed. "Just wondering."

He smiled. "Are you worried about that?"

"Oh, maybe," she shrugged.

"Why?"

She shrugged again. "I don't know."

He stopped packing and leaned against the wall, arms crossed. "Yes, you do know. Tell me."

"Well, it seems to me that she's changed her mind about you and wants you back."

"So what?"

"So she's a lot prettier and nicer than me, and I'm worried you'll go back to her."

"Do you *really* think that?"

Cal nodded.

He resumed his packing. "She is pretty and she is nice. You're right about that. Maybe that's what a lot of men look for in a woman. As for me, though, I go for spunky. And, believe me Cal, you can out-spunk Jill any day. And besides…" With a mischievous gleam in his eye, he paused for dramatic effect, then continued, "she's too old for me."

"Forty-six is too old?"

"Most assuredly!"

Cal smiled at the absurdity, but the fear wouldn't go away. "I hear France is a real romantic country."

"That's why I wish you'd come visit while I'm there. We'd be together in the world's most romantic place."

She went over to him and put her arms around him. He returned her embrace. "Well, actually," she said, "I think this room is the world's most romantic place."

"You just might be right," he agreed, as he kissed her forehead. "But don't tell the French Ambassador that. He'd be awfully disappointed that Paris would come in second."

*   *   *

It had been a long day. It really began last night with a wonderfully-romantic evening of love, an evening she would remember for a long time. *Hopefully,* she thought, *he will, too. At least, until he gets back home.* Then she got up earlier than usual this morning to take Leonard to the airport, and went directly from there to the studio to work on the television show she was doing this week—a science fiction/comedy series. This one was going to be fun, she felt. It's a shame Leonard wasn't here; he would have enjoyed watching her transformation into an alien for the show. She would see if she could get a tape of this episode for him.

Now she was back home, trying to stay awake through dinner with Mrs. Morris. It had become their tradition for Mrs. Morris to have dinner with her while Leonard was out of town. They had invited her to join them when he was home, too, but she refused, insisting on giving them their privacy.

"And, for dessert, chocolate frosted brownies," she said, bringing in a plate of the luscious treat.

"Oh, Mrs. Morris, you knew *exactly* what I needed—a healthy dose of chocolate." Cal took one off the top and savored every bite. "Oh, this is heaven."

"Have you noticed I always make something chocolate for you the first day Leonard's gone? It seems to cheer you up."

"I never noticed that. Today, though, I'm too tired to need cheering up. Maybe tomorrow. Let's see, there's a dozen. There will probably be a couple left for tomorrow."

"You know, Cal, you're really lucky. You can enjoy desserts, and snack in the evenings, and still not gain weight. It's much more difficult for most actresses."

"People tell me when I hit forty is when weight gain will happen. Luckily, I have a few more years to go yet." She thought for a minute, then, "I wonder if there's chocolate in heaven."

Mrs. Morris smiled. "It's my guess that we won't need it there."

Cal finished her brownie and stood up to take her dishes to the kitchen.

"Oh, don't bother with that, Cal. You're tired. Why don't you just go on to bed? I'll take care of everything here and lock the door behind me when I leave at 8:00."

"Okay. I'm bushed." She hugged Mrs. Morris. "Good night." Then she went upstairs, donned her nightgown, and dropped, exhausted, onto the bed. She rolled over onto Leonard's side of the bed and, within seconds, she was sound asleep.

⋆　⋆　⋆

Cal was on her way home from the studio the next evening when the power steering on her car ceased functioning. Fighting panic, she took her foot off the accelerator. As the car drifted slower and slower, she tugged hard to get it onto the side of the road, where it eventually came to a stop. Cal took the key out. She was a couple of miles from the nearest service station. What to do now? She made a vow then and there to get a car phone at the next opportunity. But, for now, she just sat in the car and debated what to do. *Sooner or later*, she reasoned, *a policeman's bound to come by and help.*

Another car pulled off and stopped behind her, then another behind that. *Oh, good,* she thought. *Lots of helpers.* Cal turned around to see if it was someone she knew. No, it was a rather seedy-looking stranger. She was glad her windows were up before the power went out. She reached down and manually locked her door. The man came and stood at her window. She motioned for him to go on, that she didn't need help; but he didn't leave. The way he was looking at her seemed absolutely *predatory* to her. There's no way she would unlock that door to him. He tried to open her door. Then he went to the other side of the car. She reached over to lock that door, but he had already started opening it. Her heart pounded hard and fast. The best alternative seemed to be for her to get out since he, apparently, was planning to get in. Perhaps he just wanted the car and had no intention of harming her. If so, he would get a surprise when he tried to drive it home. She got out of the driver's side. He left the other side and started coming back around the car toward her, a wild look in his eyes. *Oh, no,* Cal thought, *he must be on drugs or something.* She held her breath and wondered what to do now. As he came closer, she took a few steps backward.

"Leave her alone!" came a loud voice behind her. She turned to find Nate hurriedly approaching. It was then Cal realized that his was the other car that had stopped behind hers. He walked around her and grabbed the man by the collar.

"I was just going to help," the man said meekly.

"Sure you were. I'll take care of it," Nate said as he pushed him away from her.

The man went back to his own car and hastily drove off.

Cal heaved a sigh of relief. "Thanks, Nate."

"What happened to your car?"

"The power steering and brakes went out."

"I'll call a tow truck to take it to the garage, then I'll give you a ride home." He went back to his car and made a call on his cell phone. Then he came back to where she was still standing. "Do you need to be anywhere soon?"

"Home. Mrs. Morris is waiting dinner for me."

"Tell you what. I'll take you there real quick, then I'll come back here to wait for the tow truck. Do you need me to rent you another car while yours is being fixed?"

"No, I can use Len's." As soon as she said that, she regretted it. Now he knew that Leonard was out of town.

"That's good. Come on, then." He motioned for her to follow him to his car, they got in, then Cal reluctantly gave him directions as Nate drove her home.

* * *

She watched him pull back out of her driveway and leave, and decided that, yes, he must have truly reformed. Not only did he defend her from that awful-looking stranger, but he also took care of the car problem. Once at her house, he walked her to the door but made no attempt to stay.

She went inside and closed the door with a smile. He was no longer a threat. In fact, he was now an ally! Hell must've frozen over!

*   *   *

The phone rang that evening as she was getting ready for bed. It was Leonard.

"How was your flight?" she asked.

"Long, as always. And it was a 747, so we didn't get to see a movie upstairs in the first-class section. But at least the seats there are large enough."

"I hope you got some sleep on the plane. We didn't get a whole lot the night before you left, did we?"

He laughed. "Thanks for the memories."

"*Keep* remembering that so when some French woman tempts you, you'll remember what's waiting for you here."

"No problem, Cal."

"My car broke."

"What happened?"

"The power steering and brakes went out on my way home tonight."

"Oh, no. Did it cause an accident?"

"No. I got it to the side of the road and stopped. But it was scary. A real weird-looking guy stopped and looked like he was going to rob me or something. You'll never guess who chased him away."

"Who?"

"Nate! He happened to be driving along that road a little behind me and he stopped to help. He got rid of that guy, called the tow truck, and drove me home. I was really well taken care of."

"He didn't linger, did he?"

"No. That's another thing—he didn't even try to stay. I'll use your car while mine's being fixed, okay?"

"Sure. Get some gas on your way to work tomorrow. It's getting low."

"Okay. I've got to get a copy for you of the show I'm finishing now. You'll get a kick out of it. I'm playing an alien. I keep saying how cold it is on Earth, that their sun's not as warm as ours on Mercury."

"And I'm playing a pimp. What a pair we are!"

"Yeah. It seems like Halloween or something."

"Well, Cal, I've got to get to work. Just wanted to check in with you before you to go to bed."

"Okay. I miss you."

"I miss you, too. Goodnight, baby."

"G'night."

* * *

When filming was done for the day later that week, Leonard left immediately instead of engaging in banter with the director as he usually would. He had an appointment to meet with Stacy at a café near her temporary home. Sure enough, it was exactly where she said it would be. Stacy had a good sense of direction, unlike the other female in his life.

"Hi, Daddy!" she said happily as she rose from the outdoor table and rushed toward him.

He gave her a hug. "Hi, honey. You're looking good. How do you like it here?"

"Oh, it's terrific! I'm having a lot of fun. Come sit down with me and we can order something French. Everything around here's made with wine."

He joined her at the table. "I was hoping your host family would be here, too. I wanted to meet them."

"Well, they're not, but Mom will be here in a few minutes. When I told her you're coming, she wanted to come, too. My host family doesn't speak English at all. It's a good thing I know French so well. Otherwise, I'd be up a creek. I love French cuisine! That's one of the best parts of being here."

"You're sounding more like Cal every day."

She grinned. "Because the first thing I notice around here is the food?"

"That, and your tendency to flip from one subject to another so rapidly. If I didn't know better, I'd swear you were *her* daughter."

"There's a real cute boy right next door to the Dufays. His name is Philippe and he's sixteen. He has the cutest accent, a really romantic one."

"Don't get carried away."

"I'll try," she said with a sparkle in her eye.

"Are you having any trouble with the classes here, or are you fluent enough in the language to sail through school here like you do at home?"

"Oh, yeah, it's a breeze. I've taken French for three years, so I'm pretty good at it. Here she is. Over here, Mom!" she waved.

Jill spotted them and made her way to their table. She looked radiant and was very well dressed. "Hello, Stacy. Good evening, Leonard. It's good to see you again." She was wearing an exotic perfume.

He nodded, "Jill, how are you?"

"Enjoying every minute of this vacation, for which I thank you so much. We're both having the time of our lives."

"That's good. I hope you're keeping a watchful eye on Stacy."

"Oh, yes, I am."

The waiter arrived.

"Come on, Mom and Dad. Let's get sloshed on some French food."

*   *   *

As Leonard returned to his hotel room that night, he was thinking, *Cal was right about Jill, after all.* It seemed the man was always the last to know when a woman was coming on to him. The evening had started out pleasant enough, with a light meal and cordial conversation. They had taken Stacy back to her sponsors' home and met with the family. The language barrier was rather uncomfortable, even though Stacy was kept quite busy translating for both sides. But what was really bothering Leonard now was what happened after they left the Dufay home, and he and Jill were alone. She's lonely, she confided. It was a big mistake leaving him, she said. She had taken his arm as they strolled along the avenue. When their visit was over, she had kissed him goodbye.

What's going on? This is Your Life, with all these people from the past coming back to haunt us? he wondered. *First Nate, now Jill.*

He'd been good to her since their divorce—sent her checks regularly even though it wasn't required, visiting with Stacy whenever he could, sending them both to France. Maybe he had been *too* good to her. Maybe he was inadvertently giving her reason to think they had a future together. He had not known he would be on location in France until after they had agreed to the exchange-student program and encouraged Jill to go, too. If he *had* known, this awkward evening could have been prevented

Perhaps what disturbed him most was that he had, indeed, felt tempted. Jill had hinted strongly that Leonard would be welcome in her hotel room anytime, day or night. If he had been a younger man with less self control, he may have succumbed to that temptation. If Cal had not made her devotion to him absolutely clear on their last night together prior to this trip, he might have weakened.

Contrary to his screen image, Leonard was a man of relatively high moral standards, considering the Hollywood environment in which he worked and the promiscuous lifestyle that had become more and more the norm nationwide since the mid-1960s. The only times he had fallen short of his standards were with Cal and Jill, before they were married, and with Sheila Montgomery in high school. And, too, he hadn't been entirely honest with

Cal when they decided to marry. *Whether or not she would have married me a decade ago, she's totally committed to me now. That's what matters.*

And that is what gave him the strength to resist Jill's advances tonight.

* * *

"Where's the entertainment section?" Cal asked Mrs. Morris after dinner a few days later.

"They must have forgotten to give us one, but everything important is on the front page."

"I need my daily cryptogram. The sleuth in me needs to have a code to crack."

"How did work go today?"

"Oh, it went great. This week I'm a bank teller who's embezzling a couple zillion dollars. This is my first true 'bad-guy' role where I don't have any redeeming virtues. Michael wasn't real sure I could come off as bad as I should, so I'm doing my very best to do it convincingly so he'll get me more roles like this. I'm trying to remember everything Len told me and everything I've seen him do in his roles."

"I've got to admit, I can't picture you as an evil character."

"I want to be like Len and be able to play any kind of part there is. He's got to be the world's best actor. Why on earth hasn't he won any Oscars, I'd like to know? Why can't those judges see the obvious?"

"Cal," she patted her shoulder. "Leonard is a very, very good actor. But there are many good actors in the industry and only so many Oscars to go around."

"Other organizations have given him awards. If other places see his talent, why can't the Oscar folks? Just think what an Oscar would mean to him."

"It would be impressive, wouldn't it?"

"Yeah. Wish I had the power to give him one. Maybe I can have a baby boy and name him Oscar," she joked.

"Would you like to have children of your own?"

"Golly, yeah, but Len doesn't want anymore. So I pretend Stacy is mine."

"That's a very good compromise. You have been quite an influence on her through the years."

"She's a sweetie. Wish I could be with Len this week. He's going to be seeing her soon, if he hasn't already. I sure do miss that kid."

* * *

During a break in filming the next day, Cal noticed a coworker with the entertainment section of the previous night's newspaper. "When you're done, can I have that?" She looked around for a pencil so she could work the cryptogram.

Milly looked at her uneasily. "Are you sure you want it?"

"Yeah, why?"

"You don't know?"

"Know what?"

Milly reluctantly turned the paper around to show Cal. In the gossip column was a photo of Leonard walking arm-in-arm with Jill. Underneath were a couple of sentences suggesting a love triangle.

"That picture must be twelve or thirteen years old," Cal said. Then, she looked at it more closely and saw, in the background, French words on the store signs. Her heart sank. She looked again at the photo. Jill looked exquisite, as always, with every hair in place. She was glowing. Cal turned the page to the cryptogram and tried to work it, but she just couldn't concentrate on that. She was glad when she was needed on the set again. Working kept her mind off personal concerns. She gave the performance of her life that day.

*   *   *

When work was over that evening, she saw Nate on her way out the door. "How're you doing, Nate?"

"Oh, pretty good. Do you need a ride home?"

"No, thanks. My car's fixed now. It's a good thing I stopped it by turning off the ignition. They said if I had put the emergency brake on instead, I might've ruined it."

He walked with her to her car. "You look kind of down today."

"When's your next film? You're back working again, aren't you?"

"It starts in about three weeks. Can I take you out to dinner? That might cheer you up."

She thought for a minute. *Mrs. Morris probably has dinner cooking already, but dinner out would be nice for a change.* "Okay. Let me call Mrs. Morris and tell her to save tonight's dinner for tomorrow night."

"You can use my car phone."

"Okay." They went to his car. He held the door open for her while she slipped into the passenger seat and placed her phone call. He then closed her door, got into the driver's seat, and started the engine. Mrs. Morris took her suggestion graciously, expressing pleasure that tomorrow's dinner will be a cinch to prepare since it was already cooked. All she'd have to do would be to reheat it. Satisfied that all was well, Cal hung the phone back up. "Dinner's put away in the freezer."

"I know a good place," he said. "Would you like to eat French tonight?"

"*No!* Definitely not French. Anything but that."

He tried to repress a smile. "Okay. You name the place."

"How about Huck Finn's? I'm in the mood for a big, sloppy double cheeseburger. The more calories, the better."

"Will do." He pulled out of the parking lot and headed south.

"And chocolate. I need some gooey chocolate."

"How about a thick chocolate milkshake to go with the burger?"

"Yeah. That'll work."

"Becky's right. You've turned into a darn good actress. I was watching you today."

"Thanks."

"Been taking lessons?"

"Not officially. Len's taught me a lot."

"He's a good teacher."

"He's a turkey," she mumbled.

He looked over at her. "What makes you say that?"

"Oh, nothing. Guess I'm just having a bad day."

"Are you referring to that piece in the paper last night?"

"Oh, you saw it, too, huh? I bet the whole world saw that."

"Kind of shocking, isn't it?"

"I'll say!"

"Do you think they'll get back together?"

"How should I know?" she asked irritably. "I'll probably be the last to know. I don't think I'm hungry, after all. I'm too upset to eat."

They approached a red light and stopped. He turned to her. "Would you rather go to my place?"

It'd serve Len right, Cal thought. "Sure. Why not?" She hoped there would be some newspaper photographers there and the pictures would be immediately flashed all over the world, especially France.

He changed lanes, and now they proceeded eastward. As they neared his street, she started having second thoughts. How could she betray Leonard? She didn't know for sure he was being unfaithful.

The car pulled into Nate's driveway and came to a stop. He got out, but Cal hesitated, so he went around and opened her door for her.

"I can't stay long," she said as she exited the car. "I've got to learn my lines for tomorrow."

He unlocked and opened his front door. She slowly entered his house. He followed her and closed the door behind him.

Mrs. North hurried into the room. "Oh, you're home, Mr. Jenkins. Shall I tell Mrs. O'Donnell to begin dinner for you and your guest?"

He looked over at Cal. "Can I interest you in dinner now?"

"No. I'm not hungry."

"Not even for chocolate mousse?"

"Oh, well, maybe that would be okay."

He nodded to Mrs. North, "Ask her to whip up some mousse."

"Yes sir." She went to the kitchen.

"Come in here," he said as he led Cal past the sitting room into the living room.

She had never seen this part of his house before. It was quite large and beautifully decorated. "I can't believe you live in this huge house all by yourself."

"'Deed I do."

"And you decorated it?"

"No. A professional did." He put some soft music on the stereo.

"I really can't stay long," she fidgeted.

Nate took her right hand and put his other arm around her waist, leading her in a slow, lazy dance in rhythm to the music. It felt good and so soothing.

He drew her closer as they swayed to the music. Cal felt herself relaxing now and rested her head on his shoulder.

"Nice way to unwind after a hard day," he murmured.

"Yeah," she sighed.

"I wonder if Leonard and Jill are doing this right now."

She stiffened. "I don't want to think about that."

"While you're being the faithful wife, he's in romantic Paris with her. What're you going to do about that? Are you going to let him take you for granted?" He lifted her chin and looked into her eyes. "Let's give him a dose of his own medicine." Nate kissed her passionately, and she found herself kissing him back. Oh, how she wished Leonard could see this! Breathing heavily, he clutched her more tightly and kissed her neck.

That snapped her back to reality. What had she been *thinking*? What was she *doing* here? She didn't know about him, but when Leonard kissed her on the neck, it meant only one thing; and she had no intention of going that far with Nate. Cal pushed away from him. "I've got to go now. I'm sorry, Nate. I'm sorry I led you on. I've got to go."

"Please stay."

"No. I can't do this. Take me back to my car."

He looked at her with disgust, then turned off the stereo. "Okay. Let's go."

* * *

Cal drove around for a long time before going home. She didn't want to talk to anybody and was giving Mrs. Morris time to leave before she arrived home. In the meantime, she was wondering how her professional life could be doing so well when her personal life had gotten so out of control. The only reason she had encouraged Nate was to get back at Leonard. Thank goodness Leonard would never know about it. He'd never understand and she'd have a hard time explaining it to him. But, then again, if he *was* being unfaithful, it would serve him right. He *should* know about it. How could he do that? All the reassurances he gave her before his trip seemed now to be just empty words. Their night of lovemaking now felt meaningless. Cal felt so betrayed.

When she finally got home, the phone was ringing. It was Leonard.

"Did I catch you before you went to bed?" he asked.

She wondered if that was as innocent a question as it sounded. "I just got home."

"What's the matter, Cal? You sound different. Did you have a rough day?"

"Yeah, I guess you could say that. Have you seen Stacy yet?"

"Yes. We three had a nice dinner together at an outdoor café the other day."

"Three?"

"Jill joined us."

"I see Jill's looking as beautiful as ever."

"How could you see that? Have you become clairvoyant?" he mused.

"It was in the paper last night. You and Jill, arm-in-arm, in romantic Paris."

He hesitated. Then, "It's not the way it looked."

"And the caption said we're a love triangle."

"They're wrong."

Cal didn't know what else to say. She felt like either saying nothing, or saying every single thing that was on her mind. Anything between the two extremes just wouldn't do.

He repeated, "They're wrong, Cal."

No response.

"Look, Cal, she wanted to take a walk. She took hold of my arm. That's all it was, I swear."

"Right."

"You don't believe me, do you? I thought we trusted each other."

"I wish you were here right now."

"So do I."

"Then I could throw this telephone at you."

"Look at that picture again, Cal. Am I smiling? Do I look happy?"

"I don't know. I didn't look at you."

"You'll find that I *don't* look happy in that picture because I wasn't happy with the situation. I didn't even know she was going to be with us that night until I got there. Yes, Cal, I admit Jill did come on to me. But on a stack of Bibles I swear that I didn't do anything. And that's the way it'll stay—until I get home to you. Then I'll do plenty."

"Why?"

"Because I love *you*, Cal. I'd never do anything to jeopardize us. Never!"

"Really?"

"Really. Was that picture in a tabloid?"

"No. The daily newspaper. Everyone saw it."

"Damn!" he slammed the table with his fist. "Was it a gossip column, then?"

"Yeah. Donna Damond's."

"That figures. Don't believe anything in her column, Cal. I don't know why our paper runs it."

"Guess gossip sells papers."

"You're right about that. Okay now, tell me why you're just getting in. Did they have to do extra takes or what?"

"Well, no. It's… well," she stumbled. The guilt was gnawing at her, but there's no way she would give Leonard the complete rundown of her evening. He'd be furious if he knew what she had done.

"What?"

"Oh, just things, that's all."

"Cal, that's how you talk when you're trying to hide something from me. Come on, out with it."

"Well, first I was going to go out to dinner. I haven't eaten out in so long. Then I changed my mind and I listened to music for a while. Then I drove around a while."

"That's not like you. Usually you make a bee-line for home so you can have one of Mrs. Morris' dinners."

"Well, Len, let's just say I was feeling a little emotionally disturbed this evening, and let it go at that, okay?"

"All because of that picture?"

"Yeah."

"You know why they're doing this, don't you? Our images have changed. You were the cute little girl next door for a lot of years and I was the hero who gave you a home. There was very little criticism or innuendo printed about either of us then. Now you're an adult and doing roles that are less innocent, and I'm seen as the louse who dumped his wife for a younger woman. They're becoming less kind, more hurtful in what they print now. And, in order to sell papers, they're not above passing off conjecture as fact. It's just the price you're having to pay for achieving some degree of success in this business."

"So I guess we should be crying all the way to the bank, huh? As long as they spell our names right?"

"Different people have different ways of coping with it. Some people resort to suing the writers and the publications. In most cases, I think that's a waste of time."

"Yeah. Me, too."

"And you've got to admit that most publicity, even negative publicity, keeps our names before the public and helps our careers. But, Cal, just rest assured that, no matter what you see in papers, your place in my life is not threatened. You and my career come first. Stacy comes second. Jill's a nice lady, but she's not in the top ten."

"Oh, Len, I miss you. I wish I didn't have all these guest shots lined up so I could come visit."

"So you could throw something at me?"

"Well, right now that's not what I feel like doing."

"How about if we visit each other?"

"What do you mean?"

"I won't be working Friday, and maybe you can finish a little early, too. Then we can both fly to New York that night and stay in a hotel. We won't have to tell any of our friends or family that we're going to be there, so we can have the whole weekend to ourselves."

A big smile lit up her face. "That sounds like a dandy idea, Len!"

"Okay, baby. I'll make my reservations and you ask George to make yours. I'll let you know which hotel and room, and we'll meet there."

"Allllriiiight!"

*   *   *

"Well, that dear man did it again," Mrs. Morris marveled the next evening at dinner. "You miss him, he misses you, you both have schedules too busy to allow you to go to France or him to come here. So Leonard found the perfect solution, as he always seems to do."

"Yeah," Cal agreed. "He's a pretty smart guy, isn't he?"

"I hope you never doubt your love for each other. It became obvious to me shortly after I first came here."

"Really? That soon?"

She nodded knowingly. "I got a kick out of the way you two were trying to hide it."

"Guess you're a pretty smart cookie."

"And today you two care for each other even more than you did back then, though sometimes I fear you don't realize it."

"Well, it's kind of weird. Sometimes we drive each other crazy and we fight. But making up is always fun. In fact, sometimes I think we fight in order to have a reason to make up."

"It reminds me of the kind of relationship Liz and Dick were reputed to have."

"You know, I think location work is good for us. Being apart for a while gives us some breathing space. And, when we have a little rendezvous somewhere, it's so special."

"Just keep remembering those special times and what you find attractive about each other. That will help you through rocky times, which do happen in every marriage. Things sometimes get rough, but they'll always get better if you give it time."

"I can hardly wait to get to New York. I'll show Len how much more fun I am than Jill." She grinned wickedly. "He's going to be awfully tired when he gets back to France."

* * *

So that's how it works, Cal thought, as she left the studio the next day. The director had had to remind her today about the spiteful nature of her character. It seems her portrayal, while superb two days earlier, had now lost its edge. Thus, Cal discovered that when her personal life seemed to be in shambles, she gave a better performance. Apparently, Leonard was already aware of that phenomenon. That's probably why he would often provoke an argument with her right before an emotional scene. Inner turmoil must be the breeding ground for creativity. *Perhaps,* she thought, *that might be why great artists seem to be such tortured souls.*

"How can I expect viewers to be able to separate me from my characters if I can't do that myself?" she wondered. "Len does it so easily. Why can't I? Why am I such a slave to my emotions?"

After receiving counsel from her director, she made a conscious effort again to disassociate from herself as she became her character, and her performance much improved. *I've gotten too lax,* she thought. *I forgot the basics. Having roles that challenge will be a constant reminder of those basics.*

"Hi, Cal."

So engrossed had Cal been in her thoughts that she hadn't noticed Nate leaning against her car. "Hi," she answered as she fished her keys out of her purse. "Nate, do you ever have any trouble getting into character if the character isn't at all like you?"

"Sometimes. There has to be something in that character that I can identify with before I can play it. Why? Are you having trouble?"

"Yeah. I guess it's hard for me to identify with an embezzler."

"You didn't seem to have any trouble Monday. What's gone wrong?"

"I don't know." She leaned against her car, too. "An embezzler could be anyone. It's not like that's such an off-the-wall role."

"That might be part of the problem. There's no clear-cut way to play it."

"You might be right." She turned back toward the car and unlocked the door. "What're you doing here?"

"Just wanted to say hello. Got anything planned for tonight?"

"Dinner with Mrs. Morris. You want to join us? She's a great cook."

"Okay. Maybe after dinner, I can help you with your part. Are there any scenes in particular that you're having trouble with?"

"Well…" she thought for a minute. "I think the hardest scene is going to be the one we're doing tomorrow, when she's confronted by her boss and denies any wrongdoing. She intentionally lies. That's kind of complex."

"Instead of 'when she's confronted by her boss,' think of it as 'when I'm confronted by my boss.' That might make a big difference. I'll go over it with you and we'll see if that will help. Okay?"

"Sure. Are you going to follow me in your own car?"

"Yeah. I'll meet you there." They each entered their cars and headed toward her house.

*　*　*

"Well, Mrs. Morris, Cal was sure right. She said you're a great cook," he said as he folded his napkin and set it beside the plate.

"Thank you," she replied. "I'm glad you could come tonight."

"Yeah, Mrs. Morris is super," Cal said, as she rose from her chair. "If we're all finished with supper, let's work on that scene now. I need to pack my suitcase, too, so I don't have a whole lot of time."

He stood, too, as Mrs. Morris began clearing the table. "Suitcase? Where are you going?" he asked.

"Len and I are going to meet in New York for the weekend. I want to go to bed early tomorrow night since it'll be real late Friday before I get to sleep again, so that's why I need to pack tonight. Come on." She led him into the living room, where they had plenty of space.

"Okay. Where's the script?" he asked.

"Over here." She retrieved it from the hallway table, turned it to the correct page, and handed it to him.

He sat down to study the scene. "This will take a few minutes. If you want to be packing, I'll be ready by the time you're finished."

"You don't have to memorize it. Just read it."

"That's not the way I work. Take your time packing. By the time you're finished, I'll know the scene thoroughly. Go on."

"Well, okay." As she went upstairs, she thought to herself, *I'll never understand guys. All he has to do is read it.* She went into her room, got out the suitcase, and opened it on the bed. She got clothing out of her dresser and stacked it on the bed. *Will it be warm or cold in New York this time of year?* she wondered. *It could go either way. Better pack both warm and cool clothes, just in case.* She got more clothing out. With a wicked grin, she brought out the peignoir set that she had gotten in Virginia and laid it on the bed. *This'll be a weekend to remember, that's for sure. Shoes, sox, underwear, jeans, tee-shirts, a sweater. What else? Oh yeah, better pack the script for next week's show. There might be a few minutes to study it, while Len's showering or something.* She went into the study to fetch the script, then returned to the bedroom. *I'll pack my hairbrush and other last-minute things on Friday morning. Now for the hard part—getting all these things into one suitcase.* Leonard was good at it because he had traveled so much in his career, but Cal didn't have any system that worked. Her clothes always got wrinkled, no matter how she packed them. One by one, she carefully folded and placed some of the items into the suitcase. Then she remembered that Leonard rolled things together so that things that don't need to be wrinkle-free, like underwear, were in the middle, packed more tightly, and those that did, like slacks, were toward the outside. So she took everything out of the suitcase and started over. She would do almost anything to avoid having to iron in that hotel room. *We'll have a lot better things to do this weekend than ironing, that's for sure! Okay now, almost everything's in.* She carefully laid the peignoir overtop everything else and tried to close the suitcase. It would be a tight fit, she found. She sat on it, then clicked it shut. *Yay! Mission accomplished!* She put the suitcase by the bedroom door, turned off the light, then went back downstairs into the living room. "Are you ready now?" she asked.

He had been gazing out the window, and now turned to her. "I know it by heart."

"Golly, already? The whole scene?"

"That's right. Memorization has always come easy to me." He took his jacket off and draped it more carefully than usual over the arm of the sofa.

"Okay," she said. "Your character is at the desk and mine is coming in the door."

He pointed his finger at her. "No! Remember, it's '*You're* at the desk and *I'm* coming in the door.' Put yourself in your character's place and it'll be easier to think like she does."

"Oh, yeah. That's what Len says, too." She went to the doorway and rehearsal began:

She entered, then stopped cold in her tracks. "I didn't know you were here, Mr. Metcalf. I'll come back another time."

"Oh, no, Miss Hamilton. You have work to do. Go ahead and do it. Pretend I'm not here." He got up from behind his desk, walked around to the front, and sat on it.

"It's so late. Shouldn't you be getting home to your family?" she said while putting her log book into her teller drawer.

Nate broke in. "Cal, you don't look uncomfortable enough. Here you are with the evidence of the thousands of dollars you've embezzled right there in your hands; and if I see it, it'll be curtains for you. You want to get rid of it so I won't see it. You need to *look* guilty and put the log book into your drawer quickly and kind of clumsily, because you're distracted. Try it again."

"But I was being cold and calculating."

"I don't think that's the way he wants it done."

"Okay," she said as she retrieved the log book and returned to the doorway, and Nate sat at the desk.

She came into the room, then stopped suddenly. "I didn't know you were here, Mr. Metcalf." Her eyes darted from him to the teller drawer as she held the log book behind her. "I'd better come back another time."

"Oh, no, Miss Hamilton. You have work to do. Go ahead and do it. Pretend I'm not here." He moved around the desk and sat atop it.

"But it's so late. Shouldn't you be getting home to your family?" She hastily tossed her log book into her teller drawer. It fell out. She quickly retrieved it from the floor, stuffed it into the drawer and shoved it closed.

"Not at all. I wanted to discuss something with you, anyway." He reached behind him and picked up a portfolio. "Miss Hamilton, it seems that there might be a discrepancy in some of these reports. Have your accounts been balancing each day?"

She cleared her throat. "Well, of course. I always make sure they balance before I go home."

He stood up and approached her, holding a report up so she could see it. "This says otherwise. The tellers at this branch have been under investigation, and everyone else checks out. Let me see your log book."

This time, it was Cal who broke in. "At this point, it seems I should be shaking like a leaf. I don't know how to do that unless I'm really nervous."

"Not everyone shakes when they lie. You can just be fidgety, because the big boss is doubting your story."

Mrs. Morris peeked in the living room. "Excuse me, folks. If you don't need me for anything more, I'll be seeing you tomorrow. Cal, you'll find your breakfast on a covered plate in the refrigerator."

"Okay, thank you," Cal said. "Good night, Mrs. Morris."

Nate turned and waved. "Have a good evening, Mrs. Morris. Thanks for a wonderful dinner. I'll be leaving in a few minutes, too."

"You're welcome. Good night." She went back to the kitchen, retrieved her purse, and left through the back door.

"Don't go yet," Cal said to Nate. "Let's go over this scene some more. You're really helping a bunch."

"Where were we?"

Okay," Cal resumed. "I've got to be fidgety, but not shaky."

"That's right. Let's do it again. Start this time from my line, 'Not at all.'" He went back to the desk and put the portfolio back on it.

"Not at all. I wanted to discuss something with you, anyway." Reaching back, he picked up the portfolio. "Miss Hamilton, it seems that there might be a discrepancy in some of these reports. Have your accounts been balancing each day?"

She wrung her hands. "Well, of course they have. I always make sure they balance every day before I go home."

He stood up, advanced toward her and held the report up so she could see it. "This says otherwise. The tellers at this branch have been under investigation, and everyone else checks out. Let me see your log book."

"Uh, I think it's locked."

He went over and opened the drawer, retrieving the log book. He opened it.

She stepped away from him, then turned to face him with uncertainty. "Mr. Metcalf, I'll make you a deal."

"No, Cal. You're supposed to have come up with a great idea and look like you're thinking, 'Everyone's got a price, and I know what yours is.' But, instead, you're still looking defensive."

"Oh, okay. Back we go again, huh?"

"Let's go back to where I get the log book. Okay, I've opened the drawer, gotten the log book, and now I'm looking at it."

She stepped away from him, then turned around. When she faced him again, the uncertain look had left her eyes and she was now composed. "Mr. Metcalf, I'll make you a deal," she said with cool smoothness.

He put the log book down and looked at her skeptically. "And what might that be?"

"I understand you're going to be running for mayor in the next election."

"Well, as a matter of... ." Nate stopped abruptly and went over to the window. He watched Mrs. Morris' car turn the corner and disappear from sight. Then he pulled the drapes closed. He came back to Cal, putting his arms around her. His mood had changed dramatically and there was now cold contempt in his eyes. "Ten years," he uttered, barely above a whisper.

This turn of events confused Cal. "What? There's nothing about ten years in the script, and Mr. Metcalf never touches me."

"For ten years I rotted in that prison," he said, with more bitterness than Cal had ever heard from anyone anywhere. A cold chill went down her spine.

Her heart started beating fast and hard as she strained against his arms. "Nate, no. Please don't do this. You've come such a long way. Don't ruin everything now."

He pulled her in so tightly it felt as if the air had been squeezed from her lungs. "Ten long years! You're the one who put me in there, and in ten years time, you didn't come visit me even once. Becky came, but not you. You didn't give a damn about me. My career had been flying high, but it's all down the drain now because of you."

Feeling like the world's biggest fool for having believed Nate had changed, she struggled.

He once again had that look that she had feared so long ago—the look of uncontrolled rage. "Now you're going to pay for all you've put me through!" He then threw her violently onto the sofa, dropped across her and bit her hard on the neck.

"*Ow!* Stop it! Leave me alone!"

"Not until I get what I came for!"

Unable to kick him at that angle, she tried so hard to regain control of the situation. She scratched his face. She bit him. She punched him. She pulled his hair. She did everything she could think of, but to no avail. Nothing worked. Nothing!

*　*　*

Becky was putting her children to bed when the phone rang. She answered, but could barely make out what was being said. It sounded like Cal, but she was crying frantically.

"Cal? Is that you? What's the matter?"

There were words between the sobs, but they didn't make sense.

"Calm down, Cal. What happened?"

"I think he's dead," she sobbed. "I need you. Come over here."

"Who's dead? Leonard? Where are you?"

"Bethesda Hospital. The emergency room. Come quick. I need you."

"Okay. I'll be there as soon as I can get someone to stay with the kids. Hang in there. I'll be there soon."

Becky called Nate to see if he could watch the children. She just got his answering machine. She hung up and called her next-door neighbor.

* * *

Cal, pacing back and forth in the emergency room waiting area, couldn't make the tears stop. She looked at the clock. It was almost nine-thirty. She sure wished Becky would hurry up and get there. *What's taking the doctors and nurses so long?* she wondered. She was wringing her hands and looking out the window for Becky. There was no sign of her. She went back over to the admissions desk. "Any news yet? Why can't I see him?"

"Nothing more since last time. Please have a seat over there. We'll let you know when anything happens."

She started pacing again, looking up at the clock, then back at the closed double doors, behind which medical personnel had been valiantly laboring to preserve life.

Right then, the automatic door behind her swung open and Becky walked in. Cal ran to her and hugged her tightly. "I'm sorry, Becky. I didn't mean to kill him."

"Now calm down, Cal." Becky took her handkerchief out of her purse and wiped away Cal's tears. "Take slow, deep breaths. In and out. That's better." She led her distraught friend to the waiting area, away from the desk, and they sat on the divan. Becky handed Cal the hankie. "Now tell me what happened. Who died?"

"I've never been untrue to Len before and I wouldn't have been this time either except he forced me and I didn't want to do it. He did it, then he died. I think he did. I didn't mean to kill him."

"He did what? And who died?"

"Nate!"

Becky's face blanched.

Cal continued, "He was completely out at first, then he came around for a minute and said 'All I wanted from the beginning was a chance to love you,' then he started looking bad again, like he was dizzy or something, so then I called the ambulance but when they got there, I think his heart stopped again. They did the shock paddles and hooked him up to IVs, then they brought him here."

Tears made their way down Becky's cheeks. "What happened to him? He's not really dead, is he?" She took Cal firmly by the shoulders, "*Please* tell me he's not. Where is he? I've got to see him." She looked around for a nurse.

"I don't know what happened. All of a sudden, he just went to the floor."

"Where *is* he?"

Cal pointed to the double doors. "They won't let us go in. Oh, Becky, if Nate's not dead now, he *will* be if Len finds out what he did, then Len'll go to jail for sure. We can't let him know."

"Okay, okay. I've got to find out how Nate is." Becky left Cal and went to the nurse's station, showed them her ID, and talked with them for a few minutes. As the nurse picked up the phone and dialed, Becky returned to her friend's side. "She thinks he's still alive. She'll check on his condition for me. All we can do in the meantime is wait and pray." Becky took the handkerchief from Cal and wiped her own cheeks with it.

The nurse hung up the phone and walked over to the girls. She spoke directly to Becky, "They're admitting him into the third floor coronary care unit. When they have him settled and comfortable, you can go up to see him for a few minutes. We can't allow non-relatives to go with you, though. The doctor will be here to talk with you shortly."

Both girls sighed with relief. He's alive! Maybe he'll be okay after all.

As the nurse returned to her station, Cal's relief was replaced by shock. The meaning of the nurse's words had suddenly hit her. She stared at Becky. "You're *related* to Nate?" she asked.

"Well, yes."

"How're you related?"

"Cousins. His mother is my dad's sister. My parents took him in when his dad died, so he's been like a brother to me for most of our lives."

"So Nate's big-shot uncle is your *dad*? You've been his cousin all this time and you never told me? Why?"

"I thought you might have figured it out when you saw my dad at the hospital when Nate had pneumonia. Of course, that was a long time ago."

Cal stopped to think and to remember. It was over a decade ago, but she vaguely remembered an older man sitting in his room when she came to visit. Since Cal had never seen the CEO of Stagecraft Productions before or since that time, it didn't occur to her that that's who that man was.

Becky interrupted her thoughts. "I just didn't rub it in because I knew how much you hate Nate, and I was afraid that would make you hate me, too."

"No, I never hated him. Scared to death, maybe, but it wasn't really hate."

"You could've fooled me," Becky said.

A gray-haired doctor came through the double doors and approached them. "Which one of you is Mrs. Jenkins?"

Becky automatically held her hand up. "He's not married. I'm his closest relative."

"He had a myocardial infarction—a heart attack. His vital signs are back in the safe range now, but we're admitting him to the CCU upstairs, where he'll be monitored continually. Until more testing is done, I can't tell you what his prognosis is or the extent of the damage. His heart had already been compromised by rheumatic fever, but he's still relatively young, and that's working in his favor. In a few minutes, you can go to see him, but you can't stay long—just a few minutes each hour." He then looked to see if she had any questions. There being none, he then left.

Becky then stood. "I'm going to freshen up first, then go see him. Will you still be here when I get back?"

"Yeah."

Becky left.

A heart attack! Cal leaned back in the chair and pondered this with more than just a little guilt. If she hadn't put up such a fight, he might not have had a heart attack. He'd gone to bed with girls before and didn't. Why couldn't she be like all the other girls in the world, she wondered. None of this—the ten years of jail, all that resentment, the rape, the heart attack—would have happened if she had only treated him kindly from the very beginning.

*   *   *

The next day at work proved that Cal's new theory was correct. The director was very pleased with the way she portrayed Miss Hamilton in the confrontation scene. There was now plenty of turmoil in her personal life again, thanks to Nate, and she couldn't help putting a lot of emotion into her lines.

She had paid special attention this time to the method the make-up artist used to cover up the sore on her neck, and the woman let Cal take a tube of the camouflage crème home with her. That she didn't seem to think there was anything unusual about a woman showing up with a monstrous hickey on her neck while her husband's out of town simply amazed Cal. *This is sure a crazy business*, she thought.

*   *   *

Her flight got into New York about midnight, local time. She retrieved her luggage and took a cab. It was good to be back in New York. She would put all the events of the previous two days out of her mind and just enjoy this wonderful city and seeing her husband again. The less Leonard knew about that awful night, the better. She wished she had more than two days to spend here. As the cab made its way to the hotel, Cal watched the scenery go by, looking for all of the old, familiar places. Once into the hotel, she picked up the key and took the elevator to the eighth floor. Would he be there already, she wondered. He had a lot farther to go than she did. She opened the door. There he was in the chair by the lamp, reading the local newspaper. "Boy," she said, "if that isn't ever a familiar sight. I bet you aced every current-events test there was in school. How'd you get here so fast?"

Leonard put the paper down and rose to meet her. "I left very early this morning." He swept her into his arms and kissed her tenderly. "Oh, baby, I've missed you."

"Me, too, Len."

"Did you have a good flight?"

"Oh, yeah. Just not fast enough. How was yours?"

"The same. You know what else I've missed?" he asked, as he scooped her up and carried her to the bed.

"You don't know how glad I am to hear that." That was true in one way, but not in another. If he was hungry for love, that meant he hadn't been involved in any dalliances. She was glad about that, but now the very thought of making love made her stomach hurt. But this was her *husband*, she told herself. He loves her. He won't hurt her. And, besides, she didn't want to lose him to Jill.

He placed her on the bed, lay beside her, and stroked her hair. He lowered her collar and was about to kiss her neck, then, "What's this? Did you burn yourself?"

Her hand flew up to cover the sore. "Do the other side, okay?"

"What happened?" He gently pushed her hand away and took a close look at the welt. Then his puzzlement turned to fury. "It's *teeth* marks!" he roared. "What's this all about?"

"It's not what you think, Len."

"Who're you having an affair with?"

"Nobody!"

"I suppose you want me to believe you did this to yourself." He looked at her in disgust. "I've been staying on the straight and narrow for you, while you're at home carrying on. Why do I bother, tell me that! As many opportunities as I have…"

"I am *not* carrying on!" She squirmed off of the bed and went over to the other side of the room.

He followed and gripped her shoulders. "You belong to *me! No one* else has any right to you. Tell me who did this!"

She studied his face. He was burning with fury. It looked like he would jump on anything she said. "No! Let go!"

"Not until you do some explaining!"

She struggled, but couldn't free herself from his hold. "It was *Nate*, that's who! And it wasn't my idea, either!"

"Nate!?"

Cal bit her lip.

"What happened?"

Her eyes became blurry with tears. "Len, he was helping me with a scene I was having trouble with. Everything was going just fine. He was giving me some good pointers. Then, all of a sudden, it was like he switched personalities and he became like he used to be, and he attacked me. He wouldn't leave me alone, Len. No matter what I did, he wouldn't stop. He said he wouldn't go home until he got what he came for. Nothing made any sense, Len. I swear I wasn't coming on to him on purpose. Honest!"

"He better not have raped you."

She hated lying to him; but if she didn't, he was bound to take one of those guns of his and shoot Nate with it when he got back home. Then Leonard would spend the rest of his life in jail. "No."

"So he just got carried away, I guess. Was it a love scene you were working on?"

"No! That's just it. It was a confrontation scene between the bank teller and her boss. I can't think of anything in that scene that would've set him off. And it wasn't lust, anyway, Len. He was mad. Really, *really* mad! He kept talking about the ten years he rotted in jail because of me."

"So all that remorse and respect stuff was just an act. He was just waiting to get you alone when your guard was down for the best time and place to retaliate."

Whew! He finally believed her. "Yeah, it was like a nightmare. But I hurt him more than he hurt me. I fought back so hard he had a heart attack."

Leonard stopped short. "A heart attack? Really? He's in the hospital?"

"Yeah. In the CCU."

"So he's out for the count, then."

Cal looked at the floor and mumbled, "I guess so. He almost died."

"Oh, baby." He held her close. "I'm sorry I doubted you. I should've known you'd never have an affair, especially with him."

"I wouldn't cheat on you with anybody, Len." She returned his embrace, resting her head on his chest. "And you've really and truly been on the straight and narrow for me?"

"That's right. In fact, you'll be happy to know that from here, I'll be going directly to Belgium. We're finished in France."

Her relief was overwhelming. With two worries dispelled, she could now think about other things. "How's Stacy doing? How'd she look?"

"She's doing great, perky as ever and enjoying the French cuisine."

"That's my Stacy." Cal said happily as she picked up her suitcase, put it on the bed and started unpacking.

Leonard watched with amusement. "A flimsy nightgown? Cal Rhoads! What would your grandmother think?"

* * *

Taking advantage of room service and closed-cable television, Leonard and Cal spent most of the weekend secluded in their room. They both needed the break from their busy work schedules and the relaxation that an uncommitted weekend provided. It was different now than before, though. Before disrobing, Cal would turn the lights down low. "It's more romantic that way," she had said. The truth was that she didn't want Leonard to see the bruises from the assault. If he did, he might guess the truth and go after Nate with a gun.

Falling asleep in Leonard's strong arms gave Cal a feeling of peace and security once again. She needed that now, more than ever. She loved waking up in the morning beside Leonard. Sunday morning, she woke before he did. She turned toward him and studied her sleeping husband. *Still handsome as ever,* she thought. *Starting to get a little tummy on him, maybe, but he still looks awfully good to me."*

He drowsily opened his eyes.

"Did you feel me watching you?" she asked.

'Mm-hmm," he said as he put his arm around her and closed his eyes again.

"We may have different images nowadays, but you're still a hero to me," she said softly. "You've given me everything of value that I have."

"Like what?"

"A home, love, Stacy. And if it weren't for you, I bet my first film would have been my last; so you gave me a career, too."

"I take good care of you."

"You sure do," Cal sighed. "Okay, wake up," she patted his cheek, "and tell me what I do for you. I need some audience feedback."

He opened his eyes again. "No more sleep?"

"Nope. Go ahead. I'm waiting."

"Well, for one thing, you stare me awake me out of a sound sleep and demand feedback. That's what you do to me." He was definitely awake now.

"*For* you, not *to* you. Come on, get mushy."

"No hidden cameras in here, I trust?"

"Golly, I sure hope not!" She looked around, just to be sure.

"Okay, Cal." He stroked her cheek. "You keep me young. You keep life interesting and, when we're not killing each other, you give me the best loving I've ever had. How's that?"

"That's beautiful," she grinned, "like a verbal Valentine's Day card."

"Don't get used to it. Mush isn't my style."

"Yeah, I've noticed."

* * *

Leonard and Cal were repacking their suitcases. Their beautiful getaway weekend would soon be coming to an end. "I wish I could go to Belgium with you," she sighed.

"I'm not sure how long we'll be there. By the time you have a week off, I might be home."

"The show I'm doing this week is a sit-com. I'm a daffy telephone operator. You know, Len," she added, "doing a lot of TV shows of so many different types must be what it's like working for ManPower."

"What's ManPower?"

"It's a temporary service. When a business needs someone to fill in for an employee, they call ManPower. My dad used to call on them sometimes when his secretary was on vacation. I bet ManPower's employees get to be a lot of different things in a relatively short amount of time, just like me. In the last few weeks, I've been a school teacher, a bank embezzler, and now a telephone operator."

"I can just envision a businessman calling up ManPower, asking for someone to fill in for a vacationing embezzler," he laughed. "I'll tell you what, though. If you want to see an example of how to be convincing on the telephone, look at some of *The Dick Van Dyke Show* reruns. He's got to be the all-time master at that. The way he does it, you would *swear* there's someone at the other end of the line."

"Okay, I will. I wish I could be like you and make myself *look* different for my different characters."

"It's all in your mindset. It's different attitudes. Your attitude shows in your demeanor. In one show, my thoughts were those of an innocent, but earnest, cowboy. In another, I thought like a conniving, money-hungry schemer. On the screen, I became those people. It's like… what?" he thought. "Oh yes, Nate's a good example. When he's got something evil on his mind, doesn't he look different to you than he does other times?"

"That's for sure. It's like Jekyll and Hyde."

"Exactly! It's all in the mind. The mind has a powerful influence on the body. All you have to do is learn to control your mind." Leonard closed his suitcase and placed it by the door. "Well, Cal, our cab should be here soon."

They looked at each other for a moment, then came together in a passionate embrace. "I'm going to miss you, Len."

"Me, too, baby. But it'll only be for a couple more weeks."

Glancing out the window, she noted, "There's a cab waiting down there."

"We better go, then." He took their suitcases. Cal opened the door and looked around to see if they had forgotten anything. They then proceeded on their way.

*   *   *

Bertha had been a housekeeper at this hotel for thirty-six years. She took pride in her work and, through her toil, had sent six children to college and on to productive lives. Today, she was busy at her task, getting the room ready for its next guests. When all appeared sparkling once again, she reached under the bed for the check-off sheet on which to document her work. There was a mound of material beside the sheet. She pulled it out. It was a filmy blue negligee. Ordinarily, the hotel policy was to keep lost items in their lost-and-found bin and, if not claimed, give them to a charity. For an item like this, especially, they found it sometimes caused problems to simply mail it back to the guest—there were times when that was the very evidence a wife needed that her husband had checked into the hotel with another woman. In this case, however, Bertha knew that the couple staying in this room were husband and wife. They were quite well known in the New York area for their years of theatre work, so she knew this time the nightgown could be sent directly to their home address.

She chuckled as she folded the negligee neatly. "That ol' boy must still have a lot of life in him."

*   *   *

As soon as she got home, Cal called Becky. "How's Nate doing? Is he still going to be okay?"

"Looks like it. The way the doc talks, it sounds like the damage done to his heart is fixable. Sooner or later, he'll have to have surgery. He's been asking for you all weekend."

"Me? How come?" She was having conflicting feelings about seeing him, again. Cal wanted to see for herself that he was going to be all right, but the thought of being near him made her feel panicky. Nate can't hurt her anymore, she kept telling herself. She had heard that people are weak for a long time after having a heart attack. But there was something else, too. Guilt. It was killing her.

"He didn't say, but, Cal, he's kind of different now. I don't know how to describe it."

"I can't go see him, anyway. I'm not a relative."

"Oh, that rule doesn't apply anymore. He's out of the CCU and in his own private room now. It's room number 528. Dad's with him until 5:00, then I'll relieve him."

"I've got to be at the studio early in the morning. I'm doing another TV show this week."

"Well then stop by on your way home from work. It seems pretty important to him that he see you, again."

"Will you be there?"

"Either Dad or me. We're taking turns."

"Okay. I'll stop by, but just for a minute. I don't want to tire him out."

* * *

Cal discovered that she had had a different interpretation of her character than the director did. A writer once told her that the finished show incorporates the words of the writer and the vision of the director. That, she said, is why you can see the same story done by five different casts and crew, and it will seem as if you've seen five different stories. *That could explain why the only time we usually see a writer on the set is when he's also the director,* she thought. *It would probably drive him crazy to see his story interpreted in a different way than he intended it.*

While she had read eccentricity into her character when she initially studied the script, the director didn't. He wanted the character interpreted as slow-witted and moody. This completely different version of the character took Cal by surprise. She began re-reading the script during lunch break with the new characterization in mind. Once she did, it did indeed make sense.

"Moody," the director had said. As she got into position for her scene, she got herself into the proper mindset. The moodiest person she knew was Leonard. She would become a slow version of him for this role.

* * *

As she was driving home, Cal felt quite satisfied with her performance that day. She had succeeded in controlling her mind and becoming her character. Best of all, the director was pleased.

The feeling of triumph was short lived as she turned into the parking lot of Bethesda Hospital with a feeling of dread. Oh, good. There was Becky's car. She parked beside it, entered the lobby, and took the elevator to the fifth floor. As she approached room 528, she noticed Nate's name on the partially-opened door. That's odd. Why was his identity being revealed? *Why's it different now from last time?* she wondered. The answer to that came into her head at lightening speed and in Nate's own voice—"My career had been flying high, but it's all down the drain now because of you." That's what he had said on that fateful night, the memory of which filled her again with fear, guilt and remorse. Sure enough, there were no reporters here. Didn't they care? Cal sighed. Nate probably wanted her to visit so she could get a good look at how profoundly she had ruined his life. "Okay," she said to herself, "I deserve it." She stepped into the room.

Instead of resentment, though, there was a warm look of welcome in Nate's eyes as she entered. In the chair beside the bed, Becky, too, was glad to see her. She rose and motioned for her friend to take her place in the chair. "Come on in, Cal," she said. "I've warmed up the seat for you."

As she walked slowly over to the bed, Cal was relieved to see that Nate didn't look as sick as she expected him to. He was attached to an IV tube and a cardiac monitor, but he didn't look nearly as bad as he had when she had last seen him—ashen, almost lifeless, as the paramedics were putting him into the ambulance. He now reached his hand out for hers, and she took it. He drew her hand to his lips and gently kissed it. "Thank you" he said.

What? He was thanking her for ruining his life? Was he delusional or something?

"You two have a good visit," Becky said as she headed toward the door. "I'm going to get something to eat."

"*No!*" Cal called after her with desperation in her voice. "Don't go!"

"It's okay. I'm just going down the hall. There's vending machines there."

Nate released her hand. "Here, this will make you feel better." He gave Cal the call-button that had been clipped to his pillow. "All you have to do is press the button and a nurse will come right away. They've got a good response time on this floor."

Becky smiled at the absurdity and left.

Cal then realized that, if she ran, Nate couldn't come after her because he was hooked up to the cardiac monitor. She's safe. She then handed the call-button back to him. "I guess you need it more than I do." She sat in the chair.

They looked at each other for a moment. The many scratches she had put on his face that awful night seemed to be healing all right. Too bad the damage to his heart would take a whole lot longer.

"My funeral would have been today," he said softly.

"What do you mean?"

"If you hadn't done CPR on me."

"Oh."

"Why'd you do it?"

She shrugged and looked at the floor. "I don't know."

"Cal, that was the most unselfish… ." His voice cracked.

She looked back up at him to see why, and was surprised to see tears rolling down his cheeks. That took her completely by surprise. She had never seen Nate cry before. She would not have even thought he was capable of it.

He continued, "… the most unselfish thing I've ever seen anyone do in my life."

Cal looked at Nate with a question in her eyes.

"You don't know," he said with astonished wonder. "Cal, rape was just the beginning. I was going to make you suffer, *really* suffer. Then I was going to kill you. I had a gun in the pocket of my jacket. I didn't care what they did to me—I just wanted to see you dead. Cal, I'd been stalking you, I hurt you—God, what I did to you! Then you turned around and..." His voice faltered. He struggled to get the rest of the sentence out, "... saved my life." Overcome with emotion, Nate had to look away from her to keep from losing it completely.

She said softly, "You're a human being. You needed help."

After a moment, Nate looked back at her and, more composed now, reached out to her with both arms. She responded and they embraced.

"There's nothing in the world I wouldn't do for you now," he said. "Whatever you want, I'll get it for you. I owe you my life, my very soul. I know I would've been sentenced to hell if I had died then."

As he loosened his grip on her, she sat back down. Her eyes were moist, too. "I'm sorry I made you have a heart attack. I didn't mean to do that. And I'm sorry I made your life miserable for all those years. I *did* mean to do that, and I'm sorry. I was stupid."

He shook his head. "You didn't do any of those things. I did them to myself."

Cal wished she could get rid of the lump in her throat. She traced an imaginary pattern on the blanket with her finger as she asked earnestly, "Will you get completely well, do you think?"

"I don't know. I had a bum heart already. Letting myself get all worked up like that made everything a lot worse." Then he reassured her, "I guess I'm pretty harmless now. I have to take it easy and avoid stress, and the pills they put me on are doing a real number on my libido, too." Something in the doorway then got his attention, and he smiled. "Speaking of which..."

A nurse had arrived to dispense Nate's medication. She handed him the tiny paper cup with the capsules, then poured water into a glass.

"You need to get your rest," Cal said as she arose from the chair, "and I've got to go study my lines. Bye, Nate." She waved to him and made her exit, bumping into Becky in the hallway.

She put her arm around Cal's shoulder. "He wanted to talk to you alone. You're okay, aren't you?"

"Yeah. I'll be back tomorrow after work." She gave her a quick hug, then left.

* * *

That night, Cal had been curled up on the sofa, studying her script, when Luigi jumped into her lap. She stroked her furry pet. "You have such a simple life," she sighed. "As long as you have food to eat and a lap to curl up on, you're happy." Then she set the script aside and hugged him close. "Luigi, why did I have to do that? Why did I make everything so rough on Nate all those years?" She couldn't hold back her tears any longer. "He'd be healthy right now if it weren't for me. And he'd still be in lots of films and have lots of fans throwing their hotel keys at him… if it weren't for me. He'll never be the same again. I ruined his whole life and he thinks I'm wonderful. Luigi, why are people so crazy?"

Maybe mankind isn't *the highest form of animal life, after all,* she thought.

Chapter 30

After seventeen days in Belgium, Leonard's work on the film was over. Cal asked Mrs. Morris to prepare his favorite steak-and-potato dinner for his homecoming. He was quite glad to be back, and life began getting back into its routine.

Tests revealed exactly what further damage had been done to Nate's heart by the heart attack. Three weeks after the incident, he came home. Becky left her children in the care of a nanny and temporarily took up residence in Nate's house so she could take care of him herself. During his convalescence, her beloved cousin was slowly, but surely, gaining strength. He had been told that he could never again go back to very strenuous activity after such a close brush with death. He might not be so lucky the next time, they warned. Surgery had been advised; but Nate wasn't eager to go under the knife, so it was postponed indefinitely.

Becky saw to it that Nate's cook made low-fat, low-cholesterol versions of his favorite meals, and that he ate an acceptable amount. She gave him his medication, made sure nothing happened that would upset him, and urged Cal to come visit him as often as she could and to maintain an upbeat attitude for him. That would help his recovery more than anything, she said.

Cal had just arrived for a visit.

"Hi, Nate," Cal greeted, as she entered his living room. He had been sitting in the easy chair. "I brought you a cryptogram. I'm going to teach you to be a super sleuth, too, like me." She pulled a chair up to his. "You got a pencil?"

"Look at this. I'm considering taking the part of Joshua Sullivan. Tell me what you think of it." He handed the script to her.

Her eyes lit up as she took it. "A script? You're going to be in pictures, again?"

"I think so. That is, if you don't press charges against me."

"I won't," she assured him. "But you can't go back to work this soon, can you?"

"Production begins next year. I'll be ready by then."

She looked through it quickly, then gave it back. "It's too physical. You can't do that. You've got to get calmer roles, Nate. You know what the doc said. If you have another heart attack…"

"You sound like Becky."

"She cares a whole lot about you. I had no idea y'all were cousins."

"Oh, you know about that, huh? She made me promise not to tell you."

Cal distractedly leafed through the manuscript. "Did you mean what you said?"

"When? Just now?"

"After the CPR, when you came around."

"What'd I say?"

She set the script on the table. "Never mind. It's not important." Remembering again his precarious condition, Cal doubled her efforts to keep their conversations light. She smiled and asked, "You remember the day I brought my friend Sue over here? That was soon after our first picture. Doggone if you weren't the epitome of charm that day."

The memory gave him a glow of pleasure. "I remember."

"She thought you were God's gift to women. She never knew we were hurting each other, right under her nose." She grinned. "I was just waiting for one of my ribs to break. And I just *know* my fingernails must've dug a hole in your arm, but you didn't move a bit. We're *both* pretty good actors, aren't we?"

He reached over and took her hands in his. "Cal, I'm awfully sorry for everything. I'm sorry I scared you and hurt you so many times. I'm really sorry for everything. I wish I could live my life over and do it right this time." He hesitated, then continued in a more hushed, confidential tone, "When I was out, before your CPR brought me back, I saw my dad again. He died almost three decades ago, Cal, but I saw him clear as day, alive and well. It wasn't an illusion; I actually was in his presence, and some great truths suddenly came clear to me. What I used to think were important, really aren't." He looked at Cal earnestly. "I never realized before then how pure your soul is. Watching you struggling to bring me back, whispering for God to help you and pleading with me not to die, it was like I was seeing you clearly for the first time."

Cal was utterly confused. "You couldn't have seen that. Your eyes were closed and you were completely out of it."

"Believe me, I saw it. Why did you do it? You were crying, and you worked so hard to bring me back. Why?"

She fidgeted. "I don't know. It's just something I had to do."

"Could it be because you really *do* care about me?"

Cal shrugged, "Didn't matter. You didn't care about me."

"I've wanted you for *years*, Cal! You *know* I have."

"But that was just a sex thing. Becky told me once, a long time ago, that if I would just go to bed with you, you'd lose interest in me and would leave me alone. She said it was the fact that I'm the only girl who ever said no to you that was driving you crazy. She thought once I said yes, it would probably end. So I thought you just wanted me to be one of your conquests. And when you were so determined that we'd do that *Campus Dreams* scene under the sheets, I thought you just wanted to make your conquest in front of an audience and preserved on film for posterity, just to humiliate me. I didn't think I meant anything more to you than that."

"Oh, it was a *lot* more than that. I admit, it might have started that way—the thought of making such a challenging conquest *was* intriguing. There you were, obviously virgin and determined to stay that way. You weren't the slightest bit interested in even going out with me. I had never encountered that before. I think maybe it was on the tour that I started seeing things differently. For most of the tour, we got along so well. That time on the bus, you ended up asleep in my arms. You were so soft and warm. Looking down at you, all snuggled up close to me, I wanted you so badly.

"Then, when you married Leonard," he continued, "I thought the world would come to an end; and I knew that the lawsuit was the reason you did it. It all backfired on me. I started drinking a lot. I just wanted to be numb. I didn't want to feel anything anymore, but it didn't work. The pain wouldn't go away. I had been drinking when I strangled you that day. I completely lost control. When I think what could've happened, it makes me sick. Thank God for Becky and Leonard!"

"Wow. I'm sorry, Nate. I've been awful to you. It wasn't fair of me to keep trying to make you mad when I had Len to hide behind. I thought I was just playing a game. I didn't know you'd end up going through all that."

He gently embraced her and gave her a tender kiss on the cheek. "Let's start over. Let's make this Day One of our new life as friends. Okay?"

She nodded and put her arms around him, her head on his shoulder.

*   *   *

"No. You stay here today," Leonard told Cal as she headed again this morning to the front door.

"I'm just going to check in on him. He's still pretty weak."

"You've been going every day, for Pete's sake. Becky's there and she's taking good care of him. You need to stay home for a change."

"It's okay, Len. He's a lot different now. We don't have to worry about him hurting me anymore. He's turned over a whole new leaf. He's even got religion now."

"*No*, Cal! People all over the world get well without your visits. Nate can, too. Don't you *dare* go out that door!" The steely look in his eyes told her that he meant what he said.

It felt as if she was fifteen again. Once again, Leonard seemed to be the oppressive tyrant, ruling with an iron hand. And, again, it made her feel defiant—looking for alternate ways to still get her way so that he'd find out about it only *after* she had done it. "Don't you need to talk to your agent or have bills to pay or something?"

"I think you need to go with me on location to Alabama next week. You don't have anything on your calendar."

"Yeah. You go make the reservations." She sat in the living room chair and picked up a magazine while she waited for him to leave.

He took her hand and headed toward the stairs. "We'll go up to the study and make the reservations together. It'll be like an extended vacation for you. You can get some painting in."

*   *   *

Here in Alabama, she wasn't really in the mood to paint. The scenery wasn't all that breathtaking, as it had been in England, but this part of the state *did* have a homespun feel that was very comfortable. Instead of painting, Cal got a notebook and pens, and started writing.

As a child, she used to write short stories to entertain her friends. In high school, she had written a novella of a candy-striper's adventures in a large Dallas hospital, based on her own experience, but with many fun embellishments. While her parents had been delighted with her hospital volunteer work, they had even less time to spend with her there than they did at home. It was at that hospital, however, that she had learned CPR.

Cal didn't want to write a short story *or* a novella now. This time, she wanted to go for the big time. She was going to write a screenplay with characters that could be played by Leonard, Nate, and herself. Nate's character would have to be very sedate, however. She didn't want him to do anything that would compromise his health. From the time Leonard left for work each day until shortly before he was due back, she was happily writing. Cal was keeping this little project a secret so he would be pleasantly surprised when it was completed and presented to him.

On one of Leonard's off days, they donned sunglasses and hats, then went to check out the local shopping center. As they approached a hobby shop, Leonard stopped and gazed at the model railroad on display in the window. "I used to have one of those when I was a boy, only it wasn't electric," he said with a sparkle in his eyes. "Back then, kids had to use their imaginations a lot more than now."

Cal couldn't resist. She pulled out her checkbook as she entered the store.

*   *   *

Now back from their Alabama trip, Cal was enjoying a cold glass of lemonade while lounging in the new hammock Leonard had just bought and set up. "It works," she beamed up at him. "Now we need to get you one so we can be lazy together."

With a mischievous smile, he took the lemonade from her, then flipped the hammock over, dumping Cal onto the ground.

"Hey! What's that for?" she asked indignantly.

"I already have one. We need to get *you* one now."

She stubbornly got back into the hammock. "Go play with your trains," she lightheartedly scolded.

"Good idea," he chuckled, as he returned the lemonade to her.

Chapter 31

IT WAS A MONDAY AFTERNOON and Cal was getting situated on the sofa for a nap.

"*Again?*" Leonard asked. "Are you getting old or something? I think I'm going to have to trade you in for a younger woman," he teased.

"I can't help it, Len. I'm wiped out and need a nap." She pulled the pillow down and rested her head on it. "Maybe I'm getting the flu or something. My stomach's been upset a lot the last week or so, too."

"Uh-oh."

"You better stay away from me if you don't want to catch it."

"It sounds like something *you* got from *me*."

She looked up at him with concern. "Haven't you been feeling very good, either?"

"Have you been taking your pill every day?"

"Oh, that," she shrugged. "Yeah, except for when you're away on location."

"Cal," he looked at her sternly, "you know where I stand on the fatherhood issue. You're supposed to take one *every* day."

"But there's no reason to when you're out of town. I don't like to take chemicals when I don't have to."

"They're not as effective if you don't take them every day. Go to the phone right now and make an appointment with your doctor. We need to know for sure."

"But, Len, it's so unlikely."

"Do it anyway. Now!" He took her hands and pulled her to a standing position.

"Okay," she sighed as she went over to the phone and opened the directory.

* * *

The appointment came four weeks later.

As Cal left the doctor's office and walked back to her car, she couldn't help but to grin. She was finally going to be a mother. Maybe Leonard was right—she must have conceived during that weekend in New York. Now there would be a brand new chapter in her life, one that she thought would never happen. Leonard might not be happy about this but, doggone it, she was!

* * *

"That's what I was afraid of," he said grimly as he dropped heavily into the chair.

Cal sat on his lap and kissed his cheek. "Thank you for giving me what I've been wanting for so long, Len."

He didn't understand her elation. "But, Cal, don't you realize what this could mean?"

"So what if the baby's autistic? I sure don't wish that Darrell hadn't been born, do you?"

"No, but not all people with autism are as independent as he is. Some of them have retardation to a profound degree and no amount of therapy can give them a good life."

"But no matter what, this baby is our very own and will be wonderful. I'll take good care of it."

"I *hope* it'll be wonderful."

"You're not autistic, and none of your other relatives are. It looks like it's very likely our baby won't be, either."

"You're really happy about this, aren't you?"

"It's the best present anyone's ever given me," she grinned.

Knowing that, for Cal, there's no alternative but to have the baby, Leonard managed a smile. "I hope it's a girl and she's just like you."

Cal hugged his neck.

* * *

After a while, Leonard reached a point of acceptance and even came to enjoy his newfound status among the men with whom he was working. To be in his fifties with a pregnant young wife made him the Man of the Hour.

Cal kissed him goodbye and he left for the studio. As she watched his car back out of the driveway and proceed down the street and around the corner, she sighed with contentment. How wonderful life could be! Miracles do happen, and a multitude of them seemed to be happening to her now.

Cal gently patted her belly, wondering what this new little life would be like. Would it be a boy or girl? Would this child look like Len or her? With such a talented daddy and artistic mama, he or she couldn't help but to be a creative person, too. Life was so good!

She shut the door, then grinned. "I've *got* to tell Sue about this." Off she went to the phone.

PART III

Motherhood

Chapter 1

1981

Leonard was on his way home from the studio. Acting jobs were getting less plentiful for him now in youth-worshipping Hollywood. He was guest starring on *Precinct Four* this week as the prime suspect in a murder. Not the best role he's ever had, but not the worst either. How he wished he could have a series, again, in which he was part of an ensemble of good guys. It would be nice to have a predictable income now that they would soon have another mouth to feed.

Leonard had never seen Cal happier than she was now. She enjoyed looking at her silhouette in the mirror as she began rounding out, and could hardly wait to hold that little baby in her arms.

He pulled into the driveway. Cal was waiting for him at the door. *What's the occasion?* he wondered. As he got out of his car and headed toward the house, he saw that Cal's eyes were glowing with excitement. "Don't tell me it's twins," he teased, then kissed her hello.

"Nope. I was over at Becky's today and her kids were telling me all about computers. Did you know that, with a computer, you can type a whole page of paragraphs, then move them around in any order you want without having to type them again?"

"No, I didn't know that." He went into the front hallway, picked up the mail from the table, and leafed through it.

"Well, you can. And you can make as many copies of each page as you want without having to type it again, too."

Leonard kept one envelope and put the rest back down. "Is that so?"

As he went into the living room, Cal closed the front door and followed him. "Her oldest daughter, Kelsey, has a computer and she showed me how it works."

He sat in the easy chair, opened the envelope and unfolded the page. Actually *reading* that letter was not an option, he was soon to discover, as his wife was now sitting in his lap and kissing his cheek. "Now what would you want with a computer?" he asked, a bit impatiently.

Cal stopped short. "Uh, what makes you think I want one?"

"Just a hunch. I've never seen you type, Cal. I bet you don't even know how."

"I do too. I took typing in school. It was an easy A."

"But you hardly ever write letters. Why else would you use it?"

"I want it to be a surprise."

"You want *what* to be a surprise?"

"The thing I'm writing. It would go a whole lot faster with a computer."

He was thoroughly confused. "What on earth are you talking about?"

Cal sighed, got back up, went over to the end table beside the sofa, and pulled a notebook out of its drawer. "This." She brought it over and handed it to him. "I've been working on it for months while you've been out of the house."

He flipped through the pages and saw that she was handwriting a script. On the first page was the title *Mr. Jackson's Vacation.*

"That's just the first notebook. I'm halfway through another one, too, but that's upstairs."

"Well, you've achieved your goal. I *am* surprised. I didn't know you wrote plays."

"It a screenplay. I used to write stories all the time when I was a kid. I'm writing *Mr. Jackson's Vacation* for you. You're Mr. Jackson and I'm Marie. I'm writing it so you can have a romantic lead instead of being the bad guy all the time."

Oh, he thought. *She's planning for her little story to be a film.* Being her first attempt at writing anything of length, it would probably have a better chance at being an elementary-school play. He smiled at her naïveté. "Thanks, Cal, but I don't need a romantic lead. You know the director would probably change it all around, anyway."

"Then I'll direct it, too."

"The production company hires the director."

She sat back on his lap and stroked his hair. "Let's get a computer. Please? It sure would be a lot easier."

"When did you learn this?" he asked, with a half-smile.

"Learn what? Writing?"

"To use feminine wiles on me like this. That's not your style."

Cal shrugged innocently and grinned. "Becky said it works for her. She said if that doesn't do it, guilt might."

He kissed her nose. "How much do computers cost?"

"I don't know. Let's go find out."

"Don't we have to pick Stacy up at the airport this evening? We wouldn't have time to do both. I've got an early call tomorrow."

That's true, Cal realized. *It'll be so great to see Stacy and her family again.*

Leonard interrupted her thoughts, "There's going to be a get-together for the cast and crew when filming wraps Friday. I want you to come, too."

"Are you working with anyone I know?"

"You probably know some of the crew. I don't think you know any of the cast members, though. You know the makeup man, Kurt Williams."

"Oh, yeah! Good ol' Kurt! I'd like to see him, again. Remember how glamorous he made me look for the award presentations?"

"Mainly, I remember how excited you were when you opened the envelope and saw who won."

"Yeah. Miles. It's about time he got some recognition from his peers."

"I noticed he kissed you when he came up to get his award. Remember when you two were dating and you always wanted to linger on the porch for one more kiss?"

"Yeah. He was… " Cal stopped. She had almost said, "the best kisser I've ever known," but caught herself in time. She continued, "He used to be a good kisser, but it just wasn't the same this time." She sighed with resignation, "He's lost that lovin' feelin.'"

He smiled. "Glad to hear that."

*   *   *

Once they arrived at the wrap party, Cal found it to be like old-home day. Not only did she know the makeup man, but two of the cameramen, the script girl, one of the stars, and the producer, too. While many of the men were slapping Leonard on the back and dubbing him "Super Stud" for having impregnated Cal, she was off to the side, discussing business with Ned Sharp, the assistant producer.

Cal wanted to know everything he could tell her about setting up and running a production company. She plied him with question after question, many to which he had no answers. He told her what he did know about it and advised her to consult with the actual owner of one of the many production companies for more details. How incongruous it seemed to Ned that Cal was about to become a mother for the first time, yet was so concerned about business. She should be busying herself with furnishing a nursery and deciding what to name the baby, he joked.

"Oh, we've already done that," Cal said happily. "Starting a production company's my dream, and it'll happen someday. Just you wait and see."

He gave her a paternal pat on the head as he left her to join the crowd around Leonard.

*   *   *

Roles had become scarce for Cal, too, during the last few months. *It's just as well,* she thought, as she settled onto the sofa in Becky's house the next day. Being out of work gave her more time to write that script and be with her friends.

"Yeah," Becky agreed. "I guess there's not much call for expectant women on TV these days. Here, put your feet up on the hassock." She pushed it over in front of Cal, who obligingly propped her feet on it.

"It seems some people still think of me as a kid, though, just because I'm short."

"Who? Surely not Leonard."

"Ned Sharp, for one. I was asking his advice about starting a production company and he kind of pooh-poohed it. He seemed to think I couldn't do it."

"Well, why were you asking him, anyway? He doesn't run one. Why don't you ask my dad?"

"Because he's such a big shot," Cal shrugged. "He's too busy to bother with me."

"Would you like for me to set up an appointment for you to see him? I'll do that, if you want."

"Does he have time? It seems like he's always on the go."

"He'll make time. He knows you're my best friend, and he'd do it for me."

"Okay. It's a shame I'm not a regular on a soap opera. I bet writing in a pregnancy for their characters wouldn't be hard for those writers."

"That's true. They do it all the time. In fact, they could just write about your real life. That could easily read like a soap."

"Nah, that wouldn't work. I've been married to the same guy for eleven years. That's lousy soap-opera material." Cal leaned back and lovingly rubbed the dome of her belly. "When I married Len, I thought I'd never be a mama. For a guy who doesn't want kids, he sure is getting a lot of them."

"Have you decided on a name yet?" Becky asked.

"A boy would've been Len, Jr. That would've made his daddy feel ten feet tall, I bet."

Becky laughed. "He almost is already, Cal. But it's a girl. What about her name?"

"Well," she sighed contentedly, "Jill named Stacy after me. I wonder how Len would feel about us naming our baby after Jill."

"I've never heard of a second wife naming her baby after the first wife. That's totally weird."

"Oh, I don't know. Her name is kind of pretty. How's Jill Michelle Rhoads sound?"

Chapter 2

"Miss Kara Michelle Rhoads, may I introduce you to Mr. Leonard Rhoads? If you're really good, he just might let you call him Daddy," Cal said with a grin as Leonard entered the recovery room, where she and her brand new daughter were getting to know each other. With the help of local anesthesia at just the right time, labor and delivery had been much easier than Cal thought they would be.

The sight of his wife in such good spirits, with their newborn child in her arms, brought a smile of pride to his face. He drew near to the bed and gazed at Kara.

"Come on, kiddo," Cal gently rubbed the baby's cheek, "wake up for Daddy. Let him see your beautiful blue eyes."

Leonard then turned his attention to his wife. Stroking Cal's hair, he asked, "Happy?"

She took his hand and looked up at him. "She's what I've been wanting for a long time, Len. I'm *real* happy. And see? She's not autistic. You were worrying for nothing."

"You can't tell this soon. The symptoms take a while to show themselves."

"Well, she won't be. She's a beautiful, healthy little girl, just like Stacy was. Aren't you, sweetheart?" She kissed her sleeping daughter. "I wish she'd wake up. Being born is the most exciting thing that's ever happened to her and she seems bored by it. What a little party pooper!"

He chuckled. "You'll have plenty of time to play with her later, Cal. Don't worry about that."

"Who does she look like? She's got your blue eyes and my brown hair, but I can't see anything else about her that looks like any relatives."

"It's too soon to tell. Remember how different you said Stacy looked when she was a baby and you'd been gone for six weeks doing location work? They change a lot when they're little."

Just as Cal had hoped, Leonard had come to terms with fatherhood again. His fear of having an autistic child was greatly diminished once he realized the baby was a girl, because the articles he had read about autism said that it is more likely to occur in boys. So far, he seemed to be batting a thousand.

* * *

Nate and Becky emerged from the elevator that evening, and she led the way to the large window down the hall. "There she is," Becky pointed. "Right there in the second row. See?"

He joined his cousin at the window and beheld the roomful of babies in individual bassinets. Most of them were sleeping, a few were sucking their fists, a few were squalling. Each bassinet was labeled with the last name of the mother, the date of birth, and the doctor's name.

"That can't be her. It says 'Phillips', not 'Rhoads.'"

Becky wiggled her finger at the infant. "To protect against kidnappers, I'm sure. But it's her. I'd know her anywhere."

"How can you tell? They all look alike."

"You sound just like a man. Let's go see Cal."

Nate followed Becky as she hurried down the long hallway and into one of the rooms. When they entered, they saw Cal sitting up in bed, pencil in hand, carefully studying a folded-up section of newspaper.

"Hi, lady! You're skinny again," Becky greeted as she pulled up a chair. She nodded to Leonard, who was seated at the foot of Cal's bed, reading the sports section. "Hi, Leonard. Congratulations!"

"It's a girl," he responded proudly, as he set his paper down, too. "A hale and hardy one, to boot."

Nate smirked. "Becky?"

She looked back at him, then her eyes followed his pointing finger. On the other side of Cal's bed was a bassinet, with a sleeping baby in it. "Okay, so I was wrong. That other one *looked* a lot like Cal, though."

Nate went around the bed to the bassinet and studied the sleeping infant for a long moment. She had wispy brown hair and a little button nose. Nate gently touched the back of her tiny hand, "She's beautiful."

Cal's smile lit up her face. "Yeah, I kind of thought so, too. She might be little but she's got a powerful set of lungs. Just wait 'til she wakes up."

"Have you decided on a name yet?" Becky asked.

"Kara Michelle. Len and I both like that name."

"That's pretty."

Nate leaned over and gave Cal a kiss on the cheek. "Congratulations, Cal. I know you'll be a wonderful mother."

She smiled at him appreciatively.

"Okay, tell me all the details," Becky said as she pulled her chair closer to Cal's bed. "Have a seat, Nate. Was it awful, Cal? I bet it wasn't. Mine weren't."

Cal answered excitedly, "Not nearly as bad as I thought it'd be. After it was all over, I was wondering when the bad part was supposed to start. I was thinking, 'Is that all there is to it?'"

"Those old dowagers like to scare us to death with their horror stories. I don't know why they do that. How many hours were you in labor? And when did it start? Were you in the middle of something? Did they give you epidural? Give me all the details."

Nate seated himself beside Leonard, and the two men exchanged uncomfortable glances as the women compared childbirth experiences.

*   *   *

That evening, Leonard finally got to go home and catch up on the sleep he had missed. Maybe Cal was right—maybe he had been worrying for nothing. And Kara *was* a cute little thing. While Stacy had been born with blonde hair like his, Kara looked more like Cal's side of the family with her darker coloring. He could tell she would probably end up with a head full of brown curls, just like her mother.

The next day, he had to return to work. He stopped by the hospital to see Cal and Kara, then proceeded to the studio, where he was working on a mini-series. Cigars were proudly passed out to the cast and crew, with an announcement of Kara's arrival. He had to admit he didn't have some of the details (her weight and length) but was quick to point out that he knew the important things—her gender and the fact that she had blue eyes, just like his. The men slapped him on the back and shook his hand.

Two days later, he brought Cal and Kara home from the hospital, but had to go back to work after lunch. He was glad that Jessie, their housekeeper, was there to help them if anything needed to be done.

*   *   *

"Hi, Nate," Becky had said over the phone later that day. "Want to go with me to Cal's house? They got home this morning and Leonard's back to work already. I thought we could give her a hand."

"Sure," he had replied, not really knowing what he could do to be of any help, but willing to try anyway.

Now they had arrived at the Rhoads' front door and Jessie had greeted them, then led them upstairs into the study, where they found Cal typing away at the computer.

"Hey, gal, what're you doing?" Becky asked.

Cal swiveled her chair around, then her face lit up when she saw that her two best friends had come to visit. "Hi, y'all!"

"I thought you'd be spending all day just watching Kara sleep," Becky teased. "Where is she?"

"She's still napping, so that gives me time to do some writing. Is it normal for babies to sleep twenty-two hours a day, Becky? I thought I'd have more time to play with her. I don't remember Stacy sleeping this much."

"Yes, that's normal at first. In a couple months, you'll wish she slept more. Just you wait. Then you'll definitely need a nanny if you plan to do any writing or go back to work."

At that moment, they heard a lusty wail from the next room, and Cal smiled. "Speak of the devil. Now y'all get to see what she looks like awake." She arose and went into the nursery, followed by Becky and Nate. Inside the crib was her tiny, but very animated daughter, arms and legs flailing in accompaniment to her indignant cry. Cal reached in and lifted her up, then took her across the room to the change table. "You just didn't want to miss anything, did you, sweetie?" she asked gently. "You knew these people came just to see you." She cleaned the baby up, replaced her wet diaper with a dry one, then dressed her in a bright yellow romper. "Now you're all ready for company." She held Kara up to her shoulder and looked over at Becky. "I thought I would've forgotten all these things since it's been so long since Stacy was a baby, but it came back to me right away."

"I knew it would," Becky said.

"You want to hold her while I warm her bottle?" Cal asked Nate.

He was taken aback. "Me?"

"Sure. Didn't Becky let you hold her babies?"

"Well," he hesitated, "I didn't really ask to."

"Go ahead, Nate," Becky coaxed. "You won't hurt her. Babies are hardy creatures."

He slowly extended his arms and Cal put Kara into them while instructing him, "Be sure to support her head. Her neck's not strong enough to do that, yet." Then she told her baby in a mock confidential tone, "This guy is Uncle Nate, Kara. He's not really your uncle and Becky's not really your aunt, but we'll pretend they are anyway, since the only uncle you *do* have is so far away. You'll probably be seeing a lot of these folks in the next eighteen years."

Becky reached out her finger, and Kara took hold of it. "She doesn't really look like anyone yet, except she has your brown hair," she told Cal, "but that could change."

"She's the most beautiful baby I've ever seen," Nate stated.

Cal beamed.

"Now, wait a minute," Becky objected good-naturedly. "What's wrong with my kids? Weren't they cute?"

"They were cute. Kara is beautiful," he explained. "See how blue her eyes are?"

Cal agreed, "Yeah, blue like Len's."

"All babies' eyes are blue," said Becky.

"And look," he continued. "She's smiling at me. Isn't that the most beautiful smile you ever saw? She looks like a little angel."

"That's…"

"Don't say it!" Cal warned Becky.

Startled, Becky asked, "Don't say what?"

"That it's just gas. That's what mean people say when someone notices a baby smiling. Gas never made *me* want to smile. Did it you?"

Becky laughed, "You're right." Then she nudged Nate. "I think Kara likes you. She's probably trying to butter you up so you'll take her to Disneyland."

"Well, it's working. I'd take her anywhere," he said.

"Come on downstairs. I've got to rustle up some grub for this little critter," Cal said as she led the procession through the hallway and down the stairs. Nate followed slowly, not wanting to jostle Kara too much.

*　*　*

As Nate drove home, his mind went over the events of the day. Today had been the first time he had ever held a new baby. It had felt awkward at first—she looked so fragile. After a while, though, he came to enjoy it. Cal had even let him give Kara her bottle, and you would have thought the poor child hadn't eaten in a month the way she went after it! The minute she wrapped her tiny hand around his finger, he was hooked.

So little and yet so powerful, Kara Michelle Rhoads had already carved out a place for herself in Nate's heart. This little girl seemed to be exactly what Cal needed. It was obvious that motherhood agreed with Cal. She had never been happier.

Nate wondered if he was the one responsible for this child. It had been about nine months before Kara's birth that the rape and heart attack had happened. Who is this baby's father—Nate or Leonard? It was really hard to tell. Kara didn't bear much resemblance to either of them yet. The brown hair could be from either Nate or Cal. Becky had told him that you could usually tell by the baby's first birthday who its father is. She certainly should know. One of her children had been conceived when she was between marriages.

* * *

Two days later, Jessie was surprised to find Cal sitting alone on the living room sofa, looking forlorn. "What's the matter?" she asked as she began dusting the living room furniture.

"Oh, I don't know," she said with a sigh.

"Is Kara sleeping?"

"Yeah." She fidgeted for a moment, then said sadly, "I can't figure out why I'm feeling so down. Kara's here and healthy. I've finally got the baby I've wanted for years. Len's working, so he's happy. Everything's terrific. So why am I so sad? I just want to bawl."

"Postnatal depression is perfectly normal. Just rest assured that it eventually goes away and everything will be fine again. Why don't you take Kara to the park or something? That should help lift your spirits, and it'd be good for her, too."

Hmm, Cal thought. *That's not a bad idea.*

Right after Kara's next feeding, Cal took her over to the nearby park. There, she lay the baby in her portable bassinet beneath a shady tree, and relaxed on the bench beside her. It was nice to be out in the fresh air again. Watching children play on the seesaw and sliding board, she imagined Kara doing those things in a few years. All was going well until they were approached by a woman who behaved in a peculiar way. She seemed to be quite familiar with Cal, who was sure she had never seen her before. That was not an unusual situation, Cal knew; people who saw her on television or in movies often felt as if they knew her. Once the woman insisted on holding Kara, though, Cal packed up the baby and her gear and went back home. It was then that she decided it was best to keep Kara out of public, at least until she's older.

This, Cal was learning, was but one of many disadvantages of having a screen career.

Chapter 3

DURING THE PAST YEAR, Cal had seen a side of Nate she didn't know existed. Until Kara was born, she didn't realize how much he loved children. It made her wonder if he had always been so fond of them, or could the turnabout brought on by his heart attack have something to do with it? No matter. She was simply enjoying it.

Today, her precious baby was one year old. Leonard had to be away working on location for a couple more days, but Becky and Nate were there to help them celebrate. As soon as they walked in the door, Kara reacted the way she always did when Uncle Nate was around—she'd reach out for him.

His response was predictable, as well—he picked her up and held her in his arms. "How's little Kara-Mia today?" he asked, kissing her soft cheek.

"Just wait until you see the present Nate got her," said Becky as she handed both gifts to Cal. "It's gorgeous!"

They all settled into the living room, Cal and Becky on the sofa and Nate, with Kara happily on his lap, in the easy chair.

"Open Becky's first," he instructed.

Cal gladly obliged. Pulling the ribbon loose and tearing the paper off, she discovered a Busy Box, with knobs and doors that would intrigue any one-year-old. She opened the little door to find a picture of a cartoon character. Then she pushed the dome, which produced a squeak. "Hey, this could keep *me* busy for a while, too," she joked as she spun the little wheel.

Nate reached for it. Cal gave it to him, and he demonstrated its many items of interest to Kara. "See? Look at this," he said as he spun the wheel. "Now, Kara do it." He took her little hand and gave the wheel a whirl. "Good girl! Kara made it go." He then pushed the dome. The resulting squeak caused a belly laugh from the delighted child. She then flattened her hand against it and made a smaller squeak.

"Now, open Nate's," Becky urged her friend. "Just wait'll you see it."

Cal could see that this gift had been professionally wrapped in expensive paper. She carefully loosened the tape at the seams. The ribbon and paper fell away, and she lifted the lid. Inside was a baby-blue satin and lace dress with a white, scalloped collar and long, puffed sleeves. Becky was right—it was, indeed, beautiful. "Golly," Cal said, "we're going to have to take her somewhere in this. Is the king having a ball anytime soon?"

"It would be perfect to wear to church on Easter," he suggested. "Why don't we all go together?"

Cal nodded. "Yeah, let's do that. I bet she'd love the music."

"What did *you* get her, Cal?" Becky asked.

She grinned. "Come look." Cal led them to what was now the playroom. "Ta-dah!" In the middle of the room was a beautiful white and yellow rocking horse. "Her first pony. Someday, she'll go riding on a real one with Len and me. I can hardly wait."

Nate said with an amused smile, "You and your horses."

"Looks like she'll have to grow a bit before taking off on that thing," Becky noted.

"Let's have some birthday cake," said Cal as she disappeared into the kitchen. The others followed. On the table was a large plain cake and a tiny, ornately-decorated one. She opened the highchair so Nate could put Kara into it. Once the child was settled in comfortably, Cal snapped the tray in place, put a large bib on her, then put the little cake on the tray. "Go to it, kiddo!" she grinned.

As if on cue, the curious Kara put her finger in the frosting, then took a handful of cake and put it into her mouth.

Cal laughed. "We'll teach her to use a fork some other time. She can just have fun with this one."

With her other hand, Kara took another handful of cake and held it out to Nate.

"No, thanks," he laughed. "You can have that."

Cal cut pieces of the large cake and put them onto plates for the others. "After she's polished off that cake, I *know* Kara will need a bath. Then we can get a picture of her in that new dress."

* * *

This computer was sure a good investment, Cal thought as she saved her day's work to diskette. She just couldn't leave *Mr. Jackson's Vacation* alone. Every time she read through it, she thought of a better way to word a dialog or decided to add another scene. This was going to be a terrific story when she was finally done with it—if she could ever be done enough to let go of it.

"Here," Leonard said as he tossed a script on her desk. "Michael just brought this by."

She glanced at it and smiled at him. "Remember when I used to keep getting high school roles? Doggone it, that doesn't seem to be happening anymore."

"Look it over and see if you'll need any help with anything."

She dutifully thumbed through the script. In the past, Leonard had always been so helpful to her when a role called for her to use a skill she hadn't developed yet, but there weren't very many emotions she hadn't experienced by now. Cal knew that his mentoring status in her life was important to him, however, especially now that the demand for his own acting services had lessened. Why on earth did casting directors think that good roles should go only to young actors, she wondered. Leonard could act rings around any of them, but the roles he was given these days didn't utilize his talents to the fullest or give him much screen time. He could have done them in his sleep. Nevertheless, he still gave them his all.

"Here's one," she said. "Look at this page. I'm playing a secretary and my boss tells me to lie about where he is when his wife calls. How do I do that so that I'm lying to obey my boss, but the audience will know I don't like it?"

"If you were lying to her in person, you wouldn't look her in the eye. Since you're on the phone, though, you certainly won't be smiling. You'll probably be tapping your pen or drumming your fingers on the desk to indicate that you're impatient for that moment to be over."

"That's probably right, too," she smiled. "I'll probably be watching the clock because I'll want to come home and play with my baby."

"It's been a year. You've only done TV shows like this and they've all been here in town. Don't you want to do films anymore? Or plays? Plays don't make as much money, of course, but I know you love to do them."

"Maybe when Kara's older. We're always on a weird schedule when we do plays."

"True."

"I do want to make a film, though—*Mr. Jackson's Vacation*. And I want to direct it, too."

"Let me know if you need anymore help with your TV role," Leonard said as he opened a book and began reading.

*　*　*

As Kara grew, Uncle Nate figured more and more prominently in her life. This was quite fortunate, because Leonard seemed to be becoming less involved. *At least, my little girl still has a caring guy in her life, even if it is just her honorary "uncle",* Cal thought with a sigh.

Nate began making regular visits, and Kara would inevitably be waiting for him. As he approached their front door at the same time every Saturday afternoon, the bright-eyed toddler could be seen in the front picture window, standing on the sofa with her nose to the glass. They would then spend some time together, reading a story, working a children's puzzle, or whatever suited their fancy. Uncle Nate was rapidly becoming one of Kara's favorite playmates.

Chapter 4

1986

Five-year-old Kara excitedly jumped out of her mother's car when they had come to a stop in the driveway. She could hardly wait to see Aunt Becky's stepdaughter, Olivia, again. Cal and Becky called the little girls "the twins" since they were born just a few days apart in the same hospital and were inseparable whenever they both visited Becky at the same time. Kara hadn't seen her buddy since Olivia's mother had moved to Minnesota last year.

Becky opened the door wide. "Hi, Kara! Give me a hug before you go see Livie."

Kara ran up to Becky, who scooped her up into her arms and kissed her cheek.

"How've you been, little one?"

"I'm good, Aunt Becky, and you want to know a secret?" Then she whispered, "I brought a present for Livie."

"Oh, really? What'd you bring her?"

"A picture of Barney. It's all folded up and it's in my pocket."

"She'll love that. Barney's her very favorite dinosaur." Becky set her down. "She's out back on the swings."

Kara ran through the house and out the back door, as Cal hugged Becky in greeting.

"Let's go into the kitchen," Becky said, leading the way. "I haven't seen you in so long. It gets lonely around here when you go with Leonard on location."

"For once, he had a good-sized role. It sure was hot down there in Florida, but we got to live like the rich and famous—Kara and I watched kids' shows every morning from our hotel bed while Len had to go to work. Did you know Captain Kangaroo isn't on anymore?"

Becky smiled. "Maybe his grandson is, though."

Cal peeked out the back window while Becky filled a glass with ice. "How long will Livie be visiting?"

"A few more days. Her mother will be back from her cruise on the sixteenth."

Cal waved at the two little girls on the swings, then exclaimed, "She sure has grown! These kids will be teenagers before we know it."

Becky poured Dr. Pepper into the glass and handed it to her. "Wasn't it Erma Bombeck who said that teenagers are God's punishment for having enjoying sex?"

Cal laughed, "That sounds like Erma. I love her."

"Or maybe it was Bill Cosby. If Kara becomes the kind of teenager you were, you'll really have your hands full. It's a good thing she's your only child."

"Yeah, Len'll agree with that. We sure were glad when she didn't turn up autistic. We were kind of concerned about that."

Becky laughed and shook her head, "That wouldn't be very likely."

"Well, sure, it *could*'ve happened. Autism's in the family."

"Not in Kara's."

"Yes, it is. Don't you remember, Becky? Len's brother is autistic."

"Apparently, what's obvious to me isn't to you. Let me show you something. I'll be right back." Becky went into her den, got an album off the bookcase, then returned to the kitchen. She flipped the pages. "I don't think you'd believe me if I just told you. You'd have to see it for yourself. Here it is. Look at this photo and tell me what you see." She handed the album to her friend.

"Hey," Cal said, "it's a picture of Kara and another little girl playing in a sandbox. Where'd you get this? And who's the kid in front of her?"

"That's me."

Cal looked at her in confusion as she lay the album on the kitchen table and sat down. "You mean you took the picture?"

"No, I mean that's Nate and me when we were little. The kid in the back is Nate, not Kara."

Cal studied the photo more closely. "Are you sure? It looks exactly like her." After another moment of studying the picture, she added, "Oh, I *do* see one difference—Kara has curly hair and this kid doesn't. I guess I'm going to have to let her hair grow longer, so she'll look more like a girl."

It seemed to Becky that Cal had missed the significance of that picture. Either that, or she was intentionally ignoring it. Maybe she'd better spell it out. "She's looking more like Nate every time I see her. He's noticed that, too."

Cal squirmed uneasily in her chair. "Nate said that?"

"Oh, yeah. Many times. You mean he hasn't mentioned it to you?"

Cal shook her head. "Not a word."

"That's why he had the sliding board and swing set added to his back yard, Cal. And the little playhouse. It wasn't for my kids. It's for yours. He said he wants his house to be a happy place for his daughter to visit. And he probably has Mrs. Ellis make chocolate-chip cookies whenever he knows she's coming, too. He said that's Kara's favorite kind. You two *do* visit him pretty often, don't you?"

"Yeah, every now and then, and the cookie jar's usually the first thing she checks out. Most the time, though, he comes over to our house." Cal thought for a moment, then said, "But when she's around, he calls himself 'Uncle Nate.' If he thought she was his daughter, he'd want her to call him 'Daddy.' So that proves she's not..."

"That only proves that he doesn't want to cause any problems between you and Leonard." Then Becky smiled. "He still loves you, Cal. It's just a more unselfish love now."

"No, he doesn't. He doesn't love me, but he *has* sure changed a lot. I guess good things *can* come out of bad things. Having that heart attack seems to have made Nate a lot nicer. I never thought I'd live to see the day that he goes to church with us."

"Oooooh, is there something going on here? Has hell frozen over? This is the first time you've denied that he loves you without also denying that you love him. Could it be that you're finally realizing that you do?"

"No, I don't. Not any more than I would any good friend. He's almost as good a friend as you are." She could see that Becky didn't believe her. "Come on, Becky. I'm married. I can't love two guys at the same time."

"Why not?"

"Well, it's just not right. That's why."

Becky shook her head. "Cal, you'd enjoy life so much more if you'd just loosen up. You're such an oddity in this town. You're missing out on so much."

Becky and Cal went to church together. Why weren't they hearing the same things from the pulpit, Cal wondered. She took her empty glass to the sink. "Can we talk about something else?

"He loves Kara, too. He's even put her in his will."

"He's *that* sure that she's his?"

"It's obvious, Cal. Face it."

She had known that her dark-haired daughter didn't bear much resemblance to Leonard, especially once her eyes had turned brown, but Cal had made love with Leonard hundreds, maybe thousands, of times over the years and was with Nate only once. The odds of Nate being Kara's father seemed so remote. Apparently, though, this child was just meant to be. Cal sighed. "I guess it's a good thing Nate and I have similar coloring and everything, so everybody probably just figures she looks like my side of the family instead of Len's."

Becky nodded. "So how's little Lennie? Have you heard from Stacy lately?"

Relieved that the subject had changed, Cal responded, "Yeah, we called them last night. They're all doing great. Next month, they'll be coming for a visit." Cal smiled, remembering her namesake's beautiful wedding three months earlier. "This will be the first time her husband has been here." Then her smile faded and she looked at Becky earnestly. "Stacy was so happy to finally have a real sister, after all these years. Let's *not* let her know that Kara is Nate's. Okay?"

"I won't tell anyone, Cal. I just wanted to be sure *you* knew, in case it ever became important."

* * *

The revelation had shaken Cal to the foundations, but now things were starting to make sense. That night, as Leonard lay asleep beside her, Cal thought back to the time Becky and Nate had visited her at the hospital after Kara was born. Cal had chosen the rooming-in option, so that her baby would be kept in the room with her instead of in the nursery. When Nate saw Kara for the first time, he had stood over her little bassinet, gazing at her, for a long while. At the time, Cal had thought that was sweet; but now she realized that he was probably trying to determine which man the infant resembled. Once Leonard took Cal and Kara home from the hospital, Nate visited now and then. As time went on, Nate came to their house more and more often, and urged Cal and Kara to come to his. When they had visited his house, they always received a warm welcome. He never failed to have age-appropriate toys available for Kara. All this time, Cal had assumed that he had originally gotten them for Becky's children—but maybe not. He had always come by on Kara's birthday, bearing a nice gift for her. Sometimes it would be a toy; sometimes a fancy little dress. All this time, she had thought Nate was just being a good friend who had a fondness for children in general. Now she was starting to see that what he was *really* doing was participating as much as he could in his own daughter's life, while maintaining the discretion necessary.

Why hadn't Cal ever noticed before how much Kara looked like Nate? It was embarrassing that others would know something about her daughter that she didn't know. In fact, she *still* didn't see that much resemblance between Kara and Nate when they were together; but that photo made it unmistakable. She sure hoped Leonard would never see it.

He had been such a proud father at first. His enthusiasm seemed to have waned as time went on, though. *Maybe just getting "old hat" by now*, she thought. And, too, Kara's "terrible twos" had been quite trying sometimes. She could be a stubborn little thing. *Just like Len*, Cal had thought. *Just like Cal*, Leonard had thought. She didn't remember sweet-natured Stacy being particularly troublesome at that age. Maybe that was because Cal was often away working, and Jill's the one who had to deal with it. Maybe a child going through the twos would cool any man's enthusiasm for a while.

She looked over at Leonard. He was sleeping peacefully. She smiled. He was still as handsome as ever, she thought. Only now, with graying hair and a few more pounds on him, he was handsome in a different way. He looked so distinguished now. Cal turned toward him and cuddled up to her husband. He put his arm around her, and she fell asleep in the familiar comfort of his arms.

*   *   *

"Hey, partner! Gimme five!" Leonard greeted his young Stetson-topped grandson at the airport. This child had been a surprise to his parents. When Stacy had been an exchange student in France, she "viva l'amour"-ed a bit more than she should have and returned to the States pregnant. Leonard, Jill and Cal were initially distressed at this turn of events—this was certainly not the kind of education they had intended for her to get—but soon grew to accept it and were determined to help Stacy give her child as good a life as possible. As a result, Stacy gratefully named her son after her own father, and affectionately called him "Lennie."

The boy happily slapped his granddad's outstretched hand, then held his own hand out for the response slap. He then grinned at Kara. "Hi, Carrot."

"I'm *not* Carrot! I'm *Kara!*"

"He's just teasing you," Stacy said as she and her husband, Jim, joined them. "He likes to tease a lot. Lennie, stop calling her Carrot." She gave Cal, then Leonard, a hug.

Leonard said, aside to Cal, "Looks like we have another young Nate and Cal on our hands, only the genders are reversed. Remember how you used to tease him?"

"Yeah," she nodded. "Times have changed. Hey, guys, guess what. Nate and I are going to do a TV reunion special soon. Well, actually, we start taping it soon, but it'll air in the fall. If it goes over big, and I hope it doesn't, they could make it a weekly show."

"Why do you hope it doesn't?" Stacy asked as they headed toward the baggage-claim area.

"Well, Nate's a lot healthier than he was for a while, but I still worry about his heart. I don't want him overdoing it."

"Any interesting cases lately, counselor?" Leonard asked Jim Shulman, a twenty-nine-year-old junior partner in a respected Connecticut law firm. Jim seemed to be taking good care of his bright-eyed wife, who was eight years younger than he. Leonard was glad she had chosen such a mature young man.

Jim smiled, "I guess you could call this a 'hit and run' case that walked in yesterday. It's motorist versus train." Seeing that not everyone understood his humor, he added, "It takes a train a mile or two to stop."

"If it's a matter of 'might makes right', the train will win every time," Cal said.

"We didn't take the case," continued Jim. "They wanted to sue the railroad for letting their train hit the car that had gone around the lowered gates. No way were we going to take that one on!"

Leonard shook his head. "People will sue over the darnedest things."

"That's for sure," Jim agreed.

"Hey, how's your model railroad coming? Can it top mine, yet?"

"Don't think so. You've got to make allowances for the fact that I'm not retired. The money's there, but the time isn't."

"I'm not retired, either."

Cal shook her finger at Jim, in mock sternness, "And don't you forget that!"

"I might think about retiring when they bury me," Leonard added.

Jim shook his head, "I can hardly wait to retire. There's so much I want to do but just don't have the time. I wouldn't have had the time for this vacation, but my mean ol' wife made me take one." He patted Stacy's back affectionately.

"Here comes our luggage," Stacy said. "There's six burgundy pieces and they all match, so they should be easy to spot."

"Hey, y'all are getting real uptown," said Cal. "Matching luggage and everything."

Stacy intimated to Cal, "It's okay to look prosperous when we're traveling, and he's got a real fancy office, but you should see the clunker he drives to court when he's got a trial going on. His boss doesn't want the jury and spectators to think his company profits *too much*."

After Jim took the suitcases off the conveyor belt, he and Leonard carried them to the car.

*   *   *

As Cal was waiting for Stacy to come back downstairs after tucking Lennie and Kara in for the night, she thought back over her day. Lennie was certainly a smart little guy, she marveled. Almost five years old and he could already read. In fact, he had called out just about every sign between the airport and home. "Burger Bar! Safeway! O'Riley Brothers!" Sign after sign, all the way home. Sometimes, he read out a sign before anyone else had even seen it. *His autism must be a different kind than Darrell's*, she thought. *He seems even higher functioning than Darrell. His friendliness, too, knocks the autism stereotype on its ear.* While he didn't always relate to other people appropriately, he, nevertheless, didn't hesitate to try. And he had such a cute sense of humor. *"Carrot", indeed,* Cal smiled.

Once they had gotten home, Kara had taken Lennie into the media room to watch a movie with her. Cal noticed that the tape Kara put on the VCR was one of her Corky ones, again, and she knew it was because her beloved "Uncle Nate" was its star. She then overheard Kara telling Lennie something that Cal didn't know whether to believe or not. She had said that Uncle Nate was going to buy three horses so he, Cal, and Kara would all be able to ride at the same time. *He might be loaded,* Cal thought, *but Zeus had cost $200,000. Surely he wouldn't buy three such expensive animals at the same time. It sure would be nice, though, if Kara's right.* Since her horse's passing, Cal had been avoiding horses—it hurt too much because every one she saw reminded her of her beloved Zeus—but now the idea of riding again excited her.

Income from the television special will be nice for both of them. Since both she and Nate had signed to do the show, and Nate said financing had been obtained, it was definitely going to happen. The producers didn't want one of them without the other. Cal couldn't figure out why, though. Surely, their manufactured 'teenage sweethearts' image had faded by now. Granted, both Cal and Nate looked younger than they were, but neither of them could be mistaken for teenagers anymore. The idea that had excited her agent so long ago was finally coming to fruition. Their special would be in the variety-show format that had been such a hit on the grueling promotional tour they had done so long ago. Variety shows had been big business back in the 1960s, then they fell by the wayside. Now, Stagecraft Productions was hoping to bring them back to a new generation of viewers, a generation that had never heard of Ed Sullivan. Would it work? That was anyone's guess, but it should sure be fun trying. They would have big-name guest stars. Even Leonard had agreed to guest on their show. One reason Cal was excited about this venture was that it would spotlight Nate's real talent—music. Sure, they would still do a comedy sketch to open the show, but she knew it was his vocal number with proper lighting and background instrumentals that would really carry it. She would just harmonize with him. Cal realized that she never did have a soloist's voice and never tried to be one. But, doggone it, she could do a bang-up job of harmonizing.

What kind of act would Leonard do, she wondered. She smiled when "lion tamer" was the first thing to pop into her mind. Maybe he could do Shakespearean readings. *He's always enjoyed that sort of thing, but had never been given a chance to do it since his twenties. It seemed that most casting directors for movies or television saw him only as a bad guy. Why can't those people use their imaginations?* she wondered. Maybe, just maybe, if this turned into a weekly series, he would become a regular on their show. He would love steady work, again. He always had. And that would give him ample opportunity to show the world that he could do other things, too—things that have nothing to do with his bad-guy image.

"Both kids are abed, now," Stacy said as she descended the stairs. "Where are the guys?"

Cal smiled. "Does the phrase 'choo-choo' mean anything to you?"

"Yeah, that'll keep them busy all night. I have a feeling Kara and Lennie will be awake half the night, too. They were giggling over one of Lennie's unique little jokes when I turned off the light."

"I remember when you were that age. You wanted to be a cowboy," Cal recalled fondly, "just like your daddy."

"And like you, too. I didn't want to miss out on anything. I loved it when y'all took me horseback riding with you."

"That was fun, wasn't it? Except that time you pulled me off the horse and broke my collarbone," Cal teased.

"I did not. You just lost your balance."

"I know. You were light enough I *thought* I could pull you up onto that horse. I didn't account for distribution of weight, though. I learned a little about physics that day."

"Yeah," Stacy said, relaxing beside Cal on the sofa, "it seems we learn more from the bad things in life than the good ones, doesn't it?"

Cal nodded. "I guess you're right. That's one of the ways that God can take a bad thing and make a good thing out of it. I've seen it happen so many times. It's kind of like Lennie. His autism makes things different for y'all, but I wouldn't say it makes it worse. Would you?"

"I wouldn't, either. In fact, because of his special needs, we've got a family therapist available to us to help us through any crisis; and Lennie's had the best, most caring teachers I've ever known. A lot more people care about us because of him."

"If only every family could have that kind of emotional support."

* * *

The two families were having a wonderful week together. Jim and Leonard worked on the train layout while swapping advice and complaints about the local hobby dealers on both coasts. They taught Lennie the fine art of model railroading, allowing him the honor of wearing the engineer's hat and blowing the whistle. Cal and Stacy took their children to the swimming pool and the park. As they sat on the bench and watched Kara on one swing and

Lennie perseverating while sitting on another, they chatted about various aspects of their lives. Stacy's life seemed to be doing quite well. All was going relatively smoothly with her marriage, and she had accepted the semi-weekly visits to the speech therapist with equanimity. That therapy, in addition to the special-education program he's getting at preschool, she had said, would help Lennie progress more easily. "And, golly, Kara's growing so fast!"

"We didn't have to discipline you very much," Cal recalled, "but Kara can be kind of ornery when she wants to be. I was hoping Len would keep her in line like he did for me—after all, he *is* a professional bad guy—but he doesn't want to do it. And I don't have the heart. She's such a precious little thing."

"You know, when Nate came over that afternoon and Kara climbed into his lap, I was wishing that Daddy and I had had a relationship like that. I mean, Nate's so *sweet* to her, calling her his little Kara-Mia and everything. When I was little and got into Daddy's lap, I never did really feel like I had his whole attention. He always seemed kind of distracted. And I don't even remember Nate being around when I was a kid."

"Oh, he was, but we weren't friends back then like we are now. Kara's got the advantage of being born when he wasn't making movies all the time. If it's of any comfort to you, though, Len's not all that involved with Kara either. I guess he relates better to adults than to little kids."

"Yeah, probably so. Since Nate never had any kids of his own, I guess he likes to spoil yours. He must be thinking 'any kid of my buddy's is a kid of mine,' huh?" she laughed.

"I guess," Cal said uneasily. Then she pointed at the sky. "It looks like it's going to rain. Maybe we better get the troops home and see what Jessie has planned for dinner."

∗   ∗   ∗

The week had gone well. Everyone had had a good time together and now the Rhoadses had taken the Shulmans back to the airport.

Jim shook Leonard's hand and patted Cal on the back. "Thanks for having us. It was quite a relaxing vacation. I guess Stacy's right. I really needed that."

"Bye, Carrot," Lennie gleefully waved.

"Don't call me Carrot!" Kara yelled, as he giggled.

Jim took Lennie's hand and led him toward the gate. Stacy hugged Cal and Leonard goodbye, then caught up with her family.

∗   ∗   ∗

Work started almost immediately on the Mike-and-Corky special. They were quite fortunate to have gotten Bruce Taylor and his band to agree to provide the music. Marilyn Franklin, a current teen favorite, and Leonard would be their special guest stars. There were a few lesser-known, but quite talented, regulars who would fill in the other parts.

The writers had studied the original trilogy and had written a skit for the stars with a similar theme. This skit showed what would happen if Corky and Mike just happened to bump into each other at a ski resort twenty years later. Thinking they could finally reap the havoc they had planned in their youth, they were thwarted once again by Officer Stanton, who was now working as the security guard at the ski facility.

As work on this show progressed, Cal got more and more excited about it. The skit was wonderful, the duet she and Nate did later in the show was one of her favorite songs of all time, "More," and, after consistent begging from Cal, the producers let Leonard do a very moving Shakespearean soliloquy, which brought tears to Cal's eyes. Marilyn did her specialty comic act. These features, along with several other acts—an animal act, a magician, and an acrobatic act—were sure to make the show a hit, she thought. It would be a project of which they could all be proud and would probably appeal to all ages.

It took two and a half weeks to tape this one-hour show. Cal insisted on this slower pace in order to keep the work as low-stress for Nate as possible. Once it aired, they would then be very eager to receive feedback from the viewers. Perhaps they could do several specials, if the audience liked it.

Chapter 5

Nate came over to the Rhoads house to watch the television broadcast of their special with them. He brought a bottle of champagne, chilled on ice, for the occasion. As they settled into the media room to await the beginning of the show, Kara staked out her place on Nate's lap.

"As soon as the show's over, kiddo, it'll be your bedtime," Cal said.

"Aw," Kara whined. "Uncle Nate's here. Can't I stay up longer?"

"You've got school tomorrow."

Nate looked at Kara with mock surprise. "You're not old enough to go to school yet. I thought you were born just a few days ago."

She put her hands on his cheeks. "No, silly. I'm five. I'm a big girl now."

"You're growing up too fast. Stop it right now, you hear?" He took her hands in his and gave each a little kiss as she giggled.

"It's starting," Cal said as Leonard took the remote control and turned the sound up. On the screen flashed the title, *Stagecraft Presents: The Nate Jenkins–Stacy Ames Variety Hour.* Everyone settled down and all was quiet in the room as they watched the screen intently.

* * *

Late that night, Cal and Leonard were getting ready for bed. She felt as if she were floating on air. The broadcast looked great to her, and they had received quite a few phone calls afterward from their friends, congratulating them on having such a good show. If the television stations and, in turn, the studio were hearing similar comments, it looked as though there might be more specials in their future.

"You did great, Len," Cal said as she slipped into her nightgown. "It looks like we 'kids' got the best of you again, doesn't it? And this time, I wasn't as inept as I was way back then. I know more about acting now."

"From the phone calls, I'd say it was the musical number you and Nate did that was the biggest hit."

"Really? I could've sworn the skit would be, and I thought the Shakespearean soliloquy was a mighty close second." She got into bed.

"I'm betting that your prime audience will be the Baby Boomers, and they'll associate things like Shakespeare with required reading in high school. I think the music and maybe the comedy element, too, will be what carries it. No one said anything about the other acts."

"That's probably because they were our friends and we weren't in those other acts. Paul's friends probably called him to tell him how great the animal act was."

"You might be right." He turned off the overhead light and got into bed.

Cal turned the bedside lamp on so she could read a while before going to sleep. "I wonder if we can talk the producers into letting Kara do a little act, kind of like Sonny and Cher did with Chastity."

"No, I don't want you to do that."

"Why not? She's a great little storyteller. We could have a section just for kids and she can tell stories."

"No."

"Why?"

He looked at her for a minute, then said softly, "Just because."

Cal studied his face. He looked sad. "What's the matter? Aren't you happy about the show?"

"Yes, I'm very happy about the show. I just don't want Kara on national television."

"Why?"

He took a deep breath and let it out slowly. "It's hard enough that our neighbors and friends have suspicions. I don't want the whole world in on it."

"What're you talking about?"

"I'm not blind, Cal. Anyone who sees Nate and Kara can tell they're related. She looks just like him."

Her heart hurt for Leonard. "But she has my curly hair." That was small consolation, she knew. Cal wondered why Kara's resemblance to Nate was so obvious to everyone but her. She guessed she *should* be relieved that Leonard knows. Cal hated to keep secrets from her husband. "Len, you and I have done it zillions of times. Why did that one time with Nate have to be the one that got me pregnant? I don't understand."

He shrugged. "Because you were careless about taking your pills when I wasn't in town."

Cal sighed.

"Kara's crazy about him." Leonard said. "She doesn't know, does she?"

"No, of course not. And, if you don't want her to, she never will." Cal stroked his hair. "I hope you understand that it was rape, and not an affair."

"I suspected as much. I remember how bruised you were."

"You're not going to treat Kara any differently because of this, are you? Please keep being her daddy. She needs you."

"I know," he smiled. "It's not hard to love her. She might look like Nate, but she's very much like you in every other way. She has a stubborn streak that reminds me of you when you were a teenager."

"That's the part of Kara that I thought came from the Rhoads side of the family," Cal said lightheartedly. "Hey, Len," she said as her fingers brushed his hair out of his face, "was it hard to fight with me back then without squashing me like a June bug? You could've done a lot of real damage to me with your bare hands, but you never did—just some bruising is all. I think I hurt you more than you hurt me."

"I did only what was necessary to get you to realize I meant business. I didn't even mean to bruise you. It just happened."

"And you found out *I* meant business, too, didn't you?"

"Yeah. You were downright feisty." He smiled again, "Kara sure gets *that* honestly."

Cal said in a little-girl voice, "Don't call me Carrot!"

He chuckled as he wrapped his arms around her.

*   *   *

Feedback from viewers about the variety hour confirmed much of what Leonard had predicted. Their audience was, indeed, mostly comprised of people from the Baby-Boomer generation. Seeing Nate and Cal together again as Mike and Corky brought back happy memories of the 1960s and they enjoyed the comedy sketch the most. Their next-favorite act was the musical number, sung by Nate and Cal. The young special guest star was only moderately received, but they loved seeing Officer Stanton again. Many of the respondees saw the Shakespearean soliloquy as being out of character for him, though. A surprising number indicated an interest in seeing other members of the cast of the original trilogy and its sequel.

Cal and Nate attended two meetings with the producers and representatives of the show's sponsors, in which they decided to do a second special and discussed a change in format for the next show. Since he was part of the trilogy, it was decided that Leonard would be asked to return. Their guest stars would be those who were popular in the 1960s, as well as actors who had played some of the more minor roles in the trilogy but had never achieved fame. Instead of a general variety format, they would focus on music and comedy mainly with, perhaps, one novelty act. Each show would have a comedy dialog similar to the Burns-and-Allen type routine Cal and Nate had done on the tour, as well as a longer comedy sketch, based on the characters from the trilogy.

The writers, casting director, and producers were to begin right away getting these things together, and rehearsals for the next show would commence soon after that was accomplished.

* * *

"Guess what, Mama!" Kara ran into the house upon her return from the circus. "Mama, where are you?" she called.

"I'm coming. What happened?" Cal rushed into the living room.

Kara, eyes bright with excitement, handed her mother the remnants of her cotton candy. "Uncle Nate bought *three* horses and they were delivered this afternoon. Now we can all go riding together!"

"Hot diggity dog! Are you sure?"

"Yeah, and he said the little one's mine and I can name him."

Nate arrived and joined them in the living room. "Kara Michelle Rhoads, don't you *ever* jump out of the car before it's completely stopped!" he sternly reprimanded. "Never do that again!"

Suddenly contrite, Kara meekly said, "I'm sorry."

"Let me see your knees. I saw you fall." He knelt down to inspect her skinned knees.

"I'm sorry." Tears made their way down her cheek. "Don't fuss at me anymore, Uncle Nate."

He gave her a hug. "I didn't mean to make you cry, Kara-Mia. I just don't want you to get hurt. You'll always wait for the car to stop from now on?"

She nodded.

"Okay." He took a hankie from his pocket and wiped her cheeks. Then he stood back up and took her by the hand to the kitchen, where he lifted her up and set her on the counter. Nate took a paper towel and, after holding it under water and wringing it out, cleaned up Kara's knees.

"Ow!" she complained.

Cal had gone into the other room and retrieved a box of Band-Aids. She brought it into the kitchen and handed it to Nate. After drying Kara's knees with another paper towel, he then applied a Band-Aid to each one. "See why you shouldn't jump out of cars like that?"

"Yeah," Kara said softly.

He set her back onto the floor. "Did you tell your mom about the horses?"

"Oh, Nate, she did." Cal could hardly contain her enthusiasm. "Did you *really* buy three of them?"

He smiled broadly. "Two horses and a pony. If your family would like to come riding, there's one for each of you. I have all the accessories, too, so they're ready to go. I also have a large horse trailer, in case you'd like to take them out in the country to ride."

"Oooo, you're terrific!" Cal gave him a big hug. "Can I go see them now?" she asked eagerly.

"Sure. Want to come, Kara?"

"Yeah!"

"How about Leonard?" Nate asked. "He can come, too."

"He's at a meeting or something. We'll probably be back before he gets home." Cal grabbed her keys and said, "Come on, Kara. Last one to the car's a rotten egg."

Kara ran after her mother. "Mama, don't forget to stay in the car until it stops."

*　*　*

"She's beautiful!" Cal had immediately gone to the one who looked the most like her own horse of long ago. "Is she as sweet-natured as Zeus?" She gently stroked the horse's neck.

"I don't think we'll ever find another Zeus, Cal. This one is a bit more spirited. What would you like to name her?"

"*Me?* She's *your* horse."

"Name her anyway. Kara has dibs on the pony. I think I'll name the stallion Amadeus."

"See, Mama. This one's just my size, and he's all spotty."

"Those spots look just like patches, don't they?" she replied.

"That's what I'll name my horse," Kara chirped, "Patches!"

Nate smiled, "Okay, we've got Amadeus and Patches. What's the identity of this mystery lady here?" he patted the horse onto which Cal was already putting a saddle.

"Fido?" Cal grinned at him as she tightened a strap.

"No, I'm serious."

"Well, I'll just have to give her a test ride first, then maybe a good name will come to me." After she was sure everything was adjusted correctly, she mounted the regal mare and started her on a leisurely walk around the perimeter of Nate's considerable back yard. Then, they broke into a run from one end of the yard to the other, gracefully dodging the swings and sliding board. Cal then led her more slowly back to Nate and Kara, where she stopped. "She seems like an Isis to me."

Nate tried to stifle a smile. "Are you sure?"

"Why not?" she dismounted and proceeded to unstrap the saddle.

"Isis was the goddess of fertility."

"I thought she was a kid-show super-hero."

"I guess she had two jobs."

"Okay, then. How about Veronica?"

"Your character in *Henson of Manhattan*."

"Yeah. You saw that?"

He nodded. "I have the video. I was otherwise occupied at the time it was released. Remember?"

"Oh, sorry." She recalled now that he was imprisoned at the time. "I guess that name would bring back bad memories. Golly, Kara was easier to name than this horse is." Then an idea came to her. "I know. How about Rapunzel? She's got a long mane."

"Are you sure?"

"*Now* what's wrong? Is that the Greek goddess of B-movies or something?"

"No," he patted her back. "You just name her anything you want. If you like Rapunzel, then Rapunzel she'll be."

"I like Isis."

"Okay. We have Isis, Amadeus, and Patches. They are all now officially Christianed," Nate declared.

"Can I ride Patches now?" Kara asked.

Cal looked over at Nate, "You have a small saddle?"

He nodded and went to the back of the stable. He then returned with a saddle that was just the right size for Patches and put it on the pony.

Cal double-checked everything, then lifted Kara up onto the animal. "All comfy?" she asked. "Ready to go?"

"Yeah. I wanna' run like you did."

"We'll just walk today. You'll learn to run later." Cal lead the pony around the yard, as Nate walked alongside in case Kara lost her balance.

The ride delighted the child, and she was all smiles as they brought Patches back to the stable and Nate returned Kara to the ground. "Am I a cowboy like Daddy, now?" she asked.

Cal grinned, "You need a black hat to be like Daddy." She intimated to Nate, "She's been watching his old TV Westerns."

Kara tugged at his sleeve. "Do y'all have any chocolate-chip cookies?"

"After eating hotdogs and cotton candy all afternoon, you still want a cookie?" he asked. "Where are you putting all that?"

"Or maybe two of 'em. If I get too full, I can take the other one home and eat it for my bedtime snack."

He patted her curly brown hair. "Okay. Go see what's in the cookie jar."

She ran to the back door and rang the bell. Mrs. North let her in.

Nate turned to Cal. "Let's hope she has your metabolism. I can see she has your appetite."

"They can keep their icky ol' caviar. Chocolate-chip cookies is where it's at," she grinned.

Nate got the brush from the shelf and started grooming Amadeus. "So she wants to be a cowboy like her daddy."

"Well, the bad guy *does* seem to have all the fun in those shows." Then she grew more serious. "Nate, Len knows that you're her real father. He said it's obvious. But we don't want Kara to know."

This revelation startled him at first, then he relaxed and resumed brushing his horse. "I didn't even know *you* knew it."

She took another brush off the shelf and began to groom Isis. "Like everything else, I think I was the last one to notice. That seems to happen a lot with me."

"Well, Cal, this is one time I *can't* say I'm sorry. Who could ever be sorry for helping to create such a wonderful little girl? Do you realize Kara's the first person who's ever loved me for who I am and not for my celebrity status or my money?"

"Becky and your uncle do, too."

"Kara's love is so pure. She couldn't care less about fame or fortune."

"She just knows Uncle Nate's someone who will always make time for her."

"Every child needs someone like that."

Cal sighed. "That's one thing my parents never seemed to have. Time."

"I hope this hasn't caused problems between you and Leonard, though."

She sadly shook her head, "I wanted to see if the producers would let her be on our show now and then, but Len said no. He doesn't want the whole world to know that you fathered my child."

"I can't say that I blame him. Something like that would be a blow to any man's ego." He put the brush back on the shelf. "And, besides, I wouldn't want Kara going into this business, anyway. It can be an awfully hard way to make a living. I've seen people shattered by callous directors and bad reviews. She hasn't indicated any interest in show business, has she?"

"Well, no."

"Then let's leave well enough alone. Maybe she'll be one of the sane ones and decide to be a teacher or something."

Cal grinned, "Or a cowboy."

*   *   *

Leonard was agreeable to recreating his Officer Stanton role, yet again, on their second special, this time entitled *The Nate Jenkins–Stacy Ames Hour*, with the stipulation that he would also be allowed to do a five-minute spot of his choice in the second half of the show. Realizing that these specials could easily become a series, his purpose for this spot was to prevent becoming stereotyped into the Officer Stanton mold. The fact that the Shakespearean soliloquy had not gone over well because the audience considered it out of character illustrated this point. They came up with different ideas on how this five-minute spot would be carried out, some serious, some comedy; and it was decided that he and Cal would do a routine that would give the audience a lesson of some sort in a palatable form. The first of these spots would be a mini-skit in which Leonard would be the driving instructor and Cal the eager, but dim-witted, student. The very serious point made, in a humorous setting, would be the danger of not heeding railroad-crossing signals.

Guesting in this show would be Judy Majors, one of the lucky teens chosen for the original Corky film. As soon as she walked into the studio that Monday morning, Cal ran over and gave her a great big hug. "Judy! It's been so long, but you haven't changed at all. How'd you stay fifteen while the rest of us got old?" she asked. It was true. Judy still looked very much like she did then, except she had put on some weight.

"Wow, Cal!" she said happily, "you sure know how to keep your guest stars happy. And I get *paid* for it, too?" Then she continued in a stage whisper, "I hear you and that awful policeman are going to be having your fifteenth wedding anniversary soon. You sure are weird for a Hollywood couple!"

"We're just too lazy to start all over again with new spouses. So what've you been up to all these years?"

"Not more movies, that's for sure. After that one, I went back home to Florida, picked up where I left off, went on to college, and became a marine biologist. My husband got a promotion a few years ago, and his company relocated us to California. I was so surprised when your people called me and asked me to be on your show."

"Got a family?"

Judy nodded, "Six kids and I'm on my second husband now."

"Wow! Six! Are you still a marine biologist with all those kids? How on earth would you have time?"

"The older ones take care of the younger ones while I'm working. I had four with my first husband, then a few years later started on the second batch."

"I've got just one—an adorable little girl named Kara."

"Yeah, I saw that. After I read the article about them, I figured you *have* been influenced by Hollywood a little bit, anyway. But no one could blame you for that," she winked. "He could've had any of us."

"What're you talking about?"

"Didn't you see *Hollywood Update* this week? All four of you were on it."

"Isn't that a tabloid?"

"Yeah. It showed Nate and your little girl at a circus and told all about your being good friends and everything. But, like I said, no one's blaming you for slipping just a little. When it comes to Nate, I imagine any of us would've done the same if we'd had the opportunity. Don't I remember you two chasing each other around the set a lot?"

"Yeah, some. Do you still have a copy of that article?"

"Well, yeah. I might. I'll check tonight."

"Come on," Cal beckoned. "We're doing a read-through first. We get to do a twenty-minute sketch based on the trilogy. I'm so glad you can be in this one. It ought to be a lot of fun. Len's still Officer Stanton and we now-grownup kids keep bumping into him in the most unlikely places. This time, it'll be at the mall."

*   *   *

The next day Judy brought in her copy of *Hollywood Update* and handed it to Cal. On its cover were three pictures. One was a photo taken at the circus of Nate and Kara getting cotton candy from the vendor. Right below that was a picture of Nate and Cal in their *Campus Dreams* love scene. Set apart from the other two was a photo of Leonard in which he appeared to be looking on with great concern. This picture was taken from a tragic scene in *Henson of Manhattan*. In large type was the question, "Nate and Stacy's love child?" The corresponding article alluded to the fact that Nate had been seen quite often with Stacy Ames' daughter, Carol…

"They got the name wrong," Cal mumbled as she read on.

… who bears a striking resemblance to him. Wide speculation had been confirmed, it said, that Nate and Stacy have been having an affair for many years, despite the fact that she and character actor Leonard Rhoads would be celebrating their fifteenth anniversary soon. Nate, however, had remained a swinging single throughout this time.

"Me and Mama go to Uncle Nate's house and he comes over to our house, too. He bought us some horses," it quoted Kara as saying. It went on to elaborate on their visits, the equipment he had installed in his back yard for her, and the fondness that the two co-stars of *The Nate Jenkins–Stacy Ames Hour* were reported to still have for each other. "They hug a lot," Kara had said.

"They've talked to Kara," Cal said. "That reporter *had* to have gotten that information from her directly."

She took the paper over to Nate, who was conferring with the director. When he was finished there, Nate then directed his attention to Cal. "What's the matter?"

"Look." She showed him the paper.

He took it to his chair, sat and read it. Then he handed it back to Cal, "They did it again."

"Why'd you let a reporter talk to her? It had to have been there at the circus."

"I didn't see any reporter there. If she talked to anyone without my knowledge, it had to have been in the ladies' room. Sorry, Cal. I couldn't go in there with her, and she's too old for me to take into the men's room."

"This is going to kill Len."

"Does he have to see it?"

"Well, someone's bound to mention it to him."

"At least, it's good for business. Look at it that way. We can't stop people from gossiping, but we *can* take advantage of it. I bet more people will tune in to our next show because of this."

The director's assistant called everyone to the set. Rehearsals were to start momentarily.

* * *

"Damn!" Leonard slammed the tabloid down on the kitchen table. "Kara! Come here!"

A moment later, she came into the kitchen. "What, Daddy?" The angry look in his eyes startled her.

Cal joined them in the kitchen. "What's the matter, Len?" Then she noticed the tabloid on the table and her heart sank. "Oh."

"You did a bad thing, Kara," he said harshly. "You told a reporter things that are private."

Hoping to diffuse the situation a bit, Cal knelt down to Kara. "You remember talking to someone at the circus?"

"I talked to Uncle Nate a lot, and a clown, too."

"Anyone else? Maybe in the ladies' room?"

She thought a minute. "A lady was in the bathroom and she asked who my mama was. She asked me a lot of questions."

Cal nodded, "That's the one. That lady was a reporter and she wrote some bad things about us in a paper."

Leonard pulled Kara around to face him, "Don't you ever talk to any reporters again, you hear? If they ask you a question, you tell them to talk to us."

"Okay. Why did she write bad things?"

Cal stood back up. "Because bad things make people want to buy that paper. And now people are going to think Uncle Nate and I are bad people."

"Why?"

"Um," Cal hesitated. "Len, it's not Kara's fault. She didn't know any better." Then she looked back down at Kara, "You do what Daddy said, okay? If someone starts asking you questions, you tell them to talk to us."

"Okay. Can I tell that lady that you're not bad people?"

"It wouldn't do any good," Leonard said irritably. "Cal, you *know* what every one of the viewers is going to be thinking when they see the show, don't you?"

"Mama, will you take me to see that lady?"

"I hope we'll be putting on such a good show that they'll just be entertained," Cal told Leonard, hopefully.

"They're going to be feeling sorry for me, that's what! I hate that!"

"They just don't understand, but I can't think of a way to explain it to them that wouldn't make it worse."

Kara pulled on Leonard's sleeve. "Daddy, can you drive me there?"

"How could this happen?" he continued. "It wasn't supposed to be this way."

"I know, I know," Cal agreed.

"Damn!" he yelled, as he stormed out.

*   *   *

Leonard and Cal called an urgent meeting with the producer, director, writers, and Nate. The problem was discussed and various possible solutions were offered. After much debate, it was agreed by all that the best way to handle this sensitive issue would be head-on, but with humor. It would be written into the script that Officer Stanton would catch Mike gleefully trying to take liberties with Corky and would, with much ceremony, escort him to jail. Keeping Leonard's character in control of the situation would alleviate much of his anxiety about the show, and allowing Nate's character to be admittedly in the wrong should satisfy the audience's sense of justice while, at the same time, allowing the ensemble to continue working together comfortably.

They still had time to work it into the show they were rehearsing this week, and it was carried out seamlessly, much to the audience's delight and amusement.

Such a hit was this theme that they decided to do a different version of it in every show that would follow. Mike ended up in jail at the end of each Corky-and-Mike skit, with the classic "curses, foiled again" closing line.

Chapter 6

"Oh, come on, Len. He got Amadeus for you to use. Please come riding with us," Cal coaxed Leonard as he was trying to read the newspaper.

"I'm not interested."

"Kara's a pretty good little horsewoman these days. She'd love for you to see her ride her pony."

"Some other time, maybe."

"Let's take them to the country and we can race."

"I said *no*, Cal!"

She sighed, then went out the front door and joined Kara, who was waiting in the car.

*　*　*

Going riding with Kara was nice, but it just wasn't the same without Leonard. Cal missed the lighthearted races they used to have and the heart-to-heart talks that would sometimes follow. It seemed as though Leonard had once again lost the ability to feel joy. It had come back for a while when they were doing the specials and having such a fun time with them. The ratings were good and there was talk about it becoming a weekly show next season. Things seemed to be running smoothly, and yet Leonard seemed to have lapsed back into a depressed state. The only time he seemed happy was at work. When he was like this, he seemed unreachable to Cal. It was a very frustrating situation. She had asked him to see a doctor or a counselor for help with this, but he refused.

"What's the matter?" Nate asked as he, atop Amadeus, caught up with Cal and Isis. Kara and Patches were up ahead. "It looks like you're trying to figure out the mystery of the universe."

"I'm just kind of concerned about Len. I couldn't get him to come riding with us today, and it seems to be like that with everything these days except work. I can't get him to have fun anymore."

"I guess he's a workaholic. Some people are like that."

"I guess. What if they make our show weekly, Nate? That worries me."

"What's to worry about? That's a *good* problem to have."

"It'd be more stressful for you. I'm afraid your heart will give you trouble again."

"Oh, Cal. Don't be such a worrywart. I'll be okay."

"How do you know?"

"Because we have good people working on the show and they know our limitations. It'll be all right. And, besides, I've been feeling pretty good. My surgery last year fixed a lot of what was wrong with me. As long as I take reasonable precautions, I'll be fine."

"Come on, y'all," Kara called. "You're too slow."

Cal and Nate caught up with her, one on each side. Here in the country were many good places to ride. They also found an unexpected surprise—a small park that had not been used much since the larger one had been developed just a couple of miles away. It was still nice, though, and Kara had temporarily left her pony to climb on the jungle jim. Cal and Nate dismounted and sat on a grassy mound, enjoying the warm day while keeping an eye on the child.

"I wish Len had let me name her Jill," Cal said, dreamily.

He looked at her with amusement. "You wanted to name Kara Jill?"

"Yeah. Jill named her baby after me, so I thought I'd return the favor. She must think I'm awfully ungrateful since I didn't."

He smiled and shook his head.

"I hope she doesn't think I'm mad at her or anything."

"Don't worry about it, Cal." He put his arm around her comfortingly.

She watched her daughter and sighed. "I wonder what the future holds for her. I wonder what kind of life she'll have and what kind of work she'll do."

"That's the wonderful thing about it—the sky's the limit. Whatever she sets her mind to, she can do. And that kid has a lot of spunk. She'll go far in life."

She looked over at Nate and smiled. Then she rested her head on his shoulder. "I'm so glad there's a man in her life who cares so much about her. She's a lucky little girl."

It would have felt so natural to have held Cal in his arms, but Nate stopped himself. "Cal, I might have changed a lot in the last six years, but I'm not totally immune to this sort of thing. If you want to stay true to Leonard, you'd better not get too cozy."

"Oh." She sat back up. "Sorry."

"On the other hand, if you don't mind being *un*true to Leonard, you can get as cozy as you want. I'd be happy to cooperate."

"No, that's okay. You're right." Cal just wished that Leonard were as loving toward her and Kara as Nate was.

"Don't want to try for a little boy, this time?" he joked.

She playfully punched his arm.

*　　*　　*

Officer Stanton had become a favorite of the viewers. By the end of the season, he was considered one of the main stars of the show, not a supporting actor. The audience had come to accept Leonard as the different characters that he portrayed in the second half of each show, but Officer Stanton still remained their favorite.

As the cast and crew ended the taping of the last special of the season, it was almost certain that they would return that fall with a weekly slot on the TV schedule. Their sponsors had already renewed for the next year and they had picked up two more. The paychecks that the show provided were gratifying to Leonard, and having their old friends from the 1960s as guest stars had been exciting for Cal.

Everything was finished on the set. All that was left was the end-of-the-season cast party. In addition to the regular cast and crew, all of this season's guest stars and their spouses were invited, and it was becoming noisy indeed as everyone was arriving at the designated hotel suite.

Leonard joined the group of men in the center of the room as Cal went to the buffet table. Aha! They knew she was coming. Not only did they have the usual hors d'oeuvres, but there was a side table of nothing but chocolate desserts! Cal now knew where she would be spending most of the evening.

"I've heard that chocolate is an aphrodisiac," said a feminine voice from behind her. She turned around. It was Cheryl, a guest star from the show that aired last month.

"I'll vouch for that," Cal grinned. "Have some. Maybe this will turn out to be a very interesting party. We can all have a chocolate orgy."

"I'll take two, then." Cheryl picked up a petit four and a mini-éclair, and smiled at Cal as she popped the petit four into her mouth.

"Did you bring your husband?" Cal asked. "I haven't met him yet."

"Oh, he's here somewhere." She looked around for him. "There's so many people around, it's easy to get lost."

"Ah, *here's* where all the action is," said Judy as she joined them. "I think a table like this is a what my teenage son so eloquently calls a 'chick magnet.'"

"Can you believe who the hottest star is in this production? Nate might've had all the girls fantasizing when we were kids, but it looks like Leonard's the main man now," said Cheryl.

Cal smiled with pride as she looked over at her husband, deep in conversation with the executives. "He *has* aged gracefully, hasn't he? I think he's sexier now than he was back then."

"It looks like you've taken good care of him, Cal," said Judy, as she picked up a cupcake and took a bite.

"I'd *like* to think it's me, but I really think it's work that's kept him young. He's happiest when he's working."

"Aren't we all?" laughed Cheryl. "I've only gotten a couple commercials in the last year. I wish I had steady work."

"Hey, commercials would be fun. I liked TV work better than films because they didn't take as long, but commercials would take even *less* time."

"Tell you what, sister. I'll trade you two of my commercials for one season of your show. Two-for-one. Isn't that a good deal?"

Nate joined them. "Hey, ladies. Are you bartering work now?"

"Here's the reason I'm working at all, gals," Cal said. "Stagecraft didn't want me without him. Isn't that funny how I'm worth a million dollars standing beside Nate, but only about a nickel by myself?"

"It works the other way, too," he said. "Together, we're very valuable to the company. Separately, we're just as expendable as any other actors."

"Let's take a poll. I think his biggest talent is his music, don't you?" Cal asked her friends. Then she looked at Nate. "I bet if you recorded 'Moon Over Naples,' it'd be a best seller."

"With you harmonizing," he added.

"I agree with Cal. Why don't you cut a record?" Judy asked. "I bet it'd do well."

"Yeah, it would," agreed Cheryl.

"Thanks, ladies. I have something I need to discuss with Cal now, if you'd excuse us."

"Sure. Don't forget what we said. Music's where it's at," Judy said to the pair as they left and went out onto the terrace.

Once they were outside, he pushed the glass doors closed to ensure privacy.

"What's so secret?" Cal asked.

"Uncle Bob said they're planning a promotional tour for the studio during hiatus. He asked if we'd go on it. Do you have any plans for the next couple of months?"

She put her hand on his shoulder. "Nate, not another tour. I never want to go on another one of those things. And remember how sick you got after that first one?"

"That wasn't my first, but it was my last one to date."

"What would the schedule be? Would it only be a week or so?"

"He was talking about four weeks, again."

"No, Nate. Please don't do it," she pleaded. "If it made you get pneumonia that bad when you were young, what would it do to you now?"

He took her hands in his own. "You really care, don't you?"

"Of course I do. Please don't go, Nate. I don't want to, either."

"It seemed pretty important to Uncle Bob."

"Other people can go and do a good job. It doesn't have to be us, does it?"

The doors opened and Leonard looked at her coldly. "Come with me, Cal. There's somebody I want you to meet."

"Who?" she asked, as he took her hand and led her back into the room and across the floor.

They stopped near the inner doorway, where two gentlemen were taking drinks off a waiter's tray. "Cal, this is Elmer Rand and Maxwell Forster. They represent Kane Products, one of our sponsors."

She shook hands with the men and waited to see what business they wanted to discuss with her. After greeting her, they resumed their previous conversation about Mr. Forster's safari in Africa. Cal tried to look interested, but it was quite boring for her. She glanced around to see what other groups she could join.

"Gentlemen," Leonard said apologetically, "my wife and I need to be getting back home. Thank you for coming tonight. We'll be seeing you again in a few months."

After they said their farewells, Leonard led Cal back to their car and they went home.

∗   ∗   ∗

After Cal saw the governess, Miss James, to her car, she returned to the house and Leonard locked the door for the night.

"Why do you always cut our time short at parties, Len?" Cal asked. "We were just starting to have fun. Didn't you see all that chocolate?"

"I don't like parties. And I don't like the way you and Nate were fawning all over each other, either."

"What do you mean? We weren't fawning."

"What do you call it, then?" His icy stare penetrated to her bones.

She shook her head in disgust as she started up the stairs. "I don't call it anything. We're just friends. That's what friends do in Hollywood."

He turned off the downstairs lights and followed her into their bedroom. "Just friends, huh? I haven't seen you holding the hands of any of your other friends. Don't you have any other friends, Cal?"

She didn't have an answer to that. She took off her earrings.

He continued, "I'm sick and tired of you going over to Nate's house, talking about Nate to Kara, hugging Nate at work—everything's Nate, Nate, Nate—everywhere we go!"

"At least *he* cares about Kara and me," she said as she changed into her nightgown. "At least *he* takes time to be a good male role model for her. Nobody else does!"

"I've never been good with kids, Cal. You know that. When she gets older, we'll have a good relationship, like Stacy and I do."

"But she needs you *now*. You're not there for her."

"I'm home as much as you are."

"Even when you're home, you're not there for her—or for me, either, for that matter. You're so busy being wrapped up in yourself and your work, you don't have any room in your life for Kara or me. And the worst part of it is that it seems you just couldn't care less. Our needs mean nothing to you." She picked up her pillow and headed toward the door.

"Get back here!" He grabbed her by the arm and pulled her back into their room. "Don't you walk out when I'm talking to you!"

"I'm going to sleep in the guestroom. I don't want to be in here."

"No, you're not."

The couple verbally battled it out for another fifteen minutes before finally settling down to sleep.

*　*　*

"What's going on, Cal?" Nate asked over the phone the next day. "Kara called me last night and said you and Leonard were having another fight. She was really upset."

"She's right, but, doggone it, Nate. I can't be a happily-married couple all by myself. He's got to do his part."

"Would you like for Kara to stay here while you and Leonard work things out?"

"Oh, I don't know. He doesn't seem to want to work anything out."

"If you two are fighting a lot, that could be traumatic for Kara. I don't want her to be caught in the middle."

"I know."

"She'd be well cared for over here."

"I know she would be," Cal sighed. "Dadgum it, Nate. Why can't Len be like you? Why can't he care for her the way you do? It's not like she *chose* to come when she did. Why can't he see that she's the innocent party in all this?"

"I don't know, Cal. I just don't know."

"It just isn't fair."

"Why don't you two go for counseling? It'd probably do you a world of good."

"He won't go. I've tried. It's like I'm married to a stranger. He's just not himself anymore, and I don't know how to get the old Len back." Her moist eyes overflowed and she started sobbing. "I just don't know what to do, Nate."

"Ask him, won't you? Ask him if he'd agree to Kara's living here for a while. That will give you two time to do whatever you want. Maybe you both just need a break from responsibility. Now that we're not working, this is a perfect time for that."

"Okay. I'll ask," she said. "Thanks, Nate, for being such a good friend. I don't know what I'd do without you."

"It's okay, Cal. Let me know what he says."

*   *   *

She did, indeed, present the suggestion to Leonard, then braced herself for the verbal tirade that was sure to follow. She just *knew* that he'd hit the ceiling the very next time she mentioned Nate's name. It didn't happen.

"That might be a good idea," he said.

She looked at him closely, not believing he had really said that. "You really think so?"

"Maybe we need some time alone."

"So I'll take Kara and her stuff over to his house, she'll stay there for maybe a week or so, and I'll check in on her every couple of days. How's that?"

"Let's not put a time limit on it." He got up and looked out the window. "And maybe we can go away for a while. I don't have anything lined up for a few weeks." He turned to her. "Where would you like to go?"

"Away? Like out of town? I don't want to be too far from Kara."

"We *need* to be away from her, Cal. Far away for a while. She'll be in good hands. I'm sure he's got servants all over that house, probably in the yard, too. Would you like to go to New York?"

"I don't know, Len."

"Where have you wished all your life that you could go? If you could go anywhere in the whole world, where would it be?"

She thought for a moment, then an idea came to her. "When Pat Feldman was guesting on our show, he told me about his trip to Hawaii. He told me all about how wonderful it was there, and it sounded so romantic. Can we go there?"

"Okay."

"Really? Hawaii?" Her eyes grew huge.

"I don't see why not. We've got the time and the money." For the first time in ages, Cal saw a trace of a smile on her husband's face. Maybe everything would be all right, after all. He went to the phone. "I'll have George make the reservations. You tell Nate he's got a deal."

"How long do you want to be in Hawaii? Should I tell him a week?"

"Let's stay two weeks. Tell him she'll be there Friday night. I'll tell George we want to be on the first flight out on Saturday morning."

Cal couldn't believe her good fortune. Just when she thought her marriage was falling apart, things suddenly were getting much better; and she was even going to get to see Hawaii! As soon as Leonard finished talking with George, she called Nate to tell him the good news. He was quite receptive to that idea, and encouraged them to stay as long as they wanted. He assured her that he would have a bedroom ready for Kara on Friday evening. Everything would be fine, he said.

Chapter 7

KARA RAN UP THE SIDEWALK to Nate's house and rang the bell. When Mrs. North opened the door wide, the little girl ran inside, calling, "Uncle Nate? Uncle Nate? Where are you?"

"Say hello to Mrs. North, Kara!" Cal called. "Don't be rude."

"Hi, Mrs. North. Where's Uncle Nate?"

"I'm coming," he said as he descended the stairs. "How's my little Kara-Mia?"

She ran into his arms. "I'm going to be here for a whole two weeks! Mama and Daddy are going to Hawaii."

"I know, sweetheart. Come and see the bedroom Mrs. North fixed up for you." They started up the stairs, then Nate beckoned to Cal and Leonard. "Come on, you two. I want you to see it, too."

They followed Nate upstairs and into a beautifully-appointed bedroom, complete with canopy bed, matching bedside tables and dresser, a huge toy box, a desk, one upholstered chair and one rocking chair, and a shelf full of dolls and teddy bears. It was truly a dream bedroom for a little girl.

"Do you like it?" he asked Kara.

"Yeah! Can I play with these dolls?"

"Of course you can. They're yours."

She went over to the toy box and opened it. Inside were balls, puzzles, some glamorous clothes for playing dress-up, a huge box of crayons, coloring books, and toys she had never seen before. "Are these mine, too?"

"They sure are," he smiled. "Aunt Becky helped me pick them out."

Her eyes were round as saucers. "Mama, can I live here forever?"

"I don't think so, baby," Cal laughed. "But it's a great place to visit, isn't it?"

"I'll go get the suitcases." Leonard went back downstairs and out to the car. Soon, he brought Kara's luggage into the room and set them on the bed.

Cal opened the first one and started unpacking. "Can I hang her shirts in the closet here?"

Nate opened the closet wide. "There's lots of room." He helped her unpack and hang things up. "The dresser drawers are empty, too."

As soon as everything was put away, Cal knelt down and hugged her daughter. "I'm going to miss you, sweetie. What would you like me to bring you from Hawaii?"

"I don't know. What do they have there?" she asked.

Cal looked at Leonard. "All I can think of right now is pineapple. Pat said they had pineapple at every meal."

Kara wrinkled her nose. "I don't want that."

"Okay. We'll just surprise you then," Cal said.

"Okay."

"And we'll call."

"She'll be fine," Nate assured her. "You two just have a great time and don't worry for one moment about her. We're going to have fun, aren't we, Kara-Mia?"

"Yeah!"

*   *   *

This was the best vacation they had had in many a year. In town, there was music everywhere. Just a few miles north, George had found them a cabin on the beach, away from the crowd. It gave them quiet time to relax and enjoy watching the ocean while basking in the sunshine. Away from all the many concerns of daily life, Leonard was starting to get back some of his old vitality. They were sipping from tall, chilled glasses of iced tea as they lay in the chaise lounges in front of their cabin.

Cal reached over and took Leonard's hand. "I'm sure glad we came, aren't you?"

"Um-hmm," he nodded. "We needed this."

"Yeah, we sure did. Things were starting to get kind of hairy there."

"We've worked hard this year. Guess now it's time to play."

"Yeah." She sighed, then stood up. "I'm going to call and see how Kara's doing."

"No, you're not. Sit back down." He hadn't let go of her hand yet.

"She might be missing us. It'll be nice for us to hear each other's voices again."

"How can you get any rest if you insist on worrying all the time about Kara? Sit down and relax, Cal. She's fine."

"I guess he would've called if they need us for anything. I gave him our number." She settled back into the lounge. "He might've taken her somewhere, so they might not be home. They could be at Becky's."

"That's right. Want to go buy one of those slinky Hawaiian dresses? There's a luau tonight."

"Think I could pass as a wahine?"

"Let's give it a try. Come on." He got up and pulled her into an upright position. Together, they went to town to make their contribution to Honolulu's economy.

*   *   *

Not only did Leonard buy Cal a beautiful floral gown, but they went by the jeweler, too, where he presented her with a diamond pendant. Now she was all ready for the luau. She bought him a floral shirt to match her gown, knowing full well that, once they returned home, he would never touch it again. Just for now, though, they were willing to dress in the bright colors ever-present in the Hawaiian culture.

*   *   *

The two weeks went by very quickly and the couple was now returning home completely refreshed. As they closed the trunk and got into their car, they were now homebound and feeling very optimistic about their marriage.

Cal realized now that it was when they were alone that Leonard was the least depressed. Apparently, Kara served as a constant reminder to him that his wife had had a child by another man, and it was painful for him to deal with that. He took out his frustration on both Cal and Kara when it got to be too much for him. During these two weeks, Cal had been doing much soul searching and had reached a painful, though hopeful, decision. She felt it would be best for all concerned, but wasn't sure how to talk to Leonard about it without making him feel worse.

"Len, what do you think about letting Kara stay with Nate on a more permanent basis?"

This seemed to come out of nowhere, and he was confused. "What?"

"Well, it seems that the stress level is much lower between us when she's at Nate's house. And he loves having her there. As long as we can visit her and she can visit us, do you think she could live there?"

He became quiet, as if mulling over the pros and cons of such an arrangement. He pulled out a cigarette and lit it.

"I mean, I love her like crazy," Cal went on. "She's my baby and I'd hate being away from her, but it's not good for her to live in a home with so much tension in it."

"That's true."

"She was starting to have nightmares because you and I were fighting so much, and I hate that. I don't want to do that to her."

Leonard looked over at Cal and saw how earnest she was. "I wish it weren't that way, but I've got to admit that it is."

"So you're okay with that idea?"

"Let's see what Nate has to say about it."

Cal smiled gratefully at him. There was now a light at the end of the tunnel. Kara would be so happy to be a permanent member of the Jenkins household, and Leonard would be a lot calmer.

But would it tie Nate down too much? she wondered. *And what about his heart?*

* * *

"Hi, Mrs. North. Where's my little girl? We brought her something from Hawaii," Cal said loud enough, she hoped, for Kara to hear.

Kara came running down the stairs and into her mother's arms. "Hi, Mama and Daddy! What'd you bring me?"

"Oh, sweetie, I sure missed you." She hugged Kara tightly. "Did you miss me?"

"Yeah. What's in the suitcase?"

Cal turned and retrieved the instrument from its case. "This is a ukulele. It's an instrument that they play in Hawaii." She plucked the strings. "See?"

"It looks like a little guitar."

"That's right. Uncle Nate can teach you how to play it. He knows how to play stringed instruments." Then Cal looked back at Kara and hugged her again. "Oh, Kara, I love you. You're my little baby." A tear made its way down her cheek.

"No, I'm not, Mama. I'm a big girl," she said, with no understanding of the emotional roller coaster her mother was experiencing.

"Even someday when you're a gray-haired grandma, you'll still be my little baby."

"Hey, welcome home!" Nate said as he joined them in the front hallway and shook Leonard's hand. "Did you have a good vacation?"

"It was very nice," Leonard said.

Cal agreed. "It was wonderful. There's music everywhere you go in Oahu. That's such a beautiful place to visit."

After Kara went outside to show her ukulele to their gardener, the adults went into the living room, where Cal and Leonard presented their proposal to Nate. She guessed that Nate would be delighted at the prospect of Kara's being a permanent member of his home. Indeed, he was! His heart is fine, he assured her once again, so the child's being there full-time would not jeopardize his health. "In fact," he said, "she'll probably keep me healthy. There's nothing as refreshing as the innocence and honesty of a child in this artificial world we call Hollywood."

Chapter 8

Time, at first, went slowly for Cal. Not having her little girl around made home seem not quite as homey anymore. She occupied herself with her hobbies, writing and art, as she waited for work to begin on their new television series.

They would soon begin rehearsing, then taping on a weekly basis the new *Nate and Stacy Comedy Hour* for the fall. This season, Leonard's part had increased and Nate's decreased. This, Cal felt, would work well—it would lessen the strain on Nate and make Leonard feel that it was more his own show.

In the meantime, she had visited Kara daily, usually when Leonard was otherwise occupied. He had gone with her several times in the last two months, but his time now was usually spent working out details of the upcoming television season, and doing guest-starring roles on other shows now and then. Cal found that Leonard and Kara seemed to enjoy each other's company much more when they lived apart. This arrangement seemed to be working out really well. Kara was very happy in her new home, and Cal could tell that Nate loved having her there. *It's odd,* she thought. *All these years I've known Nate and it had never occurred to me what a conscientious father he could be. He simply dotes on Kara.*

It was now Mother's Day. Becky, Nate, and Kara always met Cal at church on Sundays, but this particular Sunday seemed to be a bit different. Soon after Cal had arrived, Becky had joined her in their usual pew.

"Where are Nate and Kara?" Cal asked softly, handing a hymnal to her friend.

"They'll be along in a minute," she answered.

As they waited, Cal read the announcements on the flip side of the bulletin. A few moments later, Nate came in and sat beside Becky. Cal looked around to see if Kara was dawdling in the narthex, but she was nowhere in sight. She certainly hoped she wasn't hanging around the nursery, again. Her child loved to "help" the attendants of the baby nursery. "Where's Kara?" she whispered to Nate, but he shrugged and put his finger to his lips.

The service was beginning. The minister made the announcements and welcomed the first-time visitors, then the introduction to the opening hymn began as everyone stood.

Nate reached over, took Cal by the sleeve, and pulled her over to his other side so she was now standing at the end of the pew. "What's that for?" she whispered to him.

"Keep your eyes on the aisle," he whispered back as the congregation began singing the hymn.

She obediently looked at the empty aisle beside her, then toward the back of the church. She couldn't believe her eyes, for there was tiny Kara, clad in a little white robe and solemnly carrying the candle lighter down the aisle. Her precious daughter was serving today as Acolyte for the very first time! As she passed her mother, Kara grinned at her. Then Cal watched with pride as she resumed her holy stance and approached the altar. Kara hesitated, bowed deeply to the cross, just as she had been coached, then proceeded to the candelabra to one side. She lit each candle, then went back toward the center of the altar, bowed to the cross again, then advanced to the candelabra on the other side. After lighting each of those candles, she returned to the cross for a final bow, then extinguished her candle lighter, propped it in its holder, and seated herself in the Acolyte chair to the side. Kara then looked back over at her mother, Aunt Becky, and Uncle Nate, and flashed a big smile.

Nate took a handkerchief from his pocket as he leaned over and whispered to Cal, "Happy Mother's Day. She wanted to be an Acolyte as her present to you." She took the hankie and wiped the tears from her cheeks.

Then and there, Cal realized that Kara was now enjoying a much better life that not only was a calmer and more loving environment for her, but was also giving her the religious training that was so important. Cal now knew that her daughter could continue to live with Nate, with her blessings, for as long as she wanted.

*　*　*

Cal had lately been coming over to Nate's about an hour before Kara got home from school. It was nice to be here when she got off the school bus, and it was good, too, to have some quiet time to chat with Nate. Soon, they would both be busy ten to twelve hours a day with the show and wouldn't have time for such leisurely visits. They were on the sofa in the sitting room and Nate was showing Cal some of the photos he had taken of Kara.

"This one was taken when she and Patches were both colts," he smiled. "Compare that to the one I took of them last week. Both photos are beside the same fencepost, so you can tell how much they've grown."

"What's it been, about a year? They're so much bigger now."

He nodded proudly, "They're really flourishing."

"I've been wondering something, Nate, but I didn't know a nice way to ask."

"What's that?"

"And I guess it's none of my business…"

"What?"

"The way you and Becky used to talk, I had the impression that you made it with a lot of girls in your time. And if only one time with me produced Kara, you must be a pretty potent guy. So don't you have lots of other kids out there somewhere?"

Nate laughed out loud.

Cal continued, "I was wondering why Kara's so special to you if you have all those other kids, too."

"She's an only child, as far as I know, Cal."

She looked at him skeptically.

"I wasn't as active as you thought I was," he said.

"But you said you got propositioned every day."

"Well, I did—well, maybe not *every* day, but I didn't take them up on it very often. I had a public image to maintain."

"But I *know* you did it with Mimi during that Omnus Award party."

He shrugged, "Well, yeah."

"And how about your fan club?"

His eyes lit up with a mischievous gleam.

Cal continued, "Didn't you go back and spend the night with two girls that time?"

"Do you believe everything I told you back then?"

"Well…"

"You sure are naïve!"

"I wish people would stop saying that."

"I was just trying to make you jealous. I wanted you to see how willing they were, in hopes that that would encourage you to loosen up. It didn't work, darn it."

"So Kara's your only child, really?"

"As far as I know. Seems, if there were another one, I would've been hit with a paternity suit by now."

They sat in silence for a moment, then she picked up another photo from Nate's lap.

"Cal, is Leonard treating you all right?"

"Pretty much. Why?"

"Well, I get the impression from what Kara tells me that he was abusive toward you before she moved here. I hate for you to be in a situation like that. Is he getting counseling yet?"

"No, no counseling. I doubt that he ever will. But yelling is the way we let off steam. That's just the way we are."

"You're not that way with anyone else, are you? I've never known you to yell at Kara."

"No. Just Len."

"Do you *like* living that way?"

She shrugged.

"Cal, if you ever need to get away, you're welcome to come here. This house has five bedrooms and only two are being used. There's plenty of room for you."

"I wish I could. I miss seeing Kara first thing in the morning and tucking her in at night."

He smiled proudly, "It's a wonderful feeling, Cal. She's a great little kid. You know what she told me when I tucked her in last night? She said that she wished I was her daddy."

"How do you tuck her in? Do you read her a story?"

"Sometimes. And other times, we sit in the rocking chair and I sing her to sleep. She looks like such a little angel when she's asleep."

"I know. I'm glad she's here. She seems happier now and more secure."

"I thought she would be."

Cal set the photo down and enveloped Nate in a big hug.

"Remember what I said at the park, Cal? Don't tempt me."

"I don't care. I love you, Nate."

He held her close and kissed her cheek. For many years, he had yearned to hear her say those words to him, and he didn't want anything to dilute this moment. "I love you, too" he whispered. She felt so soft and warm in his arms. It bothered Nate to know how vulnerable she was to Leonard's moods. He wanted so much to protect her, as he was protecting their daughter. "Remember, Cal, you can come here anytime—not only to visit Kara, but to live. We could be a family."

What a wonderful thought! To be with her daughter all day every day, and to be able to retreat into Nate's arms whenever she needed some tenderness would be a dream-come-true. But it wouldn't be right and she knew it. Her first allegiance was to Leonard.

Nate lifted her chin and looked her in the eye. "Would you like to do that—come live with us?"

To deal with this on an emotional level would break her heart. Instead, she answered lightheartedly, "If you can get Len to go back to Jill, you've got yourself a tenant."

He smiled and tapped her lightly on the nose. "I'll see what I can do."

The front door slammed shut, and they quickly let go of each other.

Kara came into the room. "Hi, Mama and Uncle Nate. Guess what we did today."

Nate held his arms out for Kara. "What?"

"Everybody told about their pets. I was the only one there that had a pony. Everybody else had cats and dogs. Except for a couple kids who had gerbils and one kid had a snake." She came up to get her hugs from Uncle Nate and Mama. "I'm hungry."

"Go see what Mrs. Ellis has for you in the kitchen. Maybe we can talk your mama into staying for dinner tonight."

"No, can't. Sorry," Cal said. "Len doesn't like to eat alone."

Kara handed her school things to her mother and disappeared into the kitchen.

Nate returned his focus to Cal. "So all I have to do is get Leonard and Jill back together?"

"Yeah. It's kind of like *Parent Trap*, isn't it?" Her eyes sparkled. "If anyone can do it, Mike and Corky can." She then looked at the papers that Kara had brought home from school. "Well, look at this, will you?" She held up a brightly-colored picture of a house with a "J" on the chimney. In front of the house were a man, woman and child—all holding hands. The grass was neon green, the sky soft blue, and high overhead was the bright yellow sun. To the side of the house were three horses. "Would the psychologists say a happy child drew that?"

"I think they would," Nate agreed.

*   *   *

Leonard was waiting when she got back. "Do you have to go over there every single day?" he asked.

"Yep."

"Why?"

"Because I promised Kara I would. I'm still her mother, you know." She went into the kitchen and he followed. Cal picked up a banana. "What happened at your meeting with Michael?"

"We were just hammering out details about next year and discussing the salary negotiations."

"How come Nate and I weren't in on all that?"

"I thought you didn't want to be bothered with the business side of things."

"Well, I guess not. Is that all they discussed? Nothing about the creative part of the show?"

"Just business."

"Oh." She peeled the banana and took a bite. Jessie was in the midst of cooking dinner and was trying to work around the couple. "I guess we're in your way, huh?" Cal asked Jessie.

"Only if you want dinner served tonight. With you two underfoot, it would take an extra few hours."

"Okay, okay. We can take a hint. Can't we, Len?" she said as they sauntered toward the door. Leonard then went into the media room. Cal followed.

He turned the television on and flipped it to the nightly news as he settled onto the sofa.

Cal sat beside him and asked casually, "So, what do you hear these days from Jill?"

"Jill? What am I supposed to hear from her?"

"Oh, I don't know," Cal shrugged. "I just haven't seen her since Stacy's wedding and was just wondering how she's doing. Doesn't she call anymore?"

"Sometimes."

"She sure is gorgeous. I bet she's had all sorts of guys proposing to her."

"Probably."

"She's still carrying a torch for you, though. She wants you back in the worst way."

"That's too bad. If you don't have anything specific to tell me, I'd like to hear the news."

Cal sighed and went back to the kitchen to help Jessie.

*　*　*

"I'm ready, Uncle Nate." It was a little after 8:00 p.m. and Kara, bedecked in her ankle-length nightgown, was all bathed and ready for bed.

He put his pen down and followed her up the stairs. "Would you like a story tonight?"

"No." She took his hand and lead him to the rocking chair. "Tell me about when I was a baby."

He sat and helped her onto his lap. She then rested her head on his chest as they gently rocked. "You were the most beautiful baby ever born in that hospital, Kara. Even the nurse said so. When they brought you home, I came to see you, and your mama let me hold you. You were so tiny."

"How little was I?"

He held his hands about twenty inches apart. "This big. You were about the size of that doll over there."

"Randy said that his baby brother looks like Winston Churchill. Maybe that means he'll be famous someday."

"You looked like a beautiful little princess, right from the beginning."

They rocked in silence for a moment. Then Kara patted Nate's hand. "Sing me 'Danny Boy'?"

He cradled her in his arms and softly sang the tune, for which his clear tenor voice was well suited. Nate felt Kara become more and more relaxed as they rocked. He then slowly and softly sang a few ballads, until she was sound asleep. Then he carried her to her bed, put her in gently, and covered her with the sheet. He softly kissed her forehead, then turned the light off.

He now returned downstairs to finish writing the letter.

*   *   *

"Well, I wonder what this could be about," Jill said as she set the rest of the mail aside and looked at the envelope.

"What is it, dear?" her mother asked from the recliner across the room.

"It's a letter from Nate Jenkins. He's never written to me before. I wonder how he got my address." She sat down and opened the envelope. As she unfolded the letter, a check fell into her lap. She picked it up and looked at it. "It's for a *huge* amount, Mother. What on earth..."

"Read the letter. Then we'll both know."

Jill put the check back on her lap and read the letter. Then she read it again.

"Well?" her mother asked.

She smiled slyly. "It looks like I have my own personal spy out west. Nate is thanking me for encouraging Cal to keep seeing him, those many years ago. I admit we were kind of in cahoots back then, and now he wants to return the favor."

"He's grateful enough to send you a big check? That doesn't make sense."

"That's just part of it. He's informing me that conditions are now quite favorable for me to win Leonard back. He says that Cal and Leonard are having some marital problems and, as he puts it, 'Leonard would surely welcome your comforting presence at this difficult time.' The check is to cover airline tickets, meals, accommodations, and any other expenses that may come up. Can you believe this?"

"I wonder what kind of problems they're having."

"Serious ones, he says. Remember I told you that Cal had had a baby several years ago? And remember that Leonard absolutely didn't want children because of the possibility of one being autistic? Well, this letter says that the baby isn't Leonard's. She's Nate's, and now she's living with him. That must have been quite a blow to Leonard's ego, for Cal to have another man's baby."

"Well, I guess Nate's right, then. The time is ripe for you to make your move."

Jill leaned back and mused, "So Nate finally got Cal in bed."

"Jill!"

"Well, it's true. That poor soul has been trying for years, and now he's finally succeeded. Why couldn't this have happened twenty years ago? It would've prevented a lot of heartache."

"So when will you be leaving for California?"

Jill looked at her watch.

Chapter 9

Now that school was out, other families were taking their vacations. Not so for the Rhoads or Jenkins families, nor those of the rest of the cast and crew of what had been nicknamed by them "The Nate-and-Cal Show." The writers were already busy at work, and the cast would soon be assembling to create the first show of the season. There weren't as many changes made this time, as the format toward the end of last season was working so well. The only real difference this season, other than the frequency of the shows, was the addition of a live studio audience for the Friday evening tapings. Contracts had been signed, with acceptable salaries for everyone. Sponsors were lined up and all appeared to be ready. The guest star for this opening show would be Damon Harris, who, as an adolescent, had been a sitcom regular in the 1960s, but went on to other, non-acting, pursuits after that show had ended. He would play his former character in the twenty-minute Mike-and-Corky sketch, then return during the second half of the show to do a comical monolog as the parent of teenagers (which, in reality, he now was). The trials and tribulations of raising teenagers would certainly be met with much empathy now from the Baby-Boomer audience. Wardrobe plans were being worked out and the cast had already gone in for fittings.

Certainly, once rehearsals began, Leonard would be easier to live with. He was home, between jobs, this week and didn't seem to have enough to do.

"Where do you think you're going?" he asked irritably.

"The same place I always go—to see Kara."

"Do you suppose the world would come to an end if you skipped one day?"

She shrugged, "Possibly", then looked in her purse for her car key.

He took her purse from her. "Stay home today."

"No." She reached for the bag. When he held it out of her reach, she exploded. "Len, stop that! I'm not going to be a prisoner in my own home. I'll walk, if I have to."

"Sure you will. That house is more than ten miles from here. By the time you got there, she'd be in bed asleep."

"Give me my purse!" She punched his arm.

"You're staying home today!"

She turned on her heel and went into the kitchen, where she got the key to Leonard's car off the hook. Her driver's license was in her purse but, with luck, she wouldn't need it. As she neared the door, Leonard warned, "If you go out that door, don't bother to ever come back."

She stopped dead in her tracks and turned around. Leonard was at the other end of the kitchen, but he didn't look angry anymore. Instead, he appeared to be hurt. It was getting harder and harder for Cal to figure him out these days. "Len, what's the matter? What do you have against Kara? She's a precious little girl who needs you—the way you used to be. Why can't you be like that anymore? Why are you so grouchy all the time?"

"Because you're driving me crazy, that's why."

"Here we go again. It's always my fault. Len, *you're* the one who's driving *me* crazy. I've got to get out of here."

"Why is it that a man has to be a sappy father in order to please you?"

"What do you mean?" Sensing that they were, at last, going to have a heart-to-heart talk, Cal put the key back on its hook and took Leonard's hand.

"I mean that any man who plays coochie-coo with Kara is wonderful in your eyes and I'm nothing but a jerk. It's not my nature to be that way, with little kids or anyone else. I tried taking Stacy to the zoo once and we both had a miserable time."

"You're not a jerk, Len. I just wish you'd love her, that's all. You don't have to act sappy to love a little girl."

"I do love her, Cal. I care about her, and I care about you."

"Then why can't we all live together in peace? Why can't we have a home as warm and full of love as the one she's in now?" Cal knew better than to mention Nate's name, especially at a time like this, when she wanted Leonard to open up.

"I told you before, long before Kara existed. We're both hotheads. When we're stressed out, we yell, we fight. That's no environment for a kid. You said it yourself. Just because we love Kara doesn't mean we can change our stripes."

"But, Len, we're both actors. If we can control our behavior on the set, why can't we do it at home?

"Because home is where we can be ourselves. If we had to play the part of happy characters all the time, home *and* away, we'd go nuts."

"Maybe we could go to a motel room to have our fights."

"A *motel*, Cal? We've got more class than that."

"Okay, a hotel, then. A ritzy one that has crystal goblets we can throw at each other."

He put his arm around her shoulders. "I think we'd have to have a very long-term lease, and, the way we've been lately, we wouldn't be spending much time at home."

"But, Len, you just don't understand. I didn't, either, until Kara came along. Mrs. Morris tried to tell me how strong a mother's love is, but it just didn't register with me until I experienced it for myself. The bond between a mother and her child is really, really strong. A child might do bad things, but her mother will still love her and do everything she can for her well being."

"You don't have to make a career of it, though. You have a tendency to jump in whole-hog and overdo things."

"I was that way before you married me, but you've gotten a lot more selfish than you used to be. You're the one who's changed."

"I only want you to put your role of wife ahead of your role of mother. Now that Kara's over there, that shouldn't be so hard to do."

"If it were meant to be like that, a mother's love wouldn't be so strong."

"Do you believe what the Bible says?"

"Of course I do."

"It says in there that a man and his wife are one, and *no one* is to come between them. That doesn't only refer to in-laws and friends, Cal. It also means kids."

"But little kids need their moms more than a husband does."

"No, they don't."

She was getting nowhere with this conversation, so she took the key off its hook again. "I'll be back in a while."

"You're staying here." He took hold of her arm.

"You're so darned possessive, Len. I used to put up with it because it didn't matter so much, but now it does. I'm not going to let your possessiveness keep me from being a mother to Kara. She needs me."

"And *I* need you."

"I'll be back. I'll be here all evening. And beginning with rehearsals next week, we'll be together most of the time for the next eight months. But for the next hour, I'm Kara's. 'Bye." She shook her arm loose and left.

＊　＊　＊

"Is everything all ready for next week?" Nate asked as Cal joined him in the den.

"I think so. What arrangements do you have for Kara? Should we hire a nanny?"

"I've already hired one. She'll be starting work later this week so Kara can be accustomed to her before I start being gone all day. Her name is Susie

Mae Allison, but she wants Kara to call her 'Miss Susie'. She's from the deep south, as you probably guessed."

Cal's eyes lit up. "Texas?"

"Georgia."

"Oh. Where's Kara?"

"Out back on the swings, I think." As Cal headed toward the door, Nate casually said, "Jill will be in the audience during taping next week."

She stopped and turned back around. "Jill's coming here? How do you know?"

"She called. She'd like to see a taping, so I'm getting her a ticket."

"Oh." She just stood there, not knowing what to think.

"It'll be good to see her again."

"Yeah, I guess so." After an awkward moment, she resumed out the door and into the back yard. "Hi, sweetie! How's everything going?"

"Good, Mama. Can you push me so hard that I'll go over the top? I want to swing in a circle."

Cal laughed. "I'm not that strong. You'll have to ask Daddy to do that. He's so strong he could probably push that swing over the moon."

"Eww, I'd better ask Uncle Nate, then."

Cal got on the swing beside Kara's, went as far back as she could, then swung forward with gusto. "Whee! I haven't done this in years. I'd forgotten how fun it is."

The little girl stopped her swing and watched her mother. She started giggling.

"What's the matter? Haven't you ever seen a kid swinging, before?" Cal asked happily as she went higher and higher.

"But you're too big for that," Kara giggled.

"No, I'm not. You're *never* too big to have a good time." The wind in her face felt so good. "We'll have to remind Daddy of that. He's forgotten how to have fun."

"I don't know if the swing's big enough for Daddy."

"Well, he can have fun other ways. I know, let's tie him up and make him go horseback riding with us. He used to love to do that."

"I'm afraid to tie him up, Mama. He might hit."

"Naw, he'd never hit you."

"But I don't want him to hit you."

She was almost going to say, "That's okay. I always get him back." Before she did, though, she realized that was an unwise example to set for Kara. She didn't want the child to think that hitting is acceptable behavior. Cal slowed down, then stopped her swing and looked at Kara. "I hope, when you chose a man to marry someday, he'll be one like Uncle Nate. He's real good to you, isn't he?"

"Usually."

"I thought he was *always* good to you."

"Well, he fussed at me this morning."

"Why'd he do that?"

"'Cause I didn't brush my teeth."

"He doesn't hit or yell, though, does he?"

"No. He fussed at me for going out in the street a couple days ago, too."

"Well, Kara, those things are because he loves you. You need to brush your teeth so they'll stay healthy, and you need to stay out of the street so you won't get hit by a car. It's okay for him to fuss at you about those things."

"But I don't like it when he fusses at me."

"You know what? When I was your age, my parents never fussed at me for anything, and I was a pretty rotten little kid. That's why Daddy and I yell at each other a lot. No one cared enough about us to teach us not to do that. You're going to have a better life than I am because Uncle Nate loves you enough to fuss at you sometimes."

Kara resumed swinging.

"You'll understand when you're grown up, Kara. He does that because he loves you, and the reason you don't like it is because you love him."

She sighed, "Yeah."

Cal set her swing in motion again. "Hey, I've got an idea. Let's play a joke on Uncle Nate."

"Okay." The little girl adopted her mother's mischievous grin.

"Go up to him and put your arms around him and say, 'I want to go to your fan club's meetings." The idea tickled Cal and she laughed. She was remembering when Nate had taken her to see his fan club and the members' silliness had surprised her. There were about fifteen girls there and they were all throwing themselves at him shamelessly. They seemed to Cal to have no self-respect at all, certainly not the sterling example of womanhood that Nate would want set for his little girl.

"What's a fan club?"

"It's a bunch of people who get together to talk about a movie star, and they go together to see his movies and everything."

"But I don't have to do that, Mama. He brings his movies home and we watch them on TV, except two of them that he won't let me see."

"Well, do it anyway. It's a joke. I want to see what he'll say."

"Is it a funny joke?"

"It sure is. Let's go do it now."

"Okay."

They both got off their swings and went into the house.

"Uncle Nate? Where are you?"

"In the den," he answered.

Right on cue, Kara went up to him and lovingly put her arm around his neck. He smiled and returned her embrace. "Uncle Nate, will you take me to your fan club's meeting, please?" She looked earnestly into his eyes.

What a great little actress! Cal thought, as she leaned against the doorway and tried to maintain a poker face.

"My fan club? No, Kara-Mia, you don't want to go there."

"How come?"

"Well, uh," he looked over at Cal, who absolutely couldn't hold it in any longer and was soon engulfed in a fit of laughter. He couldn't help chuckling, too. "I think you have to be eighteen to go to one of those meetings. You're too young."

"Good answer," Cal managed to say, as she wiped away tears of mirth.

"Did you put her up to this?" he asked.

"Who? Me?"

"Mama said it's a funny joke."

He patted Kara on the head and said, "We'll have to think of a funny joke to play on Mama one of these days. Tit for tat."

"Tic-tac-toe?" Kara asked.

"No, tit for tat, sweetie," Cal said gleefully. "That means I got him this time, but he thinks he'll get me next time."

"Maybe during the taping," he grinned. "Be on the lookout, Cal."

"Thank goodness it's not broadcast live."

"But the studio audience will see it."

Cal grinned, too. Just the thought of something unexpected happening during the taping of their show brought back happy memories of her years on the New York stage. Improvising in order to overcome such hurdles kept the actors on their toes, and made the evening interesting. She came to welcome such variety in their regular working conditions. She'll be prepared for it next Friday night, no matter what Nate has in mind.

*　*　*

Monday had finally arrived. Everyone greeted each other cheerfully that morning, then gathered around the large table. Coffee, Dr. Peppers, and doughnuts were set out in the middle of the table for them; and scripts were on the table in front of each chair. After introducing everyone to this week's guest star, they would have a read-through, followed by discussion. Then rehearsals would start and continue, as revisions would be made, through Wednesday. Thursday afternoon would be the dress rehearsal. Friday evening, at 7:00, the audience would be in place and their resident comedian would do the warm-up. After producing a few hardy laughs from the audience, he would then explain what they were about to see and what was expected of the audience. "Don't hold back," he would say. "If you feel like laughing, by all means go ahead. The louder, the better. If you want to 'boo' the villain, feel free. You're an important part of the show."

Indeed, it was interaction with the audience that the cast would enjoy the most. It was another "unexpected" element that they would find so stimulating. Unlike Leonard and Cal, Nate had never done formal stage acting before, but found that the experience he and Cal had had on stages throughout the eastern United States on that tour so long ago was very much like doing the show in this format—the main difference being the escalated audience participation in this one.

Right here, in front of a live audience who was so open to all aspects of humor, would be the perfect environment for the joke he and Kara had plotted for Cal. Sure, it would probably be edited out for the television audience, but that would not diminish the fun. The audience would love it.

It was opening night for the new season. The audience was in place, the warm-up done, and the first-half skit had been met with much cheering and applause from the enthusiastic audience. They were happy to see their old friends—Mike, Corky, and Officer Stanton—once again. All had gone quite well. They were now in the middle of the second half of the show. It was Nate and Cal's musical number, in which they were singing a duet, "Scarborough Fair." It was quite a serious song, one in which a giggle would definitely be out of place. It was the perfect song for Nate's plan.

As the duo harmonized beautifully, Cal noticed the audience seemed to be distracted. They were looking off toward stage left and smiling. Soon, she felt a tugging at her skirt. She tried to casually look down without breaking stride in the song, then had to do a double take. She burst out laughing, as did Nate and the audience. The song was temporarily abandoned. There at her feet was a chimpanzee, dressed in a tuxedo. In his hand was a dance card.

"I'm sorry, sir. I don't dance with strangers," Cal said apologetically to the chimp. Then, with a quick side glance toward Nate, she suggested with a grin, "Why don't you ask Doris?"

At that point, the chimp's trainer appeared stage left and beckoned the furry performer to follow him. The chimp ambled off stage. The trainer picked him up, then they both disappeared behind the curtain, followed by much applause from the audience.

Cal playfully punched Nate in the arm and said to the audience, "He *got* me. He said he would and, by golly, he did."

"Now we're even," Nate further explained. "Shall we try again, from the top?" When he noticed Cal's questioning expression, he continued, "Scarborough Fair?"

"Oh! Yeah." They got back into their positions and the band, once again, played the lead-in. They had sung only a couple of bars before Cal broke out into a giggle. The band stopped.

Nate smiled, good-naturedly, then said, "One more time. "

This time, as the musicians did the lead-in for the third time, Cal gave herself stern mental instructions to get serious. She envisioned a funeral. This time, she was able to sing the whole song all the way through without so much as a smile. At song's end, the spotlight faded on them, then illuminated the scene on the other side of the stage. This next act was Leonard and Damon's—Leonard as the late-night talk-show host and Damon as the mad-scientist guest.

* * *

The taping was at last over and the cast had gone back on stage to take their bows, thank the audience for coming, and bid them a good night. Now, they were backstage in their dressing rooms removing their makeup as the audience slowly left the studio auditorium.

There was a knock on Cal and Leonard's dressing room door. An aide opened the door a bit and peeked out. "Can I help you, ma'am?" he asked.

"Yes, please," they heard a familiar voice say. "I came to see Leonard and Cal. My name is Jill Rhoads."

Cal quickly looked up, then wondered why she was so startled. Nate had told her that Jill would be in the audience that night. She had just forgotten.

Leonard went to the door and opened it the rest of the way. "Come on in, Jill. Have a seat."

She joined them in the dressing room and sat in the overstuffed chair, across from Cal. Jill was exquisitely dressed in a light blue suit with matching shoes and handbag. "It was a wonderful show, Cal. I really enjoyed it." She crossed her legs daintily.

"Thank you. How have you been? I haven't seen you in a long time."

"Oh, just fine. I'm so glad that Stacy and Jim live nearby. I get to see them at least once a week. And Lennie is growing so fast."

"Did you come west just to see our show?" Leonard asked.

"I certainly did. I'm glad you have an audience for your show. They really seemed to be having a good time. The couple sitting beside me was from Kentucky, and they came all this way just to see it, too."

Cal smiled. "I bet they were in their late thirties or forties. It seems most of our audience is made up of people my age or older."

Jill nodded, "I think you're right. The show definitely appeals to people in that age bracket."

"That's the plan," Leonard said as he finished wiping off his stage make-up.

There was another knock on their door. The aide, once again, opened it a bit and peeked out. Then he opened it wide. Nate came in.

"Cal, you want to come with me for a few minutes? We need to decide which number we'll be doing next week."

"Can't we do that later? Jill's here."

Jill looked over at him and smiled. "Hello, Nate. I particularly enjoyed 'Scarborough Fair' tonight."

He beamed, "I think everyone did. Mr. Dibbs added a certain something to the act, didn't he?"

"I wouldn't be surprised if that stays in," Leonard said. "They might have to cut something else out so it doesn't go overtime, but that chimp might show up on TV in a couple of weeks."

Cal added as Nate took her by the arm, "It's a shame he wasn't carrying a sign with one of our sponsor's company names on it. That way, they could cut out one of their commercials instead of one of the acts." Nate then pulled her out the door and closed it behind her.

"You know, that's not a bad idea," he said as he led her down the hallway to his dressing room. "We could have Mr. Dibbs as a regular feature on our show and he could do the commercials."

"That might be the only way to get people to pay attention to them," Cal agreed. They entered his dressing room and he shut the door. She looked around as he sat in one of the chairs and motioned for her to do the same. "Where's the music?" she asked. She sat in the chair beside his.

"I can't decide which of these would be best for next week." He reached over to the table, picked up a folder, pulled three scores from it, and handed them to her. "What do you think?"

She started looking them over. "Oh, I love this one," she said as she held up "Sunrise, Sunset."

"How about the other two?"

The next one was "Somewhere, My Love," and the other was "Somethin' Stupid." "Well, I like them all. Can't we do one of these in each show?"

"Sure. Which one would you like to do next week?"

"Let's do 'Sunrise, Sunset.' That reminds me of Stacy." Cal gave the scores back to him and he returned them to the folder. She stood back up. "Is that all you needed me for? I want to get this makeup off."

He got up, retrieved a sponge from his dressing table, and handed it to her. "Here. You can sit here and get it off. Then, how about going home with me so we can tell Kara how successful her trick was? This has been such an incredible day, I'd like it to last a bit longer."

"It *has* been a great day, hasn't it?"

"I'll take you back to your house after that."

"Okay." She went over to his dressing table and removed her makeup.

* * *

"So how have you been, Leonard?" Jill had asked warmly, after Nate had taken Cal out of the room. She appreciated his doing that so she could have some time alone with Leonard.

"Much better now that we're back at work. And you?"

"Just fine. You never did like being out of work. It looks like you're more in demand than ever now. Age doesn't slow you down one bit, I see."

"Yes, this show is a once-in-a-lifetime opportunity. I'm very lucky that it came about when it did. If it weren't for the power of the Baby-Boomers, I'd probably have had to retire."

She smiled. "I guess nostalgia is a valuable commodity these days. You're absolutely incredible on the show, Leonard. You've never been better."

"Thanks." He scratched his head. "Where are you staying? Will you be here for a while?"

"At the Hilton, for a few weeks, probably." She re-crossed her legs and smoothed her skirt down. "I'm terribly sorry to hear about the problems you're having in your personal life, Leonard. I wish there were some way I could help."

"Oh, it's not so bad."

"I understand that Cal was unfaithful. That must have been devastating to you. I don't know how she could have done such a thing. Certainly, you're all the man any woman could ever want, much more so than Nate. I'm so sorry that happened to you. You deserve better."

"Well, there's a lot more to it than that, but we can't make it public for many reasons."

"All I can say is that your staying with their show just proves what a big man you are. You have the admiration of everyone who watches, I'm sure. But I've heard that Cal doesn't seem very grateful. People have told me that she's not being very sympathetic to you at all. That troubles me."

"You know how headstrong she's always been."

"But at a time like this, a man needs an understanding wife. Maybe I can help her learn how to be one."

He shook his head. "I think that would be a waste of time, Jill. She's not terribly interested in being understanding. Cal's totally absorbed in motherhood now, in addition to the show. It's like she has two full-time occupations, and I just don't fit in anywhere, except as a co-worker."

"What a shame! Her child is living with Nate, they say."

He nodded. "And she goes over there *every single day* to see her."

"She is certainly a devoted mother."

"*Too* devoted, if you ask me. Either that or she's using Kara as an excuse to see Nate every day. They've got something going, but I'm not sure exactly what."

She shook her head slowly, "You poor dear. I was afraid that would happen, that a younger man would… ."

There was a knock on the door, which the aide answered. Nate stuck his head around the door and said to the couple, "I'm going to take Cal to see Kara, then I'll bring her home. You don't need to wait for her. Just take your time and enjoy your visit. Good seeing you again, Jill. I'll see you Monday, Leonard."

"Okay. Monday," Leonard answered.

Jill waved at him as he left and the aide closed the door.

*   *   *

Cal and Nate found Kara still up, but ready for bed. Miss Susie was just rinsing the child's toothbrush off and putting it back in its holder.

"Did you see it, Kara-Mia?" he asked, expectantly.

She grinned. "Yeah. That was a funny joke, wasn't it, Mama?"

"It sure was, baby." Then she turned to Nate. "You mean Kara was in the audience, too? I didn't see her."

He nodded. "Miss Susie took her. I heard Kara laughing."

Then Cal knelt down to her daughter and gave her a hug. "Did you think of that monkey or was he Uncle Nate's idea?"

"We thought of it together. I thought of the monkey and he thought of the fancy clothes."

Nate smiled at Cal. "I wanted it to be something that would distract you from the song and make you laugh. Kara knew that animals always got your attention and suggested a horse at first. I knew we couldn't get one of them in the studio unnoticed, so we thought of smaller and smaller animals until Kara thought of a chimpanzee. She had seen one on a Jack Benny video I had. And I thought of the tuxedo and dance card." He then lightly tapped Cal's nose, "And you remembered Doris."

"Yeah. Nate, we've got to take a trip to Dallas so I can introduce you to poor Doris. She's probably nuts because I get to work with you and Sue got to meet you in your own house, and she never did any of those things."

Nate looked back at Kara. "It's getting late. Would you like Mama to help me tuck you in tonight, sweetheart?"

"Yeah. Come on, Mama." She took her mother's hand and led her to her bedroom.

Nate sat in the desk chair as Cal and Kara seated themselves in the rocker. He reached over to the bookshelf and retrieved her favorite Berenstain Bears book, then handed it to Cal.

"Is this what you'd like me to read?" she asked.

"Yeah."

Cal put her arms around Kara and opened the book in front of them. They rocked as she read the story of the Bears' trip to the farm.

*   *   *

Kara was sound asleep, and Nate and Cal were once again downstairs. "I better get a cab. If you drive me home, that'd leave Kara all alone in the house."

"Miss Susie agreed to stay until I get back. I've already talked to her. She's in the next room."

"Oh, okay." She followed Nate back outside and to his car. As they got in and he started the ignition, Cal stretched. Then she sighed contentedly. "This is the first time in a long time that I've been able to tuck her in. It's such a good feeling."

"I know."

"I wish I could do that every night. I wish Len would understand."

"Maybe Jill will help."

"How can she make him understand?"

"I'm not sure, but I have the feeling she'll be able to improve things, one way or the other. Let's hope."

"Yeah. She's a mother, a good one. Maybe she can talk some sense into him about Kara."

*   *   *

The house was dark when they returned. Leonard's car wasn't there yet. Cal unlocked the door and turned on the lights as they entered the living room.

"Would you like me to wait with you until Leonard gets back," Nate asked, "or are you okay by yourself?"

"Oh, I'm fine. No bogey-bears here tonight. Thanks, Nate."

He kissed her on the cheek, then heard a car door slam shut. "Have a good evening," he said as he left, encountering Leonard on the sidewalk. "Good show tonight, Leonard," Nate said, patting his back as they passed each other.

"Thanks, Nate. See you Monday."

Chapter 10

WORK SURE IS TAKING UP A LOT OF TIME, Cal thought. She knew a weekly show would be four times the work of a monthly one, but she didn't realize how little time that would leave for anything else. Here it was Wednesday of the second week already. Tomorrow would be the dress rehearsal for the next show. This week's guest star was Van Roman, another teen heartthrob from the 1960s. In fact, Cal had been one of his biggest fans in her youth. Now, though, she wasn't sure what she had seen in him. He had stayed in show business throughout the years, but had never matched the popularity he had had in the 1960s. Perhaps an appearance on this show would help.

Cal had noticed that Jill had been attending the rehearsals a lot, and wondered how long she would be in town. It had also not gone unnoticed by Cal that Leonard had been spending a lot of his precious-little spare time with Jill. Cal wasn't sure how she felt about this. Nate was quite pleased with the situation. She thought she should be, too, but it didn't seem to be happening that way. Could it be that Cal was just as possessive as Leonard was? *No, she thought, it's not that.* It's just that she didn't want Leonard *out* of her life; rather, she wanted him to be the loving, attentive man she had married. She wanted the Rhoads home to be just as nurturing an environment for Kara as the Jenkins home was. Did she still love Leonard, she wondered, or was he just a habit that was hard to break? She wasn't sure. Is it possible for a woman to love two men at the same time? Becky seemed to think so. If Cal loved both of them, why was she always fighting with Leonard? Yes, they were still fighting, but not as much, simply because they had much less time at home now.

Rehearsal was over for the day. Cal got into her car and drove over to Nate's house. She and Leonard had started coming to work in separate cars since they spent their evenings in different places now. Cal had dinner with Nate and Kara, while Leonard had dinner with Jill. Then, they'd both get home about 9:00. One distinct advantage of this arrangement was that Cal was now able to be with Kara at bedtime every weeknight. It seemed to make the little girl feel quite secure. Sometimes Cal would sit on Kara's bed while she read a story, and sometimes they'd rock together. Usually, Nate would be sitting beside them on the bed and Kara would reach over to hold his hand. It was obvious that this little girl felt very close to Nate. *She's a "daddy's girl" without even knowing it*, Cal mused.

How Cal wished she had had a relationship like that with her dad as she was growing up. If there had been a person like Nate in her life then, it might have made a tremendous difference. She would have had no need to act out in order to get attention. She wouldn't have been such a pain to her Uncle Antonio, and, thus, he might have welcomed her into his home when her parents died. *Yes,* Cal thought, *Kara's a very lucky little girl.*

It had been a wonderful evening, but Kara was in bed now so Cal had to be getting home. Nate walked her to her car, then she was on her way.

This time, Leonard had gotten home before she did.

"Will Jill be at the taping, again, this week?" she asked as she joined him in the living room.

He nodded. "This one and all the rest, too, probably."

"What do you mean? Forever?"

"She's decided to move back to L.A."

Uh-oh!

Cal said, only half-jokingly, "Is she muscling in on my territory? Doesn't she know you're mine?"

"I'm going to be glad to have her back in town. She's a good person to talk to."

"You can do that on the phone."

"She's just what I need right now."

"And I'm not?"

"No…. How's Kara?"

She disgustedly tossed her purse onto the table. "Living the kind of life I wish I had."

"Sure, he's got all the money in the world. He can buy her anything she wants. When that money's all gone, good ol' Uncle Bob will always come through with more."

"It's not the money. It's the atmosphere around there."

"An atmosphere that takes money to provide, I bet."

"He loves her. He reads her stories and rocks her to sleep. You should see the way she cuddles up to him. She's a lot more secure than I've *ever* been. Why can't you be like Nate?"

"See what I told you? In order to be good enough for you I have to be a sappy father. It's just not my nature, and Stacy turned out all right."

"That's because she had Jill and me around, too; and you and I weren't fighting when Stacy was in the house."

"Well, Jill's going to be around a lot more now."

"And not for Kara's benefit, I bet."

"She cares about me. She still loves me, Cal. All these years, and she still loves me and wants me back. She's been waiting all this time because she knew sooner or later you'd dump me for someone your own age."

"Well, that never happened, Len. I've never wanted to dump you. Who around here's my age, anyway?"

"Nate, and you know it."

"He's seven years older than me."

"That's close enough."

"Where's she going to live?"

"Jill?"

Cal nodded.

"Oh, I was thinking about offering her one of our bedrooms. We have plenty of room and aren't home very much, anyway."

Cal couldn't believe her ears. "In my own house? Len, how *could* you?"

"It'd save money. She said we could let Jessie go. Jill would take care of the housework and cooking again, just like in the good old days."

"She's in her fifties, for Pete's sake! This house is too big for her to take care of. She's not a young chicken anymore." Then she added, for good measure, "Like I am."

"Mrs. Morris was still doing it when she was in her sixties, and doing a good job, I might add."

"Mrs. Morris was an exceptional person."

"And so is Jill."

Cal ran upstairs and, before Leonard could stop her, went into the guest room and locked the door. She spent the night there, ignoring Leonard's rantings from the hallway.

*　*　*

"This is sick," Cal said disgustedly as she and Leonard helped Jill carry her things in. Jill was at the car, getting another armload. "Having both your wives living in the same house."

"She did the same for you. Remember?" Leonard reminded her.

"When the tabloids get hold of this story, you'll probably be known all over the world as a playboy."

He smiled for the first time in ages. "I can think of worse fates."

Cal tried to accustom herself to the new living arrangements, but it was very difficult to maintain their usual lifestyle with Jill in the very next room. All remained business-as-usual at the studio, however. In fact, her upsetting life at home gave Cal the emotional resources she needed to do an even better job on-camera. She found that acting was a panacea to life's problems because she could simply block them out during that time.

It was only when she came home from tucking Kara in on a Friday night and found Leonard leaving Jill's room, wearing only his undershorts, that Cal decided she had had enough.

* * *

It was almost midnight when Nate thought he heard a knock at the front door. He was quite surprised to find Cal on his porch, with suitcase in hand and cheeks wet with tears.

"Got room for a tenant?" she sobbed.

"Of course. Come in," he said as he took her suitcase, set it down, shut the door, then gave her a warm hug. "Please don't cry."

"I can't help it, Nate. I didn't know it'd hurt so bad."

"What happened? How'd he hurt you?"

"Not physically, but he killed me emotionally when I found him in Jill's bedroom."

He wiped her tears away, then handed her his handkerchief.

Cal continued, "He thought we'd be tickled pink to all live together, Jill and me. I could handle that, but I can't take him hopping from bedroom to bedroom. He's such a turkey. I just want to clobber him, Nate! I want to beat him up!"

"Shhh, it'll be okay, Cal." He held her as she gradually got herself back under control. All the frustrations of the past few months seemed to be hitting her at once now. Nate wished he could make her pain go away, but didn't know how. "Can I get you anything? Are you hungry?"

"No. I just need a place to stay." She dried the last of her tears. "I don't want to ever go back to that house again."

"Okay. My home is your home. You can use whichever bedroom you want."

"I'll take the guest bedroom beside Kara's."

"Okay." Nate showed her to her room and helped her unpack. When the last of her things had been put away, he asked, "Are you all right now? Is there anything more I can do for you?"

"I'm okay. Thanks, Nate."

"Try to get some sleep, okay?"

She nodded.

He kissed her on the cheek, and left. Cal watched as he returned to his own room, then she closed the door and got ready for bed. Why was she so sad, she wondered. Isn't this what she had wanted? Now she'll be living with Kara, again, and there would be no more fighting, no more yelling. She would now have the lifestyle that she had needed so badly for so long. So why was she so sad?

For six years now, Nate had been there for her—ready with a warm hug and any kind of help she needed. She loved Nate. He had been through so much because of her, but, in spite of everything, he loved her. And all this time, he had been giving her what she wanted most—a loving father for her daughter. Maybe it was time to let Kara know the truth about her relationship to her beloved Uncle Nate.

Cal turned off the light and went back into the hallway, peeking into Nate's room. He was already in bed.

"Is there something more you need?" he said.

Cal stepped in, then closed the door. She lifted the sheet and eased in beside Nate, looking into his eyes imploringly. "Hold me? I need to feel like somebody cares."

He put his arms around her and held her securely. "I do care, Cal. I care a lot." He had never felt so needed in his life. Here she was, feeling so rejected after having been betrayed by her husband, and desperately needing to be held and loved. Nate would be happy to give her that love, anytime, anyplace. He kissed her forehead and softly sang, "Home in the Meadow," as Cal fell asleep, secure and loved, in his arms.

If she hadn't been so melancholy, this would have given Nate a profound feeling of contentment—after all, this was the first time that Cal had ever come to his bed, and it was completely of her own volition—but it troubled him to see her so brokenhearted. He thought the transfer of Leonard's affections from Cal to Jill was what she had wanted, and he had gone to a great deal of trouble and expense to make that happen. Her anguish was a disappointment and a puzzlement to him. He didn't mean for it to have that affect. He sighed. Cal must love Leonard after all. Apparently, it had not been the marriage of convenience he thought it was.

*   *   *

The next morning, Cal was sitting in Nate's den, looking over Monday's script, when Mrs. North came in. "Mr. Rhoads is here to see you," she announced.

Powerful, contradicting feelings engulfed Cal. She wanted to jump for joy that he cared enough about her to come, and, at the same time, throw everything in the house at him for the transgression that had caused the parting in the first place. Nevertheless, she managed to keep a neutral appearance. "Show him in, please."

Mrs. North disappeared back down the hall.

As Leonard rushed into the room a moment later, Cal swiveled around to face him. He took hold of her arm. "I've had enough of this foolishness. You need to come home now."

"Did Jill move out?"

"Doesn't matter. You belong at home."

"Not while she's there, I don't."

He pulled her to her feet. "You're still my wife, damn it!"

"A wife is not a piece of property, Len; and I refuse to be a part of your harem. If you want Jill, live with her. If you want me, she'll have to leave."

"She has nowhere else to go."

"She has a very nice house in Connecticut, if I remember correctly."

"Well also remember this—that time years ago when a certain Cal Ames needed a place to stay. Do you remember who it was that offered her home to you? I didn't want a stranger invading our house, but she talked me into it."

"That was different."

"She cleaned up after you, she cooked for you, she bought you decent clothes. Hell, she even named her daughter after you. And now you want to throw her out of the house."

"Dadgum it, Len! I'll share anything else with her but I won't share my husband. Make up your mind. Which of us do you want? You can't have both!"

He led her over to the sofa, where they both sat. "Cal, she's been giving me what I need the most—a sympathetic ear. She cares enough to see things from my point of view. She makes me feel like a man, again."

Cal wiped a stray tear away. "Then go back to her and I hope you'll be very happy together."

"But, Cal, *you*'re the one I love. Why can't you listen the way she does? Why do we always end up arguing?"

"Jill and I are completely different kinds of people, Len. Heck, you and I have been arguing since my second day in L.A., and we never stopped. It's the way we are. I'll never be another Jill. It's just not my nature."

"And I'll never be another Nate—for the same reason."

They both stopped short, realizing the great truth that had just been uttered.

"Touché," Cal said softly.

He took hold of her shoulders. "Cal, we both have others who can give us what we need, don't we? Do you suppose we can learn to meet each other's needs ourselves?"

"Maybe, with help." She stroked his hair. "Len, I've been trying for so long to get you to go to a marriage counselor with me. Why won't you go?"

He grimaced, "It just rubs me the wrong way to tell our personal problems to a stranger. She could take it to a tabloid or something. We can work it out ourselves, Cal."

"No, we can't. We've tried. Over and over, we've tried, and it hasn't worked. We need professional help if we're ever going to be able to live together in peace. I just can't go on with things the way they are now." She put her arms around him. "Len, a professional won't tell anybody what we talk about. They've got a code of ethics like doctors do."

"She'll probably tell me I'm doing everything wrong. It's always the man's fault."

"No, she won't. If you'd rather, our counselor can be a guy. It'll be okay, Len. Honest."

"Okay, baby," he said softly, "I'll go if you come home."

She shook her head. "Once we're getting therapy and things get better, *then* I'll come home."

He hesitated for a moment, then sighed, "Okay."

"Really?" Her face lit up. "You'll *really* go with me for therapy?"

"If that's the only way to get you back home, I will."

"Does that mean you love me again?"

He held her close. "Baby, I never stopped."

*   *   *

After being assured that everything said during therapy would be held in strictest confidence, Cal and Leonard began the following Tuesday. The therapist came to the studio, where they spent their lunch break, three days a week, in discussion with him and each other. In their own dressing room, with their aide outside the door, they had complete privacy. As part of the program, both Cal and Leonard had agreed to an evaluation by a psychiatrist, who would rule out any medical problems that would interfere with the therapy. It was discovered that Leonard had been suffering from clinical depression for quite some time. A conscientious program of medication and therapy relieved those symptoms enough for the marriage counseling to be effective. It much improved life in general for Leonard and Cal, as well.

Both Cal and Leonard were 'takers' by nature, rather than 'givers.' They each needed nurturing, but, while they had been receiving that from others, *giving* it to a partner did not come naturally to either of them. They practiced the arts of listening and empathy; and, with guidance from their therapist, both learned how to give, as well as receive, the nurturing that is so necessary in a good relationship.

By the sixth week of therapy, Jill had moved back to Connecticut and Cal had long ago stopped visiting Nate's bedroom. Cal and Leonard were now ready to continue their relationship in the same house, and she moved back home. Once they had re-established their roles as husband and wife, using the new communication skills they had learned, the next task was to help Leonard accept Kara. This took longer. On an intellectual level, he understood that the conditions of her conception were not an indication that his wife had been intentionally unfaithful to him. On an emotional level, however, it was more difficult to see it that way. The fact that Cal and Nate were such close friends now troubled him enormously. Too, that Nate was apparently the ideal father to Kara while Leonard never had that ability added to Leonard's feelings of inadequacy. He knew how important it was to Cal and felt unable to fulfill her expectations. When Cal had kept trying to get him to be "more like Nate," he had felt rejected and emasculated. Kara's presence was a constant reminder to Leonard of the one area of his life in which he had considered himself a failure. This came as a revelation to Cal. She didn't realize that she had been making the problem worse, or that he had felt that he just didn't have what it took to be a good father. Together, they worked on this. Other couples would have been advised to take a parenting class. Leonard's and Cal's presence in such a class, however, would be awkward. Instead, the instructor came to their home, two evenings a week. They were taught how to relate to young children, what was reasonable to expect from them, and how to fill their physical and emotional needs. Children need not only stability, but also tenderness, they learned. They were taught how to provide both. Working through these problems took months, but the day finally came that they were able to welcome Kara back to a much calmer and more loving home.

Kara had mixed feelings about the change in her routine at this point. She dearly loved 'Uncle Nate' and his home, but she was also happy to be back with Daddy and to find him greeting her warmly. He held her in his arms and kissed her cheek for the first time. She responded by hugging his neck. "I missed you, Daddy."

"I missed you, too, pumpkin."

Because she was so thoroughly a part of Nate's world, Kara continued to live in his house most of the time. Cal did not feel she needed to visit often, however, because on alternate weekends and for two weeks in the spring, Kara was now part of the Rhoads household. Since weekends and hiatus were the only times that Cal, Leonard, or Nate had much time to spend with her, sharing these times seemed like the best way to arrange her visitations. Now Kara was an integral and welcome part of both families.

Nate was sorry that his life with Cal wasn't to be permanent. He still loved her, but his new nature allowed him to accept the fact that she needed to be back with her husband. He would rather she be living with Leonard and happy, than to be living with Nate and despondent. Nate would rock and sing his daughter to sleep, remembering fondly the nights when he would hold her mother in his arms and sing her to sleep, too. The two were so similar in many ways. He was glad that Kara was here and a very active part of his life. She filled his days with sunshine.

Who knows what the future would hold? The past had been made up of so many unexpected occurrences that the future could only be guessed. Because of Nate's successful heart surgery, it was now quite possible that he would outlive Leonard in the natural course of events. If that happened, perhaps Cal might be his again. Until then, he would take good care of their precious daughter, being the best "Uncle Nate" he could be.

And maybe, someday, Kara could be told the truth.

PART IV

Nate

Chapter 1

1987

"Uncle Nate, why are you sad?" Kara asked as they sat together in the large, thick-cushioned rocking chair late that Friday evening. The house was still except for the back and forth movement of the chair. To the left was a graceful canopied bed, partially unmade and awaiting its little occupant. To the right was a huge toy chest, neatly closed with a cushion atop that matched those of the rocker. On shelves around the room were dolls and teddy bears of all sizes, looking down at the lazily rocking pair who moved as one.

He opened his eyes and looked down at Kara, in pink pajamas and snuggled on his lap with her head resting against his chest. "I thought you were almost asleep, Kara-Mia. What makes you think I'm sad?"

"Because you went like this." She emitted a forlorn sigh. "Mama does that when she's sad."

"Oh. I guess I was thinking about your mama. Sometimes that makes me happy, and sometimes it makes me sad."

"But Mama and Daddy say that everything's good now, Uncle Nate, so you can smile real big and be happy."

Lord, how he loved this child! She may be the very image of Nate physically, but her spirit is definitely that of her mother. How much longer they would be able to keep her parentage a secret from Kara was anyone's guess. The tabloids had already figured it out and had shouted it to the world. It was amazing that apparently none of Kara's friends had mentioned it to her. Little kids must not pay attention to tabloids or parents' gossip—and thank heaven for that!

"You know those Hollywood types," those parents would say. "They don't live like normal people do." And it's true. The pressures and influences are quite different when you're in the public eye, day after day, in an industry whose end product is fantasy.

Kara was the most enduring tie between the Jenkins and Rhoads households. Another was work. Their television series was soon to wrap up its second season in a good position, rated in the top twenty. "High school sweethearts" was the public image of Cal and Nate—an image that was carefully manufactured and maintained in perpetuity by the publicity department of the studio to which they owed their allegiance, Stagecraft Productions, Inc. If only it were true!

"You're right, little one," Nate agreed. "Things are real good, aren't they? We have a hit TV show, and you visit Mama and Daddy every other weekend now. What else can we be happy about?"

Kara thought for a moment, then brightened. "That tomorrow's Saturday and I don't have to go to school. Mama said we're going to have a family picture made this weekend. She saw the one downstairs and wanted to do it, too."

"That'll be nice. Is everything going all right over there? Are they treating you well?"

"Yeah. They have swings in their back yard now, too. It has a ladder on it and I climb up to the top and hang by my hands."

He nodded, then closed his eyes. Kara might still have some steam left but Nate was played out. Friday was the day they taped their weekly show, and it was usually a very long day for him. Kara and Miss Susie were there in the audience tonight because their guest star had been a puppeteer. Nate thought she would enjoy that, and he was right. Kara would have been up this late anyway though, whether or not she attended the taping, simply because it was their tradition for her beloved Uncle Nate to tuck her in each night. No one else, except Mama, would do.

"You're going to have to go ahead to bed now. Uncle Nate's too tired to stay up much longer, okay?" he asked.

"Read me a story?"

"Tomorrow night."

She sighed. "Okay." Kara slid off his lap and climbed into her bed. She looked so tiny amidst such large fluffy pillows and the hand-embroidered quilt.

Nate pulled the sheets up to her chin, then leaned over and kissed her forehead. "Good night, Kara," he said.

"-Mia." She reached up to give him a hug.

He smiled as they embraced, "My sweet little Kara-Mia. See you in the morning, then we'll drive over to Mama and Daddy's house." He turned off the light and went to his own room.

As tired as he was, Nate knew it wouldn't take very long to drift off to sleep tonight. He took a fresh pair of pajamas out of his drawer. Until Kara had come to live with him, he had never worn so much to bed. Having that little girl around brought about many changes in his life, most of which were positive; but he had yet to feel completely comfortable in pajamas.

As Nate unbuttoned his shirt, he sighed, remembering the night almost a year ago that Cal had shown up on his doorstep, suitcase in hand.

If only Leonard hadn't agreed to counseling, Nate thought, *then Cal would've been mine. We came so close!* Those weeks she had lived here in Nate's house had been among his happiest. It felt as though they were a real family—just Nate, Cal and Kara. It felt so right. But, alas, it was not to be.

And Nate wouldn't *really* wish Cal and Leonard had divorced, not if he were perfectly honest with himself. She didn't believe in divorce. It would have made her feel like a failure. It was important to her to make her marriage work. She didn't want to be a statistic—yet another failed Hollywood marriage. For Leonard to have gone to a marriage counselor was the ultimate proof of his love, made at a tremendous sacrifice. Nothing short of the very real threat of losing Cal would have gotten him there. Now that the therapy was in the past, he was probably wondering why it had taken him so long to go.

Nate sighed again as he got into bed and turned off the light. No, he wouldn't wish divorce on Cal. He loved her too much to want that for her. But it sure would have been nice if she could have stayed here a while longer.

*   *   *

"Smile, everyone," said the photographer as she reached over and clicked the shutter, making the flash go off several times.

"Ow! That hurt my eyes," Kara said indignantly.

"Look at the camera, sweetie," said Cal, "not the light."

Most families dress up in their Sunday finest to have a professional portrait taken, silently mused the photographer. *Not the Rhoadses, though.* They preferred that their portrait be a true indication of who they were, and wore what they would normally wear on a Saturday—Leonard and Cal in jeans, and Kara in her favorite denim overalls. At least they did have matching yellow tee-shirts on for the occasion. At the last minute, Cal had stuck a red bandana into Kara's pocket, to give her that extra splash of color.

What Cal would *really* have loved would be a picture of them all on horseback, but the horses belonged to Nate and were at his house. Cal knew better than to suggest that Leonard go to Nate's.

"Daddy, can we go to Burger Bar?"

"After we're finished here," he responded, maintaining his pose for the camera.

"*Really?*" Cal asked, momentarily distracted from the task at hand. "A public place?"

"They have a drive-through, don't they?" he asked.

"But I want to go on the playground," Kara said, "and get a Kidz Meal."

Now Leonard, too, was distracted. "No, Kara. We can't go inside. We'd get mobbed."

"Awwww, Daddy," she whined.

Cal knelt down to put herself at eye level with Kara. "You remember what happened last time we went to a public place? It got wild and we got separated from each other. That was scary, wasn't it?

"Yeah."

"We don't want that to happen again, do we?"

"No."

"But I'll get you a Kidz Meal in the drive-through," Leonard assured her.

The photographer had been taking this time to adjust the lighting. "Okay, are we ready to get back on task now?" she asked.

Cal and Leonard got back into position, behind Kara.

The photographer snapped the shutter a few more times, then pulled out a long bench and lined it up at just the right angle in front of the camera. "Okay, you'll be like a toboggan team, with father in the back, then mother, then child in the front." The family followed the directions to her satisfaction, then she returned to the camera. She reached behind her and turned off the light. Then she turned a spotlight on them.

"It's show time, Len," Cal teased.

"How can we sing and dance sitting down like this?" he said, with a half smile.

"This beam of light casts an almost spiritual glow on you," the photographer said, adjusting the light so it was softer. "I think you'll like the affect. Everyone look up toward the light."

"Kara," Cal whispered. "It's okay to look at *that* light."

They complied and the photographer took a few more shots. Then she turned the spotlight off and the overhead light back on.

"I know a pose that would be great," Cal said as they all returned to a standing position while the photographer moved the bench back. "How about Kara on Len's shoulders? The shot would be head-and-shoulders of us, but whole-body of her. Can we do that?"

"Sure. Just let me make a few changes first." She raised the level of the camera on the tripod and the lights. Leonard, she noted, was a very tall man.

"Or we could be a triple-scoop ice-cream cone," Cal added.

"I beg your pardon?" the photographer asked.

"Me sitting on Len's shoulders and Kara sitting on mine."

"Don't you think Kara would get dizzy that high?" she asked Cal.

"Yeah. Maybe so."

"Up you go, Miss Rhoads," Leonard said as he hoisted Kara onto his shoulders.

"Wow!" she squealed. "I'm *really* tall now!" She held onto Daddy's hands.

"You're even taller than Daddy," Cal said happily. From his right side, she reached her arms around to embrace her husband and grinned at the camera. The flash went off.

The photographer then instructed, "Mother, you stand right in front of them, squarely facing the camera this time. The top of your head comes up to his shoulders, so that will work well."

Cal complied and the flash went off, again.

A few more poses and they were at last finished. After the family bid their goodbyes to her and were Burger Bar-bound, the photographer began getting all her equipment ready for the next session.

Her assistant poked her head in the door. "If you want to go to lunch, I'll stay and answer the phones."

"No, that's okay. I brought my lunch with me. Donna, did that little girl look familiar to you?"

She smiled, "Familiar to me and about six million other people, too. Anyone who reads the headlines at the supermarket checkout would recognize her."

"I'm not up to date on movie stars. So she's a child star? I figured one of them must be famous since the mother said something about being mobbed in public."

"Heavens, no. It's the parents who are the stars."

"*Really*? They sure don't act it. They seem too nice and were quite cooperative. But hasn't the little girl been in here before? She looks so familiar to me, and I know I didn't know her parents before."

"Yeah, a few months ago her father brought her in. Remember Nate Jenkins?"

"Her father?"

"Yeah, I'll show you." Donna looked in the file cabinet and pulled a folder out. She then opened it to reveal a few sets of proofs. Beautifully captured were a handsome middle-aged man in a well-tailored suit and a bright-eyed little girl in a pink chiffon dress, with their heads touching in a gesture of affection. "Nate and Kara Jenkins. They had their portrait taken a few months ago and chose pose number four. I thought number seven was better, myself. They ordered—let's see—one 16x20 and two 8x10's. Remember? He said he was going to give one to his cousin for Christmas and one to his uncle. He bought some of our priciest frames to go with them, too."

"If I had a memory like yours, Donna, I'd be the happiest woman in the world."

"You can tell by looking at them that they're related."

"So this older man here today must be the woman's father, instead of her husband. I called them by the wrong names."

"No, no. The man and woman today are married and have been for a number of years. The lady is teamed up with Nate in the movies and on TV."

"And elsewhere, too, it seems," she winked at her assistant knowingly.

Donna shrugged, "Well, if you can get away with it, why not? You know how movie stars are."

Chapter 2

THIS WAS THE LAST SHOW of the season and the cast and crew were more than ready for hiatus. Since they taped each show two weeks prior to its airing, their summer break was starting over a month before the school year was over.

All that was left was dress rehearsal this afternoon, then the taping tomorrow night, and their vacation would begin. The guest star this week was Harold Davis, one of Cal's cohorts in the second film of the trilogy. He had appeared as Eugene Thomas, the shyest of Corky and Mike's pals. Making a surprise cameo appearance at the very end of their main skit would be Diana Fogarty, who had played Eugene's overprotective young mother and who was now one of the busiest actresses in town. The producers of the *Nate and Stacy Comedy Hour* were quite pleased that Diana had consented to appear on the show, and felt it would be just the kick that would keep the show in viewers' minds over the summer months.

Already costumed for the opening dialog, which would lead into the skit, Cal and Nate were sitting in their own director-style chairs, waiting for everyone else to get ready to begin dress rehearsal. They were the first ones out this week. He reached over and tapped her hand, "I'm glad we're giving Harold a chance to shine again. He's got so much talent, but Stagecraft never promoted him.

"Why didn't they?" she asked. "Why are some actors spotlighted and some aren't? It doesn't seem to have anything to do with talent."

"Because he wasn't a box-office draw. Stagecraft takes a chance on more unknowns than most studios do, but it's still the bottom line that rules. A lot of very talented people never make it in this business."

Cal shook her head sympathetically.

"Here's a good example of that. Even though Uncle Bob knew that your teasing was driving me crazy, you were making a tidy profit for the company and they didn't want to give that up. So they cast you in the sequels. Money takes precedence over blood in this business."

By now most of their castmates were milling about on the set. The assistant director called everyone to their places so dress rehearsal could begin. Cal and Nate abandoned their chairs and took their places.

* * *

Cal sat at her desk, staring at the computer screen. She sighed and scratched her head.

"What's the matter? Won't it write itself?" Leonard asked, jokingly. His desk was beside hers in the study, and he had been looking over a couple of scripts.

Cal was really hoping that her screenplay, *Mr. Jackson's Vacation,* would be finished before hiatus. Her dream was for the couple to form their own production company and produce this film themselves, but Leonard had no interest in forming a company for that project or any other. He saw himself as an actor only and was happy to leave wheeling and dealing to the businessmen of the world.

"I can't decide whether to make it a 'happily-ever-after' ending or not," she answered. "What do you think?"

"Depends on whether you want it to be realistic or not. Films can be complete fantasy or more lifelike, depending on the intent of the director."

"You mean intent of the writer."

"No, Cal. The writer only provides the words. It's the director who determines what all those words are going to mean to the audience. You've had that experience, I know, where you'll think your character is to be interpreted one way and your director changes it completely."

"Yeah, that's true. So what you're saying is that it doesn't matter how I write it. Whether it's a happy or sad ending depends entirely on the director."

"More or less."

"Maybe I'll direct this film."

He chuckled at the thought. "Some writers think that's the only way to get the job done right."

"I wonder if George would do the business part of forming a production company. Then we can direct and produce it, too."

"No, Cal. He's got enough work to do already. We don't want to saddle a whole company on him. Let's leave production business to people who know what they're doing. Neither you nor I know the first thing about running a production company."

"What I need is a sugar daddy."

"We could both use one of those. Know of any?" he smiled indulgently.

She smiled back at him in what he interpreted to be agreement that the production-company idea wasn't worthy of pursuing. He was mistaken about that. She had just thought of a way to make her idea a reality, but would have to set it in motion first, *then* make it known to Leonard. Cal subscribed to the commonly-held theory that forgiveness is easier to get than permission. "Are either of those scripts any good?"

Leonard redirected his attention to the two scripts on his desk. "They're both pretty good. Since their production schedules don't overlap and will be finished before hiatus is, I'll do both."

"But do you think you should? You really ought to start taking it easier, Len. You're fifty-eight years old, for Pete's sake. Other guys your age are playing golf."

"They're wimps."

"But we have only two more months of hiatus. If you have good-sized roles in both of them, you won't have any downtime before we start back up in August.

"I don't need downtime. I love to work. Work's my play."

"Yeah, yeah, I know. When's the first one start? That one's in Oregon, right?"

"Next week and yes, in Oregon."

"I've got a guest spot while you're gone, but I'd like to go with you to the filming in Germany. I need to have access to my savings account. What bank is it in?"

"You know George will make all the arrangements and payments for you. You don't have to worry about that."

"I want to get some extra money for travel. What bank is my account in?"

"It's a trust fund in the First National Bank downtown, but you don't have to do that, Cal. George will. Just tell him how much you want and he'll get it for you out of our joint account."

"Okay."

*   *   *

Nate was surprised when Cal showed up at his house on a Wednesday morning. Mrs. North had shown her in, then announced her presence to him in her usual professional manner. *Whatever could the occasion be?* he wondered, as he went into the sitting room. He found Cal admiring the portrait of him and Kara on the wall. "Hi, Cal. What brings you here today?"

"I sure do love this picture," she said, still looking at it closely. "She looks like a little fairy princess, all dressed up like that, doesn't she?"

He smiled proudly, "Yes. She's my little princess, all right."

"And now I see what Becky meant. In this picture, you two DO look a lot alike." She sat in the closest chair. "Where's Kara?"

"Out back with her pony. This is the first time you've ever come on a Wednesday morning. Is there something on your mind? Something you want to talk about?"

"Yeah. I want to ask your advice about business."

"Shouldn't you ask Leonard about that? I'm not much into business."

"He isn't, either. And, besides, he's in Oregon, working on a film. That guy *never* slows down. He says work is play to him."

"I guess when one is that good at what he does for a living, it *would* seem like play. What kind of business did you want advice about?"

"I want to form a production company and I need a partner."

"A production company? Why? Aren't you happy with Stagecraft?" He pulled a chair closer to Cal's and sat down.

"I want to produce and direct a screenplay I'm writing, and I want to do it with my own production company. I want it to be like Desilu."

He smiled. "I didn't know you were a writer. What kind of screenplay is it?"

"A romantic comedy-adventure. It's got a role for you in it, too."

"Can I see it?"

"Sure, when it's finished. Would you be my production company partner?"

"I'll think about it. It seems we've been partners in a lot of things, lately, doesn't it?"

"Yeah, and this partnership might make you a lot of money."

"If I agree to it, it won't be because of the money. It'd be more for the artistic freedom." He leaned back and thought for a moment. "Having our own production company could free us to do any kind of projects we wanted to do. We wouldn't need Uncle Bob's approval. But we *would* have to have a good, experienced person running it and a few support people to help him."

"See," she beamed, "you know more about this than you thought you did. It'll turn out great."

"How much money will it take?"

She leaned forward, eyes aglow with excitement. "Nate, you'll never guess what I found out. I talked to the bank guy about my savings account—you know, the one Len's been managing for me since I was a teen? You'll never guess how much I have in there. I couldn't believe it, myself. I'm *loaded*, Nate!"

"So you'll be able to match whatever I put into this project?"

"Probably. I don't know how much it'll cost, but I do know that I've got zillions of dollars—well, more or less. When I bought Zeus, I had that whole amount already saved up and lots more, too. Len took that $200,000 out, then it started building back up again. Up and up and *up*, Nate!" She intentionally neglected telling Nate that the rules for that trust had changed, that as long as Leonard was alive, she couldn't take any money out without his signature; but she would cross that bridge when she got to it. Once the contracts were signed, he'd *have* to let her have the money. Leonard was a stickler for following through on promises, like contracts. "And it's all mine. It's completely separate from the joint account Len and I have."

He nodded, "It looks like Leonard's been taking good care of you. He wanted to be sure that you were financially secure, no matter what happened to him. He's a good man, Cal."

"I know."

"I'll have my manager check into a production company."

Yes sir, it looked like Cal's dream was going to come true.

*   *   *

After her guest appearance on *The Tidwells* was completed, Cal flew up to Oregon to see Leonard. He was quite happy to see her. They had room service bring their dinner up, then enjoyed a leisurely evening on the balcony, overlooking the Pacific Ocean. Hand-in-hand they sat in the lounging chairs, as the serenity of their surroundings washed over them.

"I love the waves of the ocean," Cal sighed. "It's so beautiful."

"Um-hmm," he nodded, eyes closed.

She looked over at him. "Are you falling asleep?"

"Just relaxing. How'd your week go?"

"Really well. Really, *really* well. I'm a businesswoman, Len. You'll be proud of me when I tell you."

"Oh? How'd that come about?"

"I found a partner for my production company. We're going in fifty-fifty on it. He's in charge of the business end, and I'll do the creative stuff."

"Where's your half of the money coming from?"

"My own savings account. I won't need to touch our joint account, so you don't have to worry." She went back into their room, retrieved the withdrawal slip from her purse, and brought it back to Leonard. "You need to sign this."

Now Leonard was fully awake and alert. "Cal, no. That money is for you to use after I'm gone."

This startled Cal. "Gone? Where're you going?"

"I'm talking about when I die. You'll be a widow someday, Cal, and I don't want you to have to worry about money when that happens."

"But Len…"

"Sooner or later, you've got to face that fact. I'm almost twenty years older than you, so I'm *sure* to die first."

"I'll put all my profit from the company back into that account and it'll be completely replaced someday."

"Profit? I think you're being overly optimistic."

"You don't have any faith in me."

"It's a gamble, Cal, a *big* gamble. Any business is. And we're talking big bucks here. Who's your partner? A businessman?"

"Nate."

"Now I *know* I won't sign it!" He tore the deposit slip into small pieces and tossed it over the railing.

"It's *my* money, Len. You have no right to it. I should be able to use that money any way I want."

"The only reason you have it at all is because I put it there and paid your bills myself. If you'd gotten hold of it, it'd be long gone by now."

Seething, she paced the width of the room and back, then she turned to him. "So when're you going?"

"Going where?"

"Wherever you go when I'm a widow."

"Not for a good long time, Cal. Just forget about this production company idea. It's not going to happen."

"But the contracts are already signed and everything. All that's left is the money part."

"Too bad."

"I thought you believed a person's only as good as his word. I gave my word when I signed those contracts, and now you want me to go back on my word."

"You should've thought of that before you signed the contracts."

"I thought you loved me. I see I was wrong about that."

"This has nothing to do with love and everything to do with business. Neither you nor Nate know how to run a business."

"But his uncle does and he's advising us."

"Cal, listen to me. This production company would be in direct competition with his. Just how good do you expect his advice to be?"

"Nate's like a son to him. He wouldn't steer him wrong. Nate has just as much money tied up in this as I will."

"But he has more money to draw from than you do and more where that came from. Let him put up one hundred percent of the money and I'll consider letting you be involved."

"What do you mean 'letting' me be involved? Since when do I need your permission?"

"Since the day you stepped off that plane from Dallas, that's when. I've been responsible for you since day one."

"I'm not a kid anymore, Len. You've never gotten over thinking I'm fifteen. It's not like that anymore."

"When you stop being so damn impulsive, then I can stop pulling in the reins."

"This is *not* an impulsive idea. I've been wanting us to have our own production company for years, so you can have more romantic leads. Nate said it'll give us artistic freedom."

He looked at her with disgust. "Oh, is that what he calls it?"

"What's that supposed to mean?"

"'Artistic freedom' to spend more time with my wife than he already does."

"He's not like that anymore, Len. You've seen how he is at work. He's a perfect gentleman."

"He always *has* been a slave to his image. How about when no one else is around, huh? Is he a perfect gentleman then?"

"Of course, he is!"

"You can't have the money and that's the end of it. I don't want to hear another word about it."

"Tough!"

"You can't get the money out of the bank without my signature, and I'm not signing."

"I'm going to do this, Len. I don't care what you say. And it's going to be a success, too, even if it kills me."

"You'll have to find the money somewhere else, then."

"Okay. I just might do that."

* * *

Wondering why she even bothered trying to talk any sense into such a stubborn man, Cal disgustedly returned to Los Angeles. During the plane ride home, she mapped out Plan B. She might not have access to her own money, but she *was* able to draw from their joint account. Since neither she nor Leonard were big spenders but *were* once again big earners, there was plenty of money from which to draw. Their joint savings account was connected to their joint checking account. Whenever they used up the money in checking, another thousand dollars was automatically transferred over from savings, so they would never be considered overdrawn. Before going to Nate's house, she stopped by the bank and checked on the balance in their joint savings account. Cal was pleasantly surprised to learn that, even after drawing out the amount to cover her half of the initial cost of starting the production company, there would still be plenty left.

Now that she had all the information she needed to complete the transaction, Cal took her luggage home, then drove over to Nate's house. It was getting dark as she pulled into his driveway, then hurried up to his door. This time, she used the key Nate had had made for her and let herself in. "Anyone home?" she asked. "Kara, Mama's here."

Nate came into the hallway from the den. "Hi, Cal. How was your trip?"

"I'm ready to write the check, then we'll be in business."

"So Leonard's given his approval?" he smiled.

"Well, not exactly. He won't let me use my savings account for it. He doesn't think we can run a production company. He thinks we'll lose our shirts. He has absolutely no faith in our ability. We'll show him. I've got another source I can get the money from."

"Oh, a slush fund of your own that he didn't know about, eh? My mother used to say every woman ought to have one of those."

Cal shrugged as she sat on the sofa and pulled out her checkbook. She wrote the check, tore it out, and handed it to him. "Partners!"

He looked at it as he sat beside her on the sofa, "But, Cal, this account has Leonard's name on it, too. So it's *not* just some mad money of your own."

"It's okay. There's plenty more where that came from."

Nate shook his head and held the check out to her. "I don't want to cause you two to have a big fight, Cal, and you *know* that's what's going to happen when he finds out."

"When he sees that I've drawn the money out of our joint account, he'll *have* to use the money from my own savings account to replace it. So this is the way I'm using my own money. It's just a little 'round about,' but it'll have the same ultimate results."

"Well, I don't know."

"It's okay, Nate. Don't worry about it. I can handle Len. Just use the money to buy what we need to get this thing going. That's my half."

"Are you sure?"

"Positive. You want to see my screenplay? I finished it now."

"It's finished?" His eyes lit up with anticipation. "Yes, I'd love to see it."

She hoped it didn't disappoint him. Cal went back out to the car, retrieved the script, then brought it back, handing it grandly to Nate. "Ta-dah! The first Ames-Jenkins production."

"Second."

"What?"

He looked over at her with a mischievous gleam as he took the manuscript. "Kara, remember?"

Cal laughed, "Oh, yeah. Where is that little critter, anyway?"

"In the bathtub, then it'll be her bedtime."

"I brought her something from Oregon. I'll be right back." Cal went upstairs and into the bathroom to find Kara chin deep in bubble bath. "Golly, I can hardly find you among all those bubbles! Didn't you kind of overdo it?"

"I'm pretending it's snow." She put a mound of it on her head and giggled. "Now it's a hat."

"Maybe sometime I can take you to Oregon in the winter. I bet they have real snow there. Look what I brought you." Cal reached into her pocket and pulled out two ivory and pink shells. "These were on the beach." Kara took them from her mother's hand and looked at them closely. Cal got another shell out of her pocket and handed it to her daughter. "One more. Aren't they pretty?"

"Yeah. They look like California shells."

Cal took off her jacket and sat on the edge of the tub. She took the washcloth, soaped it up, then washed Kara's back. "Did you miss me while I was gone?"

"Yeah. Uncle Nate took me to work."

"To work? Where's that?"

"The studio. He showed me cameras and lights and everything. And he showed me the room y'all were in the first time he ever saw you."

"Ahh, good ol' Stage 3."

"He said he couldn't stop staring at you and he had to wear sunglasses so you wouldn't know he was looking so much."

"I was just a kid back then. I was fifteen when I met Uncle Nate. He was the star of the movie I was in."

Kara grinned up at her mother, "Silly. Fifteen isn't a kid. That's old."

That made Cal smile. She re-soaped the washcloth and started washing Kara's face, neck, chest and arms. "You're going to be squeaky clean when I get through with you, kiddo."

"I already did that."

"You already washed yourself all over?"

"Well, not my back. But everything else."

"Oh." She rinsed off the suds.

"Guess what Melissa told me. She said Uncle Nate's my daddy."

Cal wasn't sure what to say at this. She knew Leonard wasn't ready for Kara to know the truth yet. "So what did *you* say?"

"I said huh-uh. And she said uh-huh, her mama told her so."

"Well, sweetie, some people think he's your daddy because you live with him."

"Oh, yeah."

"That's probably why." Cal pulled the plug and got the towel off the rack, and Kara got out of the tub. Her mother proceeded to dry the child.

"I love Uncle Nate," Kara said wistfully. "Can he be my daddy, too? Can I have two daddies so I can be like the other kids? They have daddies and step-daddies."

Cal shrugged, "Keep calling him Uncle Nate, okay? Daddy wants to be the only person you call Daddy."

Kara whispered in Cal's ear, "Can I call Uncle Nate 'Papa,' then?"

Oh, Cal thought, if only Kara knew about the "forgiveness easier to get than permission" theory. How could she sanction calling Nate Papa?

"Because I kind of do already," the child confessed.

"You call him Papa?"

"He said I can call him Papa Nate when we're here. He's Papa Nate and Daddy's just plain old Daddy."

She smiled, "Just so you keep them straight. And don't let Daddy hear you call Uncle Nate Papa, okay? It might hurt his feelings. We don't want to hurt Daddy's feelings because we love him, too, don't we?"

"Yeah. I have a giant Daddy and a regular Papa Nate."

As she finished drying Kara and held out her nightgown for her, Cal asked, "If Daddy's a giant and Uncle Nate's regular, what am I?"

The little girl held her arms up while her mother slipped the nightgown over her head. "Papa Nate said you're a munchkin."

"I hope he smiled when he said that."

"He laughed. And he said I'm a baby munchkin."

Cal put the towel back up on the rack. "Let's go tell him you're ready for bed now. Which of us would you like to tuck you in tonight?"

"Papa Nate. And you sit on the bed so you can hear the story, too."

"Okay."

"But I've gotta' brush my teeth first. He'll fuss at me if I don't." Kara pulled out a stool, stood on it, and got her toothbrush out of the holder.

*　*　*

Cal and Nate came back downstairs after having put Kara to bed.

"I guess I'd better go now." She gathered up her purse and started toward the door, then she remembered something and turned back toward Nate. "Did you read any of the screenplay? What'd you think of it?"

"What happens after they leave Italy?" he asked, taking her arm and leading her to the sofa, where they both sat. "Will they realize that they had that roll of film that could split the case wide open?"

Cal grinned. "That must mean you like it."

"I do, Cal. It's got a good plot that's fast-moving, but not *too* fast. I like the subplot, too. It's got adventure, romance, and humor. Why didn't you tell me you could write?"

"Showing is better than telling. If I hadn't gone into show biz as an actress, I might've ended up in the biz anyway, as a screenwriter. You want to play the lead?"

"I thought you wanted Leonard to have that role. It had his name on the front page."

"He probably wouldn't want to. He hasn't made any effort to even read it. I showed it to him and had it on the bedside table all weekend, and he didn't even look at it. That's another of my abilities he has no faith in."

"Well, okay. I will if you'll be my leading lady."

"Sure. I get to dress up all fancy and everything. And you pursue me all over Europe. That's the part I like."

"While we're smack in the middle of a spy ring, without even knowing it."

"And your reckless quest to win your lady-love messes up all those spies' elaborate schemes. I think that's so fun."

"I like the part where we jump off the ocean liner into the water and almost become an aquatic meal."

"It's kind of like you're an inadvertent James Bond. While you're completely focused on something else, you get the information back to America that they had sent those spies over to get."

"Is *that* how it ends?"

"Yeah. And you get the girl at the end, too."

He smiled. "I like that story."

"I was hoping you would." Then she grinned. "How'd you read it so fast? I was upstairs with Kara only about a half hour, at the most."

"I didn't read every word. When I look through scripts to see which ones I want to do, I use a speed-reading technique. That gives me a good idea of the story line. This will be your first directing experience. I've never done that, myself."

"Have you ever wanted to?"

He shrugged, "Not really."

It made Cal so happy that he had read and enjoyed her screenplay. She should have known he would be supportive of this effort. Leonard's lack of interest had made her start doubting her ability. She hugged Nate. "You're a good buddy, Nate." Then she started to get up.

He took her arm. "I sure missed you while you were gone, Cal. Kara did, too. I don't get to see you very much anymore, away from the studio."

"I know." She sat back down. "Len doesn't want me coming over here any more than I have to. It's kind of rough on me, too, to stay away."

He stroked her cheek, then kissed her softly on the lips. "Stay over-night?"

How sweet that felt, and how she would have loved to stay.

He took her purse off her shoulder and set it behind him, then he held her and kissed her passionately.

Cal, caught up in the heated emotion of the moment, wrapped her arms around him, too. Again they kissed, and again. She had forced herself not to ever say it again to Leonard, but she still kept wondering why he wasn't more like Nate. Certainly he could be this supportive and loving, if he'd just try. Why didn't he want to?

"You can stay," Nate said softly in her ear, "and he'll never know."

Cal couldn't resist any longer. They had been so good for so long, and she wanted him so badly. Surely one more time wouldn't hurt. She *was* on the pill, after all, and hadn't missed any doses. "Okay," she whispered.

Hand-in-hand, they went upstairs.

*   *   *

Nate woke up first the next morning to find Cal still lying beside him, with her arms around him. How he yearned to be able to give her his love, freely and openly, every day. He knew that Leonard wasn't giving her what she needed. Her husband's indifference to the thing that mattered so much to Cal was troubling to Nate. She had put so much time into her screenplay. It was her baby, something that she created all by herself and of which she was proud. Now that Nate had read it, he realized that she really did have literary talent. She was much more articulate on paper than she was orally, and she had a good head for plot development. Until they made a film of it, though, Leonard would never know about that talent. Even then, he would probably attribute any success of the film to its director, rather than its writer. For that reason, Nate was so glad that Cal would be directing it herself. Then Leonard would see how capable she really is.

Sometimes Nate wondered why he cared about Cal and Leonard's marriage. Surely, she'd be better off here than with Leonard. She loved her husband, though, and deserved no less than a happy life with him. Nate's thoughts went back to that fateful night so long ago when he had taken her in anger:

It was after he had been satisfied and slid, exhausted, off her that he started feeling a crushing pain in his chest. He stood back up, then every-thing went black. The next thing he knew, he was at a higher vantage point, looking down at his body on the floor. It looked as though he was dead. Cal knelt beside him, checked for a pulse and put her ear to his chest. At that point, she burst into tears. "Nate! Nate, don't die," she cried, as she tilted his head back, pinched his nose, then leaned over to breathe into his mouth for him. She sobbed as, over and over, she did chest compressions and blew air into his lungs, while her tears fell onto his chest and cheeks.

Now he saw his father, who had died years earlier. He was alive and well. There was a bright glow of light beside him. Wisdom and love seemed to emanate from this light. Things suddenly became clear to Nate that had only been shadows before. "Love one another, as I have loved you." "I am with you always, even unto the end of the world." "Where your treasure is, there will your heart be also."

His dad pointed behind Nate and said, "Your most important work is yet to be done, son. You must go back."

"Come on, Nate. Come on!" Cal cried. "Breathe!" Running out of breath herself, she continued her resuscitation attempts as well as she could, pumping on his chest and blowing air into his lungs.

Suddenly, he found himself back in his body as he opened his eyes to see her leaning over him.

Her relieved smile made her appear almost angelic. "Thank you, Lord," she sighed. Totally worn out, she sat back on her heels to catch her breath.

Everything looked different to him now. Life was a precious thing, to be used wisely. Friends were to be cherished and nurtured. Life was too short and precarious to waste.

Cal had looked at him for a long moment, then went to the phone and called an ambulance. The paramedics arrived within ten minutes and rushed him to the hospital, where it was determined that he had suffered a heart attack.

From that day on, he was a changed man. That heart attack turned his life around as nothing else had been able to do. It was as though he started living on that day. He had a new appreciation for life and people. Cal's act of complete unselfishness and concern had touched him deeply. An hour earlier, he had a loaded pistol in his pocket and fully intended to use it on her; but now she had saved not only his life, but his soul, too. No longer were they enemies; but, rather, from that moment on, they would be the closest of friends.

Yes, he thought, she deserved no less than a good, happy marriage. Since Leonard was the man she chose to marry and she still loved him after all these years, Nate would do all he could to help her achieve contentment with him. When Leonard wouldn't give her the affection she needed, though, Nate saw nothing wrong with giving it to her himself. *It's kind of like having a stunt double*, he kept telling himself.

Once it became apparent that Kara was indeed his child, Nate's world once again changed dramatically. Now he had a daughter. He had always enjoyed Becky's children, but having a daughter of his own was a very special thing. Here was a child who was half Nate, half Cal. He felt that God had sent Kara to him, against great odds, to give him some direction in life. For the first time, he had someone who depended on him and loved him for who he was. It's sad that Cal and Leonard's fights were so upsetting to Kara that Nate was given primary custody of her, but he was awfully glad to have her here. Now he had someone to love and care for on a daily basis.

He looked over at Cal and kissed her forehead. *If only I could have primary custody of her, too*, he thought with a sigh.

She opened her eyes.

"Good morning," he smiled.

"Good morning," she smiled back. "What time is it?"

"Oh, about eight o'clock."

She became alarmed. "Kara! I don't want her to see me in here."

"It's okay. The door's been closed all night, and she's been taught to stay out when my door's closed. She's probably downstairs, having breakfast with Miss Susie."

Her smile then returned and she hugged him tight. "We're partners in our own business now. Ames-Jenkins Productions. It's really, really happening."

"Yes, it is." He hugged her close, too.

"And *Mr. Jackson's Vacation* will be its very first film production."

"Well, if we're going to be in it, we'll have to wait until next year's hiatus to do it. Work on our TV show starts back up in six weeks, you know."

"But I've been in films that only took four weeks to do."

"That's just the part the actors are involved in. There's also pre-production and post-production work to be done. We can't put this together that fast or it'll look shoddy."

"Oh." Her face fell. "That's eleven whole months away."

"We can do other projects in the meantime, projects that neither of us appear in. That can be done without our being there for it. I asked Uncle Bob and he said we'd want to have our own studios eventually, but he'll let us use Stagecraft's buildings for now, whatever part no one else is using at the time."

"He sure is being nice about all this. Isn't he afraid we'll take business away from him? Len said that we'll be in direct competition with Stagecraft."

Nate fingered her curls. "Sounds like he has more faith in us than you thought, but I don't think we'll be much competition for a big company like Stagecraft. We don't have as many resources as they do."

"But we'll grow and get better and better."

"Maybe so. In any event, we'll be doing projects that we can be proud of, whether they make money or not. If we break even, I'll be happy."

"Artistic freedom."

"Exactly."

* * *

Cal and Nate had gotten dressed and were going to join Kara downstairs for breakfast. Since she was sure Kara would have noticed her car parked out front, she was prepared to tell a little white lie about having spent last night in one of the guestrooms because of the late hour. As she opened Nate's bedroom door and breezed out into the hallway, though, she found herself face to face with Miss Susie. Kara was right beside her.

"Mama! I didn't know you were here. How come you're in Papa Nate's room?"

"Uh," she hesitated, "we were discussing business."

Kara giggled, "In a *bedroom*? That's silly."

"There's a desk in his room, Kara," Miss Susie said as she took her hand and led the child downstairs. "People keep business papers in their desk drawers."

As they descended the staircase, Cal looked over at Nate and whispered, "Double that lady's salary, will you, Nate?"

He chuckled and put his arm around her shoulders, as they went downstairs, too.

* * *

The bank statement was on the desk and Leonard was furious. Cal had never seen him so irate before. He grabbed her roughly by the shoulders and shook her with each word, "You did *what*?"

"Well, it's the only way I could get the money, Len. You can get it back from my savings account."

"Your trust fund is not to be touched until I die. I refuse to take any money out of it."

"It didn't seem to bother you to take it out when we bought Zeus."

"That's different. There was a good reason for that." He let go of her and went toward the door, then he turned back toward her. "This is the most underhanded thing you've ever done, Cal. I can't believe you'd do it."

"There's a better reason for starting a production company than there was to buy Zeus."

"Buying that horse used the money you were saving for a house. It kept you from moving away."

"But I had enough in my account then that I could've bought *two* houses. Why didn't you tell me I had that much? Talk about underhanded..."

"You're changing the subject. We're talking about the check you wrote two weeks ago. Replacing it with money from your trust fund is out of the question, so what're you going to do about it now?"

"There I was almost twenty-one years old. I could've signed a contract for a house, but you wouldn't tell me how much money I had saved up. All you kept saying was that it wasn't enough. You lied to me!"

"No, I didn't. There's not enough money *in the world* to have made me let you live alone. You were hot property back then, like you are again now. For you to have lived alone would've been inviting trouble. Remember Sharon Tate? Something like that could've happened to you."

"I know that's not why you did it, because I could've gotten a body guard. I think you're just a power freak. You want to control everything about my life. You just want me to be your puppet."

"That's not true. I had the best intentions in the world."

"Yeah, right," she sneered as she made her way past him to the door.

He took hold of her arm as she passed by. "My intention from the first day I saw you was to protect you. We were responsible for you."

"Once I turned eighteen, you weren't."

"By then, I loved you, Cal; but the only way I could express it was by protecting you. You had to be protected not only from other people, but from yourself as well. If I hadn't been around to put the brakes on, you would've gone out in a hundred different directions, spending all your money and putting yourself in all sorts of dangerous situations. I was already married and you were so much younger than me, so I couldn't show my love for you any other way than by controlling your money. Keeping your money unavailable to you, except in small doses, kept you out of all sorts of trouble."

"You didn't love me. I don't think you ever did. I think you're just a good actor."

"Right about one thing," he let go of her arm, "and wrong about another."
"What?"

"Right—I'm a good actor. Wrong—I loved you long before you knew it and never stopped. There have been times I've wanted to wring your neck, but I've always loved you."

"How could that have happened?"

"I don't know how. I don't know why. I just know it happened, and it ruined a perfectly good marriage. If you hadn't come along, Jill and I would've probably been together until we died."

"I would say 'I'm sorry,' but that would be a lie. I love you, and I'm glad you're mine." Cal scratched her head and sat down. "But I've never been a femme fatale or anything, Len. I'm not even pretty, and Jill is. I don't understand. I was obnoxious and reacted to discipline by kicking and biting you."

"I don't know all that psychological mumbo-jumbo, Cal. I just know it happened. You made me feel alive, you were a challenge, something in me needed you. Life was entirely too tame and predictable before you came along. Once Jill realized I wouldn't let you move out of my house, she thought legally adopting you would keep our relationship platonic. She knew I'd never commit incest, and that's the very reason I refused to go along with adoption."

"Wow. If you were the lecherous sort, it sounds like I needed a body guard back then to protect me from *you*."

"Not really. I had self control. Always have. I waited until you were twenty-one."

"And, even then, it was only because of that adult role. You were just teaching me how to do a love scene the way adults do instead of like a teenager."

He smiled mischievously. "Sometimes, golden opportunities just fall into my lap. It had been a couple of months since Jill had left me, and I was hot as hell."

"But you said my taking that adult role would do more for my career than all my previous ones put together."

"Well, it *did*. You were finally allowed to grow up on screen."

Cal grinned. "And once you taught me all that good stuff, I found it was kind of fun. You're a great teacher, Len. I hope you don't teach good stuff to anyone else."

He mussed her hair and sat beside her. "It's a class of one, kid, and you graduated magna cum laude."

"Yeah, I've kept you in good condition, huh?"

"I've probably got the healthiest heart in the world."

"Well, Len, you always *have* been sexy. It looks like the forties is when most guys start getting potbellied, but you were still firm and strong. I would rather have died than admit it back then, but even when I was fifteen, I thought you looked awfully good."

Tonight, to her great surprise, Cal had inadvertently stumbled upon the proper way to discuss money with Leonard and receive forgiveness for her excesses.

* * *

It was good to have Leonard back home, especially since Cal knew that he'd be off again very soon to Germany for his last film of the year. Then, in August, it would be back to work on their television show. Things looked good for the show this year. They had lost one sponsor, but had picked up two more.

"Can we go to Burger Bar for breakfast, Daddy?" Kara asked as she climbed into bed with Cal and Leonard and wedged herself between them.

"What time is it?" he asked.

Kara looked at the digital clock. "Six oh four."

He grunted and turned over, away from the others.

"We only get up this early when we're working, sweetie," Cal said as she put her arm around her daughter. "Let's go back to sleep and talk about breakfast later."

"You were funny, Mama."

"I was?" She closed her eyes and tried to go back to sleep.

"Yeah. You and Uncle Nate, talking about business in his bedroom. That's silly," she giggled.

Cal's eyes sprang open as she quickly put her hand over Kara's mouth, but it was too late. Leonard had heard that and was turning back over. She let go of Kara and closed her eyes again, pretending to be asleep.

Leonard sat up and looked coldly at Cal.

Kara looked at him, then at her mother, then back at Leonard.

"Kara," Leonard said, "you scoot along to the media room and watch TV. Your mother and I have something to discuss."

Kara didn't move right away. "Did I do something bad?" She looked deeply troubled.

"No, it's fine. You go on downstairs and I'll take you to Burger Bar later, okay?" he said, patting her back reassuringly.

"Okay." She climbed over Cal and slid off the bed, then went downstairs. A moment later, they heard the television come on.

"Cal," Leonard said accusingly. "I know you're awake. What were you doing in his bedroom?"

She stretched and yawned, then opened her eyes.

"Well?" he said.

"We were talking about the production company. His desk is in his room. People keep business papers in desks."

"He's got an office downstairs where he could conduct business, Cal. Even I know that." Leonard got out of bed and closed the door. Then he turned back toward Cal.

"It's too early to get up, Len. I want to sleep." She turned over and closed her eyes again.

He sat on the edge of the bed and roughly pulled Cal's shoulder back toward him so that she was facing him. There was fire in his eyes. "What were you doing in his bedroom? And don't give me that bull about talking business."

"We were *too* talking about our company. Why don't you trust me?"

"Okay. I'll believe you were talking about business, but I'm sure that's not *all* you were doing. How could you do that with Kara around? You're corrupting your own daughter."

"No, I'm not. The door was closed. She didn't see any-… ." Cal stopped and bit her lip. She then tried to pull the sheet over her head, but Leonard whipped it back down and gripped her by the shoulders so tightly it hurt.

"All the promises you made during counseling were just words? They meant nothing to you?"

Cal tried to break his hold on her, but he wouldn't budge. "Leave me alone!"

He was clearly furious and trying very hard to stay under control. "If you could lie in front of the cameras the way you lie to me, you'd win an Oscar for sure!"

"I've never lied to you."

"You promised you'd stay out of his bed."

"Well," she hesitated, "I meant it at the time. That's not lying."

His grip got even tighter. "Remember telling me I couldn't have both you and Jill? The same is true in this case, Cal. You can't have both Nate and me. I'm not giving you a choice. Nate has to go, and that's that."

"You're hurting me."

He shook her hard. "He's got to go!"

"But Kara needs him, and we need him for the show. Stagecraft doesn't want me without him."

"Believe me, if it weren't for those two things, I'd move us back to New York so fast it'd make your head spin."

"So how can he 'go'?"

Leonard looked at her for a long moment. Then he released her shoulders and retrieved the address book from the bedside stand. After looking up the number, he lifted the telephone receiver and dialed. "Hi, Doc. It's Leonard Rhoads. We need to have a few more therapy sessions, starting this afternoon." He listened for a moment, then held his hand up. "I *know* it's Saturday but this is urgent." He stopped, then nodded. "We're still on hiatus, so you'll need to come here instead of the studio. Three o'clock." He listened once more. "We'll be waiting for you. Have your office bill me for double time. It'll be worth it. Bye." He replaced the receiver, then looked over at Cal.

"Wow," was all she could say.

"Wow what?"

"Double time, Len? He already charges an arm and a leg."

"He's working on short notice on a weekend. It's only fair we compensate him for it."

"I'm *that* important to you?"

"*We're* that important to me."

"Wow."

*   *   *

Once again, Leonard and Cal were having regular therapy sessions. The fact that, this time, Leonard had initiated them greatly impressed Cal. Dr. Reinhardt was non-judgmental and quite helpful. He guided their conversations to get past the surface and reveal the true roadblocks in their relationship, then led them to discover their own effective solutions. Time and the business of life had a way of distracting the couple from what they had learned, however, and the same problem in a different form could then present itself. Then it was time to take what they called "a refresher course."

Leonard and Cal had a very strong love for each other that they seemed to recognize mainly in times of extreme crisis. Making it more visible in their everyday lives was the goal. For people like Leonard and Cal, though, that wasn't easy. It was part of their profession, Leonard explained, to say words that writers put into their mouths, so just saying or hearing that phrase meant nothing to them. Nevertheless, the therapist noted that they both found it difficult to simply say "I love you" under any circumstances other than an emotionally-charged one. After a while, it became apparent to the doctor that such everyday verbal confession was not given easily by either one, so that effort was abandoned. It *was* important to both Cal and Leonard, however, that they *see* evidence of that love in each other's actions. Cal wanted Leonard to take her efforts to fulfill her professional dreams more seriously, and Leonard wanted Cal's undivided faithfulness.

These were the issues with which they would be dealing in these thrice-a-week sessions for the rest of the summer and on into the autumn.

* * *

Kara wandered into the den. Leonard was on the sofa, reading the newspaper. She sat beside him and idly traced an imaginary line on his arm from one freckle to another. "You have dots on your arm."

He smiled. "Did you pick your puzzle up off the floor like I told you to?"

"Yeah." Then she sighed, "Daddy?"

"What?"

"Why did Mama run away?"

"She didn't run away. She had to work. She'll be back."

"But it's Saturday."

"Sometimes she has to work on Saturdays. I guess you were at Nate's the last time she did, though. She's doing a TV show that's filmed outdoors. The weather wasn't just right for it until today."

"I was scared she ran away from home 'cause I was bad last time."

Leonard set the newspaper aside and lifted Kara onto his lap. "No, she didn't run away. She'll be back. And you weren't bad, either."

"But when I said it, you looked mad at Mama."

"Mama and Nate need to discuss their business in the office or on the phone. I think she knows now that his room isn't a good place for that. She'll do better next time."

"I didn't mean to make you mad."

"I'm not mad. Remember? I took you to Burger Bar for breakfast that day. I wouldn't do that if I were mad at you."

"Do you and Mama still love each other?"

"Of course we do. We'll never stop loving each other, and we love you, too, pumpkin." He kissed her cheek reassuringly.

"I miss her. I wish I could talk to her."

"As soon as they finish that scene, she'll be home. Then you can talk to her for the rest of the day, if you want."

Kara brightened. "When will she be home?"

"If everything goes well, early-afternoon. Surely by suppertime."

"Okay."

He set her back on the sofa beside him. "Are you okay now?"

"Yeah."

"So I can read my paper?"

"Yeah."

He took the newspaper and opened it to page two.

"Daddy?"

"What?" he replied while scanning the news.

"How come you're not in Germany? Mama said you were going to make a movie over there, and she was going to come visit you."

He lowered the newspaper again. "I changed my mind. I wanted to spend more time with you and Mama, instead. They're going to shoot it without me."

"They're going to shoot somebody? Like a cowboy?"

He smiled, "No. When they shoot a movie, that means they film a movie. It's not a Western. They don't make Westerns much anymore."

"Mama and I like to see you riding a horse." She leaned against his arm. "Why don't we buy a horse?"

"Because we don't need one."

"But Uncle Nate has horses and Mama and I like to ride them. Sometimes Uncle Nate and I ride them together when Mama's not around, too. He says I'm a good horsewoman."

"Nate has lots of money. Most people don't have as much as he does."

"Are we poor?"

"No, not by a long shot. If I bought horses and poured as much money into the production company as he does, though, we might be poor, especially if the production company loses money."

"I don't like the production company. People keep calling Uncle Nate all the time about it and he has to keep writing checks. I wish it would go away."

"So do I, but it was your Mama's dream to own one, so she needs to do this. If it doesn't make enough money to keep it going, it'll go out of business. Then Nate won't get a lot of calls, anymore."

"He says Mama's going to be a director."

"Oh?"

"She's going to direct the movie she wrote."

Leonard folded the newspaper and set it aside. "That ought to be interesting." The very thought of Cal as a director made him smile.

"I think she's going to be in it, too."

"Sounds like a one-woman show. She's writer, producer, director and star."

"Uncle Nate says she has a lot of talent."

"I'm sure he does."

"Do I have talent like Mama? I know I'm like you."

"Oh? How are you like me?"

"Mama says I'm stubborn like you. She says that's a Rhoads thing."

"That's odd. I thought that was an Ames thing," he mused. "Okay. Why don't you go play on the swings so Daddy can read the newspaper?"

"Okay." She got up and headed for the back door.

* * *

It had been a long day, Cal thought as she pulled into the driveway that evening. She didn't like working on Saturdays, especially when it was her weekend to have Kara. She was hoping that Leonard had spent at least *some* time with her little girl, but knew that Kara had several friends in the neighborhood that she could play with if he was busy. She went inside and called, "Anybody home?"

"In here," came Leonard's voice from the media room. The volume of the movie he was watching got softer. "You've got to see this, Cal. Come here."

She went down the hallway and into the media room. Leonard was on the sofa, with Kara right beside him, a bowl of popcorn on their laps. Cal smiled. This reminded her of the many sessions she and Leonard had had—sitting in those same positions, with their popcorn, as Leonard gave her instruction in the finer points of the performing arts.

"Mama! Look at you in this. You were playing tricks on Daddy."

Indeed, they were viewing Cal's very first film on their big screen. She sat beside Kara and took a handful of popcorn. "I was only fifteen when we made this. Did you see me handcuff Daddy to his car?"

"Yeah," Kara laughed. "And he tried to put you in jail, but you got away. You sure fooled him."

"Daddy taught me how to be an actress. Is he giving you lessons, too?"

"No," Leonard said. "She just wanted to see this film, again. Kara noticed something that I never did." With the remote control, Leonard rewound the tape until it got to a beach scene, then played it at the normal speed again. "Look in the background, in the water." It was a scene in which a very young Mike had been placating a very irritated Officer Stanton, after Corky had picked his pocket while he was mistakenly reprimanding one of her friends for something Corky had done.

Cal strained to make out what was happening in the background. "I can't tell. There's people back there. Is that what you mean? Or did you see a shark, or what?"

He adjusted the picture to zoom in on one of the swimmers.

Then she grinned, "Hey, that's me!"

"Yeah, but Corky was confined to her cabin during that scene," Leonard said, reaching over and mussing Cal's hair.

"Well, I wasn't in this scene, it was the last shot of the day, and I was hot. I had to wait for you to finish and wanted to cool off and was already in a swimsuit, anyway; so why not?"

"They should've done a close-up of you in the water. That would have added to the humor. You know, Corky escapes from solitary confinement—that sort of thing."

"Yeah," Cal laughed. "I could've been hamming it up while y'all were busy talking. You're right. That *would*'ve been neat!"

"Were y'all doing a scene about a beach today, Mama? Is that why you were working outdoors?"

"Not a beach, sweetie. I was in a garden and not having nearly as much fun as I would've at a beach."

"Is shooting all finished now?" Leonard asked.

"Yeah, *finally*! I don't think I want to do anymore appearances on this series. They're not the easiest people to work with. There seems to be a lot of infighting among the regular cast."

"Kara tells me that you're going to be directing your screenplay. I hope you realize you can't do that during the months we're working on our TV show." He paused the video and set the remote control down.

"I know. We'll do it during hiatus next year."

"I'm already obligated to do a film in May. When will yours be shot?"

"About the same time. I can write another one for you to do later."

"No, Cal," he shook his head. "Not necessary. I've got enough to keep me busy. It looks like I'll never be able to retire now. Our show has given my career the boost it needed."

"I thought you didn't want to retire. You said you weren't *ever* going to."

"That's right."

"And I wanted to."

"So what'd you do? Started a production company. Not the best way to leave a profession, Cal."

"Well, at least I will have had one of my works made into a film before I retire. I'm so excited about that, Len! Our first project will be terrific, too. We're giving a lot of talented, previously-unknown people national exposure."

"I know. You told me about that."

"What do you think of it?"

He looked at her cautiously. "You want my honest opinion?"

"When you put it that way, no. I know what you're going to say."

"What?"

"You're going to say it'll lose money."

"It probably will."

"But we have a couple known names in there, too, as a draw."

"That's wise."

"Have y'all had supper yet? I'm hungry."

"We've been waiting for you, Mama."

"Let's order in hoagies. That's my specialty," Cal suggested.

"Yeah! With a pickle on mine!" Kara replied.

Cal looked at Leonard, who responded, "I'll have the usual."

She picked up the phone and placed their order, while Leonard resumed the film.

*　*　*

The next weeks were spent preparing for the show's coming season. The writers were hard at work. The choreographer was mapping out dance steps. The director studied the first few scripts, making notes to himself in the margins. Musicians were contracted. Musical numbers were chosen further ahead than last season. Scenery was being built. Salary negotiations were being finalized. Guest stars were lined up. Wardrobe fittings were underway.

It took a multitude of professionals to bring such a show to the air.

Chapter 3

NATE HAD BROUGHT KARA over to the Rhoads house this Saturday morning. Cal went outside to meet them as Kara ran down the street to visit her friend Jason.

"Are you ready for some good news?" Nate asked with a sparkle in his eye.

"What?"

"I want you to meet the prime candidates for Ames-Jenkins' Executive Director."

Cal's heart leapt for joy.

He continued, "I've narrowed them down to three candidates and one's even from Dallas. I thought you'd like that. I know we agreed to let Uncle Bob choose this person since he knows better than we what's involved in the job, but I thought you'd want to meet them so we can make recommendations to him. Can you do that on Monday?"

"Okay. About 1:00?"

"Will do. We'll meet you in our office at the studio."

"*What* office?"

"Uncle Bob gave us a portion of the second floor. The entry is three doors down from the elevator. As soon as the graphics man comes, it'll say 'Ames-Jenkins Productions, Inc.' on the door."

"Can we make that "Rhoads-Jenkins? Len wouldn't take the money out of my account, so I guess he's a partner, too."

"We've already filed all the corporate papers under the other name. Does he want to be a visible partner?"

"What's that mean?"

"Sometimes, people are what you call 'silent partners.' They take part in it, but don't want it known."

She shrugged. "I don't know what he wants. I haven't asked him."

"Let's talk to him about it, okay?"

Kara returned, downcast. "Jason's not home."

"I'm glad he's not home. Let's show Mama what you learned this week."

He opened the trunk of his car and lifted out his guitar and her ukulele. Nate held out the uke and Kara took it.

"We don't have a piano here, Papa Nate."

"I know. That's why I brought my guitar."

She looked up at her mother. "He plays the piano and guitar and violin, all three."

"I know. Music is what he's best at. I've been telling him that for years."

"Are you ready?" he asked Kara. "One, two, three."

He strummed a few chords, then Kara caught up. After several bars, Cal grinned. It looked so cute to her to see Nate and Kara making music together. When she realized what tune they were playing, she was even more pleased. "I recognize that song. It's 'Moon Over Naples.'"

The little girl's eyes were glued to her instrument in complete concentration.

Nate began singing along, and Cal harmonized with him.

Kara looked up at them and smiled, then lost her place. She looked back at her ukulele and got back on track.

From inside the house, Leonard heard the music and came out onto the porch to see what was going on. When he saw that it was Cal and Kara helping to provide the serenade, he leaned back on the pillar and watched. As they slowed the last few notes to bring their song to a close, he applauded enthusiastically. "Bravo! Encore!"

"What's that mean?" Kara asked.

"It means you did a good job and I'd like to hear more," he explained. "Do you know any other songs?"

Kara shrugged, "Nope. This is the only one."

"We'll have to fix that, won't we?" Nate said. "I'll teach you another one next week." He put his guitar and Kara's ukulele back into the car, closed the trunk, then went up to Leonard and shook his hand. "It's been a long time since I've seen you. How're you doing these days? Are you ready for rehearsals to start back up?"

"Doing well, Nate," Leonard responded. "It's been a busy hiatus for me. I'll be glad to get back into the routine again."

"I've heard about the film. You're more in demand now than ever."

"Yes, the show's been good for my career, I've got to admit."

"Can we go inside? I want to discuss something with you."

"Sure." Leonard held the door open for everyone as they entered the house.

Cal followed the men into the living room as Kara went through the house and out the back door to play on the swings. They took their seats and Leonard looked at Nate expectantly. "Okay. Shoot."

"I understand that Cal hasn't asked you yet, but she was wondering if we ought to change the name to Rhoads-Jenkins Productions because you're helping to finance it. What do you think about that? Would you like to be a visible partner in this company?"

Leonard replied, "It wasn't my idea to help with the financing. It just happened by default."

"I'm really hoping you'll get your money back someday, Leonard. I'm sorry it started out the way it did—taking money away from you like that. That wasn't my intention."

"It's the lesser of the two evils. Cal will need the money in her trust fund someday, so I wasn't about to let her take anything out of it until then. When she does need it, it will support her for the rest of her life."

"That's a good plan."

"She'll have no reason to remarry for the purpose of financial security."

"So would you like to be a visible partner or a silent one? If visible, then we can have the company name changed. It would take quite a bit of paper-work, time, and expense, but it can be done."

Leonard waved that notion away. "No, no reason to do that. Keep it the way it is now."

"Are you sure, Len?" Cal asked.

Leonard nodded. "What do you say, Cal? Should we have Kara take mu-sic lessons?" He obviously didn't want to talk business anymore.

"She sure seemed to enjoy playing that uke," she agreed.

Nate suggested, "Maybe she can start off with the piano. That's a good basic instrument to learn."

"I'll have George arrange music lessons for her once a week, then. Do you have a piano in your house?" he asked Nate.

"Yes."

Cal added, "And Nate plays it, too, Len. He can teach her."

"He'll be busy with the show before long. It'd be good to have a profes-sional teach her." Then he addressed Nate. "I'll have George get with you to work out the details."

Nate stood back up. "Sounds good, Leonard. That's all I had to discuss, so, if you don't have anything you need me for, I'll be on my way." He went over to him and, as Leonard stood, they shook hands once again. "Have a good weekend, you two." Nate then left.

*   *   *

It was almost 1:00 on Monday afternoon and Cal was looking for the of-fice that Nate had said was theirs. "Three doors down from the second-floor elevator," she said to herself as she found what must be the appropriate door. She knocked.

The door opened, and she was greeted by Nate. "Come on in, Cal, and meet our candidates." He led her to an adjoining room. Seated around a long table were two men and a woman. There was something about the woman that looked so familiar to Cal. *Could she be a character actress?* she wondered.

"Lady and gentlemen," Nate said, "I'd like to introduce you to Stacy Ames. She's the visionary behind Ames-Jenkins Productions and without whom it would never have seen the light of day. Stacy, the man directly in front of you is Henry Mansfield. He's had experience with Marimak Productions for seven years, doing a job similar to what our Director will be doing."

Mr. Mansfield stood and reached across the table to shake Cal's hand.

"Next to him is Derrick McReynolds. He is a graduate of Lawrence University with a doctorate in communications. Fresh out of school with a lot of enthusiasm and good ideas."

He, too, stood and shook Cal's hand.

"And this young lady is from Dallas. Her name is Doris Anderson, and she…"

"*Doris!*" Cal cried, as she ran around the table to her old friend. "Is that really you? You look so different! You're all grown up now! What are you doing in California?"

The ladies hugged each other tightly as the tears of happiness started flowing.

The other two candidates looked at each other as though to say, "Looks like the new director has just been chosen, and not based on merit, either."

Nate realized reassurances were in order. "Robert Stewart will have the final say in hiring the Executive Director, gentlemen. I just wanted Stacy to meet all three of you first."

Cal wiped her tears away and went back around the table to Nate's side. "I'm sorry. I get carried away sometimes. Doris and I were high school buddies. It's been a whole lot of years." Nate pulled a chair back for her and she sat down as he returned to the chair beside hers. "Nate's right," she grinned. "I'm not the one who will decide who gets this job. Aren't you glad?"

"All three of you are well qualified for the job," Nate continued. "You're the cream of the crop. We had over two hundred applicants, and you were the top three. So, whether or not you're hired, you can rest assured that we have a great deal of respect for your abilities."

Cal looked over at Nate. She couldn't help herself—she was in awe of his diplomacy.

Nate led the discussions in which the candidates were given the opportunity to explain their visions for Ames-Jenkins Productions, relative details of their own lives, and other information that would give Nate and Cal a good picture of each person.

*   *   *

Cal wanted to be fair to each candidate, but, deep down, she was glad the session was over so she and Doris could get caught up on each other's lives. Now, in the break room, they sat across from each other at a small round table, Doris with a cup of coffee and Cal with a Dr. Pepper, which they had gotten from the vending machines. Seeing that the girls wanted to be alone, Nate had left.

"What'd you do to yourself, Doris? You look so different. You're a gorgeous blonde now!"

"Just outgrew the baby fat, I guess. I take care of myself and work out every morning. You're looking awfully good, too. I swear you haven't aged a day since you left Dallas. I still expect to see you pulling a good one on Barry."

"Poor old Barry," Cal laughed. "What ever became of him? Did he ever get over finding that gerbil in his locker?"

"He's a judge now."

"*Barry?* A judge? I can't believe it!"

"And guess what. You remember your other victim, Gaylord? He's a police officer. I wonder if you influenced these guys' career choices at all? They're probably waiting for you to come back to town so they can lock you up and throw away the key."

"I've done my good deed for humanity, then, giving Dallas a judge and a policeman," Cal grinned. "So what are you doing in California? You must've just gotten here recently, huh?"

"I've been here for about three weeks. Since my interests were in the entertainment industry, I figured L.A. would be the best place to find just the right position. I majored in drama in college and minored in business. I guess, in a way, you could say you influenced *me,* too. Watching you on the big screen and on TV shows, and hearing updates on you from Sue every now and then, sparked my interest in the industry."

"'Interest in the industry,' my foot!" Cal grinned, "You can't fool me, Doris. You wanted to be an actress, too, so you could do a love scene with Nate."

Doris smiled. "I have different goals in life now."

"Are you married and have a family? I have a little girl."

"I *was* married twice and had three children—two girls and a boy. They're grown now and my second husband and I divorced last year. Since there's no kids left at home, I went back to my maiden name."

"Len and I've been married for seventeen years."

"Never quite caught on to the way things are done in Hollywood, I see."

"Nope. There's nothing 'Hollywood' about us, except for our jobs."

Doris leaned toward Cal. "Everyone back home was absolutely *sure* you'd end up marrying Nate. I'm glad you didn't. I see he's still available."

"Yeah. He's never married, and I don't know why. He likes women, and he loves kids. He's missed out on a lot of good things in life by not getting married."

Doris reached over and patted Cal's hand. "I understand your daughter is his child. So your relationship hasn't been as platonic as you wanted Sue to believe."

Cal shrugged.

"Are you two still having an affair?"

"Doris, you're getting kind of personal here. I thought you wanted that director job," Cal said, only half jokingly.

Her friend smiled with a smugness that brought back memories of their high school days, when Doris never failed to outsmart Cal. "Like you and Nate both said, you're not the one to decide who gets the job, so I can get as personal with you as I want. Tell me, Cal, how is Nate as a lover? Is he any good?"

At first, the question shocked Cal. Then she looked around to be sure there were no eavesdroppers around. Satisfied that there weren't, she whispered conspiratorially, "He's terrific! But don't tell anybody I said so." Then she grinned, "You always *have* been able to drag secrets out of me, Doris. You'd be a good investigator. Or tabloid reporter. Oh, *please* promise me you'll never be a tabloid reporter."

"I promise. I have much higher ambitions than that."

"When we were in high school, your bedroom walls were covered with pictures of Nate. Were your husbands anything like him?"

Doris shrugged, "Not at all. They were as opposite from him as a guy can get. Maybe that's why they bit the dust. And *you* were crazy about Van Roman back then. Leonard's nothing like him, either."

"That's for sure. Len's a lot better."

"I noticed that Van was a guest star on one of your shows last season. Did you tell him that you used to have a crush on him?"

"No. He's so different now, not at all like the guy from the sixties. I mean, he's gotten *old*, for Pete's sake!"

"Now, Cal," Doris said with hands on hips. "You're one to talk. Your own husband's fourteen years older than Van is."

"How did you know that?"

She shrugged, "I just know these things. I read a lot."

"Well," she shrugged, "he's not old. Len's not like other guys. I don't think he's capable of ever getting old."

"His hair's getting gray and he's put on weight."

"But he's still full of life and strong as an ox. Heck, he's busier than I am these days. He did a *film* during hiatus, and I just did some TV guest shots. He says I keep him young."

"I believe it! Just don't give him a heart attack, you hear?"

"Oh, he's got a strong heart, too. Everything about him is strong, including his stubbornness."

"He's a guy. What do you expect? All guys are stubborn."

"Nate's not. Not anymore."

"Maybe he's one in a million, huh?"

"He sure is."

Doris finished her coffee. "I hope you're through with him, my friend, because I'm just beginning."

"What do you mean?"

She set her coffee cup down and looked at Cal as if she were a foolish child. "What I mean is that Nate Jenkins is going to be husband #3 before the year's up."

Cal smiled. For once, she felt she knew more about a subject than Doris did. "A lot of ladies have tried and failed. If anyone can get him to marry her, it'd be you; but I don't think even you can."

"Why? He's not gay, is he?"

"Heck, no! I guess he's just not the marrying kind. He's never been engaged or anything."

"Well, my dear, we'll just see about that."

∗   ∗   ∗

That evening, Cal had been telling Leonard about the events of the afternoon. He could tell by her accelerated speech patterns that seeing Doris again, after all these years, had been a tremendously emotional thing for her. He would have expected her to be ecstatically happy at seeing her old friend, but that's not the impression he was getting.

The telephone rang and she reached over and answered it.

"Hi, Cal. It's me," Nate said. "What do you think of the candidates? We didn't get to talk after they left."

"They all look pretty good to me."

"Is she the same Doris you got my autograph for all those years ago? The one you told me to take to the charity banquet?"

"Yep, the very same one."

"Why didn't you tell me she was such a knock-out?"

"Well, she wasn't then. She looks a whole lot better now. Guess she feels she has to look super good because she's a divorcee and has to make it in the business world on her own in order to support herself. Her kids are all grown, so she's not getting child support anymore."

"She must be getting a whole lot of alimony, though, to dress the way she does."

"I don't know. Maybe."

"Next time we're in a position like this, though, I wish you'd play it cool and keep a poker face. Use your acting skills, okay?"

"Yeah, I know."

"The men were sure they didn't have a chance at that job once you got so excited about Doris."

"I'm sorry. That kind of slipped out. I'll do better next time. I'm just not good at businessy things."

"So do you have any recommendations for me to present to Uncle Bob? He *would* like to know if we see anything particularly special in any of the candidates—something that he may fail to see right away."

"They all seemed pretty good. Each one had something special that they could bring to the job."

"What would you like for me to tell him about Doris? It seemed obvious to me that she was your top choice."

"Let's not push one person more than another. Whichever one he says to hire is okay with me."

"That's very mature of you, Cal. I appreciate that."

"Yeah, well…"

"They're scheduled to meet with Uncle Bob tomorrow afternoon. I'll let you know what he says."

"Okay."

"Cal?"

"What?"

"It's really happening. Your dream is coming true."

She smiled into the phone. "Yeah. It won't be long now."

"That's right. And this experience is opening up new worlds to me, too. I'm learning a lot about the business. So Ames-Jenkins has already started to do some good."

"Thanks, Nate."

"I'll see you later, then."

"Okay. Bye."

Nate hung up the phone, wondering why Cal had not tried to influence the vote in Doris' favor. Certainly, Doris was qualified. She had good education in two relevant fields and impressive work experience. Maybe Cal really was becoming as mature as it appeared.

*   *   *

Nate had to admit that he was relieved when his uncle chose Henry Mansfield as Ames-Jenkins' Executive Director. What had come as a surprise to them all, though, was that Doris immediately reapplied for employment with Ames-Jenkins, this time as the executive secretary to Henry. She seemed to be overqualified for such a position, but she insisted that she be considered. The responsibility of hiring all employees ranked below him was Henry's, so the decision would be his alone. Doris' knowledge, determination, and resourcefulness greatly impressed the new Executive Director, and he did hire her as his executive secretary. He then, with Doris' assistance, proceeded to interview and hire people to fill the remaining positions. When all was completed, there were four people on the paid staff of Ames-Jenkins Productions.

Nate was quite pleased. He felt that Henry had done a very fine job in selecting the personnel. The individuals chosen were enthusiastic and industrious. Nate took Cal to the Ames-Jenkins offices to show her what it looks like with a full staff that was busily at work, getting the company established and setting the groundwork to produce their first film. It was an exciting time for them both. The two met later that day with Leonard and had a celebratory dinner at The Polo Lounge, a restaurant in which they were bound to be seen. The resulting publicity would be good for Ames-Jenkins.

Henry was able to take over most of the day-to-day operations of the company, so Cal and Nate could now concentrate on their own work for Stagecraft.

Putting out a quality show at Stagecraft, week after week, was no small task. Thank goodness they had excellent writers and a high-enough rating that the sponsors were kept happy. The popularity of the show made it quite easy to get good guest stars.

While working on the show during the day, Nate would keep in contact with Ames-Jenkins by phone with Henry in the evenings. Henry would faithfully report to him several times a week, giving him a rundown on how everything was going and seek his advice on any complications that had troubled him. This, Nate found, was just the kind of work he enjoyed the most. He felt obligated to continue their show during the day, but his heart was really in business management. Helping to run Ames-Jenkins had become, to him, not only a business investment, but a challenging hobby as well—a hobby he enjoyed very much.

One of its fringe benefits, Nate found, was contact with Doris. She was, indeed, an extremely attractive woman, and they very much enjoyed each other's company. She would often come over to his house in the evenings and sometimes on the weekends. Her favorite hobby, and one she quickly taught to Nate, was golf. This activity, she said, enables an executive to hob-nob with other executives in a casual, non-business setting. Many corporate decisions have been made on the golf course, she told him. On alternate Saturday mornings, while Kara was visiting her mother, Nate and Doris could be found at an exclusive country club, perfecting his golfing skills.

It was on one of these Saturday mornings that Doris first brought up the subject of marriage. At first, Nate resisted the idea and laughed it off, claiming to be a confirmed bachelor. Little by little, though, he began to realize that the idea might deserve his consideration, after all. The only time prior to this that he had ever thought about marriage, it was Cal who figured prominently in those thoughts. Since her marriage to Leonard was now stronger than ever, however, Nate realized that he had better look elsewhere if he ever wanted to settle down. He saw many fine qualities in Doris. Not only was she beautiful and a very stylish dresser, but she had good organizational and social skills and would be able to maintain a healthy social life for them. She seemed very comfortable among wealth; in fact, she seemed to quite enjoy it. She never told him what her financial situation had been before coming to California, but it appeared that she was accustomed to the finer things in life. If she and Cal had lived in the same neighborhood as they were growing up, it was quite possible that she was born into such a lifestyle and thought of that as normal, the way Cal had. Doris was at her best at a high-level cocktail party or other such social occasion, knowing exactly what to say and what to do. Nate had to admit that she was more sophisticated than Cal. Yes, he thought, Doris might make a good executive wife, after all. He finally agreed to marriage, but insisted on a long engagement. A step this huge in his life was not to be taken quickly, he felt.

*　*　*

"Hi, Daddy," twenty-three-year-old Stacy said over the phone. "How would y'all like some company?"

Leonard smiled. "I presume you're talking about yourself. Is that right?"

"Well, partly. Mom and I wanted to visit our old neighborhood and see our friends, again—just the two of us. She said to tell you we can stay at a hotel if you'd rather not put her up in your house."

"Nonsense! You're both welcome here. When are you coming?"

"How about next week? My mother-in-law said she could take care of the kids that week."

"Sounds good to me. You do realize, don't you, that Cal and I are working long hours every weekday?"

"Yeah, we know that. We can visit with you two in the evenings and see our old friends during the days. I'd like to watch the taping of your show, too, if I can."

"Sure you can. Taping's always done on Fridays. Next week, our guest star will be Marti Marioni. I bet you can guess what kind of characters she and Cal will be in the skit."

"Italian?"

"You've got it! We probably won't be able to understand a single word they say."

They both chuckled.

*   *   *

Later that evening, Cal did not receive the news gladly. "She's staying *here*?" she asked incredulously.

"They both are."

"Can our marriage counselor be in the other guest room, then? In the room between ours and Jill's?"

"Oh, Cal, don't be so dramatic. It'll be all right." He couldn't understand her reluctance.

"Well, I don't know…"

"So what you're saying, then, is that I can't be trusted, even with my own daughter in the house."

Cal looked into his eyes, then realized she was overreacting. "No, I don't mean that. They can both stay here."

"You'll be happy to see Stacy again, won't you?"

"I sure will," she smiled. "We'll have a good old time. We'll have to have Kara over some that week, too. She just idolizes Stacy."

*   *   *

It seemed like they were bringing a whole entourage with them. It was Sunday afternoon, and Cal just couldn't wait any longer to show Stacy and Jill their production company. Becky picked everyone up in her van and brought them here to her father's studio, in which Ames-Jenkins was housed. Nate led the way, unlocking the doors and turning on the lights, followed by Cal and Leonard, then Kara, Stacy, Jill and Becky.

Kara ran on ahead. "Come look at this, Stacy. This room back here is where Uncle Nate sits at his big desk and does business things. He's teaching me how to use the computer, too."

Stacy followed her as Kara went behind Nate's desk and started pecking on the computer keyboard. She couldn't help but to smile at the incongruous picture tiny Kara made behind that immense walnut desk. She certainly seemed to feel at home here, though, working that computer almost like a pro. As a screechy sound began, the others in their party joined Stacy inside the door of Nate's office.

"I'm getting on the internet," Kara told them. "I'm going to e-mail Livie. She lives in Michigan and I'm going to tell her my sister's here."

Stacy looked at her father with some confusion. "Can she do that? She can not only read, but she can type, too?"

Leonard nodded, "She's a smart little kid."

Nate added, "She learned to read in preschool, and Cal and I both taught her how to use the computer. She doesn't use all her fingers like a professional typist, but she can get the job done with just a few." Then he turned to Kara, "Just make it a quick message, then log off. We have guests, Kara, and it's not polite to make them wait while you play on the computer."

"Okay," she said as she pecked away at the keyboard.

"In the meantime," Nate told the rest of them, "let's go back into the main offices and I'll show you some of the projects we're developing." He led them out of his office and down the hall into the central room.

This was Leonard's first time in the Ames-Jenkins offices, and Cal was excitedly pointing out to him where each employee sat and telling him what each one did. She was much more accustomed to the central room than she was the executive offices.

Kara soon rejoined them and took Stacy's hand as they toured the building together. When they approached the break room, she led Stacy into it and showed her the vending machines. "If you want to buy me some Hostess cupcakes, that'd be okay with me." She looked up at Stacy expectantly.

Stacy smiled at the thinly-veiled hint, then Nate appeared in the doorway.

"Uh-oh," the child mumbled.

"Kara Michelle Rhoads," he said sternly.

"But she's my *sister*," Kara explained.

He knelt down to get eye level with her and said softly, "Stacy is our guest, and we don't ask guests to buy us things. Understand?"

"Okay," she said meekly.

"If you're hungry, you tell me and I'll get you something to eat."

"Okay."

"Are you hungry?"

"Yeah."

He stood back up, got some change out of his pocket, and put three coins in the slot of the vending machine. "Did you say cupcakes? You want the orange ones?"

"No, choc'let." She pointed to the correct picture on the front of the machine.

Nate smiled as he pressed the button for the chocolate cupcakes. "Just like your mama," he said fondly. "She's a chocoholic, too."

"I think that must be a girl thing, Nate," Stacy said. "Mom and I are, too."

He smiled at her, then asked Kara, "Did you show Stacy your secret hiding place?" Nate removed the cellophane from the cupcakes and handed one to her.

"Not yet." She held the cupcake up to Stacy. "Want some?"

"No, thanks. Show me your hiding place. When I was your age, I had one, too. Mine was under the dining room table."

Kara took a bite of her cupcake, then led Stacy by the hand to a nook between the vending machines and the lounge area. "This is where I sit sometimes and no one can find me. They look and look, and I hear them calling 'Kara? Where are you?' but I stay real quiet and they don't know I'm here."

"Hmm, that *is* a cozy hiding place. You can pretend it's your little gingerbread house."

"I sometimes pretend it's a log cabin and we're surrounded by outlaws and shooting guns and everything."

Stacy smiled and patted Kara's head. "You've been watching Daddy's cowboy movies, haven't you?"

"Yeah. I pretend he's a sheriff in my log cabin and he's shooting out one window and I'm shooting out the other."

"Yes, that's true. He played sheriffs a lot."

"Daddy could whop the tar out of the bad guys."

"You can say that again," agreed Cal as she and Leonard joined them.

Becky and Jill caught up with everyone else, and Leonard put his arm around Cal's shoulders. "This is an impressive little business here. It seems to be well organized, and some of the upcoming projects might make you some money."

"Some should and others probably won't," Nate agreed. "Hopefully, the moneymakers will pay for the more altruistic ones. I'm hoping that *Mr. Jackson's Vacation* will have some of both elements in it."

"What's *Mr. Jackson's Vacation*?" Jill asked.

Nate looked over at Cal proudly. "It's a romantic adventure story that we'll be filming this summer. The leading lady will also be directing it. And, oh yes, she also *wrote* it."

Kara piped up, "Mama wrote it!"

Stacy looked over at Cal with awe. "So your story's being made into a movie? That's fantastic!"

"And you're going to direct, too?" Jill asked.

Cal shrugged, "That's what the boss says."

Stacy went over to Cal and lightheartedly compared their heights. She was about five inches taller than Cal. "Do you suppose people will follow the orders of this little bitty person?"

"If they don't, we'll fire them," Nate said with a smile. "Who would have a better idea of how the scene should be played than the very person who wrote it?"

"Yeah," Leonard mused, "It'll be interesting to see the picture when it's done." Then he mussed Cal's hair, "And I'm *very* glad to see that your expensive computer is being put to good use. Now it's tax deductible."

*　*　*

The week turned out to be much more pleasant than Cal had expected. She, Stacy and Jill spent evenings getting caught up on each other's lives and simply engaging in the "girl talk" that they all enjoyed. Since they were all mothers now, children and grandchildren were a favorite conversational topic. One subject came up that Cal laughingly related to Leonard later:

"Stacy had told us how romantic it had been when Jim asked her to marry him, then she asked me how you had proposed. Geez, what could I say?"

"I can't remember. How *did* I do it?"

"The nearest thing I can remember to a proposal is you telling me that a wife doesn't have to testify against her husband," Cal grinned, then pointed at him with mock sternness, "I saved your hide by marrying you."

Leonard was engulfed in a fit of laughter.

"I didn't know it was *that* funny," she said.

When he finally was able to control his mirth, he wiped the tears from his eyes. "I knew all along that that case would never go to trial."

Cal was confused. "You knew that *before* we were married?"

He nodded.

"Then why did we get married?"

"*Because*, Cal." He looked at her as though the answer were obvious.

"I know, I know," she sighed. "Because I was yours."

Leonard put his arm around her shoulder. "That's right, but you were too stubborn to see it. It seemed to me that the only way to get that through your head was to make it legal. You believe anything a preacher says."

Cal couldn't help but to feel disillusioned. "You mean I made the most major decision of my life based on a lie?"

"Would you have married me otherwise?"

"I don't know." She hated the feeling of having been manipulated. Then, as she was raising her fist to give Leonard an angry punch in the arm, she noticed his expression. It was one of disappointment and hurt. She stopped in midair.

"You don't love me?" he asked softly.

Her anger was gone, replaced by compassion. "Oh, Len." She hugged him. "I do love you. I just don't know if marriage would've ever occurred to me, though, because of our age difference."

"Are you sorry you married me? I'm not."

"Neither am I. It's lasted a lot longer than the threat of a trial did. But you know what?" she asked with a smile. "The minister didn't say I was your personal property. I'm *mine*."

"Then who do *I* belong to?" he asked gently.

"Me."

"Think about it a minute, Cal," he smiled, knowing he had won that debate.

Chapter 4

IT HAD BEEN ANOTHER SUCCESSFUL SEASON for the Nate-and-Cal show, and they wrapped it up with a two-hour special, co-produced by Stagecraft and Ames-Jenkins. In this final show of the season, most of the people who had appeared as teens in the very first Corky movie were brought back together. The most well-received portion of this show was the reenactment, as an elaborate skit, of the famous beach scene, a part of which included Corky's handcuffing Officer Stanton to his own police car. The fact that brawny Leonard still towered over most of the Baby-Boomers in the show helped the police-versus-kids concept remain believable. Everyone enjoyed this final show of the season, performers and audience alike.

Now another season was over, and hiatus had begun. This was what Nate and Cal had been anticipating for almost a year. They were finally able to focus their energies on the first major Ames-Jenkins cinematic production—the filming of *Mr. Jackson's Vacation* as a full-length movie. Because Nate would be playing Mr. Jackson, and knowing what a fine dancer he was, Cal then wrote in one more scene, which showcased his skill.

While bringing *Mr. Jackson's Vacation* to life was exciting for Cal, she was a bit apprehensive about it for one reason: This would be her first try at directing. She had been dealing with directors for many, many years, though, and knew which of their methods seemed to work best. She incorporated the best techniques of several of her favorite directors into her own style. Now able to see the situation from both the actor's and the director's viewpoints, Cal communicated well with the cast and crew.

Nate was experiencing some trepidation, as well. This would be the first time he had served as both producer and leading man of the same project. Excellent advice from his much-more-experienced uncle and assistance from the Ames-Jenkins employees were readily available, however, and he utilized them both quite often.

It was exhausting, but very emotionally-satisfying, for them both.

For Leonard, however, it was frustrating. He had to be in another state, working on a major film, for seven weeks. The fact that Cal and Nate would be working so closely together for many hours every day while he was away bothered him greatly, and he made sure to call Cal every night. Their telephone bill that summer was huge, but she appreciated his calls. Each evening, they discussed the glitches of the day and he frequently gave her good advice. She discovered that, for someone who had never directed, Leonard gave superb guidance.

Doris was a regular presence on the set, assisting with the production chores and anything else that Nate needed to have done. This back-up system was a great help to Nate, and he came to depend on it.

After six weeks of filming, it finally wrapped. The results were quite satisfying to both Cal and Nate as they viewed the edited version in the studio projection room late that summer and gave it their final approval. It was now exactly the way they wanted it, and it was ready for release. It would be released in mid-January, which, they felt, would give an emotional lift to movie-goers after the rush of the holidays was over.

Meanwhile, it was vacation time. While Nate and Doris took a much-needed Alaskan cruise, Kara went with Cal and Leonard to visit their friends and relatives in New York.

Chapter 5

1991

"I don't know what's wrong with the guy, Cal," Doris said as she stirred the cream into her coffee. Both women had a need to talk, so, after everyone else had left, they had come to the break room. "He says we can get married, but keeps moving the date back. If he doesn't want me, why doesn't he just say so?"

"I'm sure he wants you, Doris. Any man would."

"I don't know if he's having trouble making that final decision, or if he's just stringing me along on purpose, just to get what he can from me without having to bother with a commitment."

"He wouldn't do that."

"Well, then, what?"

Cal shrugged, "Who can figure guys out? I sure can't."

"You said once that Nate's not stubborn anymore, but I think you were wrong."

"Well, he's *not*, about most things. Just that one, and I don't know why. Maybe because he's been single so long he doesn't know how to be any other way. Len's stubborn about *everything*, and it's driving me bananas."

"You still haven't been able to get him to a doctor?"

"No, and the symptoms are getting worse. He just refuses to believe that anything would dare try to make him sick. He thinks he's Superman, I guess."

"Men!"

"And I can tell that he's not feeling good. His energy level's not what it used to be. He just says that's because he's not as young as he used to be. He's got an excuse for everything. I just don't know what to do."

Doris shrugged, "What *can* you do? He's his own man."

"That's for darn sure."

They sat in silence for a moment, then Doris asked, "Have you ever thought about asking to have primary custody of Kara given back to you?"

"Yeah, but she's so happy at Nate's, I just figured it'd be best to leave it the way it is."

"Don't you miss her a lot?"

"Now that we've stopped doing our show, I do. When I was working all week, every week, I didn't have time to miss anything."

"You have more time for her now, so why don't you ask Nate about that?"

"But having her for alternate weekends, then two weeks in the spring, makes our time together so very special. I'm not sure if Len could be a good father for a long stretch of time. He's great at it for two weeks, but I don't know if he could for much longer."

"Well, just think about it. Every little girl needs her mother."

Cal looked askance at her friend. "Is Kara causing some problems with Nate that he's not telling me about?"

"Well, now that you mention it," Doris said slowly, "having her at his house *does* keep him from having the freedom that he'd like."

"In what way? He's got a housekeeper, cook, and governess to watch after her if he has to work late."

"No, I mean *real* freedom, like freedom to do some world traveling. We'd love to go to Europe, but he doesn't feel he can with Kara in school and everything. And he can't work late because she's waiting for him every night."

"Oh," Cal said, feeling somewhat disillusioned, "I didn't know that was a problem for him."

"It puts a lot of limitations on him that a single man shouldn't have."

As Cal mulled the situation over in her mind, Doris patted her hand. "You know I wouldn't tell you this if you weren't such a good friend. I feel that friends like we are can be honest with each other."

"Yeah, I guess so."

*　*　*

Cal wasn't sure how to approach the subject with Leonard that night. She joined him on the sofa in the media room after dinner.

"I see you've taken up channel surfing," she said.

"I just haven't found anything worth watching." He flipped to yet another channel.

So much about him had changed recently. He used to watch television with a single purpose in mind. He always knew exactly what he wanted to watch and went right to it. Not anymore.

Leonard shook his head, turned the TV off, and set the remote down.

"You're not feeling very good today, are you?" she asked.

"It's probably just the flu or something."

She shook her head. "The flu only lasts a week. This has been hanging on for months."

"Why were you late coming home tonight?"

Well, she thought, that took care of how to approach the subject. "Doris and I waited until everyone else left, then we had a talk about Kara."

"Why'd you have to wait for everyone to leave?"

Cal shrugged, "I don't know. She just wanted to. I guess she doesn't feel comfortable talking about personal things when there's someone around who could overhear."

"Get up a minute," he said.

She stood up while he repositioned himself lengthwise on the sofa. She could tell he was in pain, but would never admit it. "Are you going to take a nap?" she asked.

"Just for a few minutes."

She sat back down by his feet. "Len, what do you think about us getting primary custody of Kara?"

"Oh, that would be okay, but why would we want to? She's happy where she is," he said tiredly.

"Doris said that Nate doesn't have much freedom with her around."

"Well, that would be true, especially during the school year."

"Freedom's not a problem for us."

"No, but we don't have all the staff that he does to take care of her when we're working."

She looked at his tired face. "Len, if you'd go to the doctor, he could help you get well faster so you can get back to work sooner."

"I still work."

"But when you got back from your last job, you were worn out. It took so much out of you."

"I'm not as young as I used to be."

She just couldn't understand why he refused to see the seriousness of the situation. Finally, in exasperation, Cal lamented, "Doggone it, Len! I'm so scared and you're not doing a thing about it. I've always counted on you to protect me and now, when I need you, you're acting like I don't matter."

"What're you talking about? I'll always protect you."

Her eyes got misty. "Len," she reached out and took his hand. "I'm so scared that whatever's making you feel tired all the time is going to take you away from me."

"No, it won't."

"How can you be sure unless you have it checked out? If you keep refusing to see a doctor and this does kill you, it'll be like you did it on purpose to get away from me. Like you don't love me. Like you don't care how I feel."

"It's not like that at all, baby."

"But it *seems* like it, Len. It seems like you're just pooh-poohing my concerns, like you couldn't care less about me."

He covered her hand with his own. "I care."

"No, you don't. It's just words. Words mean nothing."

"Okay," he said. "If I go see the doc, will you stop nagging?"

Finally! He was starting to come around! "Okay. You've got a deal."

He closed his eyes. "Make the appointment and I'll show up."

She leaned over and kissed his cheek. Then she got the phonebook out.

*   *   *

When Nate brought Kara over that Saturday morning for her weekend visit, he handed Kara six plush animals, then closed the trunk. "She wanted to keep some of her collection here. She's running out of space on her bed at home," he told Cal with a smile.

As Kara carried them into the house and upstairs to her room, Cal asked, "How many's she have, anyway? It must be about a hundred by now."

"I never counted." He leaned against his car. "You seem to be in a happier mood today. What happened?"

"Oh, Nate," Cal said with a grin, "he's *finally* going to see the doctor. I thought he'd *never* go but he promised he would. The appointment's Wednesday. I'm dying to find out what this bug is, and why I haven't caught it, too. I'm so happy he's going. The doc'll get him fixed up in no time. It feels like the sun's starting to shine again."

"Well, that's good. I'm sure that's a load off your mind."

"Oh, and I wanted to ask you something, too. How about if I take primary custody of Kara now so you can go to Europe?"

"*What?*" he asked.

"Well, you've been so sweet to take care of her all these years, but now I can do it so you can have more time for other things. A single guy like you needs to have some freedom."

"But I don't *want* that kind of freedom. I love Kara."

"Well, sure, and she loves you, too. But don't you want to go to Europe? That'd be hard to do during the school year."

"Who said anything about going to Europe? I've never had any desire to do that."

"But Doris said y'all would like to go there, but can't because of Kara."

"*She'd* like to, but I wouldn't. I don't like to travel. Never have."

"Oh."

"Cal, please don't take Kara away. She's my life."

"No, no, I didn't mean *all* the time. I just thought you wanted to reverse the way we've been doing it, so she'd be with *you* on alternate weekends and two weeks in the spring. But that's not what you want?"

"No. I want her to think of my house as home. I want to tuck her in at night, and I like to help her with her homework and have dinner with her. I need those things, Cal."

"Okay, okay. Let's keep it like it is, then."

Nate felt relieved. "Leonard's your sunshine. Kara's mine."

"Yeah."

*   *   *

Wednesday seemed to take months to get here, but it finally did. Cal went with Leonard to the doctor. No answers were to be had immediately, however. After the initial examination, he was referred to a specialist. It was a two-week wait for that appointment. The specialist ordered tests to be run. Leonard would rather have just forgotten the whole thing at that point, but Cal insisted that they follow through. "We're in too deep now to bail out," she said. So, just to placate her, he submitted himself to the testing. Once they got to the bottom of the cause, Cal felt, a solution would be found, then they could get back to the business of life.

It was not to be that simple.

Malignancy was found. Life, as they had known it, would never be the same again. Chemotherapy was to begin right away. Leonard was very much out of his element as a patient. It seemed very strange to Cal, too, to see him in a hospital bed.

As the days and weeks dragged by, he was in and out of the hospital, but seemed to be making no progress. There were complications and setbacks. Finally, surgery was ordered. As they wheeled him down the hall toward the operating room, Cal walked along beside him, with her hand on his shoulder. She gave him a good-luck kiss, then he was taken through the double doors. She stood and stared at the now-closed doors and tears trickled down her cheek. She turned and shuffled to the waiting room, where she was joined by Nate and Becky; and they all prayed together. It was the longest wait she had ever had in her life. Later, the physician came in and sat down by Cal. Bad news. The cancer had metastasized and become widespread. There was very little hope for Leonard's recovery. They could administer more radiation and chemotherapy. Even then, though, his chances of recovery were extremely slim. "I'm sorry," was all he could say.

After the doctor patted her shoulder and left, both Nate and Becky held Cal as she sobbed.

Chapter 6

Nate awakened to the ringing of the phone. As he groggily reached over to answer, he looked at the clock. It was 3:43.

On the other end of the line was Cal and she was crying. "He's gone, Nate," was all she could manage

That jarred him completely awake. He now understood what had happened. Leonard's battle was over. Cal was all alone and needed Nate's emotional support. After confirming her whereabouts, he reassured her that he would be there as soon as he could. He hung up, then immediately lifted the receiver again and called Becky. Yes, she said, she'll come over and keep an eye on Kara for him. While he awaited Becky's arrival, Nate got dressed.

*   *   *

When Nate arrived at the Rhoads house, Leonard's draped body was being put into an ambulance, and the doctor was on the porch with Cal. He then took a small container from his bag and handed it to her.

As Nate approached the porch, the doctor nodded to him and left. Cal was in tears, and completely distraught. They went inside, he closed the door, then held her comfortingly. "It's all over now, Cal. He's not in pain anymore."

"If only he would've gone back to the hospital, but he wouldn't. They could've made the pain better and helped him live longer." She buried her face in his shoulder and clung to him as she sobbed.

He wished there was more he could do for her than holding her and patting her back. Her heart was obviously broken and there was so little anyone could do. "Maybe it was better this way," he said soothingly. "He would've been miserable with all those tubes and needles. You know he would. He's at peace now." He pulled a handkerchief from his pocket and dried her tears with it. "He's happy now, Cal. He's happy and will never be in pain again."

"He wanted us to sleep with our arms around each other tonight, so we did. And that's the way we were when he stopped breathing."

"That's a wonderful way to go—from your arms directly into God's. You did the right thing. Don't feel bad."

"I wanted so badly to do CPR so he'd come back, but Len made me promise not to do that. It was really hard to just lie there and watch him go. I didn't *want* him to go, Nate. But at the same time, I didn't want him to suffer anymore, either. Part of me was glad that it was over and part of me wanted to pull him back."

"I know. Even though you knew this was coming, you're never really ready for it, are you?"

"No." She turned, and he released his hold on her. Cal went over to the sofa and sat down. She took a tissue from the nearby box and wiped her nose, then she took a deep breath and let it out slowly. After Nate joined her on the sofa, she said softly, "You know what made him feel the worst? It wasn't the physical pain. It was leaving me." She looked into Nate's eyes, then back down at the tissue. "A long time ago, I asked him to promise that he wouldn't die before me, and he said okay. He remembered that and said that he tried his best to live up to that promise. He looked so sad, then he said, 'Baby, I'm sorry, but I've *got* to leave you. I have no choice.' And then he said, 'But I'll be waiting for you when you get there.'" She looked back up at Nate as another tear trickled down her cheek. "Do you know what that means? It means he had faith all along, and I never knew it. I thought, since he hardly ever went to church, that religion meant nothing to him. But I was wrong." Then she wiped her cheeks dry, again. "I'm so glad I was wrong."

"There was a lot more to Leonard than most people thought. He was a good man, Cal. You were fortunate to have been married to him as long as you were."

"And Mrs. Morris said it herself. She said that she had no doubt that my parents and I will be together, again, someday. Now that applies to Len and me, too. We'll *all* be together, again, someday."

"That's right."

"I just wish it could be now. He's been given the ultimate healing, but I can't see it. It's not fair."

He wiped her cheeks again with his handkerchief. "Did you get any sleep at all last night?"

"Not much, maybe ten minutes or so."

"Would you like for me to stay and take care of things while you get some sleep?"

"I don't think I *could* sleep. I need to call Kara and Stacy and tell them, and Len's relatives in New York and everybody."

"I'll do that. Was that sleeping pills that the doctor gave you a while ago?"

Cal had set the bottle aside, but now picked it back up and looked at the label. "I think he said it's a sedative."

"Why don't you take one, then? It'll help you sleep. You'll need to be well rested so you can make good decisions later. We can both tell Kara in person and break it to her gently. She'll need us both. But I can go ahead and call Leonard's relatives in New York and Connecticut. I'll take care of things, Cal. You just need to get some rest. Come on," he stood up, took her hand and led her into the kitchen, where he filled a glass with water. She shook a tablet out of the bottle, then took it with the water. "That's good," he said. "Now come on." He then led her upstairs. "Which room do you want to sleep in?" he asked. She pointed to the room she and Leonard had shared for years. He gently pushed her into it. As she laid herself down onto Leonard's side of the bed, Nate covered her with the sheet. "Is there anything else you need before I start making phone calls? I'll call the people on the east coast first, since they're three hours ahead of us."

"I wish I could ask for something without it sounding stupid."

"What?"

"Would you sing me to sleep like you do for Kara?" she looked at him pleadingly.

"Sure," Nate said softly. He pulled a chair over beside her bed, sat in it and held her hand. "Remember when I had pneumonia and you sat by *my* bed and held *my* hand?"

She nodded.

"I'm glad I can return the favor now." He kissed her hand, then started softly singing 'Day By Day.'

She wiped her cheeks once again, then closed her eyes.

＊　＊　＊

Kara didn't need to be told. As soon as she saw Papa Nate and Mama enter her bedroom together that morning, looking so sad, she knew Daddy was in heaven now. Yesterday, she had overheard Mrs. Neal say that it looked like the end was near. It was only yesterday afternoon that Papa Nate had taken her over to see him for the last time. Daddy had patted the bed, indicating that he wanted her to sit on it right beside him.

"I have something important to tell you, Kara," he had said, as she followed his directions.

"What, Daddy?"

He gently patted her hand. "You know I love you very much?"

"Yeah, and I love you, too." She leaned down and gave him a hug.

"I know you do, but you need to know something." He took a few moments to gather his thoughts. Then he began, "You love your Uncle Nate."

"Yeah."

"Kara," he paused, then continued, "Uncle Nate is your real daddy."

Right inside the doorway, Cal's eyes misted over as she bit her lip. Nate watched Kara closely for a reaction.

"You're Daddy," Kara corrected Leonard.

"No, sweetheart. I'm married to your mother and we both love you, but Uncle Nate's your father."

"He is?"

Leonard nodded and, again, patted her hand. "But you'll always be my little girl."

Those had been Daddy's last words to her, the words she would carry in her heart and cherish for the rest of her life. She may be Papa Nate's biological daughter, but Daddy would always think of her as his little girl.

Now, Papa Nate came into her bedroom and sat on the bed beside her while Mama sat on her other side, and they very gently told her that Daddy was in heaven with God now. Together, they held her while she cried.

* * *

That afternoon, as he hung up the phone, Nate was torn. Sure, he had made plans to take Doris out tonight, but Cal and Kara needed him. Their needs were more pressing at the moment. Why couldn't Doris see that? He thought the two women were good friends. Doris' irritation when he cancelled their plans puzzled and annoyed him. She seemed unconcerned that her friend had just become a widow, after so many years of marriage. That's not the Doris he thought he knew. Up until now, she had seemed so kind and caring. How could she be so callous about Cal's situation, he wondered. Could it be that she's never loved a man as much as Cal loved Leonard and, therefore, simply couldn't understand her grief?

* * *

Nate had cancelled all his personal and professional plans for the following week so he could be with Cal and Kara. He was glad that they no longer were obligated to put out a new TV show each week. If the Nate-and-Cal show were still being taped, the first major problem would have been writing Leonard's beloved character out when he became too ill to work, and the final problem would have been putting together a show without *any* of the main three characters during this week. Thank goodness the show had had a good life of several years, then had ended gracefully when all three of them had wanted to go on to other projects. By then, Cal and Nate were very much into the production aspect of the industry as they became more and more involved in Ames-Jenkins Productions. Now, Henry, Doris, and the rest of the staff could take over their work while they took care of the funeral and other related matters.

Kara and Cal spent most of their waking hours at the funeral home for the next two days. At first, Cal and Nate had wondered if it would harm their child psychologically to be so close to the situation; but she seemed to want to be with them at this time, so they allowed her to stay. Nate alternated between being with them and being at the Rhoads house, overseeing the activity going on there. Normally quite capable of making decisions on her own, Cal was now relying on him a great deal for both advice and support. He understood that Cal couldn't be expected to be her usual self right now. She needed Nate's strength and concern, and he was very glad to give it.

The funeral on the fourth day would have pleased Leonard. It was what he would have called "SRO" in theatrical terms—standing room only. The church was packed full with their relatives, friends, and many, many of the co-workers they had had over the years. Nate had never seen Cal wear black before. Normally, black didn't suit her personality at all; but, today, it did. She seemed to feel that the light had gone out of her life. Present, too, and also dressed in black were Stacy and Jill. When Cal had first seen Jill that day, she ran to her and held her tightly as they both wept. *What an unusual relationship!* onlookers had thought. It was not very often that Wife #1 and Wife #2 would get along that well in Hollywood, but Nate understood the dynamics of that particular relationship. Both women had just lost the man they loved, so completely understood each other's grief. Too, Nate knew that Cal felt like she owed Jill a huge debt of gratitude for having opened her home to her when she was new in town, for assuming guardianship of her after Cal's parents had died, and for being the surrogate mother to her that she needed for many years. Jill knew that Cal had never intended to come between her and Leonard; she understood Cal, perhaps, better than anyone. And Nate probably understood Jill better than anyone there.

Cal asked that Jill sit beside her in the front pew. With Jill holding her left hand and Stacy holding her right, Cal felt the bond among them, their strong love for Leonard, was stronger than any of the circumstances had been. Kara had wanted to sit with Nate, so she was beside him on the second row. He reached over and took her hand in his. Beside them was Becky, along with Leonard's brother and other relatives from New York.

*   *   *

Now it was two days later. Family, friends, and acquaintances had departed to get on with their lives. At first, everything had seemed to be going smoothly for Cal. When Nate and Becky had checked in on her that morning, she assured them that she was fine and urged them not to worry about her but, rather, to get back to their own routines. That afternoon, though, Nate felt a strong compulsion to drop by again, so he did. There was no answer when he rang the bell. Both cars were in the driveway, indicating that Cal was indeed there, so he used the key she had given him earlier to let himself in. She was probably taking a nap, he thought. He'd just check, then be on his way. After looking in the rooms downstairs, he went upstairs and peeked into her bedroom. She was, indeed, asleep. "That's good," he thought. "She hasn't been getting enough rest lately." He was just about to leave when something caught his eye. There was a bottle of bourbon on her nightstand, beside an empty glass. The bottle was half full and its lid was off. That seemed quite unusual for Cal. He had hardly ever seen her drink before, and was hoping she wasn't taking up the habit now. Maybe she just needed it to help her sleep. He went quietly around to that side of her bed to put the lid back on the bottle. Then he noticed the pill bottle there, too, also with its lid off. He looked inside. It was empty. Uh-oh! When he had noticed it yesterday, there were about ten tablets left. He looked at Cal. Surely, she wouldn't do anything rash, would she? He shook her. "Cal, wake up. I need to know if you're okay." She didn't awaken. He shook her again, then again with more force. "Cal! Wake up! Cal!"

"Mmm?" she asked groggily.

"What did you do, Cal? How many pills did you take?"

"Go 'way." She turned away from him.

"Come back here." He pulled her back over toward him. "Talk to me."

She covered her face with her hands. "I'm gonna' be wi' Len." Her words were slurred.

"Oh, God!" His first instinct was to call the ambulance, but they probably wouldn't have equipment needed to pump her stomach. Driving her to the hospital himself would probably get her to help in the fastest possible way. "Come on." He pulled her up to a sitting position, then brought her to her feet. She was quite unsteady. Cal began sobbing as he helped her down the stairs, out the door, and to his car. Nate had to let go of her for a moment to open the car door and clear the passenger seat. She started sinking to the ground, but he caught her around the waist with one arm while tossing his briefcase and loose papers into the back seat with the other. Then he put her into the seat, belted her in, closed the door, and went around to the other side. He hurriedly got in, started the car and sped toward the hospital.

*   *   *

Sitting in the hospital's private waiting room was difficult for Nate. He wanted so badly to be with Cal, to hold her hand and help her through this. He had called Becky and she got there quickly. They were sitting on the vinyl chairs, trying valiantly to be patient. He had buried his face in his hands, and Becky was patting his back in consolation. "Thank goodness, you went over there when you did."

"I hope it wasn't too late."

"You said she was able to talk, so I imagine she'll be okay. She must've just taken those things soon before you got there."

"Lord, I hope so."

"Should we tell Kara, do you think?"

"I don't know. I just don't know. I don't want to upset her if Cal's going to be okay."

"But, if she's not…"

"I don't know." Then he slammed his fist on his knee. "Damn it, Becky, why did she *do* that? I thought she was okay this morning."

"I did, too. Apparently, she was just putting on an act."

He buried his face in his hands again.

Becky continued, "They were married for a lot of years, Nate. She's never had to be away from him for more than a few weeks at a time before, and when that happened, she always knew they'd be together again when filming was over. Now all that's gone. She obviously did it to be with Leonard again." Becky took Nate's hand in hers. When she had lowered his hand, she could see that his cheeks were wet.

"But she's got so much to live for," he said sadly, with a catch in his throat. "She's got Kara. And doesn't she know that I love her? Aren't we worth living for?"

Becky shook her head, "Of course, you are. Maybe we can talk her into getting some grief counseling or something. She's just not thinking straight."

A nurse approached them. "We've admitted Mrs. Rhoads to room 312. You may go see her now if you'd like."

The couple rose and quickly took the elevator to the third floor. When they found room 312, Nate hurried to Cal's side and took her hand. Her other hand had an IV tube attached to it. She was pale. "How're you feeling now? Better?" he asked.

She sighed. "I'll live."

Becky went to the other side of the bed and stroked Cal's hair. "I'll bring you a decent pair of PJs to wear when I come back next time. Those hospital gowns are the pits, aren't they?"

"Whatever," Cal said, wearily.

Becky didn't know what else to say. She didn't want to say the wrong thing and make matters worse. She looked over at Nate, hoping he'd know what to do.

He went over and closed the door to the hallway, then came back to the bedside. "Becky, how about letting Kara stay at your house for the next week or so? Cal and I have a lot of talking to do. I don't want to leave Cal alone for one minute because I'll be *damned* if I'm going to let her pull a stupid stunt like this again."

"Nate! Be kind!" Becky admonished her cousin.

He pushed Cal's legs aside and sat on the bed, facing her. "Cal, do you remember what it was like for you when your parents died? Think about it for a minute and tell me what it was like."

Cal shrugged and looked away from him. When Nate turned her face back toward him, she yelled, "I just want to die! Why didn't you leave me alone and let me die? Then Len and I would be together again and everything would be fine. You ruined it, Nate! You had no right to do that."

His eyes flashed with anger. "You're being utterly selfish, Cal! Think about how alone you felt when your parents died, then think about how Kara would feel. It'd be a hundred times worse for her. Your parents didn't leave you intentionally. Their intent was to come visit you, so you knew they loved you. If you had died of an overdose, Cal, Kara would have known that you didn't love her enough to stick around. When she graduates from high school, when she chooses a career, when she gets married and has children, you wouldn't be around to share those things with her. And she'd know that's because you didn't *want* to. You'd rather be dead, instead. Just how do you think that would make Kara feel, huh?"

Becky was appalled. "Nate, stop that! You're making her cry. She needs our sympathy at a time like this."

"She needs sympathy like a hole in the head. What she really needs is some common sense, so she'd stop feeling so damned sorry for herself."

"But I just can't live without Len!" Cal yelled at him. "Why can't you understand that?"

"You've lived without him for years, Cal," he retorted.

"You're crazy. I never have, not since I was fifteen."

"You've always done exactly what you wanted to do. Leonard's been around, but he hasn't been central to your life decisions. Hell, you didn't even let him in on the fact that he was paying half of the initial cost of Ames-Jenkins until it was too late to do anything about it."

Cal, again, turned away from him, looking up to Becky for help.

Nate continued, "You know I'm right, Cal. You just don't want to admit it."

She turned back to him with fire in her eyes. "I love Len! I might be a lousy wife, but I've always loved him."

At this, his voice softened. "He knows that, Cal. Believe me, when a person gets where he is now, a lot of things come clear to him that were fuzzy before. Leonard knows you love him. Of that, there is absolutely no doubt in his mind now. He might not have known it when he was here, but he knows it now."

It felt to Cal as if Nate had just taken a huge weight off her shoulders. "Honest?"

"I promise you."

"Does he know I feel bad about some things I did?" Cal asked earnestly.

Nate looked over at his cousin. "Becky, could we be alone, please? I won't harass her anymore. We need to talk about some things, and you need to take Kara over to your house for the next few days."

"Okay," Becky said. "Cal, please get better. We love you."

"I know." Cal patted Becky's hand. "Take good care of Kara for me, and tell her I love her, too. But please don't tell her what I did, okay?"

Becky nodded. "Okay."

"Just tell her that Cal's having a hard time right now," Nate instructed, "and I'm staying with her for a while to help her get better. That's all she needs to know."

"Okay." Becky then turned and left.

Once they were alone, Nate turned back to Cal. "You're feeling guilty about a lot of things, aren't you?"

"Yeah," she nodded. "Most of all about being unfaithful to him."

"I know. You could always justify the sneaky, underhanded things you did, like the Ames-Jenkins thing, but you had a hard time with the fact that you cheated on him."

"Well, at the time, I thought I could justify that, too. I thought it served him right because he was being such a jerk."

"But you know better now, don't you?"

"Yeah. It hurt him a lot. Sometimes, Nate, I feel like guys love better than girls do—more completely, without reservation. I don't know what's wrong with me, why I can't do that."

"For a long time, I justified it to myself, too," he confessed. "I told myself that I was just helping him to meet your physical needs."

"What do you mean?"

"Well, you know. I didn't think a man his age could do it."

A half-smile slowly crept across her face.

"What?" he asked.

"He could until he got sick."

"Really?"

She nodded. "Sure. Len can do anything. He's a stubborn guy."

They both laughed, for the first time since Leonard's illness had been diagnosed. It was so good to hear Cal laugh again!

Ignoring, for now, the fact that she had said that in the present tense, as though Leonard were still alive, he stroked her hand. "He's probably laughing now, too."

"Yeah, I bet so."

"He's probably glad you straightened out my stereotypical thinking. Boy, do I ever admire that guy!"

Then she asked again, "Does he know I feel bad about all that?"

Nate nodded. "Everything Leonard needs to know in order to be happy, he knows. Have faith, Cal. Heaven is a place where there are no more tears or unhappiness. He's not worried about those things anymore." Then he sternly pointed at her, "But don't get any bright ideas about getting there too soon yourself. We need you here. If you get there too soon, you'll have to wait in heaven's own detention hall, and that's not fun."

"I wonder what that detention hall is like? I never even got to see my own high school's detention hall, but my buddies did."

"In heaven's detention hall, there are absolutely no brownies or Dr. Peppers," he joked. "All you have to eat there is Brussels sprouts."

"Ewww."

"And licorice and prunes," he continued, listing everything he knew of that Cal disliked. "And there are no horses in detention hall. You have to walk everywhere, and everything is miles and miles away. When you're in detention hall, they won't allow you to be anywhere *near* Leonard. He'll be in another universe entirely."

"Okay, okay. You made your point."

He took her hands in his. "Promise me you won't try to get there too soon, anymore."

"Okay. I promise."

"I'm going to make sure someone's with you at all times until I'm sure you mean that."

This seemed to Cal like déjà vu, like she had already lived this moment. It sounded very much like what Leonard would have said. "Does Len know how happy he made me? How glad I was that he stuck by me during the bad times?"

Nate nodded, "He knows, Cal. He knows the utterings of your heart. And don't forget, you stuck by him when *he* was having bad times, too. When he was sick and not able to work, you took care of him, tenderly and lovingly. That's when the temptation to cheat would have been the greatest for a lot of women, but you didn't give in to it. You remained by his side, taking care of him just the way he wanted to be cared for, until he died just the way he wanted to die—in your loving arms. You made him *very* happy, Cal. Don't ever forget that."

She held out her arms to Nate, and he leaned down to receive her embrace. Nate had just told Cal what she so desperately needed to hear.

Chapter 7

AFTER THE THREE-DAY HOSPITAL STAY, during which time she was given daily grief therapy by the hospital psychologist, Cal was released to Nate's care. He wanted to keep a close watch on her and also allow them plenty of time to talk, so Nate suggested that Cal spend at least the next few days at his house, rather than her own. At first, she resisted that idea, wanting very much to be back among the things that had been a part of Leonard's life. Nate was willing to compromise—inviting Cal to bring to his house those things of Leonard's that meant the most to her—and she finally relented.

Except for driving time, they were questioned by reporters about the nature of Cal's hospital stay from the time they got down to the hospital lobby until the time they entered his house. Nate had forewarned her that this would happen and urged her to let him do the talking for both of them. She gladly agreed. In his front yard, he stopped, took one reporter's microphone, and made a statement: "Stacy is having trouble dealing with the death of her husband, Leonard Rhoads, which, I'm sure you would all agree, is quite understandable after having been married as long as they were. Now if you *really* care about her, you'll leave her alone while she grieves for Leonard and tries to get on with her life." He handed the microphone back to the reporter, then gently led Cal to the door of his house. He unlocked it and they entered. He then closed the door and all was quiet again.

Becky was waiting for them and welcomed Cal with a warm hug.

"Who's taking care of Kara?" Cal asked. "I thought she was at your house."

"She's at school right now, and one of Dad's employees will pick her up and stay with her at my house until I get back," Becky answered. "I wanted to be with you today."

Cal then looked over at Nate. "How will I get my clothes and stuff if I don't go to my house?

"Becky will get them for you. Just tell her what you want, and she'll go get it. Jessie can help her find everything."

"Okay, I want the picture of Len and me that's on our dresser."

"And I'll get you some clothes, too—your jeans and shirts and things," suggested Becky.

"Yeah."

"What else?"

"And I want to sit in Len's big chair and sleep on his side of the bed. Bring those things over."

Becky put her hands on her hips. "Come on, Cal. You know I can't do that."

She sighed. "Bring some of his videos from the media room. I want to watch him be Henson, again."

"Where are your suitcases? I'll need to put your clothes in them to bring them over."

"In the closet beside the dresser, on the floor to the right."

"Will do. I'll be back in a little while." With that, Becky took her purse and left.

Cal then went into Nate's living room and sat down. He followed. There was a newspaper folded on the end table, and she picked it up.

"Yes," he said, "you'll find a write-up about the incident in the paper. Of course, it's not very detailed because I told the hospital reps and Becky not to tell anyone about the overdose. Not letting *anyone* know is the only way we can keep Kara from knowing."

Cal nodded and looked at the article. It just said that she was rushed to the hospital for an undisclosed illness, then reviewed her stage and screen career. "I guess that *was* a pretty stupid thing I did, wasn't it?"

"The stupidest thing you've ever done in your life."

She set the newspaper aside. "Whenever I see a newspaper, I think of Len. He was always reading them, every word. He could give you the details of every world event there ever was, I bet. He even made me write a letter to the editor once."

"I remember that. That was a long time ago."

"Yeah." She got back up and wandered around the room, looking first at this, then at that. "I guess I've never taken a really good look at your place before. Usually when I came here, I was preoccupied with something else—Kara or Ames-Jenkins or something." She went into the sitting room. Nate was close behind. Cal went up to the mantel and smiled as she viewed the portraits of Kara. "She's so precious."

"She sure is."

"When's she coming back from Becky's?"

"Oh, I think we ought to give it a few days, at least. You need to have time to relax and get everything out of your system first. At least, Becky brought her to see you while you were in the hospital."

"Yeah, I'm glad of that. When I saw how worried Kara was, that's when I realized how right you were about how it would've affected her if I had died, too. I let her know everything's okay."

"She was afraid you had cancer."

Cal gazed at Nate. "Then you explained depression to her. Do you think she understood?"

"Maybe some of it. I think it's probably hard for anyone to understand if they've never experienced it."

"Len would've understood. He knew what it was like."

"I know."

She went to see up close the pictures hanging on the north wall, pictures of Nate with various celebrities with whom he had worked. "I remember when Sue and I came here, and she was so impressed with these. It looked to her like you'd met every big name in the business."

"I probably have."

"And now most of the really good ones are gone."

"That's true—Red Skelton, Bing Crosby, and Lucille Ball have died, but a few are still with us."

"You remember *The Red Skelton Show* coming on every week? I loved him. Clem Kadiddlehopper and Freddie the Freeloader were my favorites of his characters."

Nate nodded, "He was a gifted comedian."

"And he really seemed to have fun doing it, too. He laughed as much as his audience did."

"It's a lucky man who does for a living the thing he enjoys the most," Nate said wistfully.

"I wish they still had shows like that now. I wish I could rewind my life and go back to the good old days."

"If you could, what year would you rewind to?"

That was an intriguing question, Cal thought. Sorting through her memories of long ago, she finally settled on a year. "If I could, I would be twenty-two again. That was 1970."

"Was Red Skelton still on then?"

"I don't know, but that's the year Len and I got married."

"So it was a really good year for you, wasn't it?"

"Yeah, and we were both young and energetic. He had a playful side that most people didn't see." Cal smiled as she enjoyed the memory. "We'd chase each other through the house like a couple of kids. And he was forty-one back then! I guess I really *did* keep him young."

"*Leonard chased you through the house?* I just can't imagine that."

Cal nodded, "And you *know* how fast I am. It took a while for him to catch me. One time he cheated and jumped *overtop* the sofa instead of running around it. He caught me pretty quick that time, then we made love right there in the media-room," she grinned. Then she advanced to the entry of the hallway. "These double doors always looked so elegant to me. They're so tall. One time Len was carrying me on his shoulders inside our house. Our doors weren't tall like these, but Len was. I had to duck fast to keep from being hit in the face when we went through a door. That's when he decided that carrying me on his shoulders inside the house wasn't such a great idea, after all."

"It sounds like you brought a lot of joy into Leonard's life, Cal. You helped him kick back and have fun."

"Yeah, I guess I did."

"The difference between being married to Jill and being married to you must have been *tremendous!*"

"Yeah. Everybody always acts so dignified around Jill. That must've been awfully boring for Len."

"You were just what he needed."

"Maybe so," she said as she wiped a tear from her cheek.

"Crying, again."

"I know, I know. I'm sorry, but I just miss him so darned much."

"I know you do. I'm not scolding you, but just stating a fact. Cry all you want."

"I want to be able to talk about him without crying. Won't I ever get to that point, I wonder?"

Nate put his arm around her shoulders comfortingly. "Time will be your best friend. A year from now, everything will be better. Two years from now, better still."

"It makes me feel like a nut case, though, to be so darned weepy all the time, and I know it makes Becky feel uncomfortable. I wish I could stop."

"No, Cal, you shouldn't stop. It would be unhealthy to bottle it up. I've got a shoulder for you to cry on. It's up to you to give it a good workout."

"How come it doesn't make *you* feel uncomfortable? Most guys get unhinged when a lady cries."

"Because I know what it's like. Remember, we both lost parents tragically when we were young. That's not the same as losing a spouse, I know, but…"

"How long did it take you to get over that?"

"Probably about fifteen years, and that's only after several years of therapy. You see, I wasn't given the luxury of being able to grieve. Uncle Bob wouldn't allow any male tears in his house."

"And I thought he was such a nice guy."

"He meant well. Just had some misguided notions of what defined manhood. I got my own house as soon as I could."

Cal nodded with empathy. "When my folks died, I was glad to have work to go to. It helped take my mind off things. Once I was home again, Jill didn't want me to talk about Mom and Dad. I guess she thought that any mention of them would make me cry and that was a bad thing. Anytime I'd bring them up in conversation, she'd change the subject. Len didn't, though."

"She thought she was doing you a favor, but she wasn't. Not really. You *need* to talk about the person you're grieving for. That's part of the process. You have to work your way through it."

"You really *do* understand."

"I learned a lot from therapy."

"You know something? When you said you were going to watch me to be sure I don't mess up again, that reminded me so much of Len. But all the psychological jargon you use about the 'grieving process' and stuff sure doesn't sound like him."

"No, I don't imagine it would, but Leonard was a good man. He loved you a whole lot."

Cal's eyes started blurring. "I wish I could see him, just one more time." She sobbed on his shoulder.

∗   ∗   ∗

For the next few days, reporters were given no new information, but the fact that neither Cal nor Nate ever seemed to leave the house gave them new theories on which to speculate. Was the couple, once again, having an affair? That seemed quite callous so soon after Leonard's death. Perhaps their affair had never ended, they said. At night, only one bedroom light came on. One of the reporters walked all the way around the house and confirmed that no other light was on. Apparently, Nate's having been seen in public occasionally with Doris Anderson was a cover-up to what was *really* going on, they concluded.

Inside the house, though, it was a completely different story. The first night after Cal's discharge from the hospital, Becky had brought her things from home, then visited with them for a few hours and left. Cal then had told Nate goodnight and gone into the guestroom. She was then quite surprised to find him following her into the room.

"I'm going to bed now," she said, thinking maybe he didn't understand her intent.

"That's good," he nodded. "You need your sleep." He stood inside the door, watching her.

"Can't I have a little privacy so I can change into my PJs?"

"Why? It's nothing I've never seen before."

"Nate," she said irritably, "I'm in no mood for this. If you think I'm going to go to bed with you..."

He raised his hand, "I think nothing of the sort. I swore I'd keep an eye on you until you can be trusted to behave, and that's what I fully intend to do. You sleep in the bed, and I'll sleep here on the chair, but I'm not going to let you out of my sight."

"What if people find out we're sleeping in the same room? They'll gossip like crazy."

"Who cares? Keeping you alive is more important."

Cal turned her back to him and changed into her pajamas, then got into bed. True to his word, Nate raised the foot of his reclining chair and settled into it. Thus it was every night thereafter.

* * *

It was the middle of the night. The only light came from the nightlight in the hallway, illuminating the staircase. Nate awoke to Cal's voice.

"You're all well," she was saying softly.

Nate looked across the room at Cal and noted she was still lying in the bed. That was odd. He had never known her to talk in her sleep before. He got out of the chair and went quietly over to her, checking to be sure she was all right. Before falling asleep earlier that night, she had taken the framed portrait of herself and Leonard that Becky had brought her from home and hugged it close. She was still clutching that portrait in her left hand now. In the soft light, Nate could tell that her eyes were open, but focused in the distance, and she had a radiant smile. She reached out with her right hand to an object unseen by Nate, then put her arm back down.

"I love you, too," she whispered.

He looked in the direction she was looking, but no one was there. Nate then realized that Cal was apparently just having a happy dream about Leonard, and went back to his chair. As he put the recliner foot back up and spread the blanket back over his lap, he wondered if what he had witnessed was something more than a dream. Perhaps God was giving Cal what she wanted most right now—a chance to see her beloved Leonard one more time.

* * *

Mrs. Neal came into the kitchen, where Cal and Nate were going over some Ames-Jenkins paperwork. "Ms. Anderson is here to see you, Mr. Jenkins," Mrs. Neal said.

"Show her to the office, please, then come back to stay with Cal."

She nodded and disappeared.

This is getting ridiculous, Cal thought. "I'm not like a little kid who needs to be babysat, for Pete's sake."

"Then think of us as prison guards, if it makes you feel better." He set his papers down.

"Why didn't you have her come in here so I could say hello to her, too? She's my friend, too, you know."

"Because we'll be discussing business. That's best done in the office, where I have my files."

"Business, my foot. Y'all are going to be making out like crazy. I know Doris."

He smiled as he got up and passed Mrs. Neal in the entrance to the hallway. "I'll be back in a few minutes," he told her. Nate then went down the hall and into the office, where Doris was sitting at his desk. She reached out for him and he leaned over to give her a kiss.

She straightened his collar. "I just got back in town and now Mrs. Neal puts me in the office. Why are we being so formal? I thought maybe we could get in a round of golf before going out to dinner tonight. It's been quite a while."

"No, I'm afraid I won't be available for things like that anytime soon. Let's take a rain check, okay?"

"Why? What's going on?"

"Haven't you been reading the papers?"

"No. The real world bores me. Why?"

"Cal's staying here for a while until she gets better, and I'm keeping an eye on her. It'll be for only a week or two more, I imagine."

"What do you mean she's staying here?" Her voice had lost its velvety quality. "She's living with you?"

"In a manner of speaking."

"Don't you think that's unwise? People will talk, and Cal might get the wrong impression."

"No problem."

"But it *is* a problem, Nate. People will think you're taking advantage of her vulnerability."

"I'm not. I don't care what people think."

"I do."

"Why?"

She tried to make her mood sound light. "Because you're my man, that's why. I want your reputation to be spotless."

"Like yours?" he asked with a twinkle in his eye. There was a long silence, then Nate said, "Don't worry about that. My reputation went out the window long ago. Give me an update on Ames-Jenkins. Are our projects moving along all right?"

"Oh, fair. They'd have more incentive to move at a faster clip if you were there."

"Well, I'm not. The employees will just have to learn to handle things themselves. What's happening?"

"There's a glitch in the schedule for *Honor Among Thieves*. It's going longer than they anticipated. Then the Marian Williams special is having trouble getting everybody together at the same time. She definitely wants Leon Gordon on it, but he's tied up for the next few months. After that, Marian will be unavailable."

"So what's Henry doing about all this?"

"Delegating everything to other people. He's big on delegation."

"Is he giving the work to people who are qualified to handle it?"

"I guess."

"As long as it gets done and gets done right, I don't care who does it. I'm thinking maybe we ought to ask Cal to write a sequel to *Mr. Jackson's Vacation*. The original film went over fairly well, and she's going to need a project to work on."

"If you ask me, I'd say she's entirely too dependent on you. You're babying her too much."

"No, I'm not. She's just having a rough time, but things will get better. I'm helping with her therapy."

"Oh, yeah?" Doris looked at him suspiciously. "Exactly what kind of therapy?"

"Grief therapy, of course. I'm taking her to her therapy sessions with the hospital psychologist, then continuing it while she's home. You haven't been through this, Doris, so you wouldn't understand. Dealing with the death of someone you're close to isn't a simple or quick matter. It takes time and a lot of hard work."

"Why doesn't she hire a professional to do that, if she needs round-the-clock therapy? She can certainly afford it."

"There's no need to. I'm here."

Doris looked at him with skepticism.

"Is that all you came to see me about?" he asked, looking at his watch. "It's almost time for Mrs. Neal to leave, so I need to get back with Cal."

"Is this your roundabout way of saying our wedding plans are off? If you two are shacking up…"

"No. If I wanted to cancel them, I'd say so."

She crossed her arms. "Okay, then. Let's set a definite date and stick to it."

"That's up to you."

"December 12th."

"Not that soon. I'll be tied up with Cal for at least that long. I *told* you this takes time. Make it next summer."

Cal came into the room, followed by Mrs. Neal. "Go ahead and make it December 12th. I'll be okay. Hi, Doris."

"In the summer," he said again. "How about August?"

Doris went over to Cal and put her hand on her shoulder. "Cal, I bet if you started writing that sequel, that would keep your mind busy and you'd be better in no time. You'd forget all about Leonard and wouldn't need all this therapy crap."

"That'll be enough, Doris!" Nate said angrily. "If you have nothing more to say, I've got other things to do."

Doris went over to Nate, grabbed him by the neck and gave him a grand, passionate kiss, then left.

"Bye," Cal told her friend as Doris breezed past her, down the hall and out the front door, leaving the scent of her perfume behind. As the front door closed, Cal looked back at Nate, "I think what you just got was a Texas kiss."

He shook his head sadly, "She just doesn't understand."

"What did she mean about me writing a sequel? Does she want to produce a sequel to *Mr. Jackson's Vacation*?"

"It'll be a good project for you later, but not yet."

"Why not now?"

"I don't want you running away from your situation by burying yourself in work. First, work through your grief, *then* write the sequel and Ames-Jenkins will produce it."

"And this time, Len can... ." Then she caught herself. "Oh, I guess not."

"Play the lead?"

"Yeah."

He took her hand and led her to the sofa, where they both sat. "You're feeling guilty about that, too, aren't you?"

"Doggone, it! Why didn't I wait until he was free to play the lead in the first one? Why was I so darned bullheaded?"

"You said he didn't want the lead," Nate reminded her.

"I wrote it specifically for him. That made me mad that he didn't seem to care."

"But remember what he said at the premiere? What did he tell us?"

"He said it was a good movie and a good director," she said proudly.

"Meaning you."

"He said he didn't know I could direct. All during the filming, it drove him bananas that we were working together so closely on it every day while he was three states away, doing another picture. He wanted to keep an eye on us, but all he could do was call every night. He would've been even more uncomfortable about it if he had known about that tango scene we did. But he should've known how exhausting it was to direct and star in the same picture. I didn't have any energy left for hanky-panky."

"Did you ever convince him that nothing improper happened?"

"Yeah, I think so. He said I sounded awfully tired on the phone. I don't want to star and direct in the same project anymore. It took a lot out of me."

"And being on the production end, in addition to playing the lead, wasn't easy for me, either. I think we both bit off more than we could comfortably chew. It might've been a better picture if we had each done one of those things instead of wearing so many hats."

"Yeah."

"And you wanted to complete the picture in six weeks, beginning to end, counting pre-production and post-production. Remember that?" he smiled.

She nodded, "I know better now."

"We both learned as we went and it turned out all right."

"So now I can start on the sequel."

"I'll let you know when."

* * *

Kara couldn't stand it anymore. Aunt Becky had been good to her and everything, but she missed Papa Nate sorely and wanted to be sure Mama was all right; so instead of coming straight home to Aunt Becky's house from school today, she took a detour to Papa Nate's. She opened the door and peeked inside, hoping he wouldn't scold her for coming when she wasn't supposed to. She didn't see anyone. She came inside and closed the door.

"Well hello, Missy!" Mrs. Neal said as she plugged the vacuum cleaner into the living room outlet. "It's good to see you again."

"Hi, Mrs. Neal," replied Kara. She went into the living room to receive her hug from their housekeeper. "Are you doing okay?"

"Just fine, and you?"

"Well, except for Daddy dying, I guess I'm fine, too."

"He was so sick, Kara. I can't be sad that he's in heaven with his mama. Now, he's happy and healthy again."

"Yeah, I know. Where's Papa Nate and Mama?"

"They're in the kitchen. I would've asked Mrs. Davis to bake you some cookies if I had known you were going to be here today."

"I wanted to surprise my folks. See you later." Kara left the living room and went into the kitchen. Cal and Nate were sitting at the table, looking at some papers and photos. "Hi, Mama. Are you well now?" She went over to give her mother a hug.

Cal's eyes lit up. "Hi, sweetie!" She wrapped her arms around her daughter and hugged her tightly. "I didn't know you were here."

Nate looked at her sternly. "Kara Michelle Rhoads, I told you to stay at Aunt Becky's house. Why did you disobey me?"

"I just *had* to see how Mama's doing," she said pleadingly. "Please don't make me stay away from Mama when she needs me. I want to come back home. Please?"

"Let her stay, Nate. She's right. I *do* need her."

"Just how is it that you need her?"

"Because she's my baby. Every mother needs her baby. And besides, she's hurting, too, Nate. Len's her daddy. She misses him, too."

Nate couldn't conceal his smile.

Cal was confused. "What?"

"I think you're on the road to recovery, Cal. You're thinking about someone other than yourself or Leonard. You don't know how glad I am to see that."

"Hey, kid," Cal said to Kara, "you're just what we both needed. Welcome home!"

"I can stay?" she asked excitedly.

"Let's go to Aunt Becky's and get your things," Nate said. "Come on, Cal. We can finish our business later."

Indeed, it had been over a week since Cal had been discharged from the hospital and she was more than ready to welcome Kara back into her life now. Cal and Nate had had many heart-to-heart talks during that time, one of which left them *both* clinging to each other, in tears for the loved ones they had lost. He had helped her through the low times as only a caring friend could do. Cal had found herself becoming emotionally dependent on Nate, though, and realized that that was not a good situation, as he had been engaged for a long time to Doris. Cal could tell by Doris' impatience how trying that was for her. The last thing she wanted to do was to thwart their wedding plans. Nate deserved a loving wife to come home to, and she knew Doris would give him all the love he could ever need. "Or lust, anyway," she smiled to herself. And, too, Nate would certainly be the one man who could show Doris what a really loving relationship is all about. Apparently, her previous two husbands had failed to do that.

Cal wanted to move back into her own house and resume some semblance of normality, with regular visits from Kara; but Nate had reservations about leaving her unmonitored. They finally agreed that she would stay with Nate and Kara in his house for one more week, during which time she would continue her counseling sessions with the hospital psychologist. After that time, if the doctor and Nate both felt that Cal was no longer in danger of self-injury, she could move back home.

* * *

"It's time for another portrait," Nate announced the next evening during dinner. "Now that you're home again, Kara, I can make the appointment."

"I didn't know there were time restrictions on those things," Cal said as she put gravy on her mashed potatoes, chicken and green beans, then passed the gravy boat to him.

He ladled some onto his potatoes and passed it on to Kara. "Every five years or so would be about right."

"I want a copy of this one, then," Cal said as she picked up her chicken leg and took a bite. "Our mantel doesn't have anything fancy on it. Just a clock."

"Mama, why don't you marry Papa Nate, so we can all three be in the picture?"

Nate and Kara both looked to Cal for a response.

"Because Daddy didn't want me to marry anybody else. I don't want to ever be married again, anyway. It hurts too much when it's over." In spite of her cheerful facade, a tear escaped from Cal's eye. She quickly wiped it away, hoping no one noticed. "Why don't y'all take a couple instruments to the session with you? I think it'd be neat for y'all to be holding a guitar and ukulele in the picture."

"Yeah, that's a great idea! Can we?" Kara asked him eagerly.

"I'll think about it," Nate replied.

Cal put the chicken down and wiped her fingers with the linen napkin. "I need to bring my computer over to this house." Then she added, "And my printer, too."

"Why?" Nate asked.

"So I can get started on that sequel. I've been thinking about how to continue *Mr. Jackson's Vacation.* In the original one, you got the girl at the end and all seemed fine, but now, the beginning of the sequel should have something happen that gets him started on the chase again."

Nate put his fork down. "It's too soon for you to be working on writing the sequel, Cal. Let's give it another week. By then, you'll probably be ready to go back to your house, so you won't have to move your equipment."

"I want to start now. I'm ready."

Nate turned to Kara. "What time did Aunt Becky say she was picking you up tonight?"

"Seven-thirty, I think," she answered. "What time is it now?"

He looked at his watch. "You've got about twelve minutes."

As Kara rushed through the rest of her meal, Cal asked, "Where are y'all going?"

"Her church group's going roller skating," he said.

Cal brightened, "Hey, I've got a good idea. Why don't you go, too, Nate? It's been a long time since you've been skating and you've been cooped up in the house for a long time. You need a break."

"I never liked skating."

"You just don't know how. How about it, Kara? You think you can teach him?"

"Sure!" she said as she finished her dinner and scooted her chair back.

"No, ladies. I have no desire to learn."

"May I be excused, Papa Nate?"

"Go ahead," he nodded.

Kara ran upstairs to get her skates.

Nate looked over at Cal with some amusement. "What's the matter, Cal? You have that 'curses, foiled again' look."

"Oh, nothing. Do we have anymore chicken?"

He passed the platter over to her.

"So," she said pleasantly, "how's our business doing?"

"They're managing. My being away is good for them. It's forcing them to make some decisions and take some action on their own, instead of relying on me to give the orders. I should've taken time off sooner."

"Is the special shaping up okay? I thought it'd be great if Jeanette Patrick could be one of the guest stars."

"She's already been asked and accepted. There are a couple of complications, but it'll work out all right."

"I think it's about time we get our own building, don't you?"

"Why? I thought things were going well the way they were. With less overhead, there's more profit."

She shrugged, "I don't know. I guess I just thought it'd be great to have our own big sign outside in front of our own building. Then we'd know we've really made it."

He thought for a moment. "If we get a large enough building, we could rent out the extra space until we grow into it. That could be a good source of income."

"Well, I'm stuffed," Cal said as she pushed her chair back and stood up. "You've got a good cook. Her chicken's almost as good as Mrs. Morris." She then left the room and hurried down the hallway, turning into his office.

Nate got up and followed her. When he entered the office, he found Cal looking through his desk drawers. "What're you looking for?" he asked.

"I need a notebook and pen. Where do you keep them?"

He pulled open the bottom left drawer. "I don't have notebooks, but here's a legal pad. Will that do?"

"For starters. How about a couple pens?"

He opened the top center drawer and produced a pen. "How many?"

"Two."

He gave her a second one and closed the drawer.

"Thanks." She then darted out of the office and up the stairs.

"What's she up to?" he wondered as he hurried up the stairs after her.

Cal quickly tried to close her bedroom door before he got there, but she wasn't quite fast enough. He pushed it back open. "Stop following me," she said.

He came into the room. "Sorry. Got to."

She sighed, then lay on her stomach on the bed and started writing on the legal pad in front of her. The extra pen had been set aside.

"What're you doing?" he asked.

"Writing."

"Obviously. *What* are you writing? A letter?"

"I think I'll call it *Déjà-Vu, Mr. Jackson.* All I've got to do is figure out how to spell it."

"The sequel?"

"Yep."

He hurried over to her and took the pen out of her hand. "No, Cal. Not yet."

"Bye, Mama and Papa Nate. I'll see y'all later tonight," said Kara as she passed by Cal's door on her way downstairs.

"See ya, sweetie. Have fun," Cal said.

Nate added, "Be sure to thank Aunt Becky for the ride."

"Okay. Bye." Kara then went out the front door to the waiting car.

When Nate looked back down at Cal, she had already retrieved the second pen and resumed writing. "*No!*" he said, taking it out of her hand, too.

"It's *got* to be now. I'm inspired right now. Give me that." She grabbed the pen from his hand, held it tightly, and clutched the legal pad close to her body. Now she wished she had asked for five pens.

He sat on the bed beside her, holding his hand out. "Give that to me right now! You're not going to hide behind work."

"No! Go away!"

He tried to pull the legal pad out of her hands, but she was holding onto it with all her might.

"I need this, Nate. Stop it!"

"No, you don't. You'll have your chance next week, then you can use your computer." She had pulled the pen and pad underneath her, where he couldn't reach it. He grasped her by the shoulders and turned her over. He then took hold of the pad, pulled it from her hands, and threw it on the floor behind him.

She beat on his chest with both hands. "Get out of my life! You keep getting in my way! Just leave me alone!"

He grabbed her hands. "Writing would get in the way of your therapy. It's not time yet."

Cal put her feet on his chest and tried to push him away. "I don't need your stupid therapy. Just go away and leave me alone!"

He wrestled her back down into a flat position, then took the pen from her clinched fist. "I'm right, Cal. I don't care what you say. I *know* I'm right." They were both breathing heavily as they struggled against each other. Suddenly, he tossed the pen on the floor and kissed her passionately. She pushed against him one more time, then couldn't resist any longer. She clung to him as she mirrored his desire. They remained in their burning embrace for a moment, then Nate let go of her and got back up. "I'm sorry, Cal. I'm sorry. I got carried away." He picked up the pad and pens from the floor, then went over and contritely sat on the recliner.

Tears filled her eyes as she turned back over onto her stomach.

"I really mean it," he said earnestly. "I'm sorry. I didn't mean to do that."

Filled with guilty remorse, she pulled the bedspread over her head. It had been so long since she had experienced passion, and it felt so good—but it was so wrong. "I cheated on Len, again," she wailed, "and made you cheat on Doris, too."

"No, you weren't cheating. I was. I'm sorry. I won't do that anymore." How he wanted to hold her, to soothe her conscience and make everything all right for her, but he knew that any physical sign of affection now would only make things worse. He wondered what made him lose control like that and give in to his more basic urges. He needs to be the strong one, for her sake. He'll just have to be more careful in the future.

"I *need* to write. It's an emotional outlet for me." She dried her cheeks with the bedspread.

"Not yet."

Her renewed tears were now from sheer frustration. If only her car was here, Cal thought. Then she could just drive herself home. But, instead, she had to stay here in his house for another whole week. "I feel like a doggone prisoner here. I want to go home."

"The only way I'd let you go home is if I could stay *there* and keep an eye on you. The hospital released you to my care, so I have a legal obligation to be there."

That might work, Cal thought. *There's a lock on the door to the study, where the computer is.* She could sneak in there in the middle of the night and lock Nate out. "Can Kara come, too?"

He shrugged, "I don't see why not. Are you sure being around so many reminders of Leonard won't make things worse?"

"No. It'd make things better."

"I'll ask the doctor to be sure." Nate came back over to the bed and sat on it while he pulled the phonebook out and looked up the number. He then dialed.

In the meantime, Cal eased off the bed and over to the recliner, picking up the pad and pens.

*   *   *

He banged on the door. "Let me in, Cal. You *know* you're not supposed to be out of my sight."

"Shhhh, I need to concentrate," she said, without looking up from the pad on which she had begun writing the opening scene for her new *Mr. Jackson* screenplay. "I promise I won't stab myself with the pen."

"You're in *my* bedroom, Cal. I have a right to be in there."

She couldn't concentrate if he insisted on chatting. "How come this is the only room in the house with a lock on the door, anyway?"

"That one didn't have a lock, either, until Kara moved in. I wanted her to respect my privacy."

"Then you respect mine. I need peace and quiet."

"You're not going to unlock it?"

"Not yet. Maybe next week."

Okay, he thought. *There are other ways.* He took the wallet out of his pocket and a credit card out of the wallet. It took only two tries with the credit card before the door unlocked. He opened the door, returned the card to the wallet and the wallet to his pocket.

"Hey!" Cal yelled, indignantly. "You're not supposed to do that."

He came and sat beside her on the couch. It seemed odd to her that he didn't try to take the pad and pens out of her hand this time. Maybe he had given up.

"Turn to the next blank page," he instructed. "I want you to write something for me."

That aroused her curiosity. "Write what?"

"Just do it. I'll dictate it to you."

She flipped to the next page and held her pen ready to write.

"Write this down: 'I, Stacy Ames Rhoads, do hereby acknowledge the need for and give permission to…'"

"Not so fast! I'm not a secretary, you know." She began writing.

After she had gotten that much done, he continued, more slowly, "'… Nate Jenkins to dwell in my house for an undetermined length of time…'"

She wrote that, then looked up. "So the doc said it's okay for me to go back home, again?"

"As long as you're being watched."

"Why? I'm not a little kid, for Pete's sake."

"Let me put it to you this way. There were two choices when they were ready to release you from the medical wing of the hospital. You could either be released to my care, with the understanding that I would keep an eagle eye on you and take you to therapy regularly, or you could be admitted into their psychiatric unit, where they would do those things themselves. Would you rather go back to the hospital and stay in their psych ward?"

"No."

"Keep writing, then."

She sighed and, again, put pen to paper.

"'… for the purpose of monitoring my recovery. Dr. Gillihan and Mr. Jenkins will then determine when recovery is complete.' Then sign and date it."

Cal did as he said, until she got to his name. "'*Mr.* Jenkins'? When would I ever call you that?"

"Okay, write 'Nate Jenkins', then."

She substituted his first name for the title, finished the sentence, signed and dated it, then pulled the sheet off the legal pad and handed it to him. "Why do I need to do this, anyway? If the doc told you to be there with me, isn't that enough?"

"For most people, it would be; but I've seen how your mind works. As stubborn as you can be sometimes, I wouldn't put it past you to have me arrested for trespassing the first time I keep you from doing something you want to do."

"Hmm. I hadn't thought of that. That's an idea."

"Too late now." He folded the affidavit and put it in his pocket. Then he took the pad and pens from her. "You'll be able to write again next week."

* * *

The next morning, they were finally on their way back to the Rhoads house. Kara was nestled between Cal and Nate in the front seat, and the back seat and trunk were filled with their suitcases.

"We're almost home," Cal said excitedly to Kara. "I feel like I've been gone a hundred years."

"It feels to me like we're going on vacation. Even Papa Nate's got some suitcases."

"Well, that's because he's moving in with us for a little while. He seems to think I need a babysitter."

"That way you won't get lonely while I'm at school."

"Jessie keeps me company when she's not busy with stuff."

"She's *always* busy with stuff. She's always either cleaning up or polishing or ironing or cooking or something."

They rounded the corner and turned onto their street.

Cal's eyes sparkled. "Isn't that the most beautiful sight? Look at our house, sitting there so sweet. It's smiling and saying 'welcome home.'"

They pulled into the driveway and stopped.

Cal got out and opened the back door of the car. She took Kara's suitcase and handed it to her. Then she took her own two suitcases out and closed the door. While Nate got his luggage out of the trunk, Cal went to the front door of the house, set her suitcases down and unlocked the door. "I remember when your daddy carried me over the threshold the day we got married. It was a different house, but looked kind of like this one. We had so much fun that day," she said.

"How come you don't have wedding pictures like Aunt Becky does?" Kara asked, as they went inside, followed by Nate. "She's got pictures of both of her weddings, but you don't have any."

"Because we didn't have a church wedding. We went to the minister's house, instead. Aunt Becky was there. Then we went out for a terrific seafood dinner."

"I like Aunt Becky's better. She was dressed up like a queen."

"Yeah, she had pretty weddings and beautiful gowns."

"How come you weren't in Aunt Becky's first wedding book, Papa Nate?"

"I had to be away. I wanted to be there, but I couldn't." Nate hoped his daughter would never know that he had been behind bars when Becky was getting married. "Where should I put my luggage?"

"How about in the guest room?" Cal said as she ascended the stairs, followed by Kara and Nate. "I'll show you where that is." First, she put her luggage inside the room she and Leonard used to share. Then she pointed farther down the hallway, "It's two doors down. The green room."

He set his luggage down in the appropriate room.

"And this is my room, Papa Nate," Kara said as she took him by the hand and led him from his room into hers, which was directly across from Cal's room. "Daddy bought me this desk and he put it together for me."

"That's good. You can do your homework on it this week." He looked around. This room was nice, but not as large or exquisitely-furnished as the one she had in his house. Nate looked in her closet. There were only two dresses and twelve shirts hanging in there. "Where are all your clothes?" he asked.

"In here." Kara pulled open the drawers of her large dresser to expose pairs and pairs of blue jeans and overalls. "I hardly ever wear dresses when I'm here."

"Yeah, Nate," Cal added, "Kara and I dress Texas-style."

"Daddy liked me in this," she said, pulling out her floral overalls. "He said I look like a garden when I wear it." She held it against her cheek and looked forlornly at her mother. "Mama, why did Daddy have to die? Didn't he know we needed him?"

Cal put her arm around Kara's shoulders and led her to the bed, where they both sat. "He didn't want to die, sweetie. He wanted to stay with us and watch you grow up, but he was just too sick."

"But I thought he could do *anything*," she cried, tears streaming down her cheeks. "Why couldn't he get well?"

Cal couldn't hold back her tears, either. She hugged her daughter close. "He fought hard, honey. He tried so hard to live and stay active, but cancer's the only thing in the world he couldn't beat."

"I miss him. I wish I could talk to him."

"Me, too."

"I just want to beat up the doctor 'cause he didn't make him well."

Nate joined them, sitting beside Kara and patting her back. "Doctors aren't magic, Kara-Mia. They did the best they could."

"If only Daddy had gone to the doctor sooner," Cal said sadly, "they might've caught it in time. By the time he finally went, it was too late. Kara, if you ever get sick like that, you need to go to the doctor right away so he can help you get well."

"I will. Is Daddy watching us from heaven?"

"I don't know," Cal answered. "Maybe."

"Is he maybe my guardian angel now?"

Cal looked over at Nate. "I don't know that, either. Maybe we ought to go see Pastor Burnhart and ask him."

"We can ask him those things when we go to church tomorrow," Nate suggested.

"We're going back so soon?" Cal asked.

He turned to Kara. "Why don't you go call Aunt Becky and let her know we're here now, okay?"

"Okay." She went downstairs.

Nate looked back at Cal. "Think you could handle it? Just the worship service now, then getting more involved later?"

She thought for a moment, then said, "Let's get there a little late and leave right before it's over. I'm afraid if I let people talk to me, they'll say something that will make my waterworks start again. I hate that, especially in public. It makes me look like a nut case. Sometimes I think I am."

"It's *okay*, Cal. Why can't you get that through your head? People don't expect you to be the life of the party when you've just become a widow. If you shed a tear or two, big deal! It'll be good for you to be among people again. Dr. Gillihan told me to start getting you back into a routine. That's why he liked the idea of your being home again."

"I hate that word—'widow.'"

"Well, that's what you are. You've got to face it sooner or later. Leonard's gone."

She got up and went out into the hallway. Nate followed. She then went down the stairs and into the media room. Cal took out a video, put it on the big-screen VCR, then plopped down onto the sofa with the remote control.

Nate seated himself beside her. "What're you going to watch?" he asked.

She shrugged, "Just a movie."

"This is a really nice room," he said, looking around him. "It seems to have every bit of electronic equipment a person could ever want. Leonard must have been an electronics buff."

"Not for fun, though. It's all to help us study acting techniques and stuff. He took his work more seriously than anyone I've ever seen."

The opening credits were flashing on the screen and, just as Nate suspected, Leonard's name was among them. "Watching him on screen helps you when you're missing him, doesn't it?"

"Yeah."

Nate nodded, approvingly, "Yes, Leonard's gone but his work lives on forever."

"Stop saying that."

"What? That he's gone?"

"Yeah."

"Well, he *is*, you know. There's not a thing we can do to bring him back."

"I'm bringing him back right now." She turned the volume up loud enough to drown out Nate's voice.

*   *   *

That afternoon, Jessie approached the doorway of the den as Nate and Cal were arguing.

"How come you let me watch videos, but you won't let me write?" Cal was asking, indignantly.

"Because we can discuss what's going on in your mind during the videos. Creative writing is solitary work."

"You're driving me nuts!"

"It's not all that much fun for me either, Cal."

Jessie interrupted, "Doris Anderson is here to see you, Nate."

"Okay, I'll see her in the parlor, then you come back… ."

With hands on hips, Jessie made her meaning clearer, "No, I said she's *here*, right behind me. I'm not 'Jeeves, the Butler,' you know."

He could see right away that the Rhoads housekeeper wasn't nearly as proper as his was. "Come on in, Doris," he said, as he turned toward the doorway and Cal seated herself at her computer. He reached over with his left hand and held the computer's control in the "off" position so Cal couldn't turn it on while he was distracted.

Jessie retreated back down the hall, muttering to herself, "He should consider himself lucky I even announced her."

Doris joined the couple in the den. "The servant at your house told me you were here," she said, giving Nate a kiss in greeting. "Hi, Cal."

"Hi, Doris." Cal took hold of his hand and tried to pull it away from the switch. It wouldn't budge.

He corrected, "Her name is Mrs. Neal, my cook's name is Mrs. Davis, and the gardener is Mr. Murrayhill. It would be good for you to remember those names. That would be much more diplomatic than just calling them servants."

"Whatever," Doris shrugged. "What're you doing here? Shacking up at her house now or what?"

"Keeping an eye on Cal. How're things going at the office?"

"Oh, so-so. Sure would be better if you were there, though."

"I think Cal's making a lot of progress. It shouldn't be too much longer."

"You can go right now, if you want to," Cal added.

"No, I can't," Nate corrected.

"I've bought a wedding dress," Doris said, matter-of-factly, "and picked out my attendants."

"Sounds like y'all need to go pick out some china and crystal, too," Cal offered, hopefully. "I'll hold the fort down here while you go do that."

"Good try, Cal, but no dice," he said with an amused smile.

Doris fished a small box out of her purse, opened it, and took the ring from it. "Here, try this on for size."

Nate looked at the gold band she was holding. He sighed and held his left hand out to her.

Just the opportunity Cal needed! *Thanks, Doris!* she thought as she quickly turned on the computer and put her hand over the switch so Nate wouldn't turn it back off.

"Let's see," Doris cooed as she slipped the ring on his finger. "Looks like a good fit. Do you like that style?"

"It's fine. Just right. Here," he said, taking it off and handing it back to her. Then he turned back to the computer and Cal. "I told you to leave that thing off!" He tried to pull her hand away from the switch, but she held onto it with every ounce of strength that she had. "Okay then, you asked for it." He went behind Cal's desk and turned the surge protector off, rendering the computer useless.

"Nate!" Cal screamed as she got up and went around the desk.

Doris put the ring back into the box. "I need a list of your friends and relatives so I can make the guest list."

"Can we discuss this later, Doris? I'm kind of busy right now," Nate asked, hoping against hope that she would understand his situation.

Cal pushed him aside and reached for the floor switch.

"*No!*" he yelled. "Leave that alone!" Nate pulled her away from the switch. Cal started pummeling him with her fists. He grabbed her arms, then spun her around so she was facing away from him, while he was still holding her arms, which were now crossed in front of her, greatly limiting her movements. It sometimes took a strong-willed, forceful man to deal with such a headstrong woman, he realized, because she didn't always understand that he was just trying to *help* her. Why she resisted that help, he just couldn't fathom.

"Nate, for heaven's sake, leave her alone," Doris said irritably. "All she wants to do is work on her computer. What's wrong with that?"

"Yeah!" Cal agreed.

"Because she wants to use the computer to avoid facing reality. I can't let her do that."

"My lands! You've turned into a bloomin' shrink," Doris grumbled as she put the box back into her purse and snapped it shut.

As Cal struggled to get out of his hold, he shook his head, "Doris, the way you're talking, you'd think the wedding is tomorrow. We've got almost a year yet. Don't rush it."

"A year? I thought we decided on December."

"No! Not December! *August* of next year, Doris. Not a minute before," he corrected.

Cal finally worked one arm free and jabbed her elbow into his stomach. "Let me go!"

"Ow! If you stay away from the computer, I'll let you go."

"Okay. Just let go," Cal agreed.

He tentatively loosened his grip on her. After a moment's hesitation, they both dived for the floor switch simultaneously, but he got to it first, covering it with his hand.

Temporarily stymied, Cal went to 'Plan B', running out of the den and into her bedroom, then closing and locking the door.

He knew exactly what she was doing now. "Doris, look, I can't discuss this with you any longer. I'll call you when I have some time. You can see your way out." He went into the hallway and pulled his wallet out of his pocket.

With an air of disgust, Doris retreated from the room, then started down the stairs.

"And it's to be in *August*, not December," he added, emphatically.

"Good bye!" She disappeared down the stairway. Then he heard the front door open and slam shut.

Nate took the credit card out of his wallet and used it to unlock Cal's door. When he pushed the door open, his suspicions were confirmed. Cal was, indeed, in a chair, writing. "Where'd you get that notebook?"

"I can't talk now. I'm busy. If you want to chat, go catch up with Doris."

"Papa Nate," Kara called from her room. "Come look at this."

So many females in his life! Two wanted his attention while he must give it to the third, who didn't want it. "Can you show me in here?" he asked.

"Well, yeah, I guess," Kara sighed. "I might get my hands dirty, though."

He wrestled the pen and notebook out of Cal's hands. After unsuccessfully trying to get them back, she then got up and headed toward the door. Nate grabbed hold of her arm to keep her from going back to the computer. They almost bumped into Kara and the oil painting she was bringing to show them. They immediately stopped their struggle and made room for their daughter to enter the room.

"Let's see," Cal said eagerly. "This is her first painting, Nate. Len bought her a paint set and easel." As Kara turned the painting around to show them, Cal smiled broadly. "That's real pretty, sweetie. You like landscapes. I do, too."

"It's still wet, so don't touch it. Do you recognize where it is?" the budding young artist asked.

"It's part of my back yard," Nate answered. Then he pointed, "Over there's the horses' stable and the pond. Did you do that from memory, or did you use a photo?"

"I just remembered."

"You got every tree right. You've got a great memory, Kara-Mia."

Kara grinned. "Y'all really like it?"

"I sure do," Cal said. "When it dries, we'll have to frame it and hang it in the living room."

"I'll need one for my house, too," Nate added. "Why don't you do one of Mama's yard for my house?"

"See, Nate?" Cal said. "She inherited *something* good from me besides my hair. Remember those four paintings of England in our living room? I did those and Len had them framed and hung them up for me."

"I think I want to be an artist when I grow up," Kara stated.

Nate patted her curls. "You just be whatever you want to be."

Content that her creative endeavor was appreciated by experts, Kara smiled and took her painting back into her room. Cal followed, as did Nate.

"Are you finished painting for the day?" Cal asked.

"Uh-huh."

"Okay. Let me show you how to clean your brushes. Let's take them to the kitchen." She picked up both brushes and started for the stairs.

Kara set her painting down onto the desk, then followed her mother and Nate downstairs to the kitchen.

"First, we get all the excess paint off the brushes with a paper towel." Cal proceeded to do this, then tossed the paper towels into the trashcan. "Acrylic paints are water based, so you clean the brushes with regular soap and water. When you start using oil paints, it'll be different." She took the brushes to the sink, then held them under the running water. Once they were wet, she soaped her hand, then worked the soap into the brushes. "See? Once they're all sudsy, you rinse them out, dry them off, then you're ready for next time."

"Okay," the child said.

"Do you know what would happen if you didn't clean your brushes?" Cal asked.

"They'd stay dirty."

"And they'd get real hard, too, because paint hardens. You couldn't use the brushes anymore."

"Oh, okay."

Once Cal finished with the brushes and handed them back to Kara, she patted her shoulder. "Daddy would be happy that you're using the paints he bought you."

"Maybe he's watching from heaven and he sees that I am."

"If he is, I bet he has a big smile."

"Yeah. Did Daddy want me to be an artist?"

"I think he wanted you to try painting to see if you like it. He noticed that you were real good at drawing, so he probably just wanted you to enjoy art, whether or not you do it as a career."

"How come he wanted me to paint, but *he* never painted?"

"Well, you know Daddy loved me a lot, don't you?"

"Yeah."

"He loved us *both* a lot. And it made him happy when things about you were like me—like your hair and your art."

"I like to make Daddy happy."

"Yeah, me, too. I'm trying to live the way he wanted me to," Cal said softly.

"Me, too."

Nate remained in the doorway, watching this tender moment. He realized that sometimes it's better to stay on the perimeter, rather than being a part of every interaction in this house.

* * *

His efforts to keep Cal from writing were rapidly making her view Nate as 'the enemy,' rather than her friend. She simply could not understand his objections to her doing the thing she loved to do. After yet another fight about it, he agreed to call Dr. Gillihan and seek his opinion. *It really isn't necessary, though,* Nate thought. *It's obvious that writing would be a cop-out, a way to avoid dealing with her grief and working her way through it.* But, just to appease Cal, he dialed the doctor's number while she watched.

After a lengthy discussion with the doctor, Nate hung up the phone and looked at Cal with an air of resignation. "It's against my better judgment, but he said to go ahead and let you do it."

Cal's face lit up. "*Really?*"

"He said it could be a form of therapy. Maybe you're right about that. He said it depends on what it is you're writing and why."

"Hot *diggity!*" she shouted gleefully, as she jumped up and ran into the study. Nate reluctantly followed. Cal sat at her desk and turned on the computer. Nothing happened. "Oh, yeah," she remembered as she got up and went around to the floor switch. She flipped it on, then went back to her chair.

For the rest of the afternoon, Cal ecstatically worked on the opening chapter of *Déjà-Vu, Mr. Jackson*, while Nate busied himself at Leonard's desk with his briefcase full of Ames-Jenkins papers. There was a telephone on the desk, so Nate used this as his chance to get oral reports from their various managers. He suspected that Doris wasn't telling him the whole story of how things were going at the office. It turned out he was right. Nate was pleasantly surprised to learn how smoothly things were going there—that Henry had been handling things well. He was told this by three different employees, so it was bound to be true. They did report, however, that Doris hadn't been in much during the last week. *Uh-oh*, Nate thought. *She better not be busy making December wedding plans.* He told Henry to find out where she is. He then called his banker and discussed with him the possibility of the bank and production company going in together to buy a building to house Ames-Jenkins. The idea of buying one larger than they need and renting out the extra space was well-received by the bank.

By evening, Nate and Cal both looked happier than they had for quite some time.

As part of Cal's re-entry into the social world, Nate had told Jessie not to cook any dinner for them tonight. Instead, he sent the housekeeper home early and took Cal and Kara out to dinner. It had been many months since

Cal had been in a restaurant. Ever since their television series had become popular, they had avoided public places almost entirely. This time, though, it was like a breath of fresh air. Sure, some fans recognized them and asked for autographs, a couple gushing over how much they enjoyed their movies and television show; but it felt really good to Cal to be out of the confines of a house, at last. As they were finishing with dinner, she was yearning to get back to the computer so she could continue her writing. Back home they went.

On their way, she sighed, "You know, not a single person at the restaurant even mentioned Len. You'd think he hadn't ever existed, the way they were acting."

"They were probably avoiding that topic, thinking it would make you sad," Nate said.

"Well, it probably *would've*, but I still need to talk about him."

"We know that, don't we, Kara-Mia?" he asked, bringing their child into the conversation. "So let's talk about him."

Kara spoke up, "If Daddy had been with us tonight, I bet he would've ordered a big steak."

"And a baked potato with lots of butter," Cal added. "And pecan pie for dessert."

"Cholesterol City!" noted Nate. "It's a wonder his heart was so healthy."

Cal grinned at him mischievously. "Oh, I made sure he got *lots* of exercise."

"Yeah," Nate smiled back at her, knowingly, "I *bet* you did!"

"I never saw him exercise, Mama," Kara said. "Did he do jumping jacks and stuff when I wasn't around?"

Cal and Nate looked at each other, trying to stifle their grins. "Yeah. He did his exercising when you were at Papa Nate's. He liked to do that in private."

"Oh. I like to play kickball at school. That's good exercise, isn't it?"

"Yeah, sweetie. That's real good."

✳ ✳ ✳

It was eleven o'clock that evening, and Cal had finally turned off her computer. Nate had asked her to print out what she had written, which she had done. He was now reading it as she was putting her thesaurus and dictionary back on the shelf. "Sometimes I have the hardest time finding the word with just the right shade of meaning," she said.

They turned off the den lights and went into her bedroom. He sat in the chair and continued reading while she got ready for bed. By the time she was sliding in under the covers, he had finished.

"Do you realize that you were describing Leonard in the first chapter?" he asked.

"I was? How?"

He looked back down at the manuscript. "The spy you call 'Bulldozer.' You gave a perfect physical description of Leonard." Nate began reading, "'He was ruggedly handsome with blond hair and blue eyes, a large, solid man who had been everywhere and done everything.' It'll be interesting to see how his character develops as the story progresses."

She thought for a moment. "Hmm. I never thought of that. I guess 'Bulldozer' *is* a lot like Len."

"Is he going to be a good guy or a bad guy?"

"Oh, definitely a good guy. They're going to *think* he's bad, but he's not really."

Nate nodded, "Exactly like Leonard. I guess Dr. Gillihan is right. You can work through your feelings by writing, just as well as you can by speaking."

"Hey, that's what I kept trying to tell you. I *told* you it's something I *needed* to do. Why wouldn't you believe me?"

He set the manuscript down and shrugged, "I guess because, to me, writing would be work. It would take my mind off my own problems."

"Okay," she smiled victoriously, "go ahead and say it."

"Say what?"

"'I'm sorry, Cal. I was wrong. You were right.'"

He smirked, "You would really enjoy that, wouldn't you?"

"Um-hmm." He hadn't seen Cal look so serene in many months.

Nate gamely rose from the chair and walked over to the bed. He dipped down, dramatically, onto one knee and raised his hands in supplication, "Oh, fair lady, could you *ever* find it in your heart to forgive such a misguided soul as I? I don't deserve your forgiveness, but I beg you to have mercy on me, lowly as I am."

"Okay, okay," she laughed. "Sheesh! Are you *sure* you'd rather produce than act? There still seems to be some ham left in you."

"Have I groveled enough to suit you?"

"Yeah. Get up, for Pete's sake."

He got back to his feet, then sat on her bed. "So you're feeling better about things now, aren't you, after having had lots of time for writing?"

She nodded. "And I bet *you* feel better now that you're able to get back to your Ames-Jenkins work, too, aren't you?"

"I guess so. I really enjoy that kind of thing. It's kind of like a chess game, Cal. You figure out strategy—what will happen if I do this or that? How's the best way to get this accomplished? If I were younger, I'd go to college and major in business management."

"Why can't you do that now? Len always said you're never too old to learn."

"I'll learn by doing. I'm really glad you talked me into becoming involved in Ames-Jenkins. It's been so good for me. It's a lot more fulfilling than acting ever was."

"And we're giving young talent a chance to be seen nationally. That's the part I like."

"I like that, too. Uncle Bob had the same idea, but just did it a couple times. Ames-Jenkins does it regularly. If we did *just* that and nothing else, though, we'd lose our shirts; but we have enough money-making productions to offset the more benevolent ones."

He gave her a light kiss on the cheek, then arose, changed into his pajamas, and went back to his chair, where he stayed the rest of the night.

Chapter 8

AFTER SEEING KARA OFF TO SCHOOL, Cal settled back down to her computer and Nate phoned the office. Doris wasn't there, but she was bound to turn up, Henry said. In the meantime, her assistant was handling everything quite well. It was only then that Nate realized that she had an assistant. Oh yes, Henry told him, Doris had insisted on it—and it's a good thing she did. There had been many times that she was needed but not in the office, so her assistant would take over her duties until she returned.

"You mean she's disappeared before?" Nate asked.

Henry hesitated, "Well, sir, when it's really urgent, we know where we can find her. She doesn't really disappear."

"Where?"

There was an embarrassed silence, then Henry cleared his throat and said, "Your uncle's office."

"My *uncle's* office?" Nate was really confused now. "Why on earth would she be there?"

"I wouldn't presume to know, sir."

"Well, then, who *would* know?"

"There's always going to be office gossip, but you can't always take it at face value. It's pure speculation, I'm sure."

A picture was forming in Nate's mind, quite an unpleasant picture. Doris was a very spirited and ambitious individual and much more worldly than Cal would ever be. But certainly she wouldn't be having an affair with his *own uncle* when she was engaged to marry Nate, would she? What motive would she have to do that? Perhaps, he told himself, she was discussing business with him. Maybe they were ironing out the details of Ames-Jenkins' move into its own building. But, no. It couldn't be that. Nate didn't think either of them knew about that yet.

"What kind of gossip have you heard?" he asked Henry.

"If you don't mind, I'd really rather not say. I'm sure it's not valid."

"Okay. Is there any other Ames-Jenkins business that I should know about right now? If not, I have another phone call to make."

"No, sir. I don't think there's anything pressing that I can't handle myself. Things are going well."

"Okay, Henry. You're doing a good job. I'll talk to you later. Good-bye."

"Good-bye."

He hung up the phone.

Cal noticed his confused look and stopped typing. "What's the matter?"

"It seems that Doris doesn't spend a whole lot of time doing her job. But she *does* seem to pay regular visits to Uncle Bob's office. Did she ever say anything to you about that?"

"No. She hardly ever says anything about business to me."

"I *hope* this is about business. Would you do me a favor?"

"What's that?"

"The ladies in the office talk to you more freely than they would to me. Would you call one of them and find out what they know about what Doris is doing in Uncle Bob's office?"

Cal thought for a moment. "Yeah, I can do that. Should I call Nancy? She seems to have radar. She knows *everything* that's going on."

He nodded and pushed the phone over to her desk, watching as she dialed.

As she hung up, Cal didn't know what to tell Nate. She was wishing that Kara would walk in right now to distract him.

"Well? What'd she say?" he asked.

Cal shrugged, "It's just gossip, Nate. You can't believe all that stuff. It's like the tabloids. They take a teeny bit of truth and add a whole lot of lies to it."

"Tell me what she said."

"But why should I repeat gossip? That's just as bad as making it up."

"What did she say? What gossip is going around?"

She fidgeted. Doris was her friend, after all. She was the only one Nate ever even considered marrying. Cal didn't want to say or do anything that would ruin his only hope of ever marrying and having a family.

"Cal, come on," he pleaded. "Nothing's *that* bad."

She sighed, then looked into his eyes. He desperately wanted to know what was going on. To not tell him what Nancy had said would be a torment to him. "Okay, but remember, it's only a rumor. There might not be any truth to it."

"Okay."

"Nancy said that the girls in the office think that Doris and your uncle are having an affair, and some even think that she's run away with him. He's been gone for a couple days. They say she's a gold-digger. But, Nate, I know that can't be true. The boyfriends she had in school weren't necessarily rich. Some were, and some weren't. She seemed to like all guys pretty much the same. I don't think she's a gold-digger, and I *know* your uncle wouldn't do a thing like that to you. You're like a son to him. He'd never betray you."

He mulled it over.

Cal continued, "When you were sick in the hospital with pneumonia, your uncle was there. He cares a whole lot about you. He dropped everything to be with you. And he's been wonderful about letting us use his resources for Ames-Jenkins. He's given us terrific advice. That proves that he loves you. Surely, he wouldn't do a thing like this." Then she added, "And Doris wouldn't, either. She loves you, too. She already got your ring and everything."

"She doesn't believe it when I say that I'm a confirmed bachelor."

"But you need to have someone, Nate," she pleaded. "Everybody needs *someone*. You don't want to grow old alone, do you?"

"You seem to have no qualms about doing it."

Cal couldn't deny that. "Well, maybe, but I've got Kara."

"So do I."

There being no good argument for that, she turned back to her computer and started re-reading the last paragraph.

He broke her concentration, asking emotionally, "Why is it that you're still so intimidated by Leonard?"

Where on earth did that *come from?* she wondered. "He's hardly ever intimidated me."

"You're the one who's going to need someone to grow old with, but you're not even going to consider it because you say Leonard didn't want you to marry again. Now *that's* intimidation and, for Pete's sake, he's not even here!"

Cal had never heard Nate speak like this before. "I'm just being considerate of his feelings, that's all. I'm not intimidated."

"Cal, he's having a perfectly wonderful time where he is. Do you really think he's keeping score of your comings and goings? Do you honestly think they have nothing better to do in Eternity?"

She shrugged. He was asking questions to which she had no answers.

Nate continued, "I think you're just afraid, and using him as an excuse."

"This being the Hollywood culture, marriages come and go. They seem to have no meaning around here. Being married here is about the same thing as going steady back in Dallas."

"That's not necessarily so, Cal. We may be surrounded by a culture, but that doesn't always determine what individuals do or think. You and Leonard took marriage very seriously. You were role models for the people around you. You can't go through life being afraid to take a chance, Cal. There's always going to be a risk when you let yourself fall in love, but the rewards are well worth it."

"Who would want me, anyway? I've been a royal pain-in-the-neck since the day I was born."

Nate knew this wasn't the right time to profess his love for her. It was much too soon after Leonard's death. She was nowhere near ready to allow love into her life again. *Why did I even bring the subject up?* he wondered. He shuffled the Ames-Jenkins papers that were on the desk. "I'm sure you'll find someone someday, Cal. Just don't close your mind to possibilities. You were not meant to live your life alone."

"I guess…" she hesitated, then began again, "I guess you're right. I *am* afraid. But it's not just that. I feel like I'd be betraying Len if I started dating again. I mean, for so many years, he said I belonged to him. I was his, like he owned me. I tried to straighten out his thinking but, after so many years, I realized I was wasting my breath. He would never stop thinking it. He was so doggone stubborn."

"I don't think he really believed it. I think he just wanted *you* to believe it, so you wouldn't stray."

She looked at the floor with remorse. "And I strayed, anyway. I can't believe I was so heartless. I'm the one who deserved to get cancer, not him. God should've struck *me* down, not Len."

Nate set his papers down and wheeled his chair over to Cal's. He took her hands in his and softly sang "Amazing Grace." As he progressed soulfully through the verses, he saw her expression change from one of self-loathing to one of acceptance.

*   *   *

After two more weeks, Cal was finally deemed to be at a point in her healing that she could be trusted to be alone. As Nate was repacking his bags, she came into the room, sat in the chair, and watched.

Nate folded his shirt and laid it in the suitcase. "I guess you'll be glad to see me go, won't you?"

"Well," she scratched her head, "I don't know. It's been kind of nice having you around, once you let me write again."

"Are you noticing the path your Bulldozer character is taking? I showed it to your therapist, and he agreed with me that it's an indication that you were coming to terms with Leonard's death."

"Good grief, y'all read so much into everything. It's just a story, and he just happens to be kind of like Len."

"That's no coincidence, Cal. You had a need to maintain a connection to him, and Bulldozer is how you chose to do it. The therapist said that that's a perfectly acceptable way to handle those kind of feelings."

She watched as he took his slacks out of the closet and folded them. "I don't know how you could sleep in this chair," she said. "It's not all that comfy."

"Tonight, I'll probably have the first good night's sleep I've had in weeks."

Cal looked at the floor, avoiding his eyes. "You don't know how close I came to inviting you into my bed last night. I'm glad I didn't do that. I would've felt awfully guilty later."

"Why would you feel guilty?"

"I guess because it would remind me of how unfaithful I was to Len. I think I'll always feel awful about that."

Nate stopped packing, and crossed his arms. "That's in the past and over with. Nothing you say or do will change the past. And what you do in the future can never be construed as unfaithfulness to him. He's no longer around to be unfaithful to. I thought you had accepted that fact."

"Yeah, I guess. It would be cheating on Doris, too. I don't want to do that."

"Are you being facetious?"

"What do you mean?"

"Cal, you can't be that blind to what's going on."

"About Doris and your uncle, you mean?"

He nodded.

"Well," she said, uncertainly, "there's no proof."

"I talked to him on the phone this morning. He admitted himself that she's been coming on to him."

This is something that Cal just could not understand. This was probably the first chance Doris had ever had to have a husband who would be so very good to her, a sensitive husband who cared about people—and she was blowing it. *How could such a smart woman do such a stupid thing?* she wondered. The Doris she knew didn't let golden opportunities slip through her fingers like that. What on earth could've come over her? "It's just not like her at all, Nate," Cal said. "She knows you have everything she could ever want in a husband. Why would she do that? It doesn't make any sense at all."

"I might have money, but Uncle Bob has more."

"But money isn't everything. Doris knows that. You're a lot closer to her age than your uncle is."

"Marrying him could leave her a wealthy widow in short order, couldn't it?"

The thought made her wince. "He didn't go along with it, did he? I mean, they weren't having an affair or anything, were they?"

"He didn't say and I didn't ask."

"Surely, he wouldn't. Family loyalty and everything."

"I think if Doris and I are ever going to have a future together, we're going to have to start all over. You and Leonard did it, so we can, too. My moving back home will be the first step in making that happen, I think. She was probably just jealous of all the attention you were getting and she wanted to get even with me. Once I'm home, things might get back to the way they were before." He watched to see what Cal's reaction would be.

"Maybe so," she agreed.

He resumed packing. "If you have any problems with Kara, let me know. But I think everything will be fine."

"Sure, they will. Whose idea was it for her to stay here for a few more weeks? Yours, so you could have some alone-time with Doris?"

"No, the idea was entirely Kara's. She said that you need her."

"Aw, she's a sweetie."

"Well, yes, she's sweet, but I suspect the fact that she gets away with more here has something to do with it, too. Don't forget she has some Ames genes in her," Nate said with a smile. He then checked the closet and drawers to be sure everything was packed. It was. He closed his suitcase and started to pick it up.

Cal rose from the chair and went over to him with her arms outstretched. "Thanks for everything. Right when I needed it most, you let me know you cared about me. Thanks for not letting me take Kara's mom away from her. It would've been so awful for her to have lost both Len and me so close together."

He set the suitcase down and held her tightly. "If I had gotten to you too late, Cal, I think I would've died, too. Kara and I both need you. Please, please never do that again."

"I won't. I just wasn't thinking straight that day."

"Promise me that you won't pretend things are going well if they're not. If you have a problem, let's work it out together, okay?"

"Okay." She kissed his cheek, then stepped back as he took his suitcase and went toward the door. *How, in heaven's name, could Doris ever prefer his uncle to Nate?* she wondered. Bob Stewart was a nice man, but Nate was a golden one. Maybe it was more a matter of Doris' short attention span. She had had a crush on Nate since she saw him in *The Midnight Caller*, but when it came to the boys in school, she never dated the same one for more than a few months. It seemed she got bored and wanted to move on. But she had bought Nate's ring and her wedding gown and was actively making wedding plans. It just didn't make sense. Maybe the rumors weren't true—any of them.

Nate looked back at Cal, who appeared to be deep in thought. He set the suitcase down and went back to her, holding her once more. "I love you."

"I love you, too."

"If you're ever ready to take a chance on love again, I'll be waiting."

"Shucks, Nate, by then you and Doris will be celebrating your tenth anniversary," she said with a smile. As much as Cal loved him and wished she could be more than a close friend to him, she knew he was already spoken for. That made him off-limits, as far as she was concerned. And, besides, she *was* afraid—afraid of betraying Leonard, and afraid of letting herself get any more emotionally attached than she already was to someone who had a damaged heart that could cut his life short. There was no way that she was going to let herself be a widow, again. It was much too painful.

*   *   *

The first thing Nate did when he got home was to get a report on how things had been going from Mrs. Neal. After being brought up to date, he told her he was going to get some sleep and didn't want to be disturbed for anything short of a true emergency; then he retreated to his room. It felt so very good to be back in his own bed again, and he slept for an uninterrupted twelve hours.

The next day, after phoning Cal to be sure she was still doing all right, Nate paid a visit to his uncle's office. He closed the door behind him and approached the massive desk. "How much truth is there to the rumors about you and Doris, Uncle Bob?"

"I don't know, son," the stately gentleman said as he took a cigar out of his golden case and leaned back in his well-padded chair while he lit it. "What are the rumors?"

"Where were you when you were gone that week?"

"On vacation."

"She was gone the same week."

"So what are you suggesting?"

"She's a beautiful woman, and they say that she's been seen in your office a lot. Are you two really having an affair?"

"You know me, son. I don't kiss and tell."

"Stop calling me 'son'! I'm *not* your son! A father would never do that to his son."

"Do what?"

Nate paced the width of the office, then stopped and leaned over his uncle's desk. "Where did you and Doris go that week?"

Bob's formerly amused expression changed into a more serious one, and he put his cigar into the ashtray. "Okay, Nathan, I'll tell it like it is." As Nate seated himself in the chair in front of his desk, Bob leaned forward. "Your Doris, the woman that you say you love and plan to marry, has been coming on to me. I already told you that. I decided, what the hell, I'll play along and see how far she cares to take it and to see what her motives might be. She wanted to go to a spa, one of those high-dollar ones, so that's where we went. She ran the bill up pretty high. And guess what." He waited for a response from Nate, but he got none, so Bob continued, "She struck up a *friendship* of sorts with Harvey Kressler."

"Who?"

"The only fellow there whose net worth was more than mine."

They sat in silence for a moment, then Bob retrieved his cigar and took another puff. "You know what that means, don't you?"

"That Doris is a sociable person."

Bob shook his head sadly. "She's what you call 'sociable' to a select few."

Nate slammed is fist on the desk, "Damn it, Uncle Bob. How could you do this to me?"

"To see for myself what kind of woman could get you this close to the altar and to be sure she has your best interests at heart. You may not believe it right now, but I really *do* think of you as a son, and I want what's best for you."

"Like hell you do!"

"Here she is engaged to you, and willing to hop into bed with me while she had her eye on that other fellow. She's a gold-digger, can't you see that? You, me, Kressler—we're all wealthy men. She doesn't pay a bit of attention to anyone who isn't."

"You don't know her like I do."

"Look Nate," he leaned forward and pointed his cigar at him, "if you marry Doris, it will be the biggest mistake you've ever made in your life. The biggest!"

"No, not the biggest. My biggest mistake was made in 1970 and caused me to spend ten years of my life behind bars. Nothing I could ever do would top that."

"How can you say that? If you marry Doris, it would be like spending *the rest of your life* in jail."

"Because I almost *killed* Cal, Uncle Bob! That was the most demented thing I've ever done, and I'll never live long enough to forgive myself for it."

Bob leaned back and looked at Nate with more compassion. "Now *Cal's* the one you ought to marry. If you're so determined to get married, she'd be much more suited to you than Doris. Sure, Doris is slinky and sexy and tells a man everything he wants to hear, but she's a manipulator. You don't need that in your life."

"Cal's still grieving for Leonard, and I'm sure she will continue to do so for years to come. She said she never wants to marry again, because it hurts too much when it's over. Seeing the misery she's been going through, I can't say that I blame her."

"Yes, theirs was a marriage that was unusual in many ways—the length of it being one of them."

"They were completely committed to each other, and she's going to resist letting any man take his place."

"Let me tell you a story. When your Aunt Marian died, I thought I'd never be happy with another woman again. No one else interested me. If she wasn't Marian, I didn't want her. Time has a way of softening hurts, though, and within a couple of years, I was enjoying the company of women again. Of course, no one could ever take Marian's place. She was a wonderful woman. But I found that there's room in my life for other women. It'll be the same thing with Cal. It might take a year, maybe two years, but eventually she'll be ready. When she is, I don't want you to be tied down to a marriage that's all wrong for you. A divorce from Doris would cost you a fortune. She'd probably take as much of your assets as she could in settlement."

"What makes you so sure that Cal and I are right for each other?"

"Look," Bob shook his head and smiled, "I've watched you two grow up. Becky's been giving me updates on your personal life and Cal's over the years. I've watched you together, on- and off-screen. Believe me, I know a good match when I see one. Hell, you had a child together, and you're raising her together. You created a business together and are working together to make it successful. How much more evidence do you need?"

Nate nodded.

"And, just as importantly," Bob added, "she's got wealth of her own. You can be sure she's marrying you for yourself and not your money."

"Cal couldn't care less about money."

"That's exactly my point."

Nate sighed and shook his head sadly, "She doesn't want to get married, ever again."

"That's what she's thinking now. Just give it time, though. Everything will work out, I know it will."

Nate stood up and offered his hand. "I hope so, Uncle Bob. I sure hope so."

Bob arose, too, and shook his nephew's hand, giving it a pat with his other hand. "Now, I have some business to discuss with you."

"Business? With me?" Nate asked, as the two men returned to their respective chairs.

"That's right. By the end of the year, I plan to be semi-retired. By spring, I'll be completely out of it." He studied his nephew's disbelieving face, and smiled.

"But why?"

"Because I've worked almost every day of my life since I was twelve years old, and it's about time I stopped. I want to do that before my health forces me to. I want to enjoy retirement while I still can. That week at the spa made me realize the need for that."

"I think I understand, Uncle Bob. I just didn't see it coming."

"I'll continue to own fifty-one percent of the stock, but I'd like for you to take over my job. I'd know it would be in good hands, then."

"Me? CEO of Stagecraft?"

"That's right."

"But I've got all I can handle already with Ames-Jenkins."

Bob leaned back in his chair. "I would suggest that Stagecraft buy Ames-Jenkins, and consider it nothing more than a tax write-off."

Nate bristled, "Ames-Jenkins is *much* more than a tax write-off, Uncle Bob!"

"Oh, I know that. Don't get me wrong. But if you and I control Stagecraft, and Stagecraft owns A-J, but A-J isn't expected to turn a profit, that will give A-J the freedom to do all the charity work it wants to. And all the money it loses by doing so will be a tax write-off for the parent company, Stagecraft, which makes enough of a profit to maintain both companies. Don't you see?"

"So, then Ames-Jenkins wouldn't have to worry about making any money? That would *really* give us creative freedom."

"Exactly."

"The concept is good, but I don't have the money-making drive that Stagecraft needs."

"I do. I'll take care of that, off the record. I'll be a silent partner. When I'm no longer with you, the managers under me can take over. I've groomed them in my image."

"Can they carry the day-to-day load? I don't want anything to interfere with the time I always spend with Kara. She's still a child, you know. She still needs me—more than ever, in fact, since Leonard died."

"I know. The managers can handle it. They took care of things while I was away, didn't they?" Then Bob stood and came around his desk to Nate, who rose from his chair. "You don't have to make any snap decisions." He put his arm around Nate's shoulders. "Go home. Sleep on it. Talk it over with Cal. Then we can discuss it some more."

Chapter 9

CAL HAD BEEN JOINED THIS WEEKEND by Stacy and her family, and they all went to Nate's house to celebrate Kara's thirteenth birthday. Mrs. Davis had allowed the birthday-girl to plan the menu and, as a result, prepared a huge, one-of-a-kind pizza for the clan that evening for dinner. Kara had gone with Mrs. Davis to the supermarket and personally chosen everything that would go into this very special pizza—mushrooms, tomatoes, pepperoni, green peppers, red peppers, onions, celery, pineapple, ripe olives, green olives, crabmeat, shrimp, scallops, sausage, and three kinds of cheeses. Her elders weren't quite sure they wanted to eat this concoction, but felt obligated to at least try it.

As slices were served, Nate teased, "There's something you forgot to put on the pizza, Kara-Mia. Where's the popcorn?"

"Oh, Papa Nate," she grinned. "It's good, try it."

"Well, kiddo," Cal said, as she reached over and put her hand on Kara's shoulder, "you're now officially a teenager. I've heard that two-year-olds and teenagers are a lot alike. I sure hope they're wrong, because you were one sassy little two-year-old!"

Stacy put plates of pizza in front of her youngest child and herself. "Oh, I don't know," she said. "My teenager isn't so bad. The teen years are a time of inner searching, I guess."

Lennie loaded his plate up with three slices of pizza, then held his glass up. "Root beer, please." Jim reached over, retrieved the bottle of root beer, and poured it into his son's glass.

Stacy pulled a tiny, brightly-wrapped box from her pocket and handed it to Kara. "This is for my baby sister. Happy birthday, sweetheart."

Kara happily unwrapped it and removed the lid. Inside was a floral heart-shaped locket.

"It opens," Stacy said. "See whose picture is inside."

Kara opened the locket and beheld a miniature photo of Leonard. "It's Daddy!"

"Now you can keep Daddy close to your heart all the time."

Cal's eyes grew misty. "That's a great idea, Stacy. I wish I would've thought of that."

Kara took the locket out of its box, and Stacy helped her put it on. The sisters then hugged. "Thank you, Stacy. I love it."

"The present I got you isn't nearly as clever," Cal said, "but you might like them anyway." She reached under the table and brought up a large gift, wrapped in shades of purple.

Kara jumped up and went over to her mother. After ripping the paper off, she removed the lid. "It's roller skates—the kinds with the shoes attached. Hot dog, Mom! Thanks!"

"You and your buddies go skating so often, I thought you'd like some of the fancy ones," Cal said.

"They're so pretty," Kara marveled.

"And just wait 'til you see what Papa Nate got you," Cal said. "He took me along when he went shopping for it because he wanted me to tell him which brands are best."

"What is it? What? What?" Kara asked excitedly.

Nate went into the next room for a moment, then returned carrying a wooden case with three boxes stacked on top. He set them on the table in front of Kara. "For you, my love," he said, giving her a kiss on the cheek.

Cal advised, "Open the bottom one first."

She obligingly set the other boxes aside and snapped the hinges of the case open. Then she raised the top to reveal a huge array of tubed paints, complete with palette, two palette knives, linseed oil, and an assortment of brushes.

"That's a set of oil paints, Kara," her mother said. "Now that you've got acrylics down pat, he thought you were ready to start with oils."

"Wow! There're so many different colors," she marveled.

"What's in the other boxes?" asked Francie, Lennie's little sister.

Kara took the top box and opened it. It appeared to be a very large shirt.

"It's a painting smock," Nate said, "so you won't get your nice clothes dirty when you paint."

"Yeah," joined Cal, "within a few weeks, I bet you'll have paint smudges all over that sucker."

Francie handed Kara the next box, which she then opened. "Canvas boards," said Kara. She checked to see how many there were. "Five of them. Now I can paint five pictures."

"One more," said Francie as she pushed the last box toward Kara.

Opening that one, the child looked confused. "What're these?" she asked Nate.

Cal answered, "They're sheets of canvas that have been mounted onto stretcher bars. That's what professional artists paint on instead of canvas board. Papa Nate got you three of them to start with. He kind of got carried away when we were in that art supply store."

"Golly, I feel like a real artist now," Kara glowed.

"Would you like to take art lessons this summer?" Nate asked. "They offer them every year for kids your age."

She looked at her mother. "Should I?"

"Sure," Cal shrugged. "Daddy was always wanting us to learn new things. He's the one who got you started on art, so I bet he'd love for you to take art lessons."

"And maybe someday you really *will* be a professional artist," Nate said proudly.

"Golly, that'd be cool!" Kara said.

*   *   *

After much pre-production, Cal's story, *Déjà Vu, Mr. Jackson,* would begin filming on Monday. Cal was to direct and Nate would produce, but neither would appear in the picture. Instead, they chose Marian Hinshaw and Miles Mitchell for the leads. These actors were roughly the same age as Cal and Nate, who felt it was important to show moviegoers that a person's middle years can be just as adventurous and romantic as his youth was. Ames-Jenkins wanted to continue on that theme as long as they were producing. Their fellow Baby-Boomers appeared to be cooperating, as ticket sales for such films continued to be good.

Having this screenplay to write had been a real godsend for Cal. After a few weeks with her mother, Kara had gotten homesick for the Jenkins home; so Cal drove her back there. It was when Cal was then back home, without Nate or Kara, that she realized how very lonely life would be without Leonard. Thank goodness for Jessie, she thought, and for *Déjà Vu, Mr. Jackson!*

This Friday, Nate and Cal were in his office, tying up the loose ends before filming was to begin.

"It looks like everything's go for Monday," she said happily. "I'm kind of excited. I can hardly wait to start. It'll be good to see Miles, again."

"How long has it been since you've seen him?"

"In person, about fifteen years. He still looks pretty good on film, judging from those recent clips we saw of him."

"Yes, I think he'll make a good Mr. Jackson. I'm just curious to see if you'll fall in love with Mel O'Connor, who plays Bulldozer. Did you notice I didn't offer any suggestions on who to cast in that role? That's because I knew you had a definite look in mind, so I wanted you to choose the person you felt would best fit that role. Who should know better than the writer?"

"Yeah, I think Mel will be good in that part."

Nate got up and walked around his desk to where she was sitting, then sat on his desk, facing her. "How's everything going at home, Cal?"

She shrugged, "Oh, pretty good, I guess. Nothing special has been happening, except in preparation for the film."

Something caught his eye and he leaned forward to get a closer look. "Isn't that Kara's necklace you're wearing?"

Cal fingered the locket. "No, it's mine. I thought Kara's was pretty, so I started wearing mine again. Len and Jill gave it to me on my twenty-first birthday. Do you like it?"

"It's nice." He held his hand out. "May I see it?"

That seemed an odd request, but she held it out to him.

He opened the locket and saw that there were two photos in it—one of Kara and one of Leonard. He closed it back up. "Okay. That's all I wanted to know."

"My two people," she said.

"I know. Close to your heart."

"Yeah."

Just then, Doris came through the door and stopped short. "Oh, Cal. I didn't know you were here."

"Hi, Doris. Want to come watch some of the filming next week? We're all set to go."

She came the rest of the way in and sat in the chair beside Cal's. "Our little Cal, a director. I never thought I'd live to see the day."

"Hey, I've done it before. Did you see *Mr. Jackson's Vacation*?"

"No, I didn't. You directed that?"

Nate interrupted, "Not only directed, but she wrote them both, too."

"She used to write fiction all the time back home," Doris said with a sparkle in her eye. "Remember the notes from your parents to our home-room teacher?"

Cal grinned, "'Please excuse my daughter's absence from school yesterday. She had a one-day bout of Typhoid Fever.'"

"What *really* made you sick was the geography test. Once that was over, you had a miraculous recovery."

"Did your kids do stuff like that?" she asked Doris. "Kara better not have."

Doris shrugged, "If they did, I never heard about it. Hey, you remember the report you gave in English class about the Pegasus? You swore up and down that there really *was* such a animal and that you had seen one."

"Yeah, I must've been practicing to be a used-car salesman."

"No, probably not, because during Career Week, you claimed to aspire to the priesthood."

"And, doggone it," Cal said, with mock distress, "I just missed it by *this* much. If I'd made only four more points on my final priest test, I would've made it. Then you'd have to do everything I told you."

"Cal did us all a favor," Doris smiled at Nate. "Her antics made the rest of us look really good by comparison."

He went into the adjoining alcove and retrieved his golf clubs. "Are you ready?"

"Anytime you are," she replied. "Sorry we have to leave you like this, Cal, but we have a 1:30 tee-off time."

"Why don't you come, too?" he asked.

Cal hadn't expected that. "Me? I've never played golf before."

"Well, then, it's about time you do. Come on," he coaxed, "I'll let you use my clubs."

"Dadgum it, Nate," Doris protested, "don't push her if she doesn't want to."

"She needs to get out and try new things." He added, "We can tell Becky to meet us there, so we'll have a foursome."

"Hey, that sounds fun," Cal agreed. "Okay. I'll come."

As the three left his office, he turned off the light and closed the door. Nate's relationship with Doris had lost its luster since his confrontation with his uncle so long ago, and their wedding plans had been on hold indefinitely ever since—but they did still enjoy a challenging game of golf now and then.

＊　＊　＊

Even though the offer had seemed like a good one, Cal and Nate had both decided not to sell Ames-Jenkins Productions to Stagecraft. They had worked too hard to make it what it was, and they didn't want to hand control of it over to Stagecraft or anyone else.

The idea of Nate taking over his uncle's empire greatly appealed to Doris, and she did everything she could to persuade him to do it; but his heart was really with Ames-Jenkins and he chose to limit his production work to that single entity. Cal was relieved when she learned of his decision. He was doing such a good job of running the company, they didn't want to lose him.

Another consideration, one that was especially important to Cal, was that the concerns of Ames-Jenkins were small, compared with Stagecraft, and would, therefore, be less emotionally and physically taxing on him. Cal would do everything in her power to keep Nate from having another heart attack.

Chapter 10

1996

"I have an important announcement," said Bob Stewart. Immediately, the boardroom was as quiet as a library. All eyes were watching the now-retired patriarch of Stagecraft Productions. "Until this morning, I held controlling interest in this business. Now I don't. Now, I'm merely an advisor."

There were murmurs among the board members, until he resumed.

"I have given every last bit of my Stagecraft stock to my daughter, Rebecca Myers, and my nephew, Nathan Jenkins—divided equally between them. Together, they are now the largest shareholders of the company; and you must answer to them."

The executive director asked, "What changes will this cause within the company, sir?"

"None whatsoever that I can ascertain," Bob responded with a shrug. "You are still in charge of the whole shebang, your managers do the work, and all goes well. The only difference will be that it's Becky and Nate, along with all the other stockholders, that you must please—not me. If you want to contact me for any reason, you might catch me in Milan, or Paris, or perhaps Tahiti. In other words, I'm retired and it's about time I acted like it. The ball's in their court now."

*　*　*

Cal and Nate were in lounging chairs beside Becky's pool, lazily watching fifteen-year-old Kara practice her dives. Cal was noticing that, in a swimsuit, Kara seemed to have the same athletic build that she had had at that age. How different her life was from her mother's, though. Kara was much more secure and well mannered. Except for the heartbreak of losing Leonard at a relatively young age, her life was everything that Cal could have wished for her.

"I wonder how Len and I would've gotten along when I was fifteen if I was more like Kara," Cal mused. "I bet we wouldn't have had those knock-down, drag-out fights."

"Isn't it ironic," he asked Cal, "that your independence is the thing that attracted Leonard to you and yet drove him crazy?"

"I guess the same could be said about his stubbornness. At first, I admired the fact that he didn't let me push him around. When I broke a rule, he made me pay the consequences. At the same time, though, it drove me nuts that he wouldn't let me get away with the things I really *wanted* to get away with."

"Well, sometimes you did."

She tried to think of an instance where she did, but couldn't.

"How about Ames-Jenkins start-up money?" he reminded her.

"You're not *ever* going to let me forget about that, are you?

"No."

"But that didn't go the way I'd planned for it to. He held firm about not using my trust fund."

"And aren't you glad now?"

"Well, yeah."

"You just couldn't see it then, but now you understand what he was doing."

"Yeah. He said I'd have enough money to support myself for the rest of my life, and I wouldn't ever have to marry to have financial security. It was real important to him that I not marry again."

"Knowing what I do about Leonard, I think it wasn't so much his not wanting you to marry again per se, as it was not wanting you to marry *unwisely*, out of desperation for financial security. He probably wanted to be sure that, when you do marry again, it be for love and not for money."

That took Cal aback. She stopped and thought for a moment. That made such good sense, but was so different from the way she had interpreted Leonard's words. Could Nate be right?

He leaned forward and took her hands in his. "He *loved* you, Cal. Leonard wouldn't want you to live the rest of your life alone. Kara won't be with us forever. Someday, she'll have a husband and family of her own. That's when you're going to most need someone to share your life with."

She was starting to feel that her eyes had been opened for the first time. This had been a revelation to her—an absolutely liberating one!

"I'm not trying to rush you into anything like that," Nate said earnestly, "but just think about what I said, okay?"

She slowly nodded, "Okay."

Satisfied, he gave each of her hands a gentle kiss, then refocused on their daughter as Kara practiced a graceful swan dive.

＊　＊　＊

When Cal answered her phone that night, she could tell right away that Kara was really excited. Stacy had just invited her to visit her family in Connecticut so the sisters could have some time to spend together, just the two of them.

"Papa Nate said it's okay with him if it's okay with you," she said. "Please say yes, Mama. I want to go so bad."

"Let me talk to him for a minute."

Kara then put Nate on the phone. Cal was concerned about her flying cross-country alone, but Nate reassured her that he would hire someone to serve as her travel companion—flying with her to Connecticut, seeing that she's safely with Stacy, then immediately flying back to Los Angeles. The same person would then reverse the process when it's time for Kara to come back home. Perhaps, he felt, one of the Ames-Jenkins employees could be spared to serve in that capacity. Cal was agreeable to that. All the employees she had met were very kind people who would take good care of Kara.

Being so assured, Cal gave her permission for the trip to take place. When Nate relayed that bit of news to Kara, she let out a joyous "*Yahooooo!*" which made her parents, on both ends of the line, smile.

Nate then spoke into the phone again, with a grin, "Wher*ev*er did our proper daughter get her Texas mannerisms?"

＊　＊　＊

After Kara's plane had climbed into the clouds and out of sight, Cal turned away from the window. She looked sad. Nate put his arm around her shoulders as they left the airport and went to his car. "We're sure going to miss that little girl," he said.

"Yeah. I've never watched *her* leave *us* before. It's always been the other way around when we had to go away to work or something."

"But she'll have a really good time, I just know it. And she's in good hands."

"Yeah. I was about her age when I came to L.A. alone." She got into the passenger seat of the car, and he closed the door. Then, Nate went around and got into the driver's seat.

There was a long silence as they headed home, then Cal said softly, "I've got a surprise for you."

"Really? What's that?"

She took her locket and opened it, holding it out for Nate to see. He glanced over. The locket now had only one picture in it—the one of Kara.

He beamed. "You're finally letting go."

"Yeah. I guess I can handle the rest of my life without his help. He can rest in peace now."

"Cal, I'm so happy to hear you say that. It's taken a long time for you to get to this point, a *really* long time."

She took the wedding rings off her left hand, transferring them to her right. "And I guess he can get along okay without me, too."

Nate smiled to himself as he continued driving. After a short silence, he asked, "Isn't it a Rhoads tradition to take you out to dinner when there's something to celebrate?"

"Yeah, Len did that sometimes."

"Then let's go out to dinner tonight, then back to my place. I've got a surprise for you, too."

"I better tell Jessie not to make dinner, then."

He handed his cell phone to her.

*　*　*

They were now back after having enjoyed a delicious lobster and champagne dinner, followed by a concert of the Los Angeles Philharmonic Orchestra. It was a mellow, beautiful evening as they strolled up the sidewalk and entered Nate's house.

"What time was Kara's plane supposed to get to Connecticut?" she asked.

He looked at his watch. "Unless they made a stop between the airport and home, she should be at Stacy's house now. Want to give her a call?"

"Yeah, let's do. You have her number, don't you? It's programmed into our phone at home, but I don't remember what it is."

"Kara said it's in her address book on her desk." Nate said as Cal followed him upstairs and into Kara's room. He picked up and thumbed through the pink book. "Q, R, S—Here it is. Stacy Shulman." He held it open for Cal to see, "Look how organized she is—name, address, phone number, e-mail address, date of birth, and hobbies. She's got a dossier on everyone in here. The FBI could use her expertise."

"She sure is smart, and I sure miss her."

He lifted the receiver of Kara's phone and handed it to Cal. He then read the phone number out to her as she punched in the numbers.

*　*　*

After Cal had spoken with both Stacy and Kara for a while, she handed the receiver to Nate. "She wants to talk to you."

He took it and smiled into the phone. "Hey, Kara-Mia. How do you like travelling without any parents?"

"Oh, Papa Nate, it was so fun!" she bubbled over. "Cindy and I were almost the only people in the first-class section, and they treated us like we were royalty! They wanted to give me a gin and tonic, but Cindy told them I'm not old enough."

"They didn't give you any, did they?"

"No. I got a soft drink, instead."

"That's good."

"And Stacy's got the cutest little house. She calls it a ranch-style house– it's all on one floor, and has only three bedrooms."

"It's a lot different from our house, isn't it?"

"Yeah, a *lot* different. I thought lawyers were rich."

"Kara, don't let the Shulmans hear you talk like that," he said sternly.

"It's all right. I'm alone in the kitchen."

"Okay, that's good. Jim must be a *good* lawyer, rather than a wealthy one."

"And they're starting to go to bed already."

"They're three hours ahead of us, that's why. You need to go to bed when they do, so you'll be on the same schedule."

"Okay. Stacy said we're going to go to New York tomorrow to see Uncle Darrell."

"It looks like you're going to enjoy yourself."

"Yeah. I love being with Stacy. She's so cool."

"How are her kids?"

"They're fine. I'm probably going to end up hitting Lennie before I leave, though. He sure does tease a lot."

"No hitting, Kara!"

"I know, I know. I was just kidding. Francie won't let me hit him."

He smiled. "She's protective of her big brother."

"Yeah. I guess I better get to bed now. Stacy just came in here with her PJs on."

"Okay, sweetheart. Have a good time tomorrow."

"Good night, Papa. I love you."

"I love you, too, Kara-Mia. Good night." He put the receiver down and looked at Cal. "It looks like Stacy has a busy week planned for her. They're going to see Darrell tomorrow."

"Oh, good! He's such a sweet guy. I hope Stacy let him know they're coming. He doesn't like surprises."

"I'm sure she did." He then took Cal by the hand and led her down the hallway. "I have something for you. It's been here for quite a while. I've been waiting for just the right time to give it to you. After what seems like forever, I think the time has come."

Cal followed him into his room, where he took a box off his closet shelf and handed it to her. She lifted the lid to behold a mass of pink chiffon. "What is it?" She took it out and held it up. "Oh, a nightie. A really fancy one. You sure you didn't get this for Doris?"

"I bought it for you because I knew this day would get here eventually. It's my way of welcoming you back into the world. I was hoping it wouldn't end up being a wedding present when you married someone else."

"I can't think of anyone I'd rather wear it for than you. Too bad you're engaged."

"Try it on."

Her smile turned into a mischievous grin, as she turned and went into the adjoining bathroom and closed the door.

While he waited for her, he dimmed the lights and put some soft music on the sound system.

The door opened. Cal glided into the room, Loretta Young style, and put her hands in his. "I wish I had some perfume with me."

"You don't need it." He twirled her around, then held her hands again. "You're *beautiful*, Cal. I've never seen you look more beautiful than you are right now."

"No one's ever called me *that* before."

"Well, then, they were remiss because you really are." He kissed her tenderly, then led her to the bed and turned the sheets down.

Only one thing stood in Cal's way, but she had had the distinct feeling for a long time now that that wasn't a real problem. "You're never going to marry Doris, are you?" she asked.

He shook his head.

That's all she needed to know.

*   *   *

This was the most contented feeling Nate had ever had in his life. He looked over at Cal. She was sleeping so peacefully. He put his arms around her and murmured softly, "I love you, Cal."

She opened her eyes and smiled. "I love you, too." She snuggled up close to him.

He kissed her forehead and lifted her chin so they were looking into each other's eyes. "I hope you're ready for this. I hope it's not too soon, but I can't wait any longer. Will you marry me?"

"You *really* want to get married, after all these years of being single?"

He nodded. "The sooner, the better."

She was having a difficult time believing that. "Are you *sure*? I thought that's why you haven't married Doris yet—because you didn't want to give up your freedom."

He shook his head, "I've never been so sure of anything in my life."

She hugged him tightly, then looked deeply into his eyes.

He wondered if she was searching for a diplomatic way to say 'no.' Cal had matured a lot in the last few years and probably wanted to let him down easy.

After a long pause, she asked, "How does 'Cal Jenkins' sound to you?"

It was, to Nate, as though Heaven itself had opened up and all the angels were singing their Hallelujahs. He just couldn't keep the biggest, most radiant smile Cal had ever seen from dominating his face.

*　*　*

Cal had suggested they get married at their minister's house, but Nate would have none of that. This was a once-in-a-lifetime event, he had told her, and they were going to do it right. He was determined that this was going to be the biggest, grandest wedding this town had ever seen.

True to his word, Nate arranged for their church's full adult and children's choirs to sing for the ceremony. He helped Cal pick out her pale yellow wedding gown, and they chose the flowers together. Indeed, yellow irises and lilies were absolutely *everywhere*—not only on the altar, but also in the narthex and at each end of every pew. And there were guests—hundreds of them—as many as the church would hold! As Cal and Kara walked, hand-in-hand, down the aisle together toward Nate, Cal's old friend Sue caught her eye. Cal smiled at her, and Sue gave the thumbs-up sign in response. In the front pews on the bride's side were Jill, Stacy, Stacy's family, and Darrell. To Cal, they were, indeed, her own family; and it was so good to have their support today. At the altar stood a tuxedo-clad Nathan Arthur Jenkins, with that same beautiful smile he had had when she agreed to marry him. Instead of a best man, it was Becky who stood proudly beside him. Every detail of this wedding had a special significance to Nate and Cal. When she and Kara reached the altar and the minister asked who gave the bride away, Kara beamed as she said, "Daddy and I do," and put her mother's hand into her father's. Before stepping away, however, she looked up at her parents and said what was in her heart: "Mama and Papa Nate, you've both had so much sadness in your lives. Now I want you to be happy, being together always and loving each other the way you were meant to." The three came together in a spontaneous group hug. When Kara then went to sit in the front pew beside

Stacy and looked back up, she saw that Cal and Nate were both watching her with moist eyes. Never had Kara seen her parents more united, as though one, than they were at that moment.

The couple then knelt at the altar, and the choirs sang a beautiful arrangement of "O Perfect Love." Nate knew this was one of Cal's favorite hymns of all time. Then they just couldn't help it—Nate and Cal held hands and joined in on the second and third verses, asking for God's blessing on their union. By the final stanza, they both felt that they had received it.

* * *

Because the couple didn't want anything to detract from the sanctity of the marriage sacrament, reporters and media photographers had not been allowed inside the church. Right after the ceremony, however, the wedding party went outside to pose for pictures and answer a few brief questions while the guests were told to go to the nearby Country Club and start the celebration ahead of them. Many of their fans were standing outside, behind the members of the media, and showered the couple with flowers. One well-oiled fan good-naturedly yelled, "You two better find a house near a school! You're bound to have a *lot* of kids now."

"At *our* age?" Cal asked with a laugh. "I don't think so!"

They were enjoying this lighthearted interlude quite a bit; but the photographer was beckoning them back inside, so Nate gently led Cal toward the church door. Right before re-entering the church, Cal tossed her bouquet to one of her favorite reporters, a woman who had covered Ames-Jenkins stories for years and had been, herself, widowed shortly before Cal was. Getting caught up in the spirit of things, Nate lifted Cal's skirt, removed her blue garter, and tossed it at another of the reporters they had come to know, a man who was a confirmed bachelor of forty-eight. "If I can do it, *you* can do it!" the groom yelled at him. Cal and Nate then grinned at each other and went back into the church.

Becky stopped Cal inside the door. "*Now* will you admit that you love Nate?"

"Me? Why, Becky, I thought you knew that all along."

"Of course I did, but I want to hear *you* say it."

"Okay, okay." Cal grabbed Nate in a bear hug. "I love him like crazy and now he's all mine!"

Nate, seeing Sue nearby, winked, "See? I *told* you she couldn't keep her hands off me."

* * *

The fairy-tale wedding was followed by a gala reception, complete with full orchestra and dancing. Champagne was freely flowing. There was table after table of every type of hors d'oeuvres, and Cal's eyes lit up when she beheld a special table laden with the goodies that Nate knew she loved—chocolate brownies, chocolate petit fours, chocolate mini-parfaits, and an eight-tiered chocolate wedding cake! *Now* she understood why he insisted on being the one to order the cake. "Can we put whatever we don't eat today into a great big doggy-bag to take with us on our honeymoon?" she asked with a grin.

"Afraid not, Cal." He then nudged her and winked, "You better eat all you can now because we're going to have better things to do for the next few days."

And indeed they did!

*   *   *

Because Leonard's name had been on Kara's birth certificate as her father, Nate wanted to officially adopt her, changing her last name to his own. At the dinner table the night he and Cal returned from their honeymoon, he presented that idea to her.

Kara smiled, first at him, then at her mother. She was feeling very loved and cherished, but she felt a tug of conflict, too. "Okay, but can I just add Jenkins to the name I already have and be Kara Michelle Rhoads Jenkins? I want to keep Daddy's last name, too. I feel like y'all are both my dads."

Cal looked at Nate. "We've got ourselves a pretty smart kid, don't we?"

"A compassionate one, too," he nodded. "Okay, Kara-Mia. You'll have the longest name in your school."

Cal mused, "That makes your initials KMRJ, like a radio station."

"You know what I'll have a hard time getting used to?" Kara asked. "You guys sleeping in Papa Nate's room together. I'll keep expecting to see you come out of a guest room, Mama."

"It's a nice, cozy feeling having the man you love right beside you at night. Someday, you'll know what it's like."

"One thing I was wondering," Nate said to Kara. "Would you like a small photo of me to put with Leonard's in your necklace? I'd like to be in there, too."

Kara and Cal looked at each other and laughed. Kara then opened her locket and showed it to him. On the left was his photo, on the right was Leonard's. "Too late. Mama and I already thought of that."

"*Mama* did?" He looked over at Cal, who was holding her locket open to him, too. Right beside Kara's photo was his.

He was astonished. "When did you two do that?" he asked.

"On our wedding day," Cal said, "while you were getting a haircut. You'll find a couple photos missing from your album, but we figured you wouldn't mind."

Nate was profoundly gratified. It took many years for it to happen, but he knew that he had at last found true happiness. Every one of his dreams had now come true after the long, hard journey, full of unexpected twists and turns, that his life had become. He now had Cal as his very own, to have and to hold, for the rest of their lives. Kara, knowing now that he was her father—her very proud father, who loved her very much—was growing into a caring, sweet young lady. They were, at last, a real family now. Nate had satisfaction in his work for the first time in his life. Acting had pretty much been thrust upon him because of the family business, but now he realized that producing was his true calling. It was both a challenge and a joy for him to be associated with Ames-Jenkins Productions. And everything he had that was bringing him so much happiness now was his because of Cal. He owed his very life to her, and it would be his pleasure to give her all the love she could ever need for the rest of her life.

THE END